THE POEMS OF ALEXANDER POPE

VOLUME II

THE RAPE OF THE LOCK AND OTHER POEMS

The Twickenham Edition of the Poems of Alexander Pope

★

GENERAL EDITOR: JOHN BUTT

★

VOLUME I

PASTORAL POETRY and AN ESSAY ON CRITICISM. E. Audra, formerly Professor of English, Lille University, and Aubrey Williams, Professor of English, The Rice Institute, Houston, Texas.

VOLUME II

THE RAPE OF THE LOCK and other poems. Geoffrey Tillotson, Professor of English Literature, Birkbeck College, University of London.

VOLUME III i

AN ESSAY ON MAN. Maynard Mack, Professor of English and Fellow of Davenport College, Yale University.

VOLUME III ii

EPISTLES TO SEVERAL PERSONS (MORAL ESSAYS). F. W. Bateson, University Lecturer in English, Corpus Christi College, Oxford.

VOLUME IV

IMITATIONS OF HORACE and AN EPISTLE TO DR ARBUTHNOT and THE EPILOGUE TO THE SATIRES. John Butt, Regius Professor of Rhetoric and English Literature, University of Edinburgh.

VOLUME V

THE DUNCIAD. James Sutherland, Lord Northcliffe Professor of English, University College, University of London.

VOLUME VI

MINOR POEMS. Norman Ault and John Butt.

Plate 1 ARABELLA FERMOR

ALEXANDER POPE

THE RAPE OF THE LOCK

and OTHER POEMS

*

Edited by

GEOFFREY TILLOTSON

LONDON : METHUEN & CO. LTD
NEW HAVEN : YALE UNIVERSITY PRESS

First published 14 November 1940
Second Edition 1954
Third Edition, reset, 1962
Printed in Great Britain by The Broadwater Press Ltd
Welwyn Garden City, Hertfordshire
Catalogue number (Methuen) 02/4772/11/35
Reprinted 1966

PREFACE

FOR this edition, the third, the type has been reset. New editorial matter now makes its appearance for the first time. The appendix on ombre has had the benefit of Mr Dermot Morrah's kind attentions—as now revised it satisfies the criticisms that have been brought against it since it first appeared twenty years ago. Several appendixes have been abolished, their matter having been brought into the body of the book. Appendix F first appeared in the second edition. Annotations have been revised, particularly those for the *Rape of the Lock*. A new section on Isaac Watts has been inserted in the Introduction to *Eloisa to Abelard*. Plate IV is a welcome innovation. I am grateful to Miss Carol Landon for helping with the proofs and the index.

University of London, Birkbeck College. G. T.
1 December 1960.

PREFACE TO THE FIRST EDITION

FEW poets have built their poems so deliberately out of the detail of their time, place, and contemporaries as did Pope. The material in which he saw poetic value was something like the total cognizance of any 'liberally educated' man of the day. He appeals to us, therefore, *through* his contemporaries in a way that Wordsworth, for instance, does not. We push our way into the family circle. And until the family face becomes familiar, the individual features of Pope cannot be fully recognized as divine exceptions. Drawing his 'matter' from the thought and world of his day, he has been at the mercy of the permanence and impermanence latent in them. Often what he perceives is permanent ('And send the Godly in a Pett, to pray'), often it is a mixture of permanent and impermanent ('Sooner shall . . . Wits take Lodgings in the Sound of *Bow*'). It is out of regard for the cut of the cap that still fits that we seek to admire the cut of the cap that fits no longer. The danger of premature obsolescence—Swift saw that the *Dunciad* was risking it—is a danger risked in different degrees by much of Pope's poetry. Pope and contemporary readers did something by printed and manuscript annotations to stay what was slipping, and, as the Preface of the General Editor has shown, the work has gone on more systematically since. Historical study is obligatory for any student of Pope. So far as it succeeds, it explains what is obscure and often what at first deceptively looks perspicuous. Moreover, even the best things in Pope are frequently the sharper for it. (It has not been considered necessary here to pursue historical inquiry into periods later than Pope's. That the modern scholar knows that there is nothing to be known of Zoroaster (*Temple of Fame*, l. 98) does not affect the study of where Pope got what he thought was true.)

The historical method is worth applying to the manner as well as to the matter. The young Pope—and he is a poet under thirty in this volume—deliberately tried his hand at writing in each of the recognized 'kinds' of the day. The present volume shows the results in translation, imitation, mock-heroic, heroic epistle, elegy. The poems of these kinds have each their separate places in literary history, and have therefore required separate introductions. And it has seemed worth while to attempt to wear down the modern hostility to the kinds, and to such things as 'poetic diction' and rhetoric, since to understand them historically is to value them. The problem here, of course, stretches beyond a historical solution. Pope writes as he does according to principles of permanent reasonableness. If those principles are reconstructed, an underlying logic is discovered that commends them.

It is necessary to extend historical study to the smaller concern of Pope's phrasing. He not only wishes to express well what oft was thought, but to express better what oft was expressed well. His phrasing is often a flag planted on towers which others have reared. And he intends his reader to see the towers and the flag together, to mark what brick or marble it is that has been made arresting.

Some of my debts for help and advice have been specified in the notes. I wish to thank also Miss Mary Lascelles, Mr J. B. Leishman, Miss H. L. Lorimer, the Rev. G. L. Merchant (Rector of Somerton), the Rev. Norman Ramsay who kindly lent me certain relics of the Fermor family, Professor G. Sherburn, Professor D. Nichol Smith, Arthur Tillotson, Kathleen Tillotson, and Miss M. Northend who has kindly assisted with the proofs and the index.

University College, London. G. T.
26 August 1940.

CONTENTS

NOTE ON THE ILLUSTRATIONS

Plate I (frontispiece). W. Sykes's portrait of Arabella Fermor is reproduced by courtesy of the owner, the Hon. Mrs Roch, Llanarth Court, Raglan. Sykes, about whom little is known, enjoyed considerable repute as a portrait painter in the early eighteenth century, and in 1727 was one of the artists called in to value Thornhill's paintings at Greenwich Hospital. He died before June 1733, when his collection of paintings was sold. (See S. Redgrave, *Dictionary of Artists of the English School*, ed. 1878, p. 421, and *Bryan's Dictionary of Painters and Engravers*, ed. G. C. Williamson, 1905, v. 149.) His portrait of Arabella Fermor was engraved by R. Parr (Brit. Mus. Print Room, *Collectanea Biographica*, vol. 35 [1853]) and 'by C. Knight from a Drawing by Gardner . . . Published by Cadell & Davies . . . May 1. 1807' (Brit. Mus. Print Room, C. ix [sub. 2] x P. 3). The original painting measures 29 by 25 inches. For its date and inscription see pp. 98 f. below. The dress is blue.

Plate II (facing p. 215). For Gribelin's engraved headpiece to the *Temple of Fame* in 1717 see p. 244 below, note 3. The original measures $5\frac{9}{10}$ by $2\frac{7}{10}$ inches. Gribelin's career is described in DNB.

Plate III (facing p. 293). For the engraving of Eloisa see p. 314 below. The original measures $6\frac{7}{10}$ by 4 inches. For Cheron see DNB. The younger Gribelin is mentioned in DNB's account of his father, Simon.

Plate IV (facing p. 353) reproduces, with the kind permission of the Director of the City of Manchester Art Galleries, a detail from Blake's head of Pope, which was one of a series of eighteen heads of poets painted by him for the library of William Hayley at Felpham. The original consists of three sections not marked off from each other decisively, and the section depicting the Unfortunate Lady is to the left of Pope's head, being balanced on the other side by a representation of Eloisa. I do not know of any other picture of the Unfortunate Lady.

In Text (p. 79). The scene from the *Rape of the Lock*, which appears at the beginning of the poem, is reproduced by courtesy of the Trustees of the British Museum from an impression taken from the lid of a gold snuff-box engraved by Hogarth in 1717(?) (Brit. Mus.

1842–8–6–402[d]: see Austin Dobson, *William Hogarth*, ed. 1898, pp. 213 f.). Cf. Warton ed., i 317: 'An engraving of Sir Plume, with seven other figures, by Hogarth, was executed on the lid of a gold snuff-box, and presented to one of the parties concerned . . .' The print, which measures 3⅛ by 2¼ inches, was purchased at the Strawberry Hill sale in 1842, and the inscription is in the hand of Horace Walpole.

GENERAL NOTE ON THE TEXT
of this volume

THE texts chosen as the textual basis of the poems in the present volume are those of the first editions. Where Pope revised, the original readings have been corrected accordingly. These revisions have been edited to conform typographically with the context of the first edition. Pope himself happens to provide the authority for this treatment: writing to his printer, William Bowyer, about a change of format for a poem, he directs him to 'contrive the Capitals & evry thing exactly to correspond with that Edition'.[1] This is the practice I have followed as an editor, and followed not only for capitals but for such forms as 'cou'd'. My text, therefore, may be branded as eclectic, though only in so far, I hope, as such matters go.

Certain concessions have been made to the convenience of the modern reader. Long ſ has been printed as s; hyphens have been uniformly supplied in compounds; when quotation marks are used to open a quotation or a speech, closing marks have been inserted where the quotation or speech ends; apostrophes have been added where they are lacking; the occasional use of ? to close a wholly uninterrogative exclamation—e.g. 'Eloisa', l. 99: 'what sudden horrors rise?'—has been modernized to a !; 'e'er' meaning 'before' has been printed 'ere' to distinguish it from 'e'er' meaning 'ever'; the verb 'breathe', sometimes printed 'breath', has been always given its modern form. For most of these modernizations there is warrant in the editions of Pope's lifetime. I have introduced them silently, unless there is any doubt as to Pope's intentions. If such doubt exists, the available evidence is recorded in the apparatus.

The apparatus has been limited to variants that reach a certain level of interest. Where a lazy compositor setting up the first edition has omitted a stop because his composing-stick was full, I have silently supplied it from a later edition. Nor is any account taken of obvious misprints, e.g., 'vouchfafe,' even when they occur in the first edition; nor of such variants as 'opening' and 'op'ning'. The punctuation varies from edition to edition, often apparently with

1. 3 Mar. 1743/4 (*Pope's Corresp.*, iv 5c4).

no better reason than accident or the fluctuating taste of Pope or of his compositors. These changes are only recorded when they justify the space that they occupy in the apparatus.

Bibliographical descriptions of the various editions used are rendered unnecessary by the work of Professor Griffith, and the reader who requires them is referred, by means of the number following Griffith's name, to the relevant item in his *Alexander Pope A Bibliography* (University of Texas Press, vol. i, part 1, 1922; vol. i, part 2, 1927).

Pope usually printed his notes in italic. This practice has been followed throughout the present volume.

The texts of the *Works* of 1740–1 and 1743–5, so far as the poems in the present volume are concerned, are not always of convincing authority: the small changes they make may be due to the same carelessness which is evident in their retention of the misprints of 1736. Their variants have not always been accepted. Warburton claims for his edition that 'The FIRST Volume, and the original poems in the SECOND, are . . . printed from a copy corrected throughout by the Author himself . . . Which, with several additional notes in his own hand, he delivered to the Editor [i.e., Warburton] a little before his death'.[1] This means, for the present purpose, the *Rape of the Lock*, the 'Elegy to the Memory of an Unfortunate Lady', 'Eloisa to Abelard', and perhaps the *Temple of Fame*, but not, presumably, 'January and May' and the 'Wife of Bath Her Prologue'. The corrected copy would seem to have belonged to the *Works* of 1740 or 1743, so that it is only after allowing for what I have considered their misprints (presumably overlooked by the correcting Pope) that the value of the Pope–Warburton contribution can be assessed. So far as the present volume goes, that contribution is mainly one of notes. One or two new readings, however, seem to have authority and these have been introduced into the text.

1. 1751, iv.

CHRONOLOGICAL TABLE

The standard biographies are G. Sherburn's *The Early Career of Alexander Pope*, 1934, and W. J. Courthope's life in vol. v of the Elwin-Courthope edition of Pope's works, 1871–89. Sherburn's account stops at 1727.

1688 (May 21) Alexander Pope born in London of elderly parents.

*c.*1700 Pope's family moved to Binfield, in Windsor Forest, [?] to comply with anti-Catholic regulations. Ten miles away (as the crow flies), at Mapledurham, lived Martha Blount (1690–1763).
Death of Dryden.

*c.*1705 Pope started to make acquaintance with the literary society of London.

1709 (May) 'January and May' and the *Pastorals* published in the sixth part of Tonson's *Miscellanies*. Pope is already a friend of John Caryll.

1711 (May) *An Essay on Criticism* published; praised in *The Spectator* by Addison, and damned by Dennis. *The Rape of the Locke* written.

1712 (May) The 'Messiah' published by Steele in *The Spectator*. Lintott's *Miscellany* published, containing *The Rape of the Locke* (anonymously), and other poems by Pope. Pope was becoming acquainted with Swift, Gay, Parnell, and Arbuthnot, who together formed the Scriblerus Club.

1713 (March) *Windsor Forest*.
(April) Addison's *Cato* first acted, with a prologue by Pope.
Pope was contributing to Steele's *Guardian*.
(October) Proposals issued for a translation of the *Iliad*.
(29 December) 'Wife of Bath Her Prologue' published in Steele's *Miscellany*, dated 1714.
Began to take lessons in painting from Jervas.

1714 (March) *The Rape of the Lock.*
(August) Death of Queen Anne.

1715 (February) *The Temple of Fame.*
(April) *Key to the Lock* published.
(June 6) The *Iliad*, Books i–iv, published; followed two days later by Tickell's translation of *Iliad* i. During this year [?] Pope wrote his character of Addison, and became acquainted with Lady Mary Wortley Montagu.

1716 (March) *Iliad*, vol. ii.
Pope's revenge by poison on Curll the publisher [Sherburn, ch. vi, and *Pope's Prose*, pp. xciv ff.].
(April) Pope's family sold the house at Binfield, and settled at Chiswick, where their neighbour was Lord Burlington.
(July) Lady Mary sailed for Turkey.

1717 (January) *Three Hours after Marriage* by Pope, Gay, and Arbuthnot, first acted.
(June) *Iliad*, vol. iii.
The collected volume of Pope's *Works*, containing 'Verses to the Memory of an Unfortunate Lady' and 'Eloisa to Abelard'.
(October) Pope's father died.

1718 (June) *Iliad*, vol. iv.
Death of Parnell. Pope and his mother moved to Twickenham late in the year.

1719 Death of Addison.

1720 (May) *Iliad*, vols. v and vi.

1721 (September) The 'Epistle to Addison' prefixed to Tickell's edition of Addison's *Works*.
(December) The 'Epistle to Oxford' prefixed to Pope's edition of Parnell's *Poems*.

1723 (January) Pope's edition of John Sheffield, Duke of Buckingham's *Works* published, and seized by the Government on suspicion of Jacobitish passages.
(May) Pope called before the House of Lords as a witness at Atterbury's trial.

1725 (March) Pope's edition of Shakespeare published in six volumes.
(April) *Odyssey*, vols. i–iii.
Bolingbroke returned from exile, and settled near Pope at Dawley Farm, Uxbridge.

1726 (March) Theobald's *Shakespeare Restored: or, a Specimen of the Many Errors . . . Committed . . . by Mr Pope.*
(June) *Odyssey*, vols. iv–v.
Pope visited by Swift. *Gulliver's Travels* published in October.
Pope becomes friendly with Spence.

1727 (June) Pope–Swift *Miscellanies*, vols. i and ii.
Swift's second visit to Pope.

1728 (March) Pope–Swift *Miscellanies*, 'last' volume.
(May) *The Dunciad*, in three books, with Theobald as hero.

1729 (April) *The Dunciad Variorum.*

1731 (December) 'An Epistle to the . . . Earl of Burlington' [Moral Essay iv].

1732 (October) Pope–Swift *Miscellanies*, 'third' volume.
(December) Death of Gay.

1733 (January) 'An Epistle to . . . Lord Bathurst' [Moral Essay iii].
(February) The first *Imitation of Horace* [Sat. II i].
(February–May) *An Essay on Man*, Epistles i–iii.
(June) Death of Pope's mother.

1734 (January) 'An Epistle to . . . Lord Cobham' [Moral Essay i].
An Essay on Man, Epistle iv.
(July) *Imitation of Horace* [Sat. II ii].
(December) 'Sober Advice from Horace'.

1735 (January) 'An Epistle to Dr Arbuthnot'.
(February) 'Of the Characters of Women' [Moral Essay ii].
Death of Arbuthnot.
(April) The *Works*, vol. ii.
(May) Curll's edition of Pope's letters.

1737 (April) *Imitation of Horace* [Ep. II ii].
(May) Pope's edition of his letters.
Imitation of Horace [Ep. II i].
An Essay on Man attacked by Crousaz, Professor of Mathematics and Philosophy at Lausanne.

1738 (January–March) *Imitations of Horace* [Eps. I vi and I i].
(May–July) *Epilogue to the Satires*.
Warburton began his replies to Crousaz.

1740 (April) Pope's first meeting with Warburton.

1742 (March) *The New Dunciad* [i.e. Book iv].

1743 (October) *The Dunciad* in four books with Cibber enthroned in the place of Theobald.

1744 (May 30) Death of Pope.

LIST OF THE PRINCIPAL POEMS
of Pope to be found in the other volumes

ABBREVIATIONS

used in the footnotes and in the appendixes

[Unless otherwise stated, Dryden and Milton are cited from the Oxford Poets edition, Shakespeare from the Globe edition, Crashaw from L. C. Martin's edition (1927), and Montaigne from Cotton's translation (ed. 1711).]

ADDISON, *Remarks* = Remarks on Several Parts of Italy, &c. In the Years 1701, 1702, 1703. 1705.

ADD. MSS. = British Museum Additional MSS.

ATHENIAN ORACLE = The Athenian Oracle: being an entire collection of all the valuable questions and answers in the old Athenian Mercuries. 4 vols., 1703.

AUDRA = L'Influence Française dans L'Œuvre de Pope. Par E. Audra. Paris, 1931.

BABB = The Cave of Spleen, by Lawrence Babb. (R.E.S., April 1936, pp. 165–76.)

BEHN = The Works of Aphra Behn. Ed. Montague Summers. 6 vols., 1915.

BOILEAU = Œuvres Complètes. Ed. by A. Ch. Gidel. 4 vols., Paris, 1870–3.

BOND = English Burlesque Poetry, 1700–50. By R. P. Bond. Cambridge, Mass., 1932.

CROKER = Notes by Croker in the Elwin–Courthope edition of Pope's Works.

DACIER = The Life of Pythagoras. By A. Dacier. Translated. 1707.

DAVIDEIS = Cowley's Davideis. (The ed. dated 1687 included in *Works*, 1688.)

DENNIS = Remarks on Mr. Pope's Rape of the Lock. By [John] Dennis. 1728.

DENNIS, 1717 = Remarks Upon Mr. Pope's Translation of Homer. With Two Letters concerning Windsor Forest, and the Temple of Fame. By [John] Dennis. 1717.

DIOD. SIC. = The Historical Library of Diodorus the Sicilian. In Fifteen Books. Trans. by G. Booth. 1700.

Dilke = Papers of a Critic. By C. W. Dilke. 2 vols., 1875.

Dispensary = The Dispensary. A Poem [By S. Garth]. The Sixth Edition, With several Descriptions and Episodes never before Printed. 1706.

Dryden, Æneid &c. = The Works of Virgil. Trans. by Dryden, 3rd ed. 3 vols., 1709. (The copy used in Brit. Mus. C.28.f.6 which belonged to Pope in 1710, and to Gray in 1731.)

Dryden, Essays = Essays, selected and ed. W. P. Ker. 2 vols., 1900.

Dryden's Ovid's Ep. = Ovid's Epistles, Translated by Several Hands. 1680.

EC = The Works of Pope. Ed. W. Elwin and W. J. Courthope. 10 vols., 1871–89.

Five Love-Letters = Five Love-Letters From A Nun To A Cavalier. Trans. by Sir Roger L'Estrange. 2nd ed. 1701.

Fontenelle = Dialogues of the Dead. Trans. by J. Hughes. 1708.

Gabalis = The Count of Gabalis: Or, The Extravagant Mysteries of the Cabalists. [By Abbé de Villars, trans. by P. Ayres.] 1680.

Griffith = Alexander Pope. A Bibliography. By R. H. Griffith. 1 vol. in two parts, 1922, 1927.

Gould = The Works of R. Gould. 2 vols., 1709.

Herodotus = The History of Herodotus. Trans. by Isaac Littlebury. 2 vols., 1709.

History of Loreto = The History of Our B. Lady of Loreto. By O. Torsellino. Trans. by T. Price. 1608.

Holden = Pope's Rape of the Lock. Ed. by George Holden. 1909.

Hughes = Letters of Abelard and Heloise. To which is prefix'd, A Particular Account of their Lives, Amours, and Misfortunes. Trans. by J. Hughes. 4th ed., 1722.

Iliad = Pope's translation, quarto ed., 1715–20.

Johnson, Lives = The Lives of the English Poets. Ed. G. Birkbeck Hill. 3 vols., 1905.

Key = A Key to the Lock. By Esdras Barnivelt [i.e. Pope]. 1715.

Larwood = The Story of the London Parks. By J. Larwood. 2 vols. [1872].

Le Bossu = Monsieur Bossu's Treatise of the Epick Poem. Trans. by W. J. 1695.

LETTERS OF WIT = Letters of Wit, Politicks, and Morality. Trans. by H—H—, Thomas Cheek, etc. 1701.

LOVE WITHOUT AFFECTATION = Love without Affectation, In Five Letters from a Portuguese Nun, to a French Cavalier. Done into English Verse. 1709.

LUCAN = De Bello Civili (or Pharsalia).

LUCIAN = The Works. Trans. by several Eminent Hands. 4 vols., 1710–11.

MAGNUS = A Compendious History of the Goths, Swedes, & Vandals, And Other Northern Nations. By O. Magnus. Trans. by J. S. 1658.

MAY'S LUCAN = Lucan's Pharsalia: Or The Civill Warres of Rome. Trans. by Thomas May. 1627.

H. MISSON = M. Misson's Memoirs and Observations in his Travels over England. Trans. by J. Ozell. 1719.

F. M. MISSON = A New Voyage to Italy. Trans. anonymously. 4th ed. 2 vols. (each of two parts), 1714.

MOD. PHIL. = Modern Philology. Chicago. 1903– .

NICHOLS = Literary Anecdotes of the Eighteenth Century. By John Nichols. 9 vols., 1812–15.

OED = Oxford English Dictionary.

ODYSSEY = Pope's translation, octavo ed., 1725–6.

OLDMIXON = Amores Britannici. Epistles Historical and Gallant, In English Heroic Verse. By J. Oldmixon. 1703.

OVIDIUS BRIT. = Ovidius Britannicus: Or, Love Epistles. By David Crauford. 1703.

P. = Note by Pope.

E. PHILLIPS = The New World of English Words. Ed. 1706.

PLUTARCH = Plutarch's Lives. Translated by Several Hands. 5 vols., 1711.

PMLA = Proceedings and Transactions of the Modern Language Association of America. Baltimore, 1885– .

POPE'S CORRESP. = The Correspondence of Alexander Pope, ed. George Sherburn. 5 vols., 1956.

POPE'S OWN MISCELLANY = Pope's Own Miscellany. Being a Reprint of Poems on Several Occasions 1717. Ed. N. Ault. 1935.

POPE'S PROSE = Prose Works of Alexander Pope. Ed. N. Ault. Vol. i, 1936.

PREF. TO ILIAD = Preface to Pope's translation in vol. i (quarto ed.), 1715.

PRIMER = Hymns Attributed to John Dryden [The Primer, or, Office of the B. Virgin Mary . . . 1706]. Ed. by G. R. Noyes and G. R. Potter. Univ. of California, 1937.

RES = Review of English Studies, 1925– .

ROCHESTER = Collected Works of John Wilmot Earl of Rochester. Ed. John Hayward, 1926.

SAMMES = Britannia Antiqua Illustrata. By Aylett Sammes. 1676.

SEATON = Literary Relations of England and Scandinavia in the Seventeenth Century. By M. E. Seaton. 1935.

SEDLEY = Poetical and Dramatic Works of Sir Charles Sedley. Ed. V. de Sola Pinto. 2 vols., 1928.

SHERBURN = Early Career of Alexander Pope. By George Sherburn. 1934.

SPENCE = Anecdotes, Observations, and Characters of Books and Men. Collected by Joseph Spence. Ed. S. W. Singer. 1820.

A. M. SHARP = The History of Ufton Court. By A. Mary Sharp. 1892.

SPINGARN, HISTORY = A History of Literary Criticism in the Renaissance. By J. E. Spingarn. 5th impression. New York, 1925.

SPINGARN = Critical Essays of the Seventeenth Century. Ed. by J. E. Spingarn. 3 vols., 1908.

SPRAT = The History of the Royal-Society. By T. Sprat. 2nd ed., 1702.

SPURGEON = Five Hundred Years of Chaucer Criticism and Allusion. Caroline F. E. Spurgeon. 3 vols., 1925.

ST-EVREMOND = The Works. Translated. 2 vols., 1700.

TASSO = Godfrey of Bulloigne: or the Recovery of Jerusalem. Trans. by Edward Fairfax. Ed. 1726.

TEMPLE = Miscellanea. The Second Part. By Sir William Temple. Ed. 1696.

TEMPLE, INTRODUCTION = Introduction to the History of England. By Sir William Temple. 3rd ed., 1708.

TILLOTSON = On the Poetry of Pope. By Geoffrey Tillotson. 1938.

WAKEFIELD = Works of A. Pope. Ed. Gilbert Wakefield. 1794. Observations on Pope. By G. Wakefield. 1796.

WARBURTON = The Works of A. Pope. Ed. W. Warburton. 9 vols., 1751.

WARTON = An Essay on the Genius and Writings of Pope. 2 vols. Ed. 1806.

WARTON ED. = Works of A. Pope. Ed. J. Warton. 9 vols., 1797.

WATT = The Rape of the Lock. Ed. A. F. Watt [1905].

WOTTON = Reflections upon Ancient and Modern Learning. 2nd ed., 1697.

WRIGHT = Eighteenth-Century Replies to Pope's Eloisa. By Lawrence S. Wright. (Studies in Philology, xxxi, pp. 519 ff.)

TRANSLATIONS FROM CHAUCER

INTRODUCTION

I

> 'TILL Wit it self, and tuneful Numbers cease,
> Old *Chaucer* in his antique Dress shall please:

so declared a 'Gentleman of Oxford' in a poem published in 1721.[1] And the researches of scholars of his time, the reprint of Speght's text in 1687, the new (if bad) text of Urry in 1721, show that the Oxonian was not alone in his views. Dryden himself had admitted that certain 'judges . . . think I ought not to have translated Chaucer into English . . . they suppose there is a certain veneration due to his old language; and that it is little less than profanation and sacrilege to alter it'[2]—forceful words, however slyly their edge is abated by 'translated . . . into English'. And six years later, the objections to translations are put fairly, and without humour, in the excellent verses of William Harison: Dryden, he says,

> Took wond'rous Pains to do the Author Wrong,
> And set to modern Tune his antient Song.
> Cadence, and Sound, which we so prize, and use,
> Ill suit the Majesty of *Chaucer*'s Muse;
> His Language only can his Thoughts express,
> And honest *Clytus* scorns the *Persian* Dress.[3]

But there was much said and done on Dryden's side. Six years earlier than the *Fables*, Sir Thomas Pope Blount, whom no one could accuse of irreverence, had acknowledged that 'we despise [Chaucer's] old fashion'd Phrase, and Obsolete Words'[4]; and Dryden's *Preface* to the *Fables*, brilliantly supported by the translations themselves, stands like a gateway to a period of modernizing in verse which has not yet closed.[5] Dryden's work, followed by

---

1. *The Grove; Or, A Collection of Original Poems . . . By W. Walsh, Esq; Dr. J. Donne . . . And other Eminent Hands*, p. 105.
2. *Essays*, ii 266.
3. *Woodstock Park*, 1706, p. 4.
4. *De Re Poetica*, 1694, p. 42 (second series).
5. A modern version of the *Canterbury Tales* in verse appeared in 1934.

Pope's, set the fashion, and Professor Spurgeon goes so far as to say that 'it was in the dress provided by them that Chaucer was principally known to readers of the eighteenth century.'[1] 'Astrophil' in the *Gentleman's Magazine* of January 1740 devoted over thirty lines to a panegyric of Chaucer but ended by advising his readers to see him in the 'graceful polish' of Pope and Dryden; and Horace Walpole, even as late as 1781, refused a 'first edition' for a guinea, declaring that he preferred Chaucer in Dryden and Baskerville to Chaucer in his own language and black letter.[2]

In 1741 the *Canterbury Tales*, or eleven of them at least, had become available in modernized couplets in the collection supervised by George Ogle. The modernizations of the eighteenth century cannot be dismissed as hackwork: they were often done by serious poets who aimed at making an original contribution. Dryden, and Pope with Dryden as master,[3] produced original poems, and Henry Brooke was only an extreme instance when, in his translation of the 'Man of Law's Tale', he enlarged Chaucer's 35 lines on poverty to 168.[4] 'Translation' is often freely passing over into 'imitation'.[5] Dryden interpolated passages of his own—his version enlarged on Chaucer's by about one sixth.[6] Pope translates much more econo-

1. *Five Hundred Years of Chaucer Criticism and Allusion*, by Caroline F. E. Spurgeon, 1925, i xliii. I am indebted to this book for several of my instances.

2. Letter to Mason, 13 Nov. 1781. Urry's was the first text presented in roman type. It may be noted that, although black letter was tiresome to read, the spelling of the 1687 edition is almost entirely modern. Modern readers are apt to underestimate the difficulty that eighteenth-century readers found in the language of earlier English literature, not only when reading Chaucer, but when reading Shakespeare and the Elizabethans. The twentieth-century vocabulary includes many early words that the eighteenth century had forgotten. The point is well made by Spurgeon, i xli f.

3. Pope's translations borrow many phrases from Dryden's: A. Schade makes a list of those he has discovered in 'January and May' (*Ueber das Verhältniss von Pope's 'January and May' und 'The Wife of Bath. Her Prologue' zu den entsprechenden Abschnitten von Chaucer's Canterbury Tales*, in *Englische Studien*, xxv 115–23); I have reproduced the most striking in my notes, and am also indebted to this list for some other parallels.

4. Spurgeon, i xlvii.

5. For definitions of these terms, see Introduction to the *Temple of Fame*, p. 223 below.

6. Lounsbury, *Studies in Chaucer* (1892), iii 165.

mically, greatly reducing the number of lines, but his tone and much of his matter are his own. His freedom is as great as Dryden's, but it does not altogether take the form of Dryden's.

Pope made his translations as a boy: 'Mr *Dryden*'s *Fables* [1700] came out about that time, which occasion'd the Translations from Chaucer'.[1] Even with the 'Preface' to the *Fables* before him, he cannot long have hesitated in his choice of what kind of tale to translate. Dryden's weighty words might have been expected to steer him off the 'marriage group' and on to innocent pieces which, as Warton seems to suggest,[2] he was well fitted to translate. Dryden had decided to 'confine [his] choice to such tales of Chaucer as savour nothing of immodesty'. And among the names of the pieces avoided are those of the pieces Pope chose: 'If I had desired more to please than to instruct, [these] would have procured me as many friends and readers, as there are *beaux* and ladies of pleasure in the town.'[3] 'Above all', he has avoided the 'Wife of Bath Her Prologue'. Like Chaucer himself, Dryden—an old man, a Roman Catholic, looking to the grave and beyond it—cheers his spirit with a palinode. But because Pope—a young man, a Roman Catholic—paid no attention, he need not be set down as out to catch the public Dryden had piously forgone. Pope chose his pieces because they are comic pieces—comic pieces about marriage, a subject always engaging, and at that time, as it happened, very much under discussion—and because Chaucer was esteemed by Pope's age mainly as a comic poet. For the Elizabethans, as for the twentieth century, Chaucer was first of all the poet of *Troilus and Criseyde*, but for the

---

1. *Advertisement*, *Works* (1736), iii v (by 'Translations' Pope means 'January and May' and the 'Wife of Bath Her Prologue': the *Temple of Fame* is an 'imitation'). This statement must be read alongside a companion statement that 'January and May' 'was done at sixteen or seventeen Years of Age' (*id.*, 135), which would make its date 1704–5. (Pope quotes l. 302 as a prosodic instance in his letter to Walsh—dated in print as 22 Oct. 1706—which suggests that it is fresh in his memory.) In view of his statement in the *Advertisement*, Sherburn's suggestion (*Early Career*, p. 71) that 'possibly Pope's modernization of [the *Wife of Bath Her*] *Prologue* was suggested by Gay's attempt with the lady [in his comedy *The Wife of Bath*]' is weakened. Pope may, of course, have revised the poem at this time (1713) for its publication in 1714.

2. 'it were to be wish'd, Pope had exercised his pencil on the pathetic story of the Patience of Grisilda, or Troilus and Cressida . . .' (ii 7).

3. *Essays*, ii 263.

young and serious-minded Addison he is a jester and apparently nothing more, a jester whom unfortunately Time has had the laugh of:

> But Age has Rusted what the *Poet* writ,
> Worn out his Language, and obscur'd his Wit:
> In vain he jests in his unpolish'd strain,
> And tries to make his Readers laugh in vain.[1]

In the period between the comparative neglect of Chaucer in the earlier seventeenth century and the medieval revival later in the eighteenth, Chaucer is looked on as 'facetious', 'a Joking Bard', a teller of 'the *jocund* Tale', a 'laughing Sage', a storyteller who 'tell[s] his Tales with leering Glee'.[2] For Lady Mary Wortley Montagu 'ribaldry and rhyme' are 'Rever'd from Chaucer's down to Dryden's time', a view repeated in the *Grub Street Journal*.[3] The translations of the time are mainly translations of the comic poems: the 'Miller's Tale' is translated by both Samuel Cobb[4] and John Smith,[5] the 'Reve's' by Betterton,[6] the 'Shipman's' by Henry Travers.[7] Those who mimic Chaucer's style and vocabulary—Prior, Pope, Gay—write on comic themes. Chaucer, indeed, appears as part of the literary tradition which, beginning in the

1. Dryden's Miscellanies: *The Annual Miscellany*, 1694, p. 318.

2. The descriptions are those of Evelyn, *Poems By Several Hands . . . Collected by N. Tate*, 1685, p. 91; Samuel Cobb, *Poetæ Britannici*, 1700?, p. 10; William Diaper, *Dryades*, 1713, p. 2; Thomson, 'Summer', l. 1576; *The Oxford Sausage*, 1764, p. 158; and cf. also Judith Madan, 'The Progress of Poetry' in *The Flower-Piece . . . By Several Hands*, 1731, p. 134; and William Thompson, 'Garden Inscriptions' in *The Poetical Calendar*, viii, 2nd edition, 1763, p. 103.

3. Spurgeon, i 329 and iii (Appendix A, p. 86).

4. *The Carpenter of Oxford, Or, The Miller's Tale, From Chaucer. Attempted in Modern English, By Samuel Cobb . . . To which are added, Two Imitations of Chaucer . . . By Matthew Prior . . .* 1712.

5. *Poems upon Several Occasions. By Mr. Smith . . . MDCCXIII*, pp. 307 ff. Smith argues the subject of Chaucer's indecency: 'Yet Old *Chaucer* seems to plead hard for his broad gap-tooth'd Obscenities, and *Catullus* before him has done the same' (p. iv).

6. 'The Miller of Trompington, Or, the Reve's Tale from Chaucer' in Lintott's Miscellany, 1712, pp. 301 ff.

7. *Miscellaneous Poems and Translations . . . MDCCXXXI*, pp. 104 ff. (see R. P. Bond, *Studies in Philology*, xxv, p. 327).

middle ages, was not to die till well into the eighteenth century, the tradition of the indecently comic moral tale. Two of five *Miscellaneous Poetical Novels* published in 1705 employ the January–May theme: *The Unequal Marriage* and the *Cudgell'd Cuckold nicely pleas'd.* The Wife of Bath was a well-known character, apart from Chaucer. The ballad 'The Wanton Wife of Bath' is reprinted at intervals in the seventeenth century.[1] Even if Swift is ignorant of the source of the character—he may be joking—he is not ignorant of the character: 'I have heard of the Wife of Bath', he tells Gay, 'I think in Shakespeare.'[2] And the only two commentaries that Richard Brathwait finally accomplished after setting out, fifty years earlier, to comment on all the *Canterbury Tales*, are those on the 'Miller's Tale' and the 'Wife of Bath's Prologue'.[3]

The emphasis on the ribaldry, moral or unmoral, of Chaucer did not mean that his more solemn things went unregarded. It was Pepys after all who put Dryden on to translating the character of the good parson.[4] Betterton translated the rest of the 'Prologue', as well as the 'Reve's Tale'.[5] And Pope's enthusiasm for Chaucer is shown at its best in his words to Spence: 'I read Chaucer still with as much pleasure as almost any of our poets. He is a master of manners, of description, and the first tale-teller in the true enlivened natural way'.[6] And overleaf he is found according to Chaucer 'the spirit of poetry, and the descriptiveness' which he considered lacking in Gower.[7] He remembers Chaucer as the author of the line 'So pity soonest runs in gentle minds'—though he quotes it in Dryden's version.[8] He imitates the *Hous of Fame* as well as translates two

1. See Spurgeon, iii (Appendix A, pp. 54, 76).

2. Letter to Gay, 20 Nov. 1729.

3. *A Comment upon Two Tales*, ed. C. F. E. Spurgeon, Chaucer Soc., 1901.

4. Spurgeon, i 270 f.

5. 'Chaucer's Characters, or the Introduction to the Canterbury Tales' in Lintott's Miscellany, 1712, pp. 245 ff. For Pope's hand in Betterton's translations, see Caryll's letter to Pope, 23 May 1712, Johnson's *Lives*, iii 108, and Warton's edition of Pope, ii 166. An anonymous translation of 'The Court of Love', then believed to be Chaucer's, appeared in *Ovid's Art of Love* (translated), 1709, pp. 349 ff. Pope ascribed it to A. Mainwaring. (See *European Mag.*, Oct. 1787, p. 261.)

6. p. 19.

7. Cf. his letter to Judith Cowper, 26 Sept. 1723.

8. Letter to Henry Cromwell, 24 July 1711; and Dryden, *Palamon and Arcite*, ii 331 f.

comic pieces. But, of course, Chaucer was also a poet of 'humour',[1] the most brilliant teller of broad tales and, outside Shakespeare, the most brilliant presenter of broad characters; and as such he was rightly valued. But, if Pope liked Chaucer's fun, he cared to reproduce it only up to a point. As Warton noted, Pope 'has omitted or softened the grosser and more offensive passages'[2] of the 1687 text, and he was later to show contempt for those who learn 'Chaucer's worst ribaldry . . . by rote'.[3] He did not, however, escape one critic: the pious John Hughes—'too grave a poet for me,' said Swift[4] —withdrew most of his contributions from the 1714 miscellany when he learned that, *inter alia*, Pope's 'Wife of Bath Her Prologue' was to appear in it.[5] And Pope himself requested, or was made to take, his own palinode at the hands of Warburton:

> The Juvenile translations . . . it was never his intention to bring into this Edition of his Works, on account of the levity of some, the freedom of others, and the little importance of any. But these being the property of other men, the Editor had it not in his power to follow the Author's intention.[6]

II

Pope was not simply presenting Chaucerian japes to the unscholarly or the lazy. He wished to make original variations on Chaucer's theme.

In the first place there was the metre. The Oxonian spoke of Chaucer's 'tuneful Numbers', but his compliment is cancelled out forty years later when Hugh Dalrymple writes of Chaucer's 'tune-

1. Pope supports Chaucer as a poet of 'humour' against a charge which he wrongly attributed to Addison. Addison's lines on Chaucer are quoted above. They do not say that Chaucer's humour is poor; they say it has been rusted with age. Pope, who makes a further error in believing the poem only to have been published posthumously, corrects what was never wrong: '[Addison's] character of Chaucer is diametrically opposed to the truth; he blames him for want of humour' (Spence, p. 50). The ardour of 'diametrically' is interesting.

2. ii 7.

3. *Im. of Hor.*, Ep. II i, 'To Augustus', l. 37.

4. Letter to Pope, 3 Sept. 1735.

5. DNB.

6. Works, 1751, i v.

less numbers'.[1] In 1721 'tuneful Numbers' might have meant one of two things: that Chaucer's lines had what Dryden called 'the rude sweetness of a Scotch tune'[2]; or that Chaucer wrote regular verse that scribal ignorance and carelessness had broken into rudeness.[3] Scholars holding the latter view were right and Dryden was wrong, but there was little in Speght's text to point Dryden's error. Dryden and Pope—Pope speaks of Chaucer's 'unequal Measures'[4] —did not read Chaucer in a good text. But even if they had divined that Chaucer's heroic couplets were regular, they would still have wanted to translate them into their own kind of regular heroic couplets. There are one or two lines that Pope leaves almost unchanged in his translation, e.g.,

> When tender Youth has wedded stooping Age.[5]

Such lines were retained because 'by accident' Chaucer had hit on a form of line that Pope could place in his own poem, and enjoy placing.[6] But usually Pope needed, as Curll put it, to 'set [Chaucer] to Music'.[7]

The new metre is part of a larger change. Dryden had put a current criticism clearly:

> Chaucer, I confess, is a rough diamond, and must first be polished, ere he shines . . . living in our early days of poetry, he writes not always of a piece; but sometimes mingles trivial things with those of greater moment. Sometimes also, though not often, he runs riot, like Ovid, and knows not when he has said enough.[8]

1. Spurgeon, i 421.

2. *Essays*, ii 258. Thomas Yalden, in 1693, speaks of 'tuneful *Chaucer*' (*To Mr. Congreve*, in Dryden's Miscellanies, iii, p. 347).

3. Speght and Urry held this view, see Spurgeon, i xxviii, 325.

4. Note on *Im. of Hor.*, Ep. II i, 'To Augustus', l. 97.

5. 'January and May', l. 340.

6. As an instance of metrical regularization, see 'January and May', ll. 69–76. Each of these four couplets contains one Biblical instance. In Chaucer the four instances occupy 4, 3, 2½, 3½ lines each. The regularization does not stop there: Pope places the instances in chronological order.

7. *The Life of Mr. John Gay*, 1733, pp. 7 f.; where Curll quotes the 'Wife of Bath Her Prologue', ll. 100–5 with the introductory comment: '. . . *Chaucer*, whose Ditty on this Head Mr. *Pope* hath thus set to Music'. Cf. the quotation from Harison, p. 3 above.

8. *Essays*, ii 265.

This criticism comes strangely from a poet who spins Chaucer out to greater length, disregarding the current slang in which 'Canterbury tale' meant an old man's yarn.[1] But Dryden's words represent the views of Pope and explain his practice. It needed the twentieth century to see how wrong those views are, to see how often Chaucer stands outside what seems amiss in his stories, that the responsibility for redundancy and shapelessness often rests on the dramatic necessities of the tellers. Pope corrects, not Chaucer, but the Merchant and the Wife of Bath.

III

All translators, except those translating modern books, modernize. Professor Mackail's version of the *Æneid* embodies a modern conception of the archaic. But in Pope's time modernization was more complete, and little attempt was made to invent a historical equivalent. Dryden's *Æneid* had been done in the poetic idiom of the day. It was into this idiom that Pope translated Chaucer (the alternative was to mimic Chaucer's actual style and vocabulary as he did in his 'Imitations of English Poets'). So completely Popian are most of the lines of his two translations that it is a shock to find distinctively medieval matter remaining unchanged. It is a shock to find Pope's Wife referring to her pilgrimage to Jerusalem[2]—instead of to her jaunt to Tunbridge Wells. And what are Bacchus and Venus doing at the marriage of *his* January and May?[3] Pope's style is so much his own that one resents his 'translations' not being a little nearer to 'imitations'.

IV

The 'Merchant's Tale' is at bottom a *fabliau*, an anecdote with point. Pope read at the head of the story in Speght's text: 'Old January marrieth young May, and for his unequal match receiveth a foul reward.' Yet it is a commonplace that Chaucer creates the illusion that his *fabliau* puppets are human beings, individuals experiencing completely the events which the story provides them with. Chaucer can create his characters whole. He can accept them

1. See *Tatler* and Defoe, listed in Spurgeon, i 311 (bis) and 366.
2. ll. 243 f.
3. ll. 326 ff.

dressed and undressed. They do not seem actual just because, on occasions, they are stripped naked; they are stripped naked because nakedness seems merely an extension of their apparent actuality. Chaucer's story-telling seems nothing more than the happy and effortless tilting of a sunny mirror across which everything glides with equal candour—the smiles and words of Placebo, the slack skin of January's neck, the bride 'brought a-bedde as stille as stoon', the act in the tree. The story would be amusing if told in two hundred words—it would therefore have pleased Aristotle—but Chaucer does not leave it at that.

In making his modernization Pope loses much of this imperturbably honest human actuality of person, speech, and even incident. He makes the story shrink back into something more like a *fabliau*, a neatly told story with point. He tells the story as a story was told in the first decade of the eighteenth century, a date intermediary between the stories of Dryden and those of Defoe and Richardson. This procedure entails a neglect of Chaucer's depth of human actuality, but gains 'intellectually': Pope takes every opportunity for contributing satiric portrait and comment of his own.

The same kind of thing happens in the translation of the 'Wife of Bath Her Prologue'. Pope has to choose which way his modernization shall jump. He could have modernized the Wife by preserving the full flavour of her talk. This course would have meant degrading her in the social scale, making her, say, an oyster-woman. Or, conversely, he could have modernized her by allowing her to retain her social rank and consequently refining the style and flavour of her talk. Pope chose the second alternative. He modernizes the flavour but does not change the class. Some of the animal similes are omitted and 'as an horse' is diminished to 'like a dog',[1] the Christian oaths are paganized and so made more respectable, the Billingsgate abuse is toned down, the already half-veiled 'indecencies' are veiled still more, the rambling repetitions and redundancies are removed, the flashes of horror are omitted.[2] Pope sacrifices the completeness of a complicated human confession and provides instead all the ease, the gay regularity, the contemporary satire. His rhetoric is decreed by the sophistication. It satisfies in itself. To

1. l. 152.

2. E.g., see note on ll. 407–10. Dryden had omitted such horror in his Chaucer translations, see Lounsbury, op. cit., iii 169.

retort to it is to break it. One is left with a closed mind, but, for the occasion, closedness appears desirable for a mind. In reading Chaucer much of one's delight comes from other qualities—from the fluidity, the improvisation, the indiscretion, the touch-and-go, the streaming lips. In Pope the wheels of a machine fascinate by their turning. This, at least, is the effect Pope is aiming at producing. He does not here produce it uniformly. But he produces it often enough to indicate that he is foreseeing and working towards the style of *Moral Essays*, ii, 'Of the Characters of Women'.

NOTE ON THE NOTES

The text of Chaucer quoted in the notes to these two translations is that of the 1687 edition. The line numbering (sometimes limited to a number in square brackets) is that of Skeat's edition. 'Pope' signifies that Pope is making an addition of his own.

JANUARY and *MAY*;

OR, THE

Merchant's Tale:

FROM

CHAUCER.

NOTE ON THE TEXT

Unless anonymous work had already appeared, 'January and May' was, along with the *Pastorals*, the first of Pope's poems to be published. It appeared in Dryden's *Poetical Miscellanies: The Sixth Part*... 1709 which was published by Tonson on 2 May.[1] The text printed in the *Works* of 1717 makes a considerable number of verbal improvements and deletes two couplets. The *Works* of 1736 shows a further revision of some half-dozen words. The *Works* of 1741 agrees with 1736 in error but this does not necessarily nullify its few small variants (retained in 1745 and 1751) which may be Pope's and which I have accepted as his. The variants in the *Works* of 1751 are negligible, as one would expect from Warburton's statement (quoted above, p. xi).

The basis of the present text is that of 1709 altered in accordance with Pope's revisions and with the principles described in the General Note on the Text (pp. x f. above). The 1709 punctuation is more archaic than that of later editions, but has its own intelligible system. Owing to the suspect authority of 1741–51, I have considered their variant at l. 415 to spring from a compositor's aberration.

KEY TO THE CRITICAL APPARATUS

1709 = First edition, in *Poetical Miscellanies: The Sixth Part*, Griffith 1.
1717 = Works, quarto, Griffith 79.
1736 = Works, vol. iii, octavo, Griffith 418.
1741 = Works, vol. i, part 2, octavo, Griffith 521.
1745 = Works, vol. i, part 2, octavo, Griffith 611.
1751 = Works, ed. Warburton, vol. ii, Griffith 644.

1. The agreement, dated 4 March 1707/8, between Pope and Tonson is reproduced opposite p. 85 of Sherburn.

JANUARY AND MAY

THERE liv'd in *Lombardy*, as Authors write,
In Days of old, a wise and worthy Knight;
Of gentle Manners, as of gen'rous Race,
Blest with much Sense, more Riches, and some Grace.
Yet led astray by *Venus*' soft Delights,
He scarce cou'd rule some Idle Appetites;
For long ago, let Priests say what they cou'd,
Weak, sinful Laymen were but Flesh and Blood.
  But in due Time, when Sixty Years were o'er,
He vow'd to lead this Vicious Life no more.
Whether pure Holiness inspir'd his Mind,
Or Dotage turn'd his Brain, is hard to find;
But his high Courage prick'd him forth to wed,
And try the Pleasures of a lawful Bed.
This was his nightly Dream, his daily Care,
And to the Heav'nly Pow'rs his constant Pray'r,
Once, ere he dy'd, to taste the blissful Life
Of a kind Husband, and a loving Wife.

6 He cou'd not rule his Carnal Appetites; *1709*.
10 this] that *1709*.

---

title] *This Translation was done at sixteen or seventeen Years of Age* [P. 1736–51].

1–18. Chaucer 1–22.

1. Cf. Dryden, 'The Cock and the Fox', ll. 1 f.

as Authors write] Pope; in Chaucer's manner.

2. Pope follows Dryden ('Palamon and Arcite', i 1) in his translation of 'Whylome'.

3 f. Pope.

5 f. Chaucer 5 f.: And followed aye his bodily delite
On women, there as was his appetite.

7. Pope.

13. *high Courage*] Chaucer 10: 'a great corage'. Cf. ll. 170 and 331 below.

16. *Heav'nly Pow'rs*] Chaucer 14: 'our lord'.

18. After this line Pope omits Chaucer 17–22 as 'redundant'. ll. 19–21 read:
None other life (said he) is worth a beane:
For wedlocke is so easie and so cleane,
That in this world it is a paradise.

These Thoughts he fortify'd with Reasons still,
(For none want Reasons to confirm their Will)
Grave Authors say, and witty Poets sing,
That honest Wedlock is a glorious Thing:
But Depth of Judgment most in him appears,
Who wisely weds in his maturer Years.
Then let him chuse a Damsel young and fair,
To bless his Age, and bring a worthy Heir;
To sooth his Cares, and free from Noise and Strife
Conduct him gently to the Verge of Life.
Let sinful Batchelors their Woes deplore,
Full well they merit all they feel, and more:
Unaw'd by Precepts, Human or Divine,
Like Birds and Beasts, promiscuously they join:
Nor know to make the present Blessing last,
To hope the future, or esteem the past;
But vainly boast the Joys they never try'd,
And find divulg'd the Secrets they wou'd hide.
The marry'd Man may bear his Yoke with Ease,
Secure at once himself and Heav'n to please;
And pass his inoffensive Hours away,
In Bliss all Night, and Innocence all Day:

19–50. Chaucer 23–66.

19 f. Pope.

21 f. Chaucer [49 f.] mentions authorities: 'some clerkes' and Theophrastus. For Pope's use of Theophrastus see note on ll. 43–50 below. Cf. Dryden, 'Wife of Bath Her Tale', 464 f.: Philosophers have said, and Poets sing,
That a glad Poverty's an honest Thing.

28. There is no such image at this point in Chaucer, but Pope may have been adapting l. 157 where January tells his friends that he is hoar and old,
And almost (God wot) on the pits brinke.
(Pope's counterpart to this line is l. 88.)

31, 33–5. Pope.

35. Cf. Dryden, Ovid's *Metam.*, i 644: 'and hates the Joys she never try'd.'

36. Chaucer 35 f.: On brotell ground they bilden brotelnesse,
They find freelte, when they wenen secrenesse.
(Skeat reads 'sikernesse'.)

39 f. Pope.

Tho' Fortune change, his constant Spouse remains,
Augments his Joys, or mitigates his Pains.
  But what so pure, which envious Tongues will spare?
Some wicked Wits have libell'd all the Fair:
With matchless Impudence they stile a Wife
The dear-bought Curse and lawful Plague of Life:
A Bosome Serpent, a Domestick Evil,
A Night-Invasion, and a Mid-day-Devil.
Let not the Wise these slandrous Words regard,
But curse the Bones of ev'ry lying Bard.
  All other Goods by Fortune's Hand are giv'n,
A Wife is the peculiar Gift of Heav'n:
Vain Fortune's Favours, never at a Stay,
Like empty Shadows, pass, and glide away;
One solid Comfort, our Eternal Wife,
Abundantly supplies us all our Life:
This Blessing lasts, (if those who try, say true)
As long as Heart can wish—and longer too.
  Our Grandsire *Adam*, ere of *Eve* possest,
Alone, and ev'n in Paradise, unblest,
With mournful Looks the blissful Scenes survey'd,
And wander'd in the solitary Shade:
The Maker saw, took pity, and bestow'd
Woman, the last, the best reserv'd of God.

51 *1751 does not open new paragraph.* 54 empty] flitting *1709.*
64 reserv'd] Reserve *1709–17.*

43–50. Pope's own wording of the views of Theophrastus [52–60].

43. Perhaps suggested by Chaucer 51:

What force though Theophrast list to lie.

46. Cf. Dryden, *Iliad*, i 752: 'My Household Curse, my lawful Plague . . .'

51–8. Chaucer 67–74.

54. Chaucer 71: That passen as a shaddow on a wall.

55. *our Eternal Wife*] Cf. Dryden, Persius, *Sat.*, ii 29.

59–64. Chaucer 75–92. Pope omits the 'philosophy' which introduces and concludes the instance from Genesis.

64. Pope.

A Wife! ah gentle Deities, can he
That has a Wife, e'er feel Adversity?
Wou'd Men but follow what the Sex advise,
All things wou'd prosper, all the World grow wise.
Twas by *Rebecca*'s Aid that *Jacob* won
His Father's Blessing from an Elder Son:
Abusive *Nabal* ow'd his forfeit Life
To the wise Conduct of a prudent Wife:
Heroick *Judeth*, as old *Hebrews* show,
Preserv'd the *Jews*, and slew th'*Assyrian* Foe:
At *Hester*'s Suit, the Persecuting Sword
Was sheath'd, and *Israel* liv'd to bless the Lord.
These weighty Motives *January* the Sage
Maturely ponder'd in his riper Age;
And charm'd with virtuous Joys, and sober Life,
Wou'd try that Christian Comfort, call'd a Wife:
His Friends were summon'd, on a Point so nice,
To pass their Judgment, and to give Advice;
But fix'd before, and well resolv'd was he,
(As Men that ask Advice are wont to be.)
My Friends, he cry'd, (and cast a mournful Look
Around the Room, and sigh'd before he spoke:)

73 old *Hebrews*] the Scriptures *1709* [*cf. l. 684 below*].

65–8. Chaucer 93–117. The idealized couple in Chaucer break out into direct speech.

69–76. Chaucer 118–30. See Introduction, p. 9 *n.* 6 above, and Genesis xxvii, 1 Samuel xxv, and the apocryphal books, Judith and Esther.

73. *Heroick*] Pope sees Judith as an epic figure.

After l. 76 Pope omits the quotations from Seneca and Cato, and the further opinions of the Merchant [131–48].

77–84. Chaucer 149–54.

80. *Christian Comfort*] Pope.

81. Cf. Dryden, Juvenal vi 639:

The rest are summon'd, on a point so nice.

83 f. Pope, in Chaucer's manner.

85–98. Chaucer 155–70.

Beneath the Weight of threescore Years I bend,
And worn with Cares, am hastning to my End;
How I have liv'd, alas you know too well,
In worldly Follies, which I blush to tell;
But gracious Heav'n has op'd my Eyes at last,
With due Regret I view my Vices past,
And as the Precept of the Church decrees,
Will take a Wife, and live in Holy Ease.
But since by Counsel all things shou'd be done,
And many Heads are wiser still than one;
Chuse you for me, who best shall be content
When my Desire's approv'd by your Consent.
  One Caution yet is needful to be told,
To guide your Choice; This Wife must not be old:
There goes a Saying, and 'twas shrewdly said,
Old Fish at Table, but young Flesh in Bed.
My Soul abhors the tastless, dry Embrace,
Of a stale Virgin with a Winter Face;
In that cold Season Love but treats his Guest
With Beanstraw, and tough Forage, at the best.
No crafty Widows shall approach my Bed,
Those are too wise for Batchelors to wed;

101 shrewdly] wisely *1709*.

87. Chaucer 156: 'I am hore and old'.
88. See note on l. 28 above; and cf. Dryden, 'To . . . Mr. Congreve', 66:
    Already I am worn with Cares and Age.
93 f. Pope. He omits Chaucer 164 f.:
    I pray you shapeth for my mariage
    All suddainly, for I woll not abide.
99–112. Chaucer 171–86.
101–6. Chaucer 174–8:
    Old fish and young flesh woll I haue faine:
    Better is (qd. he) a Pike than a Pikereell,
    And bet than old Beefe is the tender Veell.
    I woll no woman of thirtie Winter age,
    It nis but Beanstraw and great forage.
107. Pope omits the reference to Wade's boot [180].

As subtle Clerks by many Schools are made,
Twice-marry'd Dames are Mistresses o' th' Trade:
But young and tender Virgins, rul'd with Ease,
We form like Wax, and mold them as we please.
  Conceive me Sirs, nor take my Sense amiss,
'Tis what concerns my Soul's Eternal Bliss;
Since if I found no Pleasure in my Spouse,
As Flesh is frail, and who (God help me) knows?
Then shou'd I live in lewd Adultery,
And sink downright to *Satan* when I die.
Or were I curst with an unfruitful Bed,
The righteous End were lost for which I wed,
To raise up Seed to bless the Pow'rs above,
And not for Pleasure only, or for Love.
Think not I dote; 'tis Time to take a Wife,
When vig'rous Blood forbids a chaster Life:
Those that are blest with Store of Grace Divine
May live like Saints, by Heav'ns Consent, and mine.
  And since I speak of Wedlock, let me say,
As, thank my Stars, in modest Truth I may,
My Limbs are active, still I'm sound at Heart,

121 to bless] t'adore *1709*.

113–26. Chaucer 187–212.
120. Chaucer's Merchant avows [194–6]:

Yet had I leuer hounds had me eaten,
Than that mine heritage should fall
In straunge honds. . .

127–38. Chaucer 213–24.
127 f. Dryden, 'The Cock and the Fox', 616 f.:

But since I speak of Singing let me say,
As with an upright Heart I safely may.

thank my Stars] Chaucer 213: 'God be thanked'.
129–36. Chaucer 214–22:

I feele my lims hole and sufficiaunt
To doen all that a man belongeth to:
I wot my selue best what I may do.
Though I be hore, I fare as doth a tree,
That blossometh ere that fruit ywox bee

And a new Vigour springs in ev'ry Part.
Think not my Virtue lost, tho' Time has shed
These rev'rend Honours on my Hoary Head;
Thus Trees are crown'd with Blossoms white as Snow,
The Vital Sap then rising from below:
Old as I am, my lusty Limbs appear
Like Winter Greens, that flourish all the Year.
Now Sirs you know to what I stand inclin'd,
Let ev'ry Friend with Freedom speak his Mind.
He said; the rest in diff'rent Parts divide,
The knotty Point was urg'd on either Side;
Marriage, the Theme on which they all declaim'd,
Some prais'd with Wit, and some with Reason blam'd.
'Till, what with Proofs, Objections, and Replies,
Each wondrous positive, and wondrous wise;
There fell between his Brothers a Debate,
Placebo This was call'd, and *Justin* That.
First to the Knight *Placebo* thus begun,
(Mild were his Looks, and pleasing was his Tone)
Such Prudence, Sir, in all your Words appears,
As plainly proves, Experience dwells with Years:
Yet you pursue sage *Solomon*'s Advice,

140 either] ev'ry *1709*. 145 between] betwixt *1709*.

The blossomd tree is neither drie ne dead:
I feele no where hore but on my head.
Mine heart and my lims been as greene,
As Laurell is through the yeare to seene.

Pope remembers Dryden, 'The Flower and the Leaf', 583 f.:

Ev'n when the vital Sap retreats below,
Ev'n when the hoary Head is hid in Snow.

139–46. Chaucer 225–33.

139 f. Cf. Addison, Ovid's *Metam.*, iii ('The Birth of Bacchus', 7 f.):

The Hearers into diff'rent Parts divide,
And Reasons are produc'd on either Side.

142. Chaucer 227: Some blameth it, some praiseth it certaine.

144. Pope.

147–55. Chaucer 234–46.

To Work by Counsel when Affairs are nice:
But, with the Wiseman's Leave, I must protest,
So may my Soul arrive at Ease and Rest,
As still I hold your own Advice the best.
  Sir, I have liv'd a Courtier all my Days,
And study'd Men, their Manners, and their Ways;
And have observ'd this useful Maxim still,
To let my Betters always have their Will.
Nay, if my Lord affirm'd that Black was White,
My Word was this; *Your Honour's in the right.*
Th'assuming Wit, who deems himself so wise

156–75. Chaucer 247–74:

For brother mine, take of me this motife,
I haue been now a court man all my life,
And God wot, though I now vnworthy bee,
I have stonden in full great degree
Abouten Lords in full great estate:
Yet had I neuer with none of hem debate,
I neuer hem contraried truly.
I wot well that my lord can more than I,
That he saith, I hold it firme and stable,
I say the same, or els thing semblable.
A full great foole is any counsailour,
That serueth any Lord of high honour,
That dare presume, or once thinke it,
That his counsaile should passe his lords wit,
Nay, Lords be no fooles I sweare by my fay.
Ye haue your selfe spoken here to day
So high sentence, so holy, and so well,
That I consent, and confirme every dell
Your words all, and your opinioun.
By God there nis no man in all this toun
Ne in Italie, coud better haue saied:
Christ holdeth him of this full well apaied.
And truly it is an high courage
Of any man that is stopen in age,
To take a yong wife, by my father kin:
Your heart hongeth on a jolly pin.
  Doth now in this matter right as you lest,
For finally I hold it for the best.

Pope exchanges irony for direct satire and so needs to turn back at l. 166

As his mistaken Patron to advise,
Let him not dare to vent his dang'rous Thought;
A Noble Fool was never in a Fault.
This Sir affects not you, whose ev'ry Word
Is weigh'd with Judgment, and befits a Lord:
Your Will is mine; and is (I will maintain)
Pleasing to God, and shou'd be so to Man;
At least, your Courage all the World must praise,
Who dare to wed in your declining Days.
Indulge the Vigour of your mounting Blood,
And let grey Fools be Indolently good;
Who past all Pleasure, damn the Joys of Sense,
With rev'rend Dulness, and grave Impotence.
  Justin, who silent sate, and heard the Man,
Thus, with a Philosophick Frown, began.
  A Heathen Author, of the first Degree,
(Who, tho' not *Faith*, had *Sense* as well as We)
Bids us be certain our Concerns to trust
To those of gen'rous Principles, and just.
The Venture's greater, I'll presume to say,
To give your Person than your Goods away:
And therefore, Sir, as you regard your Rest,
First learn your Lady's Qualities at least:
Whether she's chast or rampant, proud or civil;
Meek as a Saint, or haughty as the Devil;
Whether an easie, fond, familiar *Fool*,

180 Bids] Bid *1709*. 188 familiar] insipid *1709*.

176–215. Chaucer 275–321.

178 f. Chaucer 279 f.: 'Senecke among his other words wise Saith . . .'
l. 179 is Pope's addition.

186–93. Chaucer 289–99:

Wheder she be sober, wise, or dronkelew,
Or proud, or any other waies a shrew,
A chider, or a waster of thy good,
Other rich or poore, or els a man is wood:
All be it so, that no man find shall
None in this world, that trotteth hole in all,

Or such a *Wit* as no Man e'er can rule?
'Tis true, Perfection none must hope to find
In all this World, much less in Womankind;
But if her Virtues prove the larger Share,
Bless the kind Fates, and think your Fortune rare.
Ah gentle Sir, take Warning of a Friend,
Who knows too well the State you thus commend
And, spight of all its Praises, must declare,
All he can find is Bondage, Cost, and Care.
Heav'n knows, I shed full many a private Tear,
And sigh in Silence, lest the World shou'd hear:
While all my Friends applaud my blissful Life,
And swear no Mortal's happier in a Wife;
Demure and chast as any Vestal Nun,
The meekest Creature that beholds the Sun!
But, by th' Immortal Pow'rs, I feel the Pain,
And he that smarts has Reason to complain.
Do what you list, for me; you must be sage,
And cautious sure; for Wisdom is in Age:
But, at these Years, to venture on the Fair!
By him, who made the Ocean, Earth, and Air,
To please a Wife when her Occasions call,
Wou'd busie the most Vig'rous of us all.
And trust me, Sir, the chastest you can chuse
Will ask Observance, and exact her Dues.
If what I speak my noble Lord offend,

Ne man, ne beast, such as men can deuise.
But natheles, it ought inough suffice
With any wife, if so were that she had
Mo good thewes, than her vices bad:
And all this asketh leisure to enquere.

197. Chaucer 303: 'but cost and care'. Cf. Dryden, 'Secular Masque', 68.
199. Pope.
202. Pope.
207. Cf. Dryden, 'Wife of Bath Her Tale', 236:
Then tell your pain: For Wisdom is in Age.
214 f. Chaucer 321: I pray you that ye be not euill apaid.

My tedious Sermon here is at an End.
'Tis well, 'tis wondrous well, the Knight replies,
Most worthy Kinsman, faith, you're mighty wise!
We, Sirs, are Fools; and must resign the Cause
To heathnish Authors, Proverbs, and old Saws.
He spoke with Scorn, and turn'd another way—
What does my Friend, my dear *Placebo* say?
I say, quoth he, by Heav'n the Man's to blame,
To slander Wives, and Wedlock's holy Name.
At this, the Council rose, without Delay;
Each, in his own Opinion, went his Way;
With full Consent, that all Disputes appeas'd,
The Knight should marry, when and where he pleas'd.
Who now but *January* exults with Joy?
The Charms of Wedlock all his Soul imploy:
Each Nymph by turns his wav'ring Mind possest,
And reign'd the short-liv'd Tyrant of his Breast;
While Fancy pictur'd ev'ry lively Part,
And each bright Image wander'd o'er his Heart.
Thus, in some publick *Forum* fix'd on high,
A Mirrour shows the Figures moving by;
Still one by one, in swift Succession, pass

220 He spoke; and turn'd, with Scorn, another way—*1709*.
223 Who ventures Sacred Marriage to defame. *1709*.
224 rose,] broke *1709*. 233 o'er] in *1709*.

216–21. Chaucer 322–7. Pope's January speaks ironical, Chaucer's direct, scorn.

222 f. Chaucer 328 f.

224–7. Chaucer 330–2.

224. *without Delay*] Chaucer 330: 'suddainly'.

228–49. Chaucer 333–60. Pope's wording is original. With l. 228 cf. Dryden, 'Palamon and Arcite', ii 426: Who now but *Palamon* exults with joy?
and 'Cymon and Iphigenia', 322: Who now exults but *Cymon* . . .?

234–7. Chaucer 338–41:

As who so tooke a mirrour polished bright,
And set it in a common market place,

The gliding Shadows o'er the polish'd Glass.
This Lady's Charms the Nicest cou'd not blame,
But vile Suspicions had aspers'd her Fame;
That was with Sense, but not with Virtue blest;
And one had Grace, that wanted all the rest.
Thus doubting long what Nymph he shou'd obey
He fix'd at last upon the youthful *May*.
Her Faults he knew not, Love is always blind,
But ev'ry Charm revolv'd within his Mind:
Her tender Age, her Form divinely Fair,
Her easie Motion, her attractive Air,
Her sweet Behaviour, her enchanting Face,
Her moving Softness, and majestick Grace.
    Much in his Prudence did our Knight rejoice,
And thought no Mortal cou'd dispute his Choice:
Once more in haste he summon'd ev'ry Friend,
And told them all, their Pains were at an End.
Heav'n that (said he) inspir'd me first to wed,
Provides a Consort worthy of my Bed;

241 that] yet *1709*. 251 his] this *1709–36*.

Then should he see many a figure pace
By his mirrour . . .

238–41. Chaucer 345–9:

For if that one had beauty in her face,
Another stont so in the peoples grace
For her sadnesse and her benignite,
That of the people greatest voice had she.
And some were rich and had bad name.

244. After this line Pope omits Chaucer 355:

And when that he was in his bed ybrought.

246–9. Chaucer 357–60:

Her fresh beauty, and her age so tender.
Her middle small, her armes long & slender,
Her wise gouernance, and her gentlenesse,
Her womanly bearing, and her sadnesse.

Pope, here and at l. 259, is indebted to Walsh, *Eclogue* v.

250–75. Chaucer 361–410.

Let none oppose th'Election, since on this
Depends my Quiet, and my future Bliss.
  A Dame there is, the Darling of my Eyes,
Young, beauteous, artless, innocent and wise;
Chast tho' not rich; and tho' not nobly born,
Of honest Parents, and may serve my Turn.
Her will I wed, if gracious Heav'n so please;
To pass my Age in Sanctity and Ease:
And thank the Pow'rs, I may possess alone
The lovely Prize, and share my Bliss with none!
If you, my Friends, this Virgin can procure,
My Joys are full, my Happiness is sure.
  One only Doubt remains; Full oft I've heard
By Casuists grave, and deep Divines averr'd;
That 'tis too much for Human Race to know
The Bliss of Heav'n above, and Earth below.
Now shou'd the Nuptial Pleasures prove so great,
To match the Blessings of the future State,
Those endless Joys were ill exchang'd for these;
Then clear this Doubt, and set my Mind at ease.
  This *Justin* heard, nor cou'd his Spleen controul,
Touch'd to the Quick, and tickl'd at the Soul.
Sir Knight, he cry'd, if this be all you dread,
Heav'n put it past your Doubt whene'er you wed,
And to my fervent Pray'rs so far consent,
That ere the Rites are o'er, you may repent!
Good Heav'n no doubt the nuptial State approves,
Since it chastises still what best it loves.

---

261. Cf. Dryden, 'The Wife of Bath Her Tale', 320:

And nothing but the Man would serve her turn;

and Spenser, *F.Q.*, I vi 22 (3).

269. Pope.

276–98. Chaucer 411–44.

276 f. Chaucer 411: 'which that hated his folly'.

282 f. Pope.

Then be not, Sir, abandon'd to Despair;
Seek, and perhaps you'll find, among the Fair,
One, that may do your Business to a Hair;
Not ev'n in Wish, your Happiness delay,
But prove the Scourge to lash you on your Way:
Then to the Skies your mounting Soul shall go,
Swift as an Arrow soaring from the Bow!
Provided still, you moderate your Joy,
Nor in your Pleasures all your Might imploy,
Let Reason's Rule your strong Desires abate,
Nor please too lavishly your gentle Mate.
Old Wives there are, of Judgment most acute,
Who solve these Questions beyond all Dispute;
Consult with those, and be of better Chear;
Marry, do Penance, and dismiss your Fear.
So said they rose, nor more the Work delay'd;
The Match was offer'd, the Proposals made:
The Parents, you may think, wou'd soon comply;
The Old have Int'rest ever in their Eye:
Nor was it hard to move the Lady's Mind;
When Fortune favours still the Fair are kind.
I pass each previous Settlement and Deed,

295 f. Chaucer 440–3:

But wade we fro this matter to another.
The wife of Bathe, if ye vnderstand
Of mariage, which ye now haue in hand,
Declareth full well in a litle space.

Pope wishes his story to be independent of its context in the *Canterbury Tales*.

298. Pope.

299–304. Chaucer 445–51.

301–4. Pope. Cf. Dryden, 'Palamon and Arcite', iii 697 f.:

(For Women to the Brave an easie Prey,
Still follow Fortune, where she leads the Way.)

302. Pope cites this line in his discussion of prosody in the letter to Walsh, 22 Oct. 1706.

305–14. Chaucer 452–64.

305, 308. Cf. Dryden, 'Palamon and Arcite', i 14:

Too long for me to write, or you to read;
Nor will with quaint Impertinence display
The Pomp, the Pageantry, the proud Array.
The Time approach'd, to Church the Parties went,
At once with carnal and devout Intent:
Forth came the Priest, and bade th'obedient Wife
Like *Sarah* or *Rebecca* lead her Life:
Then pray'd the Pow'rs the fruitful Bed to bless,
And made all sure enough with Holiness.
    And now the Palace Gates are open'd wide,
The Guests appear in Order, Side by Side,
And, plac'd in State, the Bridegroom and the Bride.
The breathing Flute's soft Notes are heard around,
And the shrill Trumpets mix their Silver Sound;
The vaulted Roofs with ecchoing Musick ring,
These touch the vocal Stops, and those the trembling
    String.
Not thus *Amphion* tun'd the warbling Lyre,
Nor *Joab* the sounding Clarion cou'd inspire,
Nor fierce *Theodamas*, whose sprightly Strain

312 or] and *1709*.
317 f. *Between these lines 1709 reads:*
    Expensive Dainties load the plenteous Boards,
    The best Luxurious *Italy* affords:

    I pass their warlike Pomp, their proud Array;
and iii 61.

306 f. Pope.

310. Pope.

312. Chaucer 460: And bad her be like Sara and Rebeck. See textual note.

314. Chaucer 464: And made all seker inow with holines.

315–40. Chaucer 465–97.

317 f. The couplet which originally stood between these two lines (see textual notes) translated Chaucer 469 f.:
    And full of instruments and of vittaile,
    And that the most deintiest of all Itaile.

Cou'd swell the Soul to Rage, and fire the Martial Train.
  Bacchus himself, the Nuptial Feast to grace,
(So Poets sing) was present on the Place;
And lovely *Venus*, Goddess of Delight,
Shook high her flaming Torch, in open Sight,
And danc'd around, and smil'd on ev'ry Knight:
Pleas'd her best Servant wou'd his Courage try,
No less in Wedlock than in Liberty.
Full many an Age old *Hymen* had not spy'd
So kind a Bridegroom, or so bright a Bride.
Ye Bards! renown'd among the tuneful Throng
For gentle Lays, and joyous Nuptial Song;
Think not your softest Numbers can display
The matchless Glories of this blissful Day;
The Joys are such as far transcend your Rage,
When tender Youth has wedded stooping Age.
  The beauteous Dame sate smiling at the Board,
And darted am'rous Glances at her Lord;
Not *Hester*'s self, whose Charms the *Hebrews* sing,
E're look'd so lovely on her *Persian* King:
Bright as the rising Sun, in Summer's Day,
And fresh and blooming as the Month of *May*!

---

325. Cf. Dryden's 'Alexander's Feast', 160:
Cou'd swell the Soul to rage, or kindle soft Desire.

326 f. Chaucer 476 f.: Neither Theodomas yet halfe so clere
At Thebes, whan the city was in dout.

328. Cf. Dryden, 'The Cock and the Fox', 687:
Ah blissful Venus, Goddess of Delight.

329. Chaucer 483: And with her firebrond in her hond about.

335–40. Chaucer invokes Martianus Capella and his *De Nuptiis Philologiæ et Mercurii* [488 ff.].

340. Chaucer 494: Whan tender youth hath wedded stooping age.
After this line Pope omits Chaucer 495–7 in which the Merchant challenges any one to say that his description is exaggerated.

341–56. Chaucer 498–527.

342. Chaucer 499: That her to behold, it seemed a feire.
(Skeat reads fayerye.)

345 f. Chaucer 504: That she was like the bright morow of May.

The joyful Knight survey'd her by his Side,
Nor envy'd *Paris* with the *Spartan* Bride:
Still as his Mind revolv'd with vast Delight
Th'entrancing Raptures of th'approaching Night;
Restless he sate, invoking ev'ry Pow'r
To speed his Bliss, and haste the happy Hour.
Mean time the vig'rous Dancers beat the Ground,
And Songs were sung, and flowing Bowls went round;
With od'rous Spices they perfum'd the Place,
And Mirth and Pleasure shone in ev'ry Face.
Damian alone, of all the Menial Train,
Sad in the midst of Triumphs, sigh'd for Pain;
Damian alone, the Knight's obsequious Squire,
Consum'd at Heart, and fed a secret Fire.
His lovely Mistress all his Soul possest,
He look'd, he languish'd, and cou'd take no Rest:
His Task perform'd, he sadly went his Way,
Fell on his Bed, and loath'd the Light of Day.

354 flowing . . . went] Healths went nimbly *1709*.
362 take] find *1709*.

348. After this line Pope omits Chaucer 511–17, in which January, thinking of the night, fears he may prove too wild for May.

351 f. Chaucer 518 f.:

Now would to God that it were waxen night,
And that the night would last euer mo.

Cf. Dryden, Ovid's *Metam.*, ix, 'The Fable of Iphis and Ianthe', 151 f.:

Invoking *Hymen*'s Name, and *Juno*'s Pow'r,
To speed the work, and haste the happy hour.

353. Chaucer 525: 'men dauncen . . . fast'. Pope echoes Milton, *Comus*, 143:

Com, knit hands, and beat the ground,

whom Dryden had already echoed at Theocritus, *Idyllium* xviii 11.

357–66. Chaucer 528–38.

360. Cf Dryden, Ovid's *Metam.*, i 668 f.:

So burns the God, consuming in desire,
And feeding in his Breast a fruitless Fire.

362. Chaucer 533 f.: So sore hath Venus hurt him with her brand.

There let him lye, 'till his relenting Dame
Weep in her turn, and waste in equal Flame.
The weary Sun, as Learned Poets write,
Forsook th'*Horizon*, and roll'd down the Light;
While glitt'ring Stars his absent Beams supply,
And Night's dark Mantle overspread the Sky.
Then rose the Guests; and as the time requir'd,
Each paid his Thanks, and decently retir'd.
The Foe once gone, our Knight prepar'd t'undress,
So keen he was, and eager to possess:
But first thought fit th'Assistance to receive,
Which grave Physicians scruple not to give;
Satyrion near, with hot *Eringo's* stood,
Cantharides, to fire the lazy Blood,

365 his] the *1709–17*. 373 prepar'd t'] wou'd strait *1709*.
378 lazy] boiling *1709*.

366. After this line Pope omits Chaucer 539–50, an invocation of the 'auctor' (though not so marked in 1687) beginning:

O perilous fire; that in the bedstraw bredeth,
O familiar foe, that his service bedeth.
O seruaunt traytour . . .

The word 'foe' may have served to remind Pope of the phrase of Dryden which he uses at l. 373 below: see note.

367–72. Chaucer 551–60.

367. *as . . . write*] Pope.

369. Pope.

373–80. Chaucer 561–8.

373. Cf. Dryden in a similar context, 'Sigismonda and Guiscardo', 173: 'The Foe once gone . . .' See note on 383 below.

375 f. Pope.

377 f. Chaucer 563 f.:

He drinketh Ipocras, clarrie, and vernage
Of spices hot, to encrease his corage;

and Constantinus Afer's *De Coitu* is mentioned [567]. Satyrion (a kind of orchis), eringo (sea holly), and cantharides (a particular kind of dried beetle) were all held to have aphrodisiac properties. The first two figure in Otway's *Souldiers Fortune*, Act v, the third is referred to in Beaumont and Fletcher's *Philaster*, IV i.

Whose Use old Bards describe in luscious Rhymes,
And Criticks learn'd explain to Modern Times.
By this the Sheets were spread, the Bride undrest,
The Room was sprinkled, and the Bed was blest.
What next ensu'd beseems not me to say;
'Tis sung, he labour'd 'till the dawning Day,
Then briskly sprung from Bed, with Heart so light,
As all were nothing he had done by Night;
And sipt his Cordial as he sate upright:
He kiss'd his balmy Spouse, with wanton Play,
And feebly sung a lusty Roundelay:
Then on the Couch his weary Limbs he cast;
For ev'ry Labour must have Rest at last.
But anxious Cares the pensive Squire opprest,

387 sipt] supt *1709*; supp'd *1717*; sipp'd *1736–51*.

379 f. If by 'Rhymes' Pope means verses, he may refer principally to the Paris edition (1660) of Ovid's *Ars Amandi* 'Cum notis & interpretatione Gallica'. These notes furnish the basis for the commentary in *Ovid's Art of Love* (translated by Dryden, Congreve, etc.) 1709 ('*Ovid's Art of Love* having lately appear'd in *French*, with *Observations* written by the *Translator*, which have been very well receiv'd in *France*, it has been thought proper to add such of them as are most curious to this *Version* . . .', p. 57). The notes on Book ii 415 ff. discuss aphrodisiacs (pp. 276 ff. in 1660 ed., pp. 167 f. in 1709 ed.). 1660 ed. translates 'herba salax' (ii 422) as 'l'herbe lasciue *Leole ou le Satyrion*', and 1709 ed. mentions '*Eringo's* hot Salacious Root' (p. 132). Pope found 'a thousand errors in the notes to this book' (see his MS. comments reproduced in the *European Magazine*, Oct. 1787, p. 261). Since friends of his had a hand in the book, he probably knew it before publication (he supplies the names of anonymous contributors, loc. cit.).

380. After this line Pope omits Chaucer 569–73 in which the house is cleared of 'priuie friends . . . Men drinken, and the trauers drew anon.'

381–91. Chaucer 574–621.

383. Chaucer is much more communicative. Pope again recalls Dryden, 'Sigismonda and Guiscardo', 170: 'What Thoughts he had beseems not me to say.'

385. Pope adds the briskness.

386. Pope.

392–9. Chaucer 631–40. Pope omits Chaucer 622–30, a transitional passage and an address to Damian.

392. See *Rape of the Lock*, iv 1 and note.

Sleep fled his Eyes, and Peace forsook his Breast;
The raging Flames that in his Bosome dwell,
He wanted Art to hide, and Means to tell.
Yet hoping Time th'Occasion might betray,
Compos'd a Sonnet to the lovely *May*;
Which writ and folded, with the nicest Art,
He wrapt in Silk, and laid upon his Heart.
When now the fourth revolving Day was run,
('Twas *June*, and *Cancer* had receiv'd the Sun)
Forth from her Chamber came the beauteous Bride,
The good old Knight mov'd slowly by her Side.
High Mass was sung; they feasted in the Hall;
The Servants round stood ready at their Call.
The Squire alone was absent from the Board,
And much his Sickness griev'd his worthy Lord,
Who pray'd his Spouse, attended by her Train,
To visit *Damian*, and divert his Pain.
Th'obliging Dames obey'd with one Consent;
They left the Hall, and to his Lodging went;
The Female Tribe surround him as he lay,
And close beside him sate the gentle *May*:

---

395. Pope.

397. *Sonnet*] Chaucer 637: 'a complaint or a lay.'

400–17. Chaucer 641–710. Pope cuts out the direct speech.

400 f. Chaucer 641–3:

The Moone at noonetide that ilke day
(That Januarie had iwedded fresh May)
Out of Taure was in the Cankre gleden.

Pope times this as June and so when 'after a moneth or tway' [837] Chaucer reaches June ['ere the daies eight, Were passed, ere the month July befill'] Pope generalizes the date, l. 521. He takes refuge in Dryden, 'Palamon and Arcite', ii 9 f.:

But when the sixth revolving Year was run,
And *May* within the *Twins* received the Sun.

403. Pope, stating what Chaucer implies. Cf. Dryden, 'Wife of Bath Her Tale', 346: The good old Wife lay smiling by his Side.

408. In Chaucer January's first idea is that he and May shall together go and visit Damian. Then, preferring to rest, he sends May alone.

Where, as she try'd his Pulse, he softly drew
A speaking Sigh, and cast a mournful View;
Then gave his Bill, and brib'd the Powr's Divine
With secret Vows, to favour his Design.
Who studies now but discontented *May*?
On her soft Couch uneasily she lay:
The lumpish Husband snor'd away the Night,
'Till Coughs awak'd him near the Morning Light.
What then he did, I'll not presume to tell,
Nor if she thought her self in Heav'n or Hell.
Honest and dull, in Nuptial Bed they lay,
'Till the Bell toll'd, and All arose to Pray.
Were it by forceful Destiny decreed,
Or did from Chance, or Nature's Pow'r proceed,
Or that some Star, with Aspect kind to Love,
Shed its selectest Influence from above;
Whatever was the Cause, the tender Dame
Felt the first Motions of an infant Flame;
Receiv'd th'Impressions of the Love-sick Squire,
And wasted in the soft, infectious Fire.
Ye Fair draw near, let *May's* Example move

415 speaking] heaving *1741–51*. 422 I'll] I *1709–17*.
432 Receiv'd] She took *1709*. 434] *no new paragraph 1751*.

414. *as . . . Pulse*] Chaucer 691: Comforting him as goodly as she may.

416. *Bill*] So Chaucer 693.

416 f. *and brib'd . . . Design*] Pope. After this line Pope omits Chaucer 697–710, in which May returns, is subjected to January's kisses, and, excusing herself, goes to the privy where she reads and tears up 'this bill'.

418–25. Chaucer 711–22.

425. Chaucer 722: 'Till evensong ring'.

426–39. Chaucer 723–50. Pope preserves some of Chaucer's irony.

426 f. Cf. Dryden, 'Palamon and Arcite', ii 11:

> Were it by Chance, or forceful Destiny.

429. Cf. *Par. Lost*, viii 512–13 (of the marriage of Adam and Eve):

> And happie Constellations on that houre
> Shed thir selectest influence . . .

432. *Impressions*] Chaucer's word [734].

Your gentle Minds to pity those who love!
Had some fierce Tyrant in her stead been found,
The poor Adorer sure had hang'd, or drown'd:
But she, your Sexe's Mirrour, free from Pride,
Was much too meek to prove a Homicide.
  But to my Tale: Some Sages have defin'd
Pleasure the Sov'reign Bliss of Humankind:
Our Knight (who study'd much, we may suppose)
Deriv'd his high Philosophy from Those;
For, like a Prince, he bore the vast Expence
Of lavish Pomp, and proud Magnificence:
His House was stately, his Retinue gay,
Large was his Train, and gorgeous his Array.
His spacious Garden, made to yield to none,
Was compass'd round with Walls of solid Stone;
Priapus cou'd not half describe the Grace
(Tho' God of Gardens) of this charming Place:
A Place to tire the rambling Wits of *France*
In long Descriptions, and exceed *Romance*;

443 his] this *1709–17*.

435. Chaucer 742: Lo pittie renneth sone in gentle hert.
Pope quotes Dryden's version of this line (which comes four times in Chaucer) in his letter to Henry Cromwell, 24 July 1711.

439. After this line Pope omits Chaucer 751–76 in which May reads Damian's poem secretly and in reply writes a letter which 'lacked nought, but onely time & place' [754]. She manages to thrust it under his pillow without raising suspicion, and taking his hand,

hard him twist
So secretly, that no wight of it wist.

Next day Damian is fully recovered, and pays special attention to his appearance and to his duties as servant attending on May and January.

440–64. Chaucer 777–97.

450–3. Pope generalizes Chaucer's reference to the author of the *Romant of the Rose* [788] and by so doing hits at the seventeenth-century French romances: cf. *Rape of the Lock*, ii 38. As for 'long Descriptions', Boileau had laughed at them in *L'Art Poétique*, i 51 ff. See also Tillotson, pp. 60–2 and 171 f. Pope changes the order of Chaucer's references to the romances and Priapus.

Enough to shame the gentlest Bard that sings
Of painted Meadows, and of purling Springs.
  Full in the Center of the flow'ry Ground,
A Crystal Fountain spread its Streams around,
The fruitful Banks with verdant Lawrels crown'd:
About this Spring (if ancient Fame say true)
The dapper Elves their Moonlight Sports pursue;
Their Pigmy King, and little Fairy Queen,
In circling Dances gambol'd on the Green,
While tuneful Sprights a merry Consort made,
And Airy Musick warbled thro' the Shade.
  Hither the Noble Knight wou'd oft repair
(His Scene of Pleasure, and peculiar Care)
For this, he held it dear, and always bore
The Silver Key that lock'd the Garden Door.
To this sweet Place, in Summer's sultry Heat,

454 gentlest] boldest *1709*.
456 the flow'ry] this Spot of *1709*.
458 The] Its *1709*. 463 Consort] concert *1751*.
465 Knight] Lord *1709*.
467 f. held it dear . . . lock'd] kept it lock'd . . . op'd *1709*.

454 f. Cf Addison, *Letter from Italy* (*Works*, 1721, i 55):

> My humble verse demands a softer theme,
> A painted meadow, or a purling stream.

Pope had much to say later about gentle pastoralists; see e.g. 'The Three Gentle Shepherds', and 'Ep. to Dr. Arbuthnot', l. 150. The epithet 'boldest' in the 1709 text hits at Addison; see Ault, *New Light on Pope*, 1949, pp. 107 f.

460 Cf. Milton, *Comus*, 118: Trip the pert Fairies and the dapper Elves.

461 f. Cf. Dryden, 'The Wife of Bath Her Tale', 3 f.:

> The King of Elfs and little fairy Queen
> Gamboll'd on Heaths, and danc'd on ev'ry Green.

In Chaucer the fairy king is Pluto, his queen Proserpina [794 f.].

463 f. Chaucer 796: Disporten hem and maken melodie.

465–74. Chaucer 798–812.

465 ff. 'He has no where copied the free and easy versification and the narrative style of Dryden's Fables so happily as in this pleasant tale' (Warton ed.).

He us'd from Noise and Business to retreat;
And here in Dalliance spend the livelong Day,
Solus cum Sola, with his sprightly *May*.
For whate'er Work was undischarg'd a-bed,
The duteous Knight in this fair Garden sped.
  But ah! what Mortal lives of Bliss secure,
How short a Space our Worldly Joys endure?
O Fortune, fair, like all thy treach'rous Kind,
But faithless still, and wav'ring as the Wind!
O painted Monster form'd Mankind to cheat
With pleasing Poison, and with soft Deceit!
This rich, this am'rous, venerable Knight,
Amidst his Ease, his Solace and Delight,
Struck blind by thee, resigns his Days to Grief,
And calls on Death, the Wretch's last Relief.

474 In this fair Garden he perform'd and sped. *1709*.
474 f. *Between these lines 1709 reads:*
Thus many a Day, with Ease and Plenty blest,
Our gen'rous Knight his gentle Dame possest:
481 rich, this am'rous, venerable] aged *January*, this worthy *1709*.
482 his Solace] Enjoyment *1709*.

472. Chaucer 806:

And Maie his wife, & no wight but they two.

Dryden had used the Latin tag at 'The Cock and the Fox', l. 90. See also Pope's letter to Cromwell, 7 May 1709.

475–84. Chaucer 813–28.

475–80. Chaucer 813–20:

O sudden hap, O thou fortune vnstable,
Like to the Scorpion deceiuable,
That flattrest with thy head when thou wolt sting:
Thy tale is deth, thrugh thine enuenoming.
O brotell joy, O sweet poyson queint,
O monster, that so suddenly canst peint
Thy gifts, vnder the hew of stedfastnesse,
That thou deceiuest both more and lesse.

483 f. Cf. Dryden, 'Palamon and Arcite', i 416 f.:

Nor Art, nor Natures Hand can ease my Grief;
Nothing but Death, the Wretches last Relief.

The Rage of Jealousie then seiz'd his Mind,
For much he fear'd the Faith of Womankind.
His Wife, not suffer'd from his Side to stray,
Was Captive kept; he watch'd her Night and Day,
Abridg'd her Pleasures, and confin'd her Sway.
Full oft in Tears did hapless *May* complain,
And sigh'd full oft, but sigh'd and wept in vain;
She look'd on *Damian* with a Lover's Eye,
For oh, 'twas fix'd, she must possess or die!
Nor less Impatience vex'd her Am'rous Squire,
Wild with Delay, and burning with Desire.
Watch'd as she was, yet cou'd He not refrain
By secret Writing to disclose his Pain,
The Dame by Signs reveal'd her kind Intent,
'Till both were conscious what each other meant.
Ah gentle Knight, what wou'd thy Eyes avail,
Tho' they cou'd see as far as Ships can sail?
'Tis better sure, when Blind, deceiv'd to be,
Than be deluded when a Man can see!
Argus himself, so cautious and so wise,

491 full oft] for Woe *1709*. 496 He not] not He *1709–17*.

485–99. Chaucer 829–62. The jealousy in Chaucer is much more 'outragious' [843], and is described much more fully. Even when the worst fit is over, January cannot suffer May to ride, walk, or be anywhere without his holding her hand.

485. Cf. Dryden, 'Palamon and Arcite', i 464:

The Rage of Jealousie then fir'd his Soul.

493. Chaucer 850–2. Pope's wording is that of Dryden, Ovid's *Metam.*, x, 'Cinyras and Myrrha', 231: She stood resolv'd or to possess, or die.

495. Pope. In Chaucer Damian is 'the sorowfullest man That euer was' [854f.].

500–3. Chaucer 863–6:

O January, what might thee it auaile?
Tho thou mightest see, as far as ships saile:
For as good is a blind man disceiued be,
As to be disceiued, when that he may see.

504–19. Chaucer 867–87.

Was overwatch'd, for all his hundred Eyes:
So many an honest Husband may, 'tis known,
Who, wisely, never thinks the Case his own.
The Dame at last, by Diligence and Care,
Procur'd the Key her Knight was wont to bear;
She took the Wards in Wax before the Fire,
And gave th'Impression to the trusty Squire.
By means of this, some Wonder shall appear,
Which in due Place and Season, you may hear.
Well sung sweet *Ovid*, in the Days of yore,
What Sleight is that, which Love will not explore?
And *Pyramus* and *Thisbe* plainly show
The Feats, true Lovers when they list, can do:
Tho' watch'd, and captive, yet in spight of all,
They found the Art of Kissing thro' a Wall.
But now no longer from our Tale to stray;
It happ'd, that once upon a Summer's Day,
Our rev'rend Knight was urg'd to Am'rous Play:
He rais'd his Spouse ere Matin Bell was rung,
And thus his Morning Canticle he sung.
Awake my Love, disclose thy radiant Eyes;
Arise my Wife, my beauteous Lady rise!

522 rev'rend] noble *1709*.

519. *Kissing*] Chaucer has 'rowning', i.e., whispering.

520–34. Chaucer 888–904. The canticle in Chaucer runs:

Rise vp my wife, my loue, my lady free:
The turtle voice is heard my lady swete,
The winter is gone, with all his raines wete,
Come forth now with thine eyen columbine,
Now fairer been thy brests than is wine.
The garden is enclosed all about,
Come forth my white spouse out of all dout,
Thou hast me wounded in my hert, O wife:
No spot in thee nas in all thy life.
Come forth and let vs taken our disport,
I chese thee for my wife and my comfort.

521. See note on l. 401 above.

Hear how the Doves with pensive Notes complain,
And in soft Murmurs tell the Trees their Pain;
The Winter's past, the Clouds and Tempests fly,
The Sun adorns the Fields, and brightens all the Sky.
Fair without Spot, whose ev'ry charming Part
My Bosome wounds, and captivates my Heart,
Come, and in mutual Pleasures let's engage,
Joy of my life, and Comfort of my Age!
  This heard, to *Damian* strait a Sign she made
To haste before; the gentle Squire obey'd:
Secret, and undescry'd, he took his Way,
And ambush'd close behind an Arbour lay.
  It was not long ere *January* came,
And Hand in Hand, with him, his lovely Dame;
Blind as he was, not doubting All was sure,
He turn'd the Key, and made the Gate secure.
  Here let us walk, he said, observ'd by none,
Conscious of Pleasures to the World unknown:
So may my Soul have Joy, as thou, my Wife,
Art far the dearest Solace of my Life;
And rather wou'd I chuse, by Heav'n above,
To die this Instant, than to lose thy Love.
Reflect what Truth was in my Passion shown,
When Un-endow'd, I took thee for my own,
And sought no Treasure but thy Heart alone.

529 Tempests] tempest *1751*.

535–74. Chaucer 905–40.

542. Chaucer 915: And clapt to the wicket suddainly.

544. Cf. Dryden, 'The Flower and the Leaf', 142 f.:

Single, and conscious to my Self alone
Of Pleasures to th'excluded World unknown.

545. For the construction 'So may . . . as . . .' cf. Dryden, 'The Cock and the Fox', 412.

548. *die*] Chaucer 919: 'dien on a knife'.

Old as I am, and now depriv'd of Sight,
While thou art faithful to thy own true Knight,
Nor Age, nor Blindness, rob me of Delight.
Each other Loss with Patience I can bear,
The Loss of thee is what I only fear.
  Consider then, my Lady and my Wife,
The solid Comforts of a virtuous Life.
As first, the Love of Christ himself you gain;
Next, your own Honour undefil'd maintain;
And lastly that which sure your Mind must move,
My whole Estate shall gratifie your Love:
Make your own Terms; and ere to-morrow's Sun
Displays his Light, by Heav'n it shall be done.
I seal the Contract with a holy Kiss,
And will perform, by this—my Dear, and this.—
Have Comfort, Spouse, nor think thy Lord unkind;
'Tis Love, not Jealousie, that fires my Mind.
For when thy Charms my sober Thoughts engage,
And join'd to them, my own unequal Age;
From thy dear Side I have no Pow'r to part,

553 While] Whilst *1751*. 564 Heav'n] Heav'ns *1709*.
569–75 Charms my sober . . . them . . . modest] Beauty does my . . . that . . . sober *1709*.

553–6. Pope. In Chaucer January merely asks her to be true, for the three reasons which follow.

553. Cf. Dryden, 'The Cock and the Fox', 414:

While thou art constant to thy own true Knight.

555 f. Cf. Dryden, *Iliad*, vi 106 f.:

The *Grecian* Swords and Lances I can bear
But loss of Honour is my only Fear;

cf. also Dryden, Ovid's *Metam*., xiii, 'The Fable of Acis . . .', 97 f.

558. Cf. Rochester, 'Letter from Artemisa' (*Works*, p. 32):

And the cold Comforts of a Coxcomb's Life.

565. Cf. Dryden, 'The Wife of Bath Her Tale', 524:

And seal the Bargain with a Friendly Kiss.

568. In Chaucer January admits his jealousy [933].

Such secret Transports warm my melting Heart.
For who that once possest those Heav'nly Charms,
Cou'd live one Moment, absent from thy Arms?
He ceas'd, and *May* with modest Grace reply'd;
Weak was her Voice, as while she spoke she cry'd.
Heav'n knows, (with that a tender Sigh she drew)
I have a Soul to save as well as You;
And, what no less you to my Charge commend,
My dearest Honour, will to Death defend.
To you in holy Church I gave my Hand,
And join'd my Heart, in Wedlock's sacred Band:
Yet after this, if you distrust my Care,
Then hear, my Lord, and witness what I swear.
First may the yawning Earth her Bosome rend,
And let me hence to Hell alive descend;
Or die the Death I dread no less than Hell,
Sow'd in a Sack, and plung'd into a Well:
Ere I my Fame by one lewd Act disgrace,
Or once renounce the Honour of my Race.
For know, Sir Knight, of gentle Blood I came,
I loath a Whore, and startle at the Name.
But jealous Men on their own Crimes reflect,
And learn from thence their Ladies to suspect:
Else why these needless Cautions, Sir, to me?
These Doubts and Fears of Female Constancy?
This Chime still rings in ev'ry Lady's Ear,

575–608. Chaucer 941–74.
576. Cf. Dryden, *Iliad*, i 570:
Sigh'd ere she spoke, and while she spoke she cry'd.
582. In Chaucer May speaks of 'ilke tender flour' of 'wifehood' [946].
585 f. Pope.
592. Chaucer 958:
I am a gentlewoman, and no wench.
Cf. *Dispensary*, p. 114 (of women):
They like the Thing, That startle at the Name.
597 f. Chaucer 960:
And women haue reproofe of you, aye new.

The only Strain a Wife must hope to hear.
   Thus while she spoke, a sidelong Glance she cast,
Where *Damian* kneeling, worshipp'd as she past.
She saw him watch the Motions of her Eye,
And singled out a Pear-Tree planted nigh:
'Twas charg'd with Fruit that made a goodly Show,
And hung with dangling Pears was ev'ry Bough.
Thither th'obsequious Squire address'd his Pace,
And climbing, in the Summit took his Place:
The Knight and Lady walk'd beneath in View,
Where let us leave them, and our Tale pursue.
   'Twas now the Season when the glorious Sun
His Heav'nly Progress thro' the *Twins* had run;
And *Jove*, Exalted, his mild Influence yields,
To glad the Glebe, and paint the flow'ry Fields.
Clear was the Day, and *Phœbus* rising bright,
Had streak'd the Azure Firmament with Light;
He pierc'd the glitt'ring Clouds with golden Streams,
And warm'd the Womb of Earth with Genial Beams.

600 worshipp'd] rev'renc'd *1709*.

599–601. Chaucer 963–5:

And with y^{t} word she saw where Damian
Sat in the bush, and kneele he began:
And with her finger signes made she.

Chaucer explains that their signs had been rehearsed by letter. Pope remembers Milton, *Comus*, 302: 'And as I past, I worshipt.'

609–16. Chaucer 975–80:

Bright was the day, & blew the firmament,
Phebus of gold doun hath his streames sent
To gladen every flour with his warmenesse:
He was that time in Gemini, as I gesse,
But little fro his declination,
The causer of Joues exaltation.

612. Cf. Dryden, 'The Flower and the Leaf', 6:

To glad the Ground, and paint the Fields with Flow'rs.

617–25. Chaucer 981–992.

It so befel, in that fair Morning-tide,
The Fairies sported on the Garden's Side,
And, in the midst, their Monarch and his Bride.
So featly tripp'd the light-foot Ladies round,
The Knights so nimbly o'er the Greensword bound,
That scarce they bent the Flow'rs, or touch'd the Ground.
The Dances ended, all the Fairy Train
For Pinks and Daisies search'd the flow'ry Plain;
While on a Bank reclin'd of rising Green,
Thus, with a Frown, the King bespoke his Queen.
'Tis too apparent, argue what you can,
The Treachery you Women use to Man:
A thousand Authors have this Truth made out,
And sad Experience leaves no room for Doubt.
Heav'n rest thy Spirit, noble *Solomon*,
A wiser Monarch never saw the Sun:
All Wealth, all Honours, the supreme Degree
Of Earthly Bliss, was well bestow'd on thee!
For sagely hast thou said; Of all Mankind,
One only just, and righteous, hope to find:
But shoud'st thou search the spacious World around,

619 their Monarch] the Monarch 1709.

620–2. Pope. He again owes something to Dryden's fairies in the 'Wife of Bath Her Tale', 215 ff.:

He saw a Quire of Ladies in a round,
That featly footing seem'd to skim the Ground:
Thus dancing Hand in Hand, so light they were,
He knew not where they trod, on Earth or Air;

'featly' is from Shakespeare's fairies, *The Tempest*, I ii 380; and 'light-foot' had been applied to nymphs by Spenser (*Shep. Cal.*, 'June', l. 26) and to fairies by Drayton ('Surrey to Geraldine', l. 201). Chaucer (who calls the fairy royalty Pluto and Proserpina) refers the reader to Claudian for their story.

627–55. Chaucer 993–1019

631–4. Chaucer 998–1000:

O Salomon, richest of all richesse,
Fulfild of sapience, and of worldly glory,
Full worthy ben thy words in memory.

Yet one good Woman is not to be found.
  Thus says the King who knew your Wickedness;
The Son of *Sirach* testifies no less.
So may some Wildfire on your Bodies fall,
Or some devouring Plague consume you all,
As well you view the Leacher in the Tree,
And well this Honourable Knight you see:
But since he's blind and old, (a helpless Case)
His Squire shall cuckold him before your Face.
  Now, by my own dread Majesty I swear,
And by this awful Scepter which I bear,
No impious Wretch shall 'scape unpunish'd long,
That in my Presence offers such a Wrong.
I will this Instant undeceive the Knight,
And, in the very Act, restore his Sight:
And set the Strumpet here in open View,
A Warning to these Ladies, and to You,
And all the faithless Sex, for ever to be true.
  And will you so, reply'd the Queen, indeed?
Now, by my Mother's Soul, it is decreed,
She shall not want an Answer at her Need.
For her, and for her Daughters I'll ingage,
And all the Sex in each succeeding Age,
Art shall be theirs to varnish an Offence,

638 is] were *1709–17*.
661 Art shall be theirs] None shall want Arts *1709*.

641. *some Wildfire*] Chaucer 1008: 'A wild fire'. 'In imprecations [=] A name for erysipelas and various inflammatory eruptive diseases' (OED, which cites Chaucer, 'Reve's Tale', 252, and this line from Pope).

642. Cf. Dryden, 'The Wife of Bath Her Tale', 545:

And some devouring Plague pursue their Lives.

648 f. Pope.

656–99. Chaucer 1020–66.

656. Chaucer 1020: Ye shall (qd. Proserpine) and woll ye so?

661–8. Chaucer 1024–31:

That though they been in any gilt ytake
With face bolde, they shullen hemselue excuse

And fortify their Crimes with Confidence.
Nay, were they taken in a strict Embrace,
Seen with both Eyes, and pinion'd on the Place,
All they shall need is to protest, and swear,
Breathe a soft Sigh, and drop a tender Tear;
'Till their wise Husbands, gull'd by Arts like these,
Grow gentle, tractable, and tame as Geese.
What tho' this sland'rous *Jew*, this *Solomon*,
Call'd Women Fools, and knew full many a one?
The wiser Wits of later Times declare
How constant, chast, and virtuous, Women are.
Witness the Martyrs, who resign'd their Breath,
Serene in Torments, unconcern'd in Death;
And witness next what *Roman* Authors tell,
How *Arria*, *Portia*, and *Lucretia* fell.
But since the Sacred Leaves to All are free,
And Men interpret *Texts*, why shou'd not We?
By this no more was meant, than to have shown,
That Sovereign Goodness dwells in *Him* alone
Who only *Is*, and is but only *One*.

664 pinion'd on] seiz'd upon *1709*.
665 All they shall need is] They need no more but *1709*.
672 constant, chast, and virtuous] virtuous, chast, and constant *1709*.

And bear hem down that would hem accuse.
For lacke of answere, non of hem shull dien,
All had he see a thing with both his eyen,
Yet should we women so visage it hardely,
And wepe and swere and chide subtilly,
That ye shall been as leude as are gees.

669 f. Chaucer 1033 f.:

I wote well this Jewe, this Salomon,
Found of vs women, fooles many one.

674. Pope.

676. Pope gives instances of what Chaucer [1040] leaves as 'Romain jests' [i.e. *gesta*].

677 f. Pope.

But grant the worst; shall Women then be weigh'd
By ev'ry Word that *Solomon* has said?
What tho' this King (as ancient Story boasts)
Build a fair Temple to the Lord of Hosts;
He ceas'd at last his Maker to adore,
And did as much for Idol-Gods, or more.
Beware what lavish Praises you confer
On a rank Leacher, and Idolater,
Whose Reign Indulgent God, says Holy Writ,
Did but for *David's* Righteous Sake permit;
David, the Monarch after Heav'ns' own Mind,
Who lov'd our Sex, and honour'd all our Kind.
  Well, I'm a Woman, and as such must speak;
Silence wou'd swell me, and my Heart wou'd break.
Know then, I scorn your dull Authorities,
Your idle Wits, and all their Learned Lies.
By Heav'n, those Authors are our Sexe's Foes,
Whom, in our Right, I must, and will oppose.
  Nay, (quoth the King) dear Madam be not wroth;
I yield it up; but since I gave my Oath,
That this much-injur'd Knight again shou'd see;
It must be done—I am a King, said he,
And one, whose Faith has ever sacred been.
  And so has mine, (she said)—I am a Queen!

684 ancient] *Hebrew 1709* [*cf. l. 73 above*].

692 f. Pope is echoing Dryden, *Absalom and Achitophel*, i 7 ff.:

> . . . *Israel*'s Monarch, after Heaven's own heart,
> His vigorous warmth did, variously, impart
> To Wives and Slaves; And, wide as his Command,
> Scatter'd his Maker's Image through the Land.

698. *By Heav'n*] Chaucer 1064: As euer mote I hole broke my tresses.

700–9. Chaucer 1067–75.

703–5. Chaucer 1070–2:

> My word shall stand, y[t] warne I you certeine:
> I am a king, it set me not to lie.
> And I (quoth she) queen am of Fairie.

Her Answer she shall have, I undertake;
And thus an End of all Dispute I make:
Try when you list; and you shall find, my Lord,
It is not in our Sex to break our Word.
We leave them here in this Heroick Strain,
And to the Knight our Story turns again,
Who in the Garden, with his lovely *May*
Sung merrier than the Cuckow or the Jay:
This was his Song; Oh kind and constant be,
Constant and kind I'll ever prove to thee.
Thus singing as he went, at last he drew
By easie Steps, to where the Pear-Tree grew:
The longing Dame look'd up, and spy'd her Love
Full fairly perch'd among the Boughs above.
She stopp'd, and sighing, Oh good Gods, she cry'd,
What Pangs, what sudden Shoots distend my Side?
O for that tempting Fruit, so fresh, so green;
Help, for the Love of Heav'ns' immortal Queen!
Help dearest Lord, and save at once the Life
Of thy poor Infant, and thy longing Wife!
Sore sigh'd the Knight, to hear his Lady's Cry,
But cou'd not climb, and had no Servant nigh,
Old as he was, and void of Eye-sight too,

712 Who] That *1709*.

706. Chaucer 1073: Her answere she shall haue I vndertake.
707. Chaucer 1075: Forsooth I will no longer you contrary.
710–39. Chaucer 1076–1105.
710. *Heroick*] Cf. note on l. 73 above.
713. *Cuckow or the Jay*] Chaucer 1078: 'the Popingay'.
714 f. Chaucer 1079: You loue I best, and shall, and other non.
718. Pope.
724 f. Chaucer 1091–3:

I tell you well a woman in my plite,
May haue to fruite so great an appetite,
That she may dyen, but she it haue.

What cou'd, alas, the helpless Husband do?
And must I languish then (she said) and die,
Yet view the lovely Fruit before my Eye?
At least, kind Sir, for Charity's sweet sake,
Vouchsafe the Trunk between your Arms to take;
Then from your Back I might ascend the Tree;
Do you but stoop, and leave the rest to me.
  With all my Soul, he thus reply'd again;
I'd spend my dearest Blood to ease thy Pain.
With that, his Back against the Trunk he bent;
She seiz'd a Twig, and up the Tree she went.
  Now prove your Patience, gentle Ladies all,
Nor let on me your heavy Anger fall:

733 Trunk] Bole *1709*. 738 With that] This said *1709*.

729. Cf. Addison, Ovid's *Metam.*, ii ('Phaeton's Sisters Transformed ...', l. 47):
What cou'd alas! the weeping Mother do?

730 f. Pope.

732–5. Chaucer 1097–1101:
But would ye vouchsafe for Gods sake,
The pery in your armes for to take:
For well I wot that ye mistrust me,
Then would I climbe well ynough (qd. she)
So I my foote might set vpon your backe.

738 f. Chaucer 1104 f.:
He stoupeth down, & on his back she stood,
And caught her by a twist, and vp she goth.

740–7. Chaucer 1106 ff.:
Ladies I pray you that ye be not wroth,
I can nat glose, I am a rude man:
And sodainely anon this Damian
Gan pullen vp the smocke, and in the [*Skeat* he] throng
A great tent, a thrifty and a long.
She said it was the meriest fit,
That euer in her life she was at yet:
My lords tent serueth me nothing thus
It foldeth twifold by sweet Jesus,
He may not swiue not worth a leke:
And yet he is full gentill and full meke.
This is leuer to me than an euensong.

'Tis Truth I tell, tho' not in Phrase refin'd;
Tho' blunt my Tale, yet honest is my Mind.
What Feats the Lady in the Tree might do,
I pass, as Gambols never known to you:
But sure it was a merrier Fit, she swore,
Than in her Life she ever felt before.
  In that nice Moment, lo! the wondring Knight
Look'd out, and stood restor'd to sudden Sight.
Strait on the Tree his eager Eyes he bent,
As one whose Thoughts were on his Spouse intent;
But when he saw his Bosome-Wife so drest,
His Rage was such, as cannot be exprest:
Not frantick Mothers when their Infants die,
With louder Clamours rend the vaulted Skie:
He cry'd, he roar'd, he storm'd, he tore his Hair;
Death! Hell! and Furies! what dost Thou do there?
  What ails my Lord? the trembling Dame reply'd;
I thought your Patience had been better try'd:
Is this your Love, ungrateful and unkind,
This my Reward, for having cur'd the Blind?

755 louder] such loud *1709*. 756 storm'd] rag'd *1709*.

748–57. Chaucer 1110–23.

748 f. Chaucer mentions Pluto as agent: 'wondring' is Pope's addition. After this line Pope omits Chaucer 1113 f.:

And whan he had caught his sight againe,
Ne was there neuer man of thing so faine.

753. In Chaucer it is the sight that 'may not be expressed' [1118].

754 f. Chaucer 1120 f.:

And vp he yaf a roring and a cry,
As doth the mother when the child shall die.

756 f. Chaucer 1122–4:

Out helpe, alas, (harow) he gan to cry:
For sorrow almost he gan to die,
That his wife was swiued in the pery.
  O strong lady whore what doest thou?

Pope remembers Dryden, 'Palamon and Arcite', i 523:

He roar'd, he beat his Breast, he tore his Hair.

758–816. Chaucer 1124–71.

Why was I taught to make my Husband see,
By Strugling with a Man upon a Tree?
Did I for this the Pow'r of Magick prove?
Unhappy Wife, whose Crime was too much Love!
If this be Strugling, by this holy Light,
'Tis Strugling with a Vengeance, (quoth the Knight:)
So Heav'n preserve the Sight it has restor'd,
As with these Eyes I plainly saw thee whor'd;
Whor'd by my Slave—Perfidious Wretch! may Hell
As surely seize thee, as I saw too well.
Guard me, good Angels! cry'd the gentle *May*
Pray Heav'n, this Magick work the proper Way:
Alas, my Love, 'tis certain, cou'd you see,
You ne'er had us'd these killing Words to me.
So help me Fates, as 'tis no perfect Sight,
But some faint Glimm'ring of a doubtful Light.
What I have said, quoth he, I must maintain;
For, by th'Immortal Pow'rs, it *seem'd* too plain—
By all those Pow'rs, some Frenzy seiz'd your Mind,
(Reply'd the Dame:) Are these the Thanks I find?
Wretch that I am, that e'er I was so Kind!
She said; a rising Sigh express'd her Woe,
The ready Tears apace began to flow,
And as they fell, she wip'd from either Eye

774 Love] Lord *1709.*
780 *1709–36 do not open new paragraph.*

764 f. Pope. Cf. Ovid's *Ep.*, p. 225:
Who know no Crime but too much Love of thee.
766 f. Chaucer 1132: Strogle (qd. he) ye algate in it went.
768. Pope.
777. Chaucer 1139: Ye haue some glimsing, and no perfit sight.
780. Chaucer 1143: Ye mase ye mase, good sir (quoth she).
783–6. Pope.
784, 787. Cf. Dryden, 'Palamon and Arcite', i 93:
The Prince was touch'd, his Tears began to flow.

The Drops, (for Women when they list, can cry.)
  The Knight was touch'd, and in his Looks appear'd
Signs of Remorse, while thus his Spouse he chear'd:
Madam, 'tis past, and my short Anger o'er;
Come down, and vex your tender Heart no more:
Excuse me, Dear, if ought amiss was said,
For, on my Soul, amends shall soon be made:
Let my Repentance your Forgiveness draw,
By Heav'n, I swore but what I *thought* I saw.
  Ah my lov'd Lord! 'twas much unkind (she cry'd)
On bare *Suspicion* thus to treat your Bride;
But 'till your Sight's establish'd, for a while,
Imperfect Objects may your Sense beguile:
Thus when from Sleep we first our Eyes display,
The Balls are wounded with the piercing Ray,
And dusky Vapors rise, and intercept the Day:

800 are] seem *1709–17*.

792, 795. Cf. Dryden, 'The Wife of Bath Her Tale', 364:

Name but my Fault, amends shall soon be made;

and 359:

Believe me, my lov'd Lord, 'tis much unkind.

797–806. Chaucer 1153–66:

But sir, a man that waketh out of his sleep,
He may not suddenly well taken kepe
Vpon a thing, ne se it perfectly
Till that he be adawed verily.
Right so a man that long hath blinde be,
Ne may not suddainly so well ysee
First when the sight is new comen again,
As he that hath a day or two ysain.
Till that your sight istabled be awhile,
There may full many a sight you begile.
Beware I pray you, for by heauen king
Full many a man weneth to see a thing,
And it is all another than it seemeth.
He that misconceiueth oft misdemeth.

Pope's lines are strongly reminiscent of Dryden, even in the matter of the double triplets.

So just recov'ring from the Shades of Night,
Your swimming Eyes are drunk with sudden Light,
Strange Phantoms dance around, and skim before your Sight.
Then Sir be cautious, nor too rashly deem;
Heav'n knows, how seldom things are what they seem!
Consult your Reason, and you soon shall find,
'Twas You were jealous, not your Wife unkind:
Jove ne'er spoke Oracle more true than this,
None judge so wrong as those who think amiss.
With that, she leap'd into her Lord's Embrace,
With well-dissembl'd Virtue in her Face:
He hugg'd her close, and kiss'd her o'er and o'er,
Disturb'd with Doubts and Jealousies no more:
Both, pleas'd and blest, renew'd their mutual Vows,
A fruitful Wife, and a believing Spouse.
Thus ends our Tale, whose Moral next to make,
Let all wise Husbands hence Example take;
And pray, to crown the Pleasure of their Lives,
To be so well deluded by their Wives.

819 Pleasure] Pleasures *1709–17*.

807–10. Pope.

813. Chaucer 1170 f.:

> And on her wombe he stroketh her full oft:
> And to his paleis home he hath her lad.

814–16. Pope.

817–20. Pope. Chaucer [1172–4] simply says his story is ended, and calls down a blessing. Pope adapts his moral from the proverbial definition of happiness that Swift phrased so memorably in the *Tale of a Tub*, section ix: 'a perpetual Possession of being well Deceived.'

THE

WIFE of *BATH*

HER

PROLOGUE,

From *CHAUCER*.

NOTE ON THE TEXT

The Wife of Bath Her Prologue first appeared in Steele's *Poetical Miscellanies, Consisting of Original Poems and Translations. By the best Hands*, which was published by Jacob Tonson on 29 December 1713 with the date M DDC XIV which in variant copies is corrected to M DCC XIV. The *Works* of 1717 and 1736 make some revisions, but Pope does not seem to have paid much attention to the text—the misprint 'chose' for 'close' at l. 345 has an uninterrupted run from 1717 till some edition later than 1751.

The text here reprinted is that of 1714 altered in accordance with Pope's revisions and with the principles described in the General Note on the Text (pp. x f. above). The punctuation of 1714 is systematically lighter than that of later editions.

KEY TO THE CRITICAL APPARATUS

1714 = first edition, in *Poetical Miscellanies . . . Publish'd by Mr. Steele*, Griffith 24.
1717 = Works, quarto, Griffith 79.
1736 = Works, vol. iii, octavo, Griffith 418.
1751 = Works, ed. Warburton, vol. ii, Griffith 644.

THE WIFE of BATH her PROLOGUE

BEHOLD the Woes of Matrimonial Life,
And hear with Rev'rence an experienc'd Wife!
To dear-bought Wisdom give the Credit due,
And think, for once, a Woman tells you true.
In all these Trials I have born a Part;
I was my self the Scourge that caus'd the Smart;
For, since Fifteen, in Triumph have I led
Five Captive Husbands from the Church to Bed.
Christ saw a Wedding once, the Scripture says,
And saw but one, 'tis thought, in all his Days;
Whence some infer, whose Conscience is too nice,
No pious Christian ought to marry twice.
But let them read, and solve me, if they can,
The Words addrest to the *Samaritan*:
Five times in lawful Wedlock she was join'd;
And sure the certain Stint was ne'er defin'd.
Encrease and multiply was Heav'ns' Command,
And that's a Text I clearly understand.
This too, *Let Men their Sires and Mothers leave,*
And to their dearer Wives for ever cleave.
More Wives than One by *Solomon* were try'd,
Or else the Wisest of Mankind's bely'd.
I've had, my self, full many a merry Fit,

1–8. Pope combines Chaucer 1–8 with Chaucer 172–5 where the Wife enlarges on her general position to the Pardoner who has interrupted her. Pope omits this dialogue, see note on l. 55 below. At l. 7 Pope changes Chaucer's 'twelve' to 'Fifteen' for reasons that may be gathered from *Rape of the Lock*, iv 58 n. Line 8 extends the idea of Chaucer 48:

Some christen man shall wed me anon:

one of the subtleties of the Wife's attitude is that she carries on her amorous indulgence under cover of Christian sanction: cf. 27 [Chaucer 48], 277–87 [Chaucer 543–58]; 'January and May', 80, 310 etc., and *Mor. Es.*, ii 67 f.

9–16. Chaucer 9–25.

17–20. Pope omits the Wife's hit at glosers of texts [26 f.].

22. *bely'd*] = 'misrepresented', perhaps suggesting that he was wisest because most polygamous.

23. *merry Fit*] Chaucer 42.

And trust in Heav'n I may have many yet.
For when my transitory Spouse, unkind,
Shall die, and leave his woful Wife behind,
I'll take the next good Christian I can find.
Paul, knowing One cou'd never serve our Turn,
Declar'd 'twas better far to Wed, than Burn.
There's Danger in assembling Fire and Tow,
I grant 'em that, and what it means you know.
The same Apostle too has elsewhere own'd
No Precept for Virginity he found:
'Tis but a Counsel—and we Women still
Take which we like, the Counsel, or our Will.
I envy not their Bliss, if He or She
Think fit to live in perfect Chastity,
Pure let them be, and free from Taint of Vice;
I, for a few slight Spots, am not so nice.
Heav'n calls us different Ways, on these bestows
One proper Gift, another grants to those:
Not ev'ry Man's oblig'd to sell his Store,
And give up all his Substance to the Poor;
Such as are perfect, may, I can't deny;
But by your Leave, Divines, so am not I.
Full many a Saint, since first the World began,
Liv'd an unspotted Maid in spite of Man:
Let such (a God's Name) with fine Wheat be fed,
And let us honest Wives eat Barley Bread.

25 unkind,] unkind *1714*.

25. *unkind*] Pope overdoes the ironical emphasis.

28. Pope, on a hint from Chaucer 66. Cf. 'January and May', 261 and note.

29. After this line Chaucer cites the instances of Lamech, Abraham, and Jacob [53–8].

30 f. Chaucer 89 f.

32–5. Chaucer 59–76.

36–45. Chaucer 77–112. Pope omits Chaucer 113 f.

45. After this line Chaucer's Wife discusses in a vein mocking that of theologians the reasons for the creation of the organs of generation [115–38].

46–55. Chaucer 139–62. Pope omits the mention of Christ.

For me, I'll keep the Post assign'd by Heav'n,
And use the copious Talent it has giv'n;
Let my good Spouse pay Tribute, do me Right,
And keep an equal Reck'ning ev'ry Night;
His proper Body is not his, but mine;
For so said *Paul*, and *Paul*'s a sound Divine.
  Know then, of those five Husbands I have had,
Three were just tolerable, two were bad.
The three were Old, but rich and fond beside,
And toil'd most piteously to please their Bride:
But since their Wealth (the best they had) was mine,
The rest, without much Loss, I cou'd resign.
Sure to be lov'd, I took no Pains to please,
Yet had more Pleasure far then they had Ease.
  Presents flow'd in apace: With Show'rs of Gold,
They made their Court, like *Jupiter* of old.
If I but smil'd, a sudden Youth they found,
And a new Palsie seiz'd them when I frown'd.
  Ye Sov'reign Wives! give Ear, and understand;
Thus shall ye speak, and exercise Command.
For never was it giv'n to Mortal Man,
To lye so boldly as we Women can.
Forswear the Fact, tho' seen with both his Eyes,

55. *and . . . Divine.*] Pope. After this line Chaucer makes the Pardoner interrupt, whereupon a dialogue follows [163–92]. Pope rescues one or two lines for his opening paragraph, l. 6 being the closest to Chaucer.

56–63. Pope tones down Chaucer 193–216.

57. Cf. Chaucer 196: Three of hem were good, and two were bad.

59. *piteously*] Chaucer 202.

63. After this line Chaucer refers to the Dunmow flitch.

64–7. Cf. Chaucer 219–23:

> I gouerned hem so well after my law,
> That ech of hem full blissfull was and faw
> To bring me gay things home fro the fayre.
> They were full fain when I spake hem faire:
> For God it wot, I chid hem spitously.

68–73. Chaucer 224–34. Pope omits the reference to the story of the mad chough ('the cow is wood') [232].

And call *your maids* to Witness how he lies.
    Hark old Sir *Paul* ('twas thus I us'd to say)
Whence is our Neighbour's Wife so rich and gay?
Treated, caress'd, where-e'er she's pleas'd to roam—
I sit in Tatters, and immur'd at home!
Why to her House do'st thou so oft repair?
Art thou so Am'rous? and is she so fair?
If I but see a Cousin or a Friend,
Lord! how you swell, and rage like any Fiend!
But you reel home, a drunken beastly Bear,
Then preach till Midnight in your easie Chair;
Cry Wives are false, and ev'ry Woman evil,
And give up all that's Female to the Devil.
    If poor (you say) she drains her Husband's Purse;

79 Art thou so Amorous? Is she so fair? *1714.*

74–85. Chaucer 235–47.

74. Cf. Chaucer 235: Sir old keynard, is this thine aray . . ? 'keinard [=] micher, hedg-creeper' (glossary in 1687 ed.).

77. Cf. Chaucer 238: I sit at home, and haue no thriftie cloth.

79. Cf. Chaucer 240: Is she so faire? art thou so amorous? After this line Pope omits Chaucer 241 f.

82. Chaucer 246: 'as drunken as Mouse'.

84 f. Suggested by Chaucer 262 (quoted in note on ll. 86–99 below).

86–99. Chaucer 248–70:

Thou sayest to me it is a great mischiefe
To wed a poore woman, for costage:
And if that she be rich of high parage,
Then saiest thou, it is a very tourmentrie
To suffer her pride and her Melancholy.
And if that she be faire, thou very knaue,
Thou saiest that euery holour woll her haue.
She may no while in chastitie abide,
That is assailed on euery side.
Thou saist some folke desiren vs for richesse,
Some for our shape, & some for our fairnesse,
And some, for she can either sing or dance,
And some for gentlenesse or for daliance,
Some for her honds and her armes smale:
Thus goeth all to the deuill for thy tale.

If rich, she keeps her Priest, or something worse;
If highly born, intolerably vain;
Vapours and Pride by turns possess her Brain:
Now gayly Mad, now sow'rly Splenatick,
Freakish when well, and fretful when she's Sick.
If fair, then Chast she cannot long abide,
By pressing Youth attack'd on ev'ry side.
If foul, her Wealth the lusty Lover lures,
Or else her Wit some Fool-Gallant procures,
Or else she Dances with becoming Grace,
Or Shape excuses the Defects of Face.
There swims no Goose so gray, but, soon or late,
She finds some honest Gander for her Mate.
Horses (thou say'st) and Asses, Men may try,
And ring suspected Vessels ere they buy,
But Wives, a random Choice, untry'd they take;
They dream in Courtship, but in Wedlock wake.
Then, nor 'till then, the Veil's remov'd away,
And all the Woman glares in open Day.
You tell me, to preserve your Wife's good Grace,
Your Eyes must always languish on my Face,
Your Tongue with constant Flatt'ries feed my Ear,

101 ring] sound *1714*.

Thou saist Men may not keep a castle wall,
It may so long assailed be ouer all.
And if that she be foule, thou saiest that she
Coueteth euery Man that she may see.
For as a Spaniell, she woll on him lepe,
Til that she find some man that woll her chepe:
Ne none so gray Gose goth there in the lake
(As saist thou) y^t woll been without her make.

97. *excuses*] = 'serves as an excuse or exculpation for' (OED).

99. After this line Pope omits Chaucer 271–84 as 'redundant': 276 f. read:
With wild thunder dent and fire leuin
Mote thy wicked necke be all to broke.

100–2. Chaucer 285–91.

103–5. Chaucer 292.

106–17. Chaucer 293–302.

And tag each Sentence with, *My Life! my Dear!*
If, by strange Chance, a modest Blush be rais'd,
Be sure my fine Complexion must be prais'd:
My Garments always must be new and gay,
And Feasts still kept upon my Wedding-Day:
Then must my Nurse be pleas'd, and Fav'rite Maid;
And endless Treats, and endless Visits paid,
To a long Train of Kindred, Friends, Allies;
All this thou say'st, and all thou say'st are Lies.
  On *Jenkin* too you cast a squinting Eye;
What? can your Prentice raise your Jealousie?
Fresh are his ruddy Cheeks, his Forehead fair,
And like the burnish'd Gold his curling Hair.
But clear thy wrinkled Brow, and quit thy Sorrow,
I'd scorn your Prentice, shou'd you die to-morrow.
  Why are thy Chests all lockt? On what Design?
Are not thy Worldly Goods and Treasure mine?
Sir, I'm no Fool: Nor shall you, by St. *John*,
Have Goods and Body to your self alone.
One you shall quit—in spight of both your Eyes—
I heed not, I, the Bolts, the Locks, the Spies.
If you had Wit, you'd say, "Go where you will,
"Dear Spouse, I credit not the Tales they tell.
"Take all the Freedoms of a married Life;
"I know thee for a virtuous, faithful Wife."
  Lord! When you have enough, what need you care

119 can your] can our *1714*.

110–12. Pope.

115. Pope.

117. Chaucer 302: Thus saiest thou old barell full of lies.

118–23. Chaucer 303–7.

124–33. Chaucer 308–20.

126. *by St. John*] Chaucer 312:

Now by that Lord that called is sainct Jame.

132. Pope.

133. After this line Pope omits Chaucer 321 f., a summarizing couplet, as 'redundant'.

How merrily soever others fare?
Tho' all the Day I give and take Delight,
Doubt not, sufficient will be left at Night.
'Tis but a just and rational Desire,
To light a Taper at a Neighbour's Fire.
  There's Danger too, you think, in rich Array,
And none can long be modest that are gay.
The Cat, if you but singe her Tabby Skin,
The Chimney keeps, and sits content within;
But once grown sleek, will from her Corner run,
Sport with her Tail, and wanton in the Sun;
She licks her fair round Face, and frisks abroad
To show her Furr, and to be *Catterwaw'd.*
  Lo thus, my Friends, I wrought to my Desires
These three right Ancient Venerable Sires.
I told 'em, *Thus you say*, and *thus you do*—
And told 'em false, but *Jenkin* swore 'twas true.

136 give and take] take and give *1714–17*. [*Cf. Dryden, Ovid's* Art of Love, *i 69*.]

134–9. Chaucer 323–34. Pope omits Chaucer 323–8 which introduce the paragraph by way of a proverb of Ptolemy, and also 335 f. which is a summarizing couplet.

138 f. Chaucer 333 f.:

He is too great a nigard that woll werne
A man to light a candle at his Lanterne.

140–7. Chaucer 337–54.

140 f. Chaucer 337–47: Pope omits the quotation from St Paul.

142–7. Chaucer 348–54:

Thou saiest also, I was like a Cat:
But who so would senge the Cats skin,
Than would the Cat dwellen in his Inne:
And if the Cats skin be slicke and gay,
She nill nat dwell in house halfe a day,
But forth she woll or any day be dawed
To shew her skin, and gon a catrewawed.

Pope omits 355 f., a summarizing couplet, and also 357–78 which he no doubt considered redundant.

148–51. Chaucer 379–83.

151. After this line Pope omits an exclamatory couplet [384 f.].

I, like a Dog, cou'd bite as well as whine;
And first complain'd, whene'er the Guilt was mine.
I tax'd them oft with Wenching and Amours,
When their weak Legs scarce dragg'd 'em out of Doors;
And swore the Rambles that I took by Night,
Were all to spy what Damsels they bedight.
That Colour brought me many Hours of Mirth;
For all this Wit is giv'n us from our Birth:
Heav'n gave to woman the peculiar Grace
To spin, to weep, and cully Human Race.
By this nice Conduct and this prudent Course,
By Murmuring, Wheedling, Stratagem and Force,
I still prevail'd, and wou'd be in the right,
Or Curtain-Lectures made a restless Night.
If once my Husband's Arm was o'er my Side,
What? so familiar with your Spouse? I cry'd:
I levied first a Tax upon his Need,

152 f. Chaucer 386–92:

For as an horse, I couth both bite & whine,
I couth plain, though I were in the gilt,
Or else oftentime I had been spilt.
Who so first to Mill commeth, first grint,
I plained first, and so was our war istint.
They were full glad to excusen hem bliue
Of thing, that they a gilt neuer in her life.

154–65. Chaucer 393–408.

154 f. Chaucer 393 f.:

Of wenches would I beare hem on hond,
When y^{t} for sick, vnneths might they stond.

157. *bedight*] Chaucer [398] has 'dight' = lie with.

161. *cully*] = 'to make a fool of, to cheat, to deceive', a comparatively new word at the time, originating in rogues' slang. Pomfret had used it in 1699 (*OED*). Pope, like Dryden, can slip in a common word with devastating quietness.

165. Pope.

166–82. Chaucer 409–31. Pope makes some re-arrangement. He omits Chaucer 429 f.: For though he looked as wood as a Lyon,
Yet should he faile of his conclusion.

168 f. Chaucer 411 f.:

Till he had made his raunsom vnto me,
Then would I suffer him doe his nicete.

Then let him—'twas a *Nicety* indeed!
Let all Mankind this certain Maxim hold,
Marry who will, our *Sex* is to be Sold!
With empty Hands no Tassels you can lure,
But fulsom Love for Gain we can endure:
For Gold we love the Impotent and Old,
And heave, and pant, and kiss, and cling, for Gold.
Yet with Embraces, Curses oft I mixt,
Then kist again, and chid and rail'd betwixt.
Well, I may make my Will in Peace, and die,
For not one Word in Man's Arrears am I.
To drop a dear Dispute I was unable,
Ev'n tho' the Pope himself had sate at Table.
But when my Point was gain'd, then thus I spoke,
"*Billy*, my dear! how sheepishly you look!
"Approach my Spouse, and let me kiss thy Cheek;
"Thou should'st be always thus, resign'd and meek!
"Of *Job*'s great Patience since so oft you preach,
"Well shou'd you practise, who so well can teach.
" 'Tis difficult to do, I must allow,
"But I, my dearest, will instruct you how.
"Great is the Blessing of a prudent Wife,
"Who puts a Period to Domestick Strife!
"One of us two must rule, and one obey,
"And since in Man right Reason bears the Sway,
"Let that frail Thing, weak Woman, have her way.

179 Man's] their *1714*.
188 difficult to do,] something difficult *1714*.

172. *Tassels*] = tercels, peregrine falcons.

174 f. Chaucer 417 f.: And make me then a fained appetite,
And yet in Bacon had I neuer delite.

There is no gloss on 'bacon' in the 1687 edition. Pope may have omitted to use the metaphor from ignorance or choice.

183–204. Chaucer 431–50.

183. Chaucer 432: How meekly looketh wilken our sheep.

190 f. Pope.

192–4. Chaucer 440–2:

"The Wives of all my Family have rul'd
"Their tender Husbands, and their Passions cool'd.
"Fye, 'tis unmanly thus to sigh and groan;
"What? wou'd you have me to your self alone?
"Why take me Love! take all and ev'ry part!
"Here's your Revenge! you love it at your Heart.
"Wou'd I vouchsafe to sell what Nature gave,
"You little think what Custom I cou'd have!
"But see! I'm all your own—nay hold—for Shame!
"What means my Dear—indeed—you are to blame."
Thus with my first three Lords I past my Life;
A very Woman, and a very Wife!
What Sums from these old Spouses I cou'd raise,
Procur'd young Husbands in my riper Days.
Tho' past my Bloom, not yet decay'd was I,
Wanton and wild, and chatter'd like a Pye.
In Country Dances still I bore the Bell,

195 Family have] Race have ever *1714–17*.
207 old] first *1714*.
211 still I bore the Bell] most I did excell *1714*.

One of vs two mote obeien doubtles:
And sith a man is more reasonable
Than a woman is, ye must been sufferable.

195 f. Pope.

201–4. Chaucer 447–50:

For if I would sell my belchose,
I couth walke as fresh as any rose,
But I woll keep it for your owne tooth:
Ye be to blame by God, I say you sooth.

205–20. Chaucer 451–68.

205 f. Pope, in place of a colourless couplet tacking the two paragraphs together.

207–30. Chaucer 453–82. Pope omits 453 f. since the gist of it recurs at 481 f. (229 f. in Pope).

207 f. Pope, authorized by Chaucer's general meaning.

209. Pope makes the meaning clearer: in Chaucer [455] the Wife says she was 'yong', but her other statements show this to mean 'youngish', 'physically unimpaired'.

And sung as sweet as Evening *Philomel.*
To clear my Quail-pipe, and refresh my Soul,
Full oft I drain'd the Spicy Nut-brown Bowl;
Rich luscious Wines, that youthful Blood improve,
And warm the swelling Veins to Feats of Love:
For 'tis as sure as Cold ingenders Hail,
A Liqu'rish Mouth must have a Lech'rous Tail;
Wine lets no Lover unrewarded go,
As all true Gamesters by Experience know.
  But oh good Gods! whene'er a Thought I cast
On all the Joys of Youth and Beauty past,
To find in Pleasures I have had my Part,
Still warms me to the Bottom of my Heart.
This wicked World was once my dear Delight;
Now all my Conquests, all my Charms good night!
The Flour consum'd, the best that now I can

214 f. Bowl; Rich] Bowl Of *1714.* 216 Love:] Love. *1714–17.* 221 cast] cast, *1714–17.*

213 f. Pope decorates Chaucer, quoting 'L'Allegro', l. 100. A quail-pipe = 'a pipe or whistle on which the note of a quail (usually the female) can be imitated, in order to lure the birds into a net' (OED). Cf. Dryden, *Juvenal,* vi 107.

215 f. Pope. He omits the reference to Metell[i]us [460–3].

218. Chaucer 466: A licorus mouth must haue a lecherous taile.

219 f. Chaucer 467 f.:

In women vinolent is no defence,
This know lechours by experience.

'vinolent' = 'drunk, smelling of wine' (1687 gloss).

221–8. A poor equivalent for Chaucer 469–79:

  But Lord Christ, when it remembreth me
Vpon my youth, and my iolite,
It tickleth me about the hart root,
Vnto this day it doth my hart boot,
That I haue had my world as in my time:
But age alas, that all woll enuenime
Hath me bireft my beauty and my pith:
Let go, farewell, the deuill goe therewith.
The flower is gon, there nis no more to tell.
The bran (as I best can) now mote I sell.
But yet to be right mery woll I fond.

Is e'en to make my Market of the Bran.
My fourth dear Spouse was not exceeding true;
He kept, 'twas thought, a private Miss or two:
But all that Score I paid—As how? you'll say,
Not with my Body, in a filthy way—
But I so drest, and danc'd, and drank, and din'd;
And view'd a Friend, with Eyes so very kind,
As stung his Heart, and made his Marrow fry
With burning Rage, and frantic Jealousie.
His Soul, I hope, enjoys eternal Glory,
For here on Earth I was his Purgatory.
Oft, when his Shoe the most severely wrung,
He put on careless Airs, and sat and sung.
How sore I gall'd him, only Heav'n cou'd know,
And he that felt, and I that caus'd the Woe.
He dy'd when last from Pilgrimage I came,
With other Gossips, from *Jerusalem*,
And now lies buried underneath a Rood,
Fair to be seen, and rear'd of honest Wood.

228 Market] Markets *1714*. 237 eternal] perpetual *1714–17*.

229 f. See note on ll. 207–30 above.

231–52. Chaucer 483–502.

235 f. Chaucer 487 f.:

That in his owne greace I made him frie
For anger, and for very jelousie.

Pope blunts the point: the Wife in Chaucer is paying her husband back in his own coin for his paramour. Pope, however, may have expected the reader to see the point, and stress *his*.

237 f. Chaucer 489 f.:

By God, in earth I was his purgatorie,
For which I hope his soule bene in glorie.

241 f. Chaucer 493 f.:

There was none, saue God and he, that wist
In many wise, how sore that I him twist.

245 f. Pope neatly removes the obsolete allusion in Chaucer 496 to 'the Rode beem', i.e., the rood loft, by using rood in the sense of a cross on a grave. He follows this up by replacing Chaucer 502 ('He is now in his graue and in his chest') by l. 251. He invents l. 246 on the authority of Chaucer's general sense.

A Tomb, indeed, with fewer Sculptures grac'd,
Than that *Mausolus'* Pious Widow plac'd,
Or where inshrin'd the great *Darius* lay;
But Cost on Graves is meerly thrown away.
The Pit fill'd up, with Turf we cover'd o'er,
So bless the good Man's Soul, I say no more.
  Now for my fifth lov'd Lord, the last and best;
(Kind Heav'n afford him everlasting Rest)
Full hearty was his Love, and I can shew
The Tokens on my Ribs, in Black and Blue:
Yet, with a Knack, my Heart he cou'd have won,
While yet the Smart was shooting in the Bone.
How quaint an Appetite in Women reigns!
Free Gifts we scorn, and love what costs us Pains:
Let Men avoid us, and on them we leap;
A glutted Market makes Provision cheap.
  In pure good Will I took this jovial Spark,
Of *Oxford* he, a most egregious Clerk:
He boarded with a Widow in the Town,
A trusty Gossip, one dame *Alison*.
Full well the Secrets of my Soul she knew,
Better than e'er our Parish Priest cou'd do.

248 f. Artemisia, the widow of the Carian prince Mausolus, was inconsolable; 'to perpetuate his memory she built at Halicarnassus the celebrated monument, Mausoleum, which was regarded as one of the seven wonders of the world' (W. Smith, *Dictionary of Greek and Roman Biography*.., 1850, i 377). Darius I, of Persia, caused his sepulchre to be built during his life (*id.*, 942). Weever (*Ancient Funerall Monuments*, 1631, pp. 12 ff.) writes a chapter 'Of the excessiue expenses bestowed vpon Funerals in former times'.

253–62. Chaucer 503–23.

255. *hearty*] Pope misunderstood Chaucer's 'dangerous' [514] which means 'holding off', 'stand-offish' (see C. S. Lewis, *Allegory of Love*, 1936, Appendix ii), and so gives a different slant to the whole passage. (Pope reverts to 'hearty' at ll. 418 and 425 below.) The earlier husbands revenge themselves in the fifth who, to some extent, turns the tables on the Wife; he is poor, young, and independent while she is now rich, not so young, jealous, and dependently in love with him.

263–76. A straightforward version of Chaucer 525–42.

To her I told whatever cou'd befal;
Had but my Husband Pist against a Wall,
Or done a thing that might have cost his Life,
She—and my Neice—and one more worthy Wife
Had known it all: What most he wou'd conceal,
To these I made no Scruple to reveal.
Oft has he blush'd from Ear to Ear for Shame,
That e'er he told a Secret to his Dame.
   It so befell, in Holy Time of *Lent*,
That oft a Day I to this Gossip went;
(My Husband, thank my Stars, was out of Town)
From House to House we rambled up and down,
This Clerk, my self, and my good Neighbour *Alce*,
To see, be seen, to tell, and gather Tales;
Visits to ev'ry Church we daily paid,
And march'd in ev'ry holy Masquerade,
The Stations duly, and the Vigils kept;
Not much we fasted, but scarce ever slept.

269 cou'd] did *1714*. 281 *Alce*] *Alse 1751*.

277–89. Chaucer 543–62.

278. After this line Chaucer has a 'redundant' couplet [545 f.] naming March, April, and May; Pope reinstates May at l. 290 below.

279. Chaucer 550: 'thank my Stars' is Pope's inadequate version of Chaucer 553 f.:

> what wist I where my grace
> Was shapen for to been, or in what place?

281 f. *Alce . . . Tales*] Chaucer rhymes 'tales' and 'Ales' [547 f.], both of which are disyllabic. Pope knows nothing of the syllabic '-es' and so produces an impossible Christian name. With 282 cf. Chaucer 552:

> And for to see, and eke for to be seie.

Pope omits the statement that they went into the fields since Chaucer repeats it at 564.

283 f. Pope translates Chaucer's 'visitations' [555] by 'visits' and so points the contemporary satire. For the fashionable practice of paying visits see l. 115 above and *Rape of the Lock*, iii 12 and 167. The satire is continued in 'holy Masquerade' (which has no counterpart in Chaucer). Cf. *Rape of the Lock*, i 72, ii 108, etc.

285. *Stations*] Pope. Here used in the sense of a 'bi-weekly fast' (OED). This explains how l. 286 (Pope's invention) is to be understood.

At Sermons too I shone in Scarlet gay;
The wasting Moth ne'er spoil'd my best Array;
The Cause was this; I wore it ev'ry Day.
'Twas when fresh *May* her early Blossoms yields,
This Clerk and I were walking in the Fields.
We grew so intimate, I can't tell how,
I pawn'd my Honour and ingag'd my Vow,
If e'er I laid my Husband in his Urn,
That he, and only he, shou'd serve my Turn.
We strait struck Hands; the Bargain was agreed;
I still have shifts against a Time of Need:
The Mouse that always trusts to one poor Hole,
Can never be a Mouse of any Soul.
I vow'd, I scarce cou'd sleep since first I knew him,
And durst be sworn he had Bewitch'd me to him:
If e'er I slept, I dream'd of him alone,
And Dreams foretel, as Learned Men have shown:
All this I said; but Dreams, Sirs, I had none.
I follow'd but my crafty Crony's Lore,
Who bid me tell this Lye—and twenty more.
Thus Day by Day, and Month by Month we past;
It pleas'd the Lord to take my Spouse at last!
I tore my Gown, I soil'd my Locks with Dust,

291 This] The *1714–17*. Fields.] Fields, *1714*.

290–9. Chaucer 563–74.

292. *I . . . how*] Pope.

294. Chaucer 568: 'If I were widow . . .'

299. *Soul*] 'Intellectual or spiritual power; high development of the mental faculties' (OED, §3b).

300–6. Chaucer 575–84.

302. Pope omits the account of the dream, Chaucer 578–81.

305 f. Representing Chaucer 576, 583 f. After l. 306 Pope omits a connecting couplet, gaining the same technical end by inventing l. 307.

308–28. Chaucer 587–623.

309–12. Chaucer 588–92:

I wept algate and made heauy chere,
As wiues moten, for it is vsage:

And beat my Breasts, as wretched Widows—must.
Before my Face my Handkerchief I spread,
To hide the Flood of Tears I did *not* shed.
The good Man's Coffin to the Church was born;
Around, the Neighbours, and my Clerk too, mourn.
But as he march'd, good Gods! he show'd a Pair
Of Legs and Feet, so clean, so strong, so fair!
Of twenty Winters' Age he seem'd to be;
I (to say truth) was twenty more than he:
But vig'rous still, a lively buxom Dame,
And had a wond'rous Gift to quench a Flame.
A Conjurer once that deeply cou'd divine,
Assur'd me, *Mars* in *Taurus* was my Sign.
As the Stars order'd, such my Life has been:
Alas, alas, that ever Love was Sin!
Fair *Venus* gave me Fire and sprightly Grace,
And *Mars* Assurance, and a dauntless Face.
By Vertue of this pow'rful Constellation,
I follow'd always my own Inclination.
But to my Tale: A Month scarce past away,

And with my kerchefe couered my visage.
But for that I was purueyed of a make,
I wept but small, and that I vndertake.

315. *good Gods!*] Chaucer 596: 'As helpe me God'.

316. After this line Pope omits Chaucer 599:

That all my heart I yaue vnto his hold.

320. Chaucer 600–8.

321. Pope.

324. Chaucer 614 verbatim.

325 f. Chaucer 611 f. and 619:

Venus me yaue my lust and my licorousnesse
And Mars yaue me my sturdie hardinesse . . .
Yet haue I Martes marke vpon my face.

327 f. Chaucer 615 f.

328. After this line Pope omits Chaucer 617 f. and 620–6 as too outspoken and 'redundant'.

329–36. Chaucer 627–36. Chaucer's Wife gives the reason for the blow, viz. that she tore pages from her husband's book. Pope does not anticipate, whetting

With Dance and Song we kept the Nuptial Day.
All I possess'd I gave to his Command,
My Goods and Chattels, Mony, House, and Land:
But oft repented, and repent it still;
He prov'd a Rebel to my Sov'reign Will:
Nay once by Heav'n he struck me on the Face:
Hear but the Fact, and judge your selves the Case.
Stubborn as any Lionness was I:
And knew full well to raise my Voice on high;
As true a Rambler as I was before,
And wou'd be so, in spight of all he swore.
He, against this, right sagely wou'd advise,
And old Examples set before my Eyes;
Tell how the *Roman* Matrons led their Life,
Of *Gracchus*' Mother, and *Duilius*' Wife;
And close the Sermon, as beseemd' his Wit,

345 close] chose *1717–51*.

the appetite for what he withholds in l. 336 (his invention). He also omits the two later occasions [666–8, 711 f.] when the Wife again outlines the story she has not yet told.

337–54. Chaucer 637–63.

340. Pope mistakes the meaning of Chaucer 640: 'although he had it sworn'.

344. Pope cuts out Chaucer's instances from Valerius Flaccus and substitutes two of his own selection. St Jerome, who was one of the authors in the offensive volume described at l. 356 ff. below, had praised Cornelia, the mother of the Gracchi as 'pudicitiæ simul & fecunditatis exemplar' (*Sancti Eusebii Hieronymi... Operum Tomus Quartus*, Paris, 1706, ii 555); and in a section marginally headed 'Mulieres Romanæ insignes' had told the story of Bilia, the wife of Duilius, an 'exemplum pudicitiæ' (see index): 'Duellius, qui primus Romæ navali certamine triumphavit, Biliam virginem duxit uxorem, tantæ pudicitiæ, ut illo quoque sæculo pro exemplo fuerit, *QUO IMPUDICITIA* monstrum erat, non vitium. Is jam senex & trementi corpore, in quodam jurgio audivit exprobrari sibi os fœtidam, & tristis se domum contulit. Quumque uxori questus esset, quare nunquam se monuisset, ut huic vitio mederetur: Fecissem, inquit illa, nisi putassem omnibus viris sic os olere. Laudanda in utroque pudica & nobilis femina, & si ignoravit vitium viri, & si patienter tulit: & quòd maritus infelicitatem corporis sui, non uxoris fastidio, sed maledicto sensit inimici. Certè quæ secundum ducit maritum, hoc non potest dicere' (*id.*, 188).

345 f. Chaucer specifies the text [651–3].

With some grave Sentence out of Holy Writ.
Oft wou'd he say, Who builds his House on Sands,
Pricks his blind Horse across the Fallow Lands,
Or lets his Wife abroad with Pilgrims roam,
Deserves a Fool's-Cap and long Ears at home.
All this avail'd not; for whoe'er he be
That tells my Faults, I hate him mortally:
And so do Numbers more, I'll boldly say,
Men, Women, Clergy, Regular and Lay.
  My Spouse (who was, you know, to Learning bred)
A certain Treatise oft at Evening read,
Where divers Authors (whom the Dev'l confound
For all their Lies) were in one Volume bound.
Valerius, whole; and of St. *Jerome*, Part;
Chrysippus and *Tertullian*; *Ovid*'s Art;
Solomon's Proverbs, *Eloïsa*'s Loves;
And many more than sure the Church approves.
More Legends were there here, of wicked Wives,
Than good, in all the *Bible* and *Saints'-Lives*.

361 *Eloïsa's*] *Heloïsa's 1714*.

347–50. Chaucer 655–8:
Who so buildeth his house all of sallowes,
And pricketh his blind hors ouer the fallowes
And suffereth his wife for to seche hallowes,
Is worthy to be hanged on the gallowes.

351. Chaucer 659 f.: But all for nought, I set not an haw
Of his prouerbes, ne of his old saw.

354. Chaucer 663: And so doe mo (God it wote) than I.

355–76. Chaucer 669–712.

356. Pope transfers the gist of Chaucer 672 ('At which booke he lough alway full fast') from here to l. 413 below.

357 f. Pope (except for 'were . . . bound' which is Chaucer 681).

359–61. Pope cuts out the names Theophrastus and Trotula [Chaucer 671, 677].

362. Pope.

363 f. Chaucer 686–91.

Who drew the *Lion Vanquish'd*? 'Twas a *Man.*
But cou'd we Women write as Scholars can,
Men shou'd stand mark'd with far more Wickedness,
Than all the Sons of *Adam* cou'd redress.
Love seldom haunts the Breast where Learning lies,
And *Venus* sets ere *Mercury* can rise:
Those play the Scholars who can't play the Men;
And use that Weapon which they have, their Pen;
When old, and past the Relish of Delight,
Then down they sit, and in their Dotage write,
That not one Woman keeps her Marriage Vow.
(This by the Way, but to my Purpose now.)
  It chanc'd my Husband on a Winter's Night
Read in this Book, aloud, with strange Delight,
How the first Female (as the Scriptures show)
Brought her own Spouse and all his Race to Woe;
How *Samson* fell; and he whom *Dejanire*

368 cou'd] can *1717.*
370 ere *Mercury* can] when *Mercury* does *1714.*
381 How *Samson's* Heart false *Dalilah* did move,
His Strength, his Sight, his Life, were lost for Love.
Then how *Alcides* dy'd, whom *Dejanire* *1714.*

365. Pope's brilliant expansion of the Chaucerian shorthand, 'Who painteth the Lion, tell me who?' [692]. In the Æsopic fable (versified by La Fontaine, *Fables Choisies*, iii 10, and retold in *Spectator*, No. 11) the lion explains that the picture represents a lion as defeated because it was a man who painted it.

367. *mark'd*] the presence of this word may be due to a misunderstanding of Chaucer 696: 'all the marke of Adam', i.e., his sons. If so, it is by accident that l. 368 contains a correct translation of the phrase.

369 f. Chaucer 697–705. Pope's revision of l. 370 removes it still further from Chaucer's accurate astrology, which Pope probably did not understand in detail. The line makes its human point splendidly.

371 f. Pope; cf. his letter to Caryll, Jun., 8 Nov. 1712: 'I beg you to offer him my utmost service . . . with the only weapon I have, my pen'.

377–410. Chaucer 713–85. Pope (401–6) gives the stories of Lima and Lucy [747–56] without giving names.

Wrapt in th' envenom'd Shirt, and set on Fire.
How curst *Eryphile* her Lord betray'd,
And the dire Ambush *Clytemnestra* laid.
But what most pleas'd him was the *Cretan* Dame,
And Husband-Bull—Oh monstrous! fie, for Shame!
He had by Heart the whole Detail of Woe
Xantippe made her good Man undergo;
How oft she scolded in a Day, he knew,
How many Pisspots on the Sage she threw;
Who took it patiently, and wip'd his Head;
Rain follows Thunder, that was all he said.
He read how *Arius* to his Friend complain'd
A fatal *Tree* was growing in his Land,
On which three Wives successively had twin'd
A sliding Noose, and waver'd in the Wind.
Where grows this Plant (reply'd the Friend) oh where?
For better Fruit did never Orchard bear:
Give me some Slip of this most blissful Tree,
And in my Garden planted shall it be!
Then how two Wives their Lord's Destruction prove,
Thro' Hatred one, and one thro' too much Love;
That for her Husband mix'd a Poys'nous Draught;
And this for Lust an am'rous Philtre bought,
The nimble Juice soon seiz'd his giddy Head,
Frantic at Night, and in the Morning dead.
How some with Swords their sleeping Lords have slain,

385 f. Chaucer 733–6:

Of Pasiphae, that was queene of Crete,
For shreudness him thought y[t] tale was swete.
Fie, speake no more, it is a grisely thing,
Of her horrible lust and her liking.

396. Cf. 'January and May', l. 478: 'wav'ring as the Wind'.

407–10. Chaucer 765–85. Pope omits the rest of the story following on from l. 407—

And let her letchour dight hem all the night,
Whiles that the corse lay in floore vpright.

[767 f.]—and also the string of proverbs [773–85]. Both, for different reasons, were 'redundant'.

And some have hammer'd Nails into their Brain,
And some have drench'd them with a deadly Potion;
All this he read, and read with great Devotion.
  Long time I heard, and swell'd, and blush'd, and frown'd,
But when no End of these vile Tales I found,
When still he read, and laugh'd, and read again,
And half the Night was thus consum'd in vain;
Provok'd to Vengeance, three large Leaves I tore,
And with one Buffet fell'd him on the Floor.
With that my Husband in a Fury rose,
And down he settled me with hearty Blows:
I groan'd, and lay extended on my Side;
  Oh thou hast slain me for my Wealth (I cry'd)
Yet I forgive thee—Take my last Embrace.
He wept, kind Soul! and stoop'd to kiss my Face;
I took him such a Box as turn'd him blue,
Then sigh'd and cry'd, *Adieu my Dear, adieu!*
  But after many a hearty Struggle past,
I condescended to be pleas'd at last.
Soon as he said, My Mistress and my Wife,
Do what you list the Term of all your Life:
I took to Heart the Merits of the Cause,

411–24. Chaucer 786–810.

411. Chaucer 486 f.:

> Who coud wene, or who coud suppose
> The wo that in mine hart was and pine.

412–14. Chaucer 788 f.:

> And when I saw he would neuer fine
> To reden on this cursed booke all night.

413. See note on l. 356 above.

416. Chaucer makes the Wife push her husband on to the fire [793].

417. Pope omits 'as doth a wood Lioun' [794] which matches l. 337 above [Chaucer 637].

423 f. Chaucer 808–10:

> And yet eftsoones I hit him on the cheke,
> And saied: theefe, thus much am I bewreke,
> Now woll I die, I may no longer speke.

425–35. Chaucer 811–22.

And stood content to rule by wholsome Laws;
Receiv'd the Reins of Absolute Command,
With all the Government of House and Land;
And Empire o'er his Tongue, and o'er his Hand.
As for the Volume that revil'd the Dames,
'Twas torn to Fragments, and condemn'd to Flames.
  Now Heav'n on all my Husbands gone, bestow
Pleasures above, for Tortures felt below:
That Rest they wish'd for, grant them in the Grave,
And bless those Souls my Conduct help'd to save!

436–9. Pope. The Wife in Chaucer [823–8] concludes by saying that she and her husband became kind and true to each other, and, calling down a blessing on him, she announces the beginning of her tale.

THE RAPE OF THE LOCK

Rape of the Lock.

INTRODUCTION

I. THE OCCASION AND HISTORY OF THE POEM

THE families concerned in the *Rape of the Lock*—the Fermors, Petres, and Carylls[1]—were prominent members of that group of great intermarried Roman Catholic families owning land in the home counties, most of whom came within the circle of Pope's friends and acquaintances and to whom he considered his own family to belong.[2] Some time before 21 March 1712, when Pope sold his poem to Lintott, Robert, Lord Petre had cut off a lock of Arabella Fermor's hair, and John Caryll had suggested to Pope that he should write a poem to heal the estrangement that followed between the two families:

> The stealing of Miss Belle Fermor's hair, was taken too seriously, and caused an estrangement between the two families, though they had lived so long in great friendship before. A common acquaintance and well-wisher to both, desired me to write a poem to make a jest of it, and laugh them together again. It was with this view that I wrote the Rape of the Lock.[3]

The incident behind the poem has never been authoritatively tracked down to place and time. It is improbable, but possible, that it happened, as the poem states, at Hampton Court; and the counter-claims of the houses of the Fermors, Petres, or Carylls have never been substantiated.[4] Letters of 21 June[5] and 2 August 1711[6]

---

1. See Appendix A, pp. 371 ff.

2. See his note to 'Ep. to Dr. Arbuthnot', l. 381 and Sherburn's comment, *Early Career*, 30. It is perhaps worth noting that in the household of Edward Caryll of Benton in 1583 was one Mercy Pope, an honoured person blind and deaf (M. de Trenqualéon, *West-Grinstead et les Caryll* [1893] ii 91).

3. Spence, 194: 'laugh them together' shows reliance on the doctrines of Shaftesbury, whose phrase Pope borrows; cf. dedicatory epistle.

4. Since Sir George Browne and his wife were of the party and both they and the Fermors are connected with St James's, Westminster (see Appendix A, pp. 374 and 376), the incident may have happened in London.

5. Brit. Mus. Add. MS. 28227, fol. 104–5: a letter to Caryll from the Bishop of Chichester directed to Ingatestone Hall.

6. Letter from Pope to Caryll, Add. MS. 28618, fol. 7v–8r.

show that Caryll was staying at Ingatestone Hall, Lord Petre's place, in Essex. The lock may have been cut at this time and at this place. It may have been during this visit that Caryll made his proposal. More probably, however, the proposal was made after this visit, since Pope in his letter of 2 August is protesting that he can only return Caryll's kindness in

> that poor vulgar way of assuring you [I] will allways continue || Dear S^{r} || your most faithfull, affectionate Friend & oblig'd Servant.[1]

The same letter states that Pope is about to write words for a musical interlude, and this simply to gratify Steele's request, the task being otherwise much against the grain. Pope does not go on to make a contrasting reference to Caryll's commission, and this suggests that the commission had not yet been made. In suggesting the poem Caryll was acting responsibly. The related families of the Carylls and Petres were on admirable terms. Caryll is named twice, for instance, in the will of Thomas, Lord Petre (1704), once as a guardian of Robert and Mary his children.[2] And so after the death of Thomas Petre in January 1705–6, Robert, Lord Petre, the Baron of the poem, had been under Caryll's guardianship, remaining under it until March 1710 when he came of age. Caryll may have liked proposing subjects—in a letter of 19 November, 1712, Pope is found sending 'a few lines upon ye subject you were pleas'd to propose, only to prove my ready obedience . . .'[3] It is certain that Pope would have taken any proposal from Caryll seriously, even if, as in the instance of the musical interlude, he had not been attracted by it. His letters reiterate his deep indebtedness to Caryll's kindness, and he had only recently avowed his hopeless debts with special force. Caryll had asked Pope if he had bought the horse that had been considered (Pope was advised to ride for his health), and on 19 July 1711, realizing that Caryll probably meant to give one to him—which he did shortly afterwards—Pope wrote:

> I coud wish you wou'd not oblige too fast. I loue to keep pase

1. *id.*, fol. 8r.

2. J. J. Howard and H. F. Burke, *Genealogical Collections Illustrating the History of Roman Catholic Families of England . . . Part I. Fermor and Petre* (1887), 75.

3. Add. MS. 28618, fol. 10r.

wth a Freind if possible: and 'tis a rule, you know, in walking to lett ye Weakest goe foremost: Lett me first prove my self your Freind (wch I shall infallibly doe on the first Occasion that shall offerr itt self) and then S^{r} doe what you will . . .[1]

'This Verse to *C—l*, Muse! is due' may have had a meaning for Pope and Caryll that escaped the outside world. In complying with Caryll's suggestion he may consciously have been making repayment in the only way that he could.

I

Pope stated in a note to the poem in 1736 that 'The first sketch of this Poem [i.e. presumably the first version in two cantos: *The Rape of the Locke*] was written in less than a fortnight's time, in 1711 . . .' A reference in a mutilated letter from Pope to Caryll may be relevant in helping to fix this fortnight more precisely. This letter is without a date but contains Pope's epitaph on John, titular Lord Caryll, the octogenarian uncle of Pope's friend, the diplomatist, dramatist, and poet, who had been secretary to Mary, queen of James II, and had shared the royal exile at St Germains.

The death was announced to John Caryll, the nephew, in a letter dated 6 September from Louis Innis, principal of the Collège des Ecossais at Paris.[2] Lord Caryll's tombstone in the Collège records that he died on 4 September.[3] Innis, writing on the 6th, refers to that date as 'friday last . . . being the 4. instant'. Innis is therefore dating his letters in New Style, since only according to that style did 4 September 1711 fall on a Friday. Innis's letter is postmarked[4] in France $\substack{\text{SE}\\ 14}$ and we know from his next but one of 18 October that Caryll's letter acknowledging its receipt bore the date 18 September.[5] Caryll followed the English practice of dating according to Old Style. Caryll therefore received Innis's letter some

1. Add. MS. 28618, fol. 7r.

2. Add. MS. 28227, fol. 112 f. For Innis see the account in DNB, which does not mention his numerous letters preserved among the Caryll Papers (Add. MSS. 28227–9).

3. '. . . obiit in oppido S. Germani in Layâ pridie nonas Septembr. A.D. MDCCXI' (transcription in *Sussex Archaeological Society Collections*, xix, pp. 191 f.).

4. This mark must have been French since Innis's letter of 28 April 1712 (fol. 138–9) is marked with a stamp of the same design $\substack{\text{AP}\\ 29}$.

5. Add. MS. 28227, fol. 118r.

time between 3 September (i.e. 14 September N.S.) when it was stamped in France, and 18 September when he replied to it, and so probably some time during the week 11–18 September. Caryll would certainly tell the news to Pope since Pope was interested in this lingering gentleman of the mob who wrote with ease and in the honour that had befallen his friend's son John, who had inherited his great-uncle's fortune. Pope may, therefore, have learned of Lord Caryll's death at some date just before or following 18 September.[1] He then writes an epitaph. An epitaph is an occasional poem and so, if it is passed on to fellow mourners, is passed on with little delay. The letter containing this epitaph may therefore belong to late September or early October. And this fairly datable letter may contain, as well as the epitaph, the first reference to the *Rape of the Locke*. Pope writes:

> I have a little poetical present to make you, which I dare not trust by the post, and could be glad you would please to direct me a way to send it to you; for I am a little apprehensive of putting it into Lewis's [hand]s, who is too much a bookseller to be trusted with rhyme or reputation.[2]

The poetical present must have been in MS.—Pope fears the bookseller as a potential pirate. Elwin plausibly suggests that it was the *Rape of the Locke*.[3] Pope considered himself indebted to Caryll for

1. I have found no reference to Lord Caryll's death in contemporary newspapers so that Pope does not seem to have had any other channel for the news except Caryll.

2. *Pope's Corresp.*, i. 133 f.

3. The *Temple of Fame* is a possible other candidate. But it is difficult to see how that poem could endanger reputation. Moreover, the tone of Pope's words, secretive and apprehensive, is the tone in which the *Rape of the Lock* is usually referred to: even the apologies in the dedication are confiding, and there is its explicit phrase 'the Air of a Secret'. Professor Sherburn does not agree with me in accepting EC's conjecture that the 'present' is the *Rape of the Locke* (*Pope's Corresp.*, i 133); he thinks that it would not be so appropriately a 'present' as the epitaph that seems to have accompanied the letter in question. But the mention of Lewis, who, as Professor Sherburn notes, was Caryll's London agent for parcels, suggests that the MS. was of some bulk—and in any event only a bulky parcel consigned by Pope would excite the suspicious interest of the transmitter, whether Lewis or postman. Why should an epitaph require special arrangements? Being a short piece its existence would remain unsuspected—if a letter was safe without

presents and so may appropriately speak of a present in return. He uses the word for the *Rape of the Locke* later, when informing Caryll that the 'more Solemn Edition' is coming out:

> . . . it may better become me to appear as ye Offerer of an ill present, than you as ye Receiver of it.[1]

If the poetical present were the *Rape of the Locke*, as seems likely, the date of the composition of the poem falls some time earlier than this letter, the probable date of which is late September or early October.

There is no certain earlier reference. Two pieces of possible evidence, however, need to be argued aside. In a letter of 25 June 1711, to Caryll who is on his visit to Lord Petre, Pope makes a reference to his friend's host (the square brackets supply conjectures for two omissions, an accidental and a conscious one, of the copyist):

> [If] I had ye honor of being known to my Ld Petre, I shou'd be so impu[dent as to] desire his acceptance of a thing so inconsiderable as my most humble service.[2]

The phrase 'humble service' has no bearing on the *Rape of the Locke* —Pope passes straight on to defend himself to Lord Petre against Dennis's strictures on the *Essay on Criticism*. The phrase means simply 'respects', a meaning it had in the sentence preceding the one quoted where Pope tells Caryll that he had addressed his 'most humble service to Mr Southcote when I writt to his Brother'.

The second piece of evidence is that of Pope's letter to Cromwell of 15 July 1711, which contains lines obviously connected with the *Rape of the Locke*. Pope is speaking of the way Cromwell will be missed now his fortnight's visit is just over, missed not only by Pope but by the ladies, one of whom will be remembered by the trophy that Cromwell bore off in his snuff-box. Then follow these lines:

---

special arrangements so would an epitaph be. As to the term 'present', there seems no difficulty. Pope calls the *Rape of the Lock* a 'present' in his letter to Caryll at *Corresp.*, i 210, when he is sending him two advance copies of it (and Sir William Trumball, as it happens, uses the same word in thanking Pope for the copy he had received, *Corresp.*, i 212). Pope's description of the present as 'little' is an ironic reference rather to worth than bulk.

1. Add. MS. 28618, fol. 22v.
2. Add. MS. 28618, fol. 4v.

As long as Moco's [*written over a cancelled* India's] happy Tree shall grow,
While Berries crackle, or while Mills shall go;
While [*written over* As (?)] smoking Streams from Silver Spouts shall glide [*written over* flow],
Or China's Earth receive the sable Tyde;
While Coffee shall to British Nymphs be dear;
While fragrant Steams the bended Head shall chear;
Or grateful Bitters shall delight the Tast;
So long her Honour, Name, and Praise shall last![1]

Sherburn takes it that this is a quotation from the MS. *Rape of the Locke.*[2] The objections, however, are weighty. Pope's lines are surely extempore—his hesitation over the rhyme shows that, and he extemporizes verse elsewhere in the Cromwell correspondence. The theme, also, is coffee, and coffee is frequently mentioned in the correspondence. Moreover, the five of these lines which appear in the *Rape of the Locke* appear in a revised form, and do not all appear in the same passage. Finally, Cromwell has just left Pope: is it not, therefore, likely that Pope would have shown him the *Rape of the Locke* if it had been written, and so would not quote from it as if extemporizing? The probable explanation is that when Pope came to write the *Rape of the Locke* he rescued lines first intended only for Cromwell's amusement.

Some of the Caryll correspondence is lost. Pope writes on 2 August that he sent Caryll a letter 'near a week before'[3] in answer to one written by Caryll from Ingatestone. This letter, which would bear a date round about 27 July, is not extant. It may, of course, have contained a reference to the *Rape of the Locke*. But presumably if the poem had been thought of, begun, or finished by 27 July, Pope would have made some reference to it in the letter of 2 August, especially since he did not know whether his earlier letter had reached Caryll or not. No mention of the poem argues that there was not yet any poem to mention. It is not likely, therefore, that the poem was composed before 2 August. Pope told Spence that it 'was

1. Bodleian, MS. Rawl. Letters 90, fol. 39r.
2. *Best of Pope*, p. 396.
3. Add. MS. 28618, fol. 7v.

written fast'.[1] Its composition, we are told in 1736, occupied less than a fortnight. That short fast period, that fortnight, probably fell some time between 2 August and a date probably in late September, and certainly not far into October.

II

The letter of 25 June 1711 makes it clear that Pope did not know Lord Petre personally. He may or may not have known Arabella Fermor personally. Belinda has 'sable' ringlets in the poem,[2] and hair of a 'warm golden shade',[3] a 'fair auburn'[4] in the portraits. This seems the only evidence against their acquaintance and may count for little in a poem in which many details are heightened. Sir Plume, on the other hand, was acknowledged 'the very picture of the man',[5] and if Pope had known Sir George Browne well enough to reproduce his appearance and gestures, he may well have known his famous niece.[6] Warburton's note states that Pope 'sent [the poem] to the Lady, with whom he was acquainted'.[7] If Warburton is inferring this acquaintance from the dedication of 1714, his inference is no better than anyone else's, but he may of course be representing something Pope had said to him.

Pope told Spence that the poem was 'well received, and had its effect in the two families'.[8] Warburton notes that Arabella 'took it so well as to give about copies of it'. Arabella, that is, had 'vouchsafe[d] to view', and Lord Petre as well as Caryll had 'approve[d the] lays'.[9] This may well represent the effect of the poem in MS. But after its publication in May 1712 the attitude of the Fermors

1. p. 142.
2. *Rape of the Locke*, ii 84.
3. A. Mary Sharp, *History of Ufton Court* (1892), 123.
4. *id.*, 126.
5. Spence, 195.
6. EC's argument (ii 120 and cf. v 93) against their acquaintance is based on a misunderstanding of Edward Bedingfield's letter to Pope, which I examine at pp. 96 ff. below.
7. 1751 note on the motto. This note is erroneously signed 'P.' The initial is removed in the second edition (1753), which Warburton in a letter to Hurd, 30 June 1753, calls 'the correctest of all'. See EC ii 120 n. 2.
8. p. 194.
9. Canto i 4–6.

changed. In a letter to Caryll junior of 8 November 1712, Pope writes:

> Sir Plume blusters, I hear; nay, the celebrated lady herself is offended, and, which is stranger, not at herself, but me . . . Is not this enough to make . . . a writer . . . act with more reserve and write with less?[1]

Pope is himself offended—and legitimately so—by the treatment his poem is receiving. His exquisite care over it, the clever niceties of his 'jest', are being wasted on the recipients. It was enough to make him wish he had not taken such pains to adjust the angles of his smile, but had sniggered or laughed outright. Sir Plume's anger was formidable:

> Nobody but Sir George Brown was angry, and he was a good deal so, and for a long time. He could not bear, that Sir Plume should talk nothing but nonsense.[2]

He even threatened physical violence on Pope. A letter to the younger Caryll, which begins by comparing Pope's own sedentary life with Caryll's active one in the fields, goes on to more pressing matters:

> But possibly some of my good Friends, whom we have lately spoke of in our last letters may give me a more Lively Sense of things in a short time, & awaken my Intellects to a perfect Feeling of Myself & Them. Dull fellows that want Witt, (like those very dull fellows that want Lechery) may, by well-applyd Stroaks & Scourges, be fetchd up into a little of either. I therfore have some reason to hope no man that calls himself my Friend (except it be such an obstinate, refractory Person as yourself) will do me the Injury to hinder these well-meaning Gentlemen

1. EC note (vi 161) that 'The original of this letter is in the possession of Mr. Tuckwell, from whom Mr. Croker received it'. Pope thinks Arabella should have been offended 'at herself', not at him. This must mean either that she had let copies get about; or that she had behaved childishly over the loss of her lock, and really did need the moral lesson of the poem; or that she had been more seriously indiscreet—the remark of Pope's to Martha Blount ('it was but tother day I heard of Mrs Fermor's being Actually, directly, and consummatively, married'—see pp. 100 f. below) seems to imply that Arabella had something to be really offended at in herself.

2. Spence, 194 f.

> from Beating up my Understanding. Whipt wits, like whipt Creams, afford a most sweet & delectable Syllabub to the Taste of the Towne, and often please them better with the Dessert, than all the meal they had before. So, if Sir Plume should take the pains to Dress me, I might possibly make the Last Course better than the first.

He is already exquisitely sizing up his powers of torture in return:

> When a stale cold Fool is well heated, and hashed by a Satyrical Cooke, he may be tost up into a Kickshaw not disagreeable.[1]

Sir George did nothing. He may well have realized that Pope, if whipped, would spit words more venomous.[2]

The reason for Arabella's annoyance was that fools had talked and fools had heard them.[3] They had talked to the point of making Pope seek to render what amends he could. He writes in a letter to Caryll of 15 December 1713:

> I have some thoughts of dedicating [the second edition of the poem] to Mrs. Fermor by name, as a piece of justice in return to the wrong interpretations she has suffered under the score of that piece.

He tells Caryll a month later that

> A Preface which salv'd ye Lady's honour, without affixing her

1. *Pope's Corresp.*, i 163 f.

2. In his *Key to the Lock* (pp. 9 f.) Pope makes some amends to Sir George, since he shows two men each considering himself Sir Plume's original:

'Upon the Day that this Poem was published, it was my Fortune to step into the *Cocoa Tree*, where a certain Gentleman was railing very liberally at the Author, with a Passion extremely well counterfeited, for having (as he said) reflected upon him in the Character of *Sir Plume*. Upon his going out, I enquired who he was, and they told me, *a Roman Catholick Knight*.

'I was the same Evening at *Will*'s, and saw a Circle round another Gentleman, who was railing in like manner, and showing his Snuff-box and Cane to prove he was satyrized in the same Character. I asked this Gentleman's Name, and was told, he was a *Roman Catholick Lord*.'

3. Letter to Caryll of 9 January 1713–14. Add. MS. 28618, fol. 22r.

In the last paragraph of the dedicatory epistle of 1714 Pope implies that Arabella has been censured—he cannot hope, he says, that his poem will 'pass thro' the World half so Uncensured as You have done'. He cannot say that she has been uncensured but tries to cheer her by a comparison.

> Name, was also prepar'd, but by herself superseded in favour of y[e] Dedication.

'Salv'd the Lady's honour' are strong words, even when 'honour' means reputation, and even if the tone is purposely exaggerated. Clearly the scandal had gone to inordinate lengths. It cannot be wholly explained by the indecencies of the poem, as, in a chapter crowded with errors of fact, Courthope explains it:

> Probably, if 'the celebrated lady' had been left to herself, she would have read the poem without offence, but the keen eye of scandal detected one or two passages with a double meaning, which passed the bounds of decency, and candid friends no doubt told Belinda what was being said.[1]

The many indecent passages, which half conceal their indecency in wit and tenderness, were part of the jest of the poem—Caryll, said Pope, had 'desired [him] to write a poem to make a jest of [the families' estrangement].'[2] The jests of the poem were like those in Pope's letters to Caryll in substance, but were more hidden, as befitted a more public jest. They were much less blunt than those of the *Tatler* and *Spectator*, and in an age when these periodicals were addressed to the ladies of Great Britain, Pope's innuendos no doubt counted for little in Arabella's attitude to the poem. If she liked the poem in MS., she would probably have gone on liking it in print.

What upset her may well have been outside Pope's control. Belinda is represented in the poem as meditating love, as ready indeed to love the Baron, though she unaccountably rejects him—

> Oh say what stranger Cause, yet unexplor'd,
> Cou'd make a gentle *Belle* reject a *Lord*?

The tone of the poem,[3] Belinda's 'Rage, Resentment and Despair', her 'constant Care' over her beauty, the jests, passages like

1. EC v 94. These indecencies are made much of by Dennis (*Remarks*, D 2v); and see p. 198 below. Cf. Gildon, *New Rehearsal*, 1714, p. 43; J. Oldmixon, *The Catholick Poet* (1716) in which 'Pope is accused of trying "with vile smut" to charm "pretty Bell. Fermor" ' (Sherburn, *Early Career*, p. 178); and J. Ralph, *Sawney*, 1728, pp. 9f.

2. Spence, 194.

3. Dennis, making no allowances for the mock-heroic wrote: 'the *Manners* and

Already see you a degraded Toast,
And all your Honour in a Whisper lost!

and

What mov'd my Mind with youthful Lords to rome?
O had I stay'd, and said my Pray'rs at home!

—such things had been found delightful at the time when they were first read. The motto for the poem, adapted from Martial, was at first inoffensive—if it were in the MS. at all.[1] 'I was loth, Belinda, to violate your locks; but I am pleased to have granted that much to your prayers.' This made two suggestions: (1) (if the words were Pope's) that Belinda had asked him to write the poem—a suggestion which had little weight in view of

... This Verse to *C—l*, Muse! is due;

(2) (if the words were the Baron's) that Belinda, as the poem hinted elsewhere, was willing to marry him. Arabella may well have been considered as the possible bride for Lord Petre. The rape of the lock may well have been an incident in the period of circumspection—how thorough such circumspection was likely to be may be gathered from the correspondence of Caryll during 1710–11 when he was choosing a wife for his son.[2] If two such families who 'had lived so long in great friendship before'[3] are estranged through a fairly trivial incident,[4] it seems that there is thunder in the air. All

Behaviour of his fine Lady, who is so very rampant, and so very a Termagant, that a Lady in the Hundreds of *Drury* would be severely chastis'd, if she had the Impudence in some Company to Imitate her in some of her Actions' (*Remarks*, A 4r–v: cf. B 8v and C 1v).

1. Pope substituted a motto from Ovid in 1714 but brought back the Martial one in 1717 when it cannot possibly have been offensive.

2. See Add. MS. 28227, the letters from Louis Innis.

3. Spence, 194.

4. A modern representative of the Petre family, who may have inherited a sense of family and Catholic characteristics, thought the incident no more than an ordinary one, considering 'the high spirits of the old Catholic families, when cousins were gathered together in their tens and twenties' (M. D. Petre, *The Ninth Lord Petre*, 1928, p. 21). (One recalls Gay, *Mr Pope's Welcome from Greece*, ll. 119 f.:

I see the friendly *Carylls* come by dozens,
Their wives, their uncles, daughters, sons, and cousins.)

Havelock Ellis, on the other hand, might well have cited the Baron as a victim of hair-fetichism.

the fun of the poem read very differently when, less than two months before the poem was published, Lord Petre married Catherine Warmsley, a Lancashire heiress some seven or more years younger than Arabella and much richer.[1] The poem which Arabella may almost have forgotten must have seemed revived at a time when she could least welcome it, and revived in a much more powerful form. The verdict of M. D. Petre two centuries later may have been shared by some people in 1712:

> It seems a pity that the romance did not end as it should have done.[2]

Events had certainly placed Arabella in a silly position.

But the publicity of that position must not be exaggerated. The poem was anonymous; it did not mention Arabella nor any of its other characters by name, so that only those who knew it in MS. knew who was who.[3] Of course the 'fools' among that restricted group talked, and talk about print is more weighty than talk about MS. But presumably a very high proportion of those three thousand[4] who snapped up the first 1714 edition and read its dedication, must have been introduced to the identity of Belinda for the first time and no doubt were willing to remain incurious about the identity of the Baron. Spence, not less than a dozen years later, when the poem was already a classic, put down the facts of the origin of the poem 'with the air of a secret':

> I have been assured by a most intimate friend of Mr. Pope's, that

1. 'The estate at Dunkenhalgh (5,754 acres) [was] worth £10,995 a year in 1883' (GEC[okayne's] *Complete Peerage* (1895) vi 249 note a). Arabella's portion at her marriage in 1714 or 1715 was £4,500 (see Holden, p. 19).

2. op. cit., p. 21.

3. The anonymity was not guarded closely. *Spectator* 523 (30 Oct. 1712) spoke of the poem as Pope's. And *The Odes of Horace in Latin and English*, part xi (published on 20 Nov. 1712: see advertisement in the *Spectator*) contains a list of 'Books Printed for Bernard Lintott' which includes 'New Miscellany Poems by Mr *Prior*, Mr. *Pope*, *&c.* wherein is the *Rape of the Lock*, and the *Essay on Criticism*, both by Mr. *Pope*.' Since the miscellany cannot have been selling well (it is reissued in 1714) Lintott may have been trying to use Pope's name as a stimulant. He had not given Pope's name as author of the poem in the advertisements of the miscellany which appeared in the *Spectator* on May 20, 22, 24, and 31, and on June 3 and 5.

4. Letter to Caryll, 12 March 1714: Add. MS. 28618, fol. 24v.

the Peer in the Rape of the Lock was Lord Petre; the person who desired Mr. Pope to write it, old Mr. Caryl, of Sussex; and that what was said of Sir George Brown [whom Pope had himself named to him] in it, was the very picture of the man.[1]

III

In the dedication to the second edition the wounded Arabella is publicly stated by Pope to have authorized the original publication.

This dedication sorely tried Pope's skill. In a letter to Caryll of 9 January 1713–14, he writes:

> As to ye Rape of ye Lock, I belive I have managed ye Dædication so nicely y^t^ it can neither hurt ye Lady, nor ye Author. I writ it very lately, and upon great deliberation; the young Lady approves of it; and ye best advice in ye Kingdom, of ye Men of sense, has been made use of in it, even to ye Treasurers [i.e., Robert Harley, Earl of Oxford].[2]

Pope's 'deliberation' means that he felt his task to be delicate, but the dedication was approved by Arabella, who had taken the trouble to prefer it to the alternative 'preface' that did not name her.[3]

The main disclaimer in it is, like that of Boileau's prefaces to *Le Lutrin*, a disclaimer of all facts but the central one:

> As to the following Canto's, all the Passages of them are as

1. p. 195. The Petres, it seems, made no objection to the poem. The Baron himself was of an amiable disposition: on his death in 1713, Lord Berkeley of Stratton wrote in a letter of 31 March that he was 'Much lamented, tho' a Papist. I was very well acquainted with him and liked his humour extremely' (quoted in GEC[ockayne's] *Complete Peerage* (1895) vi 248 note c): Pope described him as '(by ye consent of all who have ye happiness to know him) one of those young Lords that have Wit in our Days!' (letter to Caryll, 25 June 1711: Add. MS. 28618, fol. 4v). The Baron's widow bore Pope no grudge. Her letter to Caryll of 3 Jan. 1713–14 ends with an order for the translation of Homer: 'I shall readily contribute to Mr Popes undertaking & accept the offer you make me of laying down the two guineas for me till I return itt back' (Add. MS. 28237, fol. 22).

2. Add. MS. 28618, ff. 21v–22r.

3. This 'preface' may well be the poem 'To Belinda On the Rape of the Lock' included in *Pope's Own Miscellany* (see op. cit., pp. lxxi–vii and 107 f.).

> Fabulous, as the Vision at the Beginning, or the Transformation at the End; (except the Loss of your Hair, which I always name with Reverence.) The Human Persons are as Fictitious as the Airy ones; and the Character of *Belinda*, as it is now manag'd, resembles You in nothing but in Beauty.[1]

Pope makes no mention of the occasion of his writing the poem—the plan of Caryll to heal the breach between the two families. There is no reference to Lord Petre, and nothing to connect Arabella with him for those who are not acquainted with the poem in its more personal MS. form. Such a reference was, of course, impossible: Lord Petre had died of small-pox on 22 March 1712–13.

Of the other relevant statements in the dedication those are presumably true that concern Arabella. She had the upper hand so far at least as her knowledge went, since Pope was the presenter of apologies and she the receiver of them. It is not likely that she would have consented to witness a lie or that Pope would have dared to require this of her. Arabella is called upon to witness that the poem 'was intended only to divert a few young Ladies . . .' (This, though it makes no mention of the first end of Pope's writing, was of course true—in a letter, for instance, addressed to Martha Blount on 25 May 1712, he says: 'yourself and your fair Sister must needs have been surfeited already with this Triffle.'[2]) The poem, however, became known beyond the intended circle:

> as [i.e. because] it was communicated with the Air of a Secret, it soon found its Way into the World. An imperfect Copy having been offer'd to a Bookseller, You had the Good-Nature for my Sake to consent to the Publication of one more correct . . .

There certainly must have been a danger of piracy. If the 'poetical present' was indeed the *Rape of the Locke*, Pope foresaw such a danger as soon as the poem was finished. But if the pirate had been actual he could easily have brought out the poem before 20 May 1712, when, after what Pope thought inordinate delay, it was published (it has 'been so long coming out, that the Ladies Charms

1. The phrase 'as it is now manag'd' means nothing more than 'as it is managed in my poem'; Pope is not contrasting the management of Belinda's character in 1714 with that of 1712: no such contrast was possible.

2. Bodleian MS. Res. d. 36.

might have been half decay'd, while the Poet was celebrating them, and the Printer publishing them.'[1]) The inactive pirate was almost certainly the 'unbody'd shade'—or, to use Johnson's equivalent, 'the usual process of literary transaction'[2]—which authors had been using in their prefaces since publishing began. This does not, however, mean that the poem was not in danger. The actual danger, however, was represented more soberly in Pope's words to Spence: 'Copies of the poem got about, and it was like to be printed.'[3] Pope had suggested in the dedication that the 'few young ladies', including Belinda, being women, were themselves responsible for the dangerous multiplication of copies:

> as it was communicated with the Air of a Secret, it soon found its Way into the World;

and Warburton, who may of course have had no other warrant than this dedication, states plainly in his preliminary note that Arabella 'took it so well as to give about copies of it'. If this is indeed what happened, she would feel responsible for any piracy that might occur and so would more readily consent to publication. The transition from MS. to print, when the poem is personal in origin, is so momentous that Pope must have got Arabella's permission before publication. If the letter from Caryll of 23 May 1712 is authentic (its only source is the printed *Letters*), Caryll had been sounding Lord Petre either on his own score or on Pope's. Pope did not know Lord Petre in 1711 (see the letter containing the Caryll epitaph which belongs to the autumn of 1711) and so may still have had to use Caryll as intermediary. This sounding must have been about publication. Caryll writes:

> I wrote to Lord Petre upon the subject of the Lock, some time since, but have as yet had no answer . . .

The same letter inquires if the poem is to 'come out in Lintot's Miscellany or not?' Clearly Caryll would have to be consulted about printing it. He would feel himself responsible for a poem he had proposed. Pope, of course, wanted to publish the poem—he

1. loc. cit. This may suggest also that Pope leisurely revised the poem before it was printed—he wrote the poem in a fortnight in the first place.

2. Life of Pope (*Lives*, iii 102).

3. p. 195.

acknowledges as much in the twisted opening sentence of the dedication. But, if the letter of 23 May can be trusted, he had gone to the length of offering to suppress the poem, an extreme measure that Caryll evidently saw no reason to agree to:

> I know that rather than draw any just reflection upon your self of the least shadow of ill-nature, you would freely have supprest one of the best of poems.

The suppression of the poem was of course unthinkable, and, since the danger of piracy was real, to delay its publication fretted the nerves. Arabella does not seem to have been given the choice between suppression and publication. Her only choice was between two forms of publication, authorized or pirated. There is no reason to think that she withheld her authority.

IV

When Pope is found to have made unusual provision that Arabella's copy of the printed poem should be presented as early and safely as possible, he is at least seen not to be hiding the step he has taken. As early as 11 May he wrote (from Binfield presumably) to his friend Edward Bedingfield of Gray's Inn, asking him, it seems, either to send or to deliver advance copies of the poem to Arabella and Lord Petre, both of whom he believed to be in town. In making this request of Bedingfield he seems to be ensuring special safety. He arranged to have Caryll's copy sent to him through the bookseller Lewis,[1] and this method had its risks—two years later, for example, the same arrangement resulted in a lost 'Packet' which meant that Caryll received a 'not . . . so fair' impression of the second edition of the poem instead of the 'first Impression, which I before designed you.'[2] Pope was running no risks over Arabella and Lord Petre since he could avoid them, as he could not for Caryll who was far from London and Bedingfield. Pope's letter to Bedingfield has not been found, but its contents may be guessed at from an allusion to it in a letter to Caryll and from Bedingfield's reply to it. In the letter of 28 May 1712, in which he informs Caryll of the arrangement made with Lewis for sending him a copy, Pope writes:

1. See Letter to Caryll, 28 May 1712.
2. Letter to Caryll of 12 March 1714: Add. MS. 28618, fol. 24v.

> . . . Mr Bedingfield . . . has done me ye favor to send some books of the Rape, to my Lord Petre, &. Mrs Fermore . . .[1]

Bedingfield's reply reads:

> Graysin May ye 16th 712
>
> S^{r}
>
> Last Night I had ye favour of y^{rs} of ye eleventh Instant and according to ye directions therein I have enclosed the Copy^{s} for Ld Petre and [*deletion*] for Mrs Belle Fermor—she is out of Towne and therefore all I can do is to leave her[2] pacquet at her lodgeing . . .
>
> S^{r}
>
> Y^{r} very Hum^{ble} Servt
>
> Edw: Bedingfeld.[3]

Pope presumably asks Bedingfield because Gray's Inn is only a few hundred yards from Bernard Lintott's 'at the Cross-Keys between the Two Temple Gates in Fleetstreet'. The words 'some books of the Rape' suggest that there were more than one copy for each person. The copies were probably offprints, such as Pope sent Caryll:

> I hope Lewis has convey'd you by this time the Rape of ye Locke, with what other things of mine are in Lintott's Collection; The whole Book I will put into y^{r} hands when I have ye satisfaction to meet you at Reading.[4]

Offprints were easy for Lintott to manage because the poem had its separate title-page and independent run of signatures.[5] He may not have had the complete miscellany ready since publication was not till the 20th. Bedingfield's words 'I have enclosed the Copy^{s}' suggest that Pope had prepared coverings for them, or packets which no doubt enclosed, or bore, the inscriptions which this

1. Add. MS. 28618, fol. 9r. The abbreviated title witnesses to Caryll's close interest in the poem.

2. This word is careted above the line.

3. Homer MSS. Sloane 4807, fol. 163v. EC read the date wrongly as 26 May.

4. Letter of 28 May 1712, Add. MS. 28618, fol. 9r.

5. The poem has its own running title, unlike all the other poems in the Miscellany. This may mean that it was originally designed to appear independently (see Caryll's question, p. 95 above), or that Pope foresaw the wish to give independent copies about to all the friends concerned.

method of presentation otherwise made impossible. Bedingfield was acting as promptly as Pope could have requested or desired. He was going to deliver the packets personally. Arabella's absence in the country may have spoiled Pope's plan for presenting her with her copy or copies before publication. But this promptitude and special care are not at least the marks of one who thinks his present will cause annoyance.

V

Whether or not Arabella authorized publication 'for [the poet's] Sake' cannot now be known. She may have done it, despite everything, partly for her own. Unlike Lord Petre, who sent no answer to Caryll, Arabella was willing to enter into correspondence with Pope about a poem which, if it made her look foolish, gave her the literary rank of Millamant and ascribed something like enchantment to her beauty. And to be offended with a rising poet had no doubt its social compensations:

Not all the Tresses that fair Head can boast
Shall draw such Envy as the Locke you lost.[1]

Her attitude becomes clearer, perhaps, when we find her, two years later, deliberately choosing to have her name set in front of the poem. When the result appeared—the bold capitals extending across the page—she cannot have failed to be pleased. Indeed there is evidence that she was more than pleased.

At some date not far distant from 1714 she had her portrait painted, and is shown wearing the 'sparkling *Cross*' mentioned in the poem. Perhaps this was the indispensable ornament for a Catholic lady (for example, the will of Mary Petre, the Baron's sister, dated 31 March 1713, specifies 'To my sister Petre my gold cross.')[2] But the portrait is inscribed with her name and with Pope's couplet describing the cross. There is some doubt when this in-

1. *Rape of the Locke*, ii 185 f. Cf. Parnell, 'To Mr. Pope' (*Poems*, 1722, p.106):
How flame the Glories of *Belinda*'s Hair,
Made by thy Muse the Envy of the Fair.

2. Or for any fashionable lady: cf. Gay's *Fan* (1714), i 117 f.:
Here an unfinish'd *Di'mond Crosslet* lay,
To which soft Lovers Adoration pay;
Gay, of course, may intend a cross-reference to the *Rape of the Lock(e)*.

scription was added. Miss Mary Sharp considered that it was 'probably . . . added at a later period'[1] than the portrait. The name affixed is 'Mrs Arabella Fermor' and that to the companion portrait of her husband 'Mr Perkins'. This use of her maiden name may mean that the portrait was painted before her marriage in 1714 or 1715 or, if later, that it was thought proper to affix the name by which Pope among other poets had addressed her. Miss Sharp dates the two portraits soon after her marriage,[2] but one cannot be certain. The inscription 'Mr Perkins' suggests that it was affixed while he was alive—he died in 1736. The form of the lettering suggests that an early date is probable. One may say, therefore, that if the words were inscribed during Arabella's life they are evidence of what her niece, the Abbess of a convent in Paris, thought conceit; if after her death, they are items in the evidence that the Abbess did not represent the fixed opinion of the family.

That the Abbess did so represent family opinion was the inference drawn by Dr Johnson:

> at Paris, a few years ago, a niece of Mrs. Fermor, who presided in an English Convent, mentioned Pope's work with very little gratitude, rather as an insult than an honour; and she may be supposed to have inherited the opinion of her family.[3]

This is Johnson's filling out of a note in his diary of the tour: 'Oct. 16 [1775] . . . Austin Nuns.—Grate.—Mrs. Fermor, Abbess.—She knew Pope, and thought him disagreeable.'[4] If the Abbess told him more he did not use it. Mrs Thrale accompanied Johnson, and her notes for the same day suggest there was much more: 'a great deal of Chat upon the Subject both of the Poet & the Lady'.[5] And some of the neglected material may be represented in the account of another visit paid to the convent by Mrs Thrale (now Mrs Piozzi) nine years later. This account may suggest that the Abbess had mellowed a little towards Pope in the meantime. Her evidence may be a little suspect since she seems to be enjoying the renewed rôle

1. op. cit., 120.
2. *ibid.*
3. *Lives*, iii 103.
4. Boswell's *Life*, ed. Hill-Powell (1934–50), ii 392 f.
5. *The French Journals of Mrs. Thrale and Doctor Johnson*, edited by M. Tyson and H. Guppy (1932), 120.

of literary anecdotist. Knowing her contribution to be valued—she or Mrs Piozzi thought the subject worth reintroducing—she may consciously be exercising her wit. Mrs Piozzi records that the Abbess took

> occasion to tell me, comically enough, 'That she believed there was but little comfort to be found in a house that harboured *poets* [*harbouring priests was another matter no doubt*]; for that she remembered Mr. Pope's praise made her aunt very troublesome and conceited, while his numberless caprices would have employed ten servants to wait on him; and he gave one' (said she) 'no amends by his talk neither, for he only sate dozing all day, when the sweet wine was out, and made his verses chiefly in the night; during which season he kept himself awake by drinking coffee, which it was one of the maids business to make for him, and they took it by turns.'[1]

But whether or not Mrs Piozzi's 'comically' merely records her own comment, the forceful and delightful diatribe shows at least that Arabella was proud, to the point of being tiresome, of her place in the poem; that Pope paid visits, which may have been long since the maids 'took it by turns'; and that the family resentment was either quite passed or was concealed. The exiled Prioress does not seem to be representing the opinions of the Fermors when one finds that some fifteen years earlier they had dedicated to Pope the Palladian Temple of Peace, with which the grounds of the new mansion at Tusmore had been ennobled.[2]

As for Pope and Arabella, he may not have forgiven her altogether for the trouble she had caused him, and it is clear he could not wholly approve what he knew, or had heard of her. In a letter postmarked 24 November [1714] he speaks of her to Martha Blount as follows:

> My Acquaintance runs so much in an Anti-Catholic Channel, that it was but tother day I heard of Mrs Fermor's being Actu-

1. *Observations and Reflections made in the Course of a Journey through France, Italy and Germany* (1789), i 20–1 With the latter part of this quotation cf. *Im. of Hor.*, Sat. II i 11 f.

2. Harry Paintin, *The Fermors of Oxfordshire*, Article v in *Oxford Journal Illustrated*, 4 July 1928.

ally, directly, and consummatively, married.[1] I wonder how the guilty Couple and their Accessories at Whiteknights [the home of the Englefields] look, stare, or simper, since that grand Secret came out which they so well concealed before. They conceald it as well as a Barber does his Utensils when he goes to trim upon a Sunday and his Towels hang out all the way . . .[2]

The tone is not pleasant, and Pope seems to be imputing to her some sort of misconduct. He had the grace to feel, however, that one of his most polished letters was due now that he had learned of the marriage:

> You are by this time satisfy'd how much the tenderness of one man of merit is to be prefer'd to the addresses of a thousand. And by this time, the Gentleman you have made choice of is sensible, how great is the joy of having all those charms and good qualities which have pleas'd so many, now apply'd to please one only. It was but just, that the same Virtues which gave you reputation, should give you happiness; and I can wish you no greater, than that you may receive it in as high a degree your self, as so much good humour must infallibly give it to your husband.
>
> It may be expected perhaps, that one who has the title of Poet, should say something more polite on this occasion: But I am really more a well-wisher to your felicity, than a celebrater of your beauty. Besides, you are now a married woman, and in a way to be a great many better things than a fine Lady; such as an excellent wife, a faithful friend, a tender parent, and at last as the consequence of them all, a saint in heaven. You ought now to hear nothing but that, which was all you ever desired to have (whatever others may have spoken to you) I mean *Truth*: And it is with the utmost that I assure you, no friend you have can more rejoice in any good that befalls you, is more sincerely delighted with the prospect of your future happiness, or more unfeignedly desires a long continuance of it. I beg you will think it but just, that a man who will certainly be spoken of as your admirer, after he is dead, may have the happiness to be esteem'd while he is living / Yours, etc.[3]

1. She was married to Francis Perkins of Ufton Court, Berks.
2. *Pope's Corresp.*, i 269.
3. *id.*, i 271 f.

Below the wreathing words there is self-justification. This letter he published, not of course till 1735. Meanwhile he represented her in his *Key to the Lock*, written about the time of her marriage, as pleased with her part in the poem:

> A Day or two after I was sent for, upon a slight Indisposition, to the young Lady's to whom the Poem is dedicated. She also took up the Character of *Belinda* with much Frankness and good Humour . . .[1]

VI

A year after first publication, says Pope, the poem was expanded.[2] This statement accords with that on the title-page of the poem in the *Works* of 1717 and later editions: 'Written in the Year 1712'. Here Pope is speaking approximately, splitting the difference between first writing and last revision since it is not till 8 December 1713 that he writes to Swift that he has 'finished the Rape of the Lock'. A letter to Caryll of 15 December shows that the additions had been occupying him at least for some weeks:

> I have been employed, since my being here in the country, in finishing the additions to the *Rape of the Lock*, a part of which I remember I showed you.[3]

Pope seems to have gone into the country late in November (he tells Gay on 23 October that 'I shall go into the country about a month hence'[4]), but although it was at Binfield that the additions were finished, work had been done on them earlier in London: Pope had told Caryll on 17 October that

> What Poetical News I have to tell you shall be deferr'd 'till our meeting. I shall be still att Mr Gervas's . . . except for a Fortnight at Binfield (wch some Poetical affairs of mine require) I therefore beg to know a week (or two rather) before y^u^ come up, that I may manage accordingly.[5]

1. p. 10. For the *Key*, see Ault, *Prose Works*, i lxxiii ff. and for its place in the Scriblerus programme, see Sherburn, *Early Life*, 80 f.

2. *Works*, 1736, i 141. For the extent of the additions see pp. 123 f.

3. *Pope's Corresp.*, i 205.

4. *id.*, i 195.

5. Add. MS. 28618, fol. 21r. The 'Poetical affairs' may be the additions or,

The letter of 15 December suggests that this meeting took place and that during it Pope showed Caryll what additions were then finished. The need to expand the poem with more machinery may have occurred to him at least as early as 10 June, when his *Receit to make an Epick Poem* had appeared in the *Guardian*.

The *Post Boy* of 26–8 January 1714 announced forthcoming publication:

> In a few Days will be publish'd, The Rape of the Lock; an Heroik-Comical Poem; by Mr. POPE now first publish'd complete in 5 Cantos; with 6 Copper Plates: Price 1s. . . . There will be a small Number . . . printed on fine Paper; those who are willing to have These, are desired to send in their Names to Bernard Lintott . . . No more being to be thus printed than are bespoke.

This elaborate arrangement explains why it was not till 20 February that Lintott paid Pope £15 for the poem,[1] and not till 2 March that the poem was published.[2] Some copies were ready by 25 February: in a letter of that date Pope sends Caryll two 'thô ye Poem will not be published this Week'.[3] The ruse to whet the public appetite succeeded astonishingly well. Whereas the first version, despite Addison's puff in *Spectator* 523, sold poorly—copies of the miscellany were being reissued in 1714[4]—Pope was able to announce to Caryll on 12 March that the poem

> has in four days time sold to the number of three thousand, and is already reprinted thô not in so fair a manner as the first Impression.[5]

instead or as well, they may be the *Iliad* which just at this time he was announcing his intention to translate (see Sherburn, *Early Career*, p. 113).

1. Nichols, viii 300: two years earlier, on 21 Mar. 1712, Lintott had paid £7 for the *Rape of the Locke* (*ibid.*).

2. The advertisement in the *Post Boy*, 2–4 March reads: 'This Day is publish'd, The Rape of the Lock, an Heroi-comical Poem by Mr. Pope, now first publish'd compleat; with the Addition of 3 New Cantos, adorn'd with 6 Copper Plates. Pr. 1s. Printed for Bernard Lintott . . . of whom may be had, most of this Author's Poems, separately; or, in a Collection of Miscellanies.'

3. Add. MS. 28618, fol. 22v.

4. Griffith 32: some sheets are newly set up, but not those of the *Rape of the Locke*.

5. Add. MS. 28618, fol. 24v.

The *Post Boy* of 9–11 March had announced this second edition.[1] A third edition followed in July,[2] and, speaking before the fourth, Pope places the sales at 'above 6000.'[3]

The *Key to the Lock*, by which Pope, under the name of Esdras Barnivelt, amused and benefited himself,[4] claimed for his poem a baleful political significance. He may still be said to be working in the epic tradition: the poem is shown to have a practical moral, and a political one such as that bestowed on Fénelon's *Télémaque*.

The later history of the poem is the placid one of textual improvement, except when, in 1728, Dennis published his *Remarks on Mr. Pope's Rape of the Lock*, the objections of which Pope answered on the margin of his copy.[5] When, in his later work, he refers to his poem, he does so with playful depreciation—

> A painted Mistress or a purling Stream[6]

—or with an envy of the days when, despite Caryll's commission, fancy was free:

> And all that voluntary[7] Vein,
> As when Belinda rais'd my Strain.[8]

The external history of the poem has been one of universal fame. Pope might consider his later work as a rarer achievement, but it is the *Rape of the Lock* which has charmed the crowd, at home and

1. Again announced as 'This Day . . . Publish'd' in the *Daily Courant* of 10 April, and again in the *Post Boy* of 4–6 May.

2. *Daily Courant*, 27 July: 'This Day is Publish'd, the 3d Edition of, The Rape of the Lock'.

3. *Key to the Lock*, p. v. The Key was published on 25 April 1715 (see Sherburn, *Mod. Phil.*, xxii 329) and the fourth edition of the *Rape* in the following September (Griffith 43).

4. Lintott paid him £10 15s. for it on 31 [*sic*] April 1715 (Nichols, viii 300).

5. See Appendix D, pp. 392 ff.

6. 'Epistle to Dr. Arbuthnot', l. 150.

7. Probably in the rare sense of 'growing wild or naturally; of spontaneous growth' (OED, which cites Pope's *Iliad*, xiv 396).

8. *Im. of Hor.*, Ep. I vii 49 f. In the same year comes this account from the diary of a not very literary young man, born 1691 and later to become Lord Chief Justice: 'August 22 [1716]. Read some *Spectators* and also the *Rape of the Lock*, which is a very witty poem, I think one of the best we have had come out these many years.' (*The Diary of Dudley Rider*, ed. W. Matthews, 1939, p. 300.)

abroad. It was being read by sempstresses in 1716,[1] it inaugurated a host of imitations,[2] it was anonymously translated into French prose in 1728 ('un petit Poëme Anglois de l'illustre Mr. Pope, le premier Poëte moderne de l'Angleterre'),[3] and when it was translated into Italian verse in 1739 Pope was acclaimed the greatest of living poets.[4]

1. Gay, *Trivia*, ii 562.

2. See Bond, pp. 68 ff.

3. *La Boucle de Cheveux Enlevée . . . Traduit de l'Anglois par Mr.* ** [i.e., P. F. Guyot Desfontaines]. *A Paris . . . M.DCC.XXVIII*, A 7r: the translator's preface also notes that the poem will help to remove the French prejudice, already shaken by *Gulliver's Travels*, that the English only deal in the serious and profound (A 8r).

4. *Il Riccio Rapito* [translated by A. Bonducci] *In Firenze. MDCCXXXIX*, A 1r: 'perchè il Sig. Pope si è fatta da per se stesso tale strada nel Mondo, che non vi è alcuno, che gli contrasti la stima del più gran Poeta, non solo dell'Inghilterra, ma di tutti i viventi'. Voltaire paid him the same praise 13 years before: 'I intend to send you two or three poems of Mr Pope, the best poet of England, and at present, of all the world. I hope you are acquainted enough with the English tongue, to be sensible of all the charms of his works. For my part I look on his poem call'd the essay upon criticism as superior to the art of poetry of Horace; and his rape of the lock, la boucle de cheveux, (that is a comical one) is in my opinion above the lutrin of Despreaux. I never saw so amiable an imagination, so gentle graces, so great varyety, so much wit, and so refined knowledge of the world, as in this little performance.' (*Voltaire's Correspondence*, ed. Theodore Besterman, Geneva, 1953, ii 36, letter 294 to N. C. Thierot, 26 Oct. 1726.) In 1744 the poem was translated into German verse, and in 1772 into Dutch prose. For the fortunes of the poem in Poland see S. Helsztynski's 'Pope in Poland. A Bibliographical Sketch' (*Slavonic Review*, vii, 1928–9, pp. 230 ff.). In 1778 appeared a translation excellently done from Marmontel's French version by Ignacy Bykowski, and in 1803 another, also excellent, by Niemcewicz, who translated it direct from the original. In his preface Niemcewicz writes: 'Heroic-comical works are known in many languages, but none can equal the rhymes of the English poet who in the highest degree unites wit, mirth and charm; the perfection of the original has made the translator's task the more difficult.' In 1822 the translation by Kaminski appeared, a more accurate version than Niemcewicz's but not so faithful to the spirit of the poem.

For particulars of further translations into French see Twickenham ed., v 17 f., and Audra, *Les Traductions françaises de Pope (1717–1825)*, Paris, 1931.

II: THE POEM

I

The epic, along with tragedy, has always been considered the most serious of poetic forms, but from the earliest times it has been skirted, or even intruded upon, by the comic. Homer, or some one else, had written the *Margites*, which, said Aristotle, stood in the same relation to comedies as the *Iliad* and *Odyssey* to tragedies.[1] And the *Battle of the Frogs and Mice* remains to show a trivial subject comically exalted by the epic manner, or, conversely, an exalted manner comically degraded by a trivial subject. Even in his 'serious' epics Homer did not seem entirely serious. He impaired the sacredness of his celestials, degrading gods into men at the same time that he elevated men into gods.[2] The epic continued to be regarded as comic as well as serious, sometimes by the same poet. There is the *Æneid* and, set against it, the avowedly mock-heroic *Culex* and the mock-heroic dignifying of the bees in *Georgic* iv. Set against Vida's *Christiad*, in the sixteenth century, there is his *Scacchia Ludus* with its

effigiem belli, simulataque veris
Prœlia, buxo acies fictas, et ludicra regna.[3]

Paradise Lost, in the next century, coexists with a number of comic poems which imitate the methods of the epic and so contribute to deflate its dignity. And along with mockery of the epic goes mockery of the romance, which had never been wholly separate from epic, except in the work of Lucan and Tasso.[4] 'Sir Thopas' leads to 'Nymphidia' and *Hudibras*, and in prose there had been *Don Quixote*. During the seventeenth and early eighteenth centuries, when so much reverence was being paid to the serious epic by poet and

1. *Art of Poetry*, trs. I. Bywater, 1920, p. 31.

2. Longinus, *Concerning Sublimity*, ix; cf. Davenant (Spingarn, ii 2), and *Rape of the Lock*, v 45 f.

3. Pope knew Vida early, and drew on him for onomatopœic examples in the letter to Walsh, 22 Oct. 1706. He included the *Scacchia Ludus* in his *Selecta Poemata Italorum*, 1740. For English translations see Bond, pp. 223 f. Vida is imitated in 'Upon Chesse-Play' (*Musarum Deliciæ*, 1655, pp. 41–5) which describes the play in military, but not epic, language.

4. Pope, with his eye on *Hudibras*, includes mockery of the romance in the epic mockery of the *Rape*: see iii 129 f.: 'So Ladies in Romance . . .' and ii 38.

critic, the best method of mimicking it was perfected. This process culminates in the *Rape of the Lock*. The epic, a dying mammoth, lives long enough to see its perfected self-criticism in Pope's poem.

But the triumph of the mock-heroic is not its mockery of a literary form. The mock-heroic poets laugh at the epic form but also at men. This is the reason why Addison's 'Prœlium inter Pygmæos et Grues Commissum'[1] cannot be considered in the line of development. Addison is back again at the *Battle of the Frogs and Mice* where the mockery, if it touches life at all, only touches life as it is lived in epics. It is as if the *Rape of the Lock* consisted solely of its sylphs. The best mock-heroic poets mock at the literary form for carrying the contemporary 'low' human material, but they mock more severely at the material for being so unworthy of the form. For though the mock-heroic poet adopts a different angle from the epic poet, he is standing on the same ground. Both are serious, morally interested, and in earnest. The seventeenth and eighteenth centuries considered the moral element in the epics their first glory, and they did not mock at that as they mocked at the machinery. Indeed, the literary mockery, like the gilded carriages of the time, was intended to get you somewhere worth getting to.

II

The literary mockery was found in practice to lead to complications. Boileau distinguished two bold methods: *Le Lutrin* was

> un burlesque nouveau . . . car, au lieu que dans l'autre burlesque Didon et Enée parloient comme des harengères et des crocheteurs, dans celui-ci une horlogère et un horloger parlent comme Didon et Enée.[2]

James Beattie called these two methods the burlesque and the mock-heroic respectively.[3] Burlesque can be quickly dismissed. It had been exploited in Scarron's *Virgile Travesti* (1648) and in the work of his French and English imitators. The degradation of the epic was complete when Dido spoke like a fishwife. It was, how-

1. 1699: translated anonymously as 'The Battel of the Pygmies and Cranes' in *Poems on Several Occasions . . . By Mr. Addison . . . 1719.*

2. *Œuvres*, ii 405: from the 'Au Lecteur' which appeared in the first edition (1674).

3. *Essays* (ed. 1778), p. 396.

ever, too complete: Scarron's long joke was as tediously insensitive as a schoolboy's. Boileau discredited burlesque by precept in the *Art Poétique*,[1] and by practice in *Le Lutrin*; and after him Dryden, Garth, and Pope find the mock-heroic to be the only method worthy of the serious attention of a poet.[2] But, though burlesque is inferior as a single method, it is found handy as a complication of mock-heroic. In Tassoni's *Secchia Rapita* (1622), for instance, the human characters are 'low'—citizens of Modena and Bologna warring over the theft of a bucket—but they act in the guise of epic heroes. This is the mock-heroic. But Tassoni brings in the epic gods to preside over his human action, and provides burlesque by degrading them to the level of men at their most unheavenly: Saturn, for example, has a bad cold, and Juno cannot attend an assembly of the gods because she is having her hair cut. But elsewhere Tassoni mixes the two kinds simultaneously. His low heroes, raised to epic stature, are often found breaking out into crude Italian dialects instead of grand epic speech. A similar complication exists in the *Rape of the Lock*. Clarissa and Thalestris, unlike Dido, are mere modern characters, but they are made to appear wholly heroic—indeed Clarissa's speech in Canto v minutely follows Sarpedon's speech to Glaucus in *Iliad* xii. But Sir Plume's heroics last no longer than his silence. He becomes burlesque when he bursts out into the appalling slang of 1712. In the *Rape of the Lock* the mock-heroic is established but not rigidly. The epical Belinda has hysterics, the Hector-like Baron sneezes: low figures which have been advanced into sublimity are suddenly dropped again, and dropped not only into Queen Anne courtiers, but into mere human beings at the mercy of their comic bodies. They begin as ordinary people—Belinda is asleep, the Baron has risen early—they are exalted by their epic context, and their fall is the sillier because it is from so high a perch. Pope makes much of both kinds in combination. But, unlike Tassoni, he does not go the whole hog and use full burlesque. His sylphs do not have colds, his gods are not blasphemed.

1. i 79 ff.

2. Pope's copy of the *Dispensary* (ed. 1706) is preserved in the Huntington Library: see R. K. Root, *The Poetical Career of Alexander Pope*, 1938, pp. 75 f.

III

Le Lutrin is the first modern poem to mock the whole epic form by the most ingenious means, those of diminution. Its epic is about as long as a single 'book' of an epic poem. The mockery of the complete epic form was seen to be essential to mock-heroic since the comparatively fixed structure of an epic was the most obvious thing about it, warranting the attention of Aristotle and many a later critic.[1] Principal among the latest was Le Bossu, 'the best of modern critics',[2] whose *Traité du Poëme Epique* appeared in 1675. The way the seventeenth-century critic looks at the epic decrees the way he looks at the mock-epic. The epic is seen first as a didactic poem, its chief end being the formation of the manners. Technically speaking, it must consist of a single 'fable', or action, which has its beginning, middle, and end and which covers a long time in comparison with the twenty-four hours allotted to a tragedy. The epic must arouse the emotion of wonder, particularly through its machinery (this machinery may be theological—designed to show the nature of God; or physical—representing external nature; or moral—representing virtues and vices). There are also the obvious minor elements: armies, fights, journeys by land and sea, a visit to the underworld, the arming of heroes, harangues, the manner of conducting the narration with its 'proposition' and 'invocation', its commentary on the action, its passages of historical or 'scientific' disquisition.[3] Then again the action of an epic should belong to the poet's own nation: 'One design of the *Epick Poets* before [the transgressing Davenant] was to adorn their own Countrey, there finding their *Heroes* and patterns of Virtue'[4]; and it was objected that Fénelon's *Télémaque* (1699) had no relation to France.[5]

As Boileau saw it, or came to see it, the mock-epic included as many of these epic ingredients as possible. It included them in one of two ways: either by taking them as they stood or by inverting

1. This rules out from mock-heroic John Philips's 'Splendid Shilling' (1701). Philips borrows Milton's epic style for a modern low subject but does not mimic the structure of the epic.

2. Dryden, *Essays*, i 211.

3. Homer is, for Pope, 'a historian antiquary . . . as well as a poet' (Postscript to *Odyssey*, vol. v 241).

4. Rymer (Spingarn, ii 168).

5. It was also considered to be a satire on Louis XIV and his government.

them for comic purposes. The epic moral, for instance, is not mocked at in *Le Lutrin*. Indeed its seriousness is deepened. Seventeenth-century critics saw, of course, far more moral in epic than was ever intended, and it may have been because of Le Bossu that Boileau added the explicitly moral ending to *Le Lutrin*. The first four Chants appeared in 1674 and were followed in 1683 by two more, the fifth continuing the general mock-heroics of i–iv and the sixth ending the poem with full moral statement like that of the *Epîtres*. This last Chant has little of the mock-heroic about it, but its moral and poetic grandeur are not felt to be altogether an intrusion. For all the comedy of the poem, it is, throughout its six Chants, profoundly serious, even grave. Some of the incidents may suggest Fielding's boisterousness in 'comic epic', but Boileau's farce, like Fielding's, is weighty with moral concern. The world of *Le Lutrin*, that is, is almost the world of *Hudibras*. Le Bossu, however, may have been partly responsible for the length and directness of the moral statement in *Le Lutrin*, and Pope thinks the moral of the *Rape of the Lock* important enough to 'open [it] more clearly' in the speech of Clarissa that he added in 1717.[1]

This moral element is transferred from the epic unchanged. In the same way, Boileau's machinery might almost be that of the later Latin epic. Like Lucan, he employs allegorical figures instead of gods, treating them seriously since they are the machinery of his moral as well as of his fable. These epic elements—including the native derivation of the fable, its singleness, its beginning, middle, and end—go unchanged into the mock-epic. The mockery lies elsewhere: in the diminution of size and time, in the meanness of the facts (instead of Tassoni's 'Elena transformarsi in una secchia' there is 'fait d'un vain pupitre un second Ilion'), in the low modernity of the characters and in the incongruity of the epic manner for its narration.

IV

Boileau's achievement is not the final one for the mock-heroic since Pope sees and takes the chance of going one better. *Le Lutrin*

1. See note on v 7 ff. Pope readily defends himself when Dennis charges the poem with the lack of a moral, and when it comes to Dr Johnson he not only defends Pope's moral but demonstrates its practical superiority to Boileau's: see Appendix D, pp. 394 ff. below.

is a brief dictionary of epic gesture and phrase,[1] and Pope only needed to put Boileau's method to further use. Like Boileau, he provides the epic opening of 'proposition' and 'invocation', the parody of actual epic speeches, the epic simile, the supernatural agent appearing in a dream, the allegorical figures given their appropriate setting, the battle, the learned survey of a tract of knowledge—in *Le Lutrin* it is the history of Christianity, in the *Rape of the Lock* the pre-existence and cosmology of the sylphs. There are, moreover, elements that have nothing to do with epic but belong rightly to mock-epic, which, being more 'literary' than epic (parody implies sophistication), allows the contemporary scene to intensify into actual names. Boileau names some of the books that are sent flying in his 'battle of the books', and Pope slights *Atalantis* by name[2]; Boileau hits at personal enemies—Ribou, Hainault, Barbin—and Pope at Partridge.[3]

Pope is further indebted to Boileau for his adaptation of the epic dénouement of strategy in war. The Greeks had had their wooden horse as a last and successful resort. When, in *Le Lutrin*, the battle is on the point of ending disastrously for the *trésorier*, Boileau, perhaps remembering Tassoni,[4] makes him forestall the vantages of victory by lifting his sacred hand to bless the victors, to disable them by forcing them to their knees; the *chantre* attempts flight but the 'doigts saintement allongés' pursue him till he, too, must kneel. This is the 'source' of Belinda's trick with the snuff:

> But this bold Lord, with manly Strength indu'd,
> She with one Finger and a Thumb subdu'd.

Nothing could excel the blessing in *Le Lutrin*: it seals the moral satire of the poem. Equally, nothing could excel Belinda's snuff in the *Rape of the Lock*: the contemporary reference is perfect. But the mock-heroic reference in Pope, accidentally as it were, improves on Boileau since the likeness between the blessing and the wooden horse is more difficult to trace than that between the *trésorier's*

1. See Gidel's notes, *Œuvres*, ii 413 ff.
2. Othello is mentioned, v 105 f., and a song from *Camilla* quoted, v 64; the other direct literary references are to epic. The poem provides, of course, continual literary echoes, parodies, and criticisms.
3. Tassoni had ridiculed an astrologer.
4. v xxx ff.

fingers and Belinda's finger and thumb. A comparison with Garth enforces Pope's superiority. In the *Dispensary*, just when the victorious physician is about to stab his opponent, Apollo interposes 'in form of Fee'.[1] This imitation of Homeric stratagem is good, but neglects to go one better in parody by improving on a particular stratagem.

V

Pope improves on Boileau as to fable. He makes his more homogeneous and shapely, shortens its duration to half a day, and refines its texture. This was no inevitable next step, since the English translators and adaptors of *Le Lutrin*—Crowne, Oldham, N[icholas] O[kes]—made it more gross in matter and less fine in manner. Nor had Garth taken his opportunity.

Garth is the most important poet connecting the mock-heroics of Boileau and Pope.[2] Pope early became his friend and took particular interest in the successive revisions of the *Dispensary*. Garth failed to improve on Boileau himself but he helps Pope to improve on him. The *Dispensary*, which first appeared in 1699, derives its theme from the dispute which arose between the College of Physicians and the Company of Apothecaries when the latter were ordered to dispense drugs *gratis* to the poor. Garth lacks the control necessary for fine mockery either of people or of a literary form. He has too many incidents. Indeed his poem is almost an *Endymion*, so delighted is its author to pass among 'gay gilded Meteors' and 'nimble Corruscations' in flying to the Fortunate Isles, or to travel underground among coloured ores 'glimm'ring in their dawning Beds'.[3] Alternatively, his poem sometimes reads like a satire or epistle of Boileau or Pope: at one point he even adapts a passage from Boileau's *Art Poétique* and puts it into the mouth of the Fury

1. Cf. *Hudibras*, I ii 775 ff.:

    This said, with hasty rage he snatch'd
    His gun-shot . . .
    But Pallas came, in shape of rust,
    And 'twixt the spring and hammer thrust
    Her Gorgon shield . . .

2. Dryden's 'Mac Flecknoe' is important for the *Dunciad*, but not for the *Rape of the Lock*.

3. pp. 66, 101.

Disease.[1] Far from providing the mock-heroic with its perfect form, Garth unmakes it. The charming elements jostle as in Tassoni; the less-than-perfect form of Boileau's Chant vi is made the excuse for formlessness. But one or two of Garth's original elements find their place in the *Rape of the Lock*. Garth employed for his descriptions the method of laying down parallel stripes of the beautiful and the sordid, of enforcing his scale of values by pretending not to have one. This method was more subtle than Tassoni's (familiar to English readers in *Don Juan*) of dropping flat into bathos. Garth writes:

> With that, a Glance from mild *Aurora*'s Eyes
> Shoots thro' the Chrystal Kingdoms of the Skies;
> The Savage Kind in Forests cease to roam,
> And Sots o'ercharg'd with nauseous Loads reel home.
> Light's chearful Smiles o'er th' Azure Waste are spread,
> And Miss from Inns o' Court bolts out unpaid.[2]

This is one of the descriptive-satiric methods in the *Rape of the Lock* —see, e.g., iii 19 ff.[3] It is also the key to more concentrated effects:

> To stain her Honour, or her new Brocade . . .[4]

or to that line which has troubled so many readers:

> Puffs, Powders, Patches, Bibles, Billet-doux.[5]

Pope is indebted to Garth for these and other figures. But the real virtue of Garth in the history of mock-heroic lies in fragments of his material. Among the medical lumber of his poem are satiric references to the 'beau monde' (the phrase of the time) that provide Pope with hints and materials. Science in the *Dispensary*, among more serious concerns, seeks to understand

> Why paler Looks impetuous Rage proclaim,
> And why chill Virgins redden into Flame.
> Why Envy oft transforms with wan Disguise,

1. p. 63 ff.: cf. *L'Art Poétique*, iii 311 ff. This objection was raised at the time and Garth discusses it in his preface, A 5v.

2. p. 34: contrast Dryden, *Æneid*, viii 546 ff.

3. Warton (i 232) speaks of the 'real and imaginary distresses . . . coupled together' at iv 3 ff.

4. ii 107.

5. i 138. See Appendix F below, pp. 401 ff.

And why gay Mirth sits smiling in the Eyes.
All Ice why *Lucrece*, or *Sempronia*, Fire . . .[1]

And Horoscope has his opinion sought by Iris, among others, who

. . . his Cosmetick *Wash* would try,
To make her Bloom revive, and Lovers die . . .[2]

There are other similar passages, some of them more medically outspoken.[3] And Garth's underworld has, like Virgil's, its 'Mansion of disastrous Love', but it is Virgil's with a difference:

Olivia here in Solitude he found,
Her down-cast Eyes fix'd on the silent Ground:
Her Dress neglected, and unbound her Hair,
She seem'd the mournful Image of Despair.
How lately did this celebrated *Thing*
Blaze in the Box, and sparkle in the Ring . . .[4]

Two of these lines with little change go into the *Rape of the Lock* and the spirit and material of them are Pope's, too.[5]

Like most other elements in the *Dispensary*, these amusing, exquisite, or poignant glimpses of the 'beau monde' lose their value in the general chaos of the poem. The same fate befalls the 'beauty' in Garth's poem, and here again Pope takes, and makes significant, what in Garth was only half valued. The description of the Fortunate Isles,[6] or of the gradual conversational collapse of the god of sloth—

More had he spoke, but sudden Vapours rise,
And with their silken Cords tie down his Eyes[7]

—in such descriptions Garth manipulates silken cords of his own.

1. p. 4.
2. p. 24.
3. Pope's poem has its innuendos.
4. pp. 112 f.
5. Ozell's translation of *Le Lutrin* (1708) owes something to Garth in its interpolation of a six-line passage on spleen and the fashionable world (p. 61); and, to take another instance, in its unwarranted reference to Arabian tales and the way 'fair' readers are lulled by them 'Supinely in soft Dreams' (p. 97) Ozell is helping to feminize the mock-heroic.
6. pp. 69 ff.
7. p. 13.

The trouble is, however, that they are tangled in the litter of the poem, and in a medical satire in mock-heroics should not be there at all.

VI

When Pope came to write his poem he had little left to invent. The abstract form of his poem was already three-quarters ready in *Le Lutrin*. Like Boileau, he had been given his theme, and this theme entailed a fashionable setting that had been accidentally but memorably touched on by Garth—and, outside the mock-heroic, had been brilliantly recreated by Waller and fifty other poets, by Addison and Steele and the periodical writers, and was soon to furnish the material for Gay's *Fan*.[1] In creating the unified form of the mock-epic Pope had mainly to attend to the ending.

The characteristic ending for an epic is the work of a *deus ex machina*. In Boileau it had been Piété and Thémis, who sought out de Lamoignon. In Garth it had been Harvey, who was to be found plucking simples in the Elysian Fields. The quarrels of both their poems had been readily terminable by a return to a modified status quo. There was no such solution possible in Pope's poem since the fatal scissors had severed the lock

From the fair Head, for ever and for ever![2]

Boileau had brought de Lamoignon into his poem as mediator, and Pope could have brought in Caryll whose rôle in the genesis of the poem had been similar. But he does not choose to end his poem in this way. What happened to the lock in Lord Petre's hands remains unknown. But, in the poem, it was as much an offence against poetic justice for him to keep it as it was futile for Belinda to take it back. The solution for Pope's difficulty needed to be one resembling as closely as possible the dénouement of some actual epic poem. Pope remembered a poem that had been a favourite since

1. I have seldom drawn on this poem to illustrate the *Rape of the Lock*, since it is difficult to see which way the debt lies. The debt may well have been Pope's: he refers to news about the poem in August 1713, and is found asking Gay to let him 'take along with me [into the country] your poem of the *Fan*, to consider it at full leisure' at about the time when he was engaged on the additions to the *Rape of the Locke* (letters to Gay, 23 Aug. 1713 and 23 Oct. [1713]).

2. iii 154.

childhood. Ovid had ended his *Metamorphoses* by transforming the soul of Julius Caesar into a star. Callimachus had so transformed the locks of Berenice. Pope combines the two.[1] In adapting a metamorphosis from Ovid he is still in touch with epic. Ovid's poem borders on the epic, and similar metamorphoses are found in pure epic: Le Bossu had commented on them in his *Traité*.[2]

Pope had been given his theme, complete with its setting, and seized it as an opportunity to sharpen the mock-heroic references to their final point. It was not a difficult task to intensify the mock-heroic references in number, for the simple reason that Pope followed rather than led. He used all the kinds of references used by Boileau and Garth and added to them (as Garth had added to those of Boileau)[3] by providing a voyage, Jove-like threats of torture, the genealogy of the bodkin, and so on. But the intensifying of the mock-heroic references in sharpness is the most brilliant and original thing about the *Rape of the Lock*. What Pope does is mainly to continue the process of diminution. He makes most things smaller in size and more femininely exquisite in quality, which better fulfilled the demands of mockery. He makes his hero a woman, and not simply any woman, but Belinda herself. In the old epics the heroes were god-like Hectors, in earlier mock-epics the heroes were common men: Pope completes the mockery in the mock-heroics by widening the gulf between Hector and the fat *trésorier* or Horoscope until it stretches between Hector and Belinda. From this beginning everything else follows. Instead of the rape of Helen, there was Tassoni's bucket, Boileau's pulpit, but Pope's lock of hair. Instead of the epic meals—the beefsteak in Homer, the loads of sausages in Tassoni, the piled refectory fare in Boileau—there is in Pope the lacquer and silver ceremonial of coffee. Ajax and Achilles had their great shields magnificently displayed by Homer. Garth had given Querpo a shield for the medical fracas.[4] In Pope these shields have

1. Pope was no doubt familiar with Boileau's bagatelle, 'La Métamorphose de la Perruque de Chapelain en Comète' (1664); and see Pope's *Epilogue to the Sat.*, ii 231 and note.

2. v, chr. iii.

3. Garth provides an altar built to Disease, the fire on which is lighted by prescriptions.

4. His Arms were made, if we may credit Fame,
By *Mulciber*, the Mayor of *Bromingham*.

become Belinda's tremblingly expansive petticoat. Homer, Virgil, and Tassoni have their gods and goddesses; Lucan, Tassoni, Boileau, and Garth have their personified gods and goddesses—Fame, Fate, Time, Death, Piety, Law, Envy, Sloth. But the machinery of Pope is mainly provided by the sylphs, who unite the bodily fluidity of Milton's angels with the minuteness of Shakespeare's fairies. Boileau had imitated the epic battles by a skirmish of flung books; Garth's equivalent for books had been gallipots, urinals, and brass weights, and he had made Mirmillo boast of the patients he had dispatched in a single day.[1] In Pope it is a game of cards drawn forth to combat on a velvet plain and, later, a hullabaloo mainly of fans, silks, and milliners' whalebone. Boileau had had his similes of bulls, wolf, and cranes; Garth his of Leviathan and cranes. The mock-epic was incomplete without its simile, but Pope will not admit the beast. His simile for the battle (at this point Boileau had brought out his bull) is literary:

So when bold *Homer* makes the Gods engage . . .[2]

and the subsidiary one for an incident in the battle is a gentle adaptation from Ovid's Dido:

Thus on *Meander*'s flow'ry Margin lies
Th'expiring Swan, and as he sings he dies.[3]

VII

Garth had spent some pains on providing beautiful description in his poem. An account of evening will contain such a line as

The Clouds aloft with golden Edgings glow.[4]

Of temper'd *Stibium* the bright Shield was cast,
And yet the Work the Metal far surpass'd.
A Foliage of dissembl'd *Senna* Leaves,
Grav'd round the Brim, the wond'ring Sight deceives.
Embost upon the Field, a Battel stood
Of *Leeches* spouting Hemorrhoidal Blood . . . (p. 82).

1. *Oxford* and all her passing Bells can tell,
By this Right Arm, what mighty Numbers fell.
Whilst others meanly ask'd whole Months to slay,
I oft dispatch'd the Patient in a Day . . . (p. 54).

2. v 45.
3. v 65 f.
4. p. 66.

Pope's theme justifies such poetry more than Garth's did, and in following him he was jealous of it. It is an element that has been grossly undervalued by critics who at most can speak only of 'filigree'.[1] And there have been other and graver oversights. It is seen that there is diminution, but not that there is magnification, too.[2] In the same way that the poem mixes burlesque with mock-heroic, it applies these two contrasted scales. There is a game of cards instead of a battle; but, instead of coffee pouring into a cup,

> . . . *China*'s Earth receives the smoking Tyde,[3]

a line gigantically increasing space and time. Instead of Hector there is Belinda, but her eyes radiate lightning. One is continually at a loss for definitions. And the critics also miss what an editor cannot—the way the poem beds itself in its city and in its time. The renaissance critics considered that the epic should be vast, containing the whole world.[4] The whole world is represented in Pope's poem:

> This Casket *India*'s glowing Gems unlocks,
> And all *Arabia* breathes from yonder Box.[5]

or

> The Fate of *Louis*, and the Fall of *Rome*.[6]

But the scene of the epics is empty desert beside the milieu of the *Rape of the Lock*, its close-packed London. And the epic is thing-less beside Pope's poem with its close-packed material objects. 'Coffee, tea, and Chocolate . . . are now become capital branches of this nation's commerce', wrote Defoe in 1713[7]: all three find a place in the *Rape of the Lock*. There are the white-gloved beaux, the tweezer-case, but also, flashed into the very bosom of Hampton Court, the

1. The best comment on the filigree of the poem is Beardsley's: *The Rape of the Lock . . . Embroidered with Nine Drawings by Aubrey Beardsley . . . MDCCCXCVI.* The verso of the half-title reads 'Twenty-five copies of this Book have been printed on Japanese Vellum for Sale.' The drawings should be seen in this edition.

2. This seems to have been first pointed out by W. H. Auden (*From Anne to Victoria*, ed. B. Dobrée, 1937, p. 105).

3. iii 110. Cf. 'wedg'd whole Ages in a *Bodkin*'s Eye' (ii 128).

4. See Spingarn, *History*, pp. 212 f.

5. i 133 f.

6 v 140.

7. See D. George, *England in Transition*, 1931, pp. 35 f.

coffee-house politicians with their half-closed eyes.[1] The hour that Belinda sits down to ombre is the hour

> When hungry Judges soon the Sentence sign,
> And Wretches hang that Jury-men may Dine.[2]

Nor are the intellectual interests of the time neglected. Pope's Catholic friends found phrases in the poem reminding them of the Primer[3]; Dennis discovers 'a bitter Bob for Predestinarians'[4]; there is a hit at Presbyterians[5]; contemporary educational theory is criticized by implication[6]; and the virtuosi and the casuists, both lay and ecclesiastical, are pinioned here as firmly as in the *Dunciad*:

> Dry'd Butterflies, and Tomes of Casuistry.[7]

This sort of satire was expected of the mock-heroic. As it came to be practised in the seventeenth and eighteenth centuries, the mock-heroic mocked at epic but mocked more at contemporary society. But the social mockery of the *Rape of the Lock* is not simple, does not make a pat contribution to single-mindedness. Its world is vast and complicated. It draws no line of cleavage between its 'seriousness' and its mockery. Belinda is not closed up in a rigid coterie which Clarissa and the rest of the poem mock at. Pope, fierce and tender by turns, knows no more than Hazlitt, 'whether to laugh or weep'[8] over the poem. He is aware of values that transcend his satire:

> *Belinda* smil'd, and all the World was gay[9]

and

> If to her share some Female Errors fall,
> Look on her Face, and you'll forget 'em all.[10]

---

1. iii 117 f.
2. iii 21 f.
3. Cf. the charge (*Key*, p. 26) that 'a Tendency to Popery . . . is secretly insinuated through the whole'.
4. In ii 101–10 (*Remarks*, E 1r).
5. v 121; and see n.
6. i 29 ff.
7. v 122; and see n.
8. Hazlitt, *Works*, ed. P. P. Howe, 1930, v 72. Warton (i 225, 231) twice uses the word 'poignant' to describe passages in the poem.
9. ii 52.
10. ii 17 f.

The criticism the poem provides is sometimes more a picture than a criticism. It is so elaborate, shifting, constellated, that the intellect is baffled and demoralized by the aesthetic sense and emotions. One is left looking at the face of the poem, as at Belinda's.

That Pope was aware of the complex response his poem elicits from its readers is shown by his letter to Mrs Marriot of 28 February 1713/14, which accompanies what is evidently the newly published *Rape of the Lock*, and contains the following:

> What excuse then, can I offer for the poem that attends this letter, where 'tis a chance but you are diverted from some very good action or useful reflection for more hours than one. I know it is no sin to laugh, but I had rather your laughter should be at the vain ones of your own sex than at me, and therefore would rather have you read my poem than my letter. This whimsical piece of work, as I have now brought it up to my first design, is at once the most a satire, and the most inoffensive, of anything of mine. People who would rather it were let alone laugh at it, and seem heartily merry, at the same time that they are uneasy. 'Tis a sort of writing very like tickling. I am so vain as to fancy a pretty complete picture of the life of our modern ladies in this idle town from which you are so happily, so prudently, and so philosophically retired.[1]

VIII

Finally, Pope takes over from the serious epic another element which he does not mock at: the element of serious technical care. He spent on his eight hundred lines as much devotion as, say, Milton had spent on one (or more) of the Books of *Paradise Lost*. He even plays ombre with himself till he hits on the game which suits his purpose. With the economy for which he is the supreme poet, he makes the same vehicle carry both human and epic mockery.[2] He makes the 'figures' carry the satire. The line

> Dost sometimes Counsel take—and sometimes *Tea*[3]

1. *Pope's Corresp.*, i 211.
2. See notes on i 55 f., and on v 71 ff.
3. iii 8: 'This association, of serious and comic subjects with the same verb, is one of the most diverting ingredients of comic poetry. Thus ... Phaedrus, v. 2. 8.

> Nunc conde ferrum—et linguam pariter futilem ...

is famous among grammarians as an instance of zeugma, but lying beyond its technical smartness is all the mixed power, hollowness, and public homeliness of royalty. There is more than literary surprise, than bathos, in

And send the Godly in a Pett, to pray;[1]

and the bathetic and alliteratively peppered disorder on Belinda's dressing table is fundamentally a moral disorder:

Puffs, Powders, Patches, Bibles, Billet-doux.[2]

The integrity of Pope's art is well exhibited by the additions to the second edition. He considered that the manner in which he had contrived the sylphs to 'fit so well' with 'what was published before' constituted 'one of the greatest proofs of judgment of anything I ever did'.[3] Addison, who had cited the first version of the poem as an instance of the appropriateness of pagan mythology for mock-heroic,[4] tried to dissuade him from altering a poem that was already 'a delicious little thing, and, as he expressed it, *merum sal.*'[5] According to Warburton, Pope imputed Addison's advice to ungenerous motives,[6] and his immediate revenge took the form of two stabs at *Rosamond* in which Addison had used machines facilely.[7]

Pope saw to it that the additions included specimens of all the

---

a passage which Butler, the grand exemplar of this species of festivity, seems to have had in view in [*Hudibras*] Part ii. Canto 2. ver. 660' (Wakefield's note).

1. iv 64.

2. i 138.

3. Spence, p. 142: 'the scheme of adding [the machinery] was much liked and approved of by several of my friends, and particularly by Dr. Garth: who, as he was one of the best natured men in the world, was very fond of it' (p. 195).

4. *Spectator* 523 (30 Oct. 1712): 'In Mock-Heroick Poems, the use of the Heathen Mythology is not only excusable but graceful, because it is the Design of such Compositions to divert, by adapting the fabulous Machines of the Ancients to low Subjects, and at the same time by ridiculing such kinds of Machinery in Modern Writers'.

5. Warburton, vol. iv 26.

6. *ibid.*

7. See notes on ii 90 and iv 46. Pope's notes to the later cantos of the poem show his pleasure—cf. that of the sylphs themselves at v 132—in the recurrent use of the machines: Le Bossu had affirmed that '*Machines* are to be made use of all over, since *Homer* and *Virgil* do nothing without them' (*Treatise*, p. 225).

three kinds of machine noted by Le Bossu[1]: the sylphs are 'theological' (they represent 'good' and 'bad'), 'physical' (they roll planets and attend to the weather), and 'allegorical' or 'moral' (the machines include Spleen). And if Ariel takes up a disproportionate space in Cantos i and ii—it will be recalled that Shock thought that Belinda had slept too long—it is mainly in his long speeches that Pope contrives to set the poem most firmly in its world of virgins, prudes, matrons, powders, essences, and jewels, and to deliver some of his most telling satire. Nor must it be overlooked—Pope[2] and later critics overlooked it[3]—that the additions do not provide the only machinery in the poem. They join a poem the machinery of which Addison had already commended. In the first version of the poem the Baron had worshipped 'Propitious Heav'n, and ev'ry Pow'r . . . But chiefly *Love*'; had built an altar; had devised a prayer to which 'The Pow'rs gave Ear', but only 'granted half'.[4] Moreover, though it was coffee, and not a god, which

> Sent up in Vapours to the *Baron*'s Brain
> New Stratagems, the radiant Locke to gain,[5]

the stroke which severed the lock is described as 'fatal',[6] and Fate is hymned, along with steel, in the concluding paragraph of the canto. Belinda's hysterics are in vain since

> *Fate* and *Jove* had stopp'd the *Baron*'s Ears.

Jove hangs out the golden scales so that the battle of fans and whalebone can reach an issue. And, finally, Heaven, which at the outset granted only half the Baron's prayer, consistently dooms him to lose the trophy:

> With such a Prize no Mortal must be blest,
> So Heav'n decrees! with Heav'n who can contest?[7]

1. See above, p. 109. For a discussion of contemporary views on the kinds of machinery allowable see *Englische Studien*, 73 (1938–9), pp. 45 ff.

2. See dedicatory epistle, p. 142 below.

3. Dennis is an exception, see *Remarks*, C 7v: but he makes no use of his perception.

4. *Rape of the Locke*, i 52 ff.

5. *id.*, 99 f.

6. *id.*, 117: in the 1714 version it is even more explicitly part of the machinery: Fate urg'd the Sheers' (iii 151).

7. *Rape of the Locke*, ii 91, 126, 156 f.

All this machinery is of the kind which Le Bossu had spoken of most strongly: 'The *Gods* are the *Causes* of the Actions. They make the *Plots*, and dispose the *Solution* of them too'[1]; and in his closing transformation Pope has also provided machinery of the kind which Le Bossu had described as 'requir[ing] Divine Probability'.[2] So that it is to all this august machinery that Pope added the more exquisitely mechanized sylphs and the dour goddess Spleen.[3] And it is for this reason that Dennis's charge that the machinery does not affect the action is beside the point: he is thinking only of the sylphs and is forgetting the active machines which they supplement.[4] For the same reason there is nothing to be said for Dennis's verdict that in the *Rape of the Lock* the machines are not opposed to each other.[5] Pope's sylphs are opposed to Fate[6] and are betrayed because Belinda, to the improvement of the moral satire, transgresses the one condition which gives them power, 'an inviolate Preservation of Chastity'.[7] Moreover, Pope, unlike de Villars, makes some of his sylphs 'bad', and, though the bad are not actively confronted with the good, they alternate within a split second:

> . . . that sad moment, when the *Sylphs* withdrew,
> And *Ariel* weeping from *Belinda* flew,

in that moment, the gnome Umbriel

> Repairs to search the gloomy Cave of *Spleen*.[8]

IX

By means of Pope's additions a poem of two cantos (334 lines) became a poem of five cantos (794 lines). The big changes, deserving to be called structural, mainly affect cantos i–iii and canto iv

1. *Treatise*, p. 226.
2. *id.*, 223 f. The 1714 additions provided for other machines of this kind: the metamorphoses of the tortoise and the elephant at i 135 f., and of the splenetics at iv 47 ff.
3. He also took the opportunity to increase the rôle of the original machines.
4. See Appendix D, pp. 394 and 396 f. Dr Johnson agreed with Dennis: see *Lives*, iii 235.
5. *Remarks*, C 4r–5r.
6. See, especially, iii 145 f.
7. Dedicatory epistle, p. 143.
8. iv 11 f., 16.

up to l. 92. We get, besides a few small additions, Belinda's dream of Ariel, i 20–114; the toilet, i 121–48; the voyage up the Thames and Ariel's speech to the sylphs, ii 47–142; the game of ombre, iii 25–104; the sylphs' vain attempt to divert the scissors, iii 135–46, 149–52; and Umbriel's visit to the cave of Spleen, iv 11–92. After this point till the end, a matter of 230 lines, the changes in 1714 are less vital, inclining to the ornamental (Umbriel breaking the vial, iv 141 f.; Belinda remembering Ariel's warning, iv 165 f.; Umbriel and the sprites watching the battle, v 53–6; the gnomes directing the snuff, v 83 f.; the pedigree of the bodkin, v 89–96; and the sylphs watching the flight of the lock, v 131 f.). The only other addition in this section of the poem, Clarissa's speech (v 7–36), is not made till 1717. Pope was wise not to add too much towards the end of the poem: the action of a story should speed up at the end.

It is difficult for a modern reader to realize how dazzling, after the earlier history of the mock-heroic, these additions were. But, though he cannot fail to be 'conscious of the rich Brocade' of the 1714 version, the story itself is not so proportionate in 1714 as in 1712. One reason for this is that even in 1712 its thin thread was already carrying quite a number of weights—Pope is already inserting meditations and descriptive passages, and fairly long speeches. After all, the story is a slight one to fill the 334 lines of the original version, let alone the 794 of the final one. Moreover, we have never known the 1712 version in a revised state. It contains poor passages, especially in the narrative parts[1] (the speeches did not need much revision). The revision which was given to the 1712 version is only encountered amid the new version of 1714. Without making any additions, Pope's inevitable verbal changes could have made the 1712 version *merum sal* indeed. But the first version—and verbal revision could have made no difference to this—yields most of itself at a first reading, while the second version is inexhaustible. And, without the additions, the poem could never have dropped its 'salt' so deftly and finally on the great disappearing tail of the epic poem.

1. e.g. i 13–18, 83 f.

THE *RAPE* of the *LOCKE*.

AN

HEROI-COMICAL

P O E M.

Nolueram, Belinda, *tuos violare capillos,*
Sed juvat hoc precibus me tribuisse tuis.

MART. Lib. 12. Ep. 86

NOTE ON THE TEXT

The principles set out in the General Note on the Text, pp. x f. above, have been waived, except for the modernization of ſ. The text is *literatim* that of the first and only edition (*Miscellaneous Poems And Translations. By Several Hands*, 1712; reissued 1714), except that two italic colons have been corrected to roman, and 'Their' at ii 160 has been corrected to 'There'.

NOTE ON THE NOTES

In the *Rape of the Locke* Pope's annotations have been reproduced. Other annotations are restricted to passages not found in the *Rape of the Lock*.

THE RAPE *of the* LOCKE.

CANTO I.

WHAT dire Offence from Am'rous Causes springs,
What mighty Quarrels rise from Trivial Things,
I sing—This Verse to *C—l*, Muse! is due;
This, ev'n *Belinda* may vouchsafe to view:
Slight is the Subject, but not so the Praise,
If she inspire, and He approve my Lays.
Say what strange Motive, Goddess! cou'd compel
A well-bred *Lord* t'assault a gentle *Belle?*
Oh say what stranger Cause, yet unexplor'd,
Cou'd make a gentle *Belle* reject a *Lord?*
And dwells such Rage in *softest Bosoms* then?
And lodge such daring Souls in *Little Men*?
Sol thro' white Curtains did his Beams display,
And op'd those Eyes which brighter shine than they;
Shock just had giv'n himself the rowzing Shake,
And Nymphs prepar'd their *Chocolate* to take;
Thrice the wrought Slipper knock'd against the Ground,
And striking Watches the tenth Hour resound.
Belinda rose, and 'midst attending Dames
Launch'd on the Bosom of the silver *Thames:*
A Train of well-drest Youths around her shone,
And ev'ry Eye was fixed on her alone;
On her white Breast a sparkling *Cross* she wore,
Which *Jews* might kiss, and Infidels adore.

---

11. Concanen (*Supplement to the Profound*, 1728, pp. 19 f.) after quoting Pope's *Peri Bathous* ('the whole Spirit of the *Bathos* shall be owing *to one choice Word that ends the Line*'), takes this line as his instance. Pope changes it in the edition of 1736, see *Rape of the Lock*, i 11 f.

12. Cf. Virgil, *Georgic* iv 83 (of the bees):

Ingentes animos angusto in pectore versant;

Addison's translation (*Works*, 1721, i 20):

Their little bodies lodge a mighty soul;

and *Iliad*, v 999: Whose little Body lodg'd a mighty Mind.

Her lively Looks a sprightly Mind disclose,
Quick as her Eyes, and as unfixt as those:
Favours to none, to all she Smiles extends;
Oft she rejects, but never once offends.
Bright as the Sun her Eyes the Gazers strike,
And, like the Sun, they shine on all alike.
Yet graceful Ease, and Sweetness void of Pride,
Might hide her Faults, if *Belles* had Faults to hide:
If to her share some Female Errors fall,
Look on her Face, and you'll forgive 'em all.
This Nymph, to the Destruction of Mankind,
Nourish'd two Locks, which graceful hung behind
In equal Curls, and well conspir'd to deck
With shining Ringlets her smooth Iv'ry Neck.
Love in these Labyrinths his Slaves detains,
And mighty Hearts are held in slender Chains.
With hairy Sprindges we the Birds betray,
Slight Lines of Hair surprize the Finny Prey,
Fair Tresses Man's Imperial Race insnare,
And Beauty draws us with a *single Hair*.
Th'Adventrous *Baron* the bright Locks admir'd,
He saw, he wish'd, and to the Prize aspir'd:
Resolv'd to win, he meditates the way,
By Force to ravish, or by Fraud betray;
For when Success a Lover's Toil attends,
Few ask, if Fraud or Force attain'd his Ends.
For this, e'er *Phœbus* rose, he had implor'd
Propitious Heav'n, and ev'ry Pow'r ador'd,
But chiefly *Love*—to *Love* an Altar built,
Of twelve vast *French* Romances, neatly gilt.
There lay the Sword-knot *Sylvia*'s Hands had sown,
With *Flavia*'s Busk that oft had rapp'd his own:

56. A busk is 'A strip of wood, whalebone, steel, or other rigid material passed down the front of a corset, and used to stiffen or support it' (OED): cf. Rochester, 'On a Juniper Tree cut down to make busks'. Hall, *Virgidemiarum*, IV vi 10

A Fan, a Garter, half a Pair of Gloves;
And all the Trophies of his former Loves.
With tender *Billet-doux* he lights the Pyre,
And breaths three am'rous Sighs to raise the Fire.
Then prostrate falls, and begs with ardent Eyes
Soon to obtain, and long possess the Prize:
The Pow'rs gave Ear, and granted half his Pray'r,
The rest, the Winds dispers'd in empty Air.
  Close by those Meads for ever crown'd with Flow'rs,
Where *Thames* with Pride surveys his rising Tow'rs,
There stands a Structure of Majestick Frame,
Which from the neighb'ring *Hampton* takes its Name.
Here *Britain*'s Statesmen oft the Fall foredoom
Of Foreign Tyrants, and of Nymphs at home;
Here Thou, great *Anna!* whom three Realms obey,
Dost sometimes Counsel take—and sometimes *Tea*.
  Hither our Nymphs and Heroes did resort,
To taste awhile the Pleasures of a Court;
In various Talk the chearful hours they past,
Of, who was *Bitt*, or who *Capotted* last:
This speaks the Glory of the *British Queen*,
And that describes a charming *Indian Screen*;
A third interprets Motions, Looks, and Eyes;
At ev'ry Word a Reputation dies.
Snuff, or the *Fan*, supply each Pause of Chatt,
With singing, laughing, ogling, and all that.
  Now, when declining from the Noon of Day,
The Sun obliquely shoots his burning Ray;
When hungry Judges soon the Sentence sign,
And Wretches hang that Jury-men may Dine;
When Merchants from th'*Exchange* return in Peace,

---

charged men with wearing them, and the annotation in the Warton–Singer edition (1824) extends the accusation to later centuries. Cf. John Caryll, Dryden's *Ovid's Ep.*, p. 247.

76. *Bitt*] = cheated at cards.

Capotted] = scored all the tricks at cards: see OED.

And the long Labours of the *Toilette* cease—
The Board's with Cups and Spoons, alternate, crown'd;
The Berries crackle, and the Mill turns round;
On shining Altars of *Japan* they raise
The silver *Lamp*, and fiery Spirits blaze;
From silver Spouts the grateful Liquors glide,
And *China*'s Earth receives the smoking Tyde:
At once they gratifie their Smell and Taste,
While frequent Cups prolong the rich Repast.
Coffee, (which makes the Politician wise,
And see thro' all things with his half shut Eyes)
Sent up in Vapours to the *Baron*'s Brain
New Stratagems, the radiant Locke to gain.
Ah cease rash Youth! desist e're 'tis too late,
Fear the just Gods, and think of *Scylla*'s Fate!
Chang'd to a Bird, and sent to flitt in Air,
She dearly pays for *Nisus*' injur'd Hair!
    But when to Mischief Mortals bend their Mind,
How soon fit Instruments of Ill they find?
Just then, *Clarissa* drew with tempting Grace
A two-edg'd Weapon from her shining Case;
So Ladies in Romance assist their Knight,
Present the Spear, and arm him for the Fight.
He takes the Gift with rev'rence, and extends
The little Engine on his Finger's Ends,
This just behind *Belinda*'s Neck he spread,
As o'er the fragrant Steams she bends her Head:
He first expands the glitt'ring *Forfex* wide
T'inclose the Lock; then joins it, to divide;
One fatal stroke the sacred Hair does sever
From the fair Head, for ever, and for ever!
    The living Fires come flashing from her Eyes,
And Screams of Horrow rend th'affrighted Skies.
Not louder Shrieks by Dames to Heav'n are cast,

103. *Vide* Ovid. Metam. 8. [P.]

When Husbands die, or *Lap-dogs* breath their last,
Or when rich *China* Vessels fal'n from high,
In glittring Dust and painted Fragments lie!
  Let Wreaths of triumph now my Temples twine,
(The Victor cry'd) the glorious Prize is mine!
While Fish in Streams, or Birds delight in Air,
Or in a Coach and Six the *British* Fair,
As long as *Atalantis* shall be read,
Or the small Pillow grace a Lady's Bed,
While *Visits* shall be paid on solemn Days,
When num'rous Wax-lights in bright Order blaze,
While Nymphs take Treats, or Assignations give,
So long my Honour, Name and Praise shall live!
  What Time wou'd spare, from Steel receives its date,
And Monuments, like Men, submit to Fate!
Steel did the Labour of the Gods destroy,
And strike to Dust th'aspiring Tow'rs of *Troy*;
Steel cou'd the Works of mortal Pride confound,
And hew Triumphal Arches to the ground.
What Wonder then, fair Nymph! thy Hairs shou'd feel
The conqu'ring Force of unresisted Steel?

THE RAPE *of the* LOCKE.

CANTO II.

But anxious Cares the pensive Nymph opprest,
And secret Passions labour'd in her Breast.
Not youthful Kings in Battel seiz'd alive,
Not scornful Virgins who their Charms survive,
Not ardent Lover robb'd of all his Bliss,
Not ancient Lady when refus'd a Kiss,
Not Tyrants fierce that unrepenting die,
Not *Cynthia* when her *Manteau*'s pinn'd awry,
E'er felt such Rage, Resentment, and Despair,
As Thou, sad Virgin! for thy ravish'd Hair.
While her rackt Soul Repose and Peace requires,
The fierce *Thalestris* fans the rising Fires.
O wretched Maid (she spreads her hands, and cry'd,
And *Hampton*'s Ecchoes, wretched Maid! reply'd)
Was it for this you took such constant Care,
Combs, *Bodkins*, *Leads*, *Pomatums*, to prepare?
For this your Locks in Paper Durance bound,
For this with tort'ring Irons wreath'd around?
Oh had the Youth but been content to seize
Hairs less in sight—or any Hairs but these!
Gods! shall the Ravisher display this Hair,
While the Fops envy, and the Ladies stare!
Honour forbid! at whose unrival'd Shrine
Ease, Pleasure, Virtue, All, our Sex resign.
Methinks already I your Tears survey,
Already hear the horrid things they say,
Already see you a degraded Toast,
And all your Honour in a Whisper lost!
How shall I, then, your helpless Fame defend?
'Twill then be Infamy to seem your Friend!
And shall this Prize, th'inestimable Prize,
Expos'd thro' *Crystal* to the gazing Eyes,
And heighten'd by the *Diamond*'s circling Rays,

On that Rapacious Hand for ever blaze?
Sooner shall Grass in *Hide*-Park *Circus* grow,
And Wits take Lodgings in the Sound of *Bow*;
Sooner let Earth, Air, Sea, to *Chaos* fall,
Men, Monkies, Lap-dogs, Parrots, perish all!
  She said; then raging to *Sir Plume* repairs,
And bids her *Beau* demand the precious Hairs:
(*Sir Plume*, of *Amber Snuff-box* justly vain,
And the nice Conduct of a *clouded Cane*)
With earnest Eyes, and round unthinking Face,
He first the Snuff-box open'd, then the Case,
And thus broke out—"My Lord, why, what the Devil?
"Z—ds! damn the Lock! 'fore Gad, you must be civil!
"Plague on't! 'tis past a Jest—nay prithee, Pox!
"Give her the Hair—he spoke, and rapp'd his Box.
  It grieves me much (reply'd the Peer again)
Who speaks so well shou'd ever speak in vain.
But by this Locke, this sacred Locke I swear,
(Which never more shall join its parted Hair,
Which never more its Honours shall renew,
Clipt from the lovely Head where once it grew)
That while my Nostrils draw the vital Air,
This Hand, which won it, shall for ever wear.
He spoke, and speaking in proud Triumph spread
The long-contended Honours of her Head.
  But see! the *Nymph* in Sorrow's Pomp appears,
Her Eyes half languishing, half drown'd in Tears;
Now livid pale her Cheeks, now glowing red;
On her heav'd Bosom hung her drooping Head,
Which, with a Sigh, she rais'd; and thus she said.
  For ever curs'd be this detested Day,
Which snatch'd my best, my fav'rite Curl away!
Happy! ah ten times happy, had I been,
If *Hampton-Court* these Eyes had never seen!

51. *In allusion to* Achilles's *Oath in* Homer. *Il.* 1. [P.]

Yet am not I the first mistaken Maid,
By Love of Courts to num'rous Ills betray'd.
Oh had I rather un-admir'd remain'd
In some lone *Isle*, or distant *Northern* Land;
Where the gilt *Chariot* never mark'd the way,
Where none learn *Ombre*, none e'er taste *Bohea!*
There kept my Charms conceal'd from mortal Eye,
Like Roses that in Desarts bloom and die.
What mov'd my Mind with youthful Lords to rome?
O had I stay'd, and said my Pray'rs at home!
'Twas this, the Morning *Omens* did foretel;
Thrice from my trembling hand the *Patch-box* fell;
The tott'ring *China* shook without a Wind,
Nay, *Poll* sate mute, and *Shock* was *most Unkind!*
See the poor Remnants of this slighted Hair!
My hands shall rend what ev'n thy own did spare.
This, in two sable Ringlets taught to break,
Once gave new Beauties to the snowie Neck.
The Sister-Locke now sits uncouth, alone,
And in its Fellow's Fate foresees its own;
Uncurl'd it hangs! the fatal Sheers demands;
And tempts once more thy sacrilegious Hands.
She said: the pitying Audience melt in Tears,
But *Fate* and *Jove* had stopp'd the *Baron*'s Ears.
In vain *Thalestris* with Reproach assails,
For who can move when fair *Belinda* fails?
Not half so fixt the *Trojan* cou'd remain,
While *Anna* begg'd and *Dido* rag'd in vain.
To Arms, to Arms! the bold *Thalestris* cries,
And swift as Lightning to the Combate flies.
All side in Parties, and begin th'Attack;
Fans clap, Silks russle, and tough Whalebones crack;
Heroes and Heroins Shouts confus'dly rise,
And base, and treble Voices strike the Skies.
No common Weapons in their Hands are found,
Like Gods they fight, nor dread a mortal Wound.

So when bold *Homer* makes the Gods engage,
And heavn'ly Breasts with human Passions rage;
'Gainst *Pallas*, *Mars*; *Latona*, *Hermes* Arms;
And all *Olympus* rings with loud Alarms.
Jove's Thunder roars, Heav'n trembles all around;
Blue *Neptune* storms, the bellowing Deeps resound;
Earth shakes her nodding Tow'rs, the Ground gives way,
And the pale Ghosts start at the Flash of Day!
While thro' the Press enrag'd *Thalestris* flies,
And scatters Deaths around from both her Eyes,
A *Beau* and *Witling* perish'd in the Throng,
One dy'd in *Metaphor*, and one in *Song*.
O cruel Nymph! a living Death I bear,
Cry'd *Dapperwit*, and sunk beside his Chair.
A mournful Glance Sir *Fopling* upwards cast,
Those Eyes are made so killing—was his last:
Thus on *Meander*'s flow'ry Margin lies
Th'expiring Swan, and as he sings he dies.
As bold Sir *Plume* had drawn *Clarissa* down,
Chloë stept in, and kill'd him with a Frown;
She smil'd to see the doughty Hero slain,
But at her Smile, the Beau reviv'd again.
Now *Jove* suspends his golden Scales in Air,
Weighs the Mens Wits against the Lady's Hair;
The doubtful Beam long nods from side to side;
At length the Wits mount up, the Hairs subside.
See fierce *Belinda* on the *Baron* flies,
With more than usual Lightning in her Eyes;
Nor fear'd the Chief th'unequal Fight to try,
Who sought no more than on his Foe to die.
But this bold Lord, with manly Strength indu'd,
She with one Finger and a Thumb subdu'd:
Just where the Breath of Life his Nostrils drew,

104. Homer. *Il.* 20. [P.]
126. *Vid.* Homer Iliad. 22 & Virg. Æn. 12. [P.]

A Charge of *Snuff* the wily Virgin threw;
Sudden, with starting Tears each Eye o'erflows,
And the high Dome re-ecchoes to his Nose.
Now meet thy Fate, th'incens'd Virago cry'd,
And drew a deadly *Bodkin* from her Side.
Boast not my Fall (he said) insulting Foe!
Thou by some other shalt be laid as low.
Nor think, to dye dejects my lofty Mind;
All that I dread, is leaving you behind!
Rather than so, ah let me still survive,
And still burn on, in *Cupid*'s Flames, *Alive*.
Restore the Locke! she cries; and all around
Restore the Locke! the vaulted Roofs rebound.
Not fierce *Othello* in so loud a Strain
Roar'd for the Handkerchief that caus'd his Pain.
But see! how oft Ambitious Aims are cross'd,
And Chiefs contend 'till all the Prize is lost!
The Locke, obtain'd with Guilt, and kept with Pain,
In ev'ry place is sought, but sought in vain:
With such a Prize no Mortal must be blest,
So Heav'n decrees! with Heav'n who can contest?
Some thought, it mounted to the Lunar Sphere,
Since all that Man e'er lost, is treasur'd there.
There Heroe's Wits are kept in pondrous Vases,
And Beau's in *Snuff-boxes* and *Tweezer-Cases*.
There broken Vows, and Death-bed Alms are found,
And Lovers Hearts with Ends of Riband bound;
The Courtiers Promises, and Sick Man's Pray'rs,
The Smiles of Harlots, and the Tears of Heirs,
Cages for Gnats, and Chains to Yoak a Flea;
Dry'd Butterflies, and Tomes of Casuistry.
But trust the Muse—she saw it upward rise,
Tho' mark'd by none but quick Poetic Eyes:
(Thus *Rome*'s great Founder to the Heav'ns withdrew,

159. *Vid.* Ariosto. Canto 34. [P.]

To *Proculus* alone confess'd in view.)
A sudden Star, it shot thro' liquid Air,
And drew behind a radiant *Trail of Hair.*
Not *Berenice*'s Locks first rose so bright,
The Skies bespangling with dishevel'd Light.
This, the *Beau-monde* shall from the *Mall* survey,
As thro' the Moon-light shade they nightly stray,
And hail with Musick its propitious Ray.
This *Partridge* soon shall view in cloudless Skies,
When next he looks thro' *Galilæo*'s Eyes;
And hence th'Egregious Wizard shall foredoom
The Fate of *Louis*, and the Fall of *Rome*.
Then cease, bright Nymph! to mourn the ravish'd Hair
Which adds new Glory to the shining Sphere!
Not all the Tresses that fair Head can boast
Shall draw such Envy as the Locke you lost.
For, after all the Murders of your Eye,
When, after Millions slain, your self shall die;
When those fair Suns shall sett, as sett they must,
And all those Tresses shall be laid in Dust;
This Locke, the Muse shall consecrate to Fame,
And mid'st the Stars inscribe *Belinda*'s Name!

FINIS.

THE *RAPE* of the *LOCK*.

AN

HEROI-COMICAL

P O E M.

IN FIVE CANTO'S.

Nolueram, Belinda, tuos violare capillos,
Sed juvat hoc precibus me tribuisse tuis.

MARTIAL.

NOTE ON THE TEXT

The *Rape of the Lock* appears in 1714 in octavo format, embellished with steel engravings as head- and tail-pieces, and with six plates signed 'Lud. Du Guernier inv. [*gap*] C. Du Bosc sculp.'[1] No changes of any importance occur in the second and third editions which follow before the year is out, but the 'Fourth Edition Corrected' of 1715 makes a few verbal revisions. The text printed in the *Works* of 1717 carries on this kind of revision and adds the speech of Clarissa (v 7–36). Many medial commas also appear while a few of those found in the earlier editions are deleted.

There are many later reprints and I have collated enough in them to see that they are without textual authority. The main exception is the *Works* of 1736 which contains verbal revisions. The *Works* of 1740 introduces a few misprints (so I consider them) which Warburton's text reproduces and adds to; Warburton's reading at i 89 is probably authorized by Pope. The 1740 variant at i 58 must be allowed to stand because of the similar one at *Eloisa*, 324 (discussed at p. 314 below). In view of the theological nature of this correction, the 1740 variant at i 112 may also be intentional. I have treated it, however, as a misprint.

The text here reproduced is that of the first edition changed in accordance with Pope's revisions and in accordance with the principles laid down in the General Note on the Text, pp. x f. above. Since Clarissa's speech was first added to a quarto and folio text, its typography has been accommodated to the octavo style of 1714 by reference to the text of the octavo edition of 1718 (Griffith 103).

Certain notes of Pope in 1736 (i.e., at i 11 f., 13 ff., and iii 11 f.) together with certain notes signed 'P.' in 1751 (i.e., at ii 4, iii 1, 24f., 105, 134, and iv 11) call attention to revisions. When they do no more than this I have omitted them since their information is supplied in the critical apparatus.

The title-pages of 1714–15 read: THE || *RAPE* of the *LOCK*. ||

1. For these French artists see DNB. Miss G. Lloyd Thomas has kindly lent me a copy of the large paper issue of this edition (Griffith 30): it is Pope's presentation copy to Addison's sister: on the fly-leaf Pope has written: 'To Mrs Sartre: || from her most humble Servant || A. Pope.'

AN || HEROI-COMICAL || POEM. || In FIVE CANTO'S. || [*with the motto from Ovid, and imprint.*] 1717–43 read: THE || *RAPE* of the *LOCK.* || AN || HEROI-COMICAL || POEM. || Written in the Year 1712. || [*with the motto from Martial.*] 1751 places the motto from Martial at the head of the poem: otherwise it reads as 1717–43. The Ovid is *Metam.* viii 151 (see iii 122 below, and note): the Martial is XII lxxxiv 1 f. (Teubner Series); Pope substitutes 'Belinda' for Martial's 'Polytime'.

KEY TO THE CRITICAL APPARATUS

1714*a* = First edition, octavo, Griffith 29.
1714*b* = Second edition, octavo, Griffith 34.
1714*c* = Third edition, octavo, Griffith 35.
1715 = Fourth edition corrected, octavo, Griffith 43.
1717 = Works, quarto, Griffith 79.
1736 = Works, vol. i, octavo, Griffith 413.
1740 = Works, octavo, vol. i, part 1, Griffith 510.
1743 = Works, octavo, vol. i, part 1, Griffith 582.
1751 = Works, ed. Warburton, vol. i, octavo, Griffith 643.

TO
Mrs. *ARABELLA FERMOR.*

MADAM,

It will be in vain to deny that I have some Regard for this Piece, since I Dedicate it to You. Yet You may bear me Witness, it was intended only to divert a few young Ladies, who have good Sense and good Humour enough, to laugh not only at their Sex's little unguarded Follies, but at their own. But as it was communicated with the Air of a Secret, it soon found its Way into the World. An imperfect Copy having been offer'd to a Bookseller, You had the Good-Nature for my Sake to consent to the Publication of one more correct: This I was forc'd to before I had executed half my Design, for the *Machinery* was entirely wanting to compleat it.

The *Machinery*, Madam, is a Term invented by the Criticks, to signify that Part which the Deities, Angels, or Dæmons, are made to act in a Poem: For the ancient Poets are in one respect like many modern Ladies; Let an Action be never so trivial in it self, they always make it appear of the utmost Importance. These Machines I determin'd to raise on a very new and odd Foundation, the *Rosicrucian* Doctrine of Spirits.

I know how disagreeable it is to make use of hard Words before a Lady; but 'tis so much the Concern of a Poet to have his Works understood, and particularly by your Sex, that You must give me leave to explain two or three difficult Terms.

The *Rosicrucians* are a People I must bring You acquainted with. The best Account I know of them is in a French Book call'd *Le Comte de Gabalis*, which both in its Title and Size is so like a *Novel*,

1 Regard] Value *1714–15*.

For Arabella Fermor and the history of the poem see Introduction, pp. 81 ff. above, and Appendix A, pp. 371 ff. below.

Warton (i 214) considered this letter 'far superior to any of Voiture'.

3–8. *good Sense and good Humour . . . Good-Nature*] See note on v 16, 30 f. below.

10. *Machinery*] See Introduction, pp. 121 ff. above.

17. *Rosicrucian Doctrine*] See Appendix B, pp. 378 ff. below.

24. *Title and Size*] *The Count de Soissons* and *The Count of Amboise* are two of the novels translated from the French and included in the series of 'Modern Novels' (published by Richard Bentley) in which Ayres's translation of *Gabalis* appeared. The size of them all is duodecimo.

that many of the Fair Sex have read it for one by Mistake. According to these Gentlemen, the four Elements are inhabited by Spirits, which they call *Sylphs*, *Gnomes*, *Nymphs*, and *Salamanders*. The *Gnomes*, or Dæmons of Earth, delight in Mischief; but the *Sylphs*, whose Habitation is in the Air, are the best-condition'd Creatures imaginable. For they say, any Mortals may enjoy the most intimate Familiarities with these gentle Spirits, upon a Condition very easie to all true *Adepts*, an inviolate Preservation of Chastity.

As to the following Canto's, all the Passages of them are as Fabulous, as the Vision at the Beginning, or the Transformation at the End; (except the Loss of your Hair, which I always mention with Reverence.) The Human Persons are as Fictitious as the Airy ones; and the Character of *Belinda*, as it is now manag'd, resembles You in nothing but in Beauty.

If this Poem had as many Graces as there are in Your Person, or in Your Mind, yet I could never hope it should pass thro' the World half so Uncensured as You have done. But let its Fortune be what it will, mine is happy enough, to have given me this Occasion of assuring You that I am, with the truest Esteem,

Madam,

Your Most Obedient

Humble Servant.

A. POPE.

29 in the Air] Air *1714–15*. 35 mention] name *1714–17*.

27. *Gnomes*] In *Gabalis* these, like all the other spirits, are 'good', but, living in the earth near to the Devil, they have been frightened into helping him to make 'the Soul of a man become Mortal' (p. 166). Pope makes them mischievous by nature. Gabalis calls them '*Gnomes or Pharyes*' (p. 29): cf. note on ii 74 below.

32. *Chastity*] The renunciation of 'all Carnal Commerce with Women' is the first condition for men who wish to control the sylphs (*Gabalis*, p. 25). The chastity entailed was compensated for by 'the most intimate Familiarities with these gentle Spirits', since unless the sylphs could gain an earthly lover they never achieved immortality.

37. *Belinda*] The name of a 'gentlewoman' in Etherege's *Man of Mode*, of an 'affected lady' in Congreve's *Old Bachelor*, and of several addressees in the 1712 Miscellany in which the *Rape of the Locke* appears. As so often, Pope found the opportunity for wit ready to hand. The short form of Arabella is 'Belle', which smoothly links with the fashionable 'Belinda' and allows the pun on the newly imported Gallicism, 'belle' (= pretty young lady) at i 8, i 10, and ii 16 (Pope does not use this word elsewhere in his poems).

THE RAPE *of the* LOCK.

CANTO I.

WHAT dire Offence from am'rous Causes springs,
What mighty Contests rise from trivial Things,
I sing—This Verse to *Caryll*, Muse! is due;
This, ev'n *Belinda* may vouchsafe to view:
Slight is the Subject, but not so the Praise,

2 Contests] Quarrels *1714–15* [*Pope provides for the change in his letter to Broome* (*1717 ?*) *Pope's Corresp.*, i. 394.]
3 *Caryll*] *C—l 1714–15*, *C— 1717–43*, CARYL *1751*.

The first sketch of this Poem was written in less than a fortnight's time, in 1711, *in two Canto's, and so printed in a Miscellany, without the name of the Author. The Machines were not inserted till a year after, when he publish'd it, and annex'd the foregoing Dedication.* [P. 1736: in 1751 it was much enlarged by Warburton.]

1–12. 'The custom of beginning all *Poems*, with a *Proposition* of the whole work, and an *Invocation* of some God for his assistance to go through with it, is so solemnly and religiously observed by all the ancient *Poets*, that though I could have found out a better way, I should not (I think) have ventured upon it' (Cowley, *Davideis*, i, note 1).

Pope imitates the epic 'propositions' in placing the object before the verb.

Wakefield noted the 'concourse of heavy and hissing *consonants*' in the latter half of l. 1; Tennyson considered its sibilants 'horrible' (Hallam, Lord Tennyson, *Tennyson*, 1897, ii 286). Pope's revisions show him reducing sibilants.

3. *Caryll*] See Intro., pp. 81 ff. and Appendix A, p. 375. In a letter to Caryll of 25 Feb. 1714 Pope writes: 'In this more solemn Edition [1714], I was strangely tempted to have set y^r^ Name at length, as well as I have my own; but I remember'd y^r^ desire you formerly express'd to ye contrary; besides, that it may better become me to appear as ye Offerer of an ill present, than you as ye Receiver of it'. Lucan had addressed his *Civil War* to Nero (i 33 ff.) and Statius his *Thebaid* to Domitian (i 22 ff.).

5. Cf. Virgil, *Georgic* iv 6 f.:

> In tenui labor; at tenuis non gloria, si quem
> Numina laeva sinunt, auditque vocatus Apollo.

Sedley's translation (*Works*, i 74) reads:

> The Subjects humble, but not so the Praise,
> If any Muse assist the Poets Lays.

Dryden's translation reads:

> Slight is the Subject, but the Praise not small,
> If Heav'n assist, and *Phœbus* hear my Call.

Pope combines the two for l. 5.

If She inspire, and He approve my Lays.
Say what strange Motive, Goddess! cou'd compel
A well-bred *Lord* t'assault a gentle *Belle*?
Oh say what stranger Cause, yet unexplor'd,
Cou'd make a gentle *Belle* reject a *Lord*?
In Tasks so bold, can Little Men engage,
And in soft Bosoms dwells such mighty Rage?
Sol thro' white Curtains shot a tim'rous Ray,

11 f. And dwells such Rage in softest Bosoms then?
And lodge such daring Souls in Little Men? *1714–17.*

13–18 *Sol* thro' white Curtains did his Beams display,
And op'd those Eyes which brighter shine than they;
Now *Shock* had giv'n himself the towzing Shake,
And Nymphs prepar'd their *Chocolate* to take;
Thrice the wrought Slipper knock'd against the Ground,
And striking Watches the tenth Hour resound. *1714–15.*

---

9. *unexplor'd*] undiscovered: see OED, s.v. 'explore' (sense 1*b*, which became obsolete in early nineteenth century). Cf. 'Messiah', ll. 49 ff.: '. . . the good shepherd . . . Explores the lost, the wand'ring sheep directs', and Dryden (*Fables*, 'Meleager and Atalanta', l. 200 f.):

his pointed Dart
Explores the nearest Passage to his Heart.

11. Cf. *Æneid*, i 11: . . . Tantaene animis caelestibus irae?
—'a characteristic touch of the poet's gentle nature: with an undertone of sadness too' (note in A. Sidgwick's edition, 1888). This undertone improves the mockery of Boileau's 'Tant de fiel entre-t-il dans l'âme des dévots?' (*Lutrin*, i 12) and of Pope's echo here.

Little Men] Pope is stating the mock-heroic discrepancy; he is also referring to Lord Petre's short stature (see Warton ed.).

12. See above, p. 127 *n.* 12.

13–18. The description here is of lovers in general and no discrepancy exists, as Croker supposed it did, between l. 14 and ll. 19 f. 'Those eyes' (l. 15) are the eyes of lovers, who ring the bell and knock the floor. Belinda does not enter the scene till l. 19, and then as an exception because of the action of Ariel in keeping her asleep.

13. Cf. Dryden, 'To Mr. Granville', 35:

Their Setting Sun still shoots a Glim'ring Ray.

The curtains are those of the four-poster bed.

And op'd those Eyes that must eclipse the Day;
Now Lapdogs give themselves the rowzing Shake,
And sleepless Lovers, just at Twelve, awake:
Thrice rung the Bell, the Slipper knock'd the Ground,
And the press'd Watch return'd a silver Sound.

14. Pope is using the hyperbole of the Elizabethan sonnets; cf. ii 1–4 below.

15. *Lapdogs*] See note on iii 158 below.

16. For fashionable hours of rising see *Poems of Anne Countess of Winchelsea*, ed. M. Reynolds (1903), note on pp. 420 f.; cf. Gould, ii 280:

> Who'd think, at twelve a *Clock* it shou'd be said
> That the great Lady's *soaking* in her *Bed*?

The line contains an epic reference at one remove. Horace had described the suitors of Penelope as asleep at mid-day (*Ep.*, I ii 30), but the charge was inspired by contemporary Roman lovers (see Persius, *Sat.*, iii, *passim*) rather than Homer's.

17. The triple repetition is common in epic poetry: cf. Dryden, *Æneid*, iv 989 ff. and *Iliad*, v 529 f.; and for mock heroic cf. *Dispensary*, p. 34:

> The Sage transported at th' approaching Hour,
> Imperiously thrice thunder'd on the Floor.

and p. 99:

> Thrice did the Goddess with her Sacred Wand
> The Pavement strike . . .

'Bell-hanging was not introduced into our domestic apartments till long after the date of the Rape of the Lock. There are no bells at Hampton Court, nor were there any in the first quarter of the present century at Chatsworth and Holkham. I myself, about the year 1790, remember that it was still the practice for ladies to summon their attendants to their bedchambers by knocking with a high-heeled shoe. Servants, too, were accustomed to wait in ante-rooms, whence they were summoned by hand-bells, and this explains the extraordinary number of such rooms in the houses of the last century' [Croker]. Fielding uses the arrangement for comedy, *Joseph Andrews*, Book I, ch. viii.

18. By 1700 London watches were held to be the best in the world. The 'repeater' watch was considered by the Privy Council of 1686 to have been the invention of Daniel Quare (1648–1724). The first repeaters sounded the hour and the quarters when pressure was applied to the pin which projected from the case near the pendant; but, later, Quare made the pendant itself do duty for the pin. The chime—so many for the hour and then 2, 4, or 6 for the quarter just passed—came from a bell screwed into the back of the case. The difficulty of striking a light made repeaters popular. See F. J. Britten, *Old Clocks and Watches and their Makers* (ed. 1933), pp. 326 f. and 671 f.; and D. Glasgow, *Watch and Clock Making* (1885), p. 19. Belinda presses her watch because the sunlight is only 'tim'rous'. In the *Memoirs of Martinus Scriblerus*, xi, 'repeating-watches' are grouped with 'gold Snuff-boxes' and 'Tweezer-cases' as 'Love-toys'.

In *Lutrin* i it was the clocks that had 'voix argentines': Pope is diminishing the scale.

Belinda still her downy Pillow prest,
Her Guardian *Sylph* prolong'd the balmy Rest.
'Twas he had summon'd to her silent Bed
The Morning-Dream that hover'd o'er her Head.
A Youth more glitt'ring than a *Birth-night Beau*,
(That ev'n in Slumber caus'd her Cheek to glow)
Seem'd to her Ear his winning Lips to lay,
And thus in Whispers said, or seem'd to say.
  Fairest of Mortals, thou distinguish'd Care
Of thousand bright Inhabitants of Air!
If e'er one Vision touch'd thy infant Thought,
Of all the Nurse and all the Priest have taught,

29 touch'd] touch *1751*.

21 ff. The gods sometimes communicate with the epic hero by means of apparitions during sleep, e.g. *Æneid*, iii 147 ff. In *Secchia Rapita* (iii 1 ff.) and *Lutrin* (Chant i) an apparition appears at dawn in a bedroom. The latter poem, like Lucan's *Civil War*, begins with its appearance; and almost at the beginning of the *Davideis*, Envy, disguised as Benjamin, the father of Saul, appears to Saul in a vision while he sleeps.

Ariel summons a dream in which he figures in a disguise calculated to interest Belinda. His calculation succeeds (see l. 24). His normal appearance is described at ii 70 ff. For the sylphs generally, see Appendix B, pp. 378 ff.

Morning-Dream] Cf. *Temple of Fame*, 7 f. and note; and *Lutrin*, iv 19 ff.

23. The dresses worn for the royal birthday celebrations were exceptionally splendid; cf. *Im. of Horace*, Ep. II i 332 f.

26. *said, or seem'd to say*] *The Athenian Oracle*, i 235, had answered the query '*How to know when God reveals himself in a* Dream, *and how when we only* dream, *he* reveals himself?' Pope is echoing Virgil, *Æneid*, vi 454 and *Par. Lost*, i 781 ff.

27. Cf. *Iliad*, i 229: 'the Gods distinguish'd Care'; *id.*, v 1079; and *Odyssey*, iii 481. See also n. on i 41 f. below.

28. Cf. Dennis, *The Battle of Ramillia*, 1706, p. 94:

> Of all the bright Inhabitants of Heaven.

29. *infant*] Cf. i 89 and v 93 below; it is a favourite epithet in the *Davideis*. It is unfortunate that 'e'er' echoes the rhyme word of the previous line.

30–4. The nurse and the priest were considered by seventeenth-century philosophers and educationalists as the chief inlets of superstition: cf. Dryden, *Hind and Panther*, iii 389 ff.:

> By education most have been misled . . .
> The *Priest* continues what the nurse began;

Of airy Elves by Moonlight Shadows seen,
The silver Token, and the circled Green,
Or Virgins visited by Angel-Pow'rs,
With Golden Crowns and Wreaths of heav'nly Flow'rs,
Hear and believe! thy own Importance know,
Nor bound thy narrow Views to Things below.
Some secret Truths from Learned Pride conceal'd,
To Maids alone and Children are reveal'd:
What tho' no Credit doubting Wits may give?
The Fair and Innocent shall still believe.
Know then, unnumber'd Spirits round thee fly,

Davenant (Spingarn, ii 5); Locke, *Thoughts concerning Education* (ed. 1880), pp. 117 and 167; Temple, ii 344 f.; and *Gabalis*, p. 133. On the other hand Pomfret, *Reason* (1700), p. 17 asserted:

> The Careful Nurse, and Priest is all we Need
> To Learn Opinions and our Country's Creed.

The nurse's lore is that of ll. 31 f., the priest's that of ll. 33 f.

32. See Dryden, 'Wife of Bath Her Tale', 1–23. The *Athenian Oracle* (i 397) considered the origin of fairy rings.

33. Carrying a reference to the Annunciation and to the experiences of virgin saints. The imagery is that of hymns to the Virgin Mary: see *Primer*, p. 183 and Crashaw, 'In the Glorious Assumption of our Blessed Lady. The Hymn', and 'An Ode . . . Præfixed to a little Prayer-book given to a young Gentle-Woman'.

35 f. This is the line taken by Gabalis when introducing the sylphs to de Villars.

37 f. Cf. Matthew, xi 25.

39. *doubting*] In Pope's age, as in Dryden's, much pride was taken in scepticism.

41 f. It is an old idea that supernatural beings congregate in military formation: cf. the 'hosts of heaven' of the A.V. and the 'militia caeli' of the Vulgate. For the guardianship of human by supernatural beings in military array see Sannazaro's *De Partu Virginis*, i 19 ff., and *Pope's Own Miscellany*, 'Psalm xci' 23 f.:

> I see protecting Myriads round thee fly,
> And all the bright *Militia* of the sky.

(Cf. E. Bensley, *Modern Language Review*, xi, 1916, p. 341.)

When the 'Famous Cabalist Zedechias' advised the sylphs to show themselves to convince the world, they did so with great magnificence, 'appearing in the Air in Human Shape; Sometimes ranged in Battle, Marching in good Order or standing to their Arms, or Encamped under most Majestick Pavillions'. (*Gabalis*, pp. 173 f.)

lower Sky] The militia is composed of aerial sylphs in distinction from etherial: see Appendix D, pp. 396 f. below.

The light *Militia* of the lower Sky;
These, tho' unseen, are ever on the Wing,
Hang o'er the *Box*, and hover round the *Ring*.
Think what an Equipage thou hast in Air,
And view with scorn *Two Pages* and a *Chair*.
As now your own, our Beings were of old,
And once inclos'd in Woman's beauteous Mold;
Thence, by a soft Transition, we repair
From earthly Vehicles to these of Air.
Think not, when Woman's transient Breath is fled,
That all her Vanities at once are dead:
Succeeding Vanities she still regards,

41–3. Cf. *Paradise Lost*, iv 677 f.:

> Millions of spiritual Creatures walk the Earth
> Unseen ...

44. Cf. the Earl of Dorset, *On the Countess of Dorchester ... Written in 1680*, 6f.:

> Wilt thou still sparkle in the box
> Still ogle in the ring;

Intro., p. 114; and Gould ii 338. For the Ring, see Appendix E, p. 400.

45. *Equipage*] = 'A carriage and horses, with attendant footmen' (OED): 'the Coachmaker contrives new Machines, Chairs, Flyes, *&c.* all to prompt the whimsies, and unaccountable Pride of the Gentry [which results in] uncommon Extravagancies; changing their Equipages as often as fancy, or necessity directs' (Defoe, *Complete English Tradesman*, 1726, II, part ii 149). They had been censured in *Tatler* 144, and *Spectator* 15.

46. *a Chair*] a sedan chair.

47 ff. The origin of this system of metempsychosis is Dryden, Ovid's *Metam.*, xv 229 f. and Dryden, 'Flower and Leaf', 480 ff.; and cf. Dryden, 'Epilogue to Tyranick Love', ll. 4 ff.:

> I am the Ghost of poor departed *Nelly* ...
> I'm what I was, a little harmless Devil.
> For, after death, we Sprights have just such Natures,
> We had, for all the World, when humane Creatures;
> And, therefore, I, that was an Actress here,
> Play all my Tricks in Hell, a Goblin there.

50. *Vehicles*] 'The *Platonists* doe chiefly take notice of *Three* Kindes of *Vehicles*, *Æthereal*, *Aereal*, and *Terrestrial*' (Henry More, *Immortality of the Soul*, ii 14, §1). Locke (*Essay* III x 14) had given prominence to 'aerial and ætherial vehicles' as examples of sectarian gibberish. Pope intends a pun linking vehicles and equipages.

And tho' she plays no more, o'erlooks the Cards.
Her Joy in gilded Chariots, when alive,
And Love of *Ombre*, after Death survive.
For when the Fair in all their Pride expire,
To their first Elements their Souls retire:
The Sprights of fiery Termagants in Flame
Mount up, and take a *Salamander*'s Name.
Soft yielding Minds to Water glide away,
And sip with *Nymphs*, their Elemental Tea.
The graver Prude sinks downward to a *Gnome*,
In search of Mischief still on Earth to roam.
The light Coquettes in *Sylphs* aloft repair,

58 their Souls] the Souls *1714–36*.

55 f. —*Quæ gratia currûm*
Armorumque fuit vivis, quæ cura nitentes
Pascere equos, eadem sequitur tellure repostos.

Virg. Æn. 6. [653 ff.] [P. 1736–51]. Dryden had translated thus (vi 890 f.):

The love of Horses which they had, alive,
And care of Chariots, after Death survive.

Cf. Ovid, *Metam.*, iv 445 f.

The carriages of the time were called 'chariots': Pope intends a pun, satirizing contemporary society under cover of epic quotation.

Ombre] See Appendix C, pp. 383 ff.

58. *first*] = preponderating. A person's nature was supposed to depend on the relative proportions of the four elements in the composition of his body.

59 ff. Cf. *Dispensary*, p. 3 which describes

How ductile Matter new Meanders takes.

59. 'Termagant . . . A scold; a bawling turbulent woman' (Johnson's *Dictionary*, which cites this couplet).

fiery] Pope puns on the two meanings (a) bad-tempered, (b) having a preponderating amount of fire in one's constitution: 'If we would recover that Empire over the Salamanders: we must purifie and exalt the Element of Fire which is in us . . . and make us become . . . of a Fiery Nature' (*Gabalis*, 45 f.). The heart of a dissected coquette has 'a certain Salamandrine Quality, that made it capable of living in the midst of Fire and Flame, without being consumed, or so much as singed' (*Spectator* 282).

61. Wakefield compares the transformation of Proteus, Virgil, *Georgic* iv 410: 'aut in aquas tenuis dilapsus abibit'.

62. *Tea*] Then a perfect rhyme with *away*. Cf. iii 7 f. below.

And sport and flutter in the Fields of Air.
  Know farther yet; Whoever fair and chaste
Rejects Mankind, is by some *Sylph* embrac'd:
For Spirits, freed from mortal Laws, with ease
Assume what Sexes and what Shapes they please.
What guards the Purity of melting Maids,
In Courtly Balls, and Midnight Masquerades,
Safe from the treach'rous Friend, the daring Spark,
The Glance by Day, the Whisper in the Dark;
When kind Occasion prompts their warm Desires,
When Musick softens, and when Dancing fires?
'Tis but their *Sylph*, the wise Celestials know,
Tho' *Honour* is the Word with Men below.
  Some Nymphs there are, too conscious of their Face,
For Life predestin'd to the *Gnomes*' Embrace.
These swell their Prospects and exalt their Pride,
When Offers are disdain'd, and Love deny'd.
Then gay Ideas crowd the vacant Brain;

73 the daring] and daring *1714–17*.   81 These] Who *1714–15*.

66. Cf. Tickell, 'To Apollo Making Love' (1709 Miscellany, p. 412):
[The Moth] Sports, and flutters near the treach'rous Blaze.

Fields of Air] Cf. *Æneid*, vi 888: 'Aeris in campis latis'; and Dryden, *Æneid*, i 196: 'the Fields of Air'.

69 ff. Cf. *Par. Lost*, i 423 ff.

72. *Midnight Masquerades*] *Spectator* 8 is up in arms against them: 'In short, the whole Design of this libidinous Assembly, seems to terminate in Assignations, and Intrigues'; see also *Spectator* 14.

73. *Spark*] 'A lively, showy, splendid, gay man. It is commonly used in contempt' (Johnson's *Dictionary*).

76. Cf. St-Evremond, i 437: 'You'll not pitch upon Music to soften the hardship of [dying]'.

77 f. This distinction between how the gods name a thing and how men name it has its epic source in Homer: see *Dunciad*, iv 362, and the Pope–Warburton note on it. Pope's adaptation owes something to Dryden's *Hind and the Panther*, iii 823 f.:

Immortal pow'rs the term of conscience know,
But int'rest is her name with men below.

79. 'too sensible of their beauty' [Warburton].

While Peers and Dukes, and all their sweeping Train,
And Garters, Stars, and Coronets appear,
And in soft Sounds, *Your Grace* salutes their Ear.
'Tis these that early taint the Female Soul,
Instruct the Eyes of young *Coquettes* to roll,
Teach Infant-Cheeks a bidden Blush to know,
And little Hearts to flutter at a *Beau*.
Oft when the World imagine Women stray,
The *Sylphs* thro' mystick Mazes guide their Way,
Thro' all the giddy Circle they pursue,
And old Impertinence expel by new.
What tender Maid but must a Victim fall
To one Man's Treat, but for another's Ball?
When *Florio* speaks, what Virgin could withstand,
If gentle *Damon* did not squeeze her Hand?
With varying Vanities, from ev'ry Part,

89 Infant-Cheeks] Infants Cheeks *1714–43*.

84. Cf. Dryden's *Æneid*, xii 665: '*Æneas* leads; and draws a sweeping Train'; Pope may intend a pun on the trailing robes; cf. *Spectator* 16: 'To speak truly, the young People of both Sexes are . . . wonderfully apt to shoot out into long Swords or sweeping Trains, bushy Head-dresses or full-bottom'd Periwigs'.

88. *Spectator* 46 presents an Ogling-Master who sets up to teach 'the whole Art of Ogling'; cf. *Spectator* 250 and 252.

89. i.e., with rouge.

92. *mystick*] See note on i 221 below.

94. *Impertinence*] 'Trifle: thing of no value' (Johnson's *Dictionary*).

96. *Treat*] 'An entertainment of food and drink' (OED).

99 ff. Cf. *Guardian* 106: 'As I cast my Eye upon her Bosom, it appeared to be all of Chrystal, and so wonderfully transparent, that I saw every Thought in her Heart. The first Images I discovered in it were Fans, Silks, Ribbonds, Laces, and many other Gewgaws, which lay so thick together, that the whole Heart was nothing else but a Toy-shop. These all faded away and vanished, when immediately I discerned a long Train of Coaches and six, Equipages and Liveries that ran through the Heart one after another in a very great hurry [and so on to cards, a play-house, a church, a court, a lap-dog, etc.]'. (Cf. note on iii 142 below.) As an 'example of extravagance in fitting up' a shop in 1710, Defoe gives 'a Cutler's shop, *Anglicè* a Toy-man, which are now come up to such a ridiculous expence' (*The Complete English Tradesman*, 1726, i 315). Cf. D. George, *England in Transition*, pp. 37 f.

They shift the moving Toyshop of their Heart;
Where Wigs with Wigs, with Sword-knots Sword-knots strive,
Beaus banish Beaus, and Coaches Coaches drive.
This erring Mortals Levity may call,
Oh blind to Truth! the *Sylphs* contrive it all.
Of these am I, who thy Protection claim,
A watchful Sprite, and *Ariel* is my Name.
Late, as I rang'd the Crystal Wilds of Air,

100. *moving*] changeful, unstable (OED, sense 1*c*). Cf. *Æneid*, iv 569 f.: 'varium et mutabile semper || femina'. According to the OED there had been no use of the word in this sense in the seventeenth century. Pope probably intends a joke between 'moving' and 'shifts', intensifying the mutability ascribed to women.

101 f. Cf. *Iliad*, iv 508 f.:

> Now Shield with Shield, with Helmet Helmet clos'd,
> To Armour Armour, Lance to Lance oppos'd;

id., xiii 180 ff.; Ovid, *Metam.*, ix 44 f.; *Thebaid*, viii 398 f.; and Lucan, vii 573.

Sword-knots] 'A *Beau* is known by the Decent Management of his Sword-Knot and Snuff-Box' (T. Brown, *Amusements*, 1700, p. 50). Johnson defines as 'Ribband tied to the hilt of the sword', and quotes these lines. They were sometimes the work of the beau's mistress: cf. the line which, until 1715 ed., followed ii 38 below.

drive] Another pun.

104. The supernaturals in epics, e.g., Juno in *Æneid*, vii, contrive human moods and actions.

105. *thy Protection*] = my protection of thee; for this 'pregnant' use of *protection* cf. *Iliad*, v 159: War be thy Province, thy Protection mine.

106. Modelled on Dryden's usual method of beginning a story. For a history of the Hebrew name Ariel, see Shakespeare's *Tempest*, Furness Variorum ed., 1897, pp. 6 f. Being a name variously used in magical writings for one of the spirits who control the elements or the planets it was appropriate for Pope's purposes as for Shakespeare's.

107 ff. Wakefield compares the speeches of Uriel and Gabriel, *Par. Lost*, iv 561 ff.

107 f. H. C. Wyld's *Studies in English Rhymes from Surrey to Pope*, 1923, throws no light on this rhyme; he cites Dryden's use of *stars* to rhyme with *disperse*, and Swift's use of it to rhyme with *verse* (p. 84). No doubt the rhyme *air–star* comes under Swift's ban: 'pray in [the next volume of the translation of the *Iliad*] do not let me have so many unjustifiable Rhymes to *war* . . .' (*Pope's Corresp.*, i 301).

In the clear Mirror of thy ruling *Star*
I saw, alas! some dread Event impend,
Ere to the Main this Morning Sun descend.
But Heav'n reveals not what, or how, or where:
Warn'd by thy *Sylph*, oh Pious Maid beware!
This to disclose is all thy Guardian can.
Beware of all, but most beware of Man!
He said; when *Shock*, who thought she slept too long,
Leapt up, and wak'd his Mistress with his Tongue.
'Twas then *Belinda*! if Report say true,
Thy Eyes first open'd on a *Billet-doux*;
Wounds, *Charms*, and *Ardors*, were no sooner read,

110 Morning Sun] Morning's Sun *1714–15*.
112 thy] the *1736* [the 'variant b' edition of that year, Griffith 414] *–51*.

108. *In the clear Mirror*] *The Language of the Platonists, the writers of the intelligible world of Spirits, etc.* [P. 1751].

Pope's note in 1751 is affixed to the first four words of the line (clear mirrors are common images among Platonists, e.g., John Norris, author of *The Ideal and Intelligible World*, 1701–4). Pope combines this Platonic image with astrology, perhaps on the authority of Plato's *Timæus* 41 ff. where stars and souls are connected and a mirror image is used (46). Cf. also *Davideis*, p. 62:

Shap'd in the *glass* of the divine *Foresight*.

112 ff. Warnings are common in the epics: cf., e.g., *Æneid*, ii 270 ff. where the ghost of Hector appears to Æneas on the night of the sack of Troy warning him to escape. For Pope's phrasing cf. *Iliad*, xv 232, *Odyssey*, xi 545, *Par. Lost*, viii 638, and Eusden, 'Hero and Leander' (1709 Miscellany, p. 611).

113. Wakefield compares Virgil, *Æneid*, iii 461.

115. The shock or shough was a kind of lap-dog thought to have been brought to England from Iceland: cf. R. Holme's *Academy of Armory* (1688), ii 185: '[a shough] is an Island Dog . . . of a pretty bigness: curled and rough all over, which by the reason of the length of their hair, make shew neither of face, nor of body: these Curs are much set by, with Ladys, who usually wash, comb, and trim of all the hair of their hinder parts, leaving only the fore parts, and hinder feet jagged'. For the history of the cult see Seaton, pp. 32 ff.

117 f. Report was a liar—see p. 156 below, l. 138.

119. The country girl Corinna is delighted with such a letter ('a mighty civil Letter . . . not one smutty Word in it') in Vanbrugh's *Confederacy* (1705), II. Since the vogue of Voiture, this terminology adorned the love letters of the vulgar.

But all the Vision vanish'd from thy Head.
And now, unveil'd, the *Toilet* stands display'd,
Each Silver Vase in mystic Order laid.
First, rob'd in White, the Nymph intent adores
With Head uncover'd, the *Cosmetic* Pow'rs.
A heav'nly Image in the Glass appears,
To that she bends, to that her Eyes she rears;
Th'inferior Priestess, at her Altar's side,
Trembling, begins the sacred Rites of Pride.
Unnumber'd Treasures ope at once, and here
The various Off'rings of the World appear;

121. *Toilet*] Many of the accessories of the dressing table are detailed in *Spectator* 45.

1751 has a note signed 'P.' introducing Parnell's translation of ll. 121–48 into leonine hexameters. Pope had already printed them in his 'own' miscellany. For the incident of their composition see Goldsmith, *Works*, ed. Cunningham, 1854, iv 143.

122. Cf. *Gondibert*, II vii 17, 2:

> . . . Flowers, which she in mistick order ties;

and Behn, vi 182. ('Mystic' is a favourite epithet of these two poets and of Cowley.) The furniture of an altar is arranged so as to symbolize certain mystical values.

123 ff. Warburton errs in finding here 'a small inaccuracy. [Pope] first makes his Heroine the chief Priestess, and then the Goddess herself.' Belinda is adoring her 'heavn'ly Image' in the mirror; her image is the 'Goddess', she is the chief priestess. The supposed 'small inaccuracy' is a master-stroke.

Holden notes: 'It is odd that the combing and dressing of the fateful lock is not mentioned here'. Warton, however, considered that 'The mention of the Lock, on which the poem turns, is rightly reserved to the second canto' (ii 20).

126. Cf. Sandys, Ovid's *Metam.*, xi 464: 'She reares her humid eyes'; an expression used again by Dryden, Ovid's *Metam.*, xi ('Ceyx and Alcyone') 75.

127 f. Cf. the hairdressing ceremony in Dryden's Juvenal, *Sat.* vi 631 f.:

> *Psecas*, the chief, with Breast and Shoulders bare,
> Trembling, considers every Sacred Hair.

130. This perennial observation had been recently worded in *Spectator* 69: 'The single Dress of a Woman of Quality is often the Product of an Hundred Climates. The Muff and the Fan come together from the different Ends of the Earth. The Scarf is sent from the Torrid Zone, and the Tippet from beneath the Pole. The Brocade Petticoat rises out of the Mines of *Peru*, and the Diamond Necklace out of the Bowels of *Indostan*'. Cf. Burton, *Anatomy*, III ii 2 (3).

From each she nicely culls with curious Toil,
And decks the Goddess with the glitt'ring Spoil.
This Casket *India*'s glowing Gems unlocks,
And all *Arabia* breathes from yonder Box.
The Tortoise here and Elephant unite,
Transform'd to *Combs*, the speckled and the white.
Here Files of Pins extend their shining Rows,
Puffs, Powders, Patches, Bibles, Billet-doux.
Now awful Beauty puts on all its Arms;

132. *glitt'ring Spoil*] This, in the plural, is the phrase for captive armour in Dryden's *Æneid*, ix 495.

134. Cf. Blackmore, *Creation*, vii 36:

Let all Arabia in thy garments dwell.

135 f. A small Ovidian metamorphosis.

137 f. The rhyme is imperfect; cf. i 117 f. above.

138. For discussion of this line see Appendix F below, pp. 401 ff. The line consisting almost wholly of a list of common nouns—for those listing proper nouns see below, p. 202 note on l. 47—is according to a pattern found as early as Petrarch: see sonnet, 'Amor che . . .', l. 5:

fior frondi erbe ombre antri onde aure soavi.

Cf. also Sidney, *Complete Works*, ed. A. Feuillerat, Cambridge, 1912–26, i 442:

Fire, aire, sea, earth, fame, time, place show your power,

and ii 229:

Earth, sea, ayre, fire, heav'n, hell, and gastly sprite.

The nearest approach to this pattern in Latin poetry may be Juvenal, *Sat.*, i 85 f.:

Quicquid agunt homines, votum, timor, ira, voluptas,
Gaudia, discursus, nostri est farrago libelli.

Pope was not the first to apply this satiric formula (the list with one incongruous item) to the present matter: Wakefield compares Charles Montagu, Earl of Halifax (*Supplement to the Works of the Most celebrated Minor Poets*, 1750, p. 46):

Her waiting-maids prevent the peep of day,
And, all in order, on her toilet lay
Prayer-book, patch-boxes, sermon-notes and paint,
At once t'improve the sinner and the saint.

Patches] H. Misson, p. 214, notes their excess in England.

139 ff. Arabella's beauty had already been described as 'awful', see Appendix A, p. 373.

Pope is parodying the arming of the epic hero. And cf. Dryden's *Ovid's Ep.*, p. 85:

I see fair *Helen* put on all her Charms.

The motto of the passage might be that of Keats' *Hyperion*, ii 228 f.:

The Fair each moment rises in her Charms,
Repairs her Smiles, awakens ev'ry Grace,
And calls forth all the Wonders of her Face;
Sees by Degrees a purer Blush arise,
And keener Lightnings quicken in her Eyes.
The busy *Sylphs* surround their darling Care;

. . . for 'tis the eternal law
That first in beauty should be first in might.

Dennis, who missed the epic parody, notes that Belinda's beauty, insisted on at i 14 and 27, is shown here to be mainly the result of her toilet, and that the same is true of the beauty of the lock—see iv 97 ff. (*Remarks*, pp. 11 ff.). What he intends as adverse moral criticism, still has interest for its literary perception.

140. Cf. 'the swelling and growing figures of the poets: of which *Fame*, the *Sibyl*, and the *Pestilence* of *Virgil*, with the *Satan* of *Milton*, are sublime examples' [Wakefield]; cf. also *Temple of Fame*, 258 ff.

142. Cf. Dryden, *Æneid*, vii 627:

And open all the Furies of her Face;

and Eusden, Ovid's *Metam.*, x ('Venus and Adonis'):

But when he saw the Wonders of her Face.

144. Belinda employs the juice of belladonna (deadly night-shade), which enlarges the pupil of the eye, or else she darkens the surrounding skin.

145. *Antient Traditions of the* Rabbi's *relate, that several of the fallen Angels became amorous of Women, and particularize some; among the rest* Asael, *who lay with* Naamah, *the wife of* Noah, *or of* Ham; *and who continuing impenitent, still presides over the Women's Toilets.* Bereshi Rabbi *in* Genes. *6. 2.* [P. 1736–51.]

Cf. Appendix B, pp. 378 ff. below; and Basnage, *Histoire des Juives* (translated by Thos. Taylor, 1708) which reproduces Enoch's account. Azael, or Azalzel, is there said to have 'taught Maids to Paint' (p. 312) and Naamah to have been one of the four mothers of the demons, being 'beautiful as the Angels, to whom she resigned herself' (p. 310). Pope may have known B. Bekker's *The World Bewitch'd; or, An Examination of the Common Opinions Concerning Spirits* (translated 1695), where p. 110 reads: '[Josephus] even knows the Names of those Angels that were carried to [the] excess of Letchery; *Aza* and *Azael* were the chiefest amongst them, being both enamour'd with the Beauty of *Naema*, *Cain*'s Daughter.'

Gabalis (which discusses Enoch's account, pp. 33 ff.) contains a parallel statement that Zoroaster was the son of Oromasis, whom *Gabalis* represents as a salamander, and of Vesta who was traditionally identified with Naamah.

Prof. G. Scholem informs me that the words *Bereshi Rabbi* are likely to be a mistake for *Bereshit Rabba*: '[the] theory about Naama as Noa's wife is found in that collection of Rabbinical traditions, known as the Midrash Bereshit Rabba . . . the misprint may have been in Pope's source. That it was Naama, to whose

These set the Head, and those divide the Hair,
Some fold the Sleeve, whilst others plait the Gown;
And *Betty*'s prais'd for Labours not her own.

147 whilst] while *1714–17*.

beauty the angels became victims and Asael among them, is a later cabbalistical tradition, found several times in the Zohar and not in the Book Ber. Rabba.'

146. Cf. Waller, 'The Battle of the Summer Islands', ii 37:

These share the bones, and they [= those] divide the oil.

147. There seems no great difference between 'fold' and 'plait'; the kindest periphrasis would run: 'Some arrange the hang of the sleeve while others arrange the folds of the gown.'

148. Cf. *Iliad*, ii 160: And *Troy* prevails by Armies not her own.

Betty] At this time 'Betty' was a generic name for lady's maids: cf. Pope, *Moral Essays*, i 251, and Young's *Love of Fame*, v 438. In Congreve's *Old Bachelor* there is a maid Betty as well as 'an affected Lady' Belinda.

THE RAPE *of the* LOCK.

CANTO II.

NOT with more Glories, in th' Etherial Plain,
The Sun first rises o'er the purpled Main,
Than issuing forth, the Rival of his Beams
Lanch'd on the Bosom of the Silver *Thames*.
Fair Nymphs, and well-drest Youths around her shone,
But ev'ry Eye was fix'd on her alone.
On her white Breast a sparkling *Cross* she wore,
Which *Jews* might kiss, and Infidels adore.
Her lively Looks a sprightly Mind disclose,

4 Lanch'd] Launch'd *1751*.

---

1 ff. Cf. Æneas's voyage up the Tiber (*Æneid*, vii); and Shadwell's voyage on the Thames, 'Mac Flecknoe', 38 ff. Cf. also Chaucer, 'Knight's Tale', l. 1415:

Up roos the sonne and up roos Emelye,

which Dryden's translation retained: Oldmixon, *An Essay on Criticism* (1728), p. 39, comments: 'Had *Chaucer* said, *Up rose the Sun*, and then *up rose Emily* brighter than the Sun, *Emily* and the Reader would have been entertain'd with only a common Complement . . .' Pope's mock-heroics decree his heightened phrasing.

1–18. Belinda is described in part directly—her breast is white, for instance—but in the main indirectly through her acts and the effect she produces on others.

3, 13 f. The comparisons with the sun continue that of l. 3 above. See p. 170 below, ll. 19 f. and note thereon; the use of 'burn' at l. 26 continues metaphorically the 'burning' of l. 20. And see p. 211 below, note on v 147 f.

4. E. Hatton, *View of London* (1708), ii 796, gives the authorized fares from London to Hampton Court as 6s. the whole fare, 1s. each if a company. Embarkation could be made from any of the many 'Stairs'. Miss Jeffries Davies tells me that the shore of the Thames was so dirty with coal that Belinda would doubtless have had to choose her stairs carefully. The silver Thames was nearer midstream.

Lanch'd] The spelling recalls a pronunciation that still survives in Navy circles. Cf. some old people's pronunciation of 'laundry' [*la :ndri*]. Swift has the spelling 'flanting' (*Tale of a Tub*, ed. A. C. Guthkelch and D. Nichol Smith, 1920, p. 84).

7 f. See Introduction, pp. 98 f., for Arabella Fermor's cross in her portrait.

Cf. *Secchia Rapita*, III lxv, where the ensign of Ramberto Balugola represents a child who is making a Jew kiss the cross; *Antony and Cleopatra*, II ii 244 f.; Donne's 'Loves Exchange', ll. 29 f.; and Dryden, 'Song To a Fair Young Lady', ll. 13 ff.

Quick as her Eyes, and as unfix'd as those:
Favours to none, to all she Smiles extends,
Oft she rejects, but never once offends.
Bright as the Sun, her Eyes the Gazers strike,
And, like the Sun, they shine on all alike.
Yet graceful Ease, and Sweetness void of Pride,
Might hide her Faults, if *Belles* had Faults to hide:
If to her share some Female Errors fall,
Look on her Face, and you'll forget 'em all.
  This Nymph, to the Destruction of Mankind,
Nourish'd two Locks, which graceful hung behind
In equal Curls, and well conspir'd to deck
With shining Ringlets the smooth Iv'ry Neck.
Love in these Labyrinths his Slaves detains,

22 the] her *1714–17*.

10. Note the contrast with 'fix'd', l. 6 above.

14. Cf. Matthew, v 45; Wakefield compares Quintilian, *Instit. Orat.*, I ii 14: 'ut sol, universis idem lucis calorisque largitur' and Shakespeare, *Henry V*, IV, Chorus, 43.

15, 20. I do not see any point in the repetition of 'graceful', and conclude it to be an oversight on Pope's part.

15. *Ease*] Considered as the test of good breeding; cf. 'Ep. to Dr. Arbuthnot', 196.

16. *Belles*] Cf. p. 143 above, note on l. 37.

19. Cf. Dryden, I *Conquest of Granada*, III i:

You bane, and soft destruction of mankind.

23–8. Paulus Silentiarius (*Anthologia Planudea* [Florence, 1494]: *The Greek Anthology*, ed. Loeb, i 242 f.) represents Doris as pulling out one of her golden hairs and binding the hands of the incredulous lover so tight that he moans, unable to escape. Buchanan translated this epigram, with a small original addition (*Poemata*, ed. 1676, p. 349), and Sandys employed the idea, *Song of Solomon*, iv 32. Meantime Butler (*Hudibras*, II iii 13 f.) had used a similar expression—perhaps it was an English proverb—for fishing (some fish, e.g. trout, can be caught with a line only one hair strong). Dryden intruded the Greek idea into his translation of Persius (*Sat.*, v 246 f.) but, following Butler, he may also have had fishing in mind. (Wakefield supplies instances from Milton and Waller of the connection of a woman's hair and a net.) Pope explicitly combines the Greek and the English traditions.

A. Davenport (*Notes and Queries*, cc, Jan.–Dec. 1955, p. 433) notes a further

And mighty Hearts are held in slender Chains.
With hairy Sprindges we the Birds betray,
Slight Lines of Hair surprize the Finny Prey,
Fair Tresses Man's Imperial Race insnare,
And Beauty draws us with a single Hair.
  Th' Adventrous *Baron* the bright Locks admir'd,
He saw, he wish'd, and to the Prize aspir'd:
Resolv'd to win, he meditates the way,
By Force to ravish, or by Fraud betray;
For when Success a Lover's Toil attends,
Few ask, if Fraud or Force attain'd his Ends.
  For this, ere *Phœbus* rose, he had implor'd
Propitious Heav'n, and ev'ry Pow'r ador'd,
But chiefly *Love*—to *Love* an Altar built,
Of twelve vast *French* Romances, neatly gilt.
There lay three Garters, half a Pair of Gloves;

39 There lay the Sword-knot *Sylvia*'s Hands had sown,
With *Flavia*'s Busk that oft had rapp'd his own:
A Fan, a Garter, half a Pair of Gloves; *1714.*

---

parallel in Florio's translation of an Italian proverb in *Second Frutes*, 1591, sig. Aa 4:

Ten teemes of oxen draw much lesse
Than doth one hair of Helens tresse.

For the structure of this passage and for one of its phrases cf. Dryden's translation of Virgil's *Georgics*, iii 375 ff.:

Thus every Creature, and of every Kind,
The secret Joys of sweet Coition find:
Not only Man's Imperial Race; but they
That wing the liquid Air, or swim the Sea,
Or haunt the Desart, rush into the flame:
For Love is Lord of all; and is in all the same.

32. *By Force . . . or by Fraud*] A common antithesis in the epics. Cf. Dryden's *Æneid*, i 942, ii 62, and *Odyssey*, i 385, iii 235, etc.

34. Cf. *Æneid*, ii 390: dolus, an virtus, quis in hoste requirat?

35 ff. Cf. iii 107 below; 'Mac Flecknoe', 207; *Dispensary*, p. 36, where Horoscope builds an altar to *Disease*; *Dunciad*, i 155 ff.

36 f. The Baron has taken a tip from Palamon's experience in Chaucer's 'Knight's Tale', iii.

39 f. Cf. the inventory of effects left by the deceased beau in *Tatler* 113.

And all the Trophies of his former Loves.
With tender *Billet-doux* he lights the Pyre,
And breathes three am'rous Sighs to raise the Fire.
Then prostrate falls, and begs with ardent Eyes
Soon to obtain, and long possess the Prize:
The Pow'rs gave Ear, and granted half his Pray'r,
The rest, the Winds dispers'd in empty Air.
But now secure the painted Vessel glides,
The Sun-beams trembling on the floating Tydes,
While melting Musick steals upon the Sky,
And soften'd Sounds along the Waters die.
Smooth flow the Waves, the Zephyrs gently play,
Belinda smil'd, and all the World was gay.

43 ff. Pope cleverly adapts the episode of Arruns, Chloreus, and Camilla (*Æneid*, xi 759 ff.). Dryden's translation (1144 f.) reads:

Him, the fierce Maid beheld with ardent Eyes;
Fond and Ambitious of so Rich a Prize.

See the following note.

45 f. Virg. Æn. 11 [794 f.] [P. 1736–51]:

audiit et voti Phœbus succedere partem
mente dedit, partem volucris disperit in auras.

Dryden's translation (1165 f.) reads:

Apollo heard, and granting half his Pray'r,
Shuffled in Winds the rest, and toss'd in empty Air.

Cf. also *Iliad*, xvi 306 ff., and Dryden, Ovid's *Metam.*, xi 250 f.:

This last Petition heard of all her Pray'r,
The rest dispers'd by winds were lost in Air.

'The *Poets* made always the *Winds* either to disperse the prayers that were not to succeed, or to carry away those that were' (*Davideis*, iii note 54).

48. *Tydes*] The Thames is tidal up to Teddington, or was in 1714, and so an expression which in some poems of the time would have been 'poetic diction' used for the sake of the rhyme has here a literal application. Dryden had used 'floating tides' figuratively of a mob, 'Palamon and Arcite', iii 466 f.:

The Palace-yard is fill'd with floating Tides,
And the last Comers bear the former to the Sides;

cf. also his *Albion and Albanius*, Act I, where the 'horny flood' is invited to 'swell the Moony Tide'

That on thy buxom Back the floating Gold may glide;

and Ovid, *Ars Amandi*, ii 721.

All but the *Sylph*—With careful Thoughts opprest,
Th'impending Woe sate heavy on his Breast.
He summons strait his Denizens of Air;
The lucid Squadrons round the Sails repair:
Soft o'er the Shrouds Aerial Whispers breathe,
That seem'd but *Zephyrs* to the Train beneath.
Some to the Sun their Insect-Wings unfold,
Waft on the Breeze, or sink in Clouds of Gold.
Transparent Forms, too fine for mortal Sight,
Their fluid Bodies half dissolv'd in Light.
Loose to the Wind their airy Garments flew,
Thin glitt'ring Textures of the filmy Dew;
Dipt in the richest Tincture of the Skies,
Where Light disports in ever-mingling Dies,
While ev'ry Beam new transient Colours flings,

53 f. Cf. Dryden, *Æneid*, iv i: 'But anxious Cares already seiz'd the Queen;' (which Pope had already echoed at 'January and May', 392); *Iliad*, x 1 ff.:

> All Night the Chiefs before their Vessels lay,
> And lost in Sleep the Labours of the Day:
> All but the King; with various Thoughts oppress,
> His Country's Cares lay rowling in his Breast;

and ii 1 ff.

55. *Denizens*] Used in its proper sense of 'naturalized aliens'.

56 ff. See Appendix B, pp. 381 ff.

56 f. 'The word [*shrouds*] is hardly applicable to up-river light craft. The shrouds are the large ropes which support, or "stay," the masts of a ship, and enable them to carry sail' [Holden]. But Pope is purposely raising Belinda's 'painted Vessel' to epic dignity. He is imitating Blackmore's *King Arthur* (1696), p. 4, where around Arthur's fleet Mercy, Deliverance, Pity, and Hope

> Sung on the Shrowds, or with the Streamers plaid.

57 f. Cf. ii 83 ff. below.

64. 'The gossamer, which is spun in autumn by a species of spider that has the power of sailing in the air, was formerly supposed to be the product of sunburnt dew. Thus Spenser speaks of

> ... The fine nets which oft we woven see
> Of scorched dew' [EC].

65. In *Gabalis* the sylphs are 'cloathed in divers Colours' (p. 14); cf. also *Par. Lost*, v 283 ff., 'colours dipt in Heav'n ... skie-tinctur'd grain'.

67. *flings*] A word with a significant history in English poetry: cf. *Comus*, 990 and Gray's 'Ode on the Spring', 10.

Colours that change whene'er they wave their Wings.
Amid the Circle, on the gilded Mast,
Superior by the Head, was *Ariel* plac'd;
His Purple Pinions opening to the Sun,
He rais'd his Azure Wand, and thus begun.
  Ye *Sylphs* and *Sylphids*, to your Chief give Ear,
Fays, *Fairies*, *Genii*, *Elves*, and *Dæmons* hear!
Ye know the Spheres and various Tasks assign'd,
By Laws Eternal, to th' Aerial Kind.
Some in the Fields of purest *Æther* play,
And bask and whiten in the Blaze of Day.
Some guide the Course of wandring Orbs on high,

70. The hero in epic is always taller than his followers. Cf. *Iliad*, ii 566 ff., 988 ff., and xviii 602:

August, Divine, Superior by the Head!

Par. Lost, i 589 ff.; and 1 Samuel, ix 2.

72. *azure*] Probably because Ariel demands a sky-coloured wand. A. Philips (*Pastorals*, ed. 1748, vi 124) gives Oberon an 'azure scepter, pointed with a star'.

73. *Sylphids*] The female sylph in *Gabalis* is called a *sylphide*.

74. With the exception of 'Elves' (cf. i 31 above) all these names are found in *Gabalis*: '*Fees*, or *Fairies*' (p. 179), 'This *Vesta*, being Dead, was the Tutelar Genius of *Rome*' (p. 115), and 'These *Demons* . . . were an Aerial People' (p. 92). Pope is finding difficulty in parodying *Par. Lost*, v 601:

Thrones, Dominations, Princedomes, Vertues, Powers.

75 ff. In *Gabalis* each sylph etc. has control of the element he inhabits; 'they trouble the *Air*, and the *Sea*, set the Earth in Combustion, and dispense the Fire of *Heaven*, according to their Humour' (p. 52). Cf. also *Dispensary*, pp. 66 f.

77 ff. This division of occupation is in the epic style: cf. *Æneid*, vi 642 ff., *Par. Lost*, ii 528 ff. and *Dispensary*, pp. 6 f.

78. For the epic parody, cf. *Æneid*, vi 740 f. Cf. also Dryden, *King Arthur*, Act II:

Merlin. . . . as thy Place is nearest to the Sky,
The rays will reach thee first, and bleach thy Soot.
Philadel [an 'Airy Spirit'].
In hope of that, I spread my Azure Wings . . .
I bask in Day-Light, and behold with Joy
My Scum work outward, and my Rust wear off.

Addison, translating Lucan on Phaeton (*Remarks*, p. 112) has 'the Blaze of Day'.

79. See Appendix B, pp. 381 f.; cf. *Windsor Forest*, 245.

Or roll the Planets thro' the boundless Sky.
Some less refin'd, beneath the Moon's pale Light
Pursue the Stars that shoot athwart the Night,
Or suck the Mists in grosser Air below,
Or dip their Pinions in the painted Bow,
Or brew fierce Tempests on the wintry Main,
Or o'er the Glebe distill the kindly Rain.
Others on Earth o'er human Race preside,
Watch all their Ways, and all their Actions guide:
Of these the Chief the Care of Nations own,
And guard with Arms Divine the *British Throne*.
  Our humbler Province is to tend the Fair,
Not a less pleasing, tho' less glorious Care.
To save the Powder from too rude a Gale,
Nor let th' imprison'd Essences exhale,
To draw fresh Colours from the vernal Flow'rs,
To steal from Rainbows ere they drop in Show'rs
A brighter Wash; to curl their waving Hairs,
Assist their Blushes, and inspire their Airs;
Nay oft, in Dreams, Invention we bestow,

82 Hover, and catch the shooting Stars by Night; *1714–17*.
86 o'er] on *1714–15*.

80. Cf. *Iliad*, i 671:

Who rolls the Thunder o'er the vaulted Skies.

86. *kindly Rain*] Cf. Dryden, *Georgic*, i 29.

89 f. Each nation was supposed to have its guardian angel (see Peake's *Commentary on the Bible*, ed. 1919, n. on *Daniel*, x 13). Cf. the final tableau in Dryden's *Albion and Albanius*; and the angel in Addison's *Rosamond*, III i 5 f.:

In hours of peace, unseen, unknown,
I hover o'er the *British* throne.

Dryden had discussed the august role of the guardian angels of kingdoms—'a doctrine almost universally received' (*Essays*, ii 34 ff.). He had recommended their use as machinery in modern epics.

99. *Invention*] 'the first happiness of the poet's imagination is . . . invention, or finding of the thought' (Dryden, *Essays*, i 15). Women, Pope allows, also invent, but invent only the trimmings of dresses.

To change a *Flounce*, or add a *Furbelo*.
This Day, black Omens threat the brightest Fair
That e'er deserv'd a watchful Spirit's Care;
Some dire Disaster, or by Force, or Slight,
But what, or where, the Fates have wrapt in Night.
Whether the Nymph shall break *Diana*'s Law,
Or some frail *China* Jar receive a Flaw,
Or stain her Honour, or her new Brocade,
Forget her Pray'rs, or miss a Masquerade,
Or lose her Heart, or Necklace, at a Ball;
Or whether Heav'n has doom'd that *Shock* must fall.
Haste then ye Spirits! to your Charge repair;
The flutt'ring Fan be *Zephyretta*'s Care;
The Drops to thee, *Brillante*, we consign;
And, *Momentilla*, let the Watch be thine;
Do thou, *Crispissa*, tend her fav'rite Lock;
Ariel himself shall be the Guard of *Shock*.
To Fifty chosen *Sylphs*, of special Note,

100. *Furbelo*] Johnson's *Dictionary* cites the definition translated from Trévou's dictionary: 'A piece of stuff plaited and puckered together, either below or above, on the petticoats or gowns of women'. His example is this couplet.

103. *Force, or Slight*] Cf. Spenser's *Faerie Queene*, VI vii 34–5.

105 ff. Warburton notes the 'fine satire on the female estimate of human mischances'.

106. *China*] Henry Felton (*A Dissertation*, 1713, pp. 104 ff.) speaks of 'those Modish Ladies that change their Plate for China'. Cf. *Moral Es.*, ii 268:

And Mistress of herself, tho' China fall.

113. *Drops*] 'Diamond(s) hanging in the ear', Johnson's *Dictionary*, which cites this couplet.

115. *Crispissa*] 'To crisp in our earlier writers is a common word for curl, from the Latin *crispo*' [Wakefield].

116. The reason for Ariel's special post is hinted at iii 158 and iv 75 f.

117 ff. Pope mimics the epic shield; cf. *Iliad*, vii 295 ff., xviii 551 ff., especially 701 ff. (where Vulcan, making the shield of Achilles, binds the circumference with silver), and *Æneid*, viii 447 ff. He may also have in mind the helmet of Pallas, *Iliad*, v 918 ff., and Entellus' gloves with their 'sev'n distinguish'd folds' (Dryden, *Æneid*, v 538). Thomas Hardy endorses and annotates this passage, unconsciously (*Desperate Remedies*, chr. viii): 'His clothes are something exterior to every man; but to a woman her dress is part of her body. Its motions are all present to

We trust th'important Charge, the *Petticoat*:
Oft have we known that sev'nfold Fence to fail,
Tho' stiff with Hoops, and arm'd with Ribs of Whale.
Form a strong Line about the Silver Bound,
And guard the wide Circumference around.
  Whatever Spirit, careless of his Charge,
His Post neglects, or leaves the Fair at large,
Shall feel sharp Vengeance soon o'ertake his Sins,
Be stopt in *Vials*, or transfixt with *Pins*;

---

her intelligence if not to her eyes; no man knows how his coat-tails swing. By the slightest hyperbole it may be said that her dress has sensation. Crease but the very Ultima Thule of fringe or flounce, and it hurts her as much as pinching her. Delicate antennæ, or feelers, bristle on every outlying frill. Go to the uppermost: she is there, tread on the lowest: the fair creature is there almost before you.'

'The hoop petticoat, in spite of the notion of Addison, that "a touch of his pen would make it contract like a sensitive plant" [see *Spectator*, 127], continued in fashion as an ordinary dress for upwards of threescore years, and remained the court costume till the death of Queen Charlotte' [Croker]. Addison also writes: 'It is most certain that a Woman's Honour cannot be better intrenched than after this manner, in Circle within Circle, amidst such a Variety of Outworks and Lines of Circumvallation'; cf. *Tatler* 116 and Eusden, 'Verses Spoken at... Cambridge', 1714, pp. 3 f.

Cf. the stoutness of l. 120 with the trembling expansiveness of l. 122.

120. A 'Robe of Tissue' sent by Æneas as a gift for Iulus is 'stiff with golden Wire' (Dryden, *Æneid*, i 915). The phrase 'stiff with gold' comes frequently in Pope's Homer.

123 ff. Cf. Jove's threats, *Iliad*, viii 11 ff. and 'the various Penances enjoyn'd' before a soul in Hades can be made ready for human life again (*Æneid*, vi 739 ff.). Cf. also Sandys, Ovid's *Metam.*, iv 457 ff.; and the threats of Amariel, the guardian-spirit of St Catherine, in Dryden's *Tyrannick Love*, iv i.

'Our poet still rises in the delicacy of his satire, where he employs, with the utmost judgment and elegance, all the implements and furniture of the toilette, as instruments of [the sylphs'] punishment.' (Warton, i 226). Warton might also have noted that when the emotion of pain joins the more purely aesthetic emotions, Pope achieves his best poetry.

careless of his Charge] Cf. the lines from the *State of Innocence* quoted in Dryden's preface (*Essays*, i 188):

> Seraph and cherub, careless of their charge,
> And wanton, in full ease now live at large:
> Unguarded leave the passes of the sky,
> And all dissolved in hallelujahs lie.

Or plung'd in Lakes of bitter *Washes* lie,
Or wedg'd whole Ages in a *Bodkin*'s Eye:
Gums and *Pomatums* shall his Flight restrain,
While clog'd he beats his silken Wings in vain;
Or Alom-*Stypticks* with contracting Power
Shrink his thin Essence like a rivell'd Flower.
Or as *Ixion* fix'd, the Wretch shall feel
The giddy Motion of the whirling Mill,
In Fumes of burning Chocolate shall glow,
And tremble at the Sea that froaths below!
He spoke; the Spirits from the Sails descend;
Some, Orb in Orb, around the Nymph extend,
Some thrid the mazy Ringlets of her Hair,
Some hang upon the Pendants of her Ear;
With beating Hearts the dire Event they wait,
Anxious, and trembling for the Birth of Fate.

135 In] Midst *1714–15*.

128. Cf. *Iliad*, v 1090 f. and the fate of Shakespeare's Ariel (*Tempest*, I ii 270 ff). Pope plays on the various meanings of *bodkin*: (1) here it means a blunt-pointed needle; (2) at iv 98 and v 95, a hair ornament; (3) at v 55 and 88 a dagger (with a pun on (2)).

132. *rivell'd*] 'contract[ed] into wrinkles and corrugations' (Johnson's *Dictionary*, which cites this couplet and two instances from Dryden, one applied to flowers, one to fruit).

134. Cf. iii 106 below, and *Iliad*, i 764 (of Vulcan's fall from heaven):
Breathless I fell, in giddy Motion lost.

136. Cf. Dryden's *Ovid's Ep.*, p. 48:
And trembling at the Waves which roul below.

138. Cf. the angels in *Par. Lost*, v 596.

142. Cf. *Iliad*, iv 112; And Fate now labours with some vast Event.

THE RAPE *of the* LOCK.

CANTO III.

CLOSE by those Meads for ever crown'd with Flow'rs,
Where *Thames* with Pride surveys his rising Tow'rs,
There stands a Structure of Majestick Frame,
Which from the neighb'ring *Hampton* takes its Name.
Here *Britain*'s Statesmen oft the Fall foredoom
Of Foreign Tyrants, and of Nymphs at home;
Here Thou, Great *Anna*! whom three Realms obey,
Dost sometimes Counsel take—and sometimes *Tea*.
Hither the Heroes and the Nymphs resort,
To taste awhile the Pleasures of a Court;
In various Talk th' instructive hours they past,

---

1 ff. Pope refines on the vulgar structures described in similar terms in 'Mac Flecknoe', ll. 64 ff., the *Dispensary*, pp. 1 f., 38 f. (and Blackmore's *Kit-Cats*, 1708, p. 5). For Hampton Court, see Appendix E, p. 399.

2. *rising Tow'rs*] Dryden uses the expression of Carthage (*Æneid*, iv 123 where, between 103 and 164, he uses 'rising' four times) and again in his *Ovid's Ep.*, p. 216.

5–18. Pope is enlarging on a scene he had already sketched: see Twickenham ed., vi (*Minor Poems*), p. 59:

> At length the Board in loose disjointed Chat,
> Descanted, some on this Thing, some on that;
> Some, over each Orac'lous Glass, fore-doom
> The Fate of Realms, and Conquests yet to come.

7. The English crown still kept up its absurd claim to rule France as well as Great Britain and Ireland.

8. See Introduction, pp. 118 and 120 f. above.

10 f. Pope glances at Horace's account of the function of poetry—to instruct and to please—and so laughs at the court's aping of its betters. Since the instruction, as specified, is contemptible, perhaps the 'pleasures' are also.

11. Cf. Dryden, *Æneid*, vi 720:

> While thus, in talk, the flying Hours they pass.

11 ff. 'At this Assembly [the Court of King William at Kensington], the only diversion is playing at Cards: For which purpose there are two Tables for *Basset* and three or four more for *Picket* and *Ombre*, but generally the Basset-Tables are only fill'd while the rest of the Company either sit or stand, talking on various Subjects, or justle about from one end of the Gallery [of pictures] to the other, some to admire, and most to find fault' (*Letters of Wit*, p. 214).

Who gave the *Ball*, or paid the *Visit* last:
One speaks the Glory of the *British Queen*,
And one describes a charming *Indian Screen*;
A third interprets Motions, Looks, and Eyes;
At ev'ry Word a Reputation dies.
Snuff, or the *Fan*, supply each Pause of Chat,
With singing, laughing, ogling, and all that.
 Mean while declining from the Noon of Day,
The Sun obliquely shoots his burning Ray;
The hungry Judges soon the Sentence sign,
And Wretches hang that Jury-men may Dine;
The Merchant from th' *Exchange* returns in Peace,

12 the *Ball*] a *Ball* *1714–15*.

12. *Visit*] See note on iii 167 below.

14. For Atterbury's aesthetic dissatisfaction with the mere prettiness of the fashionable Indian screens, see his letter to Pope (*Letters*, 1737, quarto, p. 231).

16. Cf. Donne, 'Ecclogue', 25 ff.:

> Then from . . . the Brides bright eyes,
> At every glance, a constellation flyes,
> And sowes the Court with starres . . .

17. 'The singular growth of the practice of taking snuff was a special feature of the reign of Queen Anne: before 1702 it was comparatively unknown' [Holden]. See note on iv 123, 126 below.

19 f. Cf. *Odyssey*, xvii 687 f.:

> 'Till now declining tow'rd the close of day,
> The sun obliquely shot his dewy ray

and Ambrose Philips's *Pastorals*, v 7 f.:

> The Sun, now mounted to the Noon of Day,
> Began to shoot direct his burning Ray.

20, 26. Belinda has already been compared to the sun (see note on ii 3, 13 f., p. 159 above) and the comparison is here continued.

21 f. Cf. *Iliad*, xvi 468 f.; *Odyssey*, xii 519:

> What-time the Judge forsakes the noisy bar

—which Boileau had interpreted as 'towards Three a Clock in the Afternoon' (*Works*, trans. 1711, ii 112 [second series]); *Dispensary*, p. 41; Wycherley's *Plain Dealer*, I i: 'You may talk, young Lawyer, but I shall no more mind you, than a hungry Judge does a Cause, after the Clock has struck One'; Congreve, *Love for Love*, I ii: 'with as much Dexterity, as a hungry Judge [dispatches] causes at Dinner-time'.

And the long Labours of the *Toilette* cease—
Belinda now, whom Thirst of Fame invites,
Burns to encounter two adventrous Knights,
At *Ombre* singly to decide their Doom;
And swells her Breast with Conquests yet to come.
Strait the three Bands prepare in Arms to join,
Each Band the number of the Sacred Nine.
Soon as she spreads her Hand, th' Aerial Guard
Descend, and sit on each important Card:
First *Ariel* perch'd upon a *Matadore*,
Then each, according to the Rank they bore;
For *Sylphs*, yet mindful of their ancient Race,
Are, as when Women, wondrous fond of Place.
Behold, four *Kings* in Majesty rever'd,
With hoary Whiskers and a forky Beard;
And four fair *Queens* whose hands sustain a Flow'r,
Th' expressive Emblem of their softer Pow'r;
Four *Knaves* in Garbs succinct, a trusty Band,

24. Cf. Dryden's *Æneid*, vii 171: 'And the long Labours of your Voyage end.'

25 ff. For ombre and the play described below, see Appendix C, pp. 383 ff. This passage (ll. 25–100) was printed as 'Description of the Game at *Ombre*. By Mr. Pope' in *A Miscellaneous Collection of Poems . . . By several Hands. Publish'd by T. M. Gent.*, Dublin, 1721.

29–98. Pope's mock-heroic treatment owes something to Dryden's account of the bees, Virgil's *Georgic*, iv 92 ff.

31 ff. A further example of the sylphs' 'humbler Province' of tending 'the Fair' (ii 91): cf. i 53 f.

34. The Gods in Virgil sit in order: Dryden's *Æneid*, x 5 f.:

. . . From first to last
The Sov'raign Senate in Degrees are plac'd.

35. Cf. Dryden's *Æneid*, v 46: And not unmindful of his ancient Race.

36. Cf. Chaucer, 'Prologue', 449 f. [of the Wife of Bath]; Butler, *Hudibras*, III i 869 ff.; and *Tatler*, 262.

37 ff. This review of the forces is epical in all but length: cf. *Iliad*, iii 175 ff. For notes on the playing cards see Appendix C, pp. 391 f.

38. *Whiskers*] 'a tuft of Hair on the Upper Lip of a Man' [E. Phillips].

39. Cf. Dryden's *Æneid*, i 439 [of Venus disguised as a huntress]: 'Her Hand sustain'd a Bow'.

Caps on their heads, and Halberds in their hand;
And Particolour'd Troops, a shining Train,
Draw forth to Combat on the Velvet Plain.
 The skilful Nymph reviews her Force with Care;
Let Spades be Trumps! she said, and Trumps they were.
 Now move to War her Sable *Matadores*,
In Show like Leaders of the swarthy *Moors*.
Spadillio first, unconquerable Lord!
Led off two captive Trumps, and swept the Board.
As many more *Manillio* forc'd to yield,
And march'd a Victor from the verdant Field.
Him *Basto* follow'd, but his Fate more hard
Gain'd but one Trump and one *Plebeian* Card.
With his broad Sabre next, a Chief in Years,
The hoary Majesty of *Spades* appears;
Puts forth one manly Leg, to sight reveal'd;
The rest his many-colour'd Robe conceal'd.
The Rebel-*Knave*, who dares his Prince engage,
Proves the just Victim of his Royal Rage.
Ev'n mighty *Pam* that Kings and Queens o'erthrew,
And mow'd down Armies in the Fights of *Lu*,
Sad Chance of War! now, destitute of Aid,
Falls undistinguish'd by the Victor *Spade*!

42 Halberds] halberts *1736–51*. 46 *Trumps!*] *Trumps*, *1714–17*.
47 *1714 do not start a new paragraph*. 59 who] that *1714–15*.

44. *Velvet Plain*] Cf. the 'verdant Field', l. 52 below. Both phrases are commonplaces of descriptive poetry, and are (Pope implies) at least as applicable to a velvet-covered card-table as to pastures.

46. Wakefield compares Genesis i 3: 'And God said, "Let there be light:" and there was light', which on the authority of Longinus (*De Sublimitate*, ix) became the most famous of all instances of the sublime.

47 f. Cf. note on iii 81 ff. below. African warrior tribes are mentioned in the *Æneid* and in Lucan's *Civil War*, iv 676 ff. Claudian's unfinished *De Bello Gildonico* deals with war in Africa. Memnon (Dryden's *Æneid*, i 1052) is called 'swarthy'.

56. Cf. 'Mac Flecknoe', l. 106: The hoary Prince in Majesty appear'd.

64. *undistinguish'd*] It is a part of the method ot tne epic poet to name only the

Thus far both Armies to *Belinda* yield;
Now to the *Baron* Fate inclines the Field.
His warlike *Amazon* her Host invades,
Th' Imperial Consort of the Crown of *Spades*.
The *Club*'s black Tyrant first her Victim dy'd,
Spite of his haughty Mien, and barb'rous Pride:
What boots the Regal Circle on his Head,
His Giant Limbs in State unwieldy spread?
That long behind he trails his pompous Robe,
And of all Monarchs only grasps the Globe?
The *Baron* now his *Diamonds* pours apace;
Th' embroider'd *King* who shows but half his Face,
And his refulgent *Queen*, with Pow'rs combin'd,
Of broken Troops an easie Conquest find.
Clubs, *Diamonds*, *Hearts*, in wild Disorder seen,
With Throngs promiscuous strow the level Green.
Thus when dispers'd a routed Army runs,

---

great. In speaking of the forces of war, whether before or after battle, he treats the common soldiers *en masse*, and says so. Cf. *Iliad*, ii 580 f.:

To count them all, demands a thousand Tongues,
A Throat of Brass, and Adamantine Lungs.

Cf. also *Iliad*, xvi 776, where Sarpedon

Lies undistinguish'd from the vulgar dead.

71 ff. 'These lines are a parody of several passages in *Virgil*. Compare the *Windsor Forest*, ver. 115' [Wakefield].

76 f. 'Embroider'd' and 'refulgent' are frequent epithets of apparel in the *Iliad*.

79. Cf. *Thebaid*, xi 597: 'arma, viri, currus'; and Dryden's *Æneid*, xi 943:

Arms, Horses, Men, on heaps together lye.

81 ff. Pope is probably referring to the rout at the defeat of Hannibal by Scipio at Zama in North Africa. Cf. Silius Italicus, *Punica*, xvii 585 ff.:

ingruit Ausonius versosque agit aequore toto
rector. iamque ipsae trepidant Carthaginis arces:
impletur terrore vago cuncta Africa pulsis
agminibus, volucrique fuga sine Marte ruentes
tendunt attonitos extrema ad litora cursus
ac Tartessiacas profugi sparguntur in oras;
pars Batti petiere domos, pars flumina Lagi;

and *Godfrey of Bulloigne*, xx, st. 56 ff.:

Of *Asia*'s Troops, and *Africk*'s Sable Sons,
With like Confusion different Nations fly,
Of various Habit and of various Dye,
The pierc'd Battalions dis-united fall,
In Heaps on Heaps; one Fate o'erwhelms them all.
The *Knave* of *Diamonds* tries his wily Arts,
And wins (oh shameful Chance!) the *Queen* of *Hearts*.
At this, the Blood the Virgin's Cheek forsook,
A livid Paleness spreads o'er all her Look;
She sees, and trembles at th' approaching Ill,
Just in the Jaws of Ruin, and *Codille*.
And now, (as oft in some distemper'd State)
On one nice *Trick* depends the gen'ral Fate.
An *Ace* of Hearts steps forth: The *King* unseen
Lurk'd in her Hand, and mourn'd his captive *Queen*.
He springs to Vengeance with an eager pace,
And falls like Thunder on the prostrate *Ace*.
The Nymph exulting fills with Shouts the Sky,
The Walls, the Woods, and long Canals reply.

84 Of . . . Habit] In . . . Habits *1714–17*.
87 tries his wily] now exerts his *1714*. 94 Fate.] Fate, *1714–15*.

The *Africk* Tyrants and the *Negro* Kings
Fell down on Heaps . . .
Their Ranks disordred be . . .
. . . quite discomfit and disperst they were.

Vida had already mocked such passages in *Scacchia Ludus*, 74 ff.

86. Cf. e.g., *Iliad* xvi 510 f.:

. . . the growing Slaughters spread
In Heaps on Heaps;

and *Odyssey*, ii 322: . . . one hour o'erwhelms them all!

92. Cf. Dryden's *Æneid*, vi 384:

Just in the Gate, and in the Jaws of Hell.

94. *Trick*] in two senses.

98. Cf. *Iliad*, xv 696:

The Victor leaps upon his prostrate Prize.

There is a reference to Jove's thunderbolts; and to the ending of the battle of the books, in *Lutrin* v, where Boileau uses the image 'l'effroyable tonnerre'.

100. Cf. Dryden's *Æneid*, xii 1344 f.:

Oh thoughtless Mortals! ever blind to Fate,
Too soon dejected, and too soon elate!
Sudden these Honours shall be snatch'd away,
And curs'd for ever this Victorious Day.
For lo! the Board with Cups and Spoons is crown'd,
The Berries crackle, and the Mill turns round.
On shining Altars of *Japan* they raise

With Groans the *Latins* rend the vaulted Sky:
Woods, Hills, and Valleys, to the Voice reply.

Woods . . . long Canals] See Appendix D, p. 396.

101 ff. Cf Dryden's *Æneid*, x 698 ff.:

O Mortals! blind in Fate . . .
The Time shall come, when *Turnus*, but in vain,
Shall wish untouch'd the Trophies of the slain:
Shall wish the fatal Belt were far away;
And curse the dire Remembrance of the Day.

blind to Fate] Cf. *Iliad*, xvi 64 and *Odyssey*, x 335.

105 ff. Pope's version of the hearty meals in the epic; see Intro., p. 116. Pope seems also to have in mind Dido's entertainment of Æneas, Dryden's *Æneid*, i 900 ff. Cf. also Nahum Tate's *Panacea: A Poem upon Tea* (1700), p. 3:

On burning Lamps a Silver Vessel plac'd,
A Table with surprising Figures grac'd,
And *china*-Bowls to feast their Sight and Tast:
The Genial Liquor, decently pour'd out,
To the admiring Guests is dealt about.
Scarce had they drank a first and second Round,
When the warm *Nectar*'s pleasing Force they found,
About their Heart enliven'd Spirits danc'd,
Then to the Brains sublimer Seat advanc'd.
(Such Transport feel young Prophets when they Dream.
Or Poets slumb'ring by *Pirene*'s Stream.)

106. The berries are first roasted (since they 'crackle') and are then ground. Cf. Pope's mock news-letter in the letter to Arbuthnot, 11 July [1714]: 'There was likewise a Side Board of Coffee which the Dean roasted with his own hands in an Engine for the purpose . . . He talked of Politicks over Coffee, with the Air & Style of an old Statesman . . .'

Pope is perhaps echoing Dryden's *Æneid*, vii 196:

The Feasts are doubl'd, and the Bowls go round.

107. *shining Altars of Japan*] = lacquered tables. Japanning had recently become so fashionable that the nobility and gentry, who previously 'were forc't to content themselves with perhaps a Screen, a Dressing-box, or Drinking bowl' could now 'be stockt with entire Furniture, Tables, Stands, Boxes' (J. Stalker

The silver Lamp; the fiery Spirits blaze.
From silver Spouts the grateful Liquors glide,
While *China*'s Earth receives the smoking Tyde.
At once they gratify their Scent and Taste,
And frequent Cups prolong the rich Repast.
Strait hover round the Fair her Airy Band;
Some, as she sip'd, the fuming Liquor fann'd,
Some o'er her Lap their careful Plumes display'd,
Trembling, and conscious of the rich Brocade.
Coffee, (which makes the Politician wise,
And see thro' all things with his half-shut Eyes)
Sent up in Vapours to the *Baron*'s Brain
New Stratagems, the radiant Lock to gain.
Ah cease rash Youth! desist ere 'tis too late,

108 Lamp; the] Lamp, and *1714–15*.
110 While] And *1714–17*. 112 And] While *1714–17*.

and G. Parker, *A Treatise of Japaning*, 1688, A iv). They name chestnut as the favourite colour in 1688.

108. For contemporary lamps and their stands see C. R. Grundy, *English Art in the XVIII Century* (1928) plates lxix f.

112. Cf. *Davideis*, p. 85:

And with long talk prolongs the hasty feast.

113 ff. More details of the humbler province of the sylphs (see ii 91 above): some are acting as table napkins.

116. Defoe praises the new brocades as 'thick and high' (*Complete English Tradesman*, 1726, II ii 155).

117 f. The coffee houses had long been the chief haunt of amateur politicians: they are satirized in *Tatlers* 155, 160, 178, and *Spectator* 403. Cf. also iii 106 *n.* above.

121. Pope's *Iliad*, xvi 847 ff. reads:

Who first, brave Hero! by that arm was slain
Who last, beneath thy Vengeance, press'd the Plain . . . ?

and adds the note: 'The Poet in a very moving and solemn way turns his Discourse to *Patroclus*. He does not accost his Muse, as it is usual with him to do, but enquires of the Hero himself who was the first, and who the last, who fell by his Hand? This Address distinguishes and signalizes *Patroclus*, (to whom *Homer* uses it more frequently, than I remember on any other occasion) as if he was some Genius or divine Being, and at the same time it is very pathetical and apt to move our Compassion. The same kind of Apostrophe is used by *Virgil* to *Camilla*:

Fear the just Gods, and think of *Scylla*'s Fate!
Chang'd to a Bird, and sent to flit in Air,
She dearly pays for *Nisus*' injur'd Hair!
But when to Mischief Mortals bend their Will,
How soon they find fit Instruments of Ill!
Just then, *Clarissa* drew with tempting Grace
A two-edg'd Weapon from her shining Case;
So Ladies in Romance assist their Knight,
Present the Spear, and arm him for the Fight.
He takes the Gift with rev'rence, and extends

125 f. Will . . . Ill!] Mind, How soon fit Instruments of Ill they find? *1714.*

130 the Spear] their Spear *1714b–15.*

Quem telo primum, quem prostremum, aspera virgo!
Dejicis? Aut quot humi morientia corpora fundis?'

122 ff. *Vide* Ovid. Metam. 8. [1 ff.] [P. 1714–51.] King Nisus, besieged in Megara by Minos, had a daughter Scylla who, seeing Minos from a watch tower, fell in love with him. The safety of Nisus and his kingdom was known to depend on a purple hair which, among 'those of honourable silver', grew on his head. Scylla plucked out this hair and took it to Minos but met with nothing but abhorrence for her impiety. After his victory he sailed away; whereupon Scylla attempted to cling to his ship till, beaten off by Nisus, who had become an osprey, she also became a bird. Virgil had alluded to the story, *Georgic* i 404 ff., and Pope adopts some words from Dryden's translation: 'injur'd' (applied to Nisus, l. 553) and 'the purple Hair is dearly paid' (l. 556). Pope draws the motto in the 1714–15 editions from the last line of Ovid's story: '*A tonso est hoc nomen adepta capillo*'. And see notes on iv 10 and v 5 f. below.

125 f. Shakespeare has 'instrument of ill' (*1 Henry VI,* III iii 65). Cf. *Absalom and Achitophel*, i 79 f.:

But, when to Sin our byast Nature leans,
The careful Devil is still at hand with means.

128. *shining Case*] See note on v 116 below; tweezer-cases for women seem to have just become fashionable: see *The Art of Dress*, 1717, p. 16:

. . . Ladies patch the Face,
And to the *Watch* now add the *Twezer Case*.

129 f. Butler in *Hudibras* makes several similar references to romances.

131 f. Cf. *Iliad*, xxiii 792 f. (when the 'Gloves of Death' have been put on, before wrestling):

Amid the Circle now each Champion stands,
And poizes high in Air his Iron Hands;

The little Engine on his Fingers' Ends,
This just behind *Belinda*'s Neck he spread,
As o'er the fragrant Steams she bends her Head:
Swift to the Lock a thousand Sprights repair,
A thousand Wings, by turns, blow back the Hair,
And thrice they twitch'd the Diamond in her Ear,
Thrice she look'd back, and thrice the Foe drew near.
Just in that instant, anxious *Ariel* sought
The close Recesses of the Virgin's Thought;
As on the Nosegay in her Breast reclin'd,
He watch'd th' Ideas rising in her Mind,
Sudden he view'd, in spite of all her Art,

132 Ends,] Ends: *1717*, ends; *1736–51*. 137 Ear,] ear; *1717–51*.

Odyssey, xviii 103; and Dryden's *Æneid*, v 543 f. (Dares has taken up the gloves of Entellus thrown down as a challenge):

> Astonish'd at their weight the Heroe stands,
> And poiz'd the pond'rous Engins in his hands.

(See also note on iii 149 below.) Johnson defines *engine* generally as 'Any mechanical complication, in which various movements and parts concur to one effect.' His second definition is 'A military machine' and his third 'Any instrument', under which he cites the present couplet. The word being applicable to a large military object or small domestic one is exactly appropriate for mock-heroic. Spenser is fond of the word in the *F.Q.*, and Butler, see *Hudibras*, I ii 113 and 353.

135 f. A thousand is a number common in epic. Cf. e.g., Rowe, 'Part of the Sixth Book of Lucan' (1709 *Miscellany*, p. 457):

> A thousand Darts upon his Buckler ring,
> A thousand Jav'lins round his Temples sing;

and again at p. 459.

136. Dryden's *Æneid* has many similar instances of the phrase 'by turns'.

139 ff. 'as Apollo leaves Hector, or Juturna Turnus' [Watt].

140. Cf. Elizabeth Singer's 'Vision' (Dryden's Miscellanies, v 1704), l. 1:

> 'Twas in the close Recesses of a Shade.

142. Cf. *Guardian* 106: 'I had Yesterday been reading and ruminating upon that Passage where *Momus* is said to have found fault with the Make of a Man, because he had not a Window in his Breast. The Moral of this Story is very obvious, and means no more than that the Heart of Man is so full of Wiles and Artifices, Treachery and Deceit, that there is no guessing at what he is from his Speeches and outward Appearances . . . I am myself very far gone in [love] for *Aurelia*, a Woman of an unsearchable Heart. I would give the World to know the Secrets of it.' Cf. note on i 99 ff. above.

An Earthly Lover lurking at her Heart.
Amaz'd, confus'd, he found his Pow'r expir'd,
Resign'd to Fate, and with a Sigh retir'd.
The Peer now spreads the glitt'ring *Forfex* wide,
T'inclose the Lock; now joins it, to divide.
Ev'n then, before the fatal Engine clos'd,
A wretched *Sylph* too fondly interpos'd;
Fate urg'd the Sheers, and cut the *Sylph* in twain,
(But Airy Substance soon unites again)
The meeting Points the sacred Hair dissever
From the fair Head, for ever and for ever!
Then flash'd the living Lightning from her Eyes,

155 Lightning] Lightnings *1714–17*.

144. *Earthly Lover*] See dedicatory epistle, ll. 30 ff.

146. *Resign'd*] the reflexive sense without the reflexive pronoun (to submit oneself to) is now rare.

149 f. The sylph is trying to imitate the angel (*Davideis*, p. 15) who puts by the spear which Saul flings at David.

149. The wooden horse is called 'the fatal Engine' in Dryden's *Æneid*, ii 345.

152. *See* Milton, *lib*. 6. [330 f.] [P. 1714–15: 1717–51 add *of* Satan *cut asunder by the Angel* Michael.] Cf. also *Iliad*, v 1109 f. Cf. also Gildon's account of the sylphs in his *Post-boy Rob'd of his Mail* (see *Notes and Queries*, cxciv, Jan.–June 1949, p. 14), where the creatures are said to come through closed doors and windows 'joyning again as soon as enter'd'.

154. *for ever and for ever!*] 'To emphasise the fact that the hair could not unite again, as the bisected sylph had done' [Holden]. This may be part of its significance now, but Pope cannot have so intended it from the start since the sylphs do not appear in the first version. The power of the words 'for ever', here twice repeated, were to strike J. H. Newman in their ecclesiastical context: 'He [i.e., Newman himself] writes the hour after he had received the Diaconate, "It is over; at first, after the hands were laid on me, my heart shuddered within me; the words 'For ever' are so terrible." The next day he says, "For ever! words never to be recalled . . ." ' (*Letters and Correspondence*, ed. Anne Mozley, 1891, i 149). In this passage Newman also uses the negative 'never', a word which Lear repeated five times over the dead body of Cordelia, and which in its form 'nevermore' seemed to Poe the saddest word in the language. Pope's poem is about the cutting off of a lock (which, it is allowed, is sufficiently vexing to a girl), but it is also about life and death.

155. Lightnings break forth from the eyes of the angry Saul (*Davideis*, p. 17).

And Screams of Horror rend th' affrighted Skies.
Not louder Shrieks to pitying Heav'n are cast,
When Husbands or when Lap-dogs breathe their last,
Or when rich *China* Vessels, fal'n from high,
In glittring Dust and painted Fragments lie!
   Let Wreaths of Triumph now my Temples twine,
(The Victor cry'd) the glorious Prize is mine!
While Fish in Streams, or Birds delight in Air,

157 to pitying] by Dames to *1714–15*.
158 Lap-dogs] Monkeys *1714* [cf. *Rape of the Locke*, i 122].

157 ff. A common device in epic. Cf. *Iliad*, xiv 456 ff.:

Both Armies join: Earth thunders, Ocean roars.
Not half so loud the bellowing Deeps resound,
When stormy Winds disclose the dark Profound;
Less loud the Winds, that from th' *Æolian* Hall
Roar thro' the Woods, and make whole Forests fall;

xv 266; and *Thebaid*, viii 406 ff.

158. Cf. Juvenal, *Sat.*, vi 653. *Tatler* 47 reports that 'The disconsolate *Maria* has three Days kept her Chamber for the Loss of the beauteous *Fidelia*, her Lap-dog'; and cf. *Tatler* 121: 'when [the fair sex] have disappointed themselves of the proper Objects of Love, as Husbands, or Children, such Virgins have exactly at such a Year, grown fond of Lap-Dogs, Parrats, or other Animals.' See Farquhar's *Sir Harry Wildair* (1701), I i: 'Shall I tell you, the Character I have heard of a fine Lady? A fine Lady can laugh at the Death of her Husband, and cry for the Loss of a Lap Dog . . .'; and also *Tatler* 40, where the adored lap-dog is 'that Shock'.

161. Watt compares Horace, *Odes*, III xxx 14 ff.

163 ff. Warburton compares Virgil, *Ecl.*, v 76 f.:

Dum iuga montis aper, fluvios dum pisces amabit,
Dumque thymo pascentur apes, dum rore cicadæ,
Semper honos nomenque tuum laudesque manebunt,

which Dryden (ll. 119 ff.) had translated:

While savage Boars delight in shady Woods,
And finny Fish inhabit in the Floods;
While Bees on Thime, and Locusts feed on Dew,
Thy grateful Swains these Honours shall renew.

(Ogilby's translation ends:

So long thy honour'd name and praise shall last;

and Sedley has the phrase 'Thy Honour, Name and Praise . . .'). Pope had a more apposite epic source in Dryden's *Æneid*, i 854 ff. [Æneas' speech to Dido, pleading for hospitality]:

Or in a Coach and Six the *British* Fair,
As long as *Atalantis* shall be read,
Or the small Pillow grace a Lady's Bed,
While *Visits* shall be paid on solemn Days,

> While rowling Rivers into Seas shall run,
> And round the space of Heav'n the radiant Sun;
> While Trees the Mountain tops with Shades supply,
> Your Honour, Name, and Praise shall never dye;

and also in ix 597 ff., in which Virgil, breaking into his narrative, promises immortality to the lamented Nisus and Euryalus:

> O happy Friends! for if my Verse can give
> Immortal Life, your Fame shall ever live:
> Fix'd as the Capitol's Foundation lies;
> And spread, where e'er the *Roman* Eagle flies!

Virgil intends his whole invocation to be soundly based, but as the centuries have passed, only the first item in it, his verse, has proved a secure stay for immortality. Pope takes what is secure (l. 163) and what is obviously not so (ll. 164–9) and sets them side by side. Virgil deserved that his promise should be sound in all its particulars—it took a long time for the Capitol and the Eagle to fail him. Pope sees to it that the particulars he takes from the world of men shall either be ephemeral things snatched up from the passing show—the small pillow, Mrs Manly's book, the last edition of which fell in 1736—or items which, though permanent, are not to the credit of man's character, but merely the result of his animal nature.

Pope also intends a parody of Philips's *Pastorals*, iii 105 ff.:

> While Mallow Kids, and Endive Lambs pursue;
> While Bees love Thyme, and Locusts sip the Dew;
> While Birds delight in Woods their Notes to strain,
> Thy Name and sweet Memorial shall remain.

Cf. also Pope's *Pastorals*, iv 84.

164. 'No gallant equipage in the Ring was complete without six grey Flanders mares and the owner's coat of arms emblazoned on the panels' (Larwood, i 93).

165. Mrs Manley's *Secret Memoirs and Manners of several Persons of Quality, of Both Sexes. From the New Atalantis, an Island in the Mediteranean*, had appeared in 1709 (2 vols.). Its libels led to her arrest, but she was released in 1710 and was soon publishing two more volumes of *Memoirs* which became vols. 3 and 4 of the *New Atalantis*.

166. Cf. Rochester, p. 78, for the fashionable small pillow on a lady's bed.

167 f. Visits were an essential part of the day's routine for a fashionable woman. They took place in the evening, and the lady was attended by servants bearing lights. During a mock-trial in *Tatler* 262, Mrs Flambeau is charged with not paying a visit, and one of the items in the defence is that 'there were no

When numerous Wax-lights in bright Order blaze,
While Nymphs take Treats, or Assignations give,
So long my Honour, Name, and Praise shall live!
What Time wou'd spare, from Steel receives its date,
And Monuments, like Men, submit to Fate!
Steel cou'd the Labour of the Gods destroy,
And strike to Dust th' Imperial Tow'rs of *Troy*;
Steel cou'd the Works of mortal Pride confound,
And hew Triumphal Arches to the Ground.
What Wonder then, fair Nymph! thy Hairs shou'd feel
The conqu'ring Force of unresisted Steel?

171 *1751 does not start a new paragraph.*
173 cou'd] did *1714–15.*

Candles lighted up'. An 'essential point' of the visit was its appointed day (*Tatler* 262)—'solemn' is therefore a pun; it includes the sense of *solemnis*, 'marked by the celebration of special observances or rites (especially of a religious character)' (OED). The visit is one of the butts of the *Tatler* and *Spectator*; and cf. Swift, *A Letter to a Very Young Lady on her Marriage.*

172. Wakefield cites Juvenal, *Sat.*, x 146:

Quandoquidem data sunt ipsis quoque fata sepulchris.

Dryden's translation, 232 f., is not echoed by Pope.

173 f. Troy was supposed to have been built by Apollo and Poseidon: cf. Addison, 'Poem to his Majesty', 38:

And laid the Labour of the Gods in dust.

'Ferrum' is often used in Latin epics as a synonym for sword, and 'steel' had already had its mock-heroic place in Mirmillo's armoury (*Dispensary*, p. 55):

Some fell by *Laudanum*, and some by *Steel.*

Imperial] a favourite word of Dryden.

176. Wakefield compares Addison's Horace, *Odes*, III iii 121:

And hew the shining fabrick to the ground.

178. Cf. Catullus, 'The Lock of Berenice', ll. 43 ff.:

ille quoque eversus mons est . . .
quid facient crines, cum ferro talia cedant?

See note on v 129 f. below. Cf. *Iliad*, v 777:

Urg'd by the Force of unresisted Fate;

and xxi 672 f.:

Yet sure He too is mortal; He may feel
(Like all the Sons of Earth) the Force of Steel.

THE RAPE *of the* LOCK.

CANTO IV.

But anxious Cares the pensive Nymph opprest,
And secret Passions labour'd in her Breast.
Not youthful Kings in Battel seiz'd alive,
Not scornful Virgins who their Charms survive,
Not ardent Lovers robb'd of all their Bliss,
Not ancient Ladies when refus'd a Kiss,
Not Tyrants fierce that unrepenting die,
Not *Cynthia* when her *Manteau*'s pinn'd awry,
E'er felt such Rage, Resentment and Despair,
As Thou, sad Virgin! for thy ravish'd Hair.
  For, that sad moment, when the *Sylphs* withdrew,
And *Ariel* weeping from *Belinda* flew,
Umbriel, a dusky melancholy Spright,
As ever sully'd the fair face of Light,

---

1. Virg. Æn. 4. [1] *At regina gravi, &c.* [P. 1736–51.] Dryden translates: But anxious Cares already seiz'd the Queen.

8. Cf. *The Art of Dress*, 1717, p. 21:

Oft have I seen a *Mantua* pinn'd amiss
Make People sneer, and almost cause a Hiss.

The mantua, mantoe or mantua-gown was 'a loose upper Garment, now generally worn by Women, instead of a straight-body'd Gown' [E. Phillips].

10. *ravish'd Hair*] Sandys's phrase at the end of his translation of the story of Nisus, *Metam.*, viii 151; see note on iii 122 ff., p. 177 above.

13 ff. The journey to the underworld is an epic commonplace. Garth concludes his poem with a subterranean journey to the Elysian Fields and, although Boileau keeps his supernaturals above ground, he employs them in grim surroundings. The subsidiary horrors in the 'antre' of Chicane (*Lutrin*, v 39 ff.), and in the lairs of Envy and Death (*Dispensary*, pp. 15 f. and 105) are like Pope's, fantastically allegorical. The source of all these is the cave which Ovid invented for Envy, *Metam.*, ii 760 ff. which Addison translated:

Shut from the Winds and from the wholesome Skies,
In a deep Vale the gloomy Dungeon lies,
Dismal and Cold, where not a Beam of Light
Invades the Winter, or disturbs the Night.

Lucian, parodying tragedy in his *Tragopodagra*, had made Gout a goddess; and R. Gould (*Works*, 1709, ii 277) had addressed Money thus:

Down to the Central Earth, his proper Scene,
Repair'd to search the gloomy Cave of *Spleen*.
  Swift on his sooty Pinions flitts the *Gnome*,
And in a Vapour reach'd the dismal Dome.
No cheerful Breeze this sullen Region knows,
The dreadful *East* is all the Wind that blows.

16 Repair'd] Repairs *1714–17*.

With *Pride* thou giv'st Birth to her *grinning Train*,
To all that is *affected*, all that's Vain;
For *Vanity* (which one whole Sex devours)
Stands waiting at her Elbow at all Hours . . .
And *Affectation* takes her very *Trace*,
When *one appears*, the *Other*'s still *in Place*.

Pomfret's vision, 'Love Triumphant over Reason', had shown a cave where there were exhibited 'The sad Effects of Female Treacheries.'

16. *Spleen*] The fashionable name—Gay speaks of 'the modish Spleen' (*The Fan*, i 120)—for an ancient malady, the incidence of which was jealously confined to the idle rich. A correspondent in *Spectator* 53 writes: 'I am a Gentleman who for many Years last past have been well known to be truly Splenetick, and that my Spleen arises from having contracted so great a Delicacy, by reading the best Authors, and keeping the most refined Company'; he therefore objects to 'Fellows in a Tavern Kitchen . . . guzzling Liquor' who presume to share this 'Distemper of the Great and the Polite'; and *Guardian* 131 cites Sir William Temple's observation that 'a *Dutchman* . . . is not delicate or idle enough to suffer from this Enemy, but *is always Well when he is not Ill, always Pleased when he is not Angry*.' Pope's account of the disease is, accordingly, 'rather fastidious', and finds no place for 'the belchings, gaseous rumblings in the viscera, gripings, heart palpitations, vomitings, spittings, etc.' which were some of the recognized symptoms (Babb, p. 173: Babb's valuable account of the malady and of Pope's use of it has furnished matter for some of the notes below).

17. Cf. *Dispensary*, p. 66:

The Bat with sooty Wings flits thro' the Grove.

18. *Vapour*] Pope puns on vapour(s) again at ll. 39 and 59 below. The spleen was also called the vapours and a misty climate was supposed to induce it.

Dome] See *Temple of Fame*, l. 65 n.

20. The east wind was considered to provoke spleen: 'the Idle Splenetick Man borrows sometimes [liveliness of face and conversation] from the Sunshine, Exercise, or an agreeable Friend . . . A Gentleman that has formerly been a very Eminent Lingerer, and something Splenetick, informs me, that in one Winter he . . . received a thousand Affronts during the North-Easterly Winds' (*Guardian*, 131).

Here, in a Grotto, sheltred close from Air,
And screen'd in Shades from Day's detested Glare,
She sighs for ever on her pensive Bed,
Pain at her Side, and *Megrim* at her Head.
Two Handmaids wait the Throne: Alike in Place,
But diff'ring far in Figure and in Face.
Here stood *Ill-nature* like an *ancient Maid*,
Her wrinkled Form in *Black* and *White* array'd;
With store of Pray'rs, for Mornings, Nights, and Noons,

24 *Megrim*] *Languor 1714.*

21 f. Burton notes that one of the symptoms of melancholy (the Elizabethan name for the spleen) is 'Solitariness, avoiding of light' (*Anatomy*, I ii 3).

Grotto] See Introduction to 'Eloisa to Abelard', pp. 307 f. below.

22. *detested*] Pope is echoing Davenant's placing of the word: cf. 'To my Friend Mr. Ogilby': '. . . in Deaths detested shade'; *The Siege of Rhodes*, *The First Entry*: '. . . Death's detested face'; and *id.*, part ii (the final scene): 'Death's detested Shade.' Cf. also *Dispensary*, p. 36: '*Hell*'s detested Womb'; Yalden, *Temple of Fame*, 1700, p. 10; and iv 147 below.

24. The organ called the spleen is at the left side of the body; megrim, or migraine, is a 'Disorder of the head' (Johnson's *Dictionary*), a severe headache: Pope places his allegorical figures accordingly.

25. *wait*] = wait on, 'to be in readiness to receive orders': this meaning is found as late as Scott (OED).

27 f. It was as painter, as well as moralist, that Pope chose the colours for Ill-nature: cf. Jonathan Richardson, *An Essay on the Theory of Painting*, 1715, p. 149: 'Perfect Black, and White are disagreeable; for which reason *a Painter should break those Extreams of Colours that there may be a Warmth, and Mellowness in his Work*'. Ill-nature was a new term at this date.

27–30. The prayers are represented as in the hand because, though damaging, they are not as damaging as the lampoons, which are precious enough for an unpleasant person to store in the bosom.

29. *Pray'rs*] Cf. *Spectator* 185: 'ILL-NATURE is another dreadful Imitator of Zeal. Many a good Man may have a natural Rancour and Malice in his Heart, which has been in some measure quelled and subdued by Religion; but if he finds any Pretence of breaking out, which does not seem to him inconsistent with the Duties of a Christian, it throws off all Restraint, and rages in its full Fury. Zeal is therefore a great Ease to a malicious Man, by making him believe he does God Service, whilst he is gratifying the Bent of a perverse revengeful Temper.'

Her Hand is fill'd; her Bosom with Lampoons.
  There *Affectation* with a sickly Mien
Shows in her Cheek the Roses of Eighteen,
Practis'd to Lisp, and hang the Head aside,
Faints into Airs, and languishes with Pride;
On the rich Quilt sinks with becoming Woe,
Wrapt in a Gown, for Sickness, and for Show.
The Fair-ones feel such Maladies as these,
When each new Night-Dress gives a new Disease.
  A constant *Vapour* o'er the Palace flies;
Strange Phantoms rising as the Mists arise;
Dreadful, as Hermit's Dreams in haunted Shades,

30. *Lampoons*] *Spectator* 23 is wholly devoted to the expression of ill-nature in lampoons and cruel personal satire.

31 ff. *Spectator* 38 had deplored Affectation by example and philosophy. Cf. also *Spectators* 460 (where Affectation is an allegorical figure in a vision) and 515.

33. *Tatler* 77, an essay on affectation (mainly that of men), notes lisping and carrying the head on one side as two marks of affectation, the former a recent fashion, the latter a fashion at the court of Alexander.

34. *Airs*] Cf. *Dunciad*, i 264: 'She [the goddess Dulness] looks, and breathes herself into their airs'.

34 ff. *Tatler* 77 exhibits valetudinarianism as a common form of affectation. *Faints into*] The OED finds this verb used only by Pope and Keats.

35–8. It was the fashion for ladies to receive visits in bed:

Chang'd is the Mode from that of former Days,
Ladies receiv'd no Visits *without Stays*

(Eusden, 'Verses Spoken . . . at Cambridge', 1714, p. 8). *Spectator* 45 makes fun of the practice, and cites an example of a lady who 'tho' willing to appear undrest, had put on her best Looks, and painted herself for our Reception. Her Hair appeared in a very nice Disorder, as the Night-Gown [i.e. dressing gown] which was thrown upon her shoulders was ruffled with great Care'.

39. *Vapour*] See note on iv 18 above.

40 ff. Hallucinations presenting gloomy or hectic phantoms were common symptoms of the spleen; see Burton's *Anatomy*, 1 iii 1 (2).

41 f. 'The poet by this comparison would insinuate, that the temptations of the mortified recluses in the Church of Rome, and the extatic visions of their female saints were as much the effects of hypocondriac disorders . . . as any of the imaginary transformations he speaks of afterwards' [Warburton]. Pope writes to Lady Mary Wortley Montagu, 3 Feb. [1716–17]: 'I am foolish again; and methinks I am imitating, in my ravings, the dreams of splenetic enthusiasts

Or bright as Visions of expiring Maids.
Now glaring Fiends, and Snakes on rolling Spires,
Pale Spectres, gaping Tombs, and Purple Fires:
Now Lakes of liquid Gold, *Elysian* Scenes,
And Crystal Domes, and Angels in Machines.
  Unnumber'd Throngs on ev'ry side are seen
Of Bodies chang'd to various Forms by *Spleen*.

---

and solitaires, who fall in love with saints, and fancy themselves in the favour of angels and spirits, whom they can never see or touch.'

43 ff. Starting from the usual hallucinatory symptoms of the spleen, Pope leads on to a satiric catalogue of the scenic effects of contemporary opera and pantomime. (Cf. *Dunciad*, iii 231 ff.) In Mountford's *Life and Death of Doctor Faustus, Made into a Farce* (1697), 'Good and bad angel descend . . . a Woman Devil rises: Fire-works about whirles round, and sinks [*sic*] . . . Throne of Heaven appears . . . Hell is discovered'; in D'Urfey's opera, *Wonders of the Sun* (1706), 'The Scene [is] a Luminous Country, adorn'd with Gorgeous Rays of the Sun'; in *The Necromancer; or, Harlequin Doctor Faustus* (9th edition, 1731), 'an Infernal Spirit rises. [There are] angels in Machines [and] pale Spectres', and the spirits of Hero and Leander appear about to cross the Styx.

Cf. also St-Evremond, ii 243: 'Let the Son of Amphiaraus make his Entrance, frighted with Visions, and demanding help against the Furies that pursue him.

> What do I see! Whence do these Flames arise!
> From gaping Tombs that seem to strike my Eyes.
> O help me to put out this cruel Fire . . .
> At me their Whips the restless Furies shake,
> Their angry Snakes a dreadful Consort make . . .'

Pope presumably also intends a particular gibe at Addison whose opera, *Rosamond*, III i, has 'a grotto, Henry asleep, a cloud descends, in it two angels'.

In l. 43 'Spires' = coils. Virgil uses 'spiris' of serpents, *Æneid*, xii 848, and Milton has 'circling spires' of the serpent-tempter, *Par. Lost*, ix 502; cf. also *Iliad*, xii 241: '[the serpent's] spires unroll'd'.

47–54. These metamorphoses represent illusions commonly suffered by the splenetic. 'The earthenware and glassware of the Cave of Spleen were commonplaces of scientific and semi-scientific literature' (Babb, p. 169, who cites instances). Melancholics, says Burton [*Anatomy*, I iii 3], often consider themselves 'pots, glasses, &c.'. Pope intends a reference to the horrors of the epic Hades, and to the fantastic metamorphoses of Ovid's poem.

47 f. Rowe's 'To Flavia', replying to Anne Lady Winchelsea's 'Spleen', alludes to

> The various Forms of the Fantastick *Spleen*;

which Pope combines with Dryden's Ovid, *Metam.*, i 1:

> Of Bodies chang'd to various Forms I sing.

Here living *Teapots* stand, one Arm held out,
One bent; the Handle this, and that the Spout:
A Pipkin there like *Homer*'s *Tripod* walks;
Here sighs a Jar, and there a Goose-pye talks;
Men prove with Child, as pow'rful Fancy works,
And Maids turn'd Bottels, call aloud for Corks.
  Safe past the *Gnome* thro' this fantastick Band,
A Branch of healing *Spleenwort* in his hand.
Then thus addrest the Pow'r—Hail wayward Queen!

57 Queen!] Queen; *1714–15*.

49 f. Cf. A. Philips's broadside, *The Tea-pot; or, The Lady's Transformation*, in which Venus 'In fit of Vapours or of Spleen' prevails on Juno to change 'a Nymph' who will have nothing to do with 'Lovers of a *Mortal* make' into a teapot. The poem is undated, but presumably follows the *Rape of the Lock*.

51. *See* Hom. *Iliad.* 18 [439 ff.], *of* Vulcan'*s Walking tripods*. [P. 1717–51.]

Pipkin] 'a small earthen boiler' (Johnson's *Dictionary*, which cites this line).

52. *Goose-pye*] *Alludes to a real fact, a Lady of distinction imagin'd herself in this condition*. [P. 1736–51.]

Blackmore, *Treatise of the Spleen and Vapours* (1725), p. 162, notes that one melancholic 'has believed himself to be a Millet-Seed, another a Goose, or a Goose-Pye' (Babb, p. 175).

53. 'The fanciful person here alluded to, was Dr. Edward Pelling [d. 1718], one of the chaplains to K. Charles II. James II. William III. and Queen Anne' (Steevens [*Supplement to Shakespeare's Plays*, 1780, ii 660] who gives particulars 'from one of the doctor's grandaughters, who is still alive, and remembers that [this] line . . . was always supposed to have reference to [this] story'). Cf. the deceit practised on Lord Nonsuch in Dryden's *Wild Gallant*.

54. The image is at least as old as Lucretius, iii 1008 ff. (Dryden's translation, ll. 218 ff.). Cf. also *Measure for Measure*, III ii 182 f.; Beaumont and Fletcher, *The Loyal Subject*, IV ii; and the sermon on *The Dignity, Use and Abuse of Glass-Bottles* (included in *Pope's Prose*, i 203 ff.). *Tatler* 47 prescribes marriage as cure for the spleen.

56. *Spleenwort*] 'Scolopendrii, *Spleen-wort* . . . Formerly . . . reckon'd . . . a Scowrer of the *spleen*' (J. Quiny, *Pharmacopœia Officinalis*, 1718).

Æneas carried the golden bough as a passport to Hades, and Celsus (*Dispensary*, p. 99), journeying to the Elysian Fields,

. . . takes *Amomum* for the Golden Bough.

Cf. also Dryden, 'Flower and the Leaf', l. 188:

A Branch of *Agnus castus* in her Hand.

57 ff. This speech, which embodies common symptoms of the spleen (see, e.g.,

Who rule the Sex to Fifty from Fifteen,
Parents of Vapors and of Female Wit,
Who give th' *Hysteric* or *Poetic* Fit,
On various Tempers act by various ways,
Make some take Physick, others scribble Plays;
Who cause the Proud their Visits to delay,
And send the Godly in a Pett, to pray.
A Nymph there is, that all thy Pow'r disdains,
And thousands more in equal Mirth maintains.
But oh! if e'er thy *Gnome* could spoil a Grace,
Or raise a Pimple on a beauteous Face,
Like Citron-Waters Matrons' Cheeks inflame,
Or change Complexions at a losing Game;
If e'er with airy Horns I planted Heads,

Babb, p. 168), is built on the model of Nisus' speech to Luna (*Æneid*, ix 404 ff.), Sidrac's to Chicane (*Lutrin*, v 63 ff.), and Horoscope's to Disease (*Dispensary*, p. 37).

58. The figures are those of *Tatler* 61. Cf. R. Gould, ii 21:

From *Fifteen* on to *Fifty* thou hast known
What Man was carnally;

and Pope's 'Wife of Bath Her Prologue', l. 7.

59–62. Melancholy was supposed to accompany creative genius: see Blackmore, loc. cit., p. 90: 'many Hysterick Women owe their good Sense, ready Wit, and lively Fancy' to the spleen (cited by Babb, p. 175; cf. p. 170). Cf. Shaftesbury, *Characteristics*, 1711, i. 162: '*Aut insanit Homo, aut versus facit.*—Hor. *Sat.* 7. Lib. 2. Composing and Raving must necessarily, we see, bear a resemblance.'

The *Tatler* and *Spectator* always treated the spleen as a malady of both sexes. Pope restricts it entirely to women (except for l. 53). Poetesses had become common enough for their skill in the 'luscious Way' of writing plays to receive serious attention in *Spectator* 51.

Tatler 47 considers 'that the Spleen is not to be cured by Medicine, but by Poetry'.

For 'Vapors' see note on iv 18 above.

63. A delayed visit is the cause of the mock trial in *Tatler* 262. *Guardian* 131 shows how the spleen delays 'Common Business.'

64. Cf. *Comus*, l. 720: 'in a pet of temperance feed on Pulse'.

68. Cf. *Moral Es.*, ii 33 ff.

69. *Citron-Waters*] 'Aqua vitæ [brandy] distilled with the rind of citrons' (Johnson's *Dictionary*). Cf. *Moral Es.*, ii 64.

70. See iii 89 ff. above.

Or rumpled Petticoats, or tumbled Beds,
Or caus'd Suspicion when no Soul was rude,
Or discompos'd the Head-dress of a Prude,
Or e'er to costive Lap-Dog gave Disease,
Which not the Tears of brightest Eyes could ease:
Hear me, and touch *Belinda* with Chagrin;
That single Act gives half the World the Spleen.
  The Goddess with a discontented Air
Seems to reject him, tho' she grants his Pray'r.
A wondrous Bag with both her Hands she binds,
Like that where once *Ulysses* held the Winds;
There she collects the Force of Female Lungs,
Sighs, Sobs, and Passions, and the War of Tongues.
A Vial next she fills with fainting Fears,
Soft Sorrows, melting Griefs, and flowing Tears.
The *Gnome* rejoicing bears her Gifts away,

87 Gifts] Gift *1714–17*.

74. Prudes dressed more quietly than the coquettes with whom *Tatler* 126 compares and contrasts them. The Puritans had introduced the practice of hiding the hair: they 'Brought in the *Fore-head Cloth* and *formal-band*' (*The Art of Dress*, 1717, p. 13). The style of the prude's head-dress must have resembled the Puritan rather than the extravagant styles discussed in *Spectator* 98.

76. Cf. Pope's 'To a Young Lady, with the Works of Voiture', l. 18:

Voiture was wept by all the brightest Eyes,

and 77 f.

78. At ii 52, Belinda's smile enlivened 'all the world'; here we are assured that when she is miserable, 'half the world'—the male half presumably—is also out of sorts.

80. 'Finely intimating that way-ward humour, which inclines people under the influence of this *queen* to mortify by refusal, even when the request is in unison with their own disposition' [Wakefield].

81–6. Cf. also *Faerie Queene*, VI viii xxiii f., where Mirabella carries a bottle (into which 'I put the tears of my contrition') and a bag (for the receipt of 'repentaunce for things past and gone').

82. Cf. *Odyssey*, x 19 ff.

85 f. Pope sometimes favours a succession of present participles used adjectivally; cf. e.g., *Iliad*, vi 374–6.

Spreads his black Wings, and slowly mounts to Day.
  Sunk in *Thalestris*' Arms the Nymph he found,
Her Eyes dejected and her Hair unbound.
Full o'er their Heads the swelling Bag he rent,
And all the Furies issued at the Vent.
Belinda burns with more than mortal Ire,
And fierce *Thalestris* fans the rising Fire.
O wretched Maid! she spread her Hands, and cry'd,
(While *Hampton*'s Ecchos, wretched Maid! reply'd)
Was it for this you took such constant Care
The *Bodkin*, *Comb*, and *Essence* to prepare;
For this your Locks in Paper-Durance bound,
For this with tort'ring Irons wreath'd around?

96 Maid!] Maid *1714–17*.

88. Cf. Sandys, Ovid's *Metam.*, xiv 123:

Through gloomy twy-light, he remounts to Day.

89. Cf. *Iliad*, xiii 817: Sunk in his sad Companion's Arms he lay.

Thalestris was the Queen of the Amazons, 'of an admirable Beauty, and strong Body, greatly honour'd in her own Country for [her] Brave and Manly Spirit' (*Diod. Sic.*, XVII viii). Cf. *Hudibras*, I ii 393.

Thalestris was Mrs Morley (see Appendix A, p. 376).

90. Unbound hair is a sign of distress in the epics; cf. Dryden, *Æneid*, iii 92:

With Eyes dejected, and with Hair unbound;

Garth had echoed this, see Introduction, p. 114 above.

95 ff. Cf. Nestor's speech to the Greeks, *Iliad*, vii 145 ff. Boileau had imitated this in the speech of Discord exhorting the three men, frightened by the owl, to return to their allotted task of setting up the pulpit (*Lutrin*, iii 125 ff.), and in the Chantre's speech, iv 77 ff.

95 f. Cf. Denham, 'Destruction of Troy', 474 f.:

. . . the womens shrieks and cries
The Arched Vaults re-eccho to the Skies.

96. 'A fine ridicule of the *echo* writings once in vogue' [Wakefield]; cf. *Hudibras*, I iii 189 ff. and the notes in Z. Grey's edition.

97 ff. Cf. *Davideis*, p. 9, and Addison, Ovid's *Metam.*, ii:

And does the Plough for this my Body tear?
This the Reward for all the Fruits I bear . . . ?

98. Cf. note on ii 128 above.

99 ff. The imagery is from incarceration and torture. 'The curl papers of ladies' hair used to be fastened with strips of pliant lead' [Croker].

For this with Fillets strain'd your tender Head,
And bravely bore the double Loads of Lead?
Gods! shall the Ravisher display your Hair,
While the Fops envy, and the Ladies stare!
Honour forbid! at whose unrival'd Shrine
Ease, Pleasure, Virtue, All, our Sex resign.
Methinks already I your Tears survey,
Already hear the horrid things they say,
Already see you a degraded Toast,
And all your Honour in a Whisper lost!
How shall I, then, your helpless Fame defend?
'Twill then be Infamy to seem your Friend!

106 All,] all *1736–51*.

101. *Fillets*] With a reference to the epic: e.g., priestesses wear fillets in the *Æneid*.

102. Cf. Gallus, *Elegy* i (translated in the 1709 Miscellany, p. 367):

With double Joy I bore the double Load,
The wanton Goddess, and the reeling God.

103 ff. Wakefield compares *Æneid*, ii 577 ff.

106. *All*,] Most editors err in deleting the comma, as a reference to sources is enough to show. Racine's *Phèdre*, III iii, reads: 'pour sauver notre honneur combattu, || Il faut immoler tout, et même la Vertu'; and Boileau's *Sat.*, x 138: 'à l'amour . . . || On doit immoler tout, jusqu'à la vertu même'. In Racine 'honneur' means personal dignity in society, in Boileau the appearance of chastity. In Pope 'honour' begins by having Racine's meaning, but when 'pleasure' is mentioned comes to mean chastity, and when 'virtue' to mean what it means in Boileau, the cynical summary coming in the word 'All'.

Garth has a speech on honour (*Dispensary*, p. 47) which contains these lines:

Bigotted to this Idol, we disclaim
Rest, Health, and Ease, for nothing but a Name.

107. Cf. *Iliad*, xxii 53 f. (Hecuba is foreseeing the death of Hector):

Methinks already I behold thee slain,
And stretch'd beneath that Fury of the Plain.

108. Cf. *Dispensary*, p. 114: And never mean the peevish Things we say.

109. Johnson's *Dictionary* defines the third meaning of 'toast' as 'A celebrated woman whose health is often drunk'; cf. *Moral Es.*, ii 282, and v 10 below.

110. Cf. Pope to Caryll, 21 Dec. 1712: 'More men's reputations I believe are whispered away, than any otherways destroyed.'

112. Cf. Sandys, Ovid's *Metam.*, v 585:

And thought it infamy to please too well.

And shall this Prize, th' inestimable Prize,
Expos'd thro' Crystal to the gazing Eyes,
And heighten'd by the Diamond's circling Rays,
On that Rapacious Hand for ever blaze?
Sooner shall Grass in *Hide*-Park *Circus* grow,
And Wits take Lodgings in the Sound of *Bow*;
Sooner let Earth, Air, Sea, to *Chaos* fall,
Men, Monkies, Lap-dogs, Parrots, perish all!

116. Cf. Dryden, *Don Sebastian*, iv: 'From those rapacious Hands . . .'

117. See Appendix E, p. 400. Lady Malapert in Southerne's *Maids last Prayer* (IV i) longs for something 'More wholesome, and diverting, than . . . the dusty Mill-Horse driving in *Hide-Park*'. The amount of dust in the Ring is frequently complained of, or noticed satirically for its contrast to fresh air, though there were organized attempts to keep it down by water-carts. As early as 1674 the 'ranger' or keeper of the Park was ordered to slake the dust of the Ring and the road leading to it (Larwood i 69 f.). Larwood (i 74) produces an unwitting annotation of this line: 'It is probable then [during the Plague] that the grass grew in the Ring, as well as in the streets of the City.'

117 ff. Cf. Virgil, *Ecl.*, i 60 ff., which Dryden translates thus:

> Th' Inhabitants of Seas and Skies shall change,
> And Fish on Shoar and Stags in Air shall range,
> The banish'd *Parthian* dwell on *Arar*'s brink,
> And the blue *German* shall the *Tigris* drink:
> E're I, forsaking Gratitude and Truth,
> Forget the Figure of that Godlike Youth.

Garth (*Dispensary*, p. 43) had already parodied this passage:

> The tow'ring *Alps* shall sooner sink to Vales,
> And *Leaches*, in our Glasses, swell to *Whales*;
> Or *Norwich* trade in Implements of Steel,
> And *Bromingham* in Stuffs and Druggets deal.

Garth may have known J. Howell, *Epistolæ Ho-Elianæ* (27 Feb. 1625):

> First shall the heaven's bright lamp forget to shine . . .
> First, wolves shall league with lambs, the dolphins fly,
> The lawyers and physicians fees deny . . .
> Ere I inconstant to my Altham prove.

118. The City with its solid brick citizens' houses had become almost wholly mercantile. 'The cleavage between the City and St. James's—"the polite end of the town"—was profound, fostered by social, political, and commercial jealousies' (*Johnson's England*, i 163). Cf. *Moral Es.*, iii 385 ff. 'The sound of Bow' adapts a proverbial phrase: Marston, *Eastward Hoe*, I i has 'out of . . . the hearing of Bow-bell'.

120. 'to keep a Monkey[,] Dog, Cat, Parrot or Thrush, has no harm in it

She said; then raging to *Sir Plume* repairs,
And bids her *Beau* demand the precious Hairs:
(*Sir Plume*, of *Amber Snuff-box* justly vain,
And the nice Conduct of a *clouded Cane*)
With earnest Eyes, and round unthinking Face,
He first the Snuff-box open'd, then the Case,
And thus broke out—"My Lord, why, what the Devil?
"Z—ds! damn the Lock! 'fore Gad, you must be civil!
"Plague on't! 'tis past a Jest—nay prithee, Pox!
"Give her the Hair"—he spoke, and rapp'd his Box.
It grieves me much (reply'd the Peer again)
Who speaks so well shou'd ever speak in vain.
But by this Lock, this sacred Lock I swear,

133 swear,] swear. *1714a.*

self, so long as we employ our Eyes only to observe the one, and our Ears only to hear the other sing, but the Heart is never to be made use of on so contemptible an Occasion' (*Don Guevara, to a Lady . . . who fell sick for the Death of a little Bitch* [*Letters of Wit*, p. 112]).

121. *Sir Plume*] Sir George Browne (see Introduction, pp. 87 ff., and Appendix A, pp. 376 f.).

123, 126. *Spectator* 138 advertises 'The Exercise of the Snuff-Box, according to the most fashionable Airs and Motions, in opposition to the Exercise of the Fan [see *Spectator* 102], will be Taught . . . at *Charles Lillie*'s Perfumer . . . There will be likewise taught *The Ceremony of the Snuff-box*, or Rules for offering Snuff to a Stranger, a Friend . . . with an Explanation of the Careless, the Scornful, the Politick, and the Surly Pinch, and the Gestures proper to each of them.' Gay notes that the snuff-box 'serves the railly'd fop for smart replies' (*The Fan*, i 122).

124. *Tatler* 103 had ridiculed the mannerisms of beaux with their canes, some of which are 'curiously clouded' and amber-headed. The snuff-box is included in the satire. Johnson defines his fourth meaning of *cloud* as to 'variegate with dark veins'.

125. *unthinking*] This late seventeenth-century coinage had been applied to 'woman' and to the 'vulgar' before Pope clapped it on to the face of Sir Plume. Isaac Watts had twice used the word in his *Horæ Lyricæ*, 1706.

127 ff. Sir Plume speaks the language of the 'common Swearer' in *Tatler* 13, and the fop in *Tatler* 110. He is an instance of Swift's discovery that 'Anger and Fury, though they add Strength to the *Sinews* of the *Body*, yet are found to relax those of the *Mind*, and to render all its Efforts feeble and impotent' (*Tale of a Tub*, ed. A. C. Guthkelch and D. Nichol Smith, 1920, p. 215).

(Which never more shall join its parted Hair,
Which never more its Honours shall renew,
Clipt from the lovely Head where late it grew)
That while my Nostrils draw the vital Air,
This Hand, which won it, shall for ever wear.
He spoke, and speaking, in proud Triumph spread
The long-contended Honours of her Head.

136 late] once *1714–15*.
139 speaking,] speaking *1714–15*.

133 ff. *In allusion to* Achilles'*s Oath* in Homer. *Il. i* [309 ff.]. [P. 1714–51.]

Now by this sacred Sceptre, hear me swear,
Which never more shall Leaves or Blossoms bear,
Which sever'd from the Trunk (as I from thee)
On the bare Mountains left its Parent Tree . . .

Cf. also *Iliad*, xv 41 ff. and Dryden's *Æneid*, ix 402:

Now by my Head, a sacred Oath, I swear.

Pope seems also to have had the whole passage in mind: cf. 406 f.:

He said, and weeping while he spoke the Word,
From his broad Belt he drew a shining Sword.

'The sacred Lock' is the phrase used at *Iliad*, xxiii 189, where Achilles cuts off his hair at the funeral of Patroclus.

135. *Honours*] See note on l. 140 below.

137. See v 81 n. This and similar pious circumlocutions for 'while I remain alive' are sacred to the epics: cf. *Æneid*, iv 336: 'dum spiritus hos regit artus.' For further parallels in the epics of Homer and Virgil, see R. S. Conway, *Virgil as a Student of Homer*, 1929, p. 7.

vital Air] Cf. Spenser, *F.Q.*, II vii 66 and Dryden, *Æneid*, i 770 and iv 42.

140. *long-contended*] The corpse of Sarpedon (*Iliad*, xvi 776) is 'long-disputed', that of Patroclus (xviii 274) 'long-contended'. At *Odyssey*, xx 400 Penelope is 'the long-contended prize'.

Honours] 'that is, *Beauties*, which make things *Honoured*; in which sense *Virgil* often uses the word, and delights in it:

Et lætos oculis afflârat Honores'

(*Davideis*, ii note 1). Cf. Dryden's *Æneid*, x 172 (of Jove):

And shook the sacred Honours of his Head,

a phrase which Dryden had parodied already in 'Mac Flecknoe', l. 134. Pope uses the phrase again at *Iliad*, xv 45 and xvii 229. He may also have in mind, for its epic value, Dryden's 'To Mr. Granville', l. 8:

The long contended Honours of the Field.

But *Umbriel*, hateful *Gnome*! forbears not so;
He breaks the Vial whence the Sorrows flow.
Then see! the *Nymph* in beauteous Grief appears,
Her Eyes half-languishing, half-drown'd in Tears;
On her heav'd Bosom hung her drooping Head,
Which, with a Sigh, she rais'd; and thus she said.
For ever curs'd be this detested Day,
Which snatch'd my best, my fav'rite Curl away!
Happy! ah ten times happy, had I been,
If *Hampton-Court* these Eyes had never seen!
Yet am not I the first mistaken Maid,
By Love of *Courts* to num'rous Ills betray'd.
Oh had I rather un-admir'd remain'd
In some lone Isle, or distant *Northern* Land;
Where the gilt *Chariot* never marks the Way,

155 marks] mark'd *1714–15*.

141 f. *These two lines are additional; and assign the cause of the different operation of the Passions of the two Ladies. The poem went on before without that distinction, as without any Machinery to the end of the Canto.* [P. 1751.]

143. Cf. *Iliad*, xxiv 959:

Sad *Helen* next in Pomp of Grief appears;

Thebaid, iv 740 f.: 'pulchro in maerore . . . Hypsipylen'; and Lucan, x 83, which Thomas May translates as

Drest in a beautious, and becomming woe.

147 ff. This speech is modelled on Achilles' lament for Patroclus, *Iliad*, xviii 107 ff.

149 f. An adaptation of Dido's cry, *Æneid*, iv 657 f.: Dryden's translation is poor at this point and Pope owes nothing to it.

154. There are several lone isles mentioned in the *Odyssey*. The North is referred to by Statius and Lucan as a place of remoteness and safety: see *Thebaid*, iii 286 ff., 351 ff., and iv 393 ff.; and cf. the complaint of the inhabitants of Ariminum (Lucan, i 248 ff.) which Thomas May translates:

. . . happier far
Might we have liv'd in farthest North, or East . . .

Cf. also C. Hopkins, 'To a Lady', Dryden's Miscellanies, v (1704), p. 121.

155. For '*Chariot*' see i 55 f. n. Cf. *Iliad*, xii 128:

Those Wheels returning ne'er shall mark the Plain.

Contemporary engravings of carriages always show them leaving deep ruts in the earth of the roads.

Where none learn *Ombre*, none e'er taste *Bohea*!
There kept my Charms conceal'd from mortal Eye,
Like Roses that in Desarts bloom and die.
What mov'd my Mind with youthful Lords to rome?
O had I stay'd, and said my Pray'rs at home!
'Twas this, the Morning *Omens* seem'd to tell;
Thrice from my trembling hand the *Patch-box* fell;
The tott'ring *China* shook without a Wind,
Nay, *Poll* sate mute, and *Shock* was most Unkind!
A *Sylph* too warn'd me of the Threats of Fate,
In mystic Visions, now believ'd too late!
See the poor Remnants of these slighted Hairs!
My hands shall rend what ev'n thy Rapine spares:
These, in two sable Ringlets taught to break,

161 seem'd to tell] did foretel *1714–15.*
167–9 these . . . Hairs! . . . Rapine spares: These] this . . . Hair! . . . own did spare. This *1714–15.*

156. *Bohea*] 'A species of tea, of higher colour, and more astringent taste, than green tea' (Johnson's *Dictionary*).

158. Cf. Waller, 'Go lovely rose', ll. 6 ff.

166. 'Nothing is more common in the poets, than to introduce omens as preceding some important and dreadful event' (Warton, i 235); Virgil has strongly described those that preceded the death of Dido.

167 ff. Cf. St-Evremond, ii 112 (quoting from 'One of our best Poets'):

> Those charming Locks the rudest Hands would spare.
> And yet they suffer in your own Despair . . .
> Is Grief so Cruel, or your Rage so Blind,
> That to your Self you must be thus unkind[?]

Cf. also Prior, *Henry and Emma*, ll. 423 f.:

> No longer shall thy comely Tresses break
> In flowing Ringlets on thy snowy Neck.

169. *sable*] According to the three extant portraits, Arabella Fermor's hair was fair auburn (see A. M. Sharp, p. 126). 'Fair Tresses' are mentioned at ii 27 above, though in that context 'Fair' may not refer to colour nor indeed 'Tresses' to Belinda's, let alone Arabella's. Black hair was most in fashion, in 1717 at least: cf. *Art of Dress*, p. 18:

> Not all your Locks are equal in Renown,
> Red yields to Fair, and Black excells the Brown.

Black lead combs were used to darken hair.

Once gave new Beauties to the snowie Neck.
The Sister-Lock now sits uncouth, alone,
And in its Fellow's Fate foresees its own;
Uncurl'd it hangs, the fatal Sheers demands;
And tempts once more thy sacrilegious Hands.
Oh hadst thou, Cruel! been content to seize
Hairs less in sight, or any Hairs but these!

172 its own] it own *1714b–15*.

171. *Sister-Lock*] Cf. Catullus, 'The Lock of Berenice', 51 f.:

> abiunctae paulo ante comae mea fata sorores
> lugebant...

174. *sacrilegious Hands*] Cf. Dryden's *Æneid*, ii 546.

175. *Cruel!*] Cf. *Æneid*, ix 483.

176. Gay cleverly works in a reference to this line in his letter of 6 July 1714, recommending Ford to visit Pope at Binfield, from whence 'Mrs Fermor is not very distant' (*Letters of ... Swift to ... Ford*, ed. D. Nichol Smith, 1935, p. 222).

THE RAPE *of the* LOCK.

CANTO V.

SHE said: the pitying Audience melt in Tears,
But *Fate* and *Jove* had stopp'd the *Baron*'s Ears.
In vain *Thalestris* with Reproach assails,
For who can move when fair *Belinda* fails?
Not half so fixt the *Trojan* cou'd remain,
While *Anna* begg'd and *Dido* rag'd in vain.
Then grave *Clarissa* graceful wav'd her Fan;
Silence ensu'd, and thus the Nymph began.
Say, why are Beauties prais'd and honour'd most,
The wise Man's Passion, and the vain Man's Toast?

7–36] *1717–51.*

---

1 ff. Pope is imitating *Æneid*, iv to which he refers at 5 f. At 2 he adapts 440 of Virgil:

Fata obstant, placidasque viri deus obstruit aures,

which Dryden (637) had translated thus:

Fate, and the God, had stop'd his Ears to Love.

5 f. Boileau, Dryden, and Garth have similes embodying material from classic legend and epic; cf. iii 121 ff. above.

7. *Clarissa*] *A new Character introduced in the subsequent Editions, to open more clearly the* MORAL *of the Poem, in a parody of the speech of Sarpedon to Glaucus in Homer.* [P. 1736 (last eleven words only)–1751.] Clarissa is a new character in the sense that she has a spoken part, but she appeared in the 1712 version at i 107 where, as in the 1714 version, iii 127, she lent the Baron her scissors.

Pope's translation of the speech in which Sarpedon incites Glaucus to join him in leading the Trojan attack on the Greek ramparts, had been part of Pope's 'Episode of Sarpedon; Translated from the Twelfth and Sixteenth Books of Homer's Iliads' (1709 Miscellany, pp. 301 ff.): see vol. vi. The version later included in the *Iliad* (xii 371 ff.) was slightly revised. Pope notes (*Iliad*, 1721, iii 216) that Denham had translated the speech (*Miscellany Poems: The First Part*, 3rd ed. 1702, pp. 188 f.): Clarissa's speech is in some ways a closer parody of Denham's version than of Pope's. Motteux had already adapted the speech (Oldmixon's *Muses Mercury*, March 1707, p. 69).

Evrard (*Lutrin*, iv) offers pacific counsel which is followed by the Chantre's cry for war.

10. Cf. Dryden, *Absal. and Achit.*, i 239:

The Young mens Vision and the Old mens Dream!

Why deck'd with all that Land and Sea afford,
Why Angels call'd, and Angel-like ador'd?
Why round our Coaches crowd the white-glov'd Beaus,
Why bows the Side-box from its inmost Rows?
How vain are all these Glories, all our Pains,
Unless good Sense preserve what Beauty gains:
That Men may say, when we the Front-box grace,
Behold the first in Virtue, as in Face!
Oh! if to dance all Night, and dress all Day,
Charm'd the Small-pox, or chas'd old Age away;
Who would not scorn what Huswife's Cares produce,
Or who would learn one earthly Thing of Use?

13. *white-glov'd Beaus*] Cf. *Tatler* 262; even this detail has its link with the epic: cf. Dryden, 'Palamon and Arcite', iii 912.

13 f. Cf. Gay's 'Toilette' (1716) 27 ff.; Cunningham compares Steele's *Theatre* 3 (9 Jan. 1720) where the 'Representatives of a *British* Audience' are 'Three of the Fair Sex [for] the Front-Boxes . . . Two Gentlemen of Wit and Pleasure for the Side-Boxes . . . Three Substantial Citizens for the Pit'; cf. v 17 below.

16, 30 f. *good Sense . . . good Humour*] Philosophic praise of these qualities is found in Montaigne, 'Of Education of Children' (*Essays*, i 219); Samuel Parker, *A Free and Impartial Censure of the Platonick Philosophie* (ed. 1667, pp. 18 ff., 23, 24: 'And therefore a peevish ill-natur'd Christian, is the greatest contradiction in the World'); Dryden (*Essays*, ii 17); Locke, *Thoughts Concerning Education* (ed. 1880, p. 118). It was the constant counsel of Shaftesbury, who claims it as 'the best Security against Enthusiasm' (*Characteristics*, 1732 ed., i 22), and so against the hysterics of l. 32 below; the *Tatler* and the *Spectator*: see especially 100 (which represents it as 'the duty of every man . . . to obtain, if possible, a disposition to be pleased'), and 424, 429, and 440 (which purport to set up an infirmary for its increase and establishment). Cf. also 'To a Young Lady with the Works of Voiture', *Moral Es.*, ii 257 ff., and Pope's letter to Arabella on her marriage.

18. A fairly common type of phrase: cf. Hopkins (1704 Miscellany, p. 188):

The first in Merit, as the first in Place;

Dryden, *Æneid*, v 744; *Iliad*, vi 637, xxiii 566, and *Odyssey*, xi 441.

20. *Small-pox*] The terrors of this disease may be gauged from the records of the Petre family: when the Hon. John Petre died in 1762 (æt. 24) the *Gent. Mag.* (p. 93) noted him as 'the 18th person of that family that has died of the small pox in 27 years.' The Lord Petre of the poem had died of it in 1713, so that this line would have especial point.

22. *Use*] In his scheme for man's happiness Pope, like Swift, placed great value as did Bacon, on ordinary usefulness.

To patch, nay ogle, might become a Saint,
Nor could it sure be such a Sin to paint.
But since, alas! frail Beauty must decay,
Curl'd or uncurl'd, since Locks will turn to grey,
Since painted, or not painted, all shall fade,
And she who scorns a Man, must die a Maid;
What then remains, but well our Pow'r to use,
And keep good Humour still whate'er we lose?
And trust me, Dear! good Humour can prevail,
When Airs, and Flights, and Screams, and Scolding fail.
Beauties in vain their pretty Eyes may roll;
Charms strike the Sight, but Merit wins the Soul.
So spoke the Dame, but no Applause ensu'd;
Belinda frown'd, *Thalestris* call'd her Prude.
To Arms, to Arms! the fierce Virago cries,

37 fierce Virago] bold *Thalestris 1714–15.*

24. Cf. *Several Letters Between Two Ladies: Wherein the Lawfulness and Unlawfulness of Artificial Beauty in Point of Conscience, are Nicely Debated* (1701); and *Athenian Oracle*, ii 32 f.

30 ff. See note on v 16 above. Cf. 'Against the Fear of Death' (1693 Miscellany, p. 118):

With shame we see our Passions can prevail,
Where Reason, Certainty, and Vertue fail;

and Pomfret, *Reason* (1700), p. 7:

Ev'n *G*[ar]*th* and *Maurus* sometimes shall prevail,
Where *Gibson*, Learned *Hannes*, and *Tyson* fail.

34. Cf. Richard Leigh, *Poems 1675*, ed. Hugh Macdonald, 1947, p. 21 (of jewels): '*Their Lustres* strike the *Eye*, but *hers* the *Heart*.'

35. *It is a verse frequently repeated in* Homer *after any speech,*

So spoke—and all the Heroes applauded.

[P. 1736–51.]

37. *From hence the first Edition goes on to the Conclusion, except a very few short insertions added, to keep the Machinery in view to the end of the poem.* [P. 1751.]

37 f. *Virago*] 'A female warriour, a woman with the qualities of a man' (Johnson's *Dictionary*, which quotes this passage). Camilla in Dryden's *Æneid* (vii 1098 and xi 768) is called 'the fierce *Virago*'. The phrase is applied to Pallas at iii 716. Cf. also *Hudibras*, I ii 367. Butler (*id.*, 380 ff.) had referred to 'authors' who

Make feeble ladies, in their works,
To fight like termagants and Turks.

And swift as Lightning to the Combate flies.
All side in Parties, and begin th' Attack;
Fans clap, Silks russle, and tough Whalebones crack;
Heroes' and Heroins' Shouts confus'dly rise,
And base, and treble Voices strike the Skies.
No common Weapons in their Hands are found,
Like Gods they fight, nor dread a mortal Wound.
  So when bold *Homer* makes the Gods engage,
And heav'nly Breasts with human Passions rage;
'Gainst *Pallas*, *Mars*; *Latona*, *Hermes* arms;

47 *Hermes*] *Hermes*, *1714*. arms] Arms *1714–15*.

40. Cf. *Dispensary*, pp. 88 f.:

And now the Signal summons to the Fray . . .
Tough Harness rustles, and bold Armour clangs.

'Women are armed with Fans as Men with Swords, and sometimes do more Execution with them' (*Spectator* 102). And see the paragraph (*id.*) on 'discharging' fans in order to make them 'crack' loud enough to resemble the 'Report of a Pocket-Pistol'. The whalebones are those of the petticoats: cf. ii 120 above.

44. *mortal*] the wound is mortal because lethal, and also because inflicted by man, not by the gods just mentioned.

45. Homer *Il.* 20 [91 ff.]. [P. 1714–51.]

First silver-shafted *Phœbus* took the Plain
Against blue *Neptune*, Monarch of the Main:
The God of Arms his Giant Bulk display'd,
Oppos'd to *Pallas*, War's triumphant Maid.
Against *Latona* march'd the Son of *May*;
The quiver'd *Dian*, Sister of the Day,
(Her golden Arrows sounding at her side)
Saturnia, Majesty of Heav'n, defy'd.
With fiery *Vulcan* last in Battle stands
The sacred Flood that rolls on golden Sands.

46. See Introduction, pp. 106 and 117.

47. The juxtaposition of proper nouns to suggest stridency and collision is the method of Ovid and Statius (and not of Homer). Cf. the battle in *Thebaid*, vii where 640 ff. read:

. . . sternunt alterna furentes
Hippomedon Sybarin, Pylium Periphanta Menoeceus,
Parthenopaeus Ityn . . .

Cf. also Virgil, *Æneid*, ix 574, 767 and x 749.

And all *Olympus* rings with loud Alarms.
Jove's Thunder roars, Heav'n trembles all around;
Blue *Neptune* storms, the bellowing Deeps resound;
Earth shakes her nodding Tow'rs, the Ground gives way;
And the pale Ghosts start at the Flash of Day!
  Triumphant *Umbriel* on a Sconce's Height
Clapt his glad Wings, and sate to view the Fight:
Propt on their Bodkin Spears, the Sprights survey
The growing Combat, or assist the Fray.
  While thro' the Press enrag'd *Thalestris* flies,
And scatters Deaths around from both her Eyes,

54 Fight:] Fight, *1714–17.* 55 Spears,] Spears *1714–15.*
58 Deaths] Death *1715, 1740–51.*

48. Cf. Dryden, *Cymon and Iphigenia*, l. 399:

> The Country rings around with loud Alarms.

51. *gives way*] a fairly common expression in Dryden's *Æneid.*

52. See Appendix D, p. 398 below. Pope has heightened Longinus' version in accordance with the later history of the idea in epic poetry. See *Æneid*, viii 246: 'trepidentque immisso lumine manes'; Ovid's *Metam.*, v 356 ff., which Sandys translates (356 f.):

> . . . the King of Shadows dreads,
> For feare the ground should split above their heads
> And let-in Day, t'affright the trembling Ghosts;

Erictho's threat, Lucan, *Civil War*, vi 742 ff.; and Addison's translation of a passage from Silius Italicus (*Remarks*, p. 248):

> Who pale with Fear the rending Earth survey,
> And startle at the sudden Flash of Day.

53–6. *These four lines added, for the reason before mentioned.* [P. 1751]: see l. 37 n. above.

53 f. Minerva *in like manner, during the Battle of* Ulysses *with the Suitors in* Odyss. [xxii 261 f.] *perches on a beam of the roof to behold it.* [P. 1736–51.]

In *Lutrin*, v, Discord hovers over the battle.

Sconce] 'A pensile candlestick' (Johnson's *Dictionary* which cites this line).

55. 'Like the heroes in Homer, when they are Spectators of a combat' (Warton, ed.): see *Iliad*, xiv 533; and cf. Dryden's *Æneid*, xii 585:

> Prop'd on his Lance the pensive Heroe stood;

and *Dispensary*, p. 99 (of the Pigmies warring against the cranes):

> The Poppets to their Bodkin Spears repair.

Bodkin] Cf. note on ii 128 above.

58. Cf. Hector (*Iliad*, viii 417 ff.); Dryden's *Æneid*, x 851:

A *Beau* and *Witling* perish'd in the Throng,
One dy'd in *Metaphor*, and one in *Song*.

Thus rag'd the Prince, and scatter'd Deaths around;

Thebaid, x 744: nunc spargit torquens volucri nova vulnera plumbo;
Vida, *Scacchia Ludus*, 563:

Funera spargebat fuscae regina cohortis;

and *Davideis*, p. 59:

An *Angel* scatters death through all the hoast.

60. Dennis had rounded on those writers of love poetry who while physically in good fettle represent themselves as dying for love in highly metaphorical style: see the preface to his *Passion of Biblis*, 1692 (*Critical Works*, ed. E.N.Hooker, 1939–43, i 2): 'in most . . . amorous Verses, there appears thro' the disguise of an affected Passion, a gaiety of Heart, a wantonness of Wit, and a Soul that's at liberty to roam about the Universe, and return home laden with rich, but far fetch'd Conceits. As merry in this respect as the Madrigals of our amorous Rake-hells; who languish in Simile, whilst they thrive in Carkass; and who eating their Half-Crowns [half a crown was usually taken to be the price of a common whore] every day thrice, decay and dye by Metaphor. In short, no sort of imagery ever can be the Language of Grief. If a Man complains in Simile, I either laugh or sleep. For this is plain, that if a man's affliction will suffer him to divert his mind by one Simile, he may as well do it by twenty, and so on to the end of the Chapter.'

Mr H. M. Reichard ('The Love Affair in Pope's *Rape of the Lock*', *PMLA*, lxix, 1954) assembles further parallels in *Tatler* 110 and *Spectator* 377: he notes (pp. 900 f.) that: 'The latter essay is an especially valuable analogue of Pope's ridicule of the clichés. To rid the language of "metaphorical deaths", Addison asks the "dying" lover to note "that all his heavy complaints of wounds and deaths rise from some little affectations of coquettry, which are improved into charms by his own fond imagination". In a jocose "Bill of Mortality" Addison illustrates how lovers may perish fancifully: "wounded by Belinda's scarlet stocking . . . smitten at the opera by the glance of an eye . . . killed by the tap of a fan on his left shoulder by Coquetilla . . . hurt by the brush of a whalebone petticoat . . . shot through the sticks of a fan . . . struck thro' the heart by a diamond necklace . . . slain by a blush from the Queen's Box . . . cut off in the twenty-first year of his age by a white-wash . . . slain by an arrow that flew out of a dimple in Belinda's left cheek . . . hurt from a pair of blue eyes . . . dispatch'd by a smile . . . murder'd by Melissa in her hair . . . drowned in a flood of tears".'

EC compare John Sheffield, Duke of Buckingham's *Essay on Poetry*, concerning the speech of heroic drama:

Or else like Bells, eternally they chime,
They *sigh* in *Simile*, and *die* in *Rhime*;

Cf. *Dispensary*, p. 93:

Stunn'd with the Blow the batter'd Bard retir'd,
Sunk down, and in a *Simile* expir'd.

O cruel Nymph! a living Death I bear,
Cry'd *Dapperwit*, and sunk beside his Chair.
A mournful Glance Sir *Fopling* upwards cast,
Those Eyes are made so killing—was his last:
Thus on *Meander*'s flow'ry Margin lies

61. Cf. Johnson's *Shakespeare*, note on *Richard III*, I ii 153: '*They kill me with a living death.* In imitation of this passage, and I suppose a thousand more;

—*a* living death *I bear,*
Says Dapperwit, and sunk beside his chair.'

62. Dapperwit is living up to his character in Wycherley's *Love in a Wood*; see, e.g., II i.

63. *Sir Fopling*] The chief character in Etherege's *Man of Mode, or Sir Fopling Flutter*, one of 'our most applauded plays' (*Spectator* 65).

64. *The Words in a Song in the Opera of* Camilla. [P. 1714–51: 1714–17 omit the first three words.] *Camilla*, the most famous opera of Marc' Antonio Buononcini, brother of Handel's rival, was first performed in England on 30 April 1706, a prologue being written by Mainwaring. It was performed fifty-four times during 1706–9. (See Burney's *General History of Music*, 1776–89, iv 201, 210.) The song referred to is sung by Tullia in Act III. Owen MacSwiney was responsible for the English version of the opera (see R. N. Cunningham, *Peter Anthony Motteux*, 1933, pp. 164 f.):

These Eyes are made so killing,
That all who look must dye;
To art I'm nothing owing,
From art I nothing want;
These graces genuin flowing
Despise the help of Paint.
'Tis Musick but to hear me,
'Tis fatal to come near me,
For death is in my Eyes.

(Repunctuated, shorn of repetitions, and arranged in metre from *Songs from the Opera of Camilla* [1706?], fol. 37.) The tunes of this opera had already been selected for parody by Richard Estcourt in his *Prunella* (1707?): see E. McA. Gagey, *Ballad Opera*, 1937, p. 21. Cf. Ozell's insertion in the battle of the books (*Boileau's Lutrin*, 1708, p. 100):

Here, At his Head Fair *Afra*'s Works let fly;
And may they prove as killing as her Eye!

65 f. Ov. Ep. [vii 1 f.]

Sic ubi fata vocant, udis abjectus in herbis,
Ad vada Mæandri concinit albus olor.

[P. 1736–51.]

Th' expiring Swan, and as he sings he dies.
  When bold Sir *Plume* had drawn *Clarissa* down,
Chloe stept in, and kill'd him with a Frown;
She smil'd to see the doughty Hero slain,
But at her Smile, the Beau reviv'd again.
  Now *Jove* suspends his golden Scales in Air,
Weighs the Men's Wits against the Lady's Hair;
The doubtful Beam long nods from side to side;
At length the Wits mount up, the Hairs subside.
  See fierce *Belinda* on the *Baron* flies,
With more than usual Lightning in her Eyes;
Nor fear'd the Chief th'unequal Fight to try,
Who sought no more than on his Foe to die.
But this bold Lord, with manly Strength indu'd,
She with one Finger and a Thumb subdu'd:
Just where the Breath of Life his Nostrils drew,
A Charge of *Snuff* the wily Virgin threw;

67 When] As *1714–15*.

71 ff. *Vid.* Homer. *Il.* 8 [1714–15 read 22] [87 ff.]. & Virg. *Æn.* 12 [725 ff.]. [P. 1714–51.] Dryden, *Æneid*, xii 1054 ff. reads:

> *Jove* sets the Beam; in either Scale he lays
> The Champions Fate, and each exactly weighs.
> On this side Life, and lucky Chance ascends:
> Loaded with Death, that other Scale descends.

The device is common in epics, see, e.g., *Iliad*, xvi 783 ff., xxii 271 ff., and *Par. Lost*, iv 996 ff. Pope mocks the epic and, at the same time, man: Jove's scales show the wits of beaux outweighed by a lock of hair.

76. Cf. i 144 above.

78. The original wit of this threadbare innuendo is renewed when the context is a battle.

79 ff. See Introduction, pp. 111 f. This kind of physical indignity overcomes Tassoni's gods and heroes: his Saturn has a cold (II xxxiii); and cf. VIII xiii.

81. Pope intends a cross reference to iv 137: the wheel has come full circle for the Baron.

Cf. Dryden, *Æneid*, x 1277 f.:

> Just where the Stroke was aim'd, th' unerring Spear
> Made way, and stood transfix'd thro either Ear.

The *Gnomes* direct, to ev'ry Atome just,
The pungent Grains of titillating Dust.
Sudden, with starting Tears each Eye o'erflows,
And the high Dome re-ecchoes to his Nose.
Now meet thy Fate, incens'd *Belinda* cry'd,
And drew a deadly *Bodkin* from her Side.
(The same, his ancient Personage to deck,
Her great great Grandsire wore about his Neck
In three *Seal-Rings*; which after, melted down,
Form'd a vast *Buckle* for his Widow's Gown:
Her infant Grandame's *Whistle* next it grew,
The *Bells* she gingled, and the *Whistle* blew;
Then in a *Bodkin* grac'd her Mother's Hairs,
Which long she wore, and now *Belinda* wears.)
Boast not my Fall (he cry'd) insulting Foe!
Thou by some other shalt be laid as low.
Nor think, to die dejects my lofty Mind;
All that I dread, is leaving you behind!
Rather than so, ah let me still survive,
And burn in *Cupid*'s Flames,—but burn alive.

87 incens'd *Belinda*] th'incens'd Virago *1714–15*.
91 after,] after *1714–15*.

83 f. *These two lines added for the above reason.* [P. 1751]: see l. 37 n. above.

85 f. A sneeze was considered by the Greeks and Romans to be a (lucky) omen. One befalls Telemachus (*Odyssey*, xvii 624 ff.) and is taken as an omen.

88. *Bodkin*] See note on ii 128 above.

89 ff. *In Imitation of the Progress of* Agamemnon's *Scepter in* Homer, *Il.* 2. [129 ff.] [P. 1714–51]: cf. also the descent of the helmet, *Iliad*, x 312 ff. EC refer to 'Sir George Etheridge To the Earl of Middleton' (Dryden's *Sylvæ*, ed. 1702, p. 224), where by similar genealogical steps a diamond bodkin is traced back through a cap ornament, a fan handle, and ear-rings.

92. *vast Buckle*] 'vast' was a fashionable word at this time, sacred to the cult of the sublime. Pope amusingly applies it to an ornament of female dress.

100. Cf. Ovid, *Ars Amandi*, ii 725 ff., and the song in Dryden's *Marriage A-La-Mode*, 'Whilst *Alexis* lay prest . . .'.

Restore the Lock! she cries; and all around
Restore the Lock! the vaulted Roofs rebound.
Not fierce *Othello* in so loud a Strain
Roar'd for the Handkerchief that caus'd his Pain.
But see how oft Ambitious Aims are cross'd,
And Chiefs contend 'till all the Prize is lost!
The Lock, obtain'd with Guilt, and kept with Pain,
In ev'ry place is sought, but sought in vain:
With such a Prize no Mortal must be blest,
So Heav'n decrees! with Heav'n who can contest?
Some thought it mounted to the Lunar Sphere,
Since all things lost on Earth, are treasur'd there.
There Heroes' Wits are kept in pondrous Vases,

---

103 f. Cf. Dryden's 'Alexander's Feast', 35 f.:

A present Deity, they shout around:
A present Deity, the vaulted Roofs rebound.

Skies are often 'vaulted' in epic, e.g. Dryden's *Æneid*, iv 962, *Iliad*, vi 431, and note on ii 80 above. Pope's *Thebais*, i 651 has 'vaulted hall'.

105. Rymer's slanging of *Othello* appeared in *A Short View of Tragedy* (1693). His running commentary on the play over-emphasizes the part of the handkerchief, and he demands why the play should not have been called the 'Tragedy of the Handkerchief' (p. 135). 'So much ado, so much stress, so much passion and repetition about an Handkerchief!' (*id.*) and 'all this outrage and clutter about it' (p. 126). Pope knew Rymer's critique—he refers to it in the notes on *Othello* in his Shakespeare (vol. vi, p. 486). He does not indicate whether or not he approves of the handkerchief scenes (III iv–x—in Pope's edition—and IV i). The 'roarings' probably refer to Othello's verbal delirium which ends in his faint (IV i). Pope's text of this speech follows Q1 with one omission. He cites later readings in a footnote with the comment '*No hint of this trash in the 1st edit.*' *Trash* was Rymer's word.

108. 'Pope seems to have taken a hint from Statius, *Thebais*, I, i, "alternaque regna profanis || Decertata odiis". In his own translation of this [he] evidently followed Caspar Barth's interpretation of "decertata", "perdita atque amissa concertando".' (E. Bensley, *Modern Language Review*), vii (1912), p. 96.

110. Cf. *Iliad*, iii 301.

112. Cf. Sandys, Ovid's *Metam.*, ii 437: 'What Woman, or, who can contend with *Jove*!' and Dryden, *State of Innocence*, 1677, p. 20: ''Twas Heav'n; and who can Heav'n withstand?'

114 ff. *Vid.* Ariosto. Canto 34. [stanzas 68 ff.] [P. 1714–51.]

Astolfo journeys to the moon in search of Orlando's lost wits, and finds

And Beaus' in *Snuff-boxes* and *Tweezer-Cases.*
There broken Vows, and Death-bed Alms are found,
And Lovers' Hearts with Ends of Riband bound;
The Courtier's Promises, and Sick Man's Pray'rs,
The Smiles of Harlots, and the Tears of Heirs,
Cages for Gnats, and Chains to Yoak a Flea;
Dry'd Butterflies, and Tomes of Casuistry.

A mighty masse of things strangely confus'd,
Things that on earth were lost, or were abus'd.

Among these are 'The vowes that sinners make, and never pay,' gifts given to princes, 'fond loves',

Large promises that Lords make, and forget...
The fruitlesse almes that men give when they die.

Here 'mans wit' is kept in jars after having been lost on earth through love, ambition, trade, service of lords, aspiration after powers magical, alchemistical or poetical. (All the above quotations are from Harington's translation ed. 1634; which Pope read early, see Spence 279.) Pope modernizes Ariosto's instances and makes them more particularly concrete. Cf. Fontenelle's use of this passage in his *Entretiens sur la Pluralité des Mondes* (1686), which was translated simultaneously by J. Glanvill and Aphra Behn in 1688.

115. *Vases*] The pronunciation of Pope's day is still current in America.

116. *Tweezer-Cases*] Cf. *Tatler* 142: 'his Tweezer-Cases are incomparable: You shall have one not much bigger than your Finger, with seventeen several Instruments in it, all necessary every Hour of the Day, during the whole Course of a Man's Life.'

119 f. Cf. Dryden, *Œdipus* III i:

The smiles of courtiers, and the harlots tears
The tradesman's oaths, and mourning of an heir.

121. *Cages for Gnats*] Cf. Theocritus, *Id.*, i 52: 'traps for locusts'.

Chains to Yoak a Flea] A slender chain is cast round a flea's neck in a Latin poem translated by John Wesley (see J. Nightingale, *A Portraiture of Methodism*, 1807, pp. 20 f.). Arbuthnot had poured Scriblerian satire on the learning of the Presbyterians as 'generally bent towards exploded Chimera's [e.g.] the *perpetuum Mobile*, the circular Shot, Philosopher's Stone, and silent Gunpowder, making Chains for Flea's, Nets for Flies, and Instruments to unravel Cobwebs, and split Hairs' (*John Bull still in his Senses*, second ed., 1712, p. 14).

122. *Dry'd Butterflies*] The 'virtuosos' of the time and their natural history collections are satirized at *Tatler* 216; cf. *Peri Bathous*, vi, *Moral Es.*, iv 10, *Dunciad*, iv 397 ff.

Casuistry] The minutely argued adaptation of ethical rules to individual cases which the Counter-Reformation had encouraged, and in England such churchmen as Jeremy Taylor, was now discredited. Cf. *Dunciad*, iv 28 and 641 f. Cf.

But trust the Muse—she saw it upward rise,
Tho' mark'd by none but quick Poetic Eyes:
(So *Rome*'s great Founder to the Heav'ns withdrew,
To *Proculus* alone confess'd in view.)
A sudden Star, it shot thro' liquid Air,
And drew behind a radiant *Trail of Hair.*
Not *Berenice*'s Locks first rose so bright,
The Heav'ns bespangling with dishevel'd Light.

130 Heav'ns . . . Light.] Skies . . . Light. *1714–15*, heav'ns . . . light, *1717*.

Pope's Corresp., i 48, a letter of 27 April 1708: 'I have nothing to say to you in this Letter; but I was resolv'd to write to tell you so. Why should not I content my self with so many great Examples, of deep Divines, profound Casuists, grave Philosophers; who have written, not Letters only, but whole Tomes and voluminous Treatises about Nothing?' The sense and some of the wording are repeated in a letter of August 1723 (?), op. cit., ii 190.

123. Cf. Isaac Watts, *Horæ Lyricæ*, 1709, p. 175:

. . . Trust the Muse,
She sings experienc'd Truth . . .

124. Cf. Denham, 'Cooper's Hill', ll. 233 f.:

. . . their airy shape
All but a quick Poetick sight escape.

125 f. See Livy, I xvi.

127. *liquid*] in the Latin sense of clear; cf. Dryden, *Æneid*, iii 571: 'liquid Air'.

127 f. Warburton compares Ovid, *Metam.*, xv 849 f.:

Flammiferumque trahens spatioso limite crinem
Stella micat.

Cf. Pope's *Thebais*, i 843 f.; and Dryden, *Æneid*, v 1092 (of Morpheus):

Descends, and draws behind a trail of Light.

129 f. For an account of Berenice see W. Smith, *Dictionary of Greek and Roman Biography and Mythology* (1844), i 482 f. Callimachus' poem on her constellated hair exists (apart from a fragment) only in the translation of Catullus. Pope mentions both these poets in his MS. annotations of Dennis's *Remarks*, see Appendix D, p. 398.

Berenice's hair had been mentioned in *Hudibras*, II iii 844, and she and 'Cosmo the Second of the Medicis' had contributed the sixth dialogue of Fontenelle's *Dialogues of the Dead*, part ii.

dishevel'd] 'applicable alike to the *lock* in question, and to the radiance of the comet's *hair*' [Wakefield].

The *Sylphs* behold it kindling as it flies,
And pleas'd pursue its Progress thro' the Skies.
This the *Beau-monde* shall from the *Mall* survey,
And hail with Musick its propitious Ray.
This, the blest Lover shall for *Venus* take,
And send up Vows from *Rosamonda*'s Lake.
This *Partridge* soon shall view in cloudless Skies,
When next he looks thro' *Galilæo*'s Eyes;
And hence th' Egregious Wizard shall foredoom
The Fate of *Louis*, and the Fall of *Rome*.
Then cease, bright Nymph! to mourn thy ravish'd Hair
Which adds new Glory to the shining Sphere!
Not all the Tresses that fair Head can boast
Shall draw such Envy as the Lock you lost.
For, after all the Murders of your Eye,
When, after Millions slain, your self shall die;
When those fair Suns shall sett, as sett they must,

141 thy] the *1714–17*.

---

131 f. *These two lines added for the same reason to keep in view the Machinery of the Poem.* [P. 1751.]

133. *the Mall*] See Appendix E, p. 399 f.

136. *Rosamonda's Lake*] See Appendix E, p. 400.

137. John Partridge *was a ridiculous Star-gazer, who in his Almanacks every year, never fail'd to predict the downfall of the Pope, and the King of* France, *then at war with the* English. [P. 1736–51.]

Partridge (1644–1715) is immortalized by Swift's practical joke: see *Predictions for the Year 1708* by *Isaac Bickerstaff*, etc.

138. Galileo improved the newly invented telescope and by its aid inaugurated a new era in the history of astronomy. Cf. *Par. Lost*, v 261 ff.

142. Cf. *The Mall* (anon.) 1709, p. 5:

Since Nature gave her such a shining Ray
That adds fresh Lustre to the Beauteous Day;

and A. Philips, *Pastorals*, iii 74:

And add new Glories to the *British* Name.

Sphere] 'This was among the words pronounced in Pope's day in continental fashion "sphare". It is found at the end of a line eight times in Pope and only once (*Es. on Man*, i 202) is it rimed otherwise' [Holden].

147 f. 'The poem concludes, as it had opened (Canto i 13,) with a comparison

And all those Tresses shall be laid in Dust;
This Lock, the Muse shall consecrate to Fame,
And mid'st the Stars inscribe *Belinda*'s Name!

FINIS.

150 Name!] Name. *1714c–15, 1736–51.*

---

of the brightness of Belinda's eyes to that of the sun' [Holden]. At ii 3, she was 'the Rival of his Beams'. Cf. *Iliad*, xx 385 f.:

> But when the Day decreed (for come it must)
> Shall lay this dreadful Hero in the Dust;

and Dryden, *Æneid*, x 543. Sidney (*Arcadia*, II chr. xii) has 'those eyes (those Sonnes)'.

148 ff. Wakefield compares Spenser, *Amoretti*, lxxv 9 ff.:

> Not so, (quod I) let baser things devize
> to dy in dust, but you shall live by fame:
> my verse your vertues rare shall eternize,
> and in the hevens wryte your glorious name;

and Cowley's paraphrase of Horace, *Odes*, iv 2 (*The Poems of Horace . . . Englished . . . by Several Hands*, ed. 1680, p. 136):

> He bids him live, and grow in fame,
> Among the Stars he sticks his name.

Cf. also Virgil, after the death of Nisus and Euryalus (*Æneid*, ix 446 f.), which Dryden had translated (ll. 597 f.):

> O happy Friends! for if my verse can give
> Immortal Life, your Fame shall ever live.

THE TEMPLE OF FAME

Plate 2 HEADPIECE FOR THE TEMPLE OF FAME

INTRODUCTION

I

THERE are three temples in Chaucer's *Hous of Fame*—those of Venus, Fame, and Rumour, and the effective presence of Venus spreads wider than her temple since, like most medieval dream-poems (including the others of Chaucer), the *Hous of Fame* is a love poem. The eagle who is carrying off Chaucer to the house of Fame announces 'mo tydinges' of 'Loves folke'[1] as reason for the journey. The house is not sighted till a thousand lines of the poem are over, though the eagle has kept Chaucer aware of his destination. And when, in the third book, the house is opened up and found to contain a miscellaneous crowd, Chaucer is frankly disappointed. Where, he asks with impatience, are the tidings of love?[2] The answer is the house of Rumour, but the poem breaks off incomplete at the point where the love tidings seem about to be delivered.

Pope's purpose was to produce something more homogeneous than Chaucer's poem. A single line wipes out the undue presence and influence of Venus, a line adapted from Dryden's 'translation' of the 'Chaucerian' *Flower and the Leaf*. For the dreaming Pope, as for Dryden,

> . . . Love it self was banish'd from my Breast.

And so Pope is principally concerned with the third Book, i.e., with the houses of Fame and Rumour. He saw in the non-amatory part of Chaucer's poem a possible basis for a *scena* peopled with heroes and typical human groups, a *scena* combining 'Description' and 'Sense',[3] the description as various—as splendid, powerful, tender, exquisite, and musical—as he could make it,[4] the sense, the 'True Wit', as 'well express'd'.[5]

---

1. ii 167.
2. iii 794 ff.
3. See 'Epistle to Dr. Arbuthnot', l. 148.
4. Gilbert Wakefield, in an excellent critical summary of the merits of the poem, writes that 'the descriptions are rich and luxuriant; and the scenery, after every allowance of originality to his predecessors, is the offspring of a very fruitful and vigorous imagination' (*Observations*, p. 131).
5. *Essay on Criticism*, l. 298.

II

There were, in 1715, certain rewards and dangers in choosing to imitate this particular poem of Chaucer. The rewards were obvious since the poem provided something for at least six noticeable interests of the age: the interests in imitation as a literary form; in imitation of Chaucer[1]; in 'visions'; in temple-poems[2]; in fame; and even in temples of Fame.

Philosophizing on Fame—not infrequently reaching the pitch of imagery, of a temple—was unusually common during the Renaissance,[3] and does not peter out in the seventeenth and eighteenth centuries so completely as has been thought.[4] Milton frequently

1. See pp. 3 ff. above.

2. There had been temples in the masques—for instance, the temple of Peace in Daniel's *Vision of the Twelve Goddesses* (1604). Davenant's masque, *The Temple of Love*, had been performed in 1634, and Motteux's opera with the same title, in 1706. A poem called *Le Temple de la Gloire* had appeared in Paris in 1646 and in the same year Philippe Habert published *Le Temple de la Mort*. Quinault's 'ballet', *Le Temple de la Paix*, was 'Dansé devant sa Majesté à Fontainebleau, le 15. d'Octobre 1685', according to the title-page of the 1686 edition. Habert's poem was translated by John Sheffield (later Duke of Buckingham) and first published as the opening poem in *A Collection of Poems . . . By several Persons* (1672). This collection was reprinted in 1673 and 1693. The 1693 edition was reissued in 1695 with a title-page beginning with the words *The Temple of Death*. The poem was also named on the title-page of the reprints of the collection in 1701, 1702, and 1716. (See A. E. Case, *A Bibliography of English Poetical Miscellanies 1521–1750* [1935], Nos. 151 a–g.) A separate reprint of the poem appeared in 1709. (For Pope's possible debt to it see note on ll. 65 ff. below.) Mrs Behn's 'translation' of Paul Tallemant's *Voyage de l'Isle d'Amour* (*Poems on Several Occasions*, 1684) has its 'Love's Temple'.

3. See J. Burckhardt's *Civilisation of the Renaissance in Italy*, translated by S. G. C. Middlemore, ed. 1890, pp. 139 ff., and the valuable paper, *Literary Fame: A Renaissance Study*, by O. Elton (*Otia Merseiana*, iv 24 ff.). Elton writes: 'The passion for personal glory is known to have dominated the Italian and to some extent the French Renaissance, increasing in intensity as time passed. The ancients were more impersonal, and even the Roman poets did not lay such a[n] emphasis, which at times was almost frantic, upon the hope of a name' (p. 39).

For the earlier treatment of the goddess Fame in literature see W. O. Sypherd, *Studies in Chaucer's Hous of Fame*, 1907.

4. E.g., by Elton, op. cit., p. 51. Elton unfortunately overlooked Pope's poem —few English scholars knew their Pope in the first three decades of the present century. The last paragraph (along with Pope's other contributions to the sub-

discussed the subject; Satan and Christ debate it at length in the third Book of *Paradise Regained*. Cowley has a pindarique called 'Life and Fame'. Davenant often reverts to the theme, and not only in the poems but in the preface to *Gondibert*. It inspired the best single stanza of Flatman,[1] and Shadwell wrote of it as Falstaff spoke of honour.[2] John Sheffield, Duke of Buckingham, discusses it in paragraphs which Pope, his posthumous editor, finds little cause to alter.[3] And the same miscellany provides in Yalden's epistolary ode 'To Mr. Congreve' a sustained excursus on the subject.[4] In prose there had been Mlle de Scudéri's *Discours de la Gloire*, anonymously translated in 1708,[5] but this is mainly concerned with personal ethics. The extreme brevity of literary fame had been pungently insisted on by Swift in the *Tale of a Tub*.[6] Addison had contributed two unusually thoughtful papers on fame to the *Spectator*.[7] Then there were the goddess's temples, literary and actual.[8] In 1625 Thomas Scot published his poem 'The House of Fame', in *The Second Part of Philomythie*. Davenant makes Gondibert visit a kind of temple of Fame which he calls, in gothic letters, 'The Monument of vanish'd Mindes'.[9] In 1700 Yalden published his

---

ject) would have provided his essay with a conclusion balancing the citations from Petrarch which open its 'modern' section.

1. 'To the Memory of . . . Orinda', stanza ii (*Poems*, 1674, pp. 2 f.).

2. See the ending of his 'On the Dutchess of New-Castle her Grace'.

3. 'On Mr. Hobs', in Dryden's *Examen Poeticum*, ed. 1706, p. 39: cf. his *Works*, 1723, p. 180.

4. pp. 199 ff.

5. *An Essay upon Glory . . . Printed for J. Morphew*.

6. See the 'Dedication to Prince Posterity'.

7. Nos. 255–256. Cf. Tickell, 'To the supposed Author of the Spectator', ll. 35 f.:

> Fame, heav'n and hell, are thy exalted theme,
> And visions such as Jove himself might dream.

8. Temples, including those to Fame, were becoming common as garden decorations; cf. Swift, 'An Epistle upon an Epistle', ll. 77 ff.:

> To *Fame* a Temple you Erect,
> A *Flora* does the Dome protect;
> Mounts, Walks, on high; and in a Hollow
> You place the *Muses* and *Apollo*;
> There shining 'midst his Train, to Grace
> Your Whimsical, Poetick Place.

9. II v st. 36. (Dryden adapts the phrase for comic purposes at 'Mac Flecknoe',

Temple of Fame. A Poem, To the Memory of the Most Illustrious Prince, William, Duke of Gloucester, which more than any other poem paves the way for Pope.[1] In 1709 the *Tatler* ran a journalistic competition

82.) Cervantes had referred to 'the Temple of Immortality' (*Don Quixote*, translated by Motteux, ed. 1712, ii 580). See note p. 233 below. Pope knew *Don Quixote* early, see his letter to Caryll, 25 Jan. 1710–11. Ben Jonson's *Masque of Queens* (1609) had had a temple of Fame as its centre. For *Le Temple de la Gloire*, see note p. 216 above.

1. Yalden, after a lyrical lament, describes 'A lonely Mansion'

> Where Fate resides, and Death in Triumph reigns . . .
>   Inglorious Crowds here undistinguish'd come
> To Nature's last Retreat, a Peaceful Tombe:
> An easie Change, to Minds that seek no more,
> But covet Rest, and dream'd out Life before;
> Those whom no Arts, no shining Actions grace,
> That liv'd obscure, and fell a worthless Race!
> Here in the Arms of kind Oblivion laid,
> Their Names forgot, they sleep beneath this Shade.

'This Scene of Horrour', however, 'but prepares the Way' to the Temple of Fame where

> Crystalline Roofs the glorious Dome adorn . . .
> On Columns rais'd in beauteous Orders plac'd,
> With Statues crown'd, Triumphal Arches grac'd . . .
> In Consort here a hundred Trumpets join,
> Return'd by Echoes thro' the vaulted Shrine:
> Loud Hymns of Praise, and joyful Pæans sound,
> That reach extreamest Earth, and Heav'ns superiour round.
>   Here Fame presides, here jealous Honour stands,
> To guard their Off-spring from the Tyrant's hands:
> To keep the Heroe's boasted Name alive,
> And make the glorious after Death survive.
> And here are Urns, but Urns with Myrtle bound,
> Adorn'd with Wreaths, with deathless Laurels crown'd:
> Whose sacred Ashes lasting Sweets diffuse,
> And Bless the Toils of the recording Muse.

Hither come ambitious crowds, but they seek fame in vain because of their 'Dulness and Sloth'.

> Deluded Wretches that consume their Days,
> In false pursuits of Fame, and courting Praise:

—these also come in vain. Then Yalden describes the shrines of (unnamed) 'Immortal Bards', and of 'fam'd Worthies of our *British* Race', the 'Kings and Heroes' who have died as famous as William now has died (pp. 10 f. Pope's debt is for manner, phrases, and versification).

to determine the heroes for a table of Fame, and in a final 'vision' showed them assembling in Fame's temple.[1] And in the same year was published an anonymous *Temple of Fame, A Poem. Inscrib'd to Mr. Congreve*, in which Fame, lacking a temple, builds one in England to celebrate the course of the war against Louis XIV, that '*Canvas-Jove*' and the 'Boy of *Spain*'.[2] *Spectator* 439 sets out with a description of Ovid's 'Palace of Fame'. And, in 1714, came the *Steeleids*, a well-written political poem which uses the courts of false and genuine Fame as the machinery for an attack on Steele and,

1. Nos. 67, 74, 81. For Pope's debt see notes to the poem.

2. The following extracts show where Pope comes into closest competition with the poem:

She spake—and strait a spacious Dome appear'd,
A Golden Roof and Brazen Pillars rear'd;
For Brass can best the hollow sounds diffuse,
And Multiply the Ecchoes of the News:
And Walls are hid with many hopeful Lye,
Which gain'd it's credit by Credulity;
Gilded with Truth; the Floor is pav'd with Eyes;
Nerves, Sinews, broken Bones, and Arteries;
The Court with one Eternal uproar Bawls,
With Scandals rushing thro' the Cranny'd walls:
A hideous din, as when the Billows Roar,
And Proudly quarel with th' insulting Shore;
A broken Tumult, deaf, confus'd and Loud;
Like Thunder rumbling in a distant Cloud . . .

(pp. 7 f.: cf. Pope, ll. 244 ff.). The goddess herself stands on a mountain beyond a wood of (named) trees, eternally green:

High o'er the Wood the Goddess rears her size,
And hides her Tow'ring forhead in the Skies:
Two Golden wings are on her Shoulders Plac'd,
To raise her Vigour and enlarge her hast:
Her better hand a Silver Trumpet bore,
To waft Report to every distant Shore;
A scarfe of Mouths across her Arms are hung,
And every Mouth is babling with a Tongue:
A Plate of yawning Ears conceals her Breast,
And a thin Vail but scarcely hides the rest.
No Peaceful Slumbers seal her wakeful Eyes,
But here and there with every blast she Flies . . .

(pp. 9 f.: cf. Pope, ll. 258 ff.).

among others, Pope.[1] Pope's *Temple of Fame* itself was followed, five weeks later, by another temple poem written to parody it.[2]

Chaucer, temples, and fame, then, were familiar, and Pope's poem met its readers more than half way. But there was one particular drawback to imitating the *Hous of Fame*. It belonged to wild medieval allegory, to a kind of poetry that a string of recent poets and critics had condemned. Pope felt the need to defend his choice. When he came to write his defence—it occupies the first two pages of his *Notes*, and is given below, at p. 251—he cannot but have felt his position a strong one. To begin with, his own pleasure in these allegories was real, so real that it was to persist. Eight years later he is found advising Judith Cowper to write a poem 'in the descriptive way . . . mixd with Vision & Moral; like the Pieces of the old Provençal Poets,[3] which abound with Fancy & are the most amusing scenes in nature'. He instances 'three or four of this kind in Chaucer', and avows his own unshaken 'inclination to tell a Fairy tale; the more wild & exotic the better'.[4] And later still he is found recalling the same fairy tale—it will never now get written—with evident indulgence: 'It . . . might not have been unentertaining'.[5] Pope's personal faith in these 'unclassical' poems was not solitary. Dryden had translated the 'Flower and the Leaf', and among other work, there had been the allegorical 'visions' in the periodicals, notably in the *Tatler* and *Spectator*. Pope's attack, therefore, is against 'Some modern Criticks' with their 'pretended Refinement of Taste'.

In defending allegory Pope is contributing to a controversy of long standing. The medieval critics—Dante, Petrarch, and Boccaccio, for example—had considered it to provide the only justi-

1. *The Steeleids, or, The Tryal of Wit . . . In Three Cantos: By John Lacey . . . 1714.* There are hits at *Windsor Forest* and the *Rape of the Lock.*

2. *Æsop at the Bear-Garden: a Vision. By Mr. Preston. In Imitation of the Temple of Fame, a Vision, By Mr. Pope . . . 1715.* The *Post Boy* (8–10 Mar. 1714–15) records it as 'This Day . . . publish'd'. Preston was the bear-ward, and the author using his name seeks to ridicule Pope's poem by quoting (sometimes in slightly altered form) lines and longer passages from it during a comic description of a bear fight. See note on ll. 435 ff. below.

3. For Pope's confusion of Provençal and Old French, see note p. 251, below.

4. Letter of 26 Sept. 1723; see the whole passage.

5. Spence, 140.

fication of poetry. This view survived strongly into the Renaissance, partly because Boiardo's *Orlando Inamorato* and Ariosto's *Orlando Furioso* 'were written before the Aristotelian canons had become a part of the critical literature of Italy'.[1] By 1715, however, poets and critics had tended more and more to believe that the extravagant medieval kind of allegory offered an unsatisfactory basis for a poem, since the Aristotelian 'fable' grounded on 'probability' lay so much nearer to human experience, to 'Nature'. It was still considered that the fable should have a moral, but the means of arriving at this moral were required to be 'Consonant to Sense and Truth', i.e., 'not Poetical upon the score of any ridiculous Fiction'.[2] The scientists supported the critics—they excused the early myths and allegories only because they had been found useful for instructing barbarous peoples. Pope's appeal to Aristotle is therefore ineffective—the *Poetics*, the concern of which in any event was with tragedy, had made no provision for anything like the *Hous of Fame*. And the appeal, later, to the *Wisdom of the Ancients* is weaker because of Bacon's statement in the *Advancement* that the moral content of the myths was often put there by those who found it,[3] and because of St-Evremond's brilliant iconoclastic essay 'Of the Wonderful that is found in the Poems of the Ancients'.[4] But Pope certainly makes a show, and he is wise in appealing mainly to the practice of poets and the pleasure of readers during several ages and over several countries, since 'Nature' which stood for probability, also stood for universality and permanence: 'The Flower & the

1. Spingarn, *History*, p. 112.

2. St-Evremond on Lucan's *Civil War* (*Works*, ii 68). Cf. i 428. The opening sentence of Pope's note suggests that he may be remembering St-Evremond's 'In short, the miraculous Spirit of the Ancients does not relish with our Age' (*id.*, 47). Among English critics who had taken the same view were Davenant ('to make great Actions credible is the principall Art of Poets'—Spingarn, ii 11); Hobbes ('the Resemblance of truth is the utmost limit of Poeticall Liberty'—*id.*, 62); Cowley ('the confused antiquated *Dreams* of senseless *Fables* and *Metamorphoses*'—*id.*, 88); and Rymer (Spenser, who unfortunately followed Ariosto rather than Tasso, lived in an age whose 'vice' it was 'to affect superstitiously the *Allegory* . . .'—*id.*, 168); and, more recently, Addison on Spenser (*Account of the Greatest English Poets*, 1694, ll. 23 ff.).

3. See Spingarn, i 8. Bacon had been preceded by Lucian (especially in his *Philopseudes*) and by Rabelais in his prologue to *Gargantua*.

4. ii 61 ff.

Leaf', he tells Judith Cowper, 'every body has been delighted with'.[1] Pope was to be justified by the future. Allegorical vision-poems were to continue popular, too popular, till well into the nineteenth century: even 'Alastor', the 'Ode to Indolence', and the 'Palace of Art' belong virtually to the same form.

Pope's commonsense reply to the critics did not end with this note. He addressed them again, along with the scientists in his note on Zembla,[2] a note which shows him to be aware of terms he had not introduced into the earlier discussion.

III

Pope had done what he could to defend allegory, but it was Chaucer's poem, not his own, which in 1715 stood in most need of the defence. The *Temple of Fame* itself had already been cleared of Chaucer's wildest 'extravagances'. In the body of the poem Pope had already shown respect for the view that ancient poets should be modernized to fit the changed times of those who were imitating them.[3] His prefatory note and his 'Advertisement' say as much, and they specify what this modernization amounts to.

Pope treats the *Hous of Fame* very freely. He does not scruple to discard all the first Book, all but a few ornamental details of the second, and much of the third. And he does what he likes with what he retains—reducing, enlarging, rearranging, enforcing, re-imagining. The *Temple of Fame* is everywhere cleared of the engaging 'Chaucerian' element of pother and hotchpotch. The comedian naïveté of the narrator, his grumblings and gapings, the icy affability of the eagle—all this is shed completely. Chaucer's thousand spinning tetrameters are reduced to half the number of weighty pentameters. For Chaucer's cinematographic speed and lightness there is Pope's Handelian tempo and harmony, for Chaucer's narrative, Pope's scene.[4]

This treatment seems to have had no precedent in non-dramatic poetry. Pope goes considerably further than Denham and Cowley

1. Letter of 26 Sept. 1723.

2. See Appendix H, p. 410.

3. One of the latest exponents of this view had been St-Evremond; see i 421 ff. and ii 47 ff.

4. For further discussion on the principles guiding Pope in the composition of this poem, see my *Pope and Human Nature*, 1958, pp. 208 ff.

had gone, who, as Dryden showed in his 'Preface to the Translation of Ovid's Epistles', had discovered this new way of translating:

> not long since . . . Sir John Denham and Mr. Cowley . . . contrive[d] another way of turning authors into our tongue, called, by the latter of them, imitation . . . I take imitation of an author, in their sense, to be an endeavour of a later poet to write like one who has written before him, on the same subject; that is, not to translate his words, or to be confined to his sense, but only to set him as a pattern, and to write, as he supposes that author would have done, had he lived in our age, and in our country.

Dryden's next words indicate that developments are possible:

> Yet I dare not say, that either of them have carried this libertine way of rendering authors (as Mr. Cowley calls it) so far as my definition reaches: for in the *Pindaric Odes*, the customs and ceremonies of ancient Greece are still preserved.

A warning, however, follows:

> But I know not what mischief may arise hereafter from the example of such an innovation, when writers of unequal parts to him shall imitate so bold an undertaking. To add and to diminish what we please, which is the way avowed by him, ought only to be granted to Mr. Cowley and that only in his translation of Pindar; because he alone was able to make him amends, by giving him better of his own, whenever he refused his author's thoughts. Pindar is generally known to be a dark writer, to want connection, (I mean as to our understanding,) to soar out of sight, and leave his reader at a gaze. So wild and ungovernable a poet cannot be translated literally; his genius is too strong to bear a chain, and Samson-like he shakes it off.[1]

For 'Cowley' read 'Pope', for 'Pindar' read 'Chaucer', and Pope's justification is eloquently complete—so complete that Pope must have found Dryden's final words inspiring rather than deterrent:

> To state it fairly; imitation of an author is the most advantageous way for a translator to show himself, but the greatest wrong which can be done to the memory and reputation of the dead . . .[2]

1. *Essays*, i 239 f.
2. *ibid.*

After all, Chaucer wrote in English and so was immune from this greatest wrong. Meanwhile the translator could show himself the most advantageous way.

IV

What Pope was doing has not been clearly understood by his critics. They therefore do not forgo the easy comparison of his poem with Chaucer's. The exception is Dennis. He is immune from the temptation because he is ignorant of Chaucer—he blames Pope as the inventor of what he borrows.[1] The later critics were familiar with the *Hous of Fame* but used it for wrong purposes. They judge these unlike poems by comparing them. 'The original vision of Chaucer,' says Dr Johnson, 'was never denied to be much improved.'[2] Joseph Warton[3] and Roscoe[4] are not so sweeping: the 'design', they say, is 'improved'.[5] Thomas Warton, who, of course, is approaching the question from Chaucer's end, comes out boldly on the other side:

> Pope has imitated this piece, with his usual elegance of diction and harmony of versification. But in the mean time, he has not only misrepresented the story, but marred the character of the poem. He has endeavoured to correct it's extravagancies, by new refinements and additions of another cast: but he did not consider, that extravagancies are essential to a poem of such a structure, and even constitute it's beauties. An attempt to unite order and exactness of imagery with a subject formed on principles so professedly romantic and anomalous, is like giving Corinthian pillars to a Gothic palace. When I read Pope's

1. Pope notes this on the margin of his copy of the *Remarks*, 1717 (*Brit. Mus.*, C. 116 b. 1 (2), p. 48) by writing 'Chaucer' against Dennis's words 'this Author' (meaning Pope). The *Remarks*, 1717, also suffer from a lack of sympathy with, and so of understanding of, the 'vision' form which Pope's note on Zembla had done its best to explain. When Dennis (p. 51) objects to the suspension of the rock of ice and its temple as 'contrary to Nature, and to the Eternal Laws of Gravitation', Pope writes ironically in the margin 'wch no dream ought to be.'

2. *Lives*, iii 226.

3. i 338.

4. *Works of Pope* (1824), ii 255

5. This is, of course, incontrovertibly true at some points: see note on ll. 259 ff. below.

> elegant imitation of this piece, I think I am walking among the modern monuments unsuitably placed in Westminster-abbey.[1]

A phrase seven pages earlier—'great strokes of Gothic imagination'—shows how well he has experienced Chaucer's poem. But to read Pope's with these strokes in mind is to look for what his legitimate plan prevented him from providing. Campbell championed Pope by refusing to allow Thomas Warton's comparison of the *Hous of Fame* with Westminster Abbey:

> The many absurd and fantastic particulars in Chaucer's 'House of Fame' will not suffer us to compare it, as a structure in poetry, with so noble a pile as Westminster Abbey in architecture.[2]

And so Pope is praised as a kind of 'Capability' Brown:

> Much of Chaucer's fantastic matter has been judiciously omitted by Pope, who at the same time has clothed the best ideas of the old poem in spirited numbers and expression.[3]

But Campbell does not see that to attempt an absolute comparison is in itself an error in critical method.

V

The critics of the poem speak of improvement or deterioration rather than of change. They are not free, therefore, to reach the point of seeing that change was inevitable, that for this poem (to use Dryden's terms[4]) metaphrase was pointless and paraphrase a waste of opportunity. Pope could only imitate and, in imitating, modernize. Modernization was inevitable not simply because St-Evremond and the rest counselled it, but because the idea of fame was different in the eighteenth century from the idea of fame in the fourteenth.

Pope is writing in the tradition of the Renaissance and so the great human figures of the past stand out more commandingly for him than for Chaucer. Fame still has some capriciousness for Pope

1. *History of English Poetry* (1774), i 396.
2. *An Essay on English Poetry; with Notices of the British Poets* (ed. 1848), pp. 132 f.
3. *id.*, 132.
4. *Essays*, i 237.

—he does not omit Chaucer's link between Fame and Fortune.[1] But for him those whom Fame exalts she exalts indeed. Chaucer's temple had its place for Achilles, Homer, Alexander, but the effect of their greatness was partly effaced by the crowds of minor, even of contemporary, names—Geoffrey of Monmouth, for example, and even 'Colle tregetour', recently identified with a contemporary juggler.[2] The figures in Chaucer's temple, like the patchwork saints in a medieval church window, lack the salience of perspective. Pope provides perspective and sees to it that he names only those figures who can stand the fierce eighteenth-century light that beats about Fame's throne. He arranges these figures 'in venerable Order',[3] with due regard for degrees of greatness.

Because of Pope's new conception of Fame, the goddess required a new temple. Chaucer's gothic was too much 'clog'd with trivial Circumstances, or little Particularities',[4] had too many

> Babewinnes and pinacles,
> Ymageries and tabernacles[5]

to suit the untrammelled nobility of Pope's goddess. Pope's temple is Palladian in its squareness and baroque in its decoration.[6] This new architecture is not chosen simply because Pope is following the counsel of the critics. He is not simply avoiding an outgrown style—indeed he retains gothic on the outside of the Northern wall since gothic is valuable for the completeness of that part of his symbolism. Far from despising gothic, he exalts it, ten years later, in his final praise of Shakespeare.[7] That praise may be also read as his praise

1. ll. 296 f.

2. iii 380 and 187. In the same way Petrarch's *Trionfo della Fama* mixed modern and ancient names.

3. l. 72.

4. Pope's prefatory note, p. 251 below.

5. iii 99 f.

6. *One Epistle to Mr. A. Pope, Occasion'd by Two Epistles Lately Published* (c. 1730), p. 15, refers jibingly to the temple of Fame as 'Fame's *Versailles*'.

7. '. . . one may look upon his works, in comparison of those that are more finish'd and regular, as upon an ancient majestick piece of *Gothick* Architecture, compar'd with a neat Modern building: The latter is more elegant and glaring, but the former is more strong and more solemn. It must be allow'd, that in one of these there are materials enough to make many of the other. It has much the greater variety, and much the nobler apartments; tho' we are often conducted

of Chaucer and of the *Hous of Fame*. The temple by which he replaces Chaucer's is no 'neat Modern building', but a structure of Palladian proportions and grandeur appropriate for the increased aristocracy of the famous names. When Inigo Jones designed a temple of Fame for Ben Jonson's *Masque of Queens*, indebtedness was acknowledged 'to that noble description made by Chaucer'. But his drawing[1] shows no sign of any debt. And if Fame needed a Palladian temple in 1609 she needed one all the more in 1715. In building it, Pope found more help in his own love of the Palladian, in the accounts of Dido's palace,[2] gorgeously translated by Dryden,[3] of Chaucer's and Dryden's temples in their *Knight's Tale*, of the temple of Fame in *Tatler* 81, and, most of all, of the palace of the fallen angels in *Paradise Lost*.[4] There were also the books of architectural engravings,[5] and a growing number of English buildings in this style, including Wren's cathedral and churches.

VI

The connotation of *fame* had changed by Pope's time, but it had not changed enough to be yet dissociated from *rumour*. That dissociation belongs to the nineteenth century.[6] For the Roman poets Fama was mainly Rumour.[7] Chaucer's Fame represents both fame and rumour, and the two temples make clear the duality of her nature. In Drayton's 'Robert Duke of Normandy' (1596–1619), Fame, 'The Secretarie of the immortall powers', is reproached by Fortune for being merely rumour. Cesare Ripa in his popular *Iconologia* distinguishes between Fama (the Rumour of Virgil),

---

to them by dark, odd, and uncouth passages. Nor does the Whole fail to strike us with greater reverence, tho' many of the Parts are childish, ill-plac'd, and unequal to its grandeur' (*The Works of Shakespeare* [1723], I xxiii f.).

1. Reproduced in J. A. Gotch's *Inigo Jones* (1928), Plate II.

2. *Æneid*, i 631 ff.

3. Dryden's *Æneid*, i 892 ff.

4. See notes on ll. 75 ff., 91, 94, 143 ff. below.

5. Palladio's *I quattro Libri dell' Architettura* was published in Venice in 1570 and frequently reprinted before 1715. The seventh edition of G. Richards's translation (fully illustrated) appeared in 1708.

6. As late as 1855 Macaulay uses *fame* for *rumour* (see OED).

7. See Pauly, *Real-Encyclopädie der classischen Altertumswissenschaft* (ed. 1909), vi, columns 1977 ff.

Fama Buona, Fama Chiara, and 'Fama cattiua di Claudiano'.[1] Thomas Scot planned his house of Fame in four storeys. 'Foure sister twins' inhabit it, the two elder, '*True fame, and good*', occupying the higher floors, and the 'youngest payre', 'false and [b]ad fame' the 'two darker roomes below'.

> False fame liues lowest, and true Fame aboue,
> Bad Fame next false, good fame next, true doth moue:
> Yet good fame somtime doth with false fame stay,
> And bad fame sometime doth with true fame play.
> But false and true (opposd) will neuer meete,
> Nor bad and good fame, one the other greete,[2]

In Milton's poem 'In Quintum Novembris' (ll. 170 ff.) Fama is Rumour, but in the sonnet 'To Mr. H. Lawes' and in *Samson Agonistes* (ll. 971 ff.) Fame represents something more permanent. In *Hudibras* Fame is distinguished as Good and Evil, but the 'tattling Gossip'[3] is mainly Rumour. For Pope the word still has both its meanings—'Fame sits aloft' directing the lies which issue from the temple of Rumour.[4] Because of this double denotation there was no question of Pope's discarding the second part of Chaucer's third Book. Dennis and Joseph Warton considered that the change to the temple of Rumour breaks the design of the poem, but did not see that, without that change, the contemporary meaning of fame is left incompletely expressed.[5] Pope, like Chaucer, has both temples,

1. *Iconologia, O Vero Descrittione d' Imagini Della Virtu, Vitij, Affetti, Passioni humane*... (1611), pp. 154 ff. In P. Tempest's translation (1709), p. 30, only the third term is used: 'Fama chiara: *Good FAME*.' (The reference to Claudian is to the *De Bello Gothico*, l. 201.)

2. *The Second Part of Philomythie*, 1625, B 2r.

3. II i 77.

4. l. 483. See my note on the line.

5. Dennis, *Remarks*, 1717, p. 48. Joseph Warton, commenting on ll. 418–21, writes: 'The scene here changes from the TEMPLE of FAME to that of Rumour. Such a change is not methinks judicious, as it destroys the unity of the subject [i.e., theme], not to mention, that the difference between Rumour and Fame is not sufficiently distinct and perceptible' (i 393 f.). Warton does not allow for Fame's being the goddess both of fame and rumour which makes distinction unnecessary after a certain point. The black trumpet of slander sounds even in the temple of Fame (l. 332), and there at times, as in the temple of Rumour,

but he is of his own age in distinguishing the two senses of fame more precisely than Chaucer. And he is of his own age again in requiring a steadier temple for Rumour, as he required a more Palladian one for fame. Fame, in her capacity as Rumour, was not quite the crazy harlotry for Pope that she was for Virgil in the first century B.C., and for Chaucer in the fourteenth. Social communications had become more serviceable, statements more readily verifiable, superstition less rank. And so, quite rightly, Pope's temple of Rumour has more staidness than Chaucer's spinning 'cage' of twigs. But Pope's temple differs from Chaucer's more than this new conception justifies. Pope describes it as a 'Structure fair', a 'Mansion'[1] which is too like a 'neat Modern building' to suit even an eighteenth-century Rumour. And it cannot be said that his temple is made mild in the interests of the general dignity of the poem since he had already designed the fierce Northern side of the temple of Fame. Pope fails in these three words. Because of them, we cannot believe his claim, as we do believe Chaucer's, that the doors are as numerous as leaves. But, apart from this, Pope's temple of Rumour has a proper disturbing mysteriousness.

VII

Pope's choice of heroes for his temple of Fame was necessarily determined by his age. The poem would otherwise have belied its title. Joseph Warton saw and allowed for this—so far at least as literary names were concerned:

> The six persons POPE thought proper to select as worthy to be placed on these pillars as the highest seats of honour, are HOMER, VIRGIL, PINDAR, HORACE, ARISTOTLE, TULLY. It is observable, that our author has omitted the great dramatic

In ev'ry Ear incessant Rumours rung,
And gath'ring Scandals grew on ev'ry Tongue.

(ll. 336 f.; cf. ll. 402 ff.). Mme du Boccage, whose translation, *Le Temple de la Renommée*, was published in 1749 (though written some ten years earlier), saw the introduction of the second temple as breaking the unity of the design, but with the scruples of a translator refrained from taking the obvious course and imposing a unity for herself by 'combining' the two temples (see the preface to her translation).

1. ll. 420, 422.

> poets of Greece. Sophocles and Euripides deserved certainly an honourable niche in the Temple of FAME, as much as Pindar and Horace. But the truth is, it was not fashionable in POPE's time, nor among his acquaintance, attentively to study these poets.[1]

It is equally observable that Warton omits Æschylus! Some of the highest pillars in the temple of Fame are held not permanently, it seems, but on leases—'Unsure the Tenure'.[2] If Pope had written his poem later in the century he might well have found a place for the 'sad Electra's poet' dear to Collins, and a place, too, for the Shakespeare, and perhaps the Milton, who are two of Gray's three instances of the progress of poesy. And Pope would also have outgrown the renaissance veneration for Cicero. Elwin's contempt is therefore irrelevant:

> The undue exaltation of antiquity is complete in the Temple of Fame. No English king, warrior, statesman, or patriot; no christian martyr or evangeliser; no poet or philosopher was deemed worthy to be ranked with the men of old. The fictitious phantoms of heathen mythology, the heroes of decayed empires, and the authors whose works are in dead languages, are the sole immortals of Pope.[3]

It is wrong to suppose that Pope celebrates the ancients because there are no great names among the moderns. In his note on allegory he speaks impartially of 'the greatest Genius's, both antient and modern'. And twenty years later he has occasion to discuss this very point when adapting Horace for his 'Epistle to Augustus'. The period after death at which 'a poet grows divine' is commonly rated at a hundred years, but rather than

> damn [him] to all Eternity at once,
> At ninety nine, a Modern, and a Dunce,[4]

ninety-nine years will do. This happens to be exactly the period intervening between Shakespeare's death and the *Temple of Fame*.

---

1. i 360 f.
2. l. 508 below.
3. EC, i 197. Elwin has, however, ground for the charge that Pope's choice of names is sometimes unsatisfactory. Pericles, for instance, is omitted.
4. ll. 59 f.

But though Dryden, as early as 1668, was hailing Shakespeare as 'the Homer, or father of our dramatic poets',[1] it was not until fifty years after the *Temple of Fame* that Dr Johnson, with an unwonted tentativeness, could truthfully say that Shakespeare 'may now begin to assume the dignity of an ancient'.[2] Meantime Shakespeare is excluded from the *Temple of Fame*. His exclusion, on the other hand, from a 'Temple of Modern Fame' in Dodsley's *Museum* is, of course, ridiculous, especially since Milton and Pope are included.[3] (But, perhaps as compensation, he and Homer head the list in a 'Ballance of Poets' with eighteen marks out of a possible twenty![4]) It is merely in a panegyric poem that Simon Harcourt shows Pope's own arrival at the temple of Fame, where

each great Ancient court[s him] to his shrine.[5]

In excluding modern names, simply because they are modern, Pope is doing what he must. But his temple finds a place for figures who undoubtedly did have a contemporary, rather than a permanent significance. Indeed, the *Temple of Fame* may be regarded as a document in the controversy of the ancients and moderns.[6] Pope is, of course, on the side of Sir William Temple and Swift, and his choice of figures for his temple of Fame owes more to Temple than to Chaucer.

Pope read Temple's essays as a boy, 'in [his] first setting out'.[7] The three companion essays on 'Ancient and Modern Learning', 'Heroick Virtue', and 'Poetry' had made use of most of the names of the 'heroes', historians, empires, and ancient 'sciences' for which Pope finds a place either in the poem or in the notes—Hercules, Theseus, Cyrus, Ninus, Sesostris, Zamolxis, Confucius, Odin, Epaminondas, Herodotus, Diodorus Siculus, Magi, Brachmans, Egypt, Chaldæa, the Scythian empire, China, astronomy, astro-

1. *Essays*, i 82.
2. *The Plays of William Shakespeare*, ed. Johnson, 1765, i, A 2r.
3. *The Museum: Or, The Literary and Historical Register*, 1746, No. xiii.
4. No. xix.
5. *Works of . . . Pope* (quarto) 1717, c3r.
6. This is the answer to Dennis's objection (*Remarks*, 1717, 71 ff.) that there are no women in the temple. (All the persons in the temple of Fame in Ben Jonson's *Masque of Queens* are women.)
7. Spence, p. 199.

logy, geometry, magic, runes, etc. Indeed, the only knowledge of antiquity made accessible to the seventeenth century and neglected by Pope was that of Mexico and Peru, which Temple had treated of in Section III of his 'Heroick Virtue'. Otherwise the temple of Fame provides an official shelter for most of the ancient names which were pushed backwards and forwards in 'the first controversy in English letters that had made anything like a public stir'.[1] Pope might have taken as his motto the penultimate sentence of Section V of Temple's 'Of Heroick Virtue', reading it as applicable to all three essays:

> Who-ever has a mind to trace the Paths of Heroick Virtue, which lead to the Temple of True Honour and Fame, need seek them no further, than in the Stories and Examples of those Illustrious Persons here assembled.[2]

This provides much of the answer to Elwin, and the rest is not difficult to find. Temple had expressly excluded 'prophets' from his survey of heroes, since prophecy is no excellence of Nature or Art, but 'an immediate Gift of God'.[3] And the *Tatler* had adopted this plan: it not only proscribed from the entries to its competition every 'Person who has not been dead an Hundred Years', but others also:

> because this is altogether a Lay-Society, and that sacred Persons move upon greater Motives than that of Fame, no Persons celebrated in holy Writ, or any Ecclesiastical Men whatsoever, are to be introduc'd here.[4]

In choosing his heroes Pope found support and suggestions in other authors than Temple. His notes record obligation to Herodotus,[5] Diodorus Siculus, and Plutarch. These historians were all available in translations. His debt to Plutarch is to a specific translation—that by several hands, which Dryden contributed to and supervised, and which appeared in 1683–6 and was republished for

1. R. C. Jebb, *Bentley* (1882), p. 84.
2. *Miscellanea* (ed. 1697), ii 287.
3. *id.*, ii 147.
4. No. 67.
5. For some remarks on Pope's acquaintance with Herodotus see J. Wells, *Studies in Herodotus* (1923), pp. 216 f.

the fourth or fifth time in 1711.[1] The attitudes struck by some of Pope's heroes are those in the engravings affixed to their lives. Another guide was Montaigne—Montaigne, who confessed that he could not write on any subject without borrowing from Plutarch.[2] Pope knew the essays early,[3] and they may have helped to fix his taste in great men. And there was Davenant, whose poems are an index to many of the 'scientific' interests of the seventeenth century. Davenant stocks his 'Monument of vanish'd Mindes' with

> Th' assembled soules of all that Men held wise,

an assembly which includes

> Others that *Egypts* chiefest Science show'd;
> Whose River forc'd Geometry on Men,
> . . . *Chaldean* Cous'ners . . .
> Who the hid bus'ness of the Stars relate;
> . . . *Persian Magi* . . . for wisdom prais'd;

'talking Greeks', Hebrews and Romans.[4] And Pope found further guidance in the bold judgements of Cowley.[5]

Pope is not only indebted to Temple for his choice of heroes but also owes to him the degrees in his hierarchy. Temple had grouped his heroes, as Pope does, according to geographical areas (the seventeenth century eagerly adopted Bodin's discovery that climate and geography account for racial characteristics[6]), and he also arranged his heroes in ascending order:

> After all that has been said of Conquerors or Conquests, this must be confessed to hold but the second Rank in the pretensions

1. In the British Museum copy the title-page of the first volume is dated M.DCC.II; the other four volumes read M DCC XI.
2. *Essays*, III v.
3. He refers to Montaigne in the letter to Henry Cromwell, 19 Oct. 1709.
4. *Gondibert* II v stanzas 36 ff. Pope may have remembered that when Don Quixote is 'enchanted' (Bk i, ch. 47) he speaks of 'all the Magick that ever its first Inventor *Zoroaster* understood', and describes himself as 'one who in spight of Envy's self, in spight of all the Magi of *Persia*, the Brachmans of *India*, or the Gymnosophists of *Ethiopia*, shall secure to his Name a place in *Temple of Immortality* . . .' (Motteux's translation, 1712, ii 577, 580).
5. See nn. on ll. 163 f. and 172–5 below.
6. See J. B. Bury, *The Idea of Progress* (1920), p. 38.

> to Heroick Virtue, and that the first has been allowed, to the wise Institution of just Orders and Laws, which frame safe and happy Governments in the world. . .[1]

And in the sequel[2] 'Of Poetry', he placed Homer and Virgil highest of all the poets:

> I am apt to believe so much of the true *Genius* of Poetry in general, and of its Elevation in these two Particulars, that I know not, whether of all the Numbers of Mankind, that live within the Compass of a Thousand Years; for one Man that is born capable of making such a Poet as *Homer* or *Virgil*, there may not be a Thousand born capable of making as great Generals of Armies, or Ministers of State, as any the most Renowned in Story.[3]

Pope follows Temple in the arrangement of his hierarchy.

VIII

The *Temple of Fame*, then, is a learned poem. Pope strenuously shared the old belief that the poet is, among other things, learned. But the *Temple of Fame* is the work of a poet in his early twenties, and, moreover, of a self-educated poet, who, in his own perhaps ambiguous words, 'had not the Happiness of an University Education'.[4] It follows that the display of learning, therefore, though it impressed Dr Johnson,[5] need not be taken too seriously. Pope's learning—to begin with, at any rate—was quick and intelligent

1. 300 f. This is Milton's arrangement, *Par. Regain'd*, iii 71 ff.

2. See pp. 147 f. Cf. Bacon, *Advancement of Learning*, I vii 1, from which Temple deviates only in inessentials. See note on l. 170 below.

3. pp. 321 f. A similar grading in Davenant's *Preface to Gondibert* is relevant here: '. . . this . . . File of Heroick Poets,—Men whose intellectuals were of so great a making . . . as perhaps they will in worthy memory outlast even Makers of Laws and Founders of Empires, and all such as must therefore live equally with them because they have recorded their names; and consequently with their own hands led them to the Temple of Fame' (Spingarn, ii 5 f.).

4. Anonymously in *Guardian*, No. 40. For Pope's view of the benefits bestowed by his irregular education see Spence, pp. 279 f.: 'Mr. Pope thought himself the better, in some respects, for not having had a regular education.—He, (as he observed in particular), read originally for the sense; whereas we are taught, for so many years, to read only for words.' (With which, by the way, cf. Wordsworth, *Prelude*, vi 95 ff.).

5. *Lives*, iii 104.

rather than solid. And so the *Temple of Fame* is the brilliant feat of the amateur. Some of the material was no doubt scrambled together too hurriedly, or pieced together too painfully, to be always accurate. Pope made a bad mistake over Odin. He writes:

And *Odin* here in mimick Trances dies[1]

and appends the following note:

> ... being subject to Fits, he persuaded his Followers, that during those Trances he receiv'd Inspirations from whence he dictated his Laws ...

Temple says nothing about Odin's trances, and the nearest thing to them seems to be the following passage from Aylett Sammes:

> Sometimes, as though he held his breath, [Odin] would fling his Body on the ground, which there lying as dead would turn into various figures, sometimes of a Bird, sometimes of a Fish, sometimes a Serpent. When he awaked, he would constantly aver he had been in forraign Countries, and had exact knowledge of what passed in them.[2]

But however much Odin suffered from fits he did not use them for messianic deception—it was Mahomet who did so. Temple's account of Mahomet comes about twenty pages after that of Odin, and Pope uses some of his words.[3] It seems that—either in actuality or in memory—the pages of his Temple blew over at this point.[4]

IX

What Pope does well in the historical section of his poem is the concentration of heroic, political, and literary character into epigram, his expression of those 'particular Thoughts' which in the *Advertisement* he claimed as 'my own'. The best instance is the lines on Alexander and Caesar.

Plutarch's 'comparison' of these heroes, if ever it existed, has

1. l. 124.
2. *Britannia Antiqua Illustrata* (1676), i 438.
3. See pp. 258 f. and 262.
4. Cf. Johnson's comment on a similar lapse in *Essay on Criticism*: 'Young men in haste to be renowned, too frequently talk of books which they have scarcely seen', *Works*, 1824, xi, 251.

been lost. The lack came to be felt all the more seriously since Alexander and Caesar were regarded as 'the greatest Men in the World'.[1] Plutarch's two orations 'concerning the Fortune or Vertue of *Alexander* the Great'[2] indicated which way his judgement might have inclined—he interprets Alexander as humane, prudent, temperate, 'of transcending Wisdom'. But the gap in the *Vitae Parallelae* remained, and as one of the candidates put it, to fill it became the 'Subject of all our Conversation'.[3] Montaigne[4] and Bacon[5] had already constructed elaborate comparisons, Bacon taking the two heroes together as his supreme instances of intellectual added to practical powers. But the most elaborate comparison is that of André Dacier, in whose French translation of the Lives, it runs to more than thirty quarto pages.[6] Pope's eight lines are his own entry into the competition. His views are virtually those of St-Evremond, but it is the literary method that is of most interest here. Pope writes:

> High on a Throne with Trophies charg'd, I view'd
> The *Youth* that all things but himself subdu'd;
> His Feet on Sceptres and *Tiara's* trod,
> And his horn'd Head bely'd the *Lybian* God.
> There *Cæsar*, grac'd with both *Minerva's*, shone;
> *Cæsar*, the World's great Master, and his own;
> Unmov'd, superior still in every State;
> And scarce detested in his Country's Fate.[7]

The two couplets on Alexander are straightforward statement but they provide only part of what Pope has to say of him. The other part is implied in the lines on Caesar. Pope does not mention that Alexander had been acclaimed as her protégé by Minerva, goddess

1. St-Evremond, i 111.
2. *Plutarch's Morals: Translated . . . By Several Hands* (4th Edition), 1704, i 439 ff.
3. St-Evremond, i 111 ff., *Comparison of Cæsar and Alexander*. The comparison had been translated as early as 1672. St-Evremond compares them again at i 188 ff.
4. *Essays*, II xxxvi.
5. *Advancemenl of Learning*, I vii 10 ff.
6. *Les Vies des Hommes Illustres de Plutarque* (ed. 1721), vi 329–63. (The translation began to appear in 1694 and was completed in 1721.)
7. ll. 151 ff.

of arms. But he implies it by saying that Caesar was graced with *both* Minervas, i.e., by Minerva in her capacities both as goddess of arms and of wisdom. The phrase is adapted from Dryden, but the emphasis, the virtual italic, is Pope's own. There is another backward glance at Alexander in the next line. As Lucian, St-Evremond, and Fontenelle had pointed out, Alexander was *not* his own master. This poetry, brief, weighty with intellectual implication, is one of the kinds in which Pope excelled. Several of the lines of the poem, like those of his actual epitaphs on friends, could stand the test of being cut on official stone.

When set against the best lines in this part of the poem, or in that similar part later where the suppliants make their requests to Fame, some of the lines describing the groups of literary statuary seem empty and pompous. But it is worth remembering that behind them stood, for Pope and for his contemporaries, the antique marbles of Rome. Pope knew these marbles from the fashionable books of engravings[1] and from the experience and collections of friends. He need have gone no further than the studio and collection of Charles Jervas, who had himself studied and copied in

1. La Chausse's *Romanum Museum* appeared in 1690, and Grævius's *Thesaurus Antiquitatum Romanarum* began to appear in 1694. (Pope wrote a Latin treatise on 'the old Buildings in Rome' founding it on Grævius—see Spence, p. 204.) Pope owned a collection of engravings entitled *Alcune Vedute di Giardini e Fontane di Roma e di Tiuoli Israell Siluestro. iu.* He executed in his 'print' hand a title-page for a similar collection bound in with it (in a nineteenth-century binding which probably replaces an earlier one): *Romae Nova Delineatio P. Schenckii.* He also provided many of the titles of the engravings with 'printed' annotations recording the heights of the obelisks and the inscriptions on the monuments. They are evidence of the neat care with which he studied the subject. (The book is now owned by J. G. Millward, Esq., to whose kindness I owe my examination of it.) Sir Godfrey Kneller (letters from whom were received early enough for them to be among the Homer MSS.) made a painting of statuary for Pope and received in return 'To Sir Godfrey Kneller, On his painting for me the Statues of Apollo, Venus and Hercules' (first published in 1727: Griffith, Add. 121a). Addison had fully described the basso relievo 'call'd *Homer*'s *Apotheosis*' with its five tiers of marble figures culminating in Jupiter, its nine Muses, its

> *Homer* . . . sitting in a Chair of State, that is supported on each Side by the Figure of a kneeling Woman. The one holds a Sword in her Hand to represent *Iliad*, or Actions of *Achilles*, as the other has an *Aplustre* to represent the *Odyssy*, or Voyage of *Ulysses*. About the Poet's Feet are creeping a Couple of Mice, as an Emblem of the *Batracho-myomachia* . . . (*Remarks*, p. 344).

Rome, and who was Pope's friend and teacher from 1713.[1] Pope considered that it was the Roman statues, 'thy well-studied marbles',[2] which had taught Jervas his 'beautiful and noble Ideas'.[3] The catalogue of Jervas's collection, sold on his death in 1740, contains several lots of statues, casts, prints, and drawings 'from the Antique' and four drawings 'Of the Hercules Farnese'.[4] The statuary of the temple of Fame is 'explained' by the epistle 'To Mr. Jervas, with Fresnoy's Art of Painting' (probably written in 1713–14) and the following lines from it may well represent the way this part of the *Temple of Fame* was composed:

> Smit with the Love of Sister-Arts we came,
> And met congenial, mingling Flame with Flame;
> Like friendly Colours found our Arts unite,
> And each from each contract new Strength and Light.
> How oft in pleasing Tasks we wear the Day,
> While Summer Suns roll unperceiv'd away?
> How oft our slowly-growing Works impart,
> While Images reflect from Art to Art?[5]

The modern reader must supply the contemporary connotation. And the untutorable disappointment which he feels over such a line as

> His Silver Beard wav'd gently o'er his Breast[6]

or

> And various Animals his Sides surround[7]

must not blind him to what is unexpectedly good in this part of the poem. In the first place Pope is able to embody literary 'allegory' in

1. See letter to Caryll, 30 April 1713.
2. 'To Mr. Jervas', l. 33.
3. Letter to Jervas, 29 Nov. 1716.
4. Lots 2009–10: *A Cagalogue Of the most Valuable Collection of Pictures, Prints, and Drawings late of Charles Jarvis, Esq; deceased . . . likewise His Marble Statues . . . With his Models and Plaisters of the most eminent Sculptors and Gravers, both Ancient and Modern. Chiefly collected by him, in a Series of Forty Years, in Rome, Lombardy, Venice, France, and Flanders . . . With sundry other valuable Remains of Antiquity.* The sale began on 11 Mar. 1739–40.
5. *The Art of Painting: By C. A. Du Fresnoy . . . Translated . . . By Mr. Dryden . . .* 1716, sig. A 6v.
6. l. 185.
7. l. 235.

his statues with a success unusual in a century when it was often tried. To take one example. The boldness which Pope's contemporaries particularly admired in Homer is enforced by being manifested in his eyes, where, since Homer was blind, one would least expect it to show:

> Tho' blind, a Boldness in his Looks appears.[1]

And, in the second place, the real subject of Pope's descriptions is not statuary but men in action, things in motion. It is the same in the description of the scenes sculptured on the west side of the temple, in which passage Pope revised his verbs to make them more lively.[2] Dennis made fun of these 'Motions of inanimate Bodies'[3] (especially of the echoes in l. 87).[4] Joseph Warton, however, contends that 'the best writers, in speaking of pieces of painting and sculpture, use the present or imperfect tense, and talk of the thing as really doing, to give a force to the description.'[5] He cites Homer and Virgil. The Homer instance is from the description of the shield of Achilles in *Iliad* xviii, a passage which Lessing was soon to make much of. Lessing's condemnation of statues in poetry does not really apply to Pope's.

X

In the later part of his poem, which may be considered as a try-out for the fourth Book of the *Dunciad*, Pope leaves the ancients and

1. l. 186. It may be noted that Joseph Warton admired the lines on Homer but thought those on Hercules and Sesostris weak (*Essay*, i 343, 350, and 364). Pope may have had in mind the Farnesian Homer, which George Vertue engraved as frontispiece to his *Homer* (1715). The eyes are large and bold and the absence of pupils which is usual in sculpture is accidentally appropriate for representing blind eyes. In this bust, however, the beard ends at the base of the neck (see l. 185). Pope owned a 'Marble Head of *Homer* by *Bernini*' which he bequeathed to Murray: see *The Life of Alexander Pope, Esq; With a True Copy of His Last Will and Testament* (1744), p. 59; and *Exhibition of 17th Century Art in Europe*, Royal Academy of Arts, London, 1938, item 940.

2. ll. 83 ff.: see textual notes.

3. *Remarks*, 1717, p. 57.

4. 'Methinks I could give a good deal, to see that Sculptor, who should pretend to carve an Eccho' (*ibid.*). Pope, of course, does not say that the echoes are represented. But the mountain's rolling into a wall implies that they existed.

5. i 344.

comes nearer to what Atterbury saw to be the true material for his genius,[1] the perception of character, especially of contemporary character.[2] (Pope, as well as Dryden, could have written

But Satire will have Room, where e're I write.)[3]

The English and the modern may not have attained to architectural status in the temple, may not be named, but they are not excluded from presenting their requests to Fame. Joseph Warton—so far behind had half a century left St-Evremond—was offended by Pope's modernity:

> Strokes of pleasantry and humour, and satirical reflections on the foibles of common life, are surely too familiar, and unsuited to so grave and majestic a poem as this hitherto has appeared to be... When I see such a line as
>
> "And at each blast a lady's honour dies",—
>
> in the TEMPLE of FAME, I lament as much to find it placed there, as to see shops, and sheds, and cottages, erected among the ruins of Dioclesian's Baths.[4]

But it is obvious that since the temple is represented as open to all comers (for Pope as for Chaucer the rock of ice is not intended as a barrier)[5] those comers will include all kinds. And since the beaux are the only group whose modernity causes them to make the request at all, Pope must show them as they are. Chaucer's group of lovers, unlike his Troilus, had not been particularized as fourteenth-century lovers. Pope legitimately takes the other course. His lovers belong to the same scene as the *Rape of the Lock*—

Sprightly our Nights, polite are all our Days.[6]

---

1. Letter to Pope, 26 Feb. 1721–2.

2. The first draft of the 'character' of Atticus ('Ep. to Dr. Arbuthnot', ll. 93 ff.) probably belongs to 1715, and l. 512 below comes from the same pen.

3. 'To Sir Godfrey Kneller', l. 94. Cf. Juvenal, *Sat.* i 30: 'Difficile est satiram non scribere'.

4. *Essay*, i 391 ff.

5. Dennis did not see this; see *Remarks*, 1717, pp. 53 f. In Gavin Douglas's *Palace of Honour* (Part III) the smooth marble rock on which the palace is built presents great difficulties for the competitors. But for Chaucer and Pope the ice is not so much slippery as subject to the weather.

6. l. 383.

One is not surprised to find them in the *Tatler*,[1] and to see them reappear later in the 'character' of Sporus.[2]

XI

There are other passages which are equally remote from their source. There are the lines on Zembla (53 ff.), one of Pope's finest pieces of description. And there is the conclusion. Pope was imitating mainly the third Book of Chaucer's poem. That Book is incomplete. Pope therefore had to provide himself with a conclusion and he did this by adapting a passage from the earlier part of the same Book, in which Chaucer represents himself as being asked why he came to the House of Fame. In his note, Pope considers that the passage transferred is, in his poem, 'more naturally made the conclusion, with the addition of a *Moral* to the whole'. In such a way—though his tone, unlike Chaucer's or Pope's, is haughty—Ovid had closed his *Metamorphoses*. Pope certainly chose his ending wisely. He knew that his particular kind of moral poetry was the best, the most original, poetry he could write. It is the same kind of moral poetry that towers in the conclusions of the various *Imitations of Horace*. Pope keeps his most resonant string for the end.

XII

The *Temple of Fame* combines two 'kinds' of poetry, the descriptive (including the 'epic') and the moral (including the satirical). The two kinds required different kinds of couplets and different verbal colourings. Wakefield considered the versification of the poem 'pure and melodious in a degree not surpassed by the best pieces of our author'.[3] But a general statement does not cover both styles. Wakefield's verdict scarcely applies to the couplets of the moral passages, which are often of the pointed kind. Indeed, several couplets in the final paragraph belong to the kind one associates with the *Moral Essays*. It is the same with the vocabulary. It falls into two kinds. For the description, Pope draws plentifully on the recognized 'poetical' words of the time. He needs them to make his temple splendid and official. He repeats words like *great*, *tow'ring*,

1. See note on ll. 378 ff. below.
2. 'Ep. to Dr. Arbuthnot', ll. 311 ff.
3. p. 131.

superior, *thousand*, *eternal*, *pompous*. (Along with these words go the scores of adjectival past participles—the past participle usually representing finality, work finished.) Then there are the other repeated 'poetical' words of another kind, e.g., *wild*, *confus'd*, *promiscuous*, *trembling*, *ambient*, *decay*, *roll*. These help to keep the poem visionary, to keep its solidity alive. (Along with these words go the scores of adjectival present participles, the present participle usually representing transcience, growth, movement.) All the words of these two groups are common in the poetry of the time. With them as norm, the passages of 'newly chosen' words have more earnestness. This newly chosen diction becomes more original as the content becomes more moral. The requests presented to Fame, the biological vicissitudes of the lies in the temple of Rumour, the confessions of the closing paragraph—in all these passages the words are new. When Pope uses a 'poetic' word here, he uses it differently. The best instance is *grace*. As verb or noun this word comes seven times[1] in the poem, and there is one *graceful*.[2] On six of the seven occasions, *grace* has the ordinary pleasant meaning. But on its last appearance it is used ironically and, because the reader has, by this time, been lulled into accepting it easily, the irony steals in slyly:

> When thus ripe Lyes are to perfection sprung,
> Full grown, and fit to grace a mortal Tongue . . .

XIII

On the half-titles of the 1717 and later editions, Pope states that the poem was 'Written in the Year 1711'. This statement does not exactly tally with the note appended to his letter to Steele of 16 November 1712[3]: Pope has been so diffident about his poem 'as to let it lie by me these two years, just as you now see it',[4] and the note comments: 'Hence it appears this Poem was writ before the Author was 22 Years old'. Since Pope became twenty-two on 21 May 1710 he cannot have written the poem before he was twenty-two if he

1. ll. 66, 72, 110, 155, 216, 226, 480.
2. l. 241.
3. *Letters of Mr. Pope* (1735) [Griffith 378], i 35 [second series] f.
4. *id.*, p. 36.

also wrote it in 1711. The date of composition cannot be arrived at exactly but there is no reason to doubt that it was substantially earlier than the *Rape of the Locke*.

Pope sent the MS. to Steele some time before 10 November 1712 when the *Spectator* recorded that Mr Pope had 'enclosed for my Perusal an admirable Poem, which, I hope, will shortly see the Light'. The poem here referred to must be the *Temple of Fame*, since that poem is the subject of Steele's letter to Pope two days later.[1] Pope mentions to Steele that he has not worked on the poem in the two years since it was written, but before the poem was ready for publication—it is noted as such by Gay on 30 December 1714[2]—it was certainly revised. Steele reported that he could see no fault among its 'thousand thousand beauties',[3] and in his reply Pope asks him 'can you [not] think it [a fault], that I have confin'd the attendance of Guardian spirits to Heaven's favourites only?',[4] a footnote adding 'This is not now to be found in the *Temple* of *Fame*, of which Poem he speaks here.'[5] In a footnote to his chapter on the *Rape of the Lock*, M. Audra connects the guardian sylphs of that poem with the discarded spirits of the *Temple of Fame* and cites Dryden as saying that these Biblical spirits might serve a modern epic in place of pagan gods.[6] M. Audra thinks that these guardian spirits served the *Temple of Fame* 'en guise de "machines" '. If this conjecture be correct, the poem as Steele saw it must have been

1. *id.*, p. 35. For particulars of an untraced letter to Steele, which empowers him to do what he pleases with a paper that Pope has written (and which has been thought to be *The Temple of Fame*, but which might perhaps equally well be some prose piece) see *Pope's Corresp.*, i 165, and *ELH* (*A Journal of English Literary History*), viii, 1941, p. 144.

2. Letter to Ford: 'Pope has been in the Country, near [*torn*] but I expect him in Town this Week to forward the Printing of his Homer, which is already begun to be printed off; he will publish his Temple of Fame as soon as he comes to Town' (*The Letters of Jonathan Swift to Charles Ford*, ed. D. Nichol Smith, 1935, p. 224).

3. op. cit., p. 35.

4. *id.*, p. 36.

5. In a letter of 6 Dec. 1712 Pope told Steele to do as he pleased with a 'paper' —presumably *The Temple of Fame* (see *The Correspondence of Richard Steele*, ed. Rae Blanchard, 1941, p. 66).

6. p. 378. The Dryden reference is to *Essays*, ii 34 ff.

very different from its final version. It is perhaps more likely that the spirits, unlike the sylphs in the *Rape of the Lock*, were of only passing importance, and confined to a couplet or two.

On 1 February 1714–15 Lintott paid Pope £32 5s. od. for the poem.[1] On the same day it was entered in the Stationers' Register.[2] The *Daily Courant*, again on the same day, announced

> This Day is Published, The Temple of Fame: A Vision by Mr. Pope. Printed for Bernard Lintott between the Two Temple-Gates in Fleetstreet.

The *Post Boy* for 3–5, for 5–8, and for 8–10 February belatedly announced the same news, adding that the price was 1s. The second edition was announced in the *Daily Courant* of 8 October:

> This Day is Published, the 2d Edition of, The Temple of Fame: A Vision. Written by Mr. Pope. Also the 4th Edition of his Rape of the Lock. . .

By 1720 or earlier Lintott was trying to sell off the remaining copies of this second edition by the help of a frontispiece which 'Lud. Cheron inv.' and 'Saml. Gribelin Junr. Sculp.'[3] There is no later separate edition.

1. Nichols, viii 300. The high prices paid by Lintott here and for the *Key to the Lock* are probably retrospective acknowledgement of the success of the *Rape of the Lock*.

2. See C. W. Dilke's MS. 'Chronology' of Pope's life (*B.M.*, 12274 i 12), p. 77.

3. See Griffith, No. 45 and *B.M.* copy, 12274.h.8. The plate bears little resemblance to the poem. It represents Fame as flying. The background is a small square undecorated temple. The headpiece (signed 'S. Gribelin') in the quarto *Works* of 1717 (sig. Z 2r) is much more appropriate: see Plate II.

NOTE ON THE TEXT

The text of the first edition is almost perfect in accuracy and was derived from Pope's doubtless exquisite MS. In the second edition the spelling and capitals are varied a little, and a *-k* is added to most epithets ending in *-ic*. There is no evidence that Pope has been consulted. I have not seen a copy of the poem as reprinted for T. Johnson in 1716 in a volume containing also the *Essay on Criticism*, *Windsor Forest*, and the *Ode for St. Cecilia's Day* [Griffith 63]. In the 1717 *Works* most of the changes introduced are important. Three new lines—on Marcus Aurelius (165–7)—are added, and two of the three couplets which follow are thoroughly revised. There are four variants in single words. At l. 349 the alexandrine is reduced to a pentameter, but the other alexandrines are allowed to remain. Some commas are added. L. 21 is indented to make a paragraph-opening.[1]

The 1718 English edition of the *Works* (there was a Dublin one also) does not incorporate the revisions of 1717 and so is textually negligible. It may have been set up from the text as it appeared in the 1716 reprint, since the publisher of that volume is the "T.J." who printed the volume of 1718. The text of the 1726 edition (*Miscellany Poems*, vol. I [Griffith 164, variant a (?)]) is puzzling. It seems to have been set up from a 1715 edition corrected in accordance with the text of 1717, but at eleven points introduces new readings: the couplet concerning lewd tales and unknown duchesses (ll. 388–9) is omitted and two paragraph-openings are reduced to the ranks. But all these changes, whether or not they were authorized by Pope, are ignored in later editions.[2]

---

1. An antiquated spelling and a bad misprint occur at ll. 508 and 512 respectively: 'Tenour' and 'are'. In the copy that Pope gave to his friend James Eckersall (*B.M.*, C. 59 i 20) neither reading has been corrected but 'ure' has been written (above the line) over the letters 'our', and 'at' similarly over 'are'. The correction 'ure' is written in a 'print' hand and is probably Pope's own work.

2. The following are the variants of 1726:

25. Then gazing up,] I look'd, and first *1726*.
30. And seem'd to distant Sight of] And distant gazers thought it *1726*.
62. Pile!] work! *1726*.
65. Dome] pile *1726*.
167. Patron] patern *1726*.

Of the four later editions, the only one of textual interest is that of the *Works* of 1736 [Griffith 418]. The importance of this text is equal to that of the 1717 edition, which it resembles again in having one or two obvious misprints (at l. 336, e.g., it reads 'year' for 'ear', a slip retained in 1741). One line (72) is changed radically. But the new readings mainly affect verbs—past tenses become present at ll. 87–8 and 319, present tenses become imperative at ll. 86 and 368, and conditional at l. 410. In changing the first person to the third in part of the last paragraph of the poem, Pope seems to dissociate himself from the company of the wits who live in vain and impecunious expectation of fame. I am not sure that the 1736 variant at l. 208 (retained in 1741–51) is not a misprint, but the general authority of the text has advised against rejection.

The text chosen as basis for the present edition is the interesting, slightly eccentric one of the first edition, which Pope almost certainly saw through the press.[1] The capitalization of this text may, of course, be put down as much to the fashion adopted in octavo books as to Pope's MS. But the spelling, italics, etc., are probably derived from Pope and represent the poem for what it always was, a poem of the early part of Pope's career. I have altered the text of the

244. *1726 does not open new paragraph.*
270. the tuneful] th' immortal *1726.*
279. fill] fill'd *1726.*
313. Fill the wide] Reach o'er the *1726.*
388 f. *om. 1726.*
392. *1726 does not open new paragraph.*

I have paid no attention to Warburton's antics at l. 86. His edition prints 'behold a sudden Thebes aspire!' but the list of errata (p. ii) directs the change to 'beholds' which had been the original reading. I have considered this direction to be due to a mistaken reading of 'behold' not as an imperative but as an indicative which ought to have been plural. But if the tense is wrong, then the pointing is wrong also—an indicative does not require an exclamation mark. The errata should have changed both readings if it changed any, and may therefore be supposed to be wholly at fault.

1. See Gay's letter to Ford, p. 243 above. One small point in the text of the first edition may be worth a note: at l. 364 occurs the exclamation 'O', whereas in the final paragraph, at ll. 517 and 524, it is spelt 'Oh'. This may mean that the passages are of different dates in the MS.: one would imagine that the final paragraph is that on which Pope before publication would have expended most pains.

first edition in accordance with Pope's later readings and with the principles described in the General Note on the Text, pp. x f. above.

The scanty verbal changes that Pope made in the notes have been adopted but the textual apparatus records only those made in the 'Advertisement'. The notes remain in 1741–51 as they were in 1736: I have not indicated their appearance later than 1736. Pope's notes are distinguished by italic. His quotations from Chaucer have been placed together in Appendix G, pp. 403 ff.

The title-page of 1715 reads: THE || TEMPLE || OF || FAME: || A VISION. [*etc.*]. 1717–51 read: THE || TEMPLE || OF FAME. || Written in the Year 1711.

KEY TO THE CRITICAL APPARATUS

1715*a* = The first edition, octavo, Griffith 36.
1715*b* = The second edition, octavo, Griffith 45.
1717 = Works, quarto, Griffith 79.
1736 = Works, vol. iii, octavo, Griffith 418.
1741 = Works, vol. 1, part ii, octavo, Griffith 521.
1745 = Works, vol. 1, part ii, octavo, Griffith 611.
1751 = Works, ed. Warburton, vol. ii, Griffith 644.

THE TEMPLE OF FAME.

Written in the Year 1711.

Advertisement.

THE *Hint of the following Piece was taken from* Chaucer'*s* House of Fame. *The Design is in a manner entirely alter'd, the Descriptions and most of the particular Thoughts my own: Yet I could not suffer it to be printed without this Acknowledgement, or think a Concealment of this Nature the less unfair for being common. The Reader who would compare this with* Chaucer, *may begin with his Third Book of* Fame, *there being nothing in the Two first Books that answers to their Title.*

4 f. *or think . . . common.*] *om. 1736–51 which replace preceding comma by a period.*

7 *Title*] title: Wherever any hint is taken from him, the passage itself is set down in the marginal notes. *1736–51.*

Cf. Introduction, p. 222 above.

3. *particular Thoughts*] thoughts on particular heroes.

3 ff. *Yet . . . common.*] Gerard Langbaine, in his *Momus Triumphans* (1687) and his *Account of the English Dramatic Poets* (1691), had attacked contemporary dramatists for unacknowledged thefts from earlier playwrights. *The Parliament of Birds* (1712) owes something to Chaucer in general idea. But Pope probably has principally in mind the debts of Yalden's *Temple of Fame* and the *Steeleids* to the *Hous of Fame*. Neither of them mentions Chaucer.

5 ff. *The Reader . . . Title*] Pope takes a few details from Book ii, and specifies two of them in his notes on 11 ff. and 428 ff. See also my note on 21 ff.

[NOTE]

S*OME modern Criticks, from a pretended Refinement of Taste, have declar'd themselves unable to relish allegorical Poems. 'Tis not easy to penetrate into the meaning of this Criticism; for if* Fable *be allow'd one of the chief Beauties, or as* Aristotle *calls it, the very* Soul *of Poetry, 'tis hard to comprehend how that Fable should be the less valuable for having a Moral. The Ancients constantly made use of Allegories: My Lord* Bacon *has compos'd an express Treatise in proof of this, entitled,* The Wisdom of the Antients; *where the Reader may see several particular Fictions exemplify'd and explain'd with great Clearness, Judgment and Learning. The Incidents indeed, by which the Allegory is convey'd, must be vary'd, according to the different Genius or Manners of different Times: and they should never be spun too long, or too much clog'd with trivial Circumstances, or little Particularities. We find an uncommon Charm in Truth, when it is convey'd by this Side-way to our Understanding; and 'tis observable, that even in the most ignorant Ages this way of Writing has found Reception. Almost all the Poems in the old* Provençal *had this Turn; and from these it was that* Petrarch *took the Idea of his Poetry. We have his* Trionfi *in this kind; and* Boccace *pursu'd in the same Track. Soon after* Chaucer *introduc'd it here, whose* Romaunt of the Rose, Court of Love, Flower and the Leaf, House of Fame, *and some others of his Writings are Masterpieces of this sort. In Epick Poetry, 'tis true, too nice and exact a Pursuit of the Allegory is justly esteem'd a Fault; and* Chaucer *had the Discernment to avoid it in his* Knight's Tale, *which was an Attempt towards an Epick*

See Intro., pp. 220 ff.

16. *old Provençal*] The Provençal poets had been introduced into English criticism by Rymer (*Short View of Tragedy,* 1693, chs. v and vi) from whom Dryden learned of them. 'Rymer knew something about Provençal poetry, and something about Chaucer, and through Dryden and Pope has made it a matter of traditional belief that Chaucer belongs, in some way or other, to "the Provençal School". Dryden seems not to have distinguished between Provençal and old French' (Ker's note, Dryden's *Essays,* ii 308). Pope follows Dryden in not discriminating.

17. *Trionfi*] Translated by Henry Parker Lord Morley in 1554. *The Temple of Fame* owes nothing to the fourth of them, the *Trionfo della Fama.*

18. *Boccace*] Canto vi of Boccaccio's *Amorosa Visione* includes a *Triumpho di Gloria.*

19 f. *Flower and the Leaf*] First suspected as apocryphal by Tyrwhitt.

Poem. Ariosto, *with less judgment, gave intirely into it in his* Orlando; *which tho carry'd to an Excess, had yet so much Reputation in* Italy, *that* Tasso (*who reduc'd Heroick Poetry to the juster Standard of the Antients*) *was forc'd to prefix to his Work a scrupulous Explanation of the Allegory of it, to which the Fable it-self could scarce have directed his Readers. Our Countryman* Spencer *follow'd, whose Poem is almost intirely allegorical, and imitates the manner of* Ariosto *rather than that of* Tasso. *Upon the whole, one may observe this sort of Writing* (*however discontinu'd of late*) *was in all Times so far from being rejected by the best Poets, that some of them have rather err'd by insisting on it too closely, and carrying it too far: And that to infer from thence that the Allegory it-self is vicious, is a presumptuous Contradiction to the Judgment and Practice of the greatest Genius's, both antient and modern.* [*P. 1715 only*]

[In 1736–51 the preceding note was reduced as follows, and appended to l. 1.]

This Poem is introduced in the manner of the Provencial *Poets, whose works were for the most part Visions, or pieces of imagination, and constantly descriptive. From these,* Petrarch *and* Chaucer *frequently borrow the idea of their poems. See the* Trionfi *of the former, and the* Dream, Flower and the Leaf, *&c. of the latter. The Author of this therefore chose the same sort of Exordium.*

---

4. *the Dream,*] Probably the 'Death of Blanche the Duchess' which in the Speght edition of 1687 is headed 'The Book commonly entitled, *Chaucer*'s *Dream*.' This edition also contains another poem (not suspected as apocryphal) which treats the same theme and is called 'Chaucer's Dream'. It immediately precedes the 'Flower and the Leaf'.

5 f. This implies Pope's reason for substituting the spring setting for Chaucer's unconventional December.

THE TEMPLE OF FAME

In that soft Season when descending Showers
Call forth the Greens, and wake the rising Flowers;
When opening Buds salute the welcome Day,
And Earth relenting feels the Genial Ray;
As balmy Sleep had charm'd my Cares to Rest,
And Love it self was banish'd from my Breast,
(What Time the Morn mysterious Visions brings,
While purer Slumbers spread their golden Wings)
A Train of Phantoms in wild Order rose,
And, join'd, this Intellectual Scene compose.

---

1 f. Cf. Dryden, *Georgics*, ii 457: 'In this soft Season', which Addison had echoed, *Letter from Italy*, l. 7; and iii 500 f.:

> But when the Western Winds with vital pow'r
> Call forth the tender Grass, and budding Flower.

3. Cf. Dryden, 'Flower and the Leaf', ll. 8 ff.: 'And Buds . . .

> Salute the welcome Sun, and entertain the Day'.

4. *relenting*] 'melt[ing] under the influence of heat' (OED). Cf. Ogilby, *Georgic* i (ed. 1684, p. 50):

> When first the Spring the Frost-bound Hills unbinds,
> And harder Gleab relents with Vernal Winds;

and Pope's *Pastorals*, i 69. 'Relent' is a favourite verb in seventeenth- and eighteenth-century poetry.

5 f. Cf. Dryden, 'Flower and the Leaf', ll. 24 f.:

> Cares had I none to keep me from my Rest,
> For Love had never enter'd in my Breast.

7 f. Morning dreams were supposed to be particularly significant. Cf. Dryden, 'Cock and the Fox', ll. 205 f.:

> Believe me, Madam, Morning Dreams foreshow
> Th' Event of Things, and future Weal or Woe;

and *Rape of the Lock*, i 20 ff.

purer Slumbers] *The Athenian Oracle*, iv 226, noted that morning dreams are less 'irregular' than 'those we have in our first Sleep . . . Because the Brain in the Morning, is not so loaden with the Fumes of the Supper's Digestion'.

9. Cf. Dryden, 'Eleonora', ll. 311 ff.:

> As gentle Dreams our waking Thoughts pursue;
> Or, one Dream pass'd, we slide into a new;
> (So close they follow, such wild Order keep,
> We think our selves awake, and are asleep:) . . .

10. *Intellectual*] 'Ideal; perceived by the intellect, not the senses' (Johnson's *Dictionary* which cites this line, and also Cowley, 'The Complaint', l. 1:

I stood, methought, betwixt Earth, Seas, and Skies;
The whole Creation open to my Eyes:
In Air self-ballanc'd hung the Globe below,
Where Mountains rise, and circling Oceans flow;
Here naked Rocks, and empty Wastes were seen,
There Tow'ry Cities, and the Forests green:
Here sailing Ships delight the wand'ring Eyes;
There Trees, and intermingl'd Temples rise:
Now a clear Sun the shining Scene displays,
The transient Landscape now in Clouds decays.
O'er the wide Prospect as I gaz'd around,

21 *1715 do not open new paragraph.*

In a deep Vision's intellectual Scene).

Cf. also Elizabeth Singer Rowe's 'Vision' (*Poetical Miscellanies*, v, 1704, p. 196):

No wild uncouth *Chimera's* intervene,
To break the perfect intellectual Scene.

11 ff. For Pope's note and quotation from Chaucer, see Appendix G, item a, p. 403.

Chaucer follows Ovid, *Metam.*, xii 39 f. which Dryden translates as:

Full in the midst of this Created Space,
Betwixt Heav'n, Earth, and Skies, there stands a Place,
Confining on all three . . .

Cf. *Dunciad*, ii 83.

13. Cf. *Par. Lost*, vii 242: And Earth self-ballanc't on her Center hung.

16 ff. Dennis (*Remarks*, 1717, pp. 48 f.) objects to minute vision from such a height. Pope is following Chaucer who is following Ovid's account of the house of Fame, *Metam.*, xii 41 f.:

unde, quod est usquam, quamvis regionibus absit,
inspicitur . . .

17 ff. Cited as an early example of the influence of Claude's paintings on English poetry in E. W. Manwaring's *Italian Landscape in Eighteenth Century England* (1925), p. 97. But the source is at least partly literary: cf. Addison's translation of Ausonius, *Ordo Urbium Nobilium*, vii [Milan] in *Remarks*, p. 51:

Here spacious Baths and Palaces are seen,
And intermingled Temples rise between.

21 ff. Cf. Dryden's Ovid, *Metam.*, xii 73 ff.:

Confus'd, and Chiding, like the hollow Roar
Of Tides, receding from th' insulted Shore:
Or like the broken Thunder, heard from far,

Sudden I heard a wild promiscuous Sound,
Like broken Thunders that at distance roar,
Or Billows murm'ring on the hollow Shoar:
Then gazing up, a glorious Pile beheld,
Whose tow'ring Summit ambient Clouds conceal'd.
High on a Rock of Ice the Structure lay,
Steep its Ascent, and slipp'ry was the Way;
The wond'rous Rock like *Parian* Marble shone,
And seem'd to distant Sight of solid Stone.
Inscriptions here of various Names I view'd,
The greater Part by hostile Time subdu'd;
Yet wide was spread their Fame in Ages past,
And Poets once had promis'd they should last.
Some fresh ingrav'd appear'd of Wits renown'd;
I look'd again, nor cou'd their Trace be found.

When *Jove* to distance drives the rowling War,

which Warton [i 340] rightly preferred to Pope's translation here. Pope, having Ovid–Dryden in mind, omitted to cite Chaucer, *Hous of Fame*, ii 525 ff.:

And what sowne is it like, qd. [the eagle]?
  Peter, lyke the beating of the see,
Qd. I, against the roches halow,
When tempests done her shippes swalow,
And that a man stand out of doute,
A myle thens, and here it route.
  Or els lyke the humbling
After the clappe of a thundring,
When Jouis hath the eyre ybete . . .

26. *ambient*] 'surrounding as a fluid; circumfused' (OED, which cites also *Par. Lost*, vi 481).

27 ff. For Pope's quotation from Chaucer, see Appendix G, item b, pp. 403 f.

28. Cf. Dryden, *Æneid*, vi 193: Smooth the Descent, and easie is the Way.

29. *Parian*] The white marble from the island of Paros, one of the Cyclades, was esteemed by the ancients for statuary. It is, therefore, frequently referred to by English poets at this time; see, e.g., 73 n. below. Pope's comparison improves on Chaucer's: ice resembles marble, and marble is a symbol of literary fame because used for statuary.

31 ff. For Pope's quotation from Chaucer and editor's comment, see Appendix G, item c, p. 404.

35 f. See Introduction, p. 217 above, on Swift.

Criticks I saw, that other Names deface,
And fix their own with Labour in their place:
Their own like others soon their Place resign'd,
Or disappear'd, and left the first behind.
Nor was the Work impair'd by Storms alone,
But felt th'Approaches of too warm a Sun;
For Fame, impatient of Extreams, decays
Not more by Envy than Excess of Praise.
Yet Part no Injuries of Heav'n cou'd feel,
Like Crystal faithful to the graving Steel:
The Rock's high Summit, in the Temple's Shade,
Nor Heat could melt, nor beating Storm invade.
There Names inscrib'd unnumber'd Ages past
From Time's first Birth, with Time it self shall last;
These ever new, nor subject to Decays,
Spread, and grow brighter with the Length of Days.
  So *Zembla*'s Rocks (the beauteous Work of Frost)
Rise white in Air, and glitter o'er the Coast;
Pale Suns, unfelt, at distance roll away,
And on th' impassive Ice the Lightnings play:
Eternal Snows the growing Mass supply,
Till the bright Mountains prop th' incumbent Sky:
As *Atlas* fix'd, each hoary Pile appears,
The gather'd Winter of a thousand Years.
  On this Foundation *Fame*'s high Temple stands;
Stupendous Pile! not rear'd by mortal Hands.
Whate'er proud *Rome*, or artful *Greece* beheld,

37 other] others *1715*.

41 ff. and 45 ff. For Pope's quotations from Chaucer, see Appendix G, items d and e, p. 404.

53 ff. For Pope's appeal to science to justify the rock of ice, see Appendix H, pp. 410 f.

62. Cf. 2 Corinthians, v 1: Dryden, *Hind and the Panther*, i 494:

Eternal house, not built with mortal hands!

and *Iliad*, xiii 35.

63 f. Cf. *Par. Lost*, i 717 ff., and Dryden, 'Palamon and Arcite', ii 450 f.

Or elder *Babylon*, its Frame excell'd.
Four Faces had the Dome, and ev'ry Face
Of various Structure, but of equal Grace:
Four brazen Gates, on Columns lifted high,
Salute the diff'rent Quarters of the Sky.
Here fabled Chiefs in darker Ages born,
Or Worthys old, whom Arms or Arts adorn,
Who Cities rais'd, or tam'd a monstrous Race;

65. *Dome*] in its meaning of (dignified) *building* (Latin, *domus*). Contrast l. 90 below.

65 ff. *The Temple is describ'd to be square, the four Fronts with open Gates facing the different Quarters of the World, as an Intimation that all Nations of the Earth may alike be receiv'd into it. The Western Front is of* Grecian *Architecture: the Dorick Order was peculiarly sacred to Heroes and Worthies. Those whose Statues are after mention'd, were the first Names of old* Greece *in Arms and Arts.* [P. 1715, 1736.]

In giving the temple four faces, Pope is imitating *Tatler* 81: 'In the Midst of these happy Fields [on the top of the mountain] there stood a Palace of a very glorious Structure: It had four great Folding-Doors, that faced the Four several Quarters of the World'; which may be indebted to the Duke of Buckingham's translation of 'Le Temple de la Mort', ll. 15 ff. (see Introduction, p. 216 n.):

Within this Vale, a famous Temple stands,
Old as the World it self, which it commands;
Round is its figure, and four Iron-Gates
Divide Mankind, by order of the Fates.
There Come in Crouds, doom'd to one common Grave,
The Young, the Old, the Monarch, and the Slave.

The Doric order was held to employ 'the heroick and gigantine manner [which] does excellently well [for ports, citadels, fortresses of towns, etc.], discovering a certain *masculine* and natural beauty, which is properly that the *French* call *la grand* [sic] *Maniere* . . . *Vitruvius* . . . compares our *Dorique* to a robust and strong Man, such as an *Hercules* might be . . .' (Evelyn, *The Whole Body of Antient and Modern Architecture*, ed. 1680, pp. 10 ff. Cf. Vitruvius, *De Architectura*, IV i).

66. *equal Grace*] Cf. Dryden, 'Palamon and Arcite', ii 526.

67 f. Cf. Dryden, *Æneid*, vi 744 f.:

Wide is the fronting Gate, and rais'd on high
With Adamantine Columns, threats the Sky.

70. *Arms or Arts*] A common phrase throughout seventeenth-century poetry, often with *and* instead of *or*. Cf. Dryden, Juvenal, *Sat.*, iii 143: 'that Town which Arms and Arts adorn'.

The Walls in venerable Order grace:
Heroes in animated Marble frown,
And Legislators seem to think in Stone.
Westward, a sumptuous Frontispiece appear'd,
On Doric Pillars of white Marble rear'd,
Crown'd with an Architrave of antique Mold,
And Sculpture rising on the roughen'd Gold.
In shaggy Spoils here *Theseus* was beheld,
And *Perseus* dreadful with *Minerva*'s Shield:
There great *Alcides* stooping with his Toil,

72 The fourfold Walls in breathing Statues grace: *1715–17.*

72. *Order*] The effigies on the walls of the palace of Virgil's Latinus are placed 'ex ordine' (*Æneid*, vii 177), to which passage Pope is indebted for the manner of decorating the outside of the temple.

73 f. Cf. Addison, *Letter from Italy*, l. 90:

And Emperors in *Parian* Marble frown;

and *Æneid*, vi 847 f.

75. *Frontispiece*] 'The principal face or front of a building; "but the term is more usually applied to the decorated entrance of a building" ' (OED).

75 ff. Cf. *Par. Lost*, i 714 ff.:

. . . Doric pillars overlaid
With Golden Architrave; nor did there want
Cornice or Freeze, with bossy Sculptures grav'n.

The whole description of the temple is greatly indebted to Milton's palace of the Fallen Angels. See later notes. Cf. also Dryden, Ovid's *Metam.*, xii 330 f.:

An ample Goblet stood, of antick Mold,
And rough with Figures of the rising Gold.

There are several earlier uses of 'rough' and 'rising' with reference to statuary and gold: see, e.g., Dryden's *Æneid*, viii 830, Addison's *Letter from Italy*, l. 73, and Pope's *Thebais*, i 536.

79. He is so represented in the engraving opposite p. 1 [second series] in Plutarch, i.

81 f. *This Figure of* Hercules *is drawn with an eye to the Position* [= posture] *of the famous Statue of* Farnese. [P. 1715, 1736.]

For Pope's acquaintance with the statue, see Introduction, pp. 237 f. The Farnesian Hercules was already famous in English literature, see, e.g., Dryden (*Essays*, ii 121) and Addison (*Remarks*, p. 349) who calls it one of 'the Four finest Figures perhaps that are now Extant'. The Hesperian fruit are the apples which the statue holds in his right hand. They have been added during restoration (probably soon after the discovery of the statue in 1540) and so may not be

Rests on his Club, and holds th' *Hesperian* Spoil.
Here *Orpheus* sings; Trees moving to the Sound
Start from their Roots, and form a Shade around:
Amphion there the loud creating Lyre
Strikes, and behold a sudden *Thebes* aspire!
Cythæron's Ecchoes answer to his Call,
And half the Mountain rolls into a Wall:
There might you see the length'ning Spires ascend,
The Domes swell up, the widening Arches bend,
The growing Tow'rs like Exhalations rise,
And the huge Columns heave into the Skies.
The Eastern Front was glorious to behold,

86 behold . . . aspire!] beholds . . . aspire; *1715–17*.
87 f. answer . . . rolls] answer'd . . . roll'd *1715–17*.

authentic. 'To mention the Hesperian apples, which the artist flung backwards, and almost concealed as an inconsiderable object, and which therefore scarcely appear in the statue, was below the notice of Pope' (Warton, i 344). Warton also considered that Pope omits 'the characteristical excellencies [of the statue], the uncommon breadth of the shoulders, the knottiness and spaciousness of the chest, the firmness and protuberance of the muscles in each limb, particularly the legs, and the majestic vastness of the whole figure . . .' (i 343). Cf. *Tatler* 81: '*Hercules* leaning an Arm on his Club.'

83 ff. See Introduction, p. 239. Cf. Horace, *Ars Poetica*, ll. 391 ff., where Orpheus and Amphion symbolize the civilizing powers of poetry in primitive times.

83 f.] Cf. Addison, 'A Song For St. Cecilia's Day', iii 9 ff.:

> When *Orpheus* strikes the trembling Lyre . . .
> The moving woods attended as he play'd,
> And *Rhodope* was left without a shade;

and Pope, *Pastorals*, ii 74.

85. *loud*] Cf. l. 127 below.

87. *Cythæron*] = Cithæron, a mountain in Boetia.

91. Cf. *Par. Lost*, i 710 f.: 'a Fabrick huge
> Rose like an Exhalation'.

93–108. Cyrus *was the Beginning of the* Persian, *as* Ninus *was of the* Assyrian *Monarchy. The* Magi *and* Chaldeans (*the chief of whom was* Zoroaster) *employ'd their Studies upon Magick and Astrology, which was in a manner almost all the Learning of the antient* Asian *People. We have scarce any Account of a moral Philosopher except* Confucius, *the great Lawgiver of the* Chinese, *who liv'd about two thousand Years ago.* [P. 1715, 1736.]

With Diamond flaming, and *Barbaric* Gold.
There *Ninus* shone, who spread th' *Assyrian* Fame,
And the Great Founder of the *Persian* Name:
There in long Robes the Royal *Magi* stand,
Grave *Zoroaster* waves the circling Wand:
The sage *Chaldæans* rob'd in White appear'd,
And *Brachmans* deep in desart Woods rever'd.
These stop'd the Moon, and call'd th' unbody'd Shades

Temple found in Cyrus 'the truest Character that can be given of Heroick Virtue' (p. 159). His history could be read in Herodotus, Book i. Temple (p. 155) gives Ninus as the greatest hero of the Assyrians.

Pope does not seem to differentiate the various groups of 'magicians'. They were believed all to belong to the same society (see, e.g., Thomas Herbert's *Some Yeares Travels*, 1677, pp. 223 f.).

94. Cf. *Par. Lost*, ii 4: '*Barbaric* Pearl & Gold'.

97. *Royal*] The magi who visited the new-born Christ were supposed to be kings, and the point is 'proved' in Hakewill's *Apology* (ed. 1635, p. 8). One of the four 'royal tutors' appointed to oversee the education of the prince destined to become king was a magus (see T. Stanley, *History of Chaldaick Philosophy*, ed. 1701, p. 31a; and cf. Selden, *De Dis Syris*, ed. 1681, p. 244).

98. Zoroaster is included in Petrarch's *Trionfo della Fama* (ii 125) as the inventor of magic. The wands or rods of the magi are familiar from Exodus, vii 12, and Dryden, *Hind and the Panther*, ii 538 f. Cf. also Addison's epilogue to Lansdowne's *British Enchanters* (1706), of the 'good Enchantress' of the play:

Let Sage *Urganda* wave the circling Wand.

99. I have found no source for the white robes of the Chaldeans. The magi (see Diogenes Laertius's survey of ancient 'philosophy' introducing his *Lives*, translated by 'several Hands' in 1696, i, p. 6), the Brahmins (Dacier's *Pythagoras*, p. 136), and the Druids (Pliny, *Nat. Hist.*, xvi 94) all wore white robes. The Egyptian priests wore linen (Herodotus, i 158). And so, since all ancient magic was supposed to be related, the Chaldeans also.

100. The Brahmins spent thirty-seven years on their education in 'Colleges, or separate abodes in Woods and Fields' (Temple, p. 9).

101. Cf. Oldham's translation (*Remains*, 1687, p. 18) of Virgil, *Eclogue* viii 69:

Charms in her wonted Course can stop the Moon.

unbody'd Shades] Cf. Philips, *Cyder* (*Whole Works*, 1720, p. 43 [second series]).

101 f. Pope seems to have in mind (1) Statius, *Thebaid*, iv 419 ff.; (2) Lucan, vi 423 ff.; (3) Lucian, especially i 377 (where 'Banquets' for ghosts are mentioned) and iv 202 ff.; and (4) Tasso, XIII ii ff., where the enchanter Ismeno calls up 'wicked Sprites' in a 'Grove':

United there the Ghosts and Goblins meet

To Midnight Banquets in the glimmering Glades;
Made visionary Fabricks round them rise,
And airy Spectres skim before their Eyes;
Of *Talismans* and *Sigils* knew the Pow'r,
And careful watch'd the Planetary Hour.
Superior, and alone, *Confucius* stood,
Who taught that useful Science, to be *good*.
  But on the South a long Majestic Race

To frolick with their Mates in silent Night...
  And there with hellish Pomp their Banquets brought
  They Solemnize, thus the vain Pagans thought...
Thither went *Ismen* old with Tresses hore...
  And there in Silence deaf, and mirksom shade,
  His Characters and Circles vain he made...
He stroke the Earth thrice with his charmed Rod,
Wherewith dead Bones he makes from Grave to rise...

103 f. For a description of the acts of the fakirs see Tavernier, *Collections of Travels . . . Being The Travels of Monsieur Tavernier Bernier* [and others], 1684, ii, pp. 97 ff. Cf. Addison's translation of Claudian's *In Rufinum*, i 123 ff., in *Remarks*, p. 3:

Ulysses here the Blood of Victims shed,
And rais'd the pale Assembly of the Dead...
The lab'ring Plow-man oft with Horror spies
Thin airy Shapes, that o'er the Furrows rise,
(A dreadful Scene!) and skim before his Eyes.

104 f. A sigil was 'an occult sign or device supposed to have mysterious powers' (OED); at a 'Planetary Hour' the planets stood in significant conjunctions. Cf. Dryden, *Palamon and Arcite*, ii 483: 'Sigils fram'd in Planetary Hours'.

107 f. Temple considers Confucius as one of the 'two great Heroes of the *Chinese* Nation . . . the most learned, wise and virtuous of all the *Chineses*. . . He writ many Tracts, and in them digested . . . all that he thought necessary or useful to Mankind . . . In short, the whole scope of all *Confutius* has writ, seems aimed only, at teaching men to live well, and to govern well; how Parents, Masters and Magistrates should rule, and how Children, Servants and Subjects should obey' (pp. 177 ff.). Temple furnishes the date 'above two thousand Years ago' (p. 178). He notes that the works of Confucius 'have lately in *France*, been printed in the Latin Tongue' (p. 179 f.).

109–118. *The Learning of the old* Egyptian *Priests consisted for the most part in Geometry and Astronomy: They also preserv'd the History of their Nation. Their greatest Hero upon Record is* Sesostris, *whose Actions and Conquests may be seen at large in* Diodorus, *&c. He is said to have caus'd the Kings he vanquish'd to draw him in his*

Of *Ægypt*'s Priests the gilded Niches grace,
Who measur'd Earth, describ'd the Starry Spheres,
And trac'd the long Records of Lunar Years.
High on his Car *Sesostris* struck my View,
Whom scepter'd Slaves in golden Harness drew:
His Hands a Bow and pointed Jav'lin hold,
His Giant Limbs are arm'd in Scales of Gold.
Between the Statues Obelisks were plac'd,

Chariot. The Posture of his Statue, in these Verses, is correspondent to the Description which Herodotus *gives of one of them remaining in his own time.* [P. 1715, 1736: 1717–26 adapt last sentence as note on l. 115.]

Concerning the Egyptian priests, see Diod. Sic., I iv and vi, Herodotus, i 139 and 191, and Wotton, p. 107.

Diodorus records of Sesostris, whom Wotton (p. 109) calls 'the only great Conqueror of [the Egyptian] Nation', that 'Although [he] was eminent in many great and worthy Actions, yet the most stately and magnificent of all, was that relating to the Princes in his Progresses . . . he receiv'd [conquered kings] with all the Marks of Honour and Respect; save that when he went into the Temple or the City, his Custom was to cause the Horses to be unharnest out of his Chariot, and in their Room Four Kings, and other Princes to draw it' (I iv; cf. Lucan x 276 f.). He records furthermore that 'In some places he set up his own Statue, carv'd in Stone (arm'd with a Bow and a Lance)' (*ibid.*). 'Two images . . . of this King, carv'd on Stone, are seen in *Ionia*. . . His Figure is five Palms in Height, holding a Bow in one Hand and an Arrow in the other, and arm'd after the Ægyptian and Æthiopian Manner' (Herodotus, i 194 f.).

110. *gilded Niches*] Cf. Lansdowne, *The British Enchanters*, II i: '*Egypt*'s Temples . . . Pompously deck'd . . . With glitt'ring Gold'. Herodotus notes the Egyptian practice of gilding their images, see, e.g., i 212. Pope may also have in mind the belief that the Egyptian priests had discovered the philosopher's stone (see Wotton, pp. 120 ff.).

112. Cf. Prior, 'Carmen Sæculare', 1700, p. 1: 'the long Records of Ages past'.

long Records] The Egyptian priests 'read to [Herodotus] from a Book, the Names of three hundred and thirty Kings who had reign'd after *Menes* [the first king of Egypt]' (i 191).

Lunar Years] 'Lunary [also called *Lunar*] Years of Thirty Days, as the *Egyptians* do account' (gloss in Diod. Sic., I ii).

116. *Scales of Gold*] Cf. Dryden, *Æneid*, ix 958, of the giant Bitias:

Nor Coat of double Mail, with Scales of Gold.

117. *Obelisks*] Herodotus mentions 'two magnificent Obeliscks which [Pheron the son of Sesostris] erected in the Temple of the Sun, each of one Stone only, a hundred Cubits in Height, and eight Cubits in Breadth' (i 198). Cf. also p. 237,

And the Learn'd Walls with Hieroglyphics grac'd.
Of *Gothic* Structure was the Northern Side,
O'er-wrought with Ornaments of barb'rous Pride.
There huge Colosses rose, with Trophies crown'd,
And *Runic* Characters were grav'd around:

---

and Diod. Sic., I iv. F. M. Misson notes of the Egyptian obelisks in Rome that 'these Monuments were erected by the *Egyptians*, both to serve for Ornaments, and to honour the Heroes of their Nation' (II pt i 105).

118. *Hieroglyphics*] '[inscriptions] in *Egyptian* Letters call'd Hieoroglifics' (Diod. Sic., I iv).

119–131. *The Architecture is agreeable to that part of the World. The Learning of the* Northern *Nations lay more obscure than that of the rest.* Zamolxis *was the Disciple of* Pythagoras, *who taught the Immortality of the Soul to the* Scythians. Odin, *or* Woden, *was the great Legislator and Hero of the* Goths. *They tell us of him that being subject to Fits, he persuaded his Followers, that during those Trances he receiv'd Inspirations from whence he dictated his Laws. He is said to have been the Inventor of the* Runic *Characters.* [P. 1715, 1736: 1717–26 insert notes at 123 and 124 on Zamolxis and Woden.]

The 'savage', 'fierce' Scythians, who inhabited 'that vast Northern Region which extends from [Norway] to the farthest Bounds of *Tartary* upon the Eastern Ocean' (Temple's *Introduction*, pp. 24 f.) are treated in section iv of his *Of Heroick Virtue*. Herodotus' fourth Book concerns the Eastern Scythians, who 'drink . . . the Blood of the first Prisoner [they take]' (i 375) and of whom Tamburlaine was the hero (Temple, p. 225), but Pope confines his attention mainly to the Western Scythians who had recently become the object of special study (see M. E. Seaton).

Among the 'great Men' who 'have come out of [Pythagoras'] School' was 'his Slave Xamolxis' (Dacier, *Pythagoras*, p. 38). Herodotus (i 392) believes that he lived much earlier than Pythagoras and that he may, or may not, have taught the idea of immortality to the Scythians. Temple (p. 231) is similarly undecided.

Long accounts of Odin are found in R. Sheringham's *De Anglorum Gentis Origine* and in Sammes, pp. 435 ff. But Pope may have read no further than Temple's essay: '*Odin* or *Woden* . . . was the first and great Hero of the Western *Scythians* . . . all agree, that this *Odin* was the first Inventer of, or at least the first Engraver of the Runick Letters or Characters . . . he instituted many excellent Orders and Laws' (pp. 234 ff.). He is one of 'The Three Saxon Gods . . . placed on Pedestals' in Dryden's *King Arthur*, I ii.

For Odin's trances see Introduction, p. 235.

121. *Colosses*] Pope may have in mind the 'high Statues . . . firmly bound fast with Lead or Iron, that they be not cast down by the violence of the Winds' which are erected on the mountains 'that divide *Sweden* from *Norway*' (Magnus, II xiii). The form *coloss*(*e*) for *colossus* was common in the seventeenth century (OED).

There sate *Zamolxis* with erected Eyes,
And *Odin* here in mimick Trances dies.
There, on rude Iron Columns smear'd with Blood,
The horrid Forms of *Scythian* Heroes stood,
Druids and *Bards* (their once loud Harps unstrung)
And Youths that dy'd to be by Poets sung.
These and a Thousand more of doubtful Fame,
To whom old Fables gave a lasting Name,
In Ranks adorn'd the Temple's outward Face;
The Wall in Lustre and Effect like Glass,
Which o'er each Object casting various Dies,
Enlarges some, and others multiplies.
Nor void of Emblem was the mystic Wall,
For thus Romantick Fame increases all.
The Temple shakes, the sounding Gates unfold,
Wide Vaults appear, and Roofs of fretted Gold:
Rais'd on a thousand Pillars, wreath'd around

123. *erected*] Cf. Sylvester's Du Bartas, *Divine Weeks*, II i 4 428: 'Heav'n-erected eyes', which became common in later poetry. Cf. l. 236 below.

125 f. In the *Hous of Fame* Chaucer places Josephus and most of the epic poets on pillars of variously graded iron, 'For Iron Martes metall is' (iii 356). Iron is used for Mars's temples in *Æneid*, vii 609 f. and the 'Knight's Tale', 1132 ff. Iron is literally appropriate for the inhabitants of a country whose 'Mines . . . very many, great, divers and very rich [are] principal[ly] Iron' (Magnus, VI i).

127 ff. *These were the Priests and Poets of those People, so celebrated for their savage Virtue. Those heroick Barbarians accounted it a Dishonour to die in their Beds, and rush'd on to certain Death in the Prospect of an After-Life, and for the Glory of a Song from their Bards in Praise of their Actions.* [P. 1715, 1736.]

Accounts of the Druids and Bards are found in Camden's *Britannia* (translated with additions by E. Gibson, 1695, columns xiii ff.) which quotes Caesar, Pliny, Lucan, and Tacitus; in Sammes, i 99 ff.; and in Temple's *Introduction*, 11 ff. Carew had introduced a 'Chorus of Druids and Rivers' into his *Cœlum Britannicum* (printed in Davenant's *Works*, 1673, 360 ff. [first series]).

The loud harps (cf. l. 85 above) are unstrung because no poems survive.

127 f. A neat development of Lucan, i 447–62.

132 ff. For Pope's quotation from Chaucer, see Appendix G, item f, p. 404.

137. Cf. *Tatler* 81: 'On a sudden, the Trumpet swell'd all its Notes into Triumph and Exultation: The whole Fabrick shook, and the Doors flew open.'

138. Cf. *Par. Lost*, i 717: 'The Roof was fretted Gold'.

With Lawrel-Foliage, and with Eagles crown'd:
Of bright, transparent Beryl were the Walls,
The Freezes Gold, and Gold the Capitals:
As Heaven with Stars, the Roof with Jewels glows,
And ever-living Lamps depend in Rows.
Full in the Passage of each spacious Gate
The sage Historians in white Garments wait;
Grav'd o'er their Seats the Form of *Time* was found,
His Scythe revers'd, and both his Pinions bound.
Within, stood Heroes who thro' loud Alarms
In bloody Fields pursu'd Renown in Arms.
High on a Throne with Trophies charg'd, I view'd

---

141. In Chaucer's temple, the outside of the walls was of beryl, the inside being plated with jewelled gold (iii 91 ff., 252 ff.).

143 f. Cf. *Par. Lost*, i 726 ff.:

> . . . from the arched roof
> Pendent by suttle Magic many a row
> Of Starry Lamps and blazing Cressets fed
> With *Naphtha* and *Asphaltus* yeilded light
> As from a sky.

146.] Cf. *Tatler* 81: 'a Band of Historians taking their Station at each Door'. The historians are not allowed to compete for places around the Tables of Fame, since they are janitors (*Tatler* 67). 'The *white garments* are suitable emblems of *pure* purpose and *undecorated* truth' (Wakefield).

147 f. The reversing of insignia or emblems indicated dishonour in heraldry etc. Comus, when ousted, enters with his rod reversed, and Thamesis has his urn reversed in Dryden's *Albion and Albanius*. Time's scythe is shown reversed in the frontispieces of Plutarch, vol. v, and of *Antiquarum Statuarum Vrbis Romae . . . M DC XXI.* Cf. also *Gondibert*, I v 61 2 f.: '*Historians . . .*

> Who thought, swift Time they could in fetters binde'.

151–6. For an analysis of the construction see Introduction, pp. 235 ff. above.

151 f. The estimate of Alexander, repeated in *Essay on Man*, i 160 and iv 220, is that of Lucian, iii 463, of Fontenelle, 1 ff., and, most strongly, of St-Evremond who often discusses Alexander and Caesar. He writes (i 189 f. and ii 27): '*Alexander* [was] Master of the World. . . *Cæsar* [was] one that better understood his own Interests, and was more Master of himself in his Passions. . . *Alexander* . . . was Taught the Knowledge of every thing in Nature, but himself . . . he had little or no Method in his Conquests, and abundance of Irregularity in his Life, for want of knowing what he owed to the Publick, to Private Men, and to himself.' Cf. also the end of Lyly's *Alexander and Campaspe*.

The *Youth* that all things but himself subdu'd;
His Feet on Sceptres and *Tiara's* trod,
And his horn'd Head bely'd the *Lybian* God.
There *Cæsar*, grac'd with both *Minerva's*, shone;
Cæsar, the World's great Master, and his own;
Unmov'd, superior still in every State;
And scarce detested in his Country's Fate.
But chief were those who not for Empire fought,

154 bely'd] express'd *1715–17*.

152. Alexander *the Great: The* Tiara *was the Crown peculiar to the* Asian *Princes: His Desire to be thought the Son of* Jupiter Ammon *caus'd him to wear the Horns of that God, and to represent the same upon his Coins, which was continu'd by several of his Successors.* [P. 1715, 1736: 1717–1726 reduce.]

See Plutarch, iv 223 ff.; Diod. Sic., XVII i–xii; and J. G. Grævius's *Thesaurus Antiquitatum Romanorum*, iv (1697), column 1557.

153. The image was perhaps suggested by Plutarch, iv 296, where Alexander and his men, entering the Persian camp, 'rode over abundance of Gold and Silver that lay scattered about'.

154. Cf. Dryden, 'Alexander's Feast', l. 28:

A Dragon's fiery Form bely'd the God.

bely = to counterfeit (not 'to disguise', as OED gives for this line).

155. See Introduction, pp. 236 f. Cf. Dryden, 'To the Earl of Roscomon', ll. 70 ff.:

Roscomon first in Fields of honour known,
First in the peaceful Triumphs of the Gown;
Who both *Minerva*'s justly makes his own.

156. Cf. Prior, 'Carmen Sæculare', 1700, p. 6 [of William III]:

How o'er Himself, as o'er the World he Reigns.

158. See Plutarch, iv 424 f. After the Civil War and Caesar's defeat of Pompey, opinion concerning him was strongly divided, since the vanquished enemy were his fellow-countrymen. As Prior put it ('Carmen Sæculare', 1700, p. 3):

Julius with Honour tam'd *Rome*'s Foreign Foes;
Too many Patriots fell e're the Dictator rose.

For this reason Temple (pp. 160 f.) denies him the rank of hero. Yet he was made Dictator for life.

159 f. Pope's estimate is Temple's: 'After all that has been said of Conquerors or Conquests, this must be confessed to hold but the second Rank in the pretensions to Heroick Virtue, and that the first has been allowed, to the wise Institution of just Orders and Laws, which frame safe and happy Governments in the world' (pp. 300 f.). 'Safety' is Temple's word, see pp. 149 and 151. For the

But with their Toils their People's Safety bought:
High o'er the rest *Epaminondas* stood;
Timoleon, glorious in his Brother's Blood;
Bold *Scipio*, Saviour of the *Roman* State,
Great in his Triumphs, in Retirement great.

163 Bold] And *1715*.

---

contemporary interest in the theory of *salus populi suprema lex* see L. I. Bredvold, *The Intellectual Milieu of John Dryden*, Ann Arbor, 1934, p. 146. Milton, *Samson Agonistes*, ll. 678 ff. makes the chorus allude to

> . . . such as thou [God of our Fathers] hast solemnly elected,
> With gifts and graces eminently adorn'd
> To some great work, thy glory,
> And people's safety . . .

161. Epaminondas 'was not only the Best and most Expert Commander of any of his own Country, but even of all the *Grecians*; and was likewise a Man of great Learning in the Liberal Sciences . . . among them [i.e., other Greek generals] some one peculiar Excellency was only remarkable in each particular Person; but in him a Constellation of Virtues were Hous'd together' (Diod. Sic., xv iv). His career as Theban general in the war against the Spartans is described at xv vi–x.

162. Timoleon *had sav'd the Life of his Brother* Timophanes *in the Battel between the* Argives *and* Corinthians; *but afterwards kill'd him when he affected the Tyranny, preferring his Duty to his Country to all the Obligations of Blood.* [P. 1715, 1736.]

Pope's note is derived from Diod. Sic., xvi x, rather than Plutarch, ii 238 ff., in which Timoleon stands by weeping while his brother is killed. In his *Timoleon Compar'd with Paulus Emilius*, Plutarch refers to Timoleon's 'just . . . punish[ment of] his Brother' as 'a truly heroick Action' (ii 237).

163 f. Cf. Cowley, 'Of Solitude': 'the Excellent *Scipio*, who was . . . the most Wise, most Worthy, most Happy, and the Greatest of all Mankind . . . after he had made *Rome* Mistress of almost the whole World, he retired himself from it by a voluntary exile, and at a private house in the middle of a wood . . . passed the remainder of his Glorious life no less Gloriously.' Scipio, surnamed Africanus, appears in the *Lives* of Plutarch, particularly in those of T. Q. Flaminius and Fabius Maximus. His expulsion of Hannibal from Italy 'rais'd again the drooping Spirits of the *Romans*, no more to be dejected; and firmly establish'd their Empire, which the Tempest of this *Punick* War had so long caus'd to fluctuate' (Plutarch, i 627). After concluding peace, he refused the honours offered him by the Roman people, retired from politics and died at his country seat in Campania.

And wise *Aurelius*, in whose well-taught Mind
With boundless Pow'r unbounded Virtue join'd,
His own strict Judge, and Patron of Mankind.
Much-suff'ring Heroes next their Honours claim,
Those of less noisy, and less guilty Fame,
Fair Virtue's silent Train: Supreme of these

165–7 *om. 1715.*
168 f. Here too the Wise and Good their Honours claim,
Much-suff'ring Heroes, of less noisy Fame, *1715.*

165–7. Marcus Aurelius is one of the heroes in Temple's list, p. 285, and was 'without Dispute', says Fontenelle's Brutus (p. 55), 'the very best Man in the *Roman* Empire'. Pope designed to have busts of him and Cicero standing along with those of Homer and Virgil in his garden (Spence, p. 273).

165. *well-taught*] One of the teachers of 'that Learned Emperor' was Sextus Chæronensis, the nephew of Plutarch, who taught him 'the *Greek* Tongue, and the Principles of Philosophy' (Dryden's 'Life of Plutarch' in Plutarch, i 3 and 31, first series). His principle of political mercy made him a successful ruler of the provinces. The wise social laws instituted by Marcus Aurelius are set out in André Dacier's life which was translated in Jeremy Collier's *The Emperor Marcus Antoninus His Conversation with Himself* (1701), xlvi ff. Pope refers to this translation at Spence, p. 293.

166. Cf. 'On the Statue of Cleopatra' (*Pope's Own Miscellany*, p. 151):

And boundless pow'r with boundless virtue join'd.

167. *His own strict Judge*] cf. *Im. of Hor.*, Ep. II ii 159. Pope took the phrase from a passage he had admired in Tickell's *On the Prospect of Peace*, 1712 (see *Pope's Corresp.*, i 157).

Patron] 'One who stands to another or others in relations analogous to those of a father; a lord or master, a protector' (OED); Pope also has in mind the secondary sense of the Latin *patronus*, 'advocate', 'pleader'.

Patron of Mankind] Pope repeats this phrase in *Im. of Hor.*, Ep. II i 1. Dryden (*Georgics*, i 33) had called Augustus 'The Patron of the World'.

168–77. All the members of this group of heroes were either executed wrongfully or committed noble suicide. Those executed jested graciously on the point of death.

169. EC note the inconsistency caused by Pope's later insertion of Marcus Aurelius, who may just be considered 'noisy' (since he was Emperor) but cannot be considered 'guilty'. Wakefield compares Pope's epitaph 'On Edmund d. of Buckingham', ll. 9 f.

170. *silent*] Cf. Bacon, *Advancement of Learning* I vii 1: 'The former [founders of states, etc.] is mixed with strife and perturbation; but the latter [inventors of

Here ever shines the Godlike *Socrates*:
He whom ungrateful *Athens* cou'd expel,
At all times Just, but when he sign'd the Shell.
Here his Abode the martyr'd *Phocion* claims,
With *Agis*, not the last of *Spartan* Names:
Unconquer'd *Cato* shews the Wound he tore,

171–3 Here ever shines the Godlike *Socrates*.
Here triumphs He whom *Athens* did expel,
In all things Just, but when he sign'd the Shell. *1715.*

new arts, etc.] hath the true character of Divine Presence, coming in *aura leni*, without noise or agitation'.

Supreme] Montaigne considers the soul of Socrates 'the most perfect that ever came to my knowledge' (*Essays*, ii 11), and calls him 'vertues chiefe favorite' (*Essays*, i 25, trans. Florio).

171. *Godlike*] 'Plato says [*Apology*, 31] he was given to the *Athenians* by the hand of GOD' (*The Memorable Things of Socrates, Written by Xenophon*, translated by E. Bysshe, 1712, p. 20).

172–5. 'Aristides, *who for his great Integrity was distinguish'd by the Appellation of* the Just. *When his Countrymen would have banish'd him by the* Ostracism, *where it was the Custom for every Man to sign the Name of the Person he voted to Exile in an Oysters Shell; a Peasant, who could not write, came to* Aristides *to do it for him, who readily sign'd his own Name.* [P. 1736: 1715 *adds* Vide Plutarch. *See the same Author of* Phocion, Agis, *&c.*: 1717–26 *reduce.*]

The incident of the shell is engraved opposite p. 432 of Plutarch, ii.

Cf. Cowley, 'Of Obscurity': 'I love and commend a true good Fame, because it is the shadow of Virtue, not that it doth any good to the Body which it accompanies . . . The best kinde of Glory . . . is that which is reflected from Honesty, such as was the Glory of *Cato* and *Aristides*, but it was harmful to them both, and is seldom beneficial to any man whilst he lives.'

174. Phocion, the Athenian statesman and general, was condemned to drink hemlock on a charge of treasonably abetting the Macedonian cause. Plutarch acknowledged that, in trusting the traitor Nicanor, he endangered the state, but never doubts that his 'chief aim was always the Weal-publick' (iv 475). His account ends: 'this Fate of *Phocion*'s, revived the Memory of *Socrates* among the *Græcians*, their Case being exactly parallel, both their Deaths being alike, the most shameful Fault, and heavy Misfortune of the People of *Athens*.'

175. Plutarch (iv 598 ff.) brackets together the lives of the 'two *Lacedemonian* Kings, *Agis* and *Cleomenes*; for they being desirous . . . to raise the People, by restoring their obsolete Laws of Equality, incurr'd the Hatred of the Rich and Powerful' (p. 601). Agis planned, and was partly able to execute, a scheme for restoring the regulations of Lycurgus which ensured the equable distribution of

And *Brutus* his ill Genius meets no more.
But in the Centre of the hallow'd Quire
Six pompous Columns o'er the rest aspire;
Around the Shrine it self of *Fame* they stand,
Hold the chief Honours, and the Fane command.
High on the first, the mighty *Homer* shone;
Eternal Adamant compos'd his Throne;
Father of Verse! in holy Fillets drest,
His Silver Beard wav'd gently o'er his Breast;
Tho' blind, a Boldness in his Looks appears,
In Years he seem'd, but not impair'd by Years.

property. In his absence on a military campaign, his work was overthrown. He was tried by mock trial and strangled.

176. Cato of Utica, like Phocion, preserved unchanged his 'Affection to the Publick Good' (Plutarch, iv 573). He felt keenly the wrong of civil war. Amid the successes of Pompey, he 'alone bewailed his Country, and curs'd that Fatal Ambition, which made so many brave *Romans* murther one another' (p. 574). After Caesar's defeat of Metellus Scipio at Thapsus, Cato resolved on suicide, but provided first for the escape of his followers. His wound was not immediately mortal; the 'Physician went to him, and would have put in his Bowels, which were not pierced, and sow'd up the Wound: *Cato* hereupon coming to himself, thrust away the Physician, pluck'd out his own Bowels, and tearing open the Wound, immediately expired' (p. 595). He is 'Unconquer'd' because he preferred his own death to Caesar's favour: '*I would not be beholding to a Tyrant*' (p. 590). Cf. citation from Cowley in note on ll. 172–5.

177. *Brutus*] See Plutarch, iv 444. The engraving facing v 578 represents the evil genius appearing to Brutus.

178 ff. *In the midst of the Temple, nearest the Throne of* Fame, *are plac'd the greatest Names in Learning of all Antiquity. These are describ'd in such Attitudes as express their different Characters. The Columns on which they are rais'd are adorn'd with Sculptures, taken from the most striking Subjects of their Works; which Sculpture bears a Resemblance in its Manner and Character, to the Manner and Character of their Writings.* [P. 1715, 1736.]

179. *pompous*] in the original sense of splendid, magnificent.

179 ff. and 182 ff. For Pope's quotations from Chaucer, see Appendix G, items g and h, pp. 404 f.

182 ff. During the battle of the books Homer was 'the special target . . . of the Moderns, who felt that, if they could succeed in discrediting him, their cause would be won' (J. B. Bury, *Idea of Progress*, 1920, p. 81). See Introduction, pp. 230 f. For Pope's prose estimate, see *Preface to Iliad*, B 1v–B 2r.

187. Cf. Dryden, *Æneid*, vi 420 f. [of Charon]:

The Wars of *Troy* were round the Pillar seen:
Here fierce *Tydides* wounds the *Cyprian* Queen;
Here *Hector* glorious from *Patroclus*' Fall,
Here dragg'd in Triumph round the *Trojan* Wall.
Motion and Life did ev'ry Part inspire,
Bold was the Work, and prov'd the Master's Fire;
A strong Expression most he seem'd t'affect,
And here and there disclos'd a brave Neglect.
A Golden Column next in Rank appear'd,
On which a Shrine of purest Gold was rear'd;
Finish'd the whole, and labour'd ev'ry Part,
With patient Touches of unweary'd Art:
The *Mantuan* there in sober Triumph sate,
Compos'd his Posture, and his Look sedate;
On *Homer* still he fix'd a reverend Eye,
Great without Pride, in modest Majesty.
In living Sculpture on the Sides were spread

He look'd in Years: yet in his Years were seen
A youthful Vigour, and Autumnal green.

For the view of Homer's vigour in advancing years cf. Longinus, chap. ix: 'I am describing an old age, but the old age of Homer'.

188 ff. 'Pope has selected from Homer only three subjects as the most interesting: Diomed wounding Venus, Hector slaying Patroclus, and the same Hector dragged along at the wheels of Achilles' chariot. Are these the most affecting and striking incidents of the Iliad? But it is highly worth remarking, that this very incident of dragging the body of Hector thrice round the walls of Troy is absolutely not mentioned by Homer . . . Virgil, for he first mentioned it [*Æneid*, i 483] [probably] adopted the circumstance from some Greek tragedy on the subject' (Warton, ed.).

194 f. Longinus (xxxviii) had cited Homer as a writer great enough to neglect trivialities. Cf. Dryden, *Essays*, ii 12 and 251; *Ess. on Crit.*, l. 141 ff.; and *Preface to Iliad*, D 2r–D 3r, E 2r.

196 ff. For Pope's quotation from Chaucer, see Appendix G, item i, p. 405. The poetical character of Virgil is that expressed by Pope in the 'Preface to Iliad' (B 2v, D 1v–D 2r), in *Ess. on Crit.* (ll. 118 ff.); in Temple (pp. 320 f.); and in Dryden (see, e.g., *Essays*, ii 197 ff.).

198. *labour'd*] having had great pains expended on its decoration.

204. *living Sculpture*] The phrase is found in Dryden, *Æneid*, vi 33.

The *Latian* Wars, and haughty *Turnus* dead;
Eliza stretch'd upon the fun'ral Pyre,
Æneas bending with his aged Sire:
Troy flam'd in burning Gold, and o'er the Throne
Arms and the Man in Golden Cyphers shone.
Four Swans sustain a Carr of Silver bright
With Heads advanc'd, and Pinions stretch'd for Flight:
Here, like some furious Prophet, *Pindar* rode,
And seem'd to labour with th' inspiring God.
A-cross the Harp a careless Hand he flings,
And boldly sinks into the sounding Strings.
The figur'd Games of *Greece* the Column grace,
Neptune and *Jove* survey the rapid Race:
The Youths hang o'er their Chariots as they run;
The fiery Steeds seem starting from the Stone;
The Champions in distorted Postures threat,
And all appear'd Irregularly great.

208 burning] burnish'd *1715–17*.

210 ff. Pindar *being seated in a Chariot, alludes to the Chariot-Races he celebrated in the* Grecian *Games. The Swans are Emblems of* Poetry, *their soaring Posture intimates the Sublimity and Activity of his Genius.* Neptune *presided over the* Isthmian, *and* Jupiter *over the* Olympian *Games.* [P. 1715, 1736.]

The late seventeenth and the eighteenth century took Pindar as a favourite instance of the sublime. Horace had called him 'Dircæum . . . cycnum' and described his verse in *Odes*, IV ii 1 ff. Boileau's *Discours sur l'Ode* (1693) had shown Pindar's 'avoiding that Methodical Order, and those exact Connexions of Sense which wou'd take away the very Soul of *Lyric* Poetry . . . these Noble Boldnesses of *Pindar*, . . . these *abrupt Senses* . . . full of Movements and Transports, wherein the Mind seem'd rather hurry'd away by the Fury of the Poetry, than guided by Reason' (translated by J. Ozell, etc., 1711–12, ii 148 f.). Boileau cites his own *Art Poétique*, in which at ii 58 ff. he had appraised the ode. For Dryden on Pindar see Introduction, p. 223 above.

215. Cf. Pope's 'Sappho to Phaon', l. 34:

And strikes with bolder rage the sounding strings.

In a letter of 28 Oct. 1710 to Cromwell, Pope cites and commends lines from Ambrose Philips's fifth Pastoral which he here seems to be imitating:

Now, lightly skimming, o'er the Strings . . .
He sinks into the Cords . . .

Here happy *Horace* tun'd th' *Ausonian* Lyre
To sweeter Sounds, and temper'd *Pindar*'s Fire:
Pleas'd with *Alcæus*' manly Rage t'infuse
The softer Spirit of the *Sapphick* Muse.
The polish'd Pillar diff'rent Sculptures grace;
A Work outlasting Monumental Brass.
Here smiling *Loves* and *Bacchanals* appear,
The *Julian* Star, and Great *Augustus* here.

---

222 ff. *This expresses the mixt Character of the Odes of* Horace. *The second of these Verses alludes to that Line of his:*

Spiritum Graiæ tenuem Camœnæ. [*Odes*, II xvi 38.]

As another which follows, to

Exegi Monumentum ære perennius. [*Odes*, III xxx 1.]

The Action of the Doves *hints at a Passage in the 4th Ode of his third Book,*

Me fabulosæ Vulture in Appulo,
Altricis extra limen Apuliæ,
  Ludo fatigatumque somno,
  Fronde nova puerum Palumbes
Texêre; mirum quod foret omnibus—
Ut tuto ab atris corpore viperis
Dormirem & ursis: ut premerer sacra
  Lauroque, collataque myrto,
  Non sine Dis animosus infans.

Which may be thus english'd;

While yet a Child, I chanc'd to stray,
And in a Desart sleeping lay;
The savage Race withdrew, nor dar'd
To touch the Muses future Bard:
But Cytheræa'*s gentle Dove*
  Myrtles *and* Bays *around me spread,*
  And crown'd your Infant Poet's Head,
Sacred to Musick *and to* Love.

[P. 1715, 1736: 1717–36 *reduce.*]

222. *Ausonian*] = Italian.

223. *temper'd*] literally from 'temperat', see following note.

224 f. Pope's account of Horace uses for original ends the material of *Epist.* I xix 22 ff. Lines 28 f. of this passage read:

temperat Archilochi Musam pede mascula Sappho,
temperat Alcæus . . .

229. Horace, *Odes*, I xii, is in praise of Augustus, its famous twelfth stanza ending:

The Doves that round the Infant Poet spread
Myrtles and Bays, hung hov'ring o'er his Head.
 Here in a Shrine that cast a dazling Light,
Sate fix'd in Thought the mighty *Stagyrite*;
His Sacred Head a radiant Zodiack crown'd,
And various Animals his Sides surround;
His piercing Eyes, erect, appear to view
Superior Worlds, and look all Nature thro'.
 With equal Rays immortal *Tully* shone,
The *Roman Rostra* deck'd the Consul's Throne:
Gath'ring his flowing Robe, he seem'd to stand,
In Act to speak, and graceful, stretch'd his Hand:
Behind, *Rome*'s *Genius* waits with *Civic* Crowns,
And the Great Father of his Country owns.

. . . micat inter omnis
Iulium sidus, velut inter ignis
luna minores.

232 ff. Pope regards him principally as the author of treatises on astronomy and natural history.

235. *various*] of different kinds.

236. *erect*] See note on l. 123 above.

238 ff. The philosophy of Cicero was held in exaggerated esteem by Renaissance scholars, and the eighteenth century had not yet revised their estimate. Pope, however, thinks of him first of all as an orator and public figure.

238. *equal*] Combining the meanings (a) equal to the rays cast around Aristotle, (b) even, equable.

239. The rostra were beaks of captured galleys used as decorations of the Roman platforms for public speaking. Cicero was an orator as well as a consul.

240 f. The attitude is that of the engraving facing Plutarch, v 291, not, as Joseph Warton (i 386) stated, that of the statue in the collection presented by the Countess of Pomfret to Oxford University (now in the Ashmolean Museum).

242 f. Alluding to Cicero's leading the conspirators who supported Catiline severally to their execution; the 'Citizens . . . receiving him . . . with Acclamations and Applauses, saluted him, *Saviour and Founder of his Country* . . . for though it might seem no wonderful thing to prevent the Design, and punish the Conspirators, yet to Defeat the greatest of all Conspiracies with so little Damage, Trouble and Commotion, was very extraordinary' (Plutarch, v 324 f.). Cato 'in an Oration to the People so highly extolled *Cicero*'s Consulate, that the greatest Honours were decreed him, and he publickly declared the Father of his Country' (p. 326).

These massie Columns in a Circle rise,
O'er which a pompous Dome invades the Skies:
Scarce to the Top I stretch'd my aking Sight,
So large it spread, and swell'd to such a Height.
Full in the midst, proud *Fame*'s Imperial Seat
With Jewels blaz'd, magnificently great;
The vivid Em'ralds there revive the Eye;
The flaming Rubies shew their sanguine Dye;
Bright azure Rays from lively Saphirs stream,
And lucid Amber casts a Golden Gleam.
With various-colour'd Light the Pavement shone,
And all on fire appear'd the glowing Throne;
The Dome's high Arch reflects the mingled Blaze,
And forms a Rainbow of alternate Rays.
When on the *Goddess* first I cast my Sight,
Scarce seem'd her Stature of a Cubit's height,
But swell'd to larger Size, the more I gaz'd,

254 Light] Lights *1715*.

245. Cf. Addison, translating Sannazaro (*Remarks*, p. 109):

And Thou, whose Rival Tow'rs Invade the Skies.

246. Wakefield compares Dryden, *State of Innocence*, IV i 7:

Their glory shoots upon my aking sense.

Cf. also Congreve, *Mourning Bride* (1710), II iii 12: '. . . my aking Sight'.

248. Cf. *Hous of Fame*, iii 270 ff., where Chaucer sees Fame

. . . al on hye, above a dees,
Sitte in a see imperial
That maad was of a rubee al,
Which that a carbuncle is y-called.

252. *lively*] Cf. *Gondibert*, II iv 45, 3 f.: a cheerful *Emrauld* . . .

Cheerful, as if the lively stone had sence.

254. Cf. *Par. Lost*, iii 362.

256 f. The rays may be alternate because bent: they travel up to the dome and then are reflected back to the eye in the form of a rainbow; or Pope may be using 'alternate' in an original sense—the colours on the pavement are mingled but in the dome they sort themselves into a series, each strip of colour alternating with the next.

259 ff. For Pope's quotation from Chaucer and editor's comment, see Appendix G, item j, p. 405.

Till to the Roof her tow'ring Front she rais'd.
With her, the Temple ev'ry Moment grew,
And ampler *Vista's* open'd to my View,
Upward the Columns shoot, the Roofs ascend,
And Arches widen, and long Iles extend.
Such was her Form, as antient Bards have told,
Wings raise her Arms, and Wings her Feet infold;
A Thousand busy Tongues the Goddess bears,
And Thousand open Eyes, and Thousand list'ning Ears.
Beneath, in Order rang'd, the tuneful Nine
(Her Virgin Handmaids) still attend the Shrine:
With Eyes on Fame for ever fix'd, they sing;
For Fame they raise the Voice, and tune the String.
With Time's first Birth began the Heav'nly Lays,
And last Eternal thro' the Length of Days.
Around these Wonders as I cast a Look,
The Trumpet sounded, and the Temple shook,
And all the Nations, summon'd at the Call,

---

266. Two of the 'ancient bards' are Virgil (*Æneid*, iv 181 ff.):

. . . cui, quot sunt corpore plumæ,
Tot vigiles oculi subter (mirabile dictu),
Tot linguæ, totidem ora sonant, tot subrigit auris;

and Chaucer, *Hous of Fame*, iii 291 ff.:

For as fele eyen hadde she
As fetheres upon foules be . . .
And soth to tellen also she
Had also fele up-stondyng eres
And tonges, as on bestes heres;
And on hir feet wexen, saugh I,
Partriches winges redely.

Pope's Fame is less grotesque than theirs.

270 ff. and 276 ff. For Pope's quotations from Chaucer, see Appendix G, items k and l, pp. 405 f.

278 ff. Cf. Mrs Behn's translation of *A Voyage to the Isle of Love* [the section headed 'The City of Love'], *Works*, vi 274:

All Nations hourly thither do resort,
To add a splendour to this glorious Court;
The Young, the Old, the Witty, and the Wise,
The Fair, the Ugly, Lavish, and Precise;

From diff'rent Quarters fill the crowded Hall:
Of various Tongues the mingled Sounds were heard;
In various Garbs promiscuous Throngs appear'd;
Thick as the Bees, that with the Spring renew
Their flow'ry Toils, and sip the fragrant Dew,
When the wing'd Colonies first tempt the Sky,
O'er dusky Fields and shaded Waters fly,
Or settling, seize the Sweets the Blossoms yield,
And a low Murmur runs along the Field.
Millions of suppliant Crowds the Shrine attend,
And all Degrees before the Goddess bend;
The Poor, the Rich, the Valiant, and the Sage,
And boasting Youth, and Narrative old Age.

Cowards and Braves, the Modest, and the Lowd,
Promiscuously are blended in the Crowd.

282 ff. Virgil uses similes of bees to describe the builders of Carthage (*Æneid*, i 430 ff.) and the souls waiting for new bodies (vi 707 ff.). Milton applies the comparison to the fallen angels entering the newly built Pandemonium (*Par. Lost*, i 768 ff.). Pope is also indebted to the bee simile in Lucan, ix 285 ff., Thomas May translating its 'laboris floriferi' as 'flowery taskes' (Milton, 'Il Penseroso', l. 143, speaks of the bee's 'flowry work'); and to the bees in *Georgics*, iv, especially in Dryden's translation.

284. *tempt*] 'to adventure oneself in or upon; to risk the perils of' (OED). Cf. *Windsor Forest*, l. 389.

285. *dusky Fields*] Cf. Dryden, 'Flower and the Leaf', l. 219 (part of another simile of bees).

shaded Waters] Cf. *Georgics*, iv 23 f.

287. Cf. Dryden, *Æneid*, xii 363: 'A rising Murmur runs along the Line'; his I *Conquest of Granada*, 1 i: 'A rising murmure ran through all the Field'; and his *Georgics*, i 491. *Run* is noted by Saintsbury as a favourite word of Dryden. Cf. l. 405 below.

288. Cf. Dryden, Ovid's *Metam.*, i 120:

No suppliant Crowds before the Judge appear'd.

289. Cf. *Hous of Fame*, iii 436 ff.: Pore and ryche . . .
. . . gonne doun on knees falle
Before this ilke noble quene.

291. Cf. Dryden, *Essays*, ii 30: 'the tattling quality of age, which, as Sir William D'Avenant says, is always narrative'. Davenant, Epilogue to *Siege of Rhodes*, 24, reads: '. . . being old and therefore Narrative'. Pope uses the epithet again in *Iliad*, iii 200, and *Odyssey*, iii 80.

Their Pleas were diff'rent, their Request the same;
For Good and Bad alike are fond of Fame.
Some she disgrac'd, and some with Honours crown'd;
Unlike Successes equal Merits found.
Thus her blind Sister, fickle *Fortune* reigns,
And undiscerning, scatters Crowns and Chains.
  First at the Shrine the Learned World appear,
And to the Goddess thus prefer their Prayer:
Long have we sought t'instruct and please Mankind,
With Studies pale, with Midnight Vigils blind;
But thank'd by few, rewarded yet by none,
We here appeal to thy superior Throne:
On Wit and Learning the just Prize bestow,
For *Fame* is all we must expect below.
  The Goddess heard, and bade the Muses raise
The Golden Trumpet of eternal Praise:

---

294 ff. For Pope's quotation from Chaucer and editor's comment, see Appendix G, item m, p. 406.

295 ff. Cf. *Hous of Fame*, iii 455 ff.:

> They hadde good fame ech deserved,
> Althogh they were diversly served;
> Right as her suster, dame Fortune,
> Is wont to serven in commune.

EC also compare Creech's translation of Juvenal, *Satire* xiii 132 ff. (*Satires*, translated by Dryden etc., ed. 1711):

> *Some* [the gods] forgive, and ev'ry Age Relates
> That *equal* Crimes have met *unequal* Fates;
> That Sins *alike*, *unlike* Rewards have found,
> And whilst *This* Villain's Crucify'd, *The other*'s Crown'd.

300. A reference to the aim of writing as remarked by Horace, *Ars Poetica*, ll. 333 ff.

306 f. Pope's poem is scenic rather than, like Chaucer's, narrative, and so he neglects Chaucer here. Chaucer's Fame sends for Eolus, who is wandering in Thrace, and who brings two trumpets, one of gold (for praise), one of black brass (for slander). In making the Muses blow the golden one, Pope symbolizes the idea, especially strong at the time of the Renaissance, that poetry conferred immortality on those whom it mentions.

Cf. Shaftesbury, *Characteristics*, 1711, i 225: 'And when the signal *Poet*, or *Herald of Fame* is once heard, the inferior Trumpets sink in Silence and Oblivion'; l. 34 above; Appendix G, item c, p. 404; and l. 128 above.

From Pole to Pole the Winds diffuse the Sound,
That fills the Circuit of the World around;
Not all at once, as Thunder breaks the Cloud;
The Notes at first were rather sweet than loud:
By just degrees they ev'ry moment rise,
Fill the wide Earth, and gain upon the Skies.
At ev'ry Breath were balmy Odours shed,
Which still grew sweeter as they wider spread:
Less fragrant Scents th' unfolding Rose exhales,
Or Spices breathing in *Arabian* Gales.
  Next these the Good and Just, an awful Train,
Thus on their Knees address the sacred Fane.
Since living Virtue is with Envy curst,
And the best Men are treated like the worst,
Do thou, just Goddess, call our Merits forth,
And give each Deed th' exact intrinsic Worth.
Not with bare Justice shall your Act be crown'd,
(Said Fame) but high above Desert renown'd:
Let fuller Notes th' applauding World amaze,
And the loud Clarion labour in your Praise.
  This Band dismiss'd, behold another Crowd

319 address] address'd *1715–17*.

313. Cf. Dryden, 'On the Death of Amyntas', l. 71:

And every Moment gains upon the Skies;

and his *Georgics*, i 500, which Pope commended in the margin of his own copy.

314 ff. Cf. Dryden, 'Astræa Redux', ll. 269 ff., and *Par. Lost*, iv 156 ff.

318 ff. For Pope's quotation from Chaucer, see Appendix G, item n, pp. 406 f.

322 f. Cf. Prior's address to Janus, 'Carmen Sæculare', 1700, p. 2:

In comely Order march each Merit forth,
Mark ev'ry Act with its intrinsic Worth.

Pope seems also to be recalling the revised version in Prior's *Poems on Several Occasions*, 1709, p. 139:

In comely Rank call ev'ry Merit forth,
Imprint on ev'ry Act its Standard Worth.

327. Cf. Addison, 'A Song, For St. Cecilia's Day', ii 5:

The Organ labours in her praise.

328 ff. For Pope's quotation from Chaucer, see Appendix G, item o, p. 407.

Prefer'd the same Request, and lowly bow'd,
The constant Tenour of whose well-spent Days
No less deserv'd a just Return of Praise.
But strait the direful Trump of Slander sounds,
Thro' the big Dome the doubling Thunder bounds:
Loud as the Burst of Cannon rends the Skies,
The dire Report thro' ev'ry Region flies:
In ev'ry Ear incessant Rumours rung,
And gath'ring Scandals grew on ev'ry Tongue.
From the black Trumpet's rusty Concave broke
Sulphureous Flames, and Clouds of rolling Smoke:
The pois'nous Vapor blots the purple Skies,
And withers all before it as it flies.
  A Troop came next, who Crowns and Armour wore,
And proud Defiance in their Looks they bore:
For thee (they cry'd) amidst Alarms and Strife,
We sail'd in Tempests down the Stream of Life;
For thee whole Nations fill'd with Flames and Blood,
And swam to Empire thro' the purple Flood.
Those Ills we dar'd thy Inspiration own,
What Virtue seem'd, was done for thee alone.
Ambitious Fools! (the Queen reply'd, and frown'd)
Be all your Acts in dark Oblivion drown'd;
There sleep forgot, with mighty Tyrants gone,
Your Statues moulder'd, and your Names unknown.
A sudden Cloud strait snatch'd them from my Sight,
And each Majestic Phantom sunk in Night.

349 What] And all that *1715*. seem'd,] seem'd *1715*.
351 drown'd] crown'd *1715*.

340. *purple*] brilliant &c. (OED, sense 3 a).
347. Pope is combining Dryden, *Æneid*, vi 133 f.:

Wars, horrid Wars I view; a field of Blood;
And *Tyber* rolling with a Purple Flood.

and the *Primer*, p. 410:

Fearless of Death he sheds his Blood,
And wades to Heaven thro' the Flood.

Then came the smallest Tribe I yet had seen,
Plain was their Dress, and modest was their Mein.
Great Idol of Mankind! we neither claim
The Praise of Merit, nor aspire to Fame;
But safe in Desarts from th' Applause of Men,
Would die unheard of, as we liv'd unseen.
'Tis all we beg thee, to conceal from Sight
Those Acts of Goodness, which themselves requite.
O let us still the secret Joy partake,
To follow Virtue ev'n for Virtue's sake.
And live there Men who slight immortal Fame?
Who then with Incense shall adore our Name?
But Mortals! know, 'tis still our greatest Pride,
To blaze those Virtues which the Good would hide.
Rise! Muses, rise! add all your tuneful Breath,
These must not sleep in Darkness and in Death.
She said: in Air the trembling Musick floats,
And on the Winds triumphant swell the Notes;
So soft, tho high, so loud, and yet so clear,
Ev'n list'ning Angels lean'd from Heaven to hear:
To farthest Shores th' Ambrosial Spirit flies,
Sweet to the World, and grateful to the Skies.

360 th'] the *1715*.
368 But Mortals!] But, Mortals *1715*.
373 on] up *1715*.

356 ff. For Pope's quotation from Chaucer and editor's comment, see Appendix G, item p, pp. 407 f.

371. Cf. Milton, 'Epitaph on the Marchioness of Winchester', l. 10:
To house with darkness, and with death.

374. One of the innumerable echoes of Denham, *Cooper's Hill*, l. 191:
Tho' deep, yet clear, tho' gentle, yet not dull.

375. Cf. 'Ode on St. Cecilia's Day', l. 130. Wakefield also compares Dryden, 'Palamon and Arcite', iii 441 f.: 'The Gods . . . leaning from their Stars'.

376. *Spirit*] 'a breath (of wind or air)' (OED, sense iv 15).

377. This line is repeated at 'Epil. to Satires', Dial. ii 245. Simon Harcourt had quoted it to end his commemorative verses before Pope's *Works* in 1717.

Next these a youthful Train their Vows exprest,
With Feathers crown'd, with gay Embroid'ry drest;
Hither, they cry'd, direct your Eyes, and see
The Men of Pleasure, Dress, and Gallantry:
Ours is the Place at Banquets, Balls and Plays;
Sprightly our Nights, polite are all our Days;
Courts we frequent, where 'tis our pleasing Care
To pay due Visits, and address the Fair:
In fact, 'tis true, no Nymph we cou'd persuade,
But still in Fancy vanquish'd ev'ry Maid;
Of unknown Dutchesses leud Tales we tell,
Yet would the World believe us, all were well.
The Joy let others have, and we the Name,
And what we want in Pleasure, grant in Fame.
The Queen assents, the Trumpet rends the Skies,
And at each Blast a Lady's Honour dies.
Pleas'd with the strange Success, vast Numbers prest
Around the Shrine, and made the same Request:
What you (she cry'd) unlearn'd in Arts to please,
Slaves to your selves, and ev'n fatigu'd with Ease,
Who lose a Length of undeserving Days;
Wou'd you usurp the Lover's dear-bought Praise?
To just Contempt, ye vain Pretenders, fall,
The People's Fable, and the Scorn of all.
Strait the black Clarion sends a horrid Sound,
Loud Laughs burst out, and bitter Scoffs fly round,

---

378 ff. For Pope's note and quotation from Chaucer, see Appendix G, item q, p. 408.

For the affectation of viciousness in dandies technically innocent, see *Tatler*, Nos. 77, 191, and 213. Cf. Introduction, pp. 239 ff.

384. Cf. *Rape of the Lock*, ii 92.

385. *Visits*] See *Rape of the Lock*, iii 167 and iv 63.

388. *unknown*] in a double sense of social and sexual knowledge.

393. Cf. *Rape of the Lock*, iii 16.

401. Cf. Spenser, 'Ruines of Rome', l. 92:

The peoples fable, and the spoyle of all.

Whispers are heard, with Taunts reviling loud,
And scornful Hisses run thro all the Croud.
Last, those who boast of mighty Mischiefs done,
Enslave their Country, or usurp a Throne;
Or who their Glory's dire Foundation laid,
On Sovereigns ruin'd, or on Friends betray'd,
Calm, thinking Villains, whom no Faith cou'd fix,
Of crooked Counsels and dark Politicks;
Of these a gloomy Tribe surround the Throne,
And beg to make th' immortal Treasons known.
The Trumpet roars, long flaky Flames expire,
With Sparks, that seem'd to set the World on fire.
At the dread Sound, pale Mortals stood aghast,
And startled Nature trembled with the Blast.
This having heard and seen, some Pow'r unknown
Strait chang'd the Scene, and snatch'd me from the Throne.
Before my View appear'd a Structure fair,
Its Site uncertain, if in Earth or Air;
With rapid Motion turn'd the Mansion round;
With ceaseless Noise the ringing Walls resound:
Not less in Number were the spacious Doors,

404 f. are . . . run] were . . . ran *1715–17*.
410 Calm,] Calm *1715a, 1736–45*. cou'd] can *1715–17*.

405. *run*] Cf. l. 287 above.

406 ff. For Pope's quotation from Chaucer and the commentary of Dilke and the editor, see Appendix G, item r, p. 408.

411. Cf. Dryden, *Absalom and Achitophel*, i 152: 'For close Designs and crooked Counsels fit'.

414. *Flake* = 'a detached portion of flame' (OED). Cf. Spenser, e.g. *F.Q.*, I xi 26 (4), and Dryden, *Georgics*, iv 254.

417. Cf. *Par. Lost*, ix 782 ff.

418 ff. For Pope's note and quotation from Chaucer, see Appendix G, item s, pp. 408 ff.

421. Cf. Denham, *Cooper's Hill*, ll. 15 ff.:

> . . . that sacred Pile, so vast so high,
> That whether 'tis a part of Earth, or Sky,
> Uncertain seems . . .

Than Leaves on Trees, or Sands upon the Shores;
Which still unfolded stand, by Night, by Day,
Pervious to Winds, and open ev'ry way.
As Flames by Nature to the Skies ascend,
As weighty Bodies to the Center tend,
As to the Sea returning Rivers roll,
And the touch'd Needle trembles to the Pole:
Hither, as to their proper Place, arise
All various Sounds from Earth, and Seas, and Skies,
Or spoke aloud, or whisper'd in the Ear;
Nor ever Silence, Rest or Peace is here.
As on the smooth Expanse of Chrystal Lakes,
The sinking Stone at first a Circle makes;
The trembling Surface, by the Motion stir'd,
Spreads in a second Circle, then a third;
Wide, and more wide, the floating Rings advance,
Fill all the wat'ry Plain, and to the Margin dance.
Thus ev'ry Voice and Sound, when first they break,
On neighb'ring Air a soft Impression make;
Another ambient Circle then they move,

425. The history of this combination of similes is as follows. Ovid (*Metam.*, xi 614 f.) compares the number of dreams in the cave of Morpheus to that of (a) ears of corn, (b) leaves, (c) grains of sand. Chaucer (*Hous of Fame*, iii 856 f.) uses (b) only, though the lack of a porter at l. 864 shows he has Ovid in mind, and he had already used (a) and (c) at ii, 183 and 190. Pope, like Chaucer, omits (a), but adds (c) to Chaucer's (b).

428 ff. For Pope's note, his quotation from Chaucer and editor's comment, see Appendix G, item t, p. 409.

429. '*Heavy Bodies* are said to move the swifter, the nearer they approach to the *Centre*' (Cowley, *Davideis*, iii, note 61).

431. Cf. Hopkins, Dryden, *Miscellany*, v (1704), p. 177:

And so the Needle trembles to the Pole.

The needle of the compass was magnetized by being touched with the lodestone.

435 ff. *Hous of Fame*, ii 280 ff. Cf. also *1 Henry VI*, I ii 133 ff. ('Glory is like a circle in the water . . .'), Donne's 'Loves Growth', ll. 21 ff., and *Ess. on Man*, iv 362 ff. *Æsop at the Bear Garden* (p. 30) provides the deviation into the indecent which explains *Dunciad*, ii 405 f.

That, in its turn, impels the next above;
Thro undulating Air the Sounds are sent,
And spread o'er all the fluid Element.
There various News I heard, of Love and Strife,
Of Peace and War, Health, Sickness, Death, and Life;
Of Loss and Gain, of Famine and of Store,
Of Storms at Sea, and Travels on the Shore,
Of Prodigies, and Portents seen in Air,
Of Fires and Plagues, and Stars with blazing Hair,
Of Turns of Fortune, Changes in the State,
The Falls of Fav'rites, Projects of the Great,
Of old Mismanagements, Taxations new—
All neither wholly false, nor wholly true.
Above, below, without, within, around,
Confus'd, unnumber'd Multitudes are found,
Who pass, repass, advance, and glide away;
Hosts rais'd by Fear, and Phantoms of a Day.

---

445. Cf. Dryden, Ovid, *Metam.*, xv, 270 f.:

And as the Fountain still supplies her store,
The Wave behind impels the Wave before.

446. *undulating*] Cf. Dryden, Ovid, *Metam.*, xii 60.

448 ff. For Pope's quotation from Chaucer, see Appendix G, item u, p. 409.

453. *Stars . . . Hair*] = comets.

454 ff. These additions to Chaucer's catalogue provide no certain help towards dating the poem. The Act of Union came in 1707, the great Whig administration fell in 1710 and the Tory in 1714. By the time of publication Pope may have revised the passage, or it may have been by accident that on its appearance it had behind it the additional force of the events of 1714: Oxford's dismissal, Queen Anne's death, the Hanoverian succession, and Bolingbroke's impeachment.

456. The period 1640–1713 is 'one of the few formative periods in English tax policy and opinion'. The customs revenue alone 'increased from under £400,000 a year in the time of Charles I to about a million and a half in 1713. The increase in rates was even greater' (W. Kennedy, *English Taxation 1640–1799*, 1913, chr. iii). As a Catholic, Pope was especially liable to taxation (see G. Sherburn, *Early Career*, p. 159).

458 ff. For Pope's quotation from Chaucer, see Appendix G, item v, pp. 409 f.

Astrologers, that future Fates foreshew,
Projectors, Quacks, and Lawyers not a few;
And Priests and Party-Zealots, num'rous Bands
With home-born Lyes, or Tales from foreign Lands;
Each talk'd aloud, or in some secret Place,
And wild Impatience star'd in ev'ry Face:
The flying Rumours gather'd as they roll'd,
Scarce any Tale was sooner heard than told;
And all who told it, added something new,
And all who heard it, made Enlargements too,
In ev'ry Ear it spread, on ev'ry Tongue it grew.
Thus flying East and West, and North and South,
News travel'd with Increase from Mouth to Mouth;
So from a Spark, that kindled first by Chance,
With gath'ring Force the quick'ning Flames advance;
Till to the Clouds their curling Heads aspire,
And Tow'rs and Temples sink in Floods of Fire.
When thus ripe Lyes are to perfection sprung,
Full grown, and fit to grace a mortal Tongue,
Thro thousand Vents, impatient forth they flow,
And rush in Millions on the World below.
Fame sits aloft, and points them out their Course,

462 f. Among the special butts of the Scriblerus Club, Swift had already attacked Partridge whom Pope names at *Rape of the Lock*, v 137; and *The Narrative of Dr. Robert Norris* had appeared in 1713.

Projector = 'promotor of bubble companies; a speculator' (OED). Ben Jonson defined it as a new word in *The Devil is an Ass*, I iii and by Pope's time investing money in companies promoted to float the wild schemes of projectors had already become a mania. Pope himself lost money when the South Sea Bubble burst in 1720.

478. Cf. Addison, 'An Account of the Greatest English Poets' (*Annual Miscellany*, 1694, p. 322):

To see the *Seraphs* sink in Clouds of Fire.

480. *grace*] See Introduction, p. 242.

483. Cf. Dryden, Ovid's *Metam.*, xii 87:

Fame sits aloft . . .

'In Ovid the scene is laid in the house of Fame. Pope lays it in the house of Rumour, and having left Fame enthroned in her own temple, he now represents

Their Date determines, and prescribes their Force:
Some to remain, and some to perish soon,
Or wane and wax alternate like the Moon.
Around, a thousand winged Wonders fly,
Born by the Trumpet's Blast, and scatter'd thro the Sky.
 There, at one Passage, oft you might survey
A Lye and Truth contending for the way;
And long 'twas doubtful, both so closely pent,
Which first should issue thro the narrow Vent:
At last agreed, together out they fly,
Inseparable now, the Truth and Lye;
The strict Companions are for ever join'd,
And this or that unmix'd, no Mortal e'er shall find.
 While thus I stood, intent to see and hear,
One came, methought, and whisper'd in my Ear;
What cou'd thus high thy rash Ambition raise?
Art thou, fond Youth, a Candidate for Praise?
 'Tis true, said I, not void of Hopes I came,

487 Around,] Around *1715*.

---

her as permanently "sitting aloft" in a totally different edifice' (EC). But Pope does not say Fame is sitting in the temple of Rumour. She can direct the course of lies from where she sits in her own temple, as in Chaucer (iii 1020 ff.):

Thus out at holes gonne wringe
Every tyding streght to Fame;
And she gan yeven eche his name . . .

489 ff. For Pope's quotation from Chaucer see Appendix G, item w, p. 410.

497 ff. *The hint is taken from a passage in another part of the third book* [778 ff.], *but here more naturally made the conclusion, with the addition of a* Moral *to the whole. In* Chaucer, *he only answers "he came to see the place*["]*; and the book ends abruptly, with his being surprized at the sight of a* Man of great authority, *and awaking in a fright.* [P. 1736.] Davenant, 'confess[ing] that the desire of Fame made [him] a writer', discusses fame and the poet in the 'Preface' to *Gondibert* (Spingarn, ii 29 ff.). Pope is indebted to *Spectators* 255–6. He often considered the subject, and acutely. His letter to Trumbull of 12 March 1713 contains a prose parallel to this passage. See also *Ess. on Crit.*, 480, 494 ff., *Ess. on Man*, iv 237 ff., and n. on *Iliad*, xvi 955, which reverts to thinking of fame as a business transaction. Ault (*New Light on Pope*, 1949, pp. 108 f.) sees the present passage as marking a point in the relations of Pope and Addison.

For who so fond as youthful Bards of Fame?
But few, alas! the casual Blessing boast,
So hard to gain, so easy to be lost:
How vain that second Life in others' Breath,
Th' Estate which Wits inherit after Death!
Ease, Health, and Life, for this they must resign,
(Unsure the Tenure, but how vast the Fine!)
The Great Man's Curse without the Gains endure,
Be envy'd, wretched, and be flatter'd, poor;
All luckless Wits their Enemies profest,
And all successful, jealous Friends at best.
Nor Fame I slight, nor for her Favours call;
She comes unlook'd for, if she comes at all:

507 they] we *1715–17*. 510 flatter'd,] flatter'd *1715*.
511 their] our *1715a–17*.

504. Wakefield quotes Garth's preface to *The Dispensary*: 'Reputation of this sort is very hard to be got, and very easie to be lost.' Cf. *Spectator* 255: 'Were not this Desire of Fame very strong, the Difficulty of obtaining it, and the Danger of losing it when obtained, would be sufficient to deter a Man from so vain a Pursuit.' Wakefield compares Otway, 'The Poet's Complaint of his Muse,' st. v.

505 ff. Cf. *Ess. on Man*, iv 237.

EC note that Pope here considers literary reputation to be vain, whereas earlier he has implied the reputation of Homer etc. to be glorious. But Pope does not consider himself on a footing with Homer. Even Wotton (p. 45) saw that 'It is almost an Heresie in Wit, among our Poets, to set up any Modern Name against *Homer* or *Virgil*, *Horace* or *Terence*.' In Simon Harcourt's verses before the 1717 *Works*, Pope is represented as arriving at the Temple of Fame and being courted by 'each great Ancient . . . to his [the ancient's] shrine.'

506 ff. Poets come into their estate (fame) on their death, but the fine (ease, health, and life itself) is vast, and the tenure unsure. Fines were levied by the landlord when the tenancy changed hands. The fine could be 'certain' or 'uncertain' and, if the latter, the opportunity was sometimes taken to make it excessive. See S. C[arter]'s *Lex Custumaria: Or, A Treatise of Copy-hold Estates*, ed. 1701, pp. 163 ff.

507. Cf. *Rape*, iv 106, and Walter Pope (T. Flatman, *Poems and Songs*, 1674, A 6v):

Prize *Gold*, before a *good name*, *ease*, *and health*.

514. 'As for gaining any [reputation], I am as indifferent in the matter as

But if the Purchase costs so dear a Price,
As soothing Folly, or exalting Vice:
Oh! if the Muse must flatter lawless Sway,
And follow still where Fortune leads the way;
Or if no Basis bear my rising Name,
But the fall'n Ruins of Another's Fame:
Then teach me, Heaven! to scorn the guilty Bays;
Drive from my Breast that wretched Lust of Praise;
Unblemish'd let me live, or die unknown,
Oh grant an honest Fame, or grant me none!

521 me,] me *1715a–17.*

Falstaff was, and may say of fame as he did of honour: "If it comes, it comes unlooked for; and there's an end on't" ' (Pope's letter to Wycherley, 20 May 1709). Cf. also Temple, cited in Appendix G, item p, p. 408 below.

518. Cf. Dryden, 'Palamon and Arcite', iii 697 f.:

(For Women to the Brave an easie Prey,
Still follow Fortune, where she leads the Way);

and the translation of Gallus, *Elegies*, i 10 (*Poetical Miscellanies*, vi, 1709):

I follow'd still where Pleasure led the Way.

519 f. Cf. Denham's 'On Mr. John Fletcher's Works', ll. 19 ff.:

. . . I need not raise
Trophies to thee from other mens dispraise;
Nor is thy Fame on lesser ruines built . . .

522. Cf. *Ess. on Crit.*, l. 521.

ELOISA TO ABELARD

Plate 3

INTRODUCTION

POPE as a young poet deliberately set out to excel in each of the forms of poetry most esteemed in his day. One of these forms was the heroic epistle. The *Heroides* were 'generally granted to be the most perfect piece of Ovid',[1] and—in the original, in translation, in paraphrase, and in burlesque—had long been accorded an almost fulsome popularity.[2] Their form, too, had been imitated

1. Dryden's *Ovid's Ep.*, A 7v.

2. Chaucer translated some passages in his *Legend of Good Women.* George Turbervile put the whole of the *Heroides* into fourteeners (1567); it is the only verse translation not in heroic couplets and, though confessedly 'basely done', was often reprinted. In his *Troia Britanica* (1609), pp. 197 ff., Thomas Heywood translated the Paris–Helen letters, and in his *ΓΥΝΑΙΚΕΙΟΝ: or, Nine Bookes of Varicus History Concerninge Women* (1624), pp. 389 ff., the 'Sappho to Phaon'. Wye Saltonstall's complete translation followed in 1636 and was often reprinted. Three years later John Sherburne published his 'verse for verse traduction'. Finally there is the translation by Dryden and others (1680). This volume was immediately burlesqued in *The Wits Paraphras'd* (see R. P. Bond, *English Burlesque Poetry, 1700–50*, 1932, p. 141). It was ridiculed also by Prior ('A Satyr on the modern Translators' in *Poems on Affairs of State*, 1697), by Oldmixon (*Amores Britannici*, 1703, A 6v) who pillories Rymer's version of 'Penelope to Ulysses' and by others, but it went on being reprinted till 1795. From the first it contained Mrs Behn's 'Paraphrase on Œnone to Paris', but by the third edition (at least) of 1683, it had been thought best to furnish also the closer version of John Cooper. (For a serious critical estimate of this volume, see W. Harte's letter: *Poetical Works of Mr. William Pattison*, 1728, pp. 46 f. [first series].) An excellent translation of 'Sappho to Phaon' comes from Fenton (*Miscellaneous Poems . . . By Several Hands . . . 1712*, pp. 230 ff.); and there is, finally, Pope's own.

Ovidius Exulans or Ovid Travestie A Mock-Poem, On Five Epistles of Ovid by 'Naso Scarronnomimus' appeared in 1673. Alexander Radcliffe's *Ovid Travestie* (1680) burlesqued five of the epistles, and by the third edition (1696) the number has grown to fifteen.

Oldmixon (op. cit., A 8r) volunteers a history of the form: 'besides the Epistles of *Ovid* and *Sabinus*, and one of *Propertius*'s [i.e., *Elegies*, IV iii], there are no such Letters in any of the Ancients; and among the Moderns, none at all, except a small Volume in *Italian*, call'd, *Epistole Eroici*, written by a nameless Author [Antonio Bruni, *Epistole Heroicke Poesie del Bruni Libri Due . . . Roma . . . MDCXLVII.*], without Spirit, Passion, Elegance or Harmony. The *French* have nothing in this kind, more than a wretched Translation of *Ovid*' (A 8r). See also Warton, i 292 ff.

and developed as a medium for original poetry. Daniel,[1] Samuel Brandon,[2] and Donne[3] produced single specimens. Drayton's *Englands Heroicall Epistles* (1597–9)—twenty-four letters arranged in pairs to and from—indicated how agreeably the moods and materials could be varied and extended.[4] Drayton's epistles were twelve times reprinted during his lifetime, a new edition was announced in the Term Catalogues for November 1689,[5] and their popularity, continued or revived, induced John Oldmixon to 'translate' them into 'correct' couplets as *Amores Britannici* (1703). In Wither's 'Elegiacall Epistle of Fidelia to her vnconstant Friend', and in William Browne's 'Fido: an Epistle to Fidelia', probably designed as sequel, the form is not so much widened as deflected nearer to the *Tristia*[6]: the persons are no longer historical and therefore the situation has to be restricted to a more ordinary circumstance. Nearer to Pope's time there were several adaptations and variations. Butler used the form for comic purposes in *Hudibras*. More 'serious' homage was that of Pomfret's 'Cruelty and Lust, An Epistolary Essay' which purports to be founded on an Angelo-Isabella incident of 1685, and in which the anonymous 'Isabella' entertains her correspondent Celia with both the passion and the discursiveness suggested by the title. Oldmixon, not content with translating Drayton, had added to his *Amores* six original epistles, choosing for his correspondents the vivid 'personalities' of Elizabeth and Essex, Mary Queen of Scots and Norfolk, Waller and Sacharissa. And in the same year David Crauford's *Ovidius Britannicus* showed the length to which variation was running. The first six of his fourteen epistles pass between Hermes and Amestris, two English 'Persons of Quality' whose 'Amour' Crauford alleges to have discovered in 'a great many Musty Papers, very difficult to be read and understood, in an old, dark Closet, that had not been

1. 'A Letter from Octavia to Marcus Antonius'.

2. Two doggerel letters, to and from Octavia and Antony, affixed to his play, *The Virtuous Octavia* (1598).

3. 'Sapho to Philænis'.

4. Dryden's *Ovid's Ep.* (A 7v) and Oldmixon (A 7v) found Ovid deficient in variety.

5. The edition announced is presumably the undated volume ('Printed for *S. Smethwick* . . . and *R. Gilford*') which is reissued ('Printed for *J. Conyers*') with the date 1697.

6. Fidelia (l. 10) speaks of writing an elegy.

opened for twenty Years before'[1]: no one in 1703, therefore, knew the story which follows in the prose form of a 52-page *roman* addressed letter-fashion 'To the Charming *Irena*'.[2] In the same way, though without the suspicion of subterfuge, six of the eight other epistles were based on fictional situations: 'Timandra to Adrastus', 'Lysander to Calista', and so on—each needs its page of 'Argument'. But his remaining two epistles, 'Phaon to Sapho' and 'Theseus to Ariadne', were replies to Ovid's and so return to the strict form. In 1713 Anne, Lady Winchelsea's 'Epistle from Alexander to Hephæstion in his Sickness' reversed Wither's variation: the persons are historical but the communication is not a love-letter.

In the meantime prose had been supplementing and encouraging the form. The *Lettres Portugaises*, published originally in Paris in 1669, and translated by Sir Roger L'Estrange as *Five Love-Letters from a Nun to a Cavalier* (1678), rapidly became popular and were soon furnished with additions and replies.[3] In 1709 they were anonymously and unappetisingly 'Done into *English* Verse'.[4] Finally, the letters of Abelard and Eloisa,[5] which, in France, had been progressively shaking off their medieval quality, appeared in John Hughes's translation (1713).[6] With them as basis, Pope writes

1. B IV.

2. Crauford seems to be the first of the well-intentioned creative forgers of the century.

3. See E. Gosse, *A Nun's Love Letters* (*Fortnightly Review*, vol. 43 new series, pp. 506 ff.). For R. M. Rilke's fine appreciation see the letter quoted in *Duino Elegies* [translated] by J. B. Leishman and Stephen Spender, 1939, pp. 149 f.: 'Marianna Alcoforado, that incomparable creature, in whose eight heavy letters woman's love is for the first time plotted from point to point, without display, without exaggeration or mitigation, as by the hand of a sibyl . . .'

4. *Love without Affectation, In Five Letters from a Portuguese Nun, to a French Cavalier.* Root, *Poetical Career of . . . Pope*, 1936, p. 98, states that these letters 'had twice been versified' by 1717. The *Post Boy*, 10–12 February 1712–13, announces 'This Day is publish'd . . . New Miscellaneous Poems, with five Love Letters from a Nun, to a Cavalier. Done into Verse. Sold by J. Morphew', and on 14–16 April a second edition is announced, printed for W. Mears. I have not seen these.

5. For the sake of uniformity, Pope's spelling of the name has been used throughout this edition, except in Appendix I. See Audra, p. 413, for the history of the spelling. Pope had already used the name in his 'Wife of Bath Her Prologue' (1714), l. 361: its 'Heloïsa' becomes 'Eloïsa' in *Works*, 1717.

6. 'This day is publish'd', *Post Boy* 28–30 July 1713. I have not been able to

his 'Eloisa to Abelard' and soon after its publication in 1717 the replies begin to arrive.[1] With Pope's poem, the heroic epistle is brought back into its strictest Ovidian definition: the persons are historical, and the woman forsaken by the man.[2]

II

Pope's material is Hughes's translation and the literature associated with his theme and his form. Prominent among this were all those French romances, letters, plays, and poems which had been teaching the English court and fashionable writers a new, tender, feverish way of experiencing passion—or, at least, a new way of wording the old passion. James Howell, in 1625, would have nothing to do with this 'kind of simpering and lank hectic Expressions',[3] but, with their recognized vocabulary,[4] they are all found in Mrs Behn's 'Paraphrase of Œnone to Paris'. Like many of the authors writing in this manner, however, Mrs Behn shows erotic experience to be subtly detailed for the mind as well as tempestuous for the senses:

> . . . how long my Maiden blushes strove
> Not to betray the easie new born Love.
> But at thy sight the kindling Fire wou'd rise,
> And I, unskil'd, declare it at my Eyes. . .
> Speechless, and panting at my feet you lay,
> And short-breath'd Sighs told what you cou'd not say . . .
> Heavens, how you swore! by ev'ry Pow'r Divine
> You wou'd be ever true! be ever mine . . .

consult an earlier edition than the fourth, 1722. Pope's correspondence with Hughes begins in 1714, and continues intermittently till Hughes's death in 1720. Addison had been indebted to the story of Eloisa and Abelard for his story of Constantia and Theodosius, *Spectator* 164.

1. See Appendix K, pp. 414 f. below for these replies.

2. See Appendix J, pp. 413 f. below for the alleged connection between 'Eloisa' and Prior's *Henry and Emma*.

3. *Epistolæ Ho-Elianæ*, ed. J. Jacobs (1890), p. 18.

4. This vocabulary is supplemented from other sources, e.g., the Roman epics and the translations of them made during the seventeenth century. In all these works 'sad', 'trembling', 'melting', 'beauteous', and similar key-words are sown as thickly as in the erotic poetry: see Tillotson, pp. 66 ff. Such vocabulary is felt to be especially appropriate in *heroic* epistles.

Quick to my Heart the perjur'd Accents ran,
Which I took in, believ'd, and was undone.[1]

Experience for the Porguguese nun is a simpler thing than this, but Pope found in Hughes's Eloisa a harp-like sensitiveness which is almost that of Rousseau's *nouvelle Héloïse*. He felt himself encouraged to make his poem the *locus classicus* of the 'romantick', of the conscious abandon of mind and body to mood and moment.

The Latin text of the letters had been published in Paris in 1616. In 1687 a letter of Roger de Rabutin, Comte de Bussy, introduced Mme de Sévigné to his version of three of them, a version not only free but, with the Portuguese nun as guide, inventive.[2] Eloisa stands frankly but austerely behind her Latin letters. But in Bussy's translation she has become the dynamo of what amounts to a 'romantick' novel; she and Abelard have been metamorphosed into French courtiers of Bussy's own time—Abelard indeed is almost a psychological self-portrait. In the work of this first translator the change from the historical Eloisa to Pope's is in essentials complete.[3]

Bussy's translation was not printed till 1697 when it appeared in the first edition of his correspondence. But it must have circulated in MS., since, in 1693, another 'translation', based on his, was published at the Hague and elsewhere. In successive editions more letters were translated or invented and the tone became more 'romantick' and sensual. It was this fashionable product that Hughes translated, making one or two puritanical omissions from the preface but none from the letters themselves, which indeed he slightly heightens.[4] Hughes provided Pope with all the data he needed.[5]

1. Dryden's *Ovid's Ep.*, pp. 100 f. These lines have no counterpart in Ovid. Mrs Behn did not know Latin. After admitting this in his preface, Dryden adds gallantly: 'But if she does not, I am afraid she has given us occasion to be asham'd who do' (a 4r).

2. For the French history of the letters I am indebted to Audra, pp. 399 ff.

3. 'Amante éplorée, religieuse déchirée entre son amour pour un homme et ses devoirs envers Dieu, l'Héloïsse de Bussy contient déjà l'essentiel de l'Eloïse de Pope' (Audra, p. 412).

4. Among the Caryll papers (Add. MS. 28,252, ff. 232–50) is an incomplete translation of Hughes's original. The letters would be of especial interest to Catholics, and in drawing on them Pope would be improving his reputation among Catholic friends.

5. The debt appears to have been first remarked by Joseph Berington in the

There is no reason to regret Pope's almost certain ignorance of the original Latin letters, which were to be published in England the year after his poem. Hughes had mentioned the Paris edition of 1616, but only to dismiss it: the original letters, he allowed, were written with 'Elegance and Beauty of Style' but 'consisting chiefly of School Divinity, and of the Learning of those Times [they are] therefore rarely to be met with but in publick Libraries, and in the Hands of some learned Men, [and] are much more known by a Translation, or rather Paraphrase of them in French'.[1] These French and English translations may be said to have shown Pope much of what he had to write about, done much of his preliminary work for him, or indicated in what spirit it should be done. There was much in Hughes, of course, which he had to reject: Hughes made no distinction between such things as 'You reign in such inward Retreats of my Soul, that I know not where to attack you' and merely contemporary elements: 'I had Wit enough to write a *Billet-doux* . . . I love you adorable Heloise!'[2] Such things, however, rolled apart as cleanly as 'Eloisa' and the *Rape of the Lock*, and Pope does not change the tone so much as keep it at its purest. But, as he well saw, an age interested in heroic epistles had so far neglected the most tempting material, these letters 'written', as Hughes had claimed, 'with the greatest Passion of any in this kind which are Extant'.[3]

preface to his *History of . . . Abeillard and Heloisa . . . with their Genuine Letters* (1784). Warton knew of the French translation, but both he and Wakefield examine only the Latin text.

Pope bases his poem mainly on Eloisa's first letter, in which she surveys the past in a fairly chronological way, but he draws freely on other letters. He rearranges freely; sometimes one passage of Hughes will be torn in two, and the pieces embodied separately in the poem (e.g., Hughes, p. 111, is used partly at ll. 119 ff. and partly at ll. 257 ff.: the quotations in the notes to the poem cannot adequately represent this kind of arrangement). Sometimes Pope enlarges what in Hughes is merely a hint—e.g., the happiness of convent life (ll. 207 ff.), the environment of the Paraclete (ll. 155 ff.), and the death scene (ll. 317 ff.). The nightmare and Eloisa's vision are built on hints in Hughes that carry Pope straight to Ovid. Pope omits one 'scene' (borrowed from the *Five Love-Letters*) that must have attracted him: Eloisa's finding solace in Abelard's portrait, which she had scarcely looked at till they parted.

1. A 3v.
2. pp. 124 f. and 79 f.
3. A 3r.

III

Hughes's letters are in prose and the change-over to verse, to couplets, meant also the change-over to tighter 'geometry' of situation. Pope's Eloisa pits one situation against another, formalizes, makes points. Pope states the contrasts in his Argument. Eloisa had always suffered from a 'sad variety of woe'[1]: but not until Pope is this variety closely co-ordinated.

> Nature stands check'd, Religion disapproves;
> Ev'n thou art cold—yet *Eloisa* loves.[2]

This 'geometry' is derived, of course, from Ovid, but Ovid's pointedness was enforced for Pope by the example of dramatic poetry, especially by the plays of Shakespeare, Corneille, and Dryden.[3] 'Eloisa to Abelard' without any change of style might have been split up and put into a rhymed play of the late seventeenth century.

This 'geometry' implies rhetoric,[4] and so 'Eloisa to Abelard' is

1. l. 36.

2. ll. 259 f.

3. The Shakespeare of the earlier histories, of the love scenes in *A Midsummer Night's Dream*, and of the play-within-the-play in *Hamlet* had posed his characters in mathematical dilemmas. And in the late plays he would sometimes reproduce the old geometry, dimmed at the edges with a far less formal rhetoric (see, e.g., *Cymbeline*, I vi 1 ff. and II i 54 ff.). Dryden, following Corneille, found in such situations the opportunity to employ the heroic couplet for constructing a kind of dramatic cat's cradle of balanced forces. Even in *All for Love*, where the style is more like that of Shakespeare's tragedies than like that of Corneille's, his eye is on pattern:

Ventidius. Was ever sight so moving! Emperor!
Dolabella. Friend!
Octavia. Husband!
Both Children. Father!

(This excerpt from Act III may be compared with 'Eloisa', ll. 153 f.) But it is in the rhymed plays that Dryden's pattern is most pronounced. The epistle, as Warton and Wordsworth saw, is really a dramatic form, a dialogue in which one person remains mute. It presents some of the difficulties of the dramatic monologue, in which everything essential to place, time, and character must be conveyed in *oratio recta*.

4. Pope plans his poem as a piece of rhetoric. The punctuation of the first edition sometimes appears to be in accordance with the rhetorical Elizabethan manner, which still survived here and there (see p. 314 below). And, like Oldmixon and the author of *Love without Affectation*, Pope reproduces contemporary

cut off from the other seventeenth-century style of erotic poetry, that of Donne who follows (with a difference) Petrarch. The style of Donne's 'Sapho to Philænis' has little to connect it with Ovid's 'Sappho to Phaon', and it is the Ovidian style that survives into the eighteenth century. The most reasoned comparison of the two styles is that of Pope's friend, William Walsh,[1] and it is significant that the preface which embodies the discussion should have been extensively quoted in Charles Gildon's preface to Crauford's *Ovidius Britannicus*. Walsh considers that Ovid, unlike Petrarch and Donne, speaks the language of Nature. Dryden in his preface had already discriminated the position: Ovid was, he allowed, too prone to wit, but

> If the Imitation of Nature be the business of a Poet, I know no Authour who can justly be compar'd with [him], especially in the Description of the Passions.[2]

In the same year as Gildon's preface, Oldmixon had defined the heroical epistle in such a way as to guard it from Ovid's 'darling sin' of cleverness:

> Passion and Nature are the distinguishing Character of such Epistles . . . the Sentiments shou'd be gallant and tender, the Language easie and musical, and nothing [shou'd] appear forc'd and affected.[3]

In such passages 'Nature' is used in the sense of what is fundament-

---

speech by curtailing 'them' into ' 'em'. The poem invites recitation, and by the 1750's most readers have it by heart (see Appendix K, p. 416). When recitation begins, the poem is found to show a new complexity, owing to the multiplication of its virtual italics. It is always a problem how Pope should be recited, but what is true of his style in general seems particularly true of the style of 'Eloisa'. There are several ways of accenting some of its lines, each way bringing out a different point, or reinforcing the same point from different angles.

> Far other dreams my erring soul employ,
> Far other raptures, of unholy joy (ll. 223 f.)

Who, after experiment, is going to say just how those lines should be accented? In the end the reader satisfies himself by combining all the separate italics in a weighty slowness.

1. *Letters and Poems, Amorous and Gallant* (1692): reprinted in Chalmers's *English Poets* (1810), vol. viii.

2. Dryden's *Ovid's Ep.*, A 5v.

3. A 8v.

al, universal, and permanent in the human mind and heart. The poets who 'followed Nature' avoided cleverness, singularity, particularity. Their heroines first of all represented sorrowing or rebellious love, and only in the second place a particular instance of sorrowing or rebellious love, or the poet's individual idea of such love or of an instance of it.[1] So there are no metaphysical disquisitions or images, no glitter of wit, no puns: Donne's compasses are excluded along with his 'unliterary' explosiveness. Any woman of Ovid's day, or Pope's, or ours, who was in Eloisa's straits would feel as she felt, in kind though not often in degree. Outside Shakespeare's plays and the novel, no woman in English literature expresses the degree of Eloisa's passion and despair—'If you search for passion,' said Byron, 'where is it to be found stronger than [here]?'[2]—but it is a 'natural' passion.

IV

Pope's passion, then, is derived from Nature and Ovid (Nature and Ovid were, he found, the same)[3] newly flushed with the experience of the time in France and England. But flushed, also, with Pope's own Roman Catholic devotion and the poetry of the mystics. It is significant that the debt to Crashaw,[4] like that to Milton,[5]

1. Contrast Browning's 'Epistle Containing the Strange Medical Experience of Karshish the Arab Physician', written when the epistle had forgotten its traditions.

2. *Letters and Journals*, ed. R. E. Prothero, iv (1900), p. 489.

3. There is an interesting letter first printed in *Pope's Correspondence*, iii 268 f., which Pope addressed on 5 Feb. 1731/2 to Dr William Cooper, who had sent him a translation into Latin hexameters of the 'Elegy on the Death of a Young Lady' (or perhaps the 'Messiah'). Pope hopes that a liking for his poems will lead his translator to a warmer liking for those of the ancient poets, and '(to give you, Sir, a proof that what you have done pleases me) I should not be sorry if you tryed your hand upon Eloisa to Abelard, since it has more of that Descriptive, &, (if I may so say) Enthusiastic Spirit, which is the Character of the Ancient Poets, & will give you more occasions of Imitating them'. It will be remembered that Pope venerated the 'fire' and 'life' he found in Homer. As Professor Sherburn says, the letter shows him making 'an interesting judgment' in considering 'Eloisa to Abelard' more like the poems of the ancients because more descriptive and enthusiastic.

4. For Pope and Crashaw see *Gentleman's Mag.*, 1786, pp. 311 f., and A. Warren, 'The Reputation of Crashaw . . .' (*Studies in Philology*, xxxi 389 ff.). Pope is also indebted to Dryden's *Tyrannic Love*: see, e.g.. note on ll. 217 ff. below.

5. l. 20.

reaches the point of a line of quotation, a debt which is considered too odd to go unspecified.[1] The 'papistical machinery', to use the phrase of William Mason, Canon of York Minster,[2] is, of course, the emphatic outward sign of the most restless of Eloisa's conflicts. It is this conflict between religious vows and paganism, between 'grace and nature, virtue and passion'[3] which, for Chateaubriand, marked her superiority over any ancient heroine.[4] From the literary point of view the conflict is central: the poem is constructed around it. And it provides opportunity for those 'layerings' of effect which are so characteristic of Pope's methods of writing.[5] It allows the Ovidian imitation to be parallel and divergent at the same time. For instance, Eloisa's vision of the nun who calls her[6] is imitated from that of Ovid's Dido who heard the same call when visiting the monument of the husband she had murdered:

> hinc ego me sensi noto quater ore citari;
> ipse sono tenui dixit 'Elissa, veni!'
> Nulla mora est, venio, venio tibi debita coniunx;[7]

which in Sherburne's translation ran:

> me thought, I heard, foure times to say,
> With trembling voyce, *Eliza*, come away.
> I come, I come, thy once vow'd wife . . .[8]

Pope keeps the frame, even the translated words, but what was pagan has become Christian (the voice is that of a sainted nun) and just because of this Eloisa is being shut again in her vocation.

Pope was not the first Ovidian imitator to add a religious con-

1. l. 212.

2. *Poems by William Whitehead*, ed. 1788, vol. iii ('To which are prefixed, Memoirs of his life and writings. By W. Mason'), p. 35.

3. Pope's 'Argument'.

4. Audra, pp. 431 f.

5. Cf. Tillotson, pp. 141 ff.

6. ll. 303 ff.

7. *Heroides*, vii 101 ff.

8. *Ovids Heroical Epistles, Englished*, 1639. Pope is also remembering Fenton's translation of 'Sappho to Phaon', ll. 185 ff.:

> Here while by Sorrow lull'd asleep I lay,
> Thus said the Guardian Nymph, or seem'd to say:
> Fly, *Sappho*, fly . . .

flict to the usual Ovidian ones. Something like the same conflict appears for a moment in Crauford. Hermes, who fell in love with Amestris only to see her unwillingly married to the Earl of her father's choice, recalls the scene in his first letter:

That Sacred place, that shou'd Confine the Soul,
And all our Thoughts, and wand'ring Hearts Controul;
Where ev'ry Act, and ev'ry Look shou'd show
That Gods are by, concern'd in what we do.
Where Silence, Pomp, and Ceremony move
The Humble Mind to a Religious Love.
Ev'n in that Holy Spot, these holier Ties,
That bound the Will, paid Homage to your Eyes:
I look'd, and in that Look ('tis strange to sense)
I both forgot, and pray'd to Heav'n at once . . .[1]

But more strongly than this, Crauford represents another similar conflict, that between official matrimonial vows and adultery. There come lines like:

And Swore Enjoyment ne'er cou'd be a Sin . . .[2]
Love, and Religion oft commence a War,
But still the last assaults you from afar . . .[3]
Let Priests, and frozen Age, make Love a Crime,
Their Trade's to *Speak*, to *Act* is Yours and mine.[4]

But in Pope the conflict is cruelly tightened. Drayton only half realized his opportunity in the John–Matilda letters,[5] nor did the conflict improve the *Lettres Portugaises* or their variation, *Love without Affectation*. In Hughes, the scales tremble and sway from time to time, but Pope goes one further and one might almost say that his poem takes place *on* the scales. Pope's Eloisa, if we can think of her as a real woman for a moment, could have solved Amestris's problems as decisively as she could have solved the choice between marriage and concubinage[6]; but, bound as she is—she is a nun, in

1. E 1r f.
2. E 6v.
3. G 4r.
4. G 7r.
5. He is content to make Matilda a nun and to make John use a small amount of religious imagery.
6. ll. 73 ff.

her cell, she is passionately, physically, in love, her lover is absent, cold, emasculated—she has only two solutions: complete acquiescence in her vows, or death, the solution which she foresees at the end of the letter.

There is also a debt to a religious poet of another persuasion. Isaac Watts' *Horæ Lyricæ* appeared in 1706, reappearing in 1709 'Altered and much Enlarged', and being frequently reprinted thereafter until well into the nineteenth century. The poems were known to Pope (as later to Gray). By birth and breeding Watts was Nonconformist, but that religion was no more cramping to an imagination which, as Dr Johnson allowed, was 'vigorous and active', than Catholicism itself would have been. Watts, haunted by the high emotions and imagery of Prophet, Psalmist, and Apocalypst, rose freely to 'Seraphical Joys of Devotion' and a 'Worship' which attained to 'Meridian Light and Meridian Fervor'. The Preface to his poems—also enlarged in 1709—is a recommendation to poets to turn from such things as 'the trifling and incredible Tales that furnish out a Tragedy', and instead to 'employ' their 'Happy Talent . . . in dressing scenes of Religion in their proper Figures of Majesty, Beauty and Terror'. It is not surprising that Southey was to remark in the 'memoir' prefixed to the 1834 edition of the lyrics that 'The condition of the souls in bliss was a favourite subject of speculation with him'. There was much in Pope's Eloisa, then, that Watts would have deplored, but his own power of rapture was not unlike hers. At a climax she cries:

In seas of flame my plunging soul is drown'd,

(l. 275), and her cry is a clear echo from Watts' 'God Incomprehensible':

I

Far in the Heav'n my God retires,
My God, the Point of my Desires,
And hides his Lovely Face;
When he descends within my view
He charms my Reason to pursue,
But leaves it tir'd and fainting in th' unequal Chase.

II

Or if I reach unusual height,
Till near his Presence brought;

Then Floods of Glory check my Flight,
Cramp the bold Pinions of my Wit
And all untune my Thought;
Plung'd in a Sea of Light I roll,
Where Wisdom, Justice, Mercy Shines;
Infinite Rays in Crossing Lines
Bear thick Confusion on my Sight, and overwhelm my Soul . . .

(1706, p. 16). That echo is a point of close resemblance, but there is a general debt also.

V

Pope found in Crashaw, in Watts, and in his own experience the means for heightening the passion and the indoor scene. The indoor scene also owes something to the Puritan Milton (to 'Il Penseroso'[1]), but the outdoor scene even more (to 'Il Penseroso', to the opening of 'L'Allegro', to *Comus*). The shrines and trembling tapers of Crashaw are housed in the dim religious walls of Milton, and those walls abut on Miltonic glooms and woods.[2] When the Rev.

1. For the disposal of the view, started by T. Warton the younger, that 'Eloisa' is the first of Pope's poems to show the influence of Milton's minor poems, see G. Sherburn, 'The Early Popularity of Milton's Minor Poems' in *Mod. Phil.*, 1919–20, pp. 259 ff. and 515 ff. 'Eloisa' is the first of Pope's poems to show the influence strongly. After 'Eloisa', eighteenth-century poetry is soaked in the Miltonic glooms. The pines and their 'brown nodding horrors' reappear (along with other relics of the heroic epistle) in Richardson's *Pamela*, vol. i, letter 32.

2. It is just possible that the rocky and gloomy landscape of 'Eloisa to Abelard' was partly inspired by the pictures of some of the female saints, e.g. Mary Magdalen. Cf. Addison's *Remarks* which recount the voyage from Marseilles to Genoa, and how Addison went ashore at Cassis where

> We were . . . shown at a distance the Desarts that have been render'd so famous by the Penance of *Mary Magdalene*, who, after her Arrival with *Lazarus* and *Joseph* of *Arimathea* at *Marseilles*, is said to have wept away the rest of her Life among these solitary Rocks and Mountains. It is so Romantic a Scene, that it has always probably given occasion to such Chimerical Relations; for 'tis perhaps of this Place that *Claudian* speaks, in the following Description.
>
> *Est locus extremum pandit qua Gallia littus*
> *Oceani prætentus aquis, quà fertur Ulysses*[.]
> *Sanguine libato populum movisse Silentûm,*
> *Illic Umbrarum tenui stridore volantûm*
> *Flebilis auditur questus; simulachra coloni*

A. H. Mills visited the Paraclete in 1768[1] he found, of course, that Pope's scenery was imaginary:

> I saw neither rocks, nor pines, nor was it a kind of ground which ever seemed to encourage such objects. On the contrary it was a vale: and mountains, like the Alps, generally produce views of [Pope's] kind.[2]

Pope's debt to Milton partly coincides with his debt to some of the recent epistles. He elaborates the scene much more than any previous writer of epistles, but he does not begin from scratch. Ovid had increased the gloom of some of his heroines by sympathetic landscape. Medea speaks of a black grove,[3] and Sappho, waking from her passionate dream, wanders in silent woods among caves hanging with rocks.[4] The general exodus of seventeenth-century lovers into *bois épais*[5] had encouraged this element in the epistles. Dryden inserts a gratuitous 'Gloomy Grove' in his translation of

---

Pallida defunctasque vident migrare figuras, &c.
Cl. In. Ruf. L.I.
A Place there lyes in *Gallia*'s utmost Bounds,
Where rising Seas insult the Frontier grounds.
Ulysses here the Blood of Victims shed,
And rais'd the pale Assembly of the Dead:
Oft in the Winds is heard a plaintive sound
Of melancholy Ghosts, that hover round;
The lab'ring Plow-man oft with Horror spies
Thin airy Shapes, that o'er Furrows rise,
(A dreadful Scene!) and skim before his Eyes.

1. Curiosity about the Paraclete had begun earlier. Lady Hertford writes to her son on 30 Oct. 1743: 'I want to know whether the Paraclete y^u pass'd by is the same where the Convent stands which was found'd by Abelard & wh. is so well known here, by Mr Popes Letter from *Eloisa*?' (Helen S. Hughes, 'More Popeana', *PMLA*, 1929, p. 1098). This article well illustrates the 'romantic' delight which women found in Pope's non-satiric, non-philosophical work.

2. *The Annual Register*, 1768 (ed. 1773), p. 174 (second series). Warton (i 303) and Wakefield similarly note that the Paraclete could not have attained the venerable romantic condition represented by Pope since it was founded by Abelard!

3. *Heroides*, xii 67.

4. *id.*, xv 135 ff.

5. See the famous song in Lully's *Amadis* (1684); cf. Spenser, 'Daphnaida', ll. 484 ff., and contrast G. Herbert, 'Holy Baptisme' (i), ll. 1 f.

Dido's description of the monument of Sychaeus,[1] and Mrs Behn, among other similar liberties, takes the poplar tree mentioned by Ovid's Œnone and endows it with an impossible shade of 'dear gloomy Boughs'.[2] Crauford cherishes this element of the macabre.[3] The glooms were certainly gathering round the forsaken lover by the time that Pope's Eloisa stares out of her gothic casement. And in the local scene and in the landscape that appears to her in her nightmare there are other than Ovidian and Miltonic elements, and elements which were to prove equally important to the poets and novelists who follow. Eloisa sees herself and Abelard wandering

Thro' dreary wastes . . .
Where round some mould'ring tow'r pale ivy creeps.[4]

The earliest ruin-and-ivy seems to be that of Katherine Philips's translation from the French, 'La Solitude de St. Amant', where there are 'old ruin'd Castle walls' with 'Ivy in the Chimney'.[5] *Windsor Forest* had had its 'broken columns [with] clasping ivy twin'd'[6] and between it and 'Eloisa' had come Garth's lines in *Claremont* (1715):

A Grott there was with hoary Moss o'ergrown,
Rough with rude Shells, and arch'd with mouldring Stone;
Sad Silence reigns within the loansome Wall;
And weeping Rills but whisper as they fall.
The clasping Ivys up the Ruin creep;
And there the Bat, and drowsie Beetle sleep.[7]

1. Dryden's *Ovid's Ep.*, p. 220.

2. *id.*, p. 103.

3. The introductory narrative to the letters of Hermes and Amestris provides a scene of 'solitary Groves' and 'gloomy Woods', though their grimness is partly undone by the addition of 'purling Streams' and 'singing Birds' (B 7v). In 'Daria to Odmar' the gloom is kept fairly dark; Daria is writing by night 'at a lonesome Lodge, at the End of [her father's] Garden', hearing wind 'Ruffling', and seeing 'wand'ring Shadows' and even 'stalking Ghosts to snowy Shrouds confin'd' (H 8r, I 2v, I 4r). At I IV f. the night-scene is realized in detail but owes nothing to Milton.

4. ll. 243 f.

5. *Poems* (1669), pp. 175 ff. Spenser (*F.Q.*, VI v 35 1 f.) had had 'a little Chappell . . . all with Yuy ouerspred' but not in ruins.

6. ll. 69 f.

7. p. 13, R. A. Aubin in his instructive *Grottoes, Geology, and the Gothic Revival*

But it was mainly from Milton that Pope learnt how to deepen the gloom, to mix grim and eerie. He needed it to match that heavy or, at times, that almost militant melancholy which is as powerful a part of Eloisa's mind as her luxury of passion.[1]

After what has been said, it is clear that there is little in the frame of 'Eloisa to Abelard' that is Pope's invention. His coda, however, is original, for an epistle. It was Pope's usual practice to end a poem with a sort of quiet personal sonnet[2] and by 1717, no doubt, such a conclusion was expected of him. But even in this, pedantically speaking, he had predecessors in the Elizabethan 'Complaint', a form which has obvious affinities with the heroic epistle. At the end of 'The Complaint of Rosamond' Daniel brings in Delia, and at the end of two of his four *Legends* (which are Complaints with a different name), Drayton brings in Idea. But Pope's characteristic coda is, for the epistle, original. To say this is only to acknowledge how little Pope cared for the kind of originality that invents new things. The originality he does care for is that which recreates older things, raising to a new power the elements that had come to be associated with the kind of poem he was writing. He was original because he crowded into his poem the best of everything that had been already achieved, and heightened it to a new best. Mason may have meant as much when he pronounced 'Eloisa to Abelard' 'such a *chef d'œuvre*, that nothing of the kind can be relished after it.'[3]

VI

But Mason spoke the enthusiasm of a past century. The modern reader is inclined to overlook or disparage 'Eloisa to Abelard'. He

(*Studies in Philology*, xxxi 408 ff.) omits to note Milton's grotto at *Comus*, l. 429, the line which Pope quotes almost without change in 'Eloisa' (l. 20). (Other omissions include Yalden's *Temple of Fame* (1700), pp. 9 ff., *Rape of the Lock*, iv 11 ff., and A. Philips's *Pastorals*, iv—see note on l. 158 below.) For a further contribution to the horror-aesthetics of the century see note on l. 134 below.

1. Audra (pp. 438 f.) has shown how sorrows multiply as the 'translators' of the letters succeed each other. In the Latin there is 1 allusion to tears, 2 to sadness, 1 to sighs; in Bussy 4 to tears and crying, 1 to sighs; in the Holland edition 5 to tears, 3 to sighs; in Pope 'c'est un déluge'—18 allusions to tears and crying, 3 to sighs. Pope feels behind him the weight of the lachrymose translators of classical epic; see Tillotson, pp. 67 ff.

2. 'au coin du tableau, tel un donateur' (Audra, p. 433).

3. Preface to W. Whitehead's *Poems*, iii 35.

does not care for rhetoric. The rhetoric of the poem is, however, justified for several reasons. In the first place, Eloisa's story, the factual material for her letter, is well known before the poem begins. Epistles which, like those of Ovid, Drayton, and Pope, have a historical basis offer technical advantages over those which, like Wither's and Crauford's, have a purely fictional basis. Ovid's epistles are called *Heroides* and Drayton's *Englands Heroicall Epistles*, since the supposed writers, as Drayton explicitly pointed out, were epic figures, figures well known in story and history. This historical derivation means that the reader, without effort, knows as much of the past as the writer and the recipient; the letter purports to be written at a crisis in familiar fortunes. The reader, therefore, expects not to be told the story and persuaded of the passions, but to see a use made of the materials that are known, to see as good a letter as possible made out of them. The writer sees the past through the present, which is not only its result but its unforeseen and unfortunate result. The act of writing is a relief,[1] and the relief is an intellectual, as well as an emotional, one: 'What Reflections did I not make?' cried Hughes's Eloisa, 'I began to consider the whole afresh'.[2]

Then again, the emotions, as well as the facts, are those of a known person. They are also those of Nature. The reader, therefore, already doubly possesses them. They are given, and have not to be proved to exist, as they have to be proved to exist, say, in Wither's epistle, or, more generally, in a nineteenth-century lyric. What is not given is the skill, the quality of the manipulation. And it will be these that will justify the poem. The reader will judge the letter as he judges a fugue on a given subject. Eloisa becomes for him the 'artist', the intellectual master co-ordinating times, places, and moods, the 'artist' of emotion rather than the experiencer of it. The rhetoric is necessary because the skill must be shown. It is assuredly not a case of *ars celare artem*. Nature and known fortunes become surprising by means of Art.

But Nature and Eloisa cannot be wholly identified. Eloisa overtops Nature in two particulars: her emotion is raised to an abnorm-

1. Cf. *Five Love-Letters*, p. 78: ''Tis not so much for your Sake that I write, as my own, for my Business is only to divert, and entertain my self.'

2. p. 100.

ally high power, and her lover is impotent. Nature may be fundamental in Eloisa as it is in Jane Austen's Marianne, but, again as in Marianne, that Nature is on fire. The feelings of mankind become strange because they have become extreme. Eloisa, like Swift's Vanessa a year or two later,[1] shows Nature self-teased almost to madness. It whispers, it speaks normally, it screams. The operatic flights outdo the rhetoric of Ovid and of the ancient guardians of Nature. Eloisa ranges heaven, earth, and hell. The human form, a in Shakespeare's *Venus and Adonis* and Chapman's poems, dilates till it is landscape:

> Back thro' the paths of pleasing sense I ran . . .[2]

or seascape:

> Thy life a long, dead calm of fix'd repose;
> No pulse that riots, and no blood that glows.
> Still as the sea, ere winds were taught to blow,
> Or moving spirit bade the waters flow . . .[3]

Until the modern reader has appreciated the battling contrarieties, general and particular, 'classical' and 'romantic', calm and rhetorical passions, he has not begun to respond to 'Eloisa to Abelard'.

The art of the poem is as triumphant as figure-skating. Dryden had commended Ovid's construction,[4] and the skilful evolution of 'Eloisa' needs no demonstration. The unification of the poem depends on Eloisa's passion. Having made religion into an erotic experience, she ends by making death one, too.[5] Her character, memories, and misfortunes decree the numerous contrasts which vary in the scale of their expression from two paragraphs[6] to two words.[7] The variations of pace are remarkable: compare, for instance, 'I have not yet forgot my self to stone'[8] with the whistling

1. The similarity between the passionate asseverations of Eloisa and Vanessa were noted by Leslie Stephen, *Swift* (1882), pp. 132 f.

2. l. 69.

3. ll. 251 ff.

4. op. cit., A 6r–v.

5. ll. 323 f. n.

6. e.g., ll. 207–48.

7. e.g., 'dear deceits' (l. 240).

8. l. 24.

speed of some of the climaxes.[1] In order that the descriptive passages should be equally rich, the plain Paraclete is described as what it is *not*, which is Crashaw's method in the poem from which Pope quotes a line.

VII

Pope's poem was published in the *Works* of 1717 and the only earlier evidence of its existence is that of a letter to Martha Blount. According to internal evidence, this letter belongs to the Holy Week of a year which Elwin and Courthope suggested to be 1716:[2]

> I am here [no place named] studying ten hours a day, but thinking of you in spight of all the learned. The Epistle of Eloise grows warm, and begins to have some Breathings of the Heart in it, which may make posterity think I was in love. I can scarce find in my heart to leave out the conclusion I once intended for it—[3]

The next mention of the poem is datable as early in June 1717, just after its publication, when Pope sends off a box of books to Turkey for Lady Mary Wortley Montagu. The box, among other things, contains

> all I am worth, that is, my Workes: There are few things in them

1. e.g., ll. 289–94. Daniel Webb (*Observations on Poetry and Music*, in *Miscellanies*, 1802, p. 205) noted that, whereas 'It is said, that monosyllables are fit to describe a slow and heavy motion; and may be happily employed to express languor and melancholy', the reverse is true of those at 'Eloisa', ll. 124 f. and 289 f. Cf. 'The Art of Painting the Passions' by Brewster Rogerson, *Journal of the History of Ideas*, xiv, 1953, pp. 92 f. where Pope's method of representing Eloisa's state of mind is related to contemporary theories about the signs of the strongly moved mind in the body, and the expression of it all in the arts:

> In *Eloisa to Abelard*, several major passions appeared in painful conflict, rising and falling with sudden transitions and violent contrasts until they subsided in gentle resignation. Pope's strategy was to paint the passions either by their outward signs or by the adaptation of his verse to their characteristic bursts and silences, and to insure the full impact of each affection by swift transition to a different but equally strong state of mind.

2. *Pope's Corresp.*, i 338. Sherburn accepts EC's date here and in *The Best of Pope*, 1929, p. 402, when he notes, 'This was apparently about the time the Popes were quitting Binfield reluctantly for Chiswick, and *Eloisa* is very likely the last of the poet's works to be written in the Forest. It contains, as a matter of fact, fully as striking images from nature as did *Windsor Forest*.'

3. *Pope's Corresp.*, i 338.

> but what you have already seen, except the Epistle of Eloisa to Abelard; in which you will find one passage, that I can't tell whether to wish you should understand, or not?[1]

The passage signified is probably the conclusion which refers pretty directly to Pope's experience of Lady Mary's absence:

> Condemn'd whole years in absence to deplore,
> And image charms he must behold no more.[2]

These references could *not* refer to Martha Blount who had never been (or was ever likely to be) absent for whole years. Some part, therefore, of this conclusion—perhaps more than the couplet quoted, since it seems indivisibly of its context—must have been written after Lady Mary's departure for Turkey in late July 1716. This means that Pope *did* 'find in [his] heart to leave out the conclusion [he] once intended for it', the conclusion that must have been specifically addressed to Martha Blount (Pope seems to be breaking it to her that a conclusion she had seen and perhaps been 'promised' is being superseded). Since the conclusion which did in fact supersede it cannot wholly have been written before late July 1716, when Lady Mary sailed for Turkey, there would seem to be a case for transferring the Holy Week of 1716 to 1717, especially since Pope's apology to Martha Blount would not be made till an approaching publication revealed something that needed an apology. The months between Holy Week 1717 and the printing of a poem which occupies the last place in the volume published on 3 June 1717 would seem to leave Pope adequate time for doing what he wanted—the poem of 366 lines was already at the stage of revision since Pope is reconsidering its *conclusion*. But though in that Holy Week he seems to be in the thick of 'Eloisa', warming it, giving it some breathings of the heart, he speaks of the poem as if it were old: '. . . the conclusion I *once* intended for it'. This must mean that the poem, passionately as it was being improved in 1717,[3] had been

1. *id.*, i 407.

2. ll. 361 f. There were other passages, of course, which Lady Mary might take personally, the chief being that exalting a loving mistress over an 'august' 'wedded dame' (ll. 73 ff.).

3. These last-moment breathings of the heart may well be mainly due to the absence of Lady Mary which stirred him deeply. Whatever one may think of his attachment to her or of the degree of sincerity in the passion he sent after her

written some fair time earlier. If I am right in dating the letter to Martha Blount as 1717, we cannot say how much earlier than 1717 that time was, except that it presumably followed 1713, the date of the translation of the letters to which Pope is indebted verbally. The odd plural '*Heloïsa*'s Loves' in his 'Wife of Bath Her Prologue'[1] —Chaucer had mentioned 'Helowis'—suggests that Pope did not know much of her story in 1714, the date of the 'Prologue'. But if the history of the poem shows Pope veering from Martha to Mary,[2] most of the personal undertone of the poem fitted each of them equally—which was as well in view of the later quarrel with Mary.

to Turkey, one cannot doubt that passion it is. For her possible influence on the cognate 'Elegy to the Memory of an Unfortunate Lady', and the dating of that poem, see my article in *RES*, Oct. 1936.

1. l. 361.

2. If the first draft had been inspired at all seriously by Lady Mary, presumably Pope would have shown it to her before she sailed—*minus* the Martha Blount conclusion, unless that conclusion contained nothing that did not equally fit Lady Mary. His letter of June 1717 suggests that this is the first she is hearing of the poem, though Pope had known her at least as early as 1715.

NOTE ON THE TEXT

'Eloisa to Abelard' first appeared in the *Works* of 1717. The volume closes with the section headed *Miscellanies*, and 'Eloisa' occupies the last place in this section. In 1719 appears *Eloisa to Abelard . . . The Second Edition* [Griffith 109]. This octavo volume is postdated M DCC XX. It is furnished with a handsome engraved frontispiece showing Eloisa seated out of doors, pen in hand (see Plate III, facing p. 293) and contains also the second edition of the 'Elegy to the Memory of an Unfortunate Lady', and several other elegiac poems by friends of Pope. After various reprints of no textual importance, the poem is slightly revised for the *Works* of 1736 and 1751.

The present text is that of 1717 revised in accordance with Pope's later readings and in accordance with the system described in the General Note on the Text, pp. x f. above. The punctuation varies in later editions—1736, for instance, is lighter in final stops, presents a few additional medial commas, and removes others. There is no proof that these new pointings are deliberate, and most of them are excluded from the critical apparatus. In the first edition Pope seems to have been using a rhetorical pointing, like that common in Elizabethan poetry. Such pointing was still the recognized equivalent of the contemporary and later italic. At ll. 72, 189, 199[1] the commas virtually italicize the preceding word and at l. 280 the period is equivalent to the contemporary and later dash. The pointing at ll. 72 and 199 presents no difficulty to the modern reader, but at ll. 189 and 280 it is likely to mislead him and the reading of later editions has been preferred. Pope's use of capitals is also interesting. They are sometimes given to a word in order to accent it and so supplement the rhetorical pointing. They are also used to call attention to Roman Catholic terminology.

L. 324 presents a difficulty: 1717–20 read 'the flying soul' and one of the two 1736 editions (Griffith 413) agrees. The other 1736 edition (Griffith 414) and the editions of 1740–51 read 'my flying soul'. This would seem a compositor's error of dittography inadvertently retained in later texts, but in view of the similar variant

1. At l. 199 the comma after 'often' may represent the omission of 'must it'.

at *Rape of the Lock*, i 58, it must be a deliberate correction in the interests of theology.

The error of 1740 at l. 37 has had too long a run and the correct reading has been restored. The form *Eloisa* has been retained: 1736–51 read *Eloïsa*.

NOTE ON THE NOTES

When a letter is quoted from Hughes without specification, Eloisa is to be understood as its writer. The figure following the name Hughes refers to the page.

A few of the parallel passages are taken without individual acknowledgement from the *Gentleman's Magazine*, 1836, pp. 240–3.

KEY TO THE CRITICAL APPARATUS

1717*a* = First edition, Works, quarto, Griffith 79.
1717*b* = First edition, Works, folio, Griffith 82.
1720 = The Second Edition, octavo, Griffith 109.
1736 = Works, octavo, vol. i, Griffith 413.
1740 = Works, octavo, vol. i, part 1, Griffith 510.
1743 = Works, octavo, vol. i, part 1, Griffith 582.
1751 = Works, octavo, ed. Warburton, vol. ii, Griffith 644.

ELOISA
TO
ABELARD

The ARGUMENT.

ABelard *and* Eloisa *flourish'd in the twelfth Century; they were two of the most distinguish'd persons of their age in learning and beauty, but for nothing more famous than for their unfortunate passion. After a long course of Calamities, they retired each to a several Convent, and consecrated the remainder of their days to religion. It was many years after this separation, that a letter of* Abelard'*s to a Friend which contain'd the history of his misfortune, fell into the hands of* Eloisa. *This awakening all her tenderness, occasion'd those celebrated letters (out of which the following is partly extracted) which give so lively a picture of the struggles of grace and nature, virtue and passion.*

7 *misfortune*] *misfortunes 1717–20.*

Pope draws on Hughes's *Preface* and introductory *History*, using several of his phrases.

2. *beauty*] For Abelard's beauty see Hughes, 13 and 196 f. In the original letters Abelard considers Eloisa as 'facie non infima', but in Hughes this has become 'if she was not a perfect Beauty, she appear'd such at least in *Abelard*'s Eyes. Her Person was well-proportion'd, her Features regular, her Eyes sparkling, her Lips Vermilion and well-formed . . .' (p. 10).

ELOISA TO ABELARD

In these deep solitudes and awful cells,
Where heav'nly-pensive, contemplation dwells,
And ever-musing melancholy reigns;
What means this tumult in a Vestal's veins?
Why rove my thoughts beyond this last retreat?
Why feels my heart its long-forgotten heat?
Yet, yet I love!—From *Abelard* it came,
And *Eloisa* yet must kiss the name.
  Dear fatal name! rest ever unreveal'd,
Nor pass these lips in holy silence seal'd.
Hide it, my heart, within that close disguise,
Where, mix'd with God's, his lov'd Idea lies.
Oh write it not, my hand—The name appears

---

1 ff. To show the writer as treasuring her lover's letter and as struggling with tears and emotion in her attempts to answer it, is a recognized opening for a heroic epistle. Cf. Hughes, 99 ff.

1 f. Cf. Broome, 'A Poem On the Seat of War in Flanders . . . Written 1710' (*Poems*, ed. 1750, p. 72):

> Ye gloomy Grots! ye awful solemn Cells,
> Where holy thoughtful *Contemplation* dwells.

9. Cf. 'that fatal Word *Adieu*' (*Ovidius Brit.*, K 5v). Wakefield compares *Æneid*, v 49 f., 'which nothing even in this poem can exceed in tenderness':

> iamque dies, nisi fallor, adest, quem semper acerbum,
> semper honoratum (sic di voluistis) habebo;

for Pope's echo of Dryden's translation of this passage, see l. 31 and note.

12. Cf. 'Thou charming Idea of a Lover', and 'you . . . the dear Idea' (Hughes, 182 f. and 197). Wakefield explains by citing Tasso, i 486 ff.:

> Her sweet Idea wandred through his Thought,
> Her Shape, her Gesture, and her Place in Mind
> He kept.

13 f. Cf. *Ovidius Brit.*, K 5v:

> My trembling Hand cou'd not my Pen contain,
> Nor all my Courage, falling Tears restrain;
> Or if I write, they wash'd it out again!

Wakefield compares Claudian, *Epithalamium Honorii et Mariæ*, 9 f.: 'nomenque beatum Injussæ scripsere manus!' In Hughes (102 and 131) Eloisa blots the paper with tears.

Already written—wash it out, my tears!
In vain lost *Eloisa* weeps and prays,
Her heart still dictates, and her hand obeys.
  Relentless walls! whose darksom round contains
Repentant sighs, and voluntary pains:
Ye rugged rocks! which holy knees have worn;
Ye grots and caverns shagg'd with horrid thorn!
Shrines! where their vigils pale-ey'd virgins keep,
And pitying saints, whose statues learn to weep!
Tho' cold like you, unmov'd, and silent grown,
I have not yet forgot my self to stone.

---

16. Cf. Hughes, 122: 'All I desire is such Letters as the Heart dictates, and which the Hand can scarce Write fast enough.'

17. *Relentless*] Crashaw has 'relentlesse rockes', 'Alexias', Elegy ii 15.
darksom] An epithet often found in Spenser; cf. l. 155 below.

18. Cf. Rochester, *Satyr against Mankind*, l. 127:

> [Man] With voluntary Pains works his Distress.

20. Cf. *Comus*, l. 429:

> By grots, and caverns shag'd with horrid shades.

See Introduction, pp. 305 f. Pope's change emphasizes the Latin connotation of Milton's *horrid*; *horridus* = bristling. Cf. *Æneid*, ix 382.

21 f. 'v[ide] D. of Wharton's "Fear of Death."

> "Where pale-ey'd griefs their wasting vigils keep."

Again, in the Tower.

> "Where kneeling statues constant vigils keep,
> And round the tombs the marble cherubs weep." '

(*Gentleman's Mag.*, 1836, p. 340: I have failed to check these references.) Cf. also Milton, 'Ode on the Morning of Christ's Nativity', l. 180: 'pale-ey'd Priest'.

22. 'A puerile conceit, from the dew, which runs down stone and metals in damp weather. *Virgil*, Geo. i 480.

> Et maestum illacrimat templis ebur æraque sudant.'

(Wakefield.) Cf. Gould, ii, p. 10:

> And thro' th' affrighted Tomb did Groans resound:
> The very Marbles wept...

24. Cf. Hughes, 129: 'O Vows! O Convent! I have not lost my Humanity under your inexorable Discipline! You have not made me Marble by changing my Habit'; and Milton, 'Il Penseroso', l. 42: 'Forget thy self to Marble'; and cf. Dryden's *Don Sebastian*, iv:

> I have not yet forgot I am a King;
> Whose Royall Office is redress of Wrongs:

All is not Heav'n's while *Abelard* has part,
Still rebel nature holds out half my heart;
Nor pray'rs nor fasts its stubborn pulse restrain,
Nor tears, for ages, taught to flow in vain.
  Soon as thy letters trembling I unclose,
That well-known name awakens all my woes.
Oh name for ever sad! for ever dear!
Still breath'd in sighs, still usher'd with a tear.
I tremble too where-e'er my own I find,
Some dire misfortune follows close behind.
Line after line my gushing eyes o'erflow,
Led thro' a sad variety of woe:

25 Heav'n claims me all in vain, while he has part, *1717–43*.

If I have wrong'd thee, charge me face to face;
I have not yet forgot I am a Soldier.

26. Wakefield compares Sedley, 'To a Devout Young Woman', ll. 1 ff.:

Phillis, this early Zeal asswage,
  You over-act your part;
The Martyrs, at your tender Age,
  Gave Heaven but half their Heart.

27 f. Cf. Hughes, 198 f.: 'We have bound our selves to severe Austerities, and must follow them, let them cost us ever so dear. . . You *Abelard*, will happily finish your Course, your Desires and Ambitions will be no Obstacle to your Salvation. *Heloise* only must lament, she only must weep without being certain whether all her Tears will be available or not to her Salvation.'

30. Cf. Hughes, 107: 'by that melancholy Relation to your Friend, you have awaken'd all my Sorrows.'

31. Cf. Dryden's *Æneid*, v 64:

(A Day for ever sad, for ever dear,).

Cf. *Odyssey*, xiv 167.

31 f. Cf. Hughes, 103: 'Shall my *Abelard* be never mention'd without Tears? Shall the dear Name be never spoken but with Sighs?'

33 f. Cf. Hughes, 100: 'I met with my Name a hundred Times; I never saw it without Fear; some heavy Calamity always followed it: I saw yours too, equally unhappy'.

36. The phrase 'variety of woe(s)' is found in Sandys' *Paraphrase upon Ecclesiastes*, iii 18, in K. Philips's *Poems* (1669), p. 7, &c.; 'sad variety of hell' in Dryden, *State of Innocence*, 1 i 6. Pomfret, 'Love Triumphant over Reason' (*Poems*, 1710, p. 20) has 'such Sad variety of Woe'.

Now warm in love, now with'ring in thy bloom,
Lost in a convent's solitary gloom!
There stern religion quench'd th' unwilling flame,
There dy'd the best of passions, Love and Fame.
  Yet write, oh write me all, that I may join
Griefs to thy griefs, and eccho sighs to thine.
Nor foes nor fortune take this pow'r away.
And is my *Abelard* less kind than they?
Tears still are mine, and those I need not spare,
Love but demands what else were shed in pray'r;
No happier task these faded eyes pursue,

37 thy] my *1740–51.*

37. Cf. Dryden's 'Palamon and Arcite', iii 795:

Now warm in Love, now with'ring in the Grave;

Steele's Miscellany, 1714, p. 268: 'wither in the Bloom'; and *Iliad*, vi 182.

38. *convent*] = monastery.

40. 'Fame' may be equated with 'ambition', as Bowles suggests. Davenant chose love and ambition as the themes of *Gondibert*: 'for Love and Ambition are too often the raging Feavers of great minds' (Spingarn, ii 14).

Eloisa, like Abelard, had had her taste of fame: '[Fulbert] had already put her to learn several Languages, which she quickly came to understand so well, that her Fame began to spread it self abroad, and the Wit and Learning of *Heloise* was every where discours'd of' (Hughes, 11).

41 ff. Cf. Hughes, 103 ff.: 'Let me have a faithful Account of all that concerns you. . . Perhaps, by mingling my Sighs with yours, I may make your Sufferings less. . . Let us not lose, thro' Negligence, the only Happiness [that is, of letter writing] which is left us, and the only one perhaps which the Malice of our Enemies can never ravish from us.'

43. *foes*] Cf. last line of n. on ll. 51 ff. below.

45 f. Cf. Hughes, 104: 'Tell me not, by way of Excuse, you will spare our Tears; the Tears of Women shut up in a melancholy Place, and devoted to Penitence, are not to be spar'd.'

47 f. Cf. Dryden's *Ovid's Ep.*, p. 42:

Still let them weep, for, loosing sight of you,
'Tis the whole business which they ought to do.

Wakefield compares Denham, 'Of Prudence', l. 94:

To live and dye is all we have to do.

EC add Prior, 'Celia to Damon', ll. 41 ff.:

. . . and These poor Eyes . . .
Shall only be of use to read, or weep.

To read and weep is all they now can do.
  Then share thy pain, allow that sad relief;
Ah more than share it! give me all thy grief.
Heav'n first taught letters for some wretch's aid,
Some banish'd lover, or some captive maid;
They live, they speak, they breathe what love inspires,
Warm from the soul, and faithful to its fires,
The virgin's wish without her fears impart,
Excuse the blush, and pour out all the heart,
Speed the soft intercourse from soul to soul,
And waft a sigh from *Indus* to the *Pole*.
  Thou know'st how guiltless first I met thy flame,

---

49 f. Cf. Hughes, 103: 'Be not then unkind, nor deny me, I beg of you, that little Relief which you only can give . . . all Sorrows divided are made lighter.'

51 ff. Cf. Hughes, 106: 'Letters were first invented for comforting such solitary Wretches as my self'. The discussion of their invention by the *Athenian Oracle* (i 338) inspired Anne, Lady Winchelsea's 'To a Friend In Praise of the Invention of Writing Letters'. *Guardian* 172 reads: 'the use of Letters [i.e., the alphabet], as significative of . . . Sounds, is such an . . . improvement . . . that I know not whether we ought not to attribute the Invention of them to the Assistance of a Power more than Human . . . By [writing] the *English* Trader may hold Commerce with the Inhabitants of the *East* or *West Indies*, without the Trouble of a Journey . . . what is spoken and thought at one Pole, may be heard and understood at the other.' Cf. also Dryden's *Ovid's Ep.*, p. 204:

Thus secrets safe to farthest Shoars may move;
By Letters Foes converse and learn to Love.

53 ff. Cf. Hughes, 105 f.: 'what cannot Letters inspire? They have Souls, they can speak, they have in them all that Force which expresses the Transports of the Heart; they have all the Fire of our Passions, they can raise them as much as if the Persons themselves were present; they have all the Softness and Delicacy of Speech.'

56. *Excuse*] in the sense of 'exempt from the need of' (OED, 13).

59 f. Cf. Hughes, 12: '[Fulbert] embrac'd [Abelard's] Proposal [to become Eloisa's tutor] with all the Joy imaginable, gave him a thousand Caresses, and desir'd he would consider him for the future as one ambitious of the strictest Friendship with him'; 'I continually call to Mind', writes Eloisa (Hughes, 137), 'that Day when you bestowed on me the first Marks of your Tenderness' (cf. 176).

When Love approach'd me under Friendship's name;
My fancy form'd thee of Angelick kind,
Some emanation of th' all-beauteous Mind.
Those smiling eyes, attemp'ring ev'ry ray,
Shone sweetly lambent with celestial day:
Guiltless I gaz'd; heav'n listen'd while you sung;
And truths divine came mended from that tongue.
From lips like those what precept fail'd to move?
Too soon they taught me 'twas no sin to love.
Back thro' the paths of pleasing sense I ran,

60. EC compare Prior, 'Celia to Damon', ll. 9 f.:

In vain I strove to check my growing Flame,
Or shelter Passion under Friendship's Name.

61 ff. Cf. Hughes, 121: 'Alas! What Folly is it to talk at this rate? I see nothing here but marks of the Deity, and I speak of nothing but Man!'

62. For this Platonic idea cf. *Ess. on Man*, ii 23 f.

63. Wakefield compares Statius, *Silvae*, IV ii 41 f.:

tranquillum vultus et maiestate serena
mulcentem radios.

64. *lambent*] The OED cites Cowley as the author who introduced the word into English. According to the same authority, Pope was the first author to soften the sense, which formerly had approximated to the Latin sense of 'licking', and to make it mean something like 'radiant', but a similar sense is found in Gould, ii 59: 'A Lambent Brightness round Her Temples play'd'.

64 ff. Cf. Hughes, 116: 'that Life in your Eyes which so admirably express'd the Vivacity of your Mind; your Conversation, with that Ease and Elegance, which gave every Thing you spoke such an agreeable and insinuating Turn.'

65. Cf. Hughes, 117: 'With what Ease did you compose Verses? . . . The smallest Song . . . had a thousand Beauties capable of making it last as long as there are Love or Lovers in the World.'

66. *He was her Preceptor in Philosophy and Divinity*. [P. 1717 folio (Griffith 82)–1751.] Cf. Hughes, 26.

Cf. Hughes, 112: 'with what Pleasure I have past whole Days in hearing you discourse'; and Dryden's 'To Kneller', l. 105:

The Fair themselves go mended from thy Hand.

69 f. Wakefield, who thought this whole paragraph 'so happily descriptive of a most delicate operation of the mind, among the very noblest efforts of English poetry', paraphrases this couplet: 'Thy holy precepts and the sanctity of thy character had made me conceive of thee as a being more venerable than man. . . But thy personal allurements soon inspired those tender feelings, which gradually conducted me from a *veneration* of the *angel* to a . . . *love* for the *man*.' I have para-

Nor wish'd an Angel whom I lov'd a Man.
Dim and remote the joys of saints I see,
Nor envy them, that heav'n I lose for thee.
How oft', when press'd to marriage, have I said,
Curse on all laws but those which love has made!
Love, free as air, at sight of human ties,

72 them,] them *1736–51*.

phrased the sense of the couplet thus in my *Pope and Human Nature*, 1958, p. 30 n.:

At first I thought you an angel, but when you taught me that loving was no sin, I retreated from my misconception and ran back happily through those paths of pleasing sense that I had first traversed in the opposite direction.

73–98. In Hughes's *History* (21 f. and 25 ff.), Eloisa's reasons against marriage are set out and discussed with the slightly vulgar relish and insistence which one associates with the *Spectator*. Pope purifies the issue, neglecting Eloisa's practical arguments (that marriage would injure Abelard's professional career) and retaining only the argument that 'true passion' (l. 79) abhors and is profaned by worldly guarantees: Eloisa wishes to be 'more free' only so as to be 'more fond' (89 f.). Cf. K. Philips on friendship, *Poems* (1669), p. 79:

All Love is sacred, and the Marriage-tie
Hath much of Honour and Divinity.
But Lust, Design, or some unworthy ends
May mingle there, which are despis'd by Friends;

and p. 94:

Nobler then Kindred or then Marriage-band,
Because more free.

With the help of the lines from Chaucer (which Spenser had echoed seriously in *F.Q.*, III i 25 (7 ff.), and Butler lightly in *Hudibras*, III i 545 ff.), Pope escapes not only the attitude of Hughes and the *Spectator*, but also that of Restoration comedy. But, on the other hand, he intends Martha Blount and/or Lady Mary Wortley Montagu to be free to understand a personal invitation.

Certainly others made free use of the passage. Ll. 91 f. were quoted by Curll in an advertisement (*Evening Post*, 17 Dec. 1717) of Rawlinson's edition of the original letters of Abelard and Eloisa; 'The warmth of this passage makes its quotation a typical "Curlicism", with unfriendly intention both to virtue and to Pope' (Sherburn, *Mod. Phil.*, xxii 332): see note on ll. 91 f. below.

73 f. Cf. Dryden, Ovid's *Metam.*, x 59:

And own no Laws, but those which Love ordains;

and *Aureng-Zebe*, II i:

'Tis true, of marriage-bands I'm weary grown;
Love scorns all ties, but those that are his own.

75 ff. *Love will not be confin'd by Maisterie:*

Spreads his light wings, and in a moment flies.
Let wealth, let honour, wait the wedded dame,
August her deed, and sacred be her fame;
Before true passion all those views remove,
Fame, wealth, and honour! what are you to Love?
The jealous God, when we profane his fires,
Those restless passions in revenge inspires;
And bids them make mistaken mortals groan,
Who seek in love for ought but love alone.
Should at my feet the world's great master fall,
Himself, his throne, his world, I'd scorn 'em all:
Not *Cæsar*'s empress wou'd I deign to prove;
No, make me mistress to the man I love;

When Maisterie comes, the Lord of Love anon
Flutters his wings, and forthwith he is gone.

Chaucer ['Franklin's Tale', 36 ff.]. [P. 1751.] Pope's text is neither that of Speght (1687) nor of Urry (1721).

77 ff. Cf. Hughes, 113 ff.: 'I knew that the Name of Wife was honourable in the World, and holy in Religion, yet the Name of your Mistress had greater Charms, because it was more free. The Bonds of Matrimony, however honourable, still bear with them a necessary Engagement. And I was very unwilling to be necessitated to love always a Man who perhaps would not always love me. I despised the Name of Wife, that I might live happy with that of Mistress. . . 'Tis not Love, but the Desire of Riches and Honour, which makes Women run into the Embraces of an Indolent Husband. Ambition, not Affection, forms such Marriages. I believe indeed they may be followed with some Honours and Advantages, but I can never think that this is the Way to enjoy the Pleasures of an affectionate Union.'

81 ff. Cf. Hughes, 115: 'This restless and tormenting Passion [i.e. ambition] punishes them for aiming at other Advantages by Love than Love it self.'

85. Cf. *Temple of Fame*, l. 156.

85 ff. Cf. Hughes, 114: 'how often I have made protestations that it was infinitely preferable to me to live with *Abelard* as his Mistress, than with any other as Empress of the World, and that I was more happy in obeying you, than I should have been in lawfully captivating the Lord of the Universe.'

Abelard had spoken similarly of his first love for Eloisa (79 f.): 'I would not have exchang'd my happy condition for that of the greatest Monarch upon Earth'.

If there be yet another name more free,
More fond than mistress, make me that to thee!
Oh happy state! when souls each other draw,
When love is liberty, and nature, law:
All then is full, possessing, and possest,
No craving Void left aking in the breast:
Ev'n thought meets thought ere from the lips it part,
And each warm wish springs mutual from the heart.
This sure is bliss (if bliss on earth there be)
And once the lot of *Abelard* and me.
  Alas how chang'd! what sudden horrors rise!

89. See note at ll. 77 ff. above.

89 f. Cf. Hughes, 107: 'We are call'd your Sisters; we call our selves your Children; and if it were possible to think of any Expressions which could signifie a dearer Relation, or a more affectionate Regard and mutual Obligation between us, we should use them'. Note change of context.

91 f. Pope is indebted to Dryden's *Absalom and Achitophel*, i 5 f.:

> When Nature prompted and no Law deni'd
> Promiscuous Use of Concubine and Bride;

the general sense of which he made more subtle by help from Denham, *Cooper's Hill*, ll. 333 f.:

> Happy when both to the same centre move,
> When kings give liberty and subjects love.

Pope adapted l. 92 for *Ess. on Man*, iii 208.

97 f. Cf. Hughes, 115: 'If there is any Thing which may properly be call'd Happiness here below, I am persuaded it is in the Union of two Persons who love each other with perfect Liberty.'

99 ff. Cf. Hughes, 118 f.: 'oh! Where is that happy Time fled?.. Where was I? Where was your *Heloise* then? What Joy should I have had in defending my Lover? I would have guarded you from Violence, tho' at the Expence of my Life; my Cries and Shrieks alone would have stopp'd the Hand—Oh! whither does the Excess of Passion hurry me? Here Love is shock'd, and Modesty, join'd with Despair, deprive me of Words: 'Tis Eloquence to be silent, where no Expressions can reach the greatness of the Misfortune'; note on ll. 177 ff. below; and Elizabeth Singer Rowe, 'Upon the Death of her Husband', ll. 56 ff.:

> The flattering vision takes its hasty flight,
> And scenes of horror swim before my sight.
> Grief and despair in all their terrors rise;
> A dying lover pale and gasping lies.

Thomas Rowe (b. 1687) died in 1715. Pope included the elegy in his 'own'

A naked Lover bound and bleeding lies!
Where, where was *Eloise*? her voice, her hand,
Her ponyard, had oppos'd the dire command.
Barbarian stay! that bloody stroke restrain;
The crime was common, common be the pain.
I can no more; by shame, by rage supprest,
Let tears, and burning blushes speak the rest.
    Canst thou forget that sad, that solemn day,
When victims at yon' altar's foot we lay?

103 stroke] hand *1717–20.*

Miscellany (1717) and among the poems appended to the Second Edition of *Eloisa* (1720).

102. *ponyard*] This weapon is mentioned by Hughes (p. 56) as feared more than poison by Abelard at St Gildas.

104. Cf. Hughes, 169 f.: 'You alone expiated the Crime common to us both' Drummond of Hawthornden, 'Flowres of Sion', vii 1:

> The Griefe was common, common were the Cryes;

Dryden's *Georgics*, iv 270:

> Their Toyl is common, common is their Sleep;

and Dryden's *Ovid's Ep.*, p. 11:

> Our first crime common; this was mine alone.

pain] = punishment (Latin *pœna*) as well as the common English meaning. The original letters read (ed. Rawlinson, 1718, p. 65): 'solus in pœna fuisti, duo in culpa . . .'

106. Cf. Dryden's *Tyrannic Love*, v i:

> I cannot speak—my tears shall speak the rest;

Settle's *Empress of Morocco*, III i:

> . . . Let my Tears and Blushes speak the rest;

and Mrs Behn, Dryden's *Ovid's Ep.*, p. 92:

> Whilst Sighs and Looks, all dying, spoke the rest.

108 ff. Since Eloisa and Abelard were professed at different times and places, Pope is here only referring to Eloisa's profession, at which Abelard was present. 'Victims' has unnecessarily been taken to mean that Abelard was also taking the vow at that time. Eloisa's conduct was far from 'solemn' and 'cold' according to Abelard's first letter: 'Speaking these Verses, she marched up to the Altar, and took the Veil with a Constancy which I could not have expected in a Woman who had so high a Taste of Pleasures which she might still enjoy' (Hughes, 93 f.). This account is modified in his second letter: 'I accompanied you with Terror to the foot of the Altar: And while you stretched out your Hand to touch the sacred

Canst thou forget what tears that moment fell,
When, warm in youth, I bade the world farewell?
As with cold lips I kiss'd the sacred veil,
The shrines all trembled, and the lamps grew pale:
Heav'n scarce believ'd the conquest it survey'd,
And Saints with wonder heard the vows I made.
Yet then, to those dread altars as I drew,
Not on the Cross my eyes were fix'd, but you;
Not grace, or zeal, love only was my call,
And if I lose thy love, I lose my all.
Come! with thy looks, thy words, relieve my woe;
Those still at least are left thee to bestow.
Still on that breast enamour'd let me lie,
Still drink delicious poison from thy eye,

Cloth, I heard you pronounce distinctly those fatal words which for ever separated you from all Men' (150 f.).

112. Cf. Prior, 'Henry and Emma', l. 337:

> Thy Limbs all trembling, and thy Cheeks all pale;

and Ovid, *Fasti*, iii 47:

> ara deæ certe tremuit pariente ministra.

113 ff. Cf. Hughes, 178: ' 'twas your Command only, and not a sincere Vocation, that shut me up in these Cloisters. I sought to give you Ease, and not to sanctify my self'.

115 ff. Cf. Hughes, 122: 'For in being Professed, I vowed no more than to be yours only. . . Why should I conceal from you the Secret of my Call? you know it was neither Zeal nor Devotion which led me to the Cloister'. Abelard writes (p. 154): 'I saw your Eyes, when you spoke your last farewell, fix'd upon the Cross'.

119 f. Cf. Hughes, 111: 'You may see me, hear my Sighs, and be a Witness of all my Sorrows, without incurring any Danger, since you can only relieve me with Tears and Words'.

122. Pope (who repeatedly describes the eye in this poem) here combines *Antony and Cleopatra*, I v 26 f.:

> . . . now I feed myself
> With most delicious poison . . .

with the common idea found, e.g., in *Ovidius Brit.*, p. 24: 'she drunk the Poyson in, and knew not if his Eyes or Tongue bewitched her Judgment most'.

Cf. also Hughes, 153: 'We cannot say Love is a Drunkenness and a Poison, 'till we are illuminated by Grace; in the mean time it is an Evil which we doat on.'

Pant on thy lip, and to thy heart be prest;
Give all thou canst—and let me dream the rest.
Ah no! instruct me other joys to prize,
With other beauties charm my partial eyes,
Full in my view set all the bright abode,
And make my soul quit *Abelard* for God.
  Ah think at least thy flock deserves thy care,
Plants of thy hand, and children of thy pray'r.
From the false world in early youth they fled,
By thee to mountains, wilds, and deserts led.
You rais'd these hallow'd walls; the desert smil'd,
And Paradise was open'd in the Wild.
No weeping orphan saw his father's stores

129 deserves] deserve *1717–20.*

125 ff. Cf. Hughes, 130: 'Teach me the Maxims of Divine Love. Since you have forsaken me I glory in being wedded to Heaven . . . tell me how this Divine Love is nourished. . . Without changing the Ardor of our Affections, let us change their Object . . . let us lift up our Hearts to God, and have no Transports but for his Glory.'

129 ff. Cf. Hughes, 110, where Eloisa is asking for a letter, not a visit: 'you neglect the innocent Sheep [the nuns], who tender as they are, would yet follow you thro' Desarts and Mountains'. On the previous page, Eloisa compares the nunnery to a plantation.

133. *He founded the Monastery.* [P. 1717–51.]

134. Paradise (the Garden of Eden) was set in the midst of desolation, and was closed after the sin committed by Adam and Eve. The Paraclete is fancied as achieving a reversal of this doom. Milton had already represented Eden as restored by Christ, and in a 'wast Wilderness', see *Paradise Regained*, i 1–7. Cf. Dryden, *Absal. and Achit.*, i 30:

And *Paradise* was open'd in his face,

which, as George Sewell pointed out (Spurgeon, i 351), Dryden had adapted from Chaucer's *Troilus*, v 817.

The sudden oasis—'beauty lying in the lap of horror'—had been strongly presented in *Par. Lost*, iv 131 ff. (cf. Isaiah, li 3) and was to endear itself to all eighteenth-century aestheticians. Mrs Radcliffe compares the palace at Carlsruhe, in its setting of forests, to 'Milton's Eden—like Paradise opened in the wild' (*Journey . . . through Holland . . .* 1795, p. 262).

135 ff. Cf. Hughes, 108: 'These Cloisters owe nothing to publick Charities; our Walls were not rais'd by the Usury of Publicans, nor their Foundations laid in

Our shrines irradiate, or emblaze the floors;
No silver saints, by dying misers giv'n,
Here brib'd the rage of ill-requited heav'n:
But such plain roofs as piety could raise,
And only vocal with the Maker's praise.
In these lone walls (their day's eternal bound)
These moss-grown domes with spiry turrets crown'd,
Where awful arches make a noon-day night,
And the dim windows shed a solemn light;
Thy eyes diffus'd a reconciling ray,
And gleams of glory brighten'd all the day.
But now no face divine contentment wears,
'Tis all blank sadness, or continual tears.
See how the force of others' pray'rs I try,
(Oh pious fraud of am'rous charity!)

141 day's] days *1717–20, 1751.*

---

base Extortion. The God whom we serve, sees nothing but innocent Riches, and harmless Votaries, whom you have placed here'; and Dryden, 'Eleonora', ll. 22 ff., especially l. 25:

Heav'n, that had largely giv'n, was largely pay'd.

136. Both verbs are found in Milton (*Par. Lost,* iii 53; *Comus,* l. 733), but this is the only instance of *irradiate* meaning 'adorn with splendour'.

137. Cf. the scores of saints' images in silver given to the Santa Casa at Loreto (*The History of Loreto, passim*).

140. *Maker's*] i.e., God's; Wakefield understands Abelard's.

142. *domes*] See *Temple of Fame*, l. 65 n.

145. Wakefield compares Dryden, 'Character of a Good Parson. Imitated from Chaucer', l. 3:

His Eyes diffus'd a venerable Grace.

146. Wakefield compares Elizabeth Singer Rowe, 'On the Creation' (Dryden's *Miscellanies*, v, 1704, p. 374):

And kind'ling Glories brighten all the Skies.

149 ff. Cf. Hughes, 110: 'But why should I intreat you in the Name of your Children? Is it possible I should fear obtaining any thing of you, when I ask it in my own Name? And must I use any other Prayers than my own, to prevail upon you?'

150. Eloisa has been trying to persuade Abelard to visit the Paraclete by pleading that the whole convent misses him; she has been relying on the power

But why should I on others' pray'rs depend?
Come thou, my father, brother, husband, friend!
Ah let thy handmaid, sister, daughter move,
And, all those tender names in one, thy love!
The darksom pines that o'er yon' rocks reclin'd
Wave high, and murmur to the hollow wind,
The wandring streams that shine between the hills,
The grots that eccho to the tinkling rills,
The dying gales that pant upon the trees,
The lakes that quiver to the curling breeze;
No more these scenes my meditation aid,
Or lull to rest the visionary maid:
But o'er the twilight groves, and dusky caves,

---

of their combined wishes. Now she throws over this argument, which was merely a pious fraud supposedly in the interests of charity (the Christian love of our fellow men), but really in her own interests, which are 'amorous'. The term 'pious fraud' seems to have originated in France during the eighteenth century: it denotes a trick to deceive in order to promote an object, especially a religious object, deemed beneficial.

152 f. The superscription of Eloisa's first letter begins '*To her Lord, her Father, her Husband, her Brother; his Servant, his Child, his Wife, his Sister*' (Hughes, 99).

154. Cf. Hughes, 125: 'If you are a Lover, a Father, help a Mistress, comfort a Child! These tender Names, cannot they move you?'; *Five Love Letters*, p. 77: 'There are a thousand tender names that I could call you now'; and 'Part of the Cento of Ausonius, Imitated' (Dryden's *Miscellany*, vi, 1709, p. 472), where, pointedly for Pope's purpose, the words are those of a bridegroom:

. . . My Love, my Life,
And ev'ry tender Name in One, my Wife.

Pope uses the line-formula again at *Odyssey*, xxii 226.

157. Pope's line is competing, successfully, with such lines as Virgil's (*Ecl.*, v 84):

saxosas inter decurrunt flumina vallis,

and with Dryden's translation of it (l. 131):

Nor winding Streams that through the Valley glide.

158. Cf. A. Philips, *Pastorals*, iv 109 f.:

Nor dropping Waters, that in Grots distil,
And with a tinkling Sound their Caverns fill.

162. 'visionary' has two meanings at this time: Dryden's 'Visionary Maid' (*Æneid*, iii 576) = 'maid seeing visions' (as here), but at 'Theodore and Honoria,' l. 280, the same phrase = 'maid seen in a vision' (cf. his *Æneid*, ii 365).

Long-sounding isles, and intermingled graves,
Black Melancholy sits, and round her throws
A death-like silence, and a dread repose:
Her gloomy presence saddens all the scene,
Shades ev'ry flow'r, and darkens ev'ry green,
Deepens the murmur of the falling floods,
And breathes a browner horror on the woods.
Yet here for ever, ever must I stay;

164. *isles*] = aisles, 'a wing or lateral division of a church' (OED); cf. *Temple of Fame*, l. 265.

165 ff. See Intro., pp. 305 ff.

'The figurative expressions, *throws*, and *breathes*, and *browner* horror, are . . . some of the strongest and boldest in the English language. The IMAGE of the Goddess MELANCHOLY sitting over the convent, and, as it were, expanding her dreadful wings over its whole circuit, and diffusing her gloom all around it, is truly sublime, and strongly conceived' (Warton, i 315).

166. Cf. Waller, 'Part of the Fourth Book of Virgil, Translated', l. 86:

A death-like quiet, and deep silence fell;

Bowles quotes Steevens's parallel from Charles Bainbrigg in *Justa Edouardo King Naufrago* (1638), p. 34:

. . . fœtor caligine mixtus
Horrorem ingeminet. . .
Terribilis requies et vasta silentia cingant.

168 f. Cf. Fenton, 'Sappho to Phaon' (*Miscellaneous Poems*, 1712, p. 239):

With him the Caves were cool, the Grove was green,
But now his Absence withers all the Scene.

169 f. Cf. I. Watts, *Horæ Lyricæ*, 1706, p. 89:

His Charms shall make my Numbers flow,
And hold the falling Floods,
While Silence sits on every Bough
And bends the List'ning Woods.

170. *Brown* shadows are found in English poetry as early as Fairfax's *Tasso*, xx 123, l. 1. For other instances see Tillotson, p. 155. 'Brown horror' is found in Dryden (e.g., *Hind and Panther*, ii 659, and *Æneid*, vii 40 f.:

. . . a Wood,
Which thick with Shades, and a brown Horror, stood).

Pope had already used the phrase at 'Thebais', l. 516.

171 ff. Cf. Hughes, 122: 'I took the Veil, and engaged my self to live for ever under your Laws[.] For in being Professed, I vowed no more than to be yours only, and I obliged my self voluntarily to a Confinement in which you desired to place me. Death only then can make me leave the Place where you have fixed me: and then too my Ashes shall rest here, and wait for yours.'

Sad proof how well a lover can obey!
Death, only death, can break the lasting chain;
And here ev'n then, shall my cold dust remain,
Here all its frailties, all its flames resign,
And wait, till 'tis no sin to mix with thine.
    Ah wretch! believ'd the spouse of God in vain,
Confess'd within the slave of love and man.
Assist me heav'n! but whence arose that pray'r?
Sprung it from piety, or from despair?
Ev'n here, where frozen chastity retires,

174 ff. Cf. Hughes, 160: 'I hope you will be contented, when you have finished this mortal Life, to be buried near me. Your cold Ashes need then fear nothing.'

177 ff. There are several parallels to this in the letters, since it is their central conflict. Cf. Hughes, 120–4: 'And tho' in this Place I ought not to retain a Wish of my own, yet I have ever secretly preserved the Desire of being beloved by you... The unhappy Consequences of a criminal Conduct, and your Disgraces, have put on me this Habit of Chastity, and not the sincere Desire of being truly penitent... Among those who are wedded to God I serve a Man... Enlighten me, O Lord! . . . I am sensible I am, in the Temple of Chastity, covered only with the Ashes of that Fire which hath consumed us. I am here, I confess, a Sinner, but one who far from weeping for her Sins, weeps only for her Lover; far from abhorring her Crimes, endeavours only to add to them; and who with a Weakness unbecoming the State I am in, please my self continually with the Remembrance of past Actions, when it is impossible to renew them'; and 174 f.: ' 'tis the last Violence to our Nature to extinguish the Memory of Pleasures, which by a sweet Habit have gain'd absolute Possession of our minds... I, who have experienced so many Pleasures in loving you, feel, in spight of my self, that I cannot repent of them, nor forbear enjoying them over again as much as is possible, by recollecting them... Whatever Endeavours I use, on whatever side I turn me, the sweet Idea still pursues me, and every Object brings to my Mind what I ought to forget. During the still Night, when my Heart ought to be quiet in the midst of Sleep . . . I cannot avoid those Illusions my Heart entertains. I think I am still with my dear *Abelard*. I see him, I speak to him, and hear him answer. Charmed with each other, we quit our Philosophick Studies to entertain our selves with our Passion. Sometimes too I seem to be a Witness of the bloody Enterprize of your Enemies; I oppose their Fury, I fill our Apartment with fearful Cries, and in the Moment I awake in Tears. Even into holy Places before the Altar I carry with me the Memory of our guilty Loves. They are my whole Business, and far from lamenting for having been seduced, I sigh for having lost them.'

178. *Confess'd*] The ordinary sense is deepened by the religious one.

Love finds an altar for forbidden fires.
I ought to grieve, but cannot what I ought;
I mourn the lover, not lament the fault;
I view my crime, but kindle at the view,
Repent old pleasures, and sollicit new:
Now turn'd to heav'n, I weep my past offence,
Now think of thee, and curse my innocence.
Of all affliction taught a lover yet,
'Tis sure the hardest science to forget!
How shall I lose the sin, yet keep the sense,
And love th' offender, yet detest th' offence?
How the dear object from the crime remove,
Or how distinguish penitence from love?

189 all] all, *1717–20.*

183. Cf. Walsh, 'Elegy To his False Mistress', ll. 27 f.:

I know I ought to hate you for your Fault;
But oh! I cannot do the thing I ought.

183 ff. Pope may owe something here to Claudius's soliloquy, *Hamlet*, III iii.

185 f. Cf. Dryden, *Don Sebastian*, v:

. . . when I behold those beauteous eyes
Repentance laggs and Sin comes hurrying on . . .
For, gazing thus, I kindle at thy sight. . .

186. Cf. Abelard (Hughes, 144): 'I mix my Tears and Sighs in the Dust, when the Beams of Grace and Reason enlighten me. Come, see me in this Posture, and solicite me to love you?'

189 f. Cf. Abelard (Hughes, 147): 'To forget, in the Case of Love, is the most necessary Penitence, and the most difficult'; *Romeo and Juliet*, I i 235:

Farewell: thou canst not teach me to forget;

and Dryden, *Tyrannic Love*, V i:

How hard it is this beauty to forget.

191. *sense*] in both meanings of 'faculty of perception' and 'faculty of sensation'.

191 ff. Cf. Abelard (Hughes, 140 f.): 'What Abhorrence can I be said to have of my Sins, if the Objects of them are always amiable to me? How can I separate from the Person I love, the Passion I must detest? . . 'Tis difficult in our Sorrow to distinguish Penitence from Love.'

192. Cf. Dryden, 'Cymon and Iphigenia', l. 367:

She hugg'd th' Offender, and forgave th' Offence.

Unequal task! a passion to resign,
For hearts so touch'd, so pierc'd, so lost as mine.
Ere such a soul regains its peaceful state,
How often must it love, how often hate!
How often, hope, despair, resent, regret,
Conceal, disdain—do all things but forget.
But let heav'n seize it, all at once 'tis fir'd,
Not touch'd, but rapt; not waken'd, but inspir'd!
Oh come! oh teach me nature to subdue,
Renounce my love, my life, my self—and you.
Fill my fond heart with God alone, for he
Alone can rival, can succeed to thee.
  How happy is the blameless Vestal's lot!

199 often,] often *1720–51.*   206 Alone] Alone, *1736–43.*

195 ff. Cf. Hughes, 129: 'A Heart which has been so sensibly affected as mine cannot soon be indifferent. We fluctuate long between Love and Hatred, before we can arrive at a happy Tranquility'; and Abelard (Hughes, 135): 'in such different Disquietudes I betray and contradict my self. I hate you; I love you.'

196. *pierc'd*] Cf. Abelard (Hughes, 142): 'my Heart is at once pierced with your Sorrows and its own'.

201 ff. 'Here is the true doctrine of the Mystics... There are many such strains in Crashaw' (Warton, ed.).

202. Cf. Hughes, 131: 'God has a peculiar Right over the Hearts of Great Men, which he has created. When he pleases to touch them, he ravishes them, and lets them not speak nor breathe but for his Glory'.

203 ff. Cf. Hughes, 125–30: 'Oh, for Pity's sake, help a Wretch to renounce her Desires, her self, and if it be possible even to renounce You! . . . I am ready to humble my self with you to the wonderful Providence of God, who does all Things for our Sanctification. . . Teach me the Maxims of Divine Love.'

206 f. Cf. Abelard (Hughes, 152): 'My Jealousie seemed to be extinguish'd: When God only is our Rival, we have nothing to fear'; and Eloisa (Hughes, 183 f.): 'When I shall have told you what Rival hath ravished my Heart from you, you will praise my Inconstancy. . . By this you may judge that 'tis God alone that takes *Heloise* from you.'

207 ff. Cf. Abelard (Hughes, 138 f., 142): 'I envy their Happiness who have never loved; how quiet and easie they are! . . . I pass whole Days and Nights alone in this Cloister, without closing my Eyes. My Love burns fiercer. amidst the happy Indifference of those who surround me'.

The world forgetting, by the world forgot.
Eternal sun-shine of the spotless mind!
Each pray'r accepted, and each wish resign'd;
Labour and rest, that equal periods keep;
'Obedient slumbers that can wake and weep';
Desires compos'd, affections ever ev'n,
Tears that delight, and sighs that waft to heav'n.
Grace shines around her with serenest beams,
And whisp'ring Angels prompt her golden dreams.
For her th' unfading rose of *Eden* blooms,

213 f. ev'n . . . heav'n] even . . . heav'n *1717–36*. even . . . heaven *1740–43*.

217 f., 219 f. *couplets in reverse order 1717–43*.

208. Cf. Horace, *Epistles*, I xi 9:

Oblitusque meorum obliviscendus et illis

which Pope quoted and adapted in his letter to Lord Marchmont, 10 Jan. 1739. Cf. also St-Evremond, i 436: 'Let those persons bury themselves alive in [the country], and renounce the World, whom the World has already renounc'd.' Neither of these 'sources' has the subtlety of the present line. In it Pope refers back to l. 190.

212. *Taken from Crashaw* ['Description of a Religious House', l. 16]. [P. 1751.]

217. Cf. Cowley, *Davideis*, p. 61:

Fair *Angels* past by next in seemly bands . . .
Some did the way with full-blown *roses* spread;
Their smell divine and colour strangely red;
Not such as our dull gardens proudly wear . . .
Such, I believe, was the first *Roses* hew,
Which at *God*'s word in beauteous *Eden* grew.

217 ff. Cf. Dryden, *Tyrannic Love*, v i:

Ætherial musick did her death prepare;
Like joyful sounds of Spousals in the Air.
A radiant light did her crown'd Temples guild,
And all the place with fragrant scents was fill'd.
The Balmy mist came thick'ning to the ground,
And sacred silence cover'd all around;

Sannazarius, *De Partu Virginis*, i 107 (of the Angel sent to Mary):

. . . explicat alas,
Ac tectis late insuetum diffundit odorem;

and Milton, *Par. Lost*, v 285 ff.

And wings of Seraphs shed divine perfumes;
For her the Spouse prepares the bridal ring,
For her white virgins *Hymenæals* sing;
To sounds of heav'nly harps, she dies away,
And melts in visions of eternal day.
  Far other dreams my erring soul employ,
Far other raptures, of unholy joy:
When at the close of each sad, sorrowing day,
Fancy restores what vengeance snatch'd away,
Then conscience sleeps, and leaving nature free,
All my loose soul unbounded springs to thee.
O curst, dear horrors of all-conscious night!
How glowing guilt exalts the keen delight!

223 ff. Cf. Hughes, 175, 197 f.: 'During the still Night, when my Heart ought to be quiet in the midst of Sleep, . . . I cannot avoid those Illusions my Heart entertains. I think I am still with my dear *Abelard*. . . I will own to you what makes the greatest Pleasure I have in my Retirement. After having pass'd the Day in thinking of you, full of the dear Idea, I give my self up at Night to sleep: Then it is that *Heloise*, who dares not without trembling think of you by Day, resigns her self entirely to the Pleasure of hearing you, and speaking to you. I see you, *Abelard*, and glut my Eyes with the sight . . . sometimes forgetting the perpetual Obstacles to our Desires, you press me to make you happy, and I easily yield to your Transports. Sleep gives you what your Enemies Rage has deprived you of; and our Souls animated with the same Passion, are sensible of the same Pleasure. But oh you delightful Illusions, soft Errors, how soon do you vanish away? At my awaking I open my Eyes and see no *Abelard*; I stretch out my Arm to take hold of him, but he is not there; I call him, he hears me not.' Cf. also Pope's 'Sappho to Phaon', ll. 143 ff.

225 f. Cf. Dryden on dreams, Chaucer's 'Cock and the Fox', ll. 337 f.:

> Sometimes we but rehearse a former Play,
> The Night restores our Actions done by Day;

and Pope's 'Sappho to Phaon', ll. 145 ff.

226. *snatch'd*] A common word in contemporary and later seventeenth-century poetry; see, e.g., Dryden's *Ovid's Ep.* Cf l. 287 below.

229. *all-conscious*] Cf. Dryden's *Ovid's Ep.*, p. 63:

> The night, and we are conscious to the rest.

conscius (common in Latin poetry) = sharing knowledge [usually of a guilty kind] with you (cf. Pope's 'Sappho to Phaon', l. 98). There is also the implied sense of Eloisa's being conscious throughout the night, i.e., being witness of her feelings. See n. on ll. 335 f.

Provoking Dæmons all restraint remove,
And stir within me ev'ry source of love.
I hear thee, view thee, gaze o'er all thy charms,
And round thy phantom glue my clasping arms.
I wake—no more I hear, no more I view,
The phantom flies me, as unkind as you.
I call aloud; it hears not what I say;
I stretch my empty arms; it glides away:
To dream once more I close my willing eyes;
Ye soft illusions, dear deceits, arise!
Alas no more!—methinks we wandring go
Thro' dreary wastes, and weep each other's woe;
Where round some mould'ring tow'r pale ivy creeps,
And low-brow'd rocks hang nodding o'er the deeps.
Sudden you mount! you becken from the skies;
Clouds interpose, waves roar, and winds arise.
I shriek, start up, the same sad prospect find,
And wake to all the griefs I left behind.
  For thee the fates, severely kind, ordain
A cool suspense from pleasure and from pain;
Thy life a long, dead calm of fix'd repose;

239 f. Wakefield compares Roscommon, 'The Dream' (*Poems*, 1717, p. 125):

Once more present the Vision to my View,
The sweet Illusion, gentle Fate, renew!

241 ff. Cf. Virgil's account of the frenzied vision of Dido, *Æneid*, iv 465 ff.:

agit ipse furentem
in somnis ferus Aeneas; semperque relinqui
sola sibi, semper longam incomitata videtur
ire viam et Tyrios deserta quaerere terra.

249. Cf. 'To a Jealous Mistress', Steele's *Miscellany*, 1714, p. 169:

No more, severely kind, affect
To put that lovely Anger on.

249–52. Cf. Hughes, 176: 'You are happy, *Abelard*, . . . and your Misfortune has been the Occasion of your finding Rest. The Punishment of your Body, has cured the deadly Wounds of your Soul. . . I am a thousand times more to be lamented than you; I have a thousand Passions to contend with. I must resist those Fires which Love kindles in a young Heart.'

No pulse that riots, and no blood that glows.
Still as the sea, ere winds were taught to blow,
Or moving spirit bade the waters flow;
Soft as the slumbers of a saint forgiv'n,
And mild as opening gleams of promis'd heav'n.
  Come *Abelard*! for what hast thou to dread?
The torch of *Venus* burns not for the dead;

258 f. *between these lines 1717–20 read:*

Cut from the root my perish'd joys I see,
And love's warm tyde for ever stopt in thee.

---

252. *glows*] A word similarly used by Donne; see *Poems*, ed. Grierson, *Elegies*, xii 37 and xiv 58. Cf. 'To a Jealous Mistress', Steele's *Miscellany*, 1714, p. 171:

If once I gaze . . . my Blood will glow.

For Pope's mock-learned note on his own use of *glow* see vol. v, *Dunciad* A, ii 175.

253 f. Cf. Dryden, Ovid's *Metam.*, i 44 f.:

Then with a Breath, he gave the Winds to blow;
And bad the congregated Waters flow.

253 ff. An echo of favourite imagery of Davenant; see 'To the King . . . 1630', ll. 1 ff. *Gondibert*, II viii 12 (2); and 'To the Queen, entertain'd at night . . .', 5 ff.:

Smooth, as the face of waters first appear'd,
Ere Tides began to strive, or Winds were heard:
Kind as the willing Saints, and calmer farre,
Than in their sleeps forgiven Hermits are.

256. Cf. Edmund Smith, 'Poem To the Memory of Mr. John Philips' (*Miscellaneous Poems*, 1712, p. 158):

How Saints aloft the Cross triumphant spread,
How op'ning Heav'ns their happy Regions show;

and Gould, ii 6:

Deluded Woman! . . . bright
As Summer's Sun, and mild as op'ning Light.

257. Cf. Hughes, p. 111: 'There is nothing that can cause you any Fear. . . You may see me, hear my Sighs . . . without incurring any Danger, since you can only relieve me with Tears and Words'.

258. Suggested by Hughes, 112: 'We leave off burning with Desire, for those who can no longer burn for us.' Wakefield notes, 'as in the case of the lamp for the entombed vestal, in ver. [261 f.].'

258 f. *variant.* Hughes, p. 33, has the same pun: Fulbert studied 'how to be revenged on . . . both [lovers] at one Stroke; which aiming at the Root of the Mischief, should for ever disable them from offending again.'

Nature stands check'd; Religion disapproves;
Ev'n thou art cold—yet *Eloisa* loves.
Ah hopeless, lasting flames! like those that burn
To light the dead, and warm th' unfruitful urn.
  What scenes appear where-e'er I turn my view!
The dear Ideas, where I fly, pursue,
Rise in the grove, before the altar rise,
Stain all my soul, and wanton in my eyes!
I waste the Matin lamp in sighs for thee,
Thy image steals between my God and me,
Thy voice I seem in ev'ry hymn to hear,

263 view!] view, *1717–43*. view? *1751*.

Pope may have withdrawn this couplet because of Concanen's citing it as an instance of his pruriency (*A Supplement to the Profound*, 1728, p. 15).

260. Cf. Hughes, 120: 'But tell me whence proceeds your Neglect of me since my being Profess'd? . . . Let me hear what is the Occasion of your Coldness'.

261 f. References to the perpetual fire in ancient tombs (e.g., in that of Tullia, daughter of Cicero) are common in seventeenth-century prose and poetry: cf. Donne, 'Epithalamion', st. xi 1 f.; *Gondibert*, II ii 87 (2); and K. Philips, 'In Memory of Mrs. Mary Lloyd', ll. 87 f. *Hudibras*, II i 309 ff. reads:

Love in your heart as idly burns
As fire in antique Roman urns,
To warm the dead, and vainly light
Those only that see nothing by't.

Browne (*Vulgar Errors*, iii 21), Cowley (*Davideis*, iv note 37), the Royal Society (see note on *Hudibras*, loc. cit., ed. Z. Grey) and the *Athenian Oracle* (i 133, and iii 207 f.) had discussed the subject. See also Pancirollas, *Rerum, Memorabilium sive Deperditarum*, 1612, p. 236, and Wilkins, *Mathematicall Magick*, 1648, pp. 232 ff.

263 ff. Cf. citation from Hughes at ll. 177 ff. above.

268. See note on ll. 277 ff.

269. 'a circumstance peculiarly tender and proper, as it refers to a particular excellence of Abelard' (Warton, i 320); cf. l. 66.

269 ff. Cf. Crashaw, 'The Weeper', st. 18 (= 24 in enlarged version):

Does thy song lull the Ayre?
Thy teares just Cadence still keeps time.
Does thy sweet breath'd *Prayer*
Vp in clouds of Incense climbe?
Still at each sigh, that is each stop:
A bead, that is a teare doth drop.

With ev'ry bead I drop too soft a tear.
When from the Censer clouds of fragrance roll,
And swelling organs lift the rising soul;
One thought of thee puts all the pomp to flight,
Priests, Tapers, Temples, swim before my sight:
In seas of flame my plunging soul is drown'd,
While Altars blaze, and Angels tremble round.
  While prostrate here in humble grief I lie,
Kind, virtuous drops just gath'ring in my eye,
While praying, trembling, in the dust I roll,
And dawning grace is opening on my soul:
Come, if thou dar'st, all charming as thou art!

280 soul:] soul. *1717–20.*

270. *too soft*] because tears of love, not of repentance (EC). Wakefield compares Sedley, 'On Don Alonzo', ll. 9 ff.:

The gentle Nymph, long since design'd
  For the proud Monsieur's Bed,
Now to a holy Jayl confin'd,
  Drops Tears with ev'ry Bead.

273 f. Cf. Dryden, *Tyrannic Love*, IV i:

And misty vapours swam before my sight;

Edmund Smith, *Phaedra and Hippolytus* (1707) I i:

all the idle Pomp,
Priests, Altars, Victims swam before my Sight;

and *Steeleids . . . By John Lacy* (1714), p. 44:

Priests, Altars, Heroes vanish all away.

275. For debt to Isaac Watts, see above, pp. 304 f.

275 ff. Bowles notes: 'How finely does this glowing imagery introduce the transition [to] While prostrate . . . drops, &c.'

276. Cf. Dryden, *State of Innocence*, V i:

Sick nature, at that instant, trembled round.

277 ff. Cf. Abelard (Hughes, 144): 'I am a miserable Sinner, prostrate before my Judge, and with my Face pressed to the Earth, I mix my Tears and Sighs in the Dust, when the Beams of Grace and Reason enlighten me. Come, see me in this Posture, and solicite me to love you[.] Come, if you think fit, and in your Holy Habit thrust your self between God and me, and be a Wall of Separation. Come, and force from me those Sighs, Thoughts, and Vows, which I owe to him only. Assist the Evil Spirits, and be the Instrument of their Malice.'

Oppose thy self to heav'n; dispute my heart;
Come, with one glance of those deluding eyes,
Blot out each bright Idea of the skies.
Take back that grace, those sorrows, and those tears,
Take back my fruitless penitence and pray'rs,
Snatch me, just mounting, from the blest abode,
Assist the Fiends and tear me from my God!
  No, fly me, fly me! far as Pole from Pole;
Rise *Alps* between us! and whole oceans roll!
Ah come not, write not, think not once of me,
Nor share one pang of all I felt for thee.
Thy oaths I quit, thy memory resign,
Forget, renounce me, hate whate'er was mine.
Fair eyes, and tempting looks (which yet I view!)
Long lov'd, ador'd ideas! all adieu!
O grace serene! oh virtue heav'nly fair!
Divine oblivion of low-thoughted care!
Fresh blooming hope, gay daughter of the sky!
And faith, our early immortality!

282. *dispute*] 'To contend with opposing arguments or assertions . . . to debate in a vehement manner' (OED).

283. Cf. Pope's 'Sappho to Phaon', l. 22.

284. Cf. Pomfret, 'Love Triumphant over Reason', l. 148:

> I'le Chase her bright *Idea* from my Breast;

and *Ess. on Crit.*, l. 485.

289. Cf. Abelard (Hughes, 146): 'Let me remove far from you, and obey the Apostle who hath said *fly*.'

289 f. Cf. Dryden, *Hind and the Panther*, ii 552 f.:

> The Gospel-sound, diffus'd from Pole to Pole,
> Where winds can carry and where waves can roll;

and Hopkins, Dryden's *Miscellany* v, 1704, p. 121:

> Drive 'em somewhere, as far as Pole from Pole,
> Let Winds between us rage, and Waters roll.

291. Note the order of the verbs.

293. Cf. Abelard (Hughes, 144 f.): 'It will always be the highest Love to shew none: I here release you of all your Oaths, and Engagements.'

298. *low-thoughted care!*] from *Comus*, l. 6.

300. 'C–T–O.' (*Gentleman's Mag.*, 1786, p. 312) compares Crashaw's 'Answer for Hope', ll. 21 f.:

Enter each mild, each amicable guest;
Receive, and wrap me in eternal rest!
See in her Cell sad *Eloisa* spread,
Propt on some tomb, a neighbour of the dead!
In each low wind methinks a Spirit calls,
And more than Echoes talk along the walls.
Here, as I watch'd the dying lamps around,
From yonder shrine I heard a hollow sound.
Come, sister come! (it said, or seem'd to say)
Thy place is here, sad sister come away!
Once like thy self, I trembled, wept, and pray'd,
Love's victim then, tho' now a sainted maid:
But all is calm in this eternal sleep;
Here grief forgets to groan, and love to weep,
Ev'n superstition loses ev'ry fear:

301 Enter] Enter, *1736–51.* 304 on] in *1717–20.*

Fair hope! our earlyer heau'n by thee
Young time is taster to eternity.

303 ff. Abelard (Hughes, 143) speaks of 'so many Voices which call me to my Duty' which provides the transition to the *Heroides*. See Intro., p. 302.

Cf. Yalden, *Temple of Fame*, 1700, p. 11:

There Ranks of unregarded Urns remain,
And shatter'd Tombs an horrid Pomp maintain:
Proud *Mausolæums* moulder there in State,
Magnificent with Heaps, in Ruins great.
With Human Bones the ghastly Pavement's spread,
The last Remains of the neglected Dead:
There dying Lamps, there solemn Tapers burn,
And long descending Vaults in endless Silence mourn.

305 f. Cf. Dryden, 'Palamon and Arcite', ii 471 ff.:

In *Venus* Temple on the Sides were seen
The broken Slumbers of inamour'd Men;
Pray'rs that ev'n spoke, and Pity seemed to call,
And issuing Sighs that smoak'd along the Wall.

309 ff. See Intro., p. 302. Cf. *Troilus and Cressida*, IV iv 50 f.:

Hark! you are call'd; some say the Genius so
Cries 'Come!' to him that instantly must die.

313. Cf. Dryden, [Lucretius] 'Against the Fear of Death', l. 182:

But all is there serene, in that eternal Sleep.

For God, not man, absolves our frailties here.
  I come, I come! prepare your roseate bow'rs,
Celestial palms, and ever-blooming flow'rs.
Thither, where sinners may have rest, I go,
Where flames refin'd in breasts seraphic glow.
Thou, *Abelard*! the last sad office pay,
And smooth my passage to the realms of day:
See my lips tremble, and my eye-balls roll,

317 I come!] ye ghosts! *1717–20.*

319. Warton (i 324) italicizes 'sinners' to show its force.

321. Cf. Virgil, *Æneid*, vi 223: 'triste ministerium'; Statius, *Thebaid*, viii 652: 'munus miserabile'; Ogilby's *Æneid*, ed. 1684, xi 26:

> And to the Dead our last sad Duties pay;

Dryden's *Æneid*, xi 322:

> Perform the last sad Office to the slain;

and Dryden's *Ovid's Ep.*, p. 238: 'The last kind Office'.

321 ff. Cf. C. Hopkins, 'Leander's Epistle to Nero' (*Art of Love*, 1709, p. 444):

> No Death can please, like Dying in thy sight.
> Oh! when I must, by Heav'ns severe Decree,
> Be snatch'd from all that's dear, be snatch'd from thee,
> May'st thou be present, to dispel my Fear,
> And soften with thy Charms the Pangs I bear.
> While on thy Lips I pour my parting Breath,
> Look thee all o'er, and clasp thee close in Death;
> Sigh out my Soul upon thy panting Breast...

Pope considered this poem 'excellent' (see *European Mag.*, Oct. 1787, p. 261).

322. Cf. *Aureng-Zebe*, IV i 9 f.:

> I thought, before you drew your latest breath,
> To smooth your passage, and to soften death;

and Dryden, *Æneid*, iii 693.

323 f. Cf. Oldham's translation of Bion's 'Lamentation for Adonis', ll. 89 ff.:

> Kiss, while I watch thy swimming eye-balls roul,
> Watch thy last gasp, and catch thy flying soul.

(Pope's copy of Oldham, now in the Brit. Mus., is dated by him 1700); Dryden's *Æneid*, iv 983 f.:

> while I in death
> Lay close my Lips to hers; and catch the flying Breath.

Pope improves the erotic suggestions by echoing Marlowe, *Faustus*, V i 110:

> [Helen's] lips suck forth my soul;

Dryden's *Cleomenes*, IV (end):

Suck my last breath, and catch my flying soul!
Ah no—in sacred vestments may'st thou stand,
The hallow'd taper trembling in thy hand,
Present the Cross before my lifted eye,
Teach me at once, and learn of me to die.
Ah then, thy once-lov'd *Eloisa* see!
It will be then no crime to gaze on me.
See from my cheek the transient roses fly!
See the last sparkle languish in my eye!
Till ev'ry motion, pulse, and breath, be o'er;
And ev'n my *Abelard* be lov'd no more.
O death all-eloquent! you only prove
What dust we doat on, when 'tis man we love.
Then too, when fate shall thy fair frame destroy,

324 my flying] the flying *1717–36* [*Griffith 413*]: (*1736* [*Griffith 414*] *reads as 1740–51.*)
334 be lov'd] belov'd *1717–43*.

sucking in each other's breath;

his *Don Sebastian*, III; and Rochester's 'Imperfect Enjoyment' ('Naked she lay...'), l. 6:

She clips me to her Breast, and sucks me to her Face.

326 f. Warton (i 325) italicizes *trembling*, *Present*, and *lifted* as 'particularly beautiful'. Wakefield notes the 'happiness' of 'human' (l. 358).

328. Cf. Crashaw, 'A Hymn to . . . Sainte Teresa', l. 54; Wakefield compares Thomas Rowe, 'An Ode To Delia', vi 12 ff.:

the destin'd hour of fate!
Whene'er it comes, may'st thou be by,
Support my sinking frame, and teach me how to die.

334. In the letters (Hughes, 163) Eloisa leaves the question open: 'Life without my *Abelard*, is an unsupportable Punishment, and Death a most exquisite Happiness, if by that Means I can be united with him'.

335 f. Cf. Abelard (Hughes, 160): 'You shall see me, to strengthen your Piety by the Horror of this Carcase, and my Death then more Eloquent than I can be, will tell you what you love, when you love a Man'; Raleigh, *Hist. of the World* (ed. 1687, p. 813): 'O Eloquent, Just and Mighty Death! whom none could advise, thou hast persuaded'; and Crashaw, 'Vpon Mr. Staninough's Death', ll. 29 f.:

. . . All daring Dust and Ashes; onely you
Of all interpreters read nature true.

For the construction cf. also: 'all-conscious' (l. 229).

(That cause of all my guilt, and all my joy)
In trance extatic may thy pangs be drown'd,
Bright clouds descend, and Angels watch thee round,
From opening skies may streaming glories shine,
And Saints embrace thee with a love like mine.
May one kind grave unite each hapless name,
And graft my love immortal on thy fame.
Then, ages hence, when all my woes are o'er,

---

343. Abelard *and* Eloisa *were interr'd in the same grave, or in monuments adjoining, in the Monastery of the* Paraclete: *He died in the year* 1142, *she in* 1163. [P. 1717–51.]

The dates here are those of Hughes's *History*, p. 63. Cf. Hughes, 66: ' 'Tis said she desired to be buried in the same Tomb with her *Abelard*, tho' that probably was not executed. *Francis D'Amboise* says, he saw at the Convent the Tombs of the Founder and Foundress near together.' Cf. *Encycl. Brit.* (ed. 13): 'First buried at St Marcel, his remains soon after were carried off in secrecy to the Paraclete, and given over to the loving care of Heloise, who in time came herself to rest beside them (1164). The bones of the pair were shifted more than once afterwards, but they were marvellously preserved even through the vicissitudes of the French Revolution, and now they lie united in the well-known tomb in the cemetery of Père-la-Chaise at Paris.'

name] 'for *person*, as in Revel. iii 4. "Thou hast a few *names* even in Sardis;" and elsewhere in the *Scriptures*' (Wakefield).

344. In the original letters Eloisa bears Abelard's fame constantly in mind, and it was mainly not to hinder his achieving or maintaining it that she did not want marriage. In Hughes and Pope this preoccupation has almost vanished.

345 ff. 'C-T-O.' (*Gentleman's Magazine*, 1786, p. 312) compares Crashaw, 'Alexias', Elegy, i 25 ff.:

> And sure where louers make their watry graues
> The weeping mariner will augment the waues.
> For who so hard, but passing by that way
> Will take acquaintance of my woes, & say
> Here 't was the roman MAID found a hard fate
> While through the world she sought her wandring mate.
> Here perish't she, poor heart, heauns, be my vowes
> As true to me, as she was to her spouse;

and Aphra Behn, 'Voyage to the Isle of Love' (*Works*, vi 283):

> Eternal Powers! when ere I sing of Love,
> And the unworthy Song immortal prove;
> To please my wandering Ghost when I am Dead,
> Let none but Lovers the soft stories read;
> Praise from the Wits and Braves I'le not implore;

When this rebellious heart shall beat no more;
If ever chance two wandring lovers brings
To *Paraclete*'s white walls, and silver springs,
O'er the pale marble shall they join their heads,
And drink the falling tears each other sheds,
Then sadly say, with mutual pity mov'd,
Oh may we never love as these have lov'd!
From the full quire when loud *Hosanna*'s rise,
And swell the pomp of dreadful sacrifice,
Amid that scene, if some relenting eye
Glance on the stone where our cold reliques lie,
Devotion's self shall steal a thought from heav'n,
One human tear shall drop, and be forgiv'n.
And sure if fate some future Bard shall join
In sad similitude of griefs to mine,
Condemn'd whole years in absence to deplore,
And image charms he must behold no more,
Such if there be, who loves so long, so well;
Let him our sad, our tender story tell;
The well-sung woes will sooth my pensive ghost;

365 will] shall *1717–20.*

Listen, ye Lovers all, I ask no more;
That where Words fail, you may with thought supply,
If any ever lov'd like me, or were so blest as I.

350. Cf. Dryden's *Ovid's Ep.*, p. 12:

[I] drunk the tears that trickled from my eyes.

352. Several of Ovid's women end their epistles by foretelling their deaths and conjecturing an epitaph or valedictory summary.

354. *dreadful sacrifice*] the technical term for the celebration of the Eucharist. Steevens (cited by Wakefield) compares *The History of Loreto*, p. 278: 'The Priest, who . . . assisted the Card[inal] in tyme of the dreadfull Sacrifice . . .'

358. See note on l. 326 f.

360. Cf. *Odyssey*, xix 400:

And sad similitude of woes ally'd.

361 f. Lady Mary Wortley Montagu in 1717 was absent from England, having accompanied her husband who was ambassador to Turkey. See Intro., pp. 311 f.

365. Cowley has the phrase 'well-sung name' in 'The Given Love' (ix 2).

He best can paint 'em, who shall feel 'em most.

---

366. The idea is as old as Aristotle (*Art of Poetry*, trans. I. Bywater, 1920, p. 61). Pope, who knew Quintilian well (witness, e.g., his use of him in *An Essay on Criticism*), here recalls the *Inst. Orat.*, x vii 15: 'Pectus est enim, quid disertos facit, et vis mentis.' Cf. Addison's ending of *The Campaign*:

And those who paint 'em truest, praise 'em most.

(Johnson's comment [*Lives*, ii 129] on Pope's debt is pedantic since 'paint' is not intended to have strong force as an image.) Cf. also *Ovidius Brit.* (I 5v):

My faithful Maid can best my Sorrows tell;
For I'm too much oppress'd to Paint them well.

ELEGY TO THE MEMORY OF AN UNFORTUNATE LADY

Plate 4 THE UNFORTUNATE LADY

INTRODUCTION

I

POPE'S letters up to 1717 show that he had every incentive to write an obituary elegy,[1] except that of an actual bereavement. Together with Caryll, he had devoted—and was to go on devoting—time, sympathy, and money to two unfortunate ladies, Mrs Weston[2] and Mrs Cope.[3] And Pope was being more particularly and romantically pained by the heroic dangers which his beloved Lady Mary was undergoing in the East.[4]

---

1. For the contemporary connotation of 'elegy' see J. Trapp, *Lectures on Poetry . . . Translated from the Latin, With additional Notes* (1742), pp. 163 ff., and Shenstone's essay, *Works*, 1764, i 3 ff. For Coleridge's definition of 'elegy' see *Table Talk and Omniana*, 1917, pp. 280 f.

2. Mrs Weston was separated from her husband, John Weston of Sutton, Surrey, and from 1711 onwards won the active protection of Caryll and Pope (some of which she did not wholly appreciate). Pope writes to Caryll on 2 Aug. 1711: 'I cannot but joyn with you in a high concern for a Person of so much merit, as I'm daily more & more convinced by her Conversation that she is; whose ill Fate it has been to be cast as a Pearl before Swine. And he [i.e., Sir William Goring, her guardian] who put so valuable a Present into so ill hands [i.e. Weston's] shall (I own to you) never have my good opinion, tho he had that of all ye world besides. God grant he may never be my Friend! and guard all my friends from such a Guardian!' (Add. MS. 28,618, fol. 8r). On 25 May 1712 Mrs Weston went to seek refuge with her aunt Lady Aston 'with that mixture of expectation & anxiety with wch people usually goe into unknown or half discover'd Countries' (Pope to Caryll, 28 May). Pope's letter to her, printed in the authorized *Letters* of 1737 (quarto ed., Griffith 454) with the title '*To the same Lady*' (i.e., the same '*unfortunate Lady*' who had figured in the title of the preceding letter) shows her contemplating entry into a convent, a step which she did not take. She died at Guildford in 1724. For the story in full see Dilke, i 131 ff.

3. Mrs Cope's husband, an army captain, had bigamously married while stationed at Port Mahon, and was proof against her two importuning visits. Mainly through the offices of Pope, she was able to live in France till, in 1728, she died of cancer. Caryll, her first cousin, introduced her to Pope in 1711, who reported that he had 'heard more Witt and sense in two hours [from her], than allmost all the sex euer spoke in their whole Lives' (Pope to Caryll, 19 July 1711: Add. MS. 28,618, fol. 7r). For her story in full see Dilke, i 141 ff.

4. Pope pictures her absence as death (see especially the letter to her of 18

Aug. 1716). Moreover she is herself playing with death and in her letter of 16 Jan. 1717 writes what amounts to dying requests:

> . . . I think . . . I ought to bid adieu to my friends with the same solemnity as if I was going to mount a breach, at least, if I am to believe the information of the people here, who denounce all sorts of terrors to me; and, indeed, the weather is at present such, as very few ever set out in. I am threatened at the same time, with being frozen to death, buried in the snow, and taken by the Tartars, who ravage that part of Hungary I am to pass. . . How my adventures will conclude, I leave entirely to Providence; if comically, you shall hear of them. —Pray be so good as to tell Mr. [Congreve?] I have received his letter. Make him my adieus: if I live, I will answer it. The same compliment to my Lady R [Rich?]. (*Works*, ed. W. Moy Thomas, i 270.)

Pope is charged to make vicarious and perhaps ultimate adieus. In his reply on 3 February to what must have been another and lost letter of the same trend, Pope shows how much he has taken her danger to heart, or, if sincerity is denied him, how much, at least, he is writing about it:

> Madam,—I wish I could write any thing to divert you, but it is impossible in the unquiet state I am put into by your letter: it has grievously afflicted me, without affectation; and I think you would hardly have writ it in so strong terms, had you known to what degree I feel the loss of those I value (it is only decency that hinders me from saying, of her I value). From this instant you are doubly dead to me; and all the vexation and concern I endured at your parting from England was nothing to what I suffer the moment I hear you have left Vienna. . . If this falls into any other hands, it will say nothing I shall be ashamed to own, when either distance or death (for ought I can tell) shall have removed you for ever from the scandal of so mean an admirer. (*id.*, i 424.)

There is one letter which may have important bearing on the 'Elegy'. It is that which Lady Mary wrote to Pope from Adrianople with the date 1 April 1717:

> I dare say you expect at least something very new in this letter, after I have gone a journey not undertaken by any Christian for some hundred years. The most remarkable accident that happened to me was my being very near overturned into the Hebrus; and, if I had much regard for the glories that one's name enjoys after death, I should certainly be sorry for having missed the romantic conclusion of swimming down the same river in which the musical head of Orpheus repeated verses so many ages since; [here are quoted lines 523 and 528 of Virgil's fourth *Georgic*]. Who knows but some of your bright wits might have found it a subject affording many poetical turns, and have told the world, in an heroic elegy, that,
>
> "As equal were our souls, so equal were our fates?"
>
> I despair of ever having so many fine things said of me, as so extraordinary a death would have given occasion for. (*id.*, i 300 f.)

Lady Mary had 'beauty, titles, wealth, and fame' (l. 70); for other links with the poem, see my article, 'Lady Mary Wortley Montagu and Pope's Elegy . . .', in *RES*, XII, 1936, pp. 401 ff. Whether or not Pope had already written his 'Elegy'

Pope, however, lacked his corpse, and the literal Caryll had to ask twice for the identity of the unfortunate lady about whom he dimly remembered hearing something: 'I think you once gave me her history, but it is now quite out of my head'.[1] How Pope put him off in the end is not preserved in writing. To him and to equally curious biographers and editors the poem itself provides the answer:

> How lov'd, how honour'd once, avails thee not,
> To whom related, or by whom begot.[2]

Pope remained silent: in the eighteenth century at least, it was in the interests of the poem that it should be believed to spring from an actual sorrow. Warton believes that 'If this ELEGY be so excellent, it may be ascribed to this cause, that the occasion of it was real...'[3] Pope does not obtrude the element of story. He wanted just enough 'fact' to float the emotions. Dr Johnson, who too readily believed

---

by the date on which he received this letter—I have argued, *id.*, pp. 408 ff., that the poem may have been written just in time for the 1717 *Works*—he had already the cue for passionate elegy.

For the possible links between Lady Mary and the note signed 'P.' which Warburton affixed to the poem in 1751, see *id.*, pp. 402 ff. The page numeral 206 is left floating in 1751. I consider it to refer to that volume (vii) of 1751 which contains the 'Letters to Several Ladies', where on p. 206 Pope, C[ongreve], and the Duke of B[uckingham] are found addressing the travelling Lady Mary with extravagant devotion. But if this is the intention in 1751, Warburton defeats it in 1753, when, in the edition of that year, he inserts the words 'quarto Edition' after the page numeral (I was wrong, *id.*, p. 403, in giving Bowles as the first editor to make this insertion). The insertion is carelessly done: there is no section headed 'Letters to several Ladies' in the quarto, and p. 206 merely concerns Pope's house at Twickenham. Sense can only be made of the insertion if 'Letters to several Ladies, p. 206' is read as 'Letters to several Persons, p. 86': on p. 86 of the quarto comes the letter to the 'unfortunate Lady' who in the preceding letter had been called 'Mrs. W.' The note, however, must remain inscrutable as well as inaccurate since, despite its 'P.', it cannot wholly be Pope's: Pope would not refer to himself as 'Mr. Pope', nor would he use the expression 'seems to' (if he wanted to deceive, this would have defeated his object by showing him to want to).

1. Caryll to Pope, 16 July 1717: the second inquiry follows on 18 Aug. 1717, Caryll hoping to learn of her orally at their next meeting.

2. ll. 71 f. For the history of the conjectures of biographers and editors, see Dilke, i 128 ff. and EC, ii 201 ff.

3. i 249; cf. Dr Johnson on 'Eloisa', *Lives*, iii 235.

the fabrication of Ruffhead, considered the 'facts' contradictory:

> History relates that she was about to disparage herself by a marriage with an inferior; Pope praises her for the dignity of ambition, and yet condemns the unkle to detestation for his pride: the ambitious love of a niece may be opposed by the interest, malice, or envy of an unkle, but never by his pride. On such an occasion a poet may be allowed to be obscure, but inconsistency never can be right.[1]

'History' here can be dismissed as equivalent to Ruffhead. Nor is Johnson's 'inconsistency' more formidable. It disappears when the lady's ambition is understood to resemble that of the angels to which it is compared, an ambition to satisfy the will to independence; and when the uncle-guardian's pride is understood to be his pride in exacting obedience.

II

The personal incentives existed beside the literary ones. Pope knew well the temperate elegies (and heroic epistles)[2] of the Roman poets—of Ovid, Tibullus, and Propertius. Then again, there were the laments in the epics.[3] And more than laments: Lucan's *Civil War*, viii 712 ff. assembles several of the elements in Pope's 'Elegy'—Codrus, the single friend, performs by moonlight the funeral of the headless Pompey; he discovers nearby a forsaken pyre which provides him with fuel (he addresses its ghost as 'Neglected ghost, deare to no friend'[4]); he contrasts the pomp of official obsequies and 'polisht Marbles'[5] with the simple fate of Pompey's 'so sacred ashes'[6]; he praises Pompey as a world power[7] who would need the world for grave; he buries him, marking the stone which covers his ashes with a brief epitaph, and cursing Egypt, Pompey's betrayer, to barrenness.[8]

---

1. *Lives*, iii 226.
2. See Introduction to 'Eloisa', pp. 293 ff. above.
3. See notes on ll. 47 ff. and 79 f. below.
4. May's translation, P 1v.
5. *id.*, P 3r: cf. Pope, l. 60.
6. *id.*, P 1v: cf. Pope, l. 68.
7. Cf. Pope, l. 33.
8. Cf. Pope, ll. 69 ff. and 29 ff.

Beside the epic there was drama, and especially—in the first fifteen years of the century—the 'she-tragedies' of Rowe, several of which centred in a woman's pathetic fortunes, and ended with her tender valedictions. Pope's interest in the work of his friend extended as far as his suggesting Mary Queen of Scots as a suitable theme.[1] There is little verbal debt to Rowe in Pope's 'Elegy' (or in 'Eloisa'),[2] but Rowe, who broaches or effects the suicide of several heroines, talks much of ghosts, of heaven, and of retreat to foreign lands.

Pope was also well aware of the many unfortunate ladies in the popular literature of the time—in ballads, romances, and novels. One ballad, which the British Museum catalogue dates as 'c. 1690', begins its title with: *The Unfortunate Lady; or The Young Lover's fatal Tragedy: who lately hang'd her self for the Love of a Young Gentleman, whom her Parents would not suffer her to have. . .* And, among recent novelties, there were the blood-stained swords, suicidal princesses, and phantoms of the *Persian Tales*.[3]

III

Pope considered that 'Most little poems should be written by a plan: this method is evident in Tibullus, and Ovid's Elegies, and almost all the pieces of the ancients'.[4] And, following his own plan, Pope has worked a great deal into his poem: the theatrical opening of scene and gesture,[5] the theological queries, the gnomic verses on ambition and the stay-at-home soul, the curse, the unpaid rites and their cynical compensations, the epitaph (which Greene detached and set to a canon in C minor[6]), the personal coda. The kind of dic-

1. Oldmixon had already provided her with a heroic epistle, see p. 294 above.

2. There are some (perhaps accidental) verbal similarities between Pope's 'Elegy' and Rowe's translation of the passage from Lucan outlined above (Rowe's *Lucan's Pharsalia. Translated* . . . appeared in 1718).

3. For King's and Ambrose Philips's translations of these in 1714 see my article, *T.L.S.*, 29 Aug. 1935, and the addenda by R. H. Griffith (16 Nov. 1935) and by D. B. Macdonald (14 Dec. 1935).

4. Spence, p. 1. Dryden was of the opposite opinion so far as Tibullus and Propertius were concerned (see *Essays*, i 235).

5. 'This ELEGY opens with a striking abruptness, and a strong image' (Warton, i 246).

6. *Catches and Canons for Three and Four Voices . . . Compos'd by Dr. Greene. Lon-*

tion used varies with the changing plan.[1] Particularly evident are the patches of diction and imagery that are derived from Elizabethan sonnets and from the panegyrics of the metaphysical poets of the seventeenth century.[2] It is by such short-hand means that Pope persuades the reader that it is not merely Mrs X who is dead, but a goddess, the ideal of a hundred poets.

That many readers found the poem extraordinarily affecting there is ample evidence until well into the nineteenth century. From this evidence a letter of the philosopher Hume is of special interest: on 15 October 1754 Hume is apprising Spence of the worth of the blind poet, Thomas Blacklock:

> I soon found him to possess a very delicate Taste, along with a passionate Love of Learning. . . I repeated to him Mr. Pope's Elegy to the Memory of an unfortunate Lady, which I happen'd to have by heart: And though I be a very bad Reciter, I saw it affected him extremely. His eyes, indeed, the great Index of the Mind, cou'd express no Passion: but his whole Body was thrown into Agitation: That Poem was equally qualified, to touch the Delicacy of his Taste, and the Tenderness of his Feelings.[3]

---

don. Printed for I. Walsh in Catherine Street in the Strand (n.d.). Under the year 1741 Griffith (No. 542) lists this setting, printed without date on a 'folio half-sheet broad-sheet', and decorated with a picture representing 'a church and burial place . . . a full-length portrait of Pope (?), standing and pointing to a tomb.' The broadsheet is dedicated to Greene, and the canon is stated as having been written in 1729.

1. For Pope's method of correcting the diction of an elegy, see Spence, pp. 23 f.

2. For Pope's connection with the metaphysical poets, see F. R. Leavis, *Revaluation*, 1936, pp. 69 ff.

3. Spence, p. 448. (I do not reproduce the italics.)

NOTE ON THE TEXT

The present text is based on that of the first edition (*Works* 1717). Apart from the title, the only signs of verbal revision occur at ll. 2 and 22. I have disregarded Warburton's evidence that Pope ended by revoking the former of these revisions, since it seems to have become a principle of his that sibilants should be excised where convenient. On the other hand, the latter of the two revisions has been adopted though there is only Warburton as its authority. Warburton's new system of punctuation has been disregarded.

The title in 1717–20 reads: VERSES || To the MEMORY of an || UNFORTUNATE LADY. 1736–51 substitute ELEGY for VERSES.

KEY TO THE CRITICAL APPARATUS

1717 = the first edition, Works, quarto and folio, Griffith 79 and 82.
1720 = *Eloisa to Abelard . . . The Second Edition*, octavo, Griffith 109 [the 'Elegy' occupies second place in this volume].
1736 = Works, vol. i, octavo, Griffith 413.
1740 = Works, vol. i, part 1, octavo, Griffith 510.
1743 = Works, vol. i, part 1, octavo, Griffith 582.
1751 = Works, vol. i, ed. Warburton, Griffith 643.

ELEGY

To the MEMORY of an UNFORTUNATE LADY.

ELEGY TO THE MEMORY OF AN UNFORTUNATE LADY

WHAT beck'ning ghost, along the moonlight shade
Invites my step, and points to yonder glade?
'Tis she!—but why that bleeding bosom gor'd,
Why dimly gleams the visionary sword?
Oh ever beauteous, ever friendly! tell,
Is it, in heav'n, a crime to love too well?

2 step] steps *1717–20, 1751.*

---

title] *See the Duke of Buckingham's verses to a Lady designing to retire into a Monastery* [i.e., convent] *compared with Mr. Pope's Letters to several Ladies, p. 206. She seems to be the same person whose unfortunate death is the subject of this poem.* [P. 1751.]

For the interpretation of this note see Introduction, p. 355 above.

1–4. Ghosts beckon who have something to impart: cf. *Hamlet*, I iv 57 ff. Thomas Warton (*Observations on the Faerie Queene*, 1754, p. 166) compares Jonson, 'Elegie on the Lady Jane Pawlet', ll. 1 ff.:

What gentle Ghost, besprent with *April* deaw,
  Hayles me, so solemnly, to yonder Yewgh?
And beckning wooes me . . . ?

The ghost of the unfortunate lady carries a visionary counterpart of the sword with which she killed herself. Cf. St-Evremond, *Dialogue of the Dead* (*Works*, ii 474): '*Lucretia* . . . came thundering down to the Infernal Mansions, with her Hair all flowing about her Shoulders, the Bloody Poniard in her Hand'.

1. *moonlight shade*] Cf. *Rape of the Locke*, ii 177 and *Rape of the Lock*, i 31.

2–6. That the wound has been carried over unhealed into the ghostly body suggests that heaven has failed to honour the virtue of the unfortunate lady.

4. Cf. *Iliad*, x 578 ff.:

Just then a deathful Dream *Minerva* sent;
A warlike Form appear'd before his Tent,
Whose visionary Steel his Bosom tore.

5–14. Cf. Settle, *Empress of Morocco*, IV iii:

  Have I for this a too fair Saint admir'd? . . .
And bounded my Ambition in your Arms?
And must I die as depos'd Angels fell;
'Cause they aspir'd, and lov'd their Heav'n too well?

6. i.e., are you excluded from heaven because you have committed suicide which is only the result of your great love? Later, ll. 23 ff., the poet thinks that 'perhaps' she was snatched to heaven as being too pure for earth.

Cf. Crashaw, 'Alexias', Elegy, iii 20:

Vnlesse it be a crime to' haue lou'd too well;

To bear too tender, or too firm a heart,
To act a Lover's or a *Roman*'s part?
Is there no bright reversion in the sky,
For those who greatly think, or bravely die?
  Why bade ye else, ye Pow'rs! her soul aspire
Above the vulgar flight of low desire?
Ambition first sprung from your blest abodes;
The glorious fault of Angels and of Gods:
Thence to their Images on earth it flows,
And in the breasts of Kings and Heroes glows!
Most souls, 'tis true, but peep out once an age,

Ovid's Ep., p. 20: My only Crime is, loving you too well,
But sure some Merit in that Crime does dwell:

and it is the frequent cry of Ovid's forsaken women that they have 'loved too well'; cf. also *Othello*, v ii 344, 'Ode on St. Cecilia's Day', l. 96, etc.

8. *To act a . . . Roman's part*] to commit suicide.

13 ff. Dryden had expressed this idea in *Absalom and Achitophel*, i 304 ff.: 'Ambition',

on Earth a Vitious Weed,
Yet, sprung from High is of Cœlestial Seed;
In God 'tis Glory: And when Men Aspire,
'Tis but a Spark too much of Heavenly Fire.
Th'Ambitious Youth, too Covetous of Fame,
Too full of Angels Metal in his Frame . . .

He also describes ambition as a 'godlike fault' (*King Arthur*, I i). Cf. Wolsey in Shakespeare's *Henry VIII*, III ii 440 ff. (which Pope comma's as a 'shining passage' in his edition); *Paradise Lost* helped to foster the idea of the glorious fault. Wakefield compares *E. on Crit.*, l. 159 ('gloriously offend') in the notes to which he gives the history of such 'bold' expressions.

blest abodes] Denham also has this expression and he too rhymes it with 'the Gods' ('To . . . Edward Howard', l. 22).

17 ff. Cf. Montaigne, 'Of Virtue' (*Essays*, ii 560): 'It accidentally happens even to us, who are but abortive Births of Men, sometimes to dart out our Souls, when rous'd by the Discourses or Examples of others, much beyond their ordinary Stretch . . . but this Whirlwind once blown over, we see that they insensibly flag, and slacken'; Dryden (*Essays*, i 5): 'the souls of other men shine out at little crannies . . . but your Lordship's soul is an entire globe of light, breaking out on every side'; Dryden, 'To her Grace the Dutchess of Ormond', 118 f.:

. . . imprison'd in so sweet a Cage,
A Soul might well be pleas'd to pass an Age;

and *Moral Es.*, i 55 f.

Dull sullen pris'ners in the body's cage:
Dim lights of life that burn a length of years,
Useless, unseen, as lamps in sepulchres;
Like Eastern Kings a lazy state they keep,
And close confin'd to their own palace sleep.
From these perhaps (ere nature bade her die)
Fate snatch'd her early to the pitying sky.
As into air the purer spirits flow,
And sep'rate from their kindred dregs below;

22 to] in *1717–43*.

19 f. Cf. 'Eloisa', ll. 261 f.

21 f. Cf. 'Ep. to Dr. Arbuthnot', l. 220.

A Description of the Grand Signor's Seraglio [by Robert Withers], 1650, describes at length the huge, guarded palace of the Turkish emperors, and how they give audience on 'a *Sofa* spread with very sumptuous Carpets of gold, and of Crimson velvet' and only 'upon a Sunday or upon a Tuesday: (for those are the days appointed . . .) to the end he may not be troubled at other times' (pp. 4 and 30); 'oftentimes the King is amongst [the sultanas] a whole day together, eating, sporting, and sleeping, of which there is no notice taken, nor may any one look into his actions: where, amongst themselves, they make him delicate, and sumptuous banquets, (over, and above the ordinary meals of dinner, and supper)' (p. 123). Pope may also be indebted to Xenophon's moral comparison between Agesilaus and the Persian king, *Agesilaus*, ix.

22. This cadence of sound and syntax is often found in lines concerned with sleep: cf. *Davideis*, p. 5:

And undisturb'd by *Moons* in silence sleep;

Dryden and Garth had parodied this, 'Mac Flecknoe', l. 73:

And, undisturb'd by Watch, in silence sleep,

and *Dispensary*, p. 104:

And undisturb'd by Form, in Silence sleeps;

Dryden had also copied the line solemnly in 'Epitaph on Sir Palmes Fairborne's Tomb', i f.:

Ye Sacred Relicks which your Marble keep,
Here, undisturb'd by Wars, in quiet sleep.

and in his I *Conquest of Granada*, 1 (ad fin.):

While he secure in your protection, slept.

25 f. The image is from chemistry.

26–30. *kindred . . . Race . . . brother*] for a tracing of thought that springs out of the metaphor *kindred* see my *Pope and Human Nature*, 1958, pp. 203 f.

So flew the soul to its congenial place,
Nor left one virtue to redeem her Race.
 But thou, false guardian of a charge too good,
Thou, mean deserter of thy brother's blood!
See on these ruby lips the trembling breath,
These cheeks, now fading at the blast of death:
Cold is that breast which warm'd the world before,
And those love-darting eyes must roll no more.
Thus, if eternal justice rules the ball,
Thus shall your wives, and thus your children fall:
On all the line a sudden vengeance waits,
And frequent herses shall besiege your gates.
There passengers shall stand, and pointing say,

---

27 f. Cf. Spenser, 'Ruins of Time', ll. 288 ff., and *Dunciad*, i 267 f. The doctrine is that of Plato's *Timæus*.

28. Cf. Juvenal, *Sat.*, iv 2 f.:

> ... monstrum nullâ virtute redemptum
> A vitiis ...

which Duke had translated:

> Without one Virtue to redeem his Fame.

29. Cf. Dryden, Ovid's *Amores*, II xix 37:

> But thou dull Husband of a Wife too fair.

Pope's guardian may have been suggested by Mrs Weston's experience: see Introduction, p. 353 above.

33. This kind of 'metaphysical' image (found in Spenser and the sonneteers as well as in Donne) occurs at *Rape of the Lock*, ii 52, and 'Ep. to Miss Blount, with the Works of Voiture', l. 80.

34. *love-darting eyes*] Cf. *Comus*, l. 753.

35. T. Earle Welby, *Popular History of English Poetry* (n.d.), p. 148, speaks of 'the falsely precise "ball" ... the earth's shape is wholly irrelevant'. But Pope has in mind the orb, the emblem of the world, which is often placed in the hand of statues of Justice. Cf. Pope's 'Two Chorus's to the Tragedy of Brutus', i 25:

> Ye Gods! what justice rules the ball?

35 ff. For the principle governing this intrusion of heroic diction see the third essay in my *Augustan Studies*, 1961.

38. Cf. Dryden, *Æneid*, ii 491:

> The Streets are fill'd with frequent Funerals;

and Dryden, Juvenal, *Sat.*, i 182:

> And Litters thick besiege the Donor's Gate;

and x 386:

> Sad Pomps, a Threshold throng'd with daily Biers.

(While the long fun'rals blacken all the way)
Lo these were they, whose souls the Furies steel'd,
And curs'd with hearts unknowing how to yield.
Thus unlamented pass the proud away,
The gaze of fools, and pageant of a day!
So perish all, whose breast ne'er learn'd to glow
For others' good, or melt at others' woe.
  What can atone (oh ever-injur'd shade!)
Thy fate unpity'd, and thy rites unpaid?

---

40. Cf. Defoe, *Complete English Tradesman*, II ii 168: 'Undertakers for Funerals, and the usage of Burying with Coaches, tho' the party lies Dead but two Doors off from the Church, with all the frightful Geugaws of Funeral Pomp, and the growing Extravagances of new Customs in Funerals, how wonderful a Foppery!'

blacken] The word had been used for dense, joyful crowds by Dryden, *Absalom and Achitophel*, i 272, and by A. Philips, 'An Epistle to . . . Halifax', l. 52: Pope improves the total sense by combining density with mourning.

41 f. Cf. Achilles in the *Iliad*, xxii 447 f.:

> The Furies that relentless Breast have steel'd,
> And curs'd thee with a Heart that cannot yield;

cf. also ix 754 f.; xvi 244 ff.; and *Odyssey*, v 245. Wakefield compares Horace, *Odes*, I vi 6 and Dryden, *Æneid*, xi 472:

> Or Conquer'd, yet unknowing how to yield.

44. Cf. *Pope's Corresp.*, i 375 (letter to Martha Blount of November 1716): 'Let your faithless Sister triumph in her ill-gotten Treasures; let her put on New Gowns to be the Gaze of Fools, and Pageant of a Birth-night!' If I am right in supposing the poem to have been written just in time for inclusion in the *Works* of 1717 (see above, p. 355), Pope recalls this letter when writing it. But it would seem more usual for a poet to recall his verse rather than his prose. It is possible that the poem was only *completed* in 1717, and that some of its couplets or even paragraphs were composed earlier.

45 f. 'From a fragment of *Sir Edward Hungerford*, according to a writer in the Gentleman's Magazine, for 1764.

> The soul by pure religion taught *to glow*
> *At others' good, or melt at others' woe*.'

(Wakefield; I have failed to check this reference.) Cf. *Odyssey*, xviii 269 f.:

> Yet taught by time, my heart has learn'd to glow
> For others good, and melt at others woe;

cf. also *Æneid*, i 630: 'non ignara mali miseris succurrere disco'.

47 ff. Cf. the lament of Euryalus's mother at the news of the death of her son whose body remains with the enemy (*Æneid*, ix 485 ff.).

No friend's complaint, no kind domestic tear
Pleas'd thy pale ghost, or grac'd thy mournful bier;
By foreign hands thy dying eyes were clos'd,
By foreign hands thy decent limbs compos'd,
By foreign hands thy humble grave adorn'd,
By strangers honour'd, and by strangers mourn'd!
What tho' no friends in sable weeds appear,
Grieve for an hour, perhaps, then mourn a year,
And bear about the mockery of woe
To midnight dances, and the publick show?
What tho' no weeping Loves thy ashes grace,
Nor polish'd marble emulate thy face?
What tho' no sacred earth allow thee room,
Nor hallow'd dirge be mutter'd o'er thy tomb?
Yet shall thy grave with rising flow'rs be drest,
And the green turf lie lightly on thy breast:
There shall the morn her earliest tears bestow,
There the first roses of the year shall blow;
While Angels with their silver wings o'ershade

---

49. *kind domestic tear*] Milton's formula, e.g. *Sam. Agon.*, l. 1695: 'tame villatic Fowl'.

51 f. Ovid's Ariadne (*Ovid's Ep.*, p. 47) foresees the same fate:

Poor *Ariadne*, thou must perish here,
Breath out thy Soul in strange and hated Air,
Nor see thy pittying Mother shed one Tear:
Want a kind hand which thy fix'd eyes may close,
And thy stiff Limbs may decently compose;

and cf. Dryden, *Æneid*, ix 645 ff., and *Odyssey*, xi 529 f. It was 'An ancient custome for the neerest in blood or affection to close the eyes of the dying' (Sandys, Ovid's *Metam.*, 1632, p. 309 n.).

57 f. Cf. *Hamlet*, I ii 85 f.

60. *emulate*] Dryden is fond of this word in the *Æneid*, and Pope in the *Iliad*.

62. The priest 'mutter'd' the marriage service in Dryden, 'Sigismonda and Guiscardo', l. 165.

63. *rising flow'rs*] Cf. *Temple of Fame*, l. 2.

64. *Sit tibi terra levis* was so common on Roman gravestones that it was often abbreviated to S.T.T.L. Pope is adding the final touches to his Roman elegy. Wakefield cites parallels from English poetry.

67. The angel Gabriel takes a 'shining Pair' of 'Silver Wings' in Tasso, I xiv I.

The ground, now sacred by thy reliques made.
So peaceful rests, without a stone, a name,
What once had beauty, titles, wealth, and fame.
How lov'd, how honour'd once, avails thee not,
To whom related, or by whom begot;
A heap of dust alone remains of thee;
'Tis all thou art, and all the proud shall be!
Poets themselves must fall, like those they sung;
Deaf the prais'd ear, and mute the tuneful tongue.
Ev'n he, whose soul now melts in mournful lays,
Shall shortly want the gen'rous tear he pays;
Then from his closing eyes thy form shall part,
And the last pang shall tear thee from his heart,
Life's idle business at one gasp be o'er,
The Muse forgot, and thou belov'd no more!

---

68. 'The expression has reference to ver. 61. "No sacred earth allowed her room", but her remains have "made sacred" the common earth in which she was buried' (EC).

74. Pope reverts to l. 43: the lady's proud persecutors will die as she has died.

75. Wakefield compares Herrick, 'A Meditation for his Mistresse', ll. 20 f.:

> But die you must (faire Maid) ere long,
> And He, the maker of this Song.

76. *tuneful tongue*] Cf. Pope's 'Ep. to Robert Harley Earl of Oxford', l. 2. 'Ear' and 'tongue' are used both literally and metaphorically, the ear standing for the poet's power of judging verbal 'music' and the tongue for 'singing' it.

78. *want*] in the sense of 'lack' and also of 'need'.

gen'rous tear] Cf. *Davideis*, p. 54.

79 f. Cf. 'Eloisa', ll. 333 f. and *Iliad*, xxii 483 ff.:

> Divine *Patroclus!* Death has seal'd his Eyes;
> Unwept, unhonour'd, uninterr'd he lies!
> Can his dear Image from my Soul depart,
> Long as the vital Spirit moves my Heart?

APPENDIXES

APPENDIX A

PERSONS CONCERNED

THE families of the Petres, the Carylls, and the Fermors were connected by marriage and friendship. John Caryll, grandfather of Pope's friend, married Lady Catherine Petre (1603–81), the daughter of the second Lord Petre; and William Petre (1602–77), the brother of this Catherine, had married Lucy Fermor (d. 1679), the daughter of Sir Richard Fermor of Somerton, Oxon., and sister of Arabella's great-grandfather, Henry Fermor. The Caryll correspondence in the British Museum preserves several examples of affectionate letters from the Petre family and in 1749 and 1757 from one of the Fermors. Caryll is usually called cousin by the Petres and the indebtedness of the young Lord Petre to his guardian may be gauged from the letter of 13 March 1710–11 which, on coming of age, he writes to Caryll:

> Dr Cousin . . . I cant but reflect *Mon cher Tuteur* of the time that is now approaching when I shall beg as a particular favour ye continuance of that fatherly Care and assistance you have been pleas'd to take upon you hitherto by way of trust as to every thing that regarded me . . . I can assure you that nobody can have a more real esteem nor a more[1] sincere affection and kindness for you than || Dr Couzen || Your Obedient humble || Servant & Affectionnate || Kinsman || Petre.[2]

The following are brief biographies of the persons represented in the poem. They do not usually repeat material incorporated in the Introduction.

(1) ARABELLA FERMOR was the daughter of Henry Fermor of Tusmore and Somerton, Oxon., and of Ellen, second daughter and co-heir of Sir George Browne of Wickhambreux, Kent.[3] The history of the family is recorded in its fullest form by J. C. Blomfield, *The Deanery of Bicester* (Part iv, *History of Middleton and Somerton* [1888], pp. 102 ff. and Part iii, *History of Cottisford, Hardwick and Tusmore* [1887], pp. 63 ff.). Some time before 1612 Sir Richard Fermor, Arabella's great-great-grandfather,[4] had bought the Somerton estate from Sir John Spencer. After Sir Richard's death in 1642, his son Henry migrated to Tusmore where the descendants of the family remained till 1806. In 1857 the property was sold to the Earl of Effingham. It had been magnificently improved in the 1760's and '70's by William Fermor who, along with the contemporary

1. mo *deleted before this word.*

2. Add. MS. 28227, fol. 473r–v.

3. A miniature portrait in enamel of Ellen Fermor, representing her as a shepherdess with a crook, was executed by Boit and is preserved in the University Galleries, Oxford. The miniature is described and reproduced in G. C. Williamson's *History of Portrait Miniatures* (1904), ii 62 and Plate 85.

4. The curious might compare *Rape of the Lock*, v 90.

Lord Petre, had been an original member of the Committee elected in 1787 to ameliorate the condition of the English Roman Catholics.

Records of Catholic families during the persecutions are scarce and any that were kept in the chapel at Tusmore perished when it was burned down in the 1830's (Blomfield, loc. cit., Part iii, 84). I have not discovered any record of Arabella's birth. According to the genealogy reproduced by J. J. Howard and H. F. Burke—*Genealogical Collections Illustrating the History of Roman Catholic Families in England. Based on the Lawson Manuscript* . . . Part i. Fermor and Petre (1887)—she was the fourth child and third daughter. But this genealogy is untrustworthy. It gives the date of Arabella's marriage (1714 or 1715) as 1736 (which is the date of her husband's death) and may be proved inaccurate at other relevant points.

There is more reliable evidence elsewhere. Family deeds of the Fermors were produced in the de Scales Peerage case. When Sir Charles Robert Tempest in 1857 brought forward his claim to the barony of de Scales, evidence was given by Clement Uvedale Price, the solicitor of the Ramsay family, descendants of the Fermors. These deeds were known to Howard and Burke (who refer to them on p. 7) but their genealogical evidence remained unused until Holden's edition of the *Rape of the Lock* (1909). These deeds establish that James was the eldest-born child of Henry Fermor[1]; that Arabella was his eldest daughter[2]; that the other daughters were, in order, Winifred, Mary, Ursula, Anne, Henrietta, Hellen, and Elizabeth; and that there was a second son Henry. The deeds and inscriptions from funeral monuments which were quoted in the case do not mention dates of birth. But Arabella had become twenty-one on or before 11 July 1713 since her 'portion is become payable'.[3] She cannot, therefore, have been born later than 11 July 1692. And she cannot have been born earlier than 29 March 1687 since it is implied in an indenture drawn up by her father on 29 March 1700 that she had not yet reached the age of thirteen.[4] On 25 March 1693 we find from the register of the English Convent in Paris that she arrived there on that day, brought by her grandmother Lady Browne, whose three daughters Barbara, Nanny, and Elizabeth were already in residence.[5] English

1. 'Henry Fermor . . . att his death [on 3 Feb. 1702–3] left (besides James Fermor his eldest sonn) eight younger children' (*Minutes of Evidence taken before the Committee for Privileges* [concerning] *the Petition of Sir Charles Robert Tempest* [to succeed to] *the Style and Title of Lord de Scales . . . Ordered to be Printed 6th February, 1857*, p. 266).

2. 'Arabella Fermor (eldest sister of the said James Fermor)' (*id.*, p. 264).

3. *id.*, p. 266.

4. *id.*, pp. 211 ff.

5. *Un Couvent de Religieuses Anglaises à Paris de 1634 à 1884* . . . Par L'Abbé F.-M.-Th. Cédoz (1891), pp. 169 f. (I am indebted to the kindness of the Reverend Mother, the Priory of Our Lady of Good Counsel, for the loan of this book.)

girls sometimes came to the convent 'very young'[1]: 'Miss Petre, eldest daughter to Mr. Petre of Fithlass . . . is not quite six years old'[2] and another child is 'about four years old'.[3] These records suggest that the date for Arabella's birth may be narrowed to something like 1688–90. She spent nine years in the convent absenting herself for considerable periods in order to 'perfect her French' in other houses. She returned to England with Lady Browne in 1704.[4]

Two possible sources for the date of Arabella's birth have been unfortunately destroyed. Mary Russell Mitford wrote in 1852:

> [In Ufton Church] her monument may still be seen amongst many others of her husband's family and her name is still shown with laudable pride and interest in . . . the Parish Register.[5]

The church was completely rebuilt in 1872 and the monument no longer exists. The pages in the register covering 1637–1743 have been cut out.[6]

Arabella is not mentioned among the thirty-two ladies complimented in *The London Belles: or, a Description of the most celebrated Beauties of the Metropolis of Great Britain*, an anonymous poem of 1707, but she comes second among the ladies complimented in *St. James's Park: A Satyr* (anon.), 1708. After a mention of Bedingfield comes this:

> So *Farmer*, with a modest Lustre shines,
> Like Silver Oar dispers'd in baser Mines?[7]
> A pleasing Strife arises in her Face,
> 'Twixt White and Red, to give the greater Grace,
> That Beauty may in all her Colours play,
> Awful, to fright the Coward Hearts away.[8]

She is accorded Elizabethan homage in *The Mall: or, the Reigning Beauties* (anon.), 1709, again being the second lady mentioned:

> Thus *Farmer*'s Neck with easie Motion turns;
> The Purpling Flood in Circling Currents runs:
> Her Snowey Breasts those lovely Mounts arise,
> And with surprizing Pleasure seize our Eyes.
> Between these Hills flows *Heliconian* Dew,

---

1. C. S. Durrant, *A Link between Flemish Mystics and English Martyrs* (1925), p. 432.
2. *id.*, p. 433.
3. *ibid.*
4. Cédoz, op. cit., p. 169.
5. *Recollections of a Literary Life*, 1852, iii 96.
6. I am indebted for this information to the Rev. S. E. Chavasse, rector of Ufton. The excision was probably made for the de Scales case: it seems that the pages were produced in court.
7. i.e., among inferior ladies in the park.
8. p. 14.

Which makes the Poet's Raptures ever new,
To these the Gods their powerful Thunder owe,
Venus her Beauty, and her *Son* his *Bow*.

She reappears in *The Celebrated Beauties*, a poem published along with Pope's *Pastorals* in the 1709 miscellany:

F—rm—r's a Pattern for the Beauteous Kind,
Compos'd to please, and ev'ry way refin'd;
Obliging with Reserve, and Humbly Great,
Tho' Gay, yet Modest, tho' Sublime, yet Sweet;
Fair without Art, and graceful without Pride,
By Merit and Descent to deathless Fame ally'd.

Pope's friend, Parnell, some time before her marriage addressed verses to her: 'On Mrs. A. F. Leaving London.' They were not included in Pope's collection of Parnell's poems (1722), and seem to have appeared for the first time in *The Posthumous Poems* of Parnell, 1758.

We know that the Fermors had a house in town: the will of Henry Fermor dated 25 January 1702–3 and proved 8 June 1703 bequeathes to 'Hellen my dear wife' £300 and 'the use and occupation of one Dozen of Silver Spoones . . . and all my Bedding Linnen Hangings Pewter Cabinetts China Ware Household-stuff and implements of Household whatsoever which shall be at the time of my decease in the Parish of St James and any other Parish or Place in the County of Middlesex . . .' (The will contains no reference to separate children other than the heir James.) The possibility that the lock was cut in one of the town houses of the Fermors or the Petres must not be overlooked.

In late 1714 or early 1715 Arabella was married to Francis Perkins (born 30 August 1683[1]) of Ufton Court, Berks. The evidence for dating the marriage most nearly happens to be Pope's own letter to M. Blount (see Introduction, p. 102 above) which can be dated from internal evidence as late 1714 or early 1715. Arabella is named as the wife of Francis Perkins in a post-nuptial settlement of 2 June 1715.[2] 'There is a tradition that it was for Arabella that Ufton Court was very much refashioned and enlarged'.[3] Here, according to Miss Mitford, she 'received the wits of that Augustan Age—Pope, Steele, Arbuthnot, Bolingbroke'.[4] A son Francis was born in 1716, then five more children, the only daughter,

1. See Parish Register of Ufton.

2. Produced in the de Scales case, op. cit., pp. 283 ff.: the marriage portion was £4,500. Francis allotted to Arabella as jointure the rent (£600 p.a.) of certain farms, etc.

3. See A. Mary Sharp, p. 126.

4. *Recollections* (1852), iii 95 f. F. Turner, *Berkshire Bachelor's Diary*, 1932, says there is no evidence of these visits. The visits described by the Abbess (see Introduction, pp. 99 f. above) may have been to Tusmore.

Arabella, dying in infancy. Arabella's husband was buried on 9 April 1736,[1] and the *Gentleman's Magazine*, May 1736, records:

> April . . . 10. *Fran. Perkins*, Esq; of *Berksh.* 2000 *l. per Ann.* He married the celebrated Mrs *Arabella Fermor.*

By his will of 6 October 1734 (proved 26 May 1736) he left to 'my Loving Wife' (among money and other things)

> all her wearing Apparrell Gold watch and Jewells and her Dressing Plate with the ffurniture of her Closet and Chamber.

Arabella was buried on 9 March 1737–8.[2] Miss Sharp records that in 1892 there were three portraits of Arabella in existence, all of which she reproduces. Pope seems to refer to one of these in his epistle *To Mr. Jervas*, l. 62. One of them is reproduced in the present volume.

(2) JOHN CARYLL (1666?–1736) was the son of Richard Caryll of West Grinstead, Sussex, and nephew of John Caryll (1625–1711), poet, playwright, English agent at Rome, and secretary to Mary, queen of James II (see DNB). His uncle's estate at West Harting was forfeited to the Crown following the discovery of complicity in the assassination plot of 1696, life interest in it being granted to Lord Cutts. John Caryll, the nephew, redeemed it in the same year at the price of £6,000. Four years later, on his father's death, he came into the property at West Grinstead. Pope had known Caryll at least as early as 1709.[3] and he became his longest correspondent, their letters running from 1711 to 1735. He befriended Gay as well as Pope. Pope may have owed to him his introduction to Steele who had been Lord Cutts's secretary during the negotiations of 1696.

(3) ROBERT, LORD PETRE. Robert, seventh Lord Petre, the Baron of the poem, was baptised at Ingatestone, the family seat in Essex, on 17 March 1689–90. He succeeded to the title on the death of his father Thomas in January 1705–6. He married, on 1 March 1711–12, Catherine Warmsley, or Walmsley (1697–1785), daughter of Bartholomew, and sister and sole heir of Francis Warmsley of Dunkenhalgh in Lancashire. Lord Petre died of small-pox in his house in Arlington Street on 22 March 1712–13, and was buried at Ingatestone. His son was born on 3 June following. His widow married Charles, Lord Stoughton on 22 April 1733. (He seems to have been a suitor at the time that she chose Lord Petre.)[4] Catherine died on 31 January 1785, and was buried at Ingatestone.

1. Parish Register of Ufton, produced in court by the Rev. Frederic Christie in the de Scales case, op. cit., p. 278.
2. Parish Register of Ufton, produced in the de Scales case, op. cit., p. 278.
3. See Dilke, i 173.
4. See the pretty anecdote, M. D. Petre's *Ninth Lord Petre* (1928), p. 21.

By the Baron's will, dated 20 March 1712–13 and administered 3 April 1713, Caryll is nominated one of the two 'guardians of Lady Catherine Petre', who was under age.[1] She subscribed to Pope's *Iliad*.

The *Rape of the Lock* was not the first great poem to be connected with the Petre family. Spenser's *Prothalamion* had celebrated the marriage of William Petre, later second Lord Petre, to Catherine, second daughter of the Earl of Worcester, along with that of Catherine's sister to Sir Henry Guildford.

(4) Mrs MORLEY. The first editor to identify Thalestris was Warton. His note (i 284) reads:

> '... Thalestris was Mrs. Morly; Sir Plume was her brother, Sir George Brown, of Berkshire.' Copied from a MS. in a book presented by R. Lord Burlington, to Mr. William Sherwin.

It is true that Sir George's sister Elizabeth married John Morley the famous land-jobber (see DNB). But Sir Plume's wife was Gertrude Morley and since, in the poem, Thalestris seeks 'her *Beau*' Sir Plume (iv 122) it seems more likely that Thalestris is the wife rather than the sister of Sir George Browne. Gertrude Morley may not have wholly relinquished her maiden name after marriage. F. Brown (op. cit., iii 66) records her will as that of 'Dame Gertrude Browne, alias Morley'.

(5) SIR GEORGE BROWNE and LADY BROWNE. Sir George Browne, the cousin of Arabella Fermor's mother, succeeded to the baronetcy in or about 1692, after the death of his two elder brothers. On 2 May 1699, in Charterhouse Chapel,[2] he married Gertrude Morley, spinster, sister of John Morley, the 'land-jobber' later to be Pope's friend (see DNB). In the register they are both referred to as 'of St. James, Westminster', Sir George being located 'in Bury streete'. Gertrude's will was administered on 2 July 1720.[3] On 5 February 1721–2 he married Prudence, daughter of Charles Thorold of Harmeston, co. Linc., in Gray's Inn chapel. The register names both of them as of Covent Garden.[4] She died on 19 December 1725 (for her will see F. Brown, op. cit., p. 66). Sir George died on 20 February 1729–30 and was buried on the 24th 'in the Church-Porch' of St Paul's, Covent Garden.[5] By his first wife he had three sons, John (fifth Baronet ob. s.p. 1775), Anthony, and James.

1. J. J. Howard and H. F. Burke, *Genealogical Collections* . . . Part i (1887). Fermor and Petre, p. 75.
2. F. Collins, *Registers . . . of Charterhouse Chapel* (1892), p. 10.
3. Frederick Brown, *Abstracts of Somersetshire Wills*, iii (1889), p. 66.
4. J. Foster, *Registers of Gray's Inn* (1889), p. xxii.
5. W. H. Hunt, *Registers of St Paul's Church, Covent Garden* (1908), iv 317.

The descent of Sir George Browne (*Sir Plume*) and the connection between the Fermors and the Brownes may be tabulated, in a selective form,[1] thus:

Anthony Browne, 1st Lord Montague = (second wife) Magdalen, daughter of William, Lord Dacre
c. 1528–1592

Sir George Browne of Wickhambreux, Co. Kent = (second wife) Mary, daughter of Sir Robert Tirwhit of Kettleby, Co. Linc., Kt.

George of Caversham, Oxon. d. 9 Feb. 1663–4 = Ellinor, daughter of Sir Richard Blount of Mapledurham, Oxon., Knight

George, eldest surviving son, created Knight of the Bath on the Coronation of Chas. II, d. 7 Dec. 1678 = Elizabeth, daughter of Sir Francis Englefield, of Englefield, Berks.

John created Bart., 10 May 1665 = Elizabeth Vandersteck (née Bradley)

Winifred; Eleanor d. 1741 (co-heirs) = Henry Fermor d. 1702

Arabella (*Belinda*)

Sir Antony d. sine prole 1688

Sir John succeeded to Baronetcy, d. sine prole, circa 1692

Sir George succeeded to Baronetcy (*Sir Plume*) = (1) (1699) Gertrude Morley (2) (Feb. 1721–2) Prudence Thorold of Harmeston, Lincs.

1. For a full genealogical table see F. Brown, *Abstracts of Somersetshire Wills*, iii (1889), p. 67. It is interesting to note the appearance of other families with which Pope was closely connected.

(6) 'CLARISSA'. In the *Key to the Lock* (1715, p. 10) Pope implies that other characters in the poem represent real people. When Esdras Barnivelt is attending Arabella Fermor in his professional capacity as apothecary, she claims that she is Belinda; and

> At the same time others of the Characters were claim'd by some Persons in the Room.

Chalestris may have been meant, and Clarissa, but no record or legend of Tlarissa's identity has survived.

APPENDIX B
SYLPHS
I

In the second edition of the *Rape of the Lock*, Pope enlarged the two cantos to five (a more suitable number after the six cantos of *Le Lutrin* and the *Dispensary*) and did this mainly by adding to the machinery. 'And that sort of Machinery which his judgment taught him was only fit for his use, his admirable invention supplied. There was but one System in all nature which was to his purpose, the *Rosicrucian Philosophy*.'[1] This philosophy, 'first enunciated in Germany in the *Fama Fraternitatis*, 1614, [and] expounded in England by Robert Fludd and John Heydon',[2] had recently been used for the purposes of erudite and erotic amusement in *Le Comte de Gabalis*, a series of five discourses written by the Abbé de Montfaucon de Villars, and published in 1670 (reprinted 1700). These discourses were known to English readers in the translations of Philip Ayres and A. Lovell, both published in 1680. Twelve years later, unsold sheets of Ayres's version were bound up in Bentley's series of 'Modern Novels'.[3] It would have been a weakness

1. Warburton, note on i 20.

2. *Sir William Temple's Essays* . . . ed. J. E. Spingarn (1909), p. 88 n.

3. A new translation was published soon after the appearance of the *Rape of the Lock* in 1714, 'Printed for B. Lintott and E. Curll'. The 'Translator's Preface' notes that 'The present Revival of it, was occasion'd by *The Rape of the Lock*; in the Dedication of which Poem Mr. *Pope* has given us his Opinion, *That the best Account he knew of the* Rosicrucian *System, is in this Tract*: Which we doubt not will be a sufficient Recommendation of it to the Publick.' (A2r). The *Rape of the Lock*, though announced in January, did not appear till 2 March and on 18 March *The Evening Post* announced:

> *Next Tuesday will be publish'd, a beautiful Edition (to bind up with Mr. Pope's Rape of the Lock) of,*
>
> *]The Count de Gabalis: Being a Diverting History of the Rosicrucian Doctrine of Spirits, viz, Sylphs, Salamanders, Gnomes, and Dæmons: Shewing their various Influence upon Human Bodies. Done from the Paris Edition, publish'd by the Abbot de Villars, to which is prefix'd M. Bayle's Account

in Pope's poem if he had had to invent these machines, since the serious epic took its machinery from established mythology,[1] and since 'Truth, or at least . . . that which passes for such'[2] is best parodied by something else in the same ambiguous category. The 'mythology' of the Rosicrucians was known well enough to count as established. Joseph Warton collected earlier allusions to the sylphs in Temple, Dryden, Mme de Sévigné, and Le Sage[3]; and to these may be added Bayle,[4] Lady Chudleigh,[5] and the *Athenian Oracle*.[6] Pope's choice was right for another reason. The salaciously naïve de Villars had introduced the sprites mainly as lovers, so that they well fitted the sophisticated world of Pope's poem.

Pope owed to *Gabalis* the right to assume the existence of this particular system of elemental sprites:

> the *Elements* are inhabited by most Perfect Creatures; from the Knowledge and Commerce of whom, the Sin of the Unfortunate *Adam*, has excluded all his too Unhappy Posterity. This immense Space, which is between the Earth, and the *Heavens*, has more Noble Inhabitants, than *Birds* and *Flyes:* This vast Ocean has also other Troops, besides *Dolphins* and *Whales:* The Profundity of the Earth, is not only for *Moles*; And the *Element* of *Fire*, (more Noble than the other Three) was not made to be Unprofitable and Voyd.
>
> The *Air* is full of an innumerable Multitude of People, having Human Shape, somewhat Fierce in appearance, but Tractable upon experience . . . Their Wives, and their Daughters have a kind of Masculine Beauty, such as we describe the *Amazons* to have . . . the *Seas* and *Rivers* are Inhabited, as well as the *Air:* The Antient *Sages* have called these kind of People *Undians* or *Nymphs*. They have but few Males amongst them; but the Women are there

---

> of this Work, and of the Sect of Rosicrusians. This Piece has been very scarce for many Years, and is not now to be had in French, the Book from which this Translation is made being communicated by a Person of Honour. Printed for E. Curll against St. Dunstan's Church, Fleetstreet.

This announcement, however, was also premature, and not till 6 April did the *Evening Post* announce 'This Day is publish'd . . .' Pope alludes to this edition in a letter to Caryll, 19 Nov. [1714]: 'The book of Count Gabalis is genuine. Who translated it, I know not—I suppose at the instigation of none but the bookseller who paid for it'. EC (vi 222) annotate: 'The advertisement states that it was "made English from the Paris edition, by Mr. Ozell".' The advertisements at the end of the second edition of the *Temple of Fame* record the '2^d Edition'.

1. Cf. Warburton, note on i 20.
2. *Spectator* 523.
3. *Works of Pope*, i 286.
4. His account was translated in the 1714 *Gabalis*: see note above.
5. A letter dated 1702 (*Whartoniana*, 1727, ii 111).
6. iii 297. Charles Gildon had made amusing use of them in the second volume of his *Post-Boy Rob'd of his Mail* (see *Notes and Queries*, 8 Jan. 1949, p. 14).

in great Numbers: Their Beauty is marvellous; and the Daughters of Men have nothing in them, comparable to these.

The Earth is filled almost to the Center with *Gnomes* or *Pharyes*; a People of small Stature; the Guardians of Treasures, of Mines, and of Precious Stones. They are Ingenious, Friends of Men, and easie to be commanded...

As for the *Salamanders*, the Inhabitants of the Region of *Fire* . . . the *Idea*, which the ignorant Painters and Sculpters have given them [is wrong]: The Wives of the *Salamanders* are Fair; nay, rather more Fair, than all others, seeing they are of a purer Element . . .[1]

Obviously Pope is deeply indebted to such passages, but he strengthens the appeal to 'established' mythology by adopting whatever he can use from other mythologies (especially when such adoption improves the epic mimicry) and by grafting the whole heterogeneous system on 'all the Nurse and all the Priest have taught'.[2] The opinion, called a 'foolish' one by Burton, that 'angels and devils are nought but souls of men departed',[3] allows him, as it had allowed Dryden,[4] to give his sprites an appropriate pre-existence as human beings: and in taking over this item Pope improves the mock-heroics—the Elysian shades of Virgil and Ovid had found congenial destinies.[5] Pope also borrows the opinion that transmigrated souls protect their friends on earth, and conspire against their enemies: he makes the sylphs guardians of maidens; and this again carries its epic reference since the epic heroes were provided with their divine guardians.[6] De Villars denounces the Rabbinical theory that some of the angels consorted with women and so effected their own fall: they were not angels, he says, but sylphs—sylphs who needed such contact to make them immortal[7]; De Villars also mentions that 'Certain *Gnomes*, desirous of becoming Immortal had a mind to gain the good Affections of our *Daughters;* and had brought abundance of Precious Stones, of which they are the Natural Guardians'.[8] Pope identifies the sylphs with the fallen angels, and, on the Rabbinical authority which de Villars decried, allots them the supervision of the toilet.[9] In *Gabalis* all the sprites are 'good', but Pope, following the traditional categories of spirits, makes the gnomes 'bad',[10] wickedly contriving such vexations as are exemplified at iv 67 ff.; this, again, makes them

1. pp. 26 ff. (Quotations are from Ayres's translation.)

2. i 30. By this stroke he connects the machinery with the beliefs of his own country, a connection required of an epic poet.

3. *Anatomy*, I ii I (2).

4. See note on i 47 ff. above.

5. See note on i 55 f. above.

6. Dryden had argued that guardian angels of the Book of Daniel x 13 and 20 would provide excellent machines for a Christian epic (*Essays*, ii 34).

7. p. 34.

8. pp. 33 f.

9. See note on i 145 above.

10. See p. 122 above.

more like the factious celestials of the epics.[1] The sylphs in *Gabalis* can change their shape and sex at will, and in adopting this detail Pope is also adopting from epic: Milton's angels 'Can either Sex assume, or both'.[2] Like Milton's angels, again, his sylphs are invulnerable, since if their bodies are divided they can, in the words of Burton, 'with admirable celerity . . . come together again'.[3]

On one occasion de Villars displays his sylphs overwhelmingly on parade:

> The Famous Cabalist *Zedechias*, was moved in his Spirit, in the Reign of your King *Pepin*, to Convince the World, that the *Elements* are Inhabited by all these People, whose Nature I have been describing to you. The Expedient to bring all this about, was in this manner; He advised the *Sylphs*, to shew themselves in the Air to all the World. They did it with great Magnificence: These Creatures appearing in the Air, in Human Shape; Sometimes ranged in Battle, Marching in good Order, or standing to their Arms, or Encamped under most Majestick Pavillions: At other times, on Airy Ships of an Admirable Structure, whose Flying Navy was tost about at the Will of the *Zephirus*'s . . . The People presently believed, that they were *Sorcerers*, who had gotten a Power in the Air, there to exercise their Conjurations, and to make it Hail upon their Corn-Fields . . . Being transported with the Fury which Inspired them with such Imaginations, they dragged these *Innocents* to Punishment. It is incredible, what a great Number of [sylphs] were made to suffer by Fire, and Water, all over this Kingdom.[4]

Pope borrows the idea of regimentation: he writes 'The light *Militia* of the lower Sky', 'The lucid Squadrons', 'th' Aerial Guard', 'her Airy Band', 'Propt on their Bodkin Spears'.[5] He is, however, more scientifically interested than de Villars in the cosmic conditions of the sylphs and his fancy builds scrupulously on contemporary science as it was brilliantly presented in Fontenelle's *Pluralité des Mondes*: cf. with ii 77–86 the following quotations from Glanvill's translation, second ed., 1695:

> the Earth which is solid, is covered from the surface 20 Leagues upwards, with a kind of Down, which is the Air . . . Beyond the Air is the Celestial Matter, incomparably more pure and subtile . . . This pale Light which comes to us from the Moon [is reflected light] . . . the Neighbouring Worlds sometimes send Visits to us, and that in a very magnificent and splendid manner: There come Comets to us from thence, adorn'd with Bright shining Hair, Venerable Beards, or Majestick Tails . . . Comets are nothing but Planets, which belong

1. '[a judicious writer] could not have failed to add the opposition of ill spirits to the good' (Dryden, *Essays*, ii 36).
2. *Par. Lost*, i 424.
3. *Anatomy*, I ii I (2).
4. pp. 173 ff.
5. i 42, ii 56, iii 31 and 113, v 55.

to a Neighbouring Vortex,[1] they move towards the out-side of it; but perhaps this Vortex being differently press'd by those Vortex's which encompass it, it is rounder above than it is below, and it is the lower part that is still towards us. These Planets which have begun to move in a Circle above, are not aware that below their Vortex will fail 'em, because it is as it were broken. Therefore to continue the Circular Motion, it is necessary that they enter into another Vortex, which we will suppose is ours, and that they cut through the outsides of it. They appear to us very high, and are much higher than *Saturn*, and according to our System, it is absolutely necessary they should be so high . . . Their Beards and their Tails . . . are not real, they are *Phænomena*, and but meer Appearances . . . our Air consists of thicker and grosser Vapours than the Air of the Moon . . . The Rainbow . . . is not known to them in the Moon; for if the Dawn is an effect of the grossness of the Air and Vapours, the Rainbow is form'd in the Clouds, from whence the Rain falls; [The inhabitants of the moon] have neither Thunder nor Lightning . . . how glorious are their days, the sun continually shining?[2]

II

Pope's sylphs are, of course, more vividly realized than those of de Villars, and, in the same way as he rifles other systems to enrich the Rosicrucian mythology, he rifles earlier English poets to enrich the sylphs. He takes hints and words from the Ariel of Shakespeare (perhaps as he appears in Dryden's version of the *Tempest*), the fairies and angels of Milton, and the fairies and demons of Dryden.[3] Pope associates the sylphs and sylphids with their short vowel *i*. In his letter to Walsh on versification he had quoted Quintilian's remarks on vowels, which include 'E *plenior litera est*, I *angustior*' (EC vi 59). Two of his sylphs are called Brillante and Crispissa, and the short *i* narrows the lip movements of several lines; for instance:

Thin glitt'ring Textures of the filmy Dew;
Dipt in the richest Tincture of the Skies . . .
Or dip their Pinions in the painted Bow . . .
Some thrid the mazy Ringlets of her Hair . . .

The vowel springs most plentifully when Ariel threatens torments:

. . . transfixt with *Pins* . . .
. . . *Stypticks* . . .
Shrink his thin Essence like a rivell'd Flower.

1. This theory of Descartes of the planetary vortices was demolished by Newton (see Jebb, *Bentley*, p. 25).

2. pp. 32, 42, 141 ff., 74, 81 f.

3. See notes to the poem. Professor L. C. Martin (*RES*, xx, 1944, 299 ff.) has shown that Pope may be indebted also to Lucretius' account of the 'simulacra' to which we owe our sensations.

Or as *Ixion* fix'd, the Wretch shall feel
The giddy Motion of the whirling Mill.

Other poets besides Pope have associated their fairies with the short *i*. There are the names (Pip, Trip, Skip, Fib, Tib, etc.) of Drayton's fairies,[1] and those of Herrick's fairy saints (Tit, Nit, Is, Will o' the Wispe, Frip, Trip, Fill, Fillie).[2] The associations of Pope's fairies reach forward to the insects in the satires and to such a phrase as 'the Cynthia of this minute.'[3]

Pope's originality most obviously shows itself in the way he particularizes the notions he has borrowed (see, e.g., the account of the sylphs' guardianship of maidens, i 71 ff.), and in the feminine satire which salts much of what he says of them and much of what he makes them say. In other poets fairies are country creatures.

APPENDIX C

OMBRE

I

OMBRE (pronounced Omber), 'the most delightful and entertaining of all Games, to those who have any thing in them, of what we call the Spirit of Play',[4] had been introduced into England during the seventeenth century (Waller has a poem 'Written on a Card that Her *Majesty* tore at Omber'), and attained full vogue early in the eighteenth century. The game was Spanish in origin, and 'has in it a great deal of the Gravity peculiar to that Nation'.[5] The version of the game played in England is that described in Richard Seymour's *Court Gamester* (1719 etc.). Seymour derived his description from *Le Royal Jeu de l'Hombre et du Piquet* (Paris, 1685, etc.). His *Compleat Gamester* (fifth edition, 1734) reprints almost verbatim the account in the *Court Gamester*. The rules for the game are elaborate and most of them are set out by Lord Aldenham in the third edition of his *Ombre* (Roxburghe Club, 1902). Lord Aldenham is concerned with the game in general rather than with the particular form of it played in Queen Anne's reign, and so for the purposes of the *Rape of the Lock* it is better to rely on William Pole's account,[6] which is based on Seymour.

Ombre was played with a pack of forty cards, that is, with the full pack minus all the 8's, 9's, and 10's. The scale of values for the cards depended (a) on their colour, (b) on whether or not they were trumps. The status of the red cards when not trumps was, in descending order, King, Queen, Knave, Ace, 2, 3, 4, 5, 6,

1. *Nymphidia*, ll. 171–6.
2. 'The Fairy Temple', ll. 34–8.
3. *Moral Essays*, ii 20.
4. Richard Seymour, *Court-Gamester*, ed. 1720, p. 2.
5. *id.*, p. 1.
6. *Macmillan's Magazine*, Dec. 1873–Jan. 1874: reprinted in Hoffman's *Cyclopædia of Card and Table Games*, 1891, pp. 138–52.

7; and for black cards when not trumps, King, Queen, Knave, 7, 6, 5, 4, 3, 2. The two black Aces were always trumps, the Ace of Spades, called Spadille,[1] always ranking highest, and the Ace of Clubs, called Basto, always ranking third highest. These Aces, together with one other card which varied for different trumps, were called Matadors. The following table indicates the values of the cards for different trumps:

red (Hearts, Diamonds)			black (Clubs, Spades)		
Ace of Spades	(Spadille)	Matadors	Ace of Spades	(Spadille)	Matadors
7	(Manille)	Matadors	2	(Manille)	Matadors
Ace of Clubs	(Basto)	Matadors	Ace of Clubs	(Basto)	Matadors
Ace	(Punto)		King		
King			Queen		
Queen			Knave		
Knave			7		
2			6		
3			5		
4			4		
5			3		
6					

There was no Punto if the trump was black, and so only eleven trumps as against twelve if the suit was red. The holder of a Matador was not obliged to follow suit when trumps were played unless the card led were a higher Matador than the one he held. If, in this situation, he had no other trumps, he had to play his Matador.

The deal, according to Seymour, was settled in one of two ways:

> One Person taking the Pack, turns up a Card . . . and afterwards gives a Card a-piece round, and whoever has the highest Card of that Suit . . . is the first Dealer. Another way is, by giving Cards round, and whoever has the first black Ace, deals first.[2]

The dealer first placed five points in the pool.[3] He then began dealing on his right and went anti-clockwise. Each player received nine cards in three batches of three ('Each Band the number of the Sacred Nine'). The remaining thirteen cards became the stock. Each deal started a new game and the dealer in the later games was always the player on the right hand of the previous dealer.

When the cards were dealt, the players decided on the Ombre. The Ombre

1. The usual form of the word was *Spadille* (Spanish, *espadilla*, a diminutive of *espada*, a sword). Garth (*Dispensary*, p. 72) and Pope introduced a second *i* for phonetic reasons.

2. op. cit., p. 13.

3. For a full account of the method of scoring see Aldenham, op. cit., pp. 9, 20, 31 ff.

(Spanish *hombre*, man) was the principal player who took on the other two, undertaking to win the game independently, i.e., by making more tricks than either of the others. (Belinda 'Burns to encounter two adventurous Knights . . . singly'). To do this Ombre would need to make five tricks[1] if one of his opponents made four, but only four if his opponents made three and two respectively. The player on the right of the dealer had the first chance of being Ombre. If he liked his chances he asked 'Do you give me leave?', if not, he said 'Pass'. If he asked leave, he did not disclose the trumps he favoured. If he said 'Pass', the second player, i.e., the one on his right, had the chance of being Ombre. If he in his turn passed, it was the chance of the youngest player. If he, too, had an unfavourable hand, the deal was over, the pool gaining accordingly. If the eldest hand asked leave and the others did not consider their chances superior, they acquiesced by saying 'Pass'. But if the second player considered his hand to warrant it, he could take on the position of Ombre. If so, he undertook to play a more difficult game, i.e. to play with his hand as it stood, without discarding. This was called playing *sans prendre*. If the eldest hand wished, he might then retrieve his lost position as Ombre but only if he also undertook to play *sans prendre*. (If, as soon as he saw his cards, the eldest player liked them well enough to undertake to play *sans prendre*, his claim to be Ombre could not be disputed.) If the eldest player said 'Pass' and the second player then asked leave, the youngest could challenge the second player in the same way.

In a straightforward game, after the acquiescence of the opponents, the Ombre declared Trumps. 'It is necessary', says Seymour, 'to be very exact in naming the Trump' since a player might show the cards he discarded, leaving his opponents to infer what were Trumps and 'sometimes in that Case, a Man may put out a Trump to deceive others'.[2] Belinda is as exact as he could wish: '*Let Spades be Trumps!* she said, and Trumps they were'. After declaring Trumps, the Ombre discarded from his hand whatever cards he did not like, placing them on the pool-dish and taking from the stock the same number of new cards. This done, the second player settled with the youngest as to which should have the first chance of what remained in the stock (they were friends first, united against the Ombre, and only in the second place enemies), for there might not be enough to satisfy the full needs of both. There was no obligation for them to discard.

The play then followed as in Whist, the eldest hand leading and the others following in the order of the dealing. If the Ombre won the game, he was said to have got Sacada (meaning 'a thing carried off'). (The use of this term may not have been common in 1714—Seymour does not mention it.) If either or both of his opponents equalled the tricks falling to the Ombre, he was said to be bested or to lose a Puesta (i.e. the stake) to the pool. When either of the opponents won

1. He was then said to 'sweep the board'. Pope's use of this expression at iii 50 is, if he intends it technically, premature.

2. op. cit., pp. 8 f.

the game, he was said to give Codille to the Ombre (Belinda only just escapes 'the Jaws of Ruin, and *Codille*'), who paid the stake to him.

II

Belinda's game was demonstrated by Mrs Battle for Elia's benefit. Peacock in *Gryll Grange* (1860) makes Miss Ilex criticize it as inaccurate, but the criticism is due to a confusion between Tredrille and Ombre. The game provided by Pope runs so as best to serve the purposes of the poem. Pope makes the game an imitation of an epic contest, keeping the third player out of sight, and achieving a victory for Belinda by a narrow margin—at the end of the eighth round she knows that it is neck or nothing. Pope does not describe everything as will be seen by a comparison between his account of the game in the poem and the account given above. I supply the missing parts as far as they can be supposed or inferred since Pope's contemporaries would suppose or infer for themselves. These readers knew the laws of the game before they read the account in Pope and had something like the eye of Seymour who quotes his lines *in extenso*, introducing them with

> THUS have I given all the Laws relating to *Ombre*, yet cannot conclude this Article, without transcribing from Mr. POPE's *Rape of the Lock*, the beautiful Description he has given, of the Manner of playing this Game, in the following excellent Lines.[1]

Mr Dermot Morrah, to whom I am greatly indebted for help in my reconstruction of Belinda's game in its present form, has noted one particular difficulty. People did not sit down to play a single deal, which lasts at most five minutes: and indeed when Belinda turns to play she 'swells her breast with conquests still to come' (l. 28). This suggests that we ought to postulate several deals. If so they might come between ll. 44 and 45 or between ll. 100 and 101, or both. Nevertheless, I cannot but think that Pope intends a single deal, so smooth and seemingly complete is the course of the play. I prefer to think that for once Belinda breaks off the rubber after her first tremendous victory. Perhaps the play was interrupted by the arrival of the refreshments.

Her game was reconstructed on paper by Pole and Aldenham in the works already mentioned. Mr Edward G. Fletcher in *The University of Texas Bulletin* for 8 July 1935 criticized their reconstructions on two grounds: (a) that ll. 37–44 imply that all the Kings, Queens, and Knaves take an active part in the game, whereas in Pole and Aldenham the Queen of Clubs remains in the stock; (b) that l. 79 calls for the playing of clubs in tricks vi and vii. Fletcher's first objection is almost certainly valid since Pope is speaking after the cards have been dealt and after the discard. The second objection is also valid since l. 79 can

1. op. cit., p. 67. Later editions and *Compleat Gamester* show slight verbal changes. The lines also appear in T. M.'s *Miscellaneous Collection of Poems, Songs and Epigrams. By Several Hands. Dublin, 1721*, i 99 ff.

scarcely refer to the whole of the Baron's counter-attack, which began with v (at l. 67), but only to vi and vii. Fletcher's two versions of the game provide for Belinda's playing the Queen of Clubs in vii, which overcomes both his objections. His versions, however, are marred by the play assigned to Sir Anonym (Pole's name for the third player) who is left both a fool and a knave—he throws away the Knave of Clubs in iv when his hand still includes the six, he plays red cards as if their values were not in reverse order and he dishonourably does not follow suit in v. The version of the play given below is based on Pole's version corrected in accordance with Fletcher's so as to bring the Queen of Clubs into the play, but differing from that version in not maligning the character and brain of Sir Anonym.[1]

---

1. Fletcher partly corrected his version of Pole's game in the *Texas Bulletin*, 8 July 1936. And we have since had an article, 'The Game of Ombre in *The Rape of the Lock*' from Professor W. K. Wimsatt (*RES*, n.s. 1, 1950, pp. 136 ff.). He has taken the stand that Pope, writing a poem, used only certain features of the game, and that what he omitted from his account is not relevant: he speaks of a 'degree of technical imprecision, or incompleteness, which is permitted by the dramatic demands of Pope's description', and continues:

> Of the forty cards in the Ombre pack, Pope tells us the location of nineteen: i.e. all ten Spades; the Ace (Basto), King, and Knave of Clubs; the King, Queen, and Knave of Diamonds; the King, Queen, and Ace of Hearts. The eight other cards in the players' hands include at least one more Club, one more Diamond, and one more Heart. But beyond that we can say little. That is, we do not know what the third player played on the third, fifth, sixth, seventh, eighth, and ninth tricks, nor what Belinda played on the sixth and seventh. One may suppose that after the drawing from the stock the three players usually held most and often all of the court cards. But surely they did not always hold all of them. In this hand we cannot be sure of the whereabouts of the two court cards not mentioned, the Queen of Clubs, and the Knave of Hearts. 'Within the limits of freedom allowed by Pope,' says Mr Fletcher, 'I shall *arbitrarily* assign cards and plays to each player.' So in Pole's account one finds the phrase 'We will suppose', in Tillotson, 'may be supposed', in Case, 'may have looked something like this'. But these arbitrary suppositions deal precisely with what the poem leaves unstated and unimplied and what is therefore no part of the pattern of the poem's artistic necessity. As Mr. Tillotson has well said, the third player's hand 'is left in shadow'. 'The technically clever thing' about Pope's treatment, says Mr Morrah, is that he has thrown 'every possible ray of limelight away from Sir Anonym'. He has thus turned the usually triangular situation of Ombre into the conventional epic duel, a 'straight fight between Belinda and the Baron'. The reconstruction of this game of cards, 'filling in the colours and all the lights and shades', as Lord Aldenham put it, may be an agreeable speculation for a player of Ombre, but is scarcely a rewarding enterprise for a critic of the poem. Not

It is Sir Anonym who deals, since Belinda has and takes the first choice of being Ombre. The hands dealt to the three players may be supposed as follows:

Belinda	*The Baron*	*Sir Anonym*
Spadille	Knave of Spades	6 of Spades
Basto	7 ,, ,,	3 ,, ,,
2 of Spades	5 ,, ,,	Knave of Hearts
King of Clubs	4 ,, ,,	2 ,, ,,
——	King of Diamonds	3 ,, ,,
5 of Hearts	——	4 ,, ,,
5 ,, Clubs	7 of Hearts	6 ,, ,,
3 ,, ,,	4 ,, Clubs	——
2 ,, Diamonds	2 ,, ,,	6 of Clubs
3 ,, ,,	4 ,, Diamonds	5 ,, Diamonds

Belinda finds she has three Matadors and a King which justifies her in asking leave. Pope has so arranged her hand that she knows from the start that she can win four tricks but that she may fail to make a fifth. He has provided her with opponents who divide their good cards in such a way that the Baron's hand is strong and that of Sir Anonym weak. It is to their interest that their hands should have this discrepancy since it is their first object to see that the Ombre does not win; once that is secured it is to the interest of the weaker opponent to make sure that his partner does not give Codille. He would rather that the Ombre were bested by a tie with the stronger opponent.

When Belinda asks leave, her opponents both pass, not being able to risk playing *sans prendre*. She then declares Spades to be trumps, her 2 of Spades thereby becoming Manille. She then discards five of her cards and takes five from the stock. The Baron, who has four trumps and a King, discards four cards and takes four from the stock. Sir Anonym, with his very weak hand, must aim at taking one and only one trick, in the hope of dividing the other eight equally between Belinda and the Baron. But even this is beyond him on the cards he

---

total reconstruction, but appearance or probability, is what has a bearing on the elements of skill and fate in this game of Ombre and hence on its dramatic and poetic interpretation.

Professor Wimsatt has made out a strong case, but it is not altogether water-tight. Pope himself had to design the play as a complete game, and set out a pack of cards on the table before him. Because he did not find it expedient to describe every move in it did not mean that he did not make them, or that his first readers, knowing about ombre, did not infer them, vaguely but with some degree of fulness. I still think that there is usefulness in a reconstruction of the game, more or less as Pope must have constructed it on the table, so that the modern reader may be furnished with something like the knowledge of it that Pope's contemporaries had. He can then return to the text and re-read Pope's account with the same sort of 'background' knowledge Pope's first readers had.

holds. His best chance is to discard his two singletons in Clubs and Diamonds, when he may possibly either (a) draw a Matador, which will give him a certain trick, or (b) be left with a void in either Clubs or Diamonds and the remote possibility of ruffing that suit before his small trumps fall. But in fact he draws the Knave of Clubs and 7 of Diamonds and is no better off than before. After the discard the cards might stand as follows:

Belinda	*The Baron*	*Sir Anonym*
Ace of Spades (Spadille)	Queen of Spades	6 of Spades
2 ,, ,, (Manille)	Knave ,, ,,	3 ,, ,,
Ace of Clubs (Basto)	7 ,, ,,	Knave of Clubs
King of Spades	5 ,, ,,	7 of Diamonds
King of Hearts	4 ,, ,,	Knave of Hearts
Queen ,, ,,	King ,, Diamonds	2 ,, ,,
King of Clubs	Queen ,, ,,	3 ,, ,,
Queen ,, ,,	Knave ,, ,,	4 ,, ,,
6 of Diamonds	Ace of Hearts	6 ,, ,,

The players do not know what are the two cards left in the stock (in fact, the Ace of Diamonds and the 7 of Clubs).

Belinda starts the play by leading her Matadors so as to draw out the trumps of her opponents:

I. *Spadillio* first, unconquerable Lord!
Led off two captive Trumps, and swept the Board.

Belinda leads Spadille; the Baron plays the 4 and Sir Anonym the 3 of Spades.

II. As many more Manillio forc'd to yield,
And march'd a Victor from the verdant Field.

Belinda leads Manille; the Baron plays the 5 and Sir Anonym the 6 of Spades.

III. Him *Basto* follow'd, but his Fate more hard
Gain'd but one Trump and one *Plebeian* card.

Belinda leads Basto which counts as a trump card, the third highest; the Baron must, therefore, play the 7 of Spades; Sir Anonym throws away, say the 7 of Diamonds.

IV. With his broad Sabre next, a Chief in Years,
The hoary Majesty of *Spades* appears . . .
The Rebel-*Knave*, that dares his Prince engage,
Proves the just Victim of his Royal Rage.
Ev'n mighty *Pam* that Kings and Queens o'erthrew,
And mow'd down Armies in the Fights of *Lu*,
Sad chance of War! now, destitute of Aid,
Falls undistinguish'd by the Victor *Spade*!

Belinda leads the King of Spades; the Baron follows with his Knave and Sir Anonym, who wishes to keep his run of Hearts unbroken, plays the Knave of Clubs. This card was called Pam in the game of five-card Loo or Lu (see Hoffmann's *Cyclopædia of Card and Table Games*, p. 122). In this game Pam is 'a sort of paramount trump, taking precedence even of the ace of the trump suit'.

v. 'Belinda', says Pole, 'must now be getting anxious. She has made her four certain tricks, and one more will win her the game. She is almost sure that the Baron has one trump remaining, though conceivably it is one of the two cards left undrawn from the stock, but if one of her Kings makes (by his having one of the suit), it is sufficient. It is immaterial what she leads, and she tries the Club.'[1] But (since 'Fortune will have a hand in small things as well as great'[2])

Now to the *Baron* Fate inclines the Field.
His warlike *Amazon* her Host invades,
Th' Imperial Consort of the Crown of *Spades*.
The *Club*'s black Tyrant first her Victim dy'd . . .

Belinda leads with the King of Clubs; the Baron plays his Queen of Spades, using his trump since he cannot follow suit; Sir Anonym throws away, say the 6 of Hearts.

vi. The *Baron* now his *Diamonds* pours apace;
Th' embroider'd *King* who shows but half his Face,

vii. And his refulgent *Queen*, with Pow'rs combin'd,
Of broken Troops an easie Conquest find.

The Baron leads with the King and then the Queen of Diamonds; Sir Anonym follows with his 4 and 3 of Hearts, and Belinda plays her 6 of Diamonds and Queen of Clubs. Reviewing the whole of the Baron's counter-attack, Pope names the fallen:

Clubs, *Diamonds*, *Hearts*, in wild Disorder seen,
With Throngs promiscuous strow the level Green.

viii. The *Knave* of *Diamonds* tries his wily Arts,
And wins (oh shameful Chance!) the *Queen* of *Hearts*,

Sir Anonym playing the 2 of Hearts. With only one trick remaining, Belinda has indeed cause for anxiety:

At this, the Blood the Virgin's Cheek forsook,
A livid Paleness spreads o'er all her Look;

The card in her hand, the King of Hearts, is the highest of its suit. But the Baron's last card may be another Diamond. (All the trumps have been played, and he has already trumped Clubs.) In that case Belinda cannot escape with the partial reverse of a Beste, as she would if Sir Anonym took the last trick, and pay her losses not to the Baron but to the pool, where she would have a chance of winning them back in the next deal; for Sir Anonym has already ceased to follow suit to Diamonds. The only alternative to complete victory is total defeat:

1. Hoffmann's *Cyclopædia*, p. 151.
2. Seymour, op. cit., p. 43.

> She sees, and trembles at th' approaching Ill,
> Just in the Jaws of Ruin, and *Codille*.

Mr Morrah writes:

> The inference that the Baron's last card, if not a Heart, must be a Diamond is direct from Pope's text. The rest of the above argument assumes, but I think also justifies, your distribution of the cards. I *could* rearrange Sir Anonym's hand so as to make a Beste possible, i.e. so far as Belinda can tell, without seeing the Baron's card—A, 2, 3 of Diamonds in place of three of the small Hearts would do the trick—but I think it would fit the last-quoted couplet less well. With your distribution Belinda *knows* it is neck or nothing.

IX. But both the Baron's and Sir Anonym's cards are Hearts, the Ace and Knave respectively.

> An *Ace* of Hearts steps forth: The *King* unseen
> Lurk'd in her Hand, and mourn'd his captive *Queen*.
> He springs to Vengeance with an eager pace,
> And falls like Thunder on the prostrate *Ace*.

Instead of the ruin she feared, Belinda receives the contents of the pool, five points from each of the players, and four more from each of the players for 'honours' (having had three Matadors and one trump card following them in sequence). She has therefore won eighteen points, beside the contents of the pool which, if this is the first and only game, consists of five points. No wonder, then, her cries penetrate far into the gardens:

> The Nymph exulting fills with Shouts the Sky,
> The Walls, the Woods, and long Canals reply.

III

The accuracy of Pope's description of the cards—they are Court Cards in the style of Rouen (c. 1567)[1]—can be tested by reference to those issued by L. Hewson in 1678,[2] and by Bamford, c. 1750.[3] The knaves all wear short tunics ('Garbs succinct', iii 41): Wakefield compares 'The servants or *knaves* of the ancients, [who] when bent on expedition and activity, were accustomed to fasten their flowing garments higher on the body with their girdles: See *Horace*, Sat. ii 8. 10. Luke xvii 8.' Pope would appreciate a mock-heroic link with the ancients. The legs of the King of Clubs are wide apart and unnaturally parallel (see iii 72), and 'None of the other Kings in the English pack holds the orb'[4] (iii 74). 'As

1. W. G. Benham, *Playing Cards* (British ed., 1931) p. 29.
2. Reproduced opposite p. 180 in Catherine P. Hargrave's *History of Playing Cards* (1930).
3. Reproduced, along with earlier uncoloured Court Cards, in Benham, op. cit., pp. 28 ff.
4. *id.*, 115.

for "his haughty mien" and his "barbarous pride" they have . . vanished in present day English packs'.[1] The King of Diamonds is represented in profile: see iii 76. At iii 67 Pope calls the Queen of Spades a 'warlike *Amazon*': Benham notes that this card is called ' "Queen of Swords", sometimes Penthesilea, Queen of the Amazons, in French packs'.[2] *Spades* means *swords* (*espadas* in Spanish) and 'The "broad sabre" noted by the observant Alexander Pope (iii 55) . . . emphasises the fact that the King of Spades is still the King of Swords'[3]: Benham reproduces an uncoloured English King of Spades of c. 1675 which shows 'the real weapon, which impressed Pope'—in Bamford's version it has 'become attenuated'.[4] Pope represents the Knave of Diamonds as 'try[ing] his wily Arts' (iii 87): Benham comments:

> Both in England and France the Knave of Diamonds had a bad reputation[.] In cartomancy he is a card of ill omen . . . Pope . . . refers to his 'wily arts', but he may have thought of 'The Knave of Diamonds' as suggestive of a sharper.[5]

APPENDIX D

POPE'S REPLY TO DENNIS'S *REMARKS* 1728

I

DENNIS'S *Remarks on Mr. Pope's Rape of the Lock* (1728) takes the form of seven letters to a friend who, apparently, has been disturbed by the admiration accorded the poem by a certain "Mrs. *S*—'.[6] The first four letters are dated early in May 1714. The rest are undated. The pamphlet was written, says Dennis, 'towards the latter End of the Reign of Queen ANNE',[7] i.e., about the time of the remarks on Pope's Homer, *Windsor Forest*, and the *Temple of Fame*. But this dating cannot be strictly correct since at C 5v, in a letter dated 9 May 1714, Dennis cites the line

> Or o'er the Glebe distil the kindly Rain

in its 1717 form (1714–15 had read 'Or on . . .'), and since at E 2r the line

> What mighty Contests rise from trivial things

is given in its 1717 form (for 'Contests' 1712–15 had read 'Quarrels' and Dennis had cited this version earlier at C 7v). In the main he seems to be quoting from one or other of the first two editions of 1714. The *Remarks*, then, were at least

1. *ibid.*
2. *id.*, p. 42.
3. *id.*, p. 97.
4. *id.*, pp. 30, 31, 39.
5. *id.*, p. 113.
6. See E 2r and E 4v.
7. A 2r.

touched up in or after 1717, and since the quotations are embedded in arguments, those arguments themselves are probably of the same date. No new text of the poem appeared after 1717 and before 1728 when the *Remarks* were published, so that no certain date later than 1717 can be proved for the revision of the pamphlet. It is probable, however, that Dennis revised it immediately before publication. The probability of this revision robs of some of its terror the statement that the *Remarks* had been held back '*in Terrorem*'.[1]

The reason for publishing the fourteen-year-old pamphlet was, of course, the *Dunciad*. Dennis's holding back *in terrorem* 'had so good an Effect, that [Pope] endeavour'd for a time to counterfeit Humility and a sincere Repentance'.[2] Now that the deteriorating behaviour of 'Mr. *A. P—E*' has culminated so outrageously in the *Dunciad*, Dennis feels that the blow must fall. The blow, however, had

> very little force, and . . . no effect; for the opinion of the publick was already settled, and it was no longer at the mercy of criticism.[3]

If the pamphlet had been sound in argument and fact its pedantry would have had its importance, since the *Rape of the Lock* exists in a context of pedantry. Pope had his eye on the rules for epic, and since Dennis was arguing from these rules, his attack was potentially serious. But there are two great flaws in his pamphlet. Dennis fails to see that the poem is not an epic but a mock-epic, and so is out to provide a contrast to epic at the same time that it imitates it. He fails also to see that any new poem must to some extent modify the rules, especially when it is a poem doing several things at the same time—following a given story, satisfying a social occasion, satirizing society as well as epic. Much of his criticism is automatically silenced by reference to these two principles. This appendix, therefore, is confined to a discussion of the *Remarks* at the most interesting points where Pope annotated his own copy. This copy is preserved in the British Museum—pressmark C 116. b. 2(6)[4]—among many other attacks—C 116 b. 1, 3, and 4—most of them similarly annotated and all of them, it seems, originally collected and bound by Pope.[5] EC's annotations of the *Remarks*[6] are inadequate and inaccurate. The pages have been trimmed by a binder so that words and parts of words are lost. In transcribing the annotations I have used < > to indicate words careted above the line of writing, || to indicate the end of a line, and + to indicate the survival of doubtful or half letters. Comments and conjectures are placed inside square brackets.

1. A 2v.
2. *ibid.*
3. Johnson, *Lives*, iii 104.
4. Misnumbered by Crocker, a former owner, as 7.
5. See Ruffhead, *Life* (1769), pp. 194 f. Two further volumes are in the Dyce Collection at S. Kensington.
6. Mainly at ii 132 f.

(a) Underneath the heading 'LETTER I.' Pope writes 'Proving that Boileau did not call his Lutrin ⟨Poeme⟩ Heroicomique, that Bossu dos not say ‖ the Machines [*gap of* 2$\frac{3}{4}$″] and that Butler ‖ y^{e} Notes to his own Hudibras'.[1] Probably some words—perhaps 'that' or 'y^{t}' and 'wrote'—have been lost in the trimming after 'say' and 'Butler'. The gap following 'Machines' may have been left to be filled in later with a statement of what Bossu said, since Pope has written 'Bossu' in the margin opposite part of Dennis's remark that 'what [Pope] calls his *Machinery* has no Manner of Influence upon what he calls his *Poem*, not in the least promoting, or preventing, or retarding the Action of it.'[2] See Introduction, p. 123 above.

(b) On B 1v Dennis speaks of 'the fantastical Composition of the Word Heroi-Comical'. Pope writes 'Boi' opposite this: Boileau first called his poem 'poëme-héroïque' on its title-page but in the edition of 1701 changed it to 'poëme héroï-comique' (see *Œuvres*, ii 413).

(c) On B 1v Dennis trivially remarks that Pope need not have troubled in his dedicatory epistle to acquaint Miss Fermor with the news that he published the poem before he had thought of the machinery (he is misrepresenting what Pope did say) since she could see this from the poem itself. Pope again appeals to *Le Lutrin*: 'Boileau did so ‖ Vid. prim. ed.' Boileau in the *Au Lecteur* prefixed to the editions of 1674 and 1675 had written:

> Voilà toute l'histoire de la bagatelle que je donne au public. J'aurois bien voulu la lui donner achevée; mais des raisons très-secrètes, et dont le lecteur trouvera bon que je ne l'instruise pas, m'en ont empêché. Je ne me serois pourtant pas pressé de le donner imparfait, comme il est, n'eût été les misérables fragmens qui en ont couru.[3]

(d) On B 3r underneath 'LETTER II.', Pope has written 'Mr Dennis's positive word that the Rape of ye Lock *can* be nothing but a triffle ‖ and that the Lutrin cannot be so, however it may appear ‖'. During the course of this letter Pope underlines certain words in order to enforce the element of inane dogmatism in Dennis's assertions. The charge that the *Rape of the Lock*, unlike *Le Lutrin*, had no moral was a serious one since Le Bossu had made the moral the principal end of an epic. Pope vindicates his poem by the ingenious device of giving alternatives for some of the words in Dennis's statement of Boileau's moral and so adapting it to suit his own poem. Dennis had written of *Le Lutrin*, ''Tis indeed a noble and important satirical Poem, upon the Luxury, the Pride, the Divisions, and Animosities of the Popish Clergy'.[4] Against the last two words Pope writes 'female sex'. On the next page Dennis states:

1. B 1r.
2. B 1v–B 2r.
3. *Œuvres*, ii 405.
4. B 4v.

The Moral is, *That when Christians, and especially the Clergy, run into great Heats about religious Trifles, their Animosity proceeds from the Want of that Religion which is the Pretence of their Quarrel.*

Pope has written 'Ladies' over '*Clergy*', underlined '*religious*', written 'sense' over '*Religion*' and underlined '*Religion*' with a sweep that begins under the preceding words and ends under the following one. (He may be indicating by this that his adaptation should end at '*Religion*', since sense was scarcely the pretence of the quarrel between the Fermors and the Petres.)

(e) On B 4v when Dennis quotes two lines from *Le Lutrin* to show how Boileau 'seems to have given broad Hints at what was his real Meaning', Pope has written in the margin 'Clarissas Speach'. If this portion of the pamphlet were actually written in May 1714, Dennis could not be blamed for having failed to allow for that speech (v 9–34), since it was not added to the poem till 1717. According to the note signed 'P.' in Warburton's edition of 1751, Clarissa was introduced 'to open more clearly the MORAL of the Poem.' Pope (or Warburton) may have written this note in order to show awareness of the standards of Le Bossu or more specifically to silence Dennis's objection. Dr Johnson considered Pope's moral superior to Boileau's:

> The purpose of [Pope] is, as he tells us, to laugh at 'the little unguarded follies of the female sex.' It is therefore without justice that Dennis charges *The Rape of the Lock* with the want of a moral, and for that reason sets it below *The Lutrin*, which exposes the pride and discord of the clergy. Perhaps neither Pope nor Boileau has made the world much better than he found it; but if they had both succeeded, it were easy to tell who would have deserved most from publick gratitude. The freaks, and humours, and spleen, and vanity of women, as they embroil families in discord and fill houses with disquiet, do more to obstruct the happiness of life in a year than the ambition of the clergy in many centuries. It has been well observed that the misery of man proceeds not from any single crush of overwhelming evil, but from small vexations continually repeated.[1]

(f) On B 5v Dennis cites '*several* ridiculous Incidents in the *Lutrin*' which surprise the reader into the laughter requisite for an alleged comic poem, adding "And whereas there are a thousand such in *Hudibras*; There is not so much as *one*, nor the *Shadow of one*, in the *Rape of the Lock*'. Over the last four words of the last of Dennis's three examples of comic incidents from *Le Lutrin*—'The Battle in the Bookseller's Shop'—Pope has written 'of men & women for ye loss of a Lock'.

(g) The third Letter is largely an argument against cosmetics, to which Belinda had been made indebted for the last fractions of her beauty. Dennis ranks himself among those 'who have a Taste of *Nature*'.[2] He blames Pope also

1. *Lives*, iii 234.
2. B 7r and again at B 8r.

for insulting Belinda by making her a virago—he does not see that it is for the purposes of the mock-heroic that she imitates the screaming heroes of Homer. Pope is quick to misrepresent Dennis's well-meaning but ambiguous words and underlines 'those who have a Taste of Nature' (B 8r), writing in the margin a comment I find unintelligible: 'love [*or* Jove] a W. i [+ half a minuscule]'. The nature of this comment is presumably indicated by Pope's subtitle to the heading 'LETTER III.': '⟨Where it⟩ appears to [*this word has two thin lines drawn slantingly across it*] Demonstration that no ⟨handsome⟩ Lady ought to dress herself, and no ‖ modest one to cry out—or be angry.'[1]

(h) On C 1r Dennis notes that there are no woods near Hampton Court for Belinda's cries to echo in. Pope writes 'Hampton ‖ Court has [+ *part of another letter*] Wood'. I am indebted to Mr Edward Yates, F.S.A., for the following communication, dated 29 Sept. 1936:

> The suite now occupied by Mrs R. Keith on the top floor at the S.E. angle of Wren's building is said to contain the rooms [where the rape of the lock took place] and looking out from these over the House Park as I did last year the trees of the triple avenues planted by Charles II and those bounding the Great Fountain Garden some of which were also planted by Charles II and were moved outward by William III (see Defoe) certainly now give the impression of a thick wood and even in Pope's time their growth may have been sufficient to produce the same effect.
>
> Trees bounding the Course in the House Park appear as a wood in early engravings and are near enough—given poet's licence . . .

See Mr Yates's *Hampton Court*, 1935, chs. vii and viii.

(i) Reverting on C 5r to his charge that the machinery of the *Rape of the Lock* does not influence the action, Dennis writes

> There is no Opposition of the *Machines* to one another in this *Rape of the Lock*. *Umbriel* the *Gnome* is not introduc'd till the Action is over, and till *Ariel* and the Spirits under him, have quitted *Belinda*.

Pope underlines several words in this passage and writes in the margin 'because they [+ *a stroke for an* f, p, *or* long s] ‖ a Gnome & E [+ o *or* a] ‖ Lover pre [+ *half a round letter*] ‖'. Perhaps the whole sentence read originally 'because they send a Gnome & Earthly Lover prevents'. In any case the references are to iv 11–16 and iii 139–46. Pope does not silence Dennis by indicating how the machines are opposed. (See Introduction, p. 123 above.) He confines his annotation to sylphs and gnomes.

(j) At C 5r–v Dennis quotes most of Ariel's speech to the sylphs describing their kinds (ii 73–90), and asks 'Did you ever hear before that the Planets were roll'd by the aerial Kind?' Pope underlines *aerial* and writes against this query 'expresly ‖ otherwise ‖'. His meaning is made clearer by his annotations of the

---

1. B 6r.

lines Dennis had quoted. Pope seems to have hesitated in this annotation. He has asterisked '*aerial*' in l. 76 and set in the margin what may be either an answering asterisk or a deletion mark. This is followed by the blotted word 'for'. In the following line

Some in the Fields of purest Æther *play,*

he has set a '1' against 'Æther' and in the margin written '1. ætheri[al]'. After the next three lines, where Dennis has left out some relevant lines, Pope has written '2. aerial ‖ beneath y[e] ‖ moon ‖'. After the final line, 90, he has continued the quotation with a significant italicizing: '*Our* humbler province'. Dennis here makes a fair point. The sylphs in *Gabalis* had been introduced as 'Aerial Substances',[1] and since their business was mainly with human beings they were not given functions in the ether.[2] Pope gives them such functions in order to include them in Le Bossu's category of 'Physical' machines[3] but he appears not to allow for this enlargement in his general term. He would, however, be roughly within his rights if lines 77–80 were understood as a parenthesis ('You know the tasks assigned to the sylphs of the air—there is, of course, a superior kind of sylph, not aerial but etherial, who rolls the planets . . .'); or if 'Aerial' were understood loosely ('You know the tasks assigned to sylphs, those airy insubstantial beings: some inhabit the ether . . .') If Pope intended this second alternative he is using 'Aerial' in the sense that it bears in Hobbes:

> As for the matter, or substance of the Invisible Agent . . . it was the same with that of the Soule of man; and . . . the Soule of man, was of the same substance, with that which appeareth in a Dream, to one that sleepeth; or in a Looking-glasse, to one that is awake . . . Ghosts . . . *Imagines*, and *Umbræ* . . . Spirits, that is, this aëriall bodies.[4]

But if Dennis had made his objection while the poem was still in MS., Pope no doubt would have removed the ambiguous word.

(k) On C 7r Dennis objects that the machines are not drawn from a single system; the sylphs, gnomes, and salamanders are Rosicrucian, the fairies, genii, and dæmons (of ii 74) are

> Beings which are unknown to those Fanatick Sophisters . . . *Spleen* and the *Phantoms* about, are deriv'd from the Powers of *Nature*, and are of a separate System. And *Fate* and *Jove* . . . belong to the Heathen Religion.

Dennis apparently only knows the Rosicrucian theory from Pope's dedicatory epistle: de Villars's system had included fairies, genii (to some extent), and

1. p. 14.

2. Although de Villars asserts that 'This immense Space, which is between the Earth and the *Heavens*, has more Noble Inhabitants, than *Birds* and *Flyes*' he goes on to imply limitation: 'The *Air* is full of [sylphs]' (p. 27).

3. See Introduction, p. 121 above.

4. *Leviathan*, 1651, p. 53.

dæmons.[1] Pope's marginal defence only covers two items: against the reference to Spleen and the phantoms he writes 'allegorical' (i.e. belonging to Le Bossu's moral, not physical, category), and against the last words of the passage quoted he writes 'and to Poetry' (cf. the *Preface* to the *Iliad*: '[Homer's] Gods continue to this Day the Gods of Poetry').[2] Pope did not, however, need to defend himself. In a mock-epic the more of the recognized machines that are mocked at, the better.

(l) Letter v, in Pope's estimation, 'sheweth: that the Rosicrucian Doctrine is not the Christian, ‖ and that Callimachus and Catullus were [fools *deleted*] a couple of fools'.[3] The latter half of this subtitle refers to iii 171–8 and is explained at D 3v, where Pope writes '‖ [Se *or* Vid]e Callimachus. ‖ [Se *or* Vid]e Catullus.' against Dennis's outburst 'who the Devil, besides this Bard, ever made a Wonder of [the force of steel in cutting off a lock of hair]?' Catullus' poem on Berenice's hair was a translation of a poem of Callimachus.

(m) On D 4v Dennis asks concerning Umbriel, 'Now to what Purpose does this fantastick Being take this Journey? Why, to give *Belinda* the Spleen.' That journey was, he considered, 'impertinent'. Pope's marginal comment is 'e[?] yt makes ‖ o [*or* s] to Alecto ‖ [*a dot belonging to a lost* i *or* j] gate Amata' which may have read originally 'ye same y^{t} makes Juno go to Alecto to instigate Amata'. The reference is to *Æneid*, vii 323 ff. On the next page Dennis exclaims, 'How absurd . . . to take a Journey down to the *central Earth*, for no other Purpose than to give [Belinda] the *Spleen*, whom [Umbriel] left and found in the Height of it?' Pope's comment is final: 'So was Ama ‖ before Fœmi ‖ ardentem cu ‖ iræqꝫ coque ‖' which must formerly have read 'So was Amata before Fœmineæ ardentem curæqꝫ iræqꝫ coquebant' (*Æneid*, vii 345). See Pope's note on iv 141.

(n) On D 7v Dennis's comment on v 45–52 reads:

> the latter Part of it is not taken from *Homer*, but from his most impertinent Imitator Monsieur *De la Motte*, and neither the one nor the other Trifler seem to have known any thing in this Passage, of the Solemnity, and the dreadful Majesty of *Homer*.

Pope's annotation reads '‖ ginus'; he is referring to the *De Sublimitate*, Section ix, where Longinus quotes *Iliad*, xx 61–5 in a version different from the accepted one. Dennis had twice cited this passage in his *Grounds for Criticism in Poetry* (*Works*, ed. E. N. Hooker, i (1939) 356, 367).

(o) On D 8v Dennis quotes v 99–102, which end:

> . . . ah! let me still survive,
> And burn in *Cupid's* Flames, but burn alive.

1. See note on ii 74.
2. C 1r.
3. C 7v.

and asks ridiculously, 'Now, Sir, who ever heard of a dead Man that burnt in *Cupid's* Flames?' Pope writes under the 'burn in' of the offending line 'still burn on' and underlines 'but burn'. By this he means to indicate the reading of the line in the edition of 1712 where the meaning was the same and not too subtle for Dennis: 'And still burn on, in *Cupid's* Flames *Alive*.'

(p) On E 2v Dennis objects that the active verb *sing* (i 3) 'has no Accusative Case depending on it'. Pope refers him to 'Virgils ‖ Georg. ‖' i.e., to *Georgic* i 1–5 where the construction 'Quid . . . canere' exactly resembles his own. Lines 1 f. are, of course, two noun-clauses, both objects of the verb.

II

These annotations show Pope's precise command of the literary learning on which so much of the mockery of his poem depends, his capacity to annotate with intense economy and to prick Dennis's various bubbles. They justify the motto from Job, xxxi 35, which he affixed to this collection of attacks against himself:

> Behold it is my desire, that mine ‖ Adversary had written a Book. ‖ Surely I would take it on my ‖ Shoulder, and bind it as a crown ‖ unto me. ‖[1]

APPENDIX E

PLACES MENTIONED IN THE RAPE OF THE LOCK

HAMPTON COURT. 'The modern portion of Hampton Court, and the East and South fronts, were built by William III, who frequently resided there. Queen Anne only went there occasionally' (Croker). Holden quotes Hutton's *Hampton Court*: '[in Anne's reign] it would be difficult to say whether it was better known as the home of statesmen or the resort of wits'. Hutton explains Anne's preference for Windsor and Kensington by her connecting Hampton Court with the death of the Duke of Gloucester (the only child of hers to survive infancy).

The eastern façade of William III's new building at Hampton Court faces on to a semi-circular ornamental garden. Beyond this garden, and running east and west, is a 'long canal'. Two other canals run north and south. See E. Yates, *Hampton Court*, 1935, chs. vii and viii.

For the 'woods' (iii 100) at Hampton Court, see Appendix D, p. 396.

THE MALL. Charles II improved St James's Park by the addition of lines of trees, a canal, and the Mall. From the time when he made the Park public, the Mall rivalled the Ring as a fashionable resort. It was an enclosed walk running

1. Brit. Mus., C. 116. b. 1: the recto of the flyleaf preceding tract i.

parallel to the front of St James's Palace, and partly devoted at first to the game of pall-mall (a kind of croquet). H. Misson (p. 181) describes the Mall as 'mark'd with Figures to [the length of] 880 Paces', which is annotated in English measure, as 'About 1424 Foot'. Sir Simon Addlepate in Wycherley's *Love in a Wood* (II i) sends for fiddlers 'to serenade the whole Park to-night'. They come and play, and there is dancing. Larwood (ii 111) notes that such impromptu music and dancing were not uncommon.

THE RING. The open-air pleasures of the Restoration court were mainly those of promenading the Mall in St James's Park, and of driving round the Ring (called also the Tour or Circus) in Hyde Park. The Ring was north of the eastern end of what is now the Serpentine, and being on high ground had views of open country on almost all sides. It measured 'two or three hundred Paces [in] Diameter', had 'a sorry Kind of Ballustrade, or rather . . . Poles plac'd upon Stakes, but three Foot from the Ground; and the Coaches drive round and round this' (H. Misson, 126). Another foreigner observes that 'the coaches drive slowly round, some in one direction, others the opposite way, which . . . produces a rather pretty effect, and proves clearly that they only come there in order to see and to be seen' (quoted by Larwood, i 59). Even during William's reign, when it was supposed to suffer from the general decline of gaiety, a French observer noted that he had 'often computed near 500 Coaches, that vie one with another for splendor and equipage' (*Letters of Wit*, p. 215). Under Anne its popularity again increased, and in 1709 was published *The Circus . . . A Satyr on the Ring in Hyde Park.* In 1736 it ceased to exist when the Serpentine came to occupy much of its site.

ROSAMONDA'S LAKE. Rosamonda's Lake, an oblong pond near the south-west corner of St James's Park, was 'long consecrated to disastrous love, and *elegiac* poetry' (Warburton, *Letters*, 1805, p. 151). *Almonds for Parrots* [anon], 1708, p. 7, presents other evidence:

> But stay my Muse, let's view that noted Pond
> That bears the Name of beauteous *Rosamond*,
> Where Herds of happy Shes sometimes repair,
> To take the Breezes of the Evening Air,
> And hide themselves there from the num'rous Train
> Of noisy, senseless, self-conceited Men:
> There Musick gently sooth[es] their Lovers Ear,
> And lulls to Rest the Courtier's Thoughts of Care.
> The busy, young Impertinent comes here,
> Buzzing about his Nonsense ev'ry where,
> 'Till all the shady, dark Retirement round,
> Is like a Publick Fair or Market found,
> Where Women do exchange themselves for gold,
> As Beasts at *Smithfield* are both bought and sold.

See Kip's drawing in the Crace Collection (Brit. Museum) P xii, dated in MS. 1726.

APPENDIX F

Puffs, Powders, Patches, Bibles, Billet-doux (i 138)

OWING to the lapse of centuries this brilliant line has caused much puzzlement. A recent writer in *Notes and Queries* (21 Jan. 1950) placed a finger on the crux of the difficulty by suggesting that 'Bibles' should be singular. My reply rejecting the proposal is adapted here by permission of the editor of that periodical. My reasons for rejection are as follows:

(*a*) Pope was very careful over the printing of his poems where important matters like singulars and plurals were concerned—otherwise why trouble to print at all? He was not very careful over matters of smaller importance, when they were indeed of smaller importance, matters perhaps such as 'commas and points' (*Epistle to Dr. Arbuthnot*, l. 161), but over his words he was, of course, meticulous. That the reading as it stands was passed by him as correct many times over is strong *prima facie* evidence of its genuineness.

(*b*) If 'Bible' gives us a line of good English, it does not give us a line of very good English nor of good Popian English. When Pope compiles a list of nouns, he tends to make them all either plural or singular: e.g.,

> *Fays*, *Fairies*, *Genii*, *Elves*, and *Daemons* hear! (ii 74)

and

> With singing, laughing, ogling, and all that (iii 18).

When he gives us a list of nouns in the singular he usually gives each of them an article: e.g.,

> A Nest, A Toad, A Fungus, or a Flow'r. (*Dunciad*, iv 400)

When he mixes, as he sometimes does, nouns singular and plural he gives the singular noun(s) an article, e.g.:

> Sighs, Sobs, and Passions, and the War of Tongues. (iv 84)

This usage is in the interests of the best English. If he had wanted 'Bible' to be a singular, he would, therefore, have preferred to write:

> Puffs, Powders, Patches, a Bible, Billet-doux,

which, of course, the metre would not have permitted. Meeting that rhythmical obstruction, Pope would, I think, have remoulded his line so as to find a place for the article before a singular noun.

The reading 'Bible' looks less attractive still when, prompted by the rhyme, we remember that 'Billet-doux' is plural. In the English of Pope's time and for long afterwards, there were at least three plurals for this gallicism, of which the two commonest are 'billets-doux' and 'billet-doux'. The sense usually prompted the correct pronunciation: [*bili du*:] when singular and [*bili du*:*z*] when plural. At ii 41, though spelt like the singular, the word is again plural:

> With tender *Billet-doux* he lights the Pyre.

Dryden provides a handy instance of this plural, and like Pope in the rhyme position: at the beginning of his Epilogue to *King Arthur* he writes:

> I've had to-day a Dozen *Billet-Doux*
> From *Fops*, and *Wits*, and *Cits*, and *Bow-Street Beaux*.

Instances of 'billet-doux' used as a plural are given in *The Stanford Dictionary of Anglicised Words and Phrases*, ed. Fennell, 1892.

(c) The reading 'Bibles' receives some backing from the relation of the line to the source of its element of parody. Pope planned his line as a parody of Milton's line

> Rocks, Caves, Lakes, Fens, Bogs, Dens, and shades of death.

(*d*) The sense, too, demands 'Bibles'. Belinda's dressing-table has plenty of everything. Our difficulty over 'Bibles' is, at bottom, a material one. A Bible we think of as a big book. But in Pope's day, more Bibles were printed in sizes which the trade at the present day might describe as 'bijou' than larger Bibles of the sort we know as 'family Bibles'. During the years 1700–4, according to the *Historical Catalogue of the Printed Editions of Holy Scripture in the Library of the British and Foreign Bible Society*, compiled by T. H. Darlow and H. F. Moule, I 246–51, nine 12mos were printed as against three each of folios, 4tos, and 8vos. An average measurement for these 12mos is about 120 mm. by 50 mm. The British Museum has a Bible published in 1683, which I have seen. It was printed by 'C. Bill, H. Hills, and Tho. Newcomb, Printers to the Kings most Excellent Majesty'. Its measurements are 2½ in. wide, 5 in. high, and 2 in. thick. Bibles in sizes such as these were printed small so as to be carried about. They were often bound ornamentally, and with clasps. A young lady might well possess several, acquired probably as gifts, which, if they were bound prettily, would afford, as occasions changed, a choice as to colour or style. Two or three of these small books on the crowded, if not untidy dressing-table of an unthinking Belinda would bulk no more inconveniently than two or three pretty prayer books on a modern dressing-table. She might, moreover, find them useful for keeping ribbons straight.

Modern scholars know of course that Arabella Fermor, whom Pope names as the original of his Belinda, was a Catholic. This was also known, possibly but not certainly, to such of his readers as knew Arabella Fermor or of her. Her concern with Bibles, therefore, would have been less than that of a Protestant girl. But this knowledge as to Arabella Fermor is not necessarily to the point when we are speaking of Belinda. Because Arabella Fermor was a Catholic it does not follow that Belinda was. In Belinda, Pope is satirizing English young ladies generally. The principles of Nature which guided him on most occasions would have prevented his limiting his poem to a small coterie, especially when its divergencies from the generality were on points not germane. When religion is in question, Belinda is first of all an English young lady, and so more a Protestant than a Catholic. When Pope allows himself a tilt at the failure of fashionable people to understand the difference between a box of patches and what

Sterne called an 'instrumental part . . . of religion', he chooses to write

Puffs, Powders, Patches, Bibles, Billet-doux

rather than

Puffs, Powders, Patches, Primers, Billet-doux

or than

Puffs, Powders, Patches, Missals, Billet-doux.

I do not know why he did not write

Puffs, Powders, Patches, Prayer-books, Billet-doux,

but I shall be surprised if there is not a sufficient reason. It may have been more fashionable in 1714 to carry Bibles than prayer-books.

THE TEMPLE OF FAME

APPENDIX G

POPE'S PARALLEL PASSAGES FROM THE *HOUS OF FAME*

THESE passages from the *Hous of Fame* first appeared in the *Works* of 1736. They have been listed by letter for convenience of cross-reference from the notes printed with the poem. The line references in round brackets are to the *Temple of Fame*, and those in square brackets to the *Hous of Fame* (Skeat's edition). It cannot be said definitely from what text Pope derived his notes since he edits them as he pleases.

a. (ll. 11 ff.) *These verses are hinted from the following of* Chaucer, *Book* 2

Tho beheld I fields and plains,
Now hills, and now mountains,
Now valeis, and now forestes,
And now unneth great bestes,
Now rivers, now citees,
Now towns, now great trees,
Now shippes sayling in the see. [389 ff.].

b. (ll. 27 ff.) Chaucer'*s third book of* Fame

It stood upon so high a rock,
Higher standeth none in Spayne—
What manner stone this rock was,
For it was like a lymed glass,
But that it shone full more clere;
But of what congeled matere
It was, I niste redily;

But at the last espied I,
And found that it was every dele,
A rock of ise, and not of stele. [26 ff.]

c. (ll. 31 ff.) *Tho saw I all the hill y-grave*
With famous folkes names fele,
That had been in much wele
And her fames wide y-blow;
But well unneth might I know,
Any letters for to rede
Ther names by, for out of drede
They weren almost off-thawen so,
That of the letters one or two
Were molte away of every name,
So unfamous was woxe her fame;
But men said, what may ever last. [iii 46 ff.]

In adapting the last line Pope changes 'men' to 'poets'. Cf. 306 f. and note.

d. (ll. 41 ff.) *Tho gan I in myne harte cast,*
That they were molte away for heate,
And not away with stormes beate. [iii 58 ff.]

e. (ll. 45 ff.) *For on that other side I sey*
Of that hill which northward ley,
How it was written full of names
Of folke, that had afore great fames,
Of old time, and yet they were
As fresh, as men had written hem there
The self day, or that houre
That I on hem gan to poure:
But well I wiste what it made;
It was conserved with the shade
(All the writing that I sye)
Of the castle that stoode on high,
And stood eke in so cold a place,
That heate might it not deface. [iii 61 ff.]

f. (ll. 132 ff.) *It shone lighter than a glass,*
And made well more than it was,
As kind thing of Fame is. [iii 199 ff.]

g. (ll. 179 ff.) *From the dees many a pillere,*
Of metal that shone not full clere, &c.
Upon a pillere saw I stonde
That was of lede and iron fine,

Him of the sect Saturnine,
The Ebraicke Josephus *the old*, &c.
Upon an iron piller strong,
That painted was all endlong,
With tygers blood in every place,
The Tholosan *that hight* Stace,
That bare of Thebes *up the name*, &c. [iii 331 ff.]

h. (ll 182 ff.) *Full wonder hye on a pillere*
Of iron, he the great Omer,
And with him Dares *and* Titus, *&c.* [iii 375 ff.]

i. (ll. 196 ff.) *There saw I stand on a pillere*
That was of tinned iron cleere,
The Latin *poet* Virgyle,
That hath bore up of a great while
The fame of pious Eneas:
And next him on a pillere was
Of copper, Venus *clerke* Ovide,
That hath sowen wondrous wide
The great God of Love's fame—
Tho saw I on a pillere by
Of iron wrought full sternly,
The great Poet Dan Lucan,
That on his shoulders bore up then
As hye as that I might see,
The fame of Julius *and* Pompee.
And next him on a pillere stode
Of sulphur, like as he were wode,
Dan Claudian, *sothe for to tell,*
That bare up all the fame of hell, &c. [iii 391 ff.]

j. (ll. 259 ff.) *Methought that she was so lite,*
That the length of a cubite,
Was longer than she seemed be;
But thus soone in a while she,
Her selfe tho wonderly straight,
That with her feet she th' earth reight,
And with her head she touchyd heaven— [iii 279 ff.]

Cf. *Æneid*, iv 176 f. and Ovid, *Metam.*, ix 139. Warton notes three other instances in Virgil of dilating figures [i 388 f.].

Chaucer introduces Fame before describing the figures on the pillars. Pope improves on this by inverting the order.

k. (ll. 270 ff.) *I heard about her throne y-sung*

That all the palays walls rung,
So sung the mighty muse, she
That cleped is Calliope,
And her seven sisters eke— [iii 307 ff.]

I ii 313 ff. are also part of Pope's source:

And evermo, eternally,
They songe of Fame, as tho herd I:—
'Heried be thou and thy name,
Goddesse of renoun and of fame!'

l. (ll. 276 ff.)

I heard a noise approchen blive,
That far'd as bees done in a hive,
Against her time of out flying;
Right such a manere murmuring,
For all the world it seemed me.
Tho gan I look about and see
That there came entring into th' hall,
A right great company withal;
And that of sundry regions,
Of all kind of conditions,—&c. [iii 431 ff.]

m. (ll. 294 ff.)

And some of them she granted sone,
And some she warned well and fair,
And some she granted the contrair—
Right as her sister dame Fortune
Is wont to serve in commune. [iii 448 ff.]

EC note that neither Chaucer nor Pope 'touch upon the truth that the same person is commonly both lauded and denounced', and cite *Samson Agonistes*, ll. 971 ff.

n. (ll. 318 ff.)

Tho came the third companye,
And gan up to the dees to hye,
And down on knees they fell anone,
And saiden: We ben everichone
Folke that han full truely
Deserved Fame right-fully,
And prayen you it might be knowe
Right as it is, and forth blowe.
I grant, quoth she, for now me list
That your good works shall be wist,
And yet ye shall have better loos,
Right in despite of all your foos,
Than worthy is, and that anone.
Let now (quoth she) thy trump gone—

And certes all the breath that went
Out of his trump's mouth smel'd
As men a pot of baume held
Among a basket full of roses— [iii 567 ff.]

o. (ll. 328 ff.) *Therewithal there came anone*
Another huge companye,
Of good fclke—
What did this Eolus, *but he*
Tooke out his trump of brass,
That fouler than the devil was:
And gan this trump for to blowe,
As all the world should overthrowe.
Throughout every regione
Went this foul trumpet's soune,
Swift as a pellet out of a gunne,
When fire is in the powder runne.
And suche a smoke gan out wende,
Out of the foul trumpets ende—&c. [iii 516 ff.]

p. (ll. 356 ff.) *I saw anone the fifth route*
That to this lady gan loute,
And downe on knees anone to fall,
And to her they besoughten all,
To hiden their good works eke;
And said, they yeve not a leke
For no fame ne such renowne;
For they for contemplacyoune,
And Goddes love had it wrought,
Ne of fame would they ought.
What, quoth she, and be ye wood?
And ween ye for to do good,
And for to have it of no fame?
Have ye despite to have my name?
Nay ye shall lien everichone:
Blowe thy trump, and that anone
(Quoth she) thou Eolus, *I hote.*
And ring these folkes workes by rote,
That all the world may of it heare;
And he gan blow their loos so cleare,
In his golden clarioune,
Through the World went the soune,
All so kindly, and eke so soft,
That their fame was blowen aloft. [iii 613 ff.]

Chaucer has two groups embodying the virtue of modest goodness, granting fame to the first, and withholding it from the second. Pope dispenses with the second group probably for a technical reason—he does not wish to repeat the formula already used at 318–41, reserving its reappearance for a more interesting occasion (ll. 378–405). (In the same way he omits Chaucer's second group of military adventurers who seek fame successfully.) He may wish to suggest that men of modest virtue are so rare (see ll. 356 and 366) that all who are really so are likely to become famous. Cf. Temple, p. 160: 'true Honour has something in it so humorous, as to follow commonly those, who avoid and neglect it, rather than those who seek and pursue it'; and the last two lines of Swift's 'Ode to the Athenian Society':

> . . . Men, who liv'd and dy'd without a Name,
> Are the chief Heroes in the sacred List of Fame.

The idea as it applied to the rose had been used symbolically in Waller's 'Go, Lovely Rose' (which Pope echoed at *Rape of the Lock*, iv 158 and which Gray was to echo at *Elegy*, ll. 55 f.).

q. (ll. 378 ff.) *The reader might compare these twenty eight lines following which contain the same matter with eighty four of* Chaucer, *beginning thus,*

> Tho came the sixth companye,
> And gan faste to Fame crye, *&c.* [iii 637 ff.]

being tco prolix to be here inserted.

r. (ll. 406 ff.)

> *Tho came another companye,*
> *That had y-done the treachery,* &c. [iii 721 ff.]

'Pope . . . wisely gave no more [than this quotation] for the single fact that it was the *treacherous* that were advanced is all that Pope had to suggest his own description. He obviously applies & illustrates the treachery—No one, I think, can doubt that these illustrations are from King William & the revolution party —Usurper of a throne &c &c[.] Pope was at the time of writing deep in with Swift & the tories—had . . . naturally quarreled with Addison—& here is something like proof that he was willing to go all lengths with the tories. The death of the Queen & the accession of the Whigs, probably cooled his ardour . . .' (C. W. Dilke's MS. note, *B.M.* 12274, i 15, opposite p. 164.)

EC note that Pope has Virgil in mind as well as Chaucer; see his description of the criminals in Hades (*Æneid*, vi 580 ff.). Pope imitates l. 825 of Dryden's translation of this passage:

> Expel their Parents, and usurp the Throne.

s. (ll. 418 ff.) *The Scene here changes from the temple of* Fame *to that of* Rumour, *which is almost entirely* Chaucer'*s. The particulars follow.*

> *Tho saw I stonde in a valey,*
> *Under the castle fast by*
> *A house, that* Domus Dedali
> *That* Labyrinthus *cleped is,*

Nas made so wonderly, I wis,
Ne half so queintly y-wrought;
And evermo, as swift as thought,
This queint house about went,
That never more it still stent—
And eke this house hath of entrees
As many as leaves are on trees,
In summer, when they ben grene;
And in the roof yet men may sene
A thousand holes and well mo,
To letten the soune out go;
And by day in every tide
Ben all the doors open wide,
And by night each one unshet;
No porter is there one to let,
No manner tydings in to pace:
Ne never rest is in that place. [iii 828 ff.]

t. (ll. 428 ff.) *This thought is transferr'd hither out of the third book of Fame, where it takes up no less than 120 Verses, beginning thus,*

Geffray, *thou wottest well this*, &c.

[*third* is an error for *second* which 1741 and 1751 retain. The lines referred to are 221 ff.] Cowley had already imitated these similes, *Davideis*, p. 47

u. (ll. 448 ff.)

Of werres, of peace, of marriages,
Of rest, of labour, of voyages,
Of abode, of dethe, and of life,
Of love and hate, accord and strife,
Of loss, of lore, and of winnings,
Of hele, of sickness, and lessings,
Of divers transmutations
Of estates and eke of regions,
Of trust, of drede, of jealousy,
Of wit, of winning, and of folly,
Of good, or bad government,
Of fire, and of divers accident. [iii 871 ff.]

v. (ll. 458 ff.)

But such a grete Congregation
Of folke as I saw roame about,
Some within, and some without,
Was never seen, ne shall be eft—
And every wight that I saw there
Rowned everich in others ear
A new tyding privily.

Or else he told it openly
Right thus, and said, Knowst not thou
That is betide to night now?
No, quoth he, tell me what?
And then he told him this and that, &c.
—Thus north and south
Went every tiding fro mouth to mouth,
And that encreasing evermo,
As fire is wont to quicken and go
From a sparkle sprong amiss,
Till all the citee brent up is. [iii 944 ff.]

w. (ll. 489 ff.) *And sometime I saw there at once,*
A lesing and a sad sooth saw
That gonnen at adventure draw
Out of a window forth to pace—
And no man, be he ever so wrothe,
Shall have one of these two, but bothe, &c. [iii 998 ff.]

APPENDIX H

ZEMBLA: THE POET AND THE SCIENTIST

(*Temple of Fame*, ll. 53–60)

Tho a strict Verisimilitude be not requir'd in the Descriptions of this visionary and allegorical kind of Poetry, which admits of every wild Object that Fancy may present in a Dream, and where it is sufficient if the moral Meaning atone for the Improbability: Yet Men are naturally so desirous of Truth, that a Reader is generally pleas'd, in such a Case, with some Excuse or Allusion that seems to reconcile the Description to Probability and Nature. The Simile here is of that sort, and renders it not wholly unlikely that a Rock *of* Ice *should remain for ever, by mentioning something like it in the Northern Regions, agreeing with the Accounts of our modern Travellers.* [P. 1715.]

See Introduction, p. 222 above. Pope is anxious to show the scientific critics of allegory that even the shell of allegory is not always without factual evidence. It was part of the programme of the Royal Society to invite the co-operation of seamen and travellers in adding to their Natural History collections: 'It is certain that many things, which now seem *miraculous*, would not be so, if once we come to be fully acquainted with their *compositions*, and *operations*' (Sprat, p. 214). Dryden shows a similar anxiety when introducing 'Iris . . . on a very large Machine' at the end of Act I of *Albion and Albanius*: 'This was really seen the 18th. of *March*, 1684. by Capt. *Christopher Gunman*, on Board his R.H. Yacht, then in *Calais Pierre*: He drew it as it then appear'd, and gave a Draught of it to us . . .'

Pope tells Caryll (21 Dec. 1712) that, to suit the season, he has been reading 'those books which treat of the descriptions of the Arctic regions, Lapland, Nova Zembla, and Spitzberg'. There were several such descriptions in English and French: see *Literature on the Polar-Regions* by J. Chavanne, A. Karpf, and F. Ritter (Vienna, 1878). But Pope's source seems to have been the illustrated 1711 edition of *An Account Of several Late Voyages and Discoveries*. Section iii of this book, *Captain J. Wood's Attempt to Discover a North-East Passage to China*, contains a description of 'Snowy Clifts' of Nova Zembla (p. 189, first series). But Pope's detail comes from Section iv, *F. Marten's Observations made in Greenland and other Northern Countries*, which is brilliant with imagery. The icebergs Pope has in mind are those fixed on the shore: 'Near to the Land . . . some greater Ice-Mountains are seen . . . that stand firm on the shoar, and never melt at bottom, but increase every year higher and higher, by reason of the Snow that falls on them, and then Rains that freezes [*sic*] and then Snow again alternately; and after this manner the Icy-hills increase yearly, and are never melted by the heat of the Sun at the Top . . . I once saw one of these pieces [broken off from an ice-hill] that was curiously workt and carved, as it were, by the Sea, like a Church with arched Windows and Pillars . . . The true Rocks look'd fiery, and the Sun shin'd pale upon them, the Snow giving the Air a bright reflection. . . Where the Ice is fixed upon the Sea, you see a snow-white brightness in the Skies, as if the Sun shined, for the Snow is reflected by the Air' (pp. 44 ff., 23, 40 second series). Martens' voyage being in the summer, he often describes the perpetual sunlight. The tops of the mountains were often hidden in fog or cloud. By 'Lightnings' Pope probably means the phenomena of light described by Martens on pp. 53 f. (second series). Cf., however, Magnus, i chr. 6: 'There appeares often in the North parts, in clear weather, all the night, in *September*, continual Lightnings, that threaten rather then hurt the Beholders of them'.

Dryden refers to 'the distant sun' in *King Arthur*, III ii, where '*The Scene Changes to a Prospect of Winter in Frozen Countries*'. Cf. also Pope's *Thebais*, i 812. Pope refers again to Zembla at *Dunciad*, i 74, and *Essay on Man*, ii 224.

ELOÏSA AND ABELARD

APPENDIX I

ABAILARD AND HÉLOÏSE

ABAILARD was born in Brittany in the year 1079, the eldest son of a knight. His father intended him for the military life, but he became instead the most famous scholar of his generation, ousting the dialectical reputation of William de Champeaux at Paris and later damaging the theological reputation of Anselm of Laon. When nearly forty he changed a life of continence for one of passionate love for Héloïse, the eighteen-year-old niece of Fulbert, canon of the cathedral at Paris. Abailard gained her love under the guise of resident tutor, thoroughly trusted by Fulbert. Abailard's students were more awake than Fulbert: they detected the passion through the deterioration of Abailard's lectures. When Héloïse conceived, Abailard removed her secretly to Brittany. A son was born and christened Astrolabe. Fulbert's sense of outrage was seemingly pacified by Abailard's promise to marry Héloïse. For a long time she refused to agree to the marriage, since marriage would ruin Abailard's career in the church, but finally yielded and returned to Paris for a secret wedding. Fulbert's anger, however, showed itself again, and Abailard took Héloïse to the nunnery at Argenteuil, near Paris, where she became a nun. Fulbert then confined his attention to Abailard. He paid ruffians to enter Abailard's lodging and emasculate him. Abailard retired to the convent of St Dénys near Paris and professed himself. His unpopular displeasure over the licentiousness and worldly glory of the monastery led to his taking up lecturing again, and again with the old success. His treatise on the Unity and the Trinity of God brought him under an official charge of heresy. The result of this charge was a virtual imprisonment in the abbey of St Médard until the Pope ordered him back to St Dénys. Here a renewal of his unpopularity prompted his escape to a cell at Provins whence he solicited and obtained permission to set up a monastery in solitude. He built himself a mud oratory on the deserted banks of the Arduzon. When this became known, students flocked to join him, and he resumed his lecturing as a means of livelihood. The students replaced his mud and wattle by a building of wood and stone large enough to answer their needs, and this convent was dedicated to the Paraclete as a perpetuation of the aid of the Comforter in softening the hardships of Abailard. But continued molestation either by enemies or by the fear of them, led Abailard to accept the abbacy of St Gildas in Brittany. Here administrative troubles made his life a torment. He reproved the morals of the monks and this provoked the old hostility which expressed itself in poisoning his drink and the posting of assassins. He seems to have borne a charmed life. On the expulsion of the nuns from the abbey of Argenteuil, he invited Héloïse and some others to occupy the Paraclete and visited them until these visits caused scandal. It was from St Gildas that Abailard addressed a letter to an unfortunate friend, describing his own career in adversity as a means of comforting by contrast. This account, if all her first letter is genuine, Héloïse read by chance. So their correspondence began. Abailard's difficulties at St Gildas led to his resigning the abbacy some time in 1131 or 1132. From this point onwards there are few documents relating to Abailard's life. He probably spent most of his time in Paris, lecturing, until in 1140 the Council of Sens met to pronounce against the heterodoxy of his writings. The plans of the bishops were temporarily foiled by Abailard's appeal to the Pope. Innocent II, however, confirmed the attitude of the Council by excommunicating Abailard and by burning his books. Abailard made his peace with St Bernard, his chief antagonist, and was allowed to retire to Cluny where the unassertiveness and holiness of his life marked him out as perhaps already in failing health. For the sake of a better climate, Abailard left Cluny for Châlons-sur-Saône where he died on 21 April

1142. His body was removed to the Paraclete by Peter, Abbot of Cluny, and Héloïse received 'the body of our master'. Twenty-two years later Héloïse was buried in the same crypt though not in the same tomb. Seven centuries later their dust was mingled in a common grave in the cemetery of Père Lachaise in Paris.

APPENDIX J

ELOISA TO ABELARD AND PRIOR'S *HENRY AND EMMA*

THERE does not seem much point in linking together 'Eloisa and Abelard' and Prior's *Henry and Emma* (1709). In 1728 Ralph charged Pope with trying to outdo Prior's success:

> . . . In *Prior*'s Verse
> *Henry* and *Emma* charm the finest Tastes;
> The racking *Trial*, the dissembled Guilt,
> The weeping Maid, her Sighs, her Tears, her firm,
> Unbated Love, melt ev'ry Soul, and claim
> A simpathizing Tear.—SAWNEY beheld
> The Labour, heard the Praise; fair *Heloise* now
> Employs his Thought, and furnishes his Rhyme;
> Her tender Wailings, and repentant Pangs
> Her frantick Flame, oppos'd to *Emma*'s Warmth,
> To *Emma*'s Woe must shine; But Innocence
> And Virtue were forgot, and 'tis the Nun,
> The enamour'd, raging, longing Nun that gives
> The Verse a Name: Extract her tender Thought
> Her hot Desires, and all the rest will shrink
> From Fame, like Parchment shriv'ling in the Blaze.

(*Sawney. An Heroic Poem. Occasion'd by the Dunciad . . . 1728*, pp. 11 f.). Delacour, writing two years later, used some of Ralph's words to reverse his judgment: 'I think [*Eloisa*] even excels Mr. *Prior*'s *Henry* to [*sic*] *Emma*, which did charm the finest Tastes Abroad and at Home' (*Abelard to Eloisa, In Answer to Mr. Pope*'s *fine Piece . . . Dublin* . . . MDCCXXX, A 3r). Savage repeated the idea of Pope's indebtedness to Prior (Johnson, *Lives*, iii 105). But before any of these critics wrote, Prior in *Alma* had already hailed *Eloisa*:

> O ABELARD, ill-fated Youth,
> Thy Tale will justify this Truth:
> But well I weet, thy cruel Wrong
> Adorns a nobler Poet's Song.
> *Dan* POPE for thy Misfortune griev'd,
> With kind Concern, and Skill has weav'd

A silken Web; and ne'er shall fade
It's Colors: gently has He laid
The Mantle o'er thy sad Distress:
And VENUS shall the Texture bless.
He o'er the weeping Nun has drawn,
Such artful Folds of Sacred Lawn,
That LOVE with equal Grief and Pride,
Shall see the Crime, He strives to hide:
And softly drawing back the Veil,
The God shall to his Vot'ries tell
Each conscious Tear, each blushing Grace,
That deck'd Dear ELOISA's Face.
  Happy the Poet, blest the Lays,
Which BUCKINGHAM has deign'd to praise.

(*Poems on Several Occasions*, 1718, pp. 349 f.). Pope considered that *Alma*, 'abating its excessive scepticism', was Prior's most enviable work (Ruffhead, *Life of Pope*, 1769, p. 482) but, on the authority of Bathurst, he 'was not pleased with [the lines on himself]' (Warton, i 301)—perhaps the last line of the passage quoted has something to do with his displeasure. Shenstone discusses the point that Pope did not repay his 'poetical obligation' to Prior (*Works*, 1764, ii 177), a discussion which T. Evans carries further (Prior's *Poetical Works*, 1779, i 381). Pope, however, found Prior's lines useful for setting against a paraphrase of Ralph's charge in the *Testimonies of Authors* prefixed to the *Dunciad*.

APPENDIX K

'ELOISA TO ABELARD'

Replies, Imitations, and Parodies

SEE Wright, pp. 532 f.: 'During the sixty years after the appearance of Pope's Eloisa, there was a fairly steady interest in the story of Abelard and Heloise. There were occasional replies to Eloisa, and there was a considerable demand for editions of Hughes. But between 1782 and 1795, there were six new "replies" and several editions of at least two of these "replies". Also, the demand for Hughes increased, and beginning with 1787, not only Pope's "Eloisa", but also five replies to it were regularly printed with the prose of Hughes. Though no new replies appeared during the early years of the nineteenth century, there were printed between 1800 and 1824 at least seventeen editions of the enlarged Hughes. . . Then, there was no further edition of the letters of Abelard and Heloise in England in any form until Hughes's version was reprinted in the *Temple Classics* series in 1901. . . The story of the love of Abelard and Heloise is essentially romantic; and Pope and his imitators emphasise the romantic possibilities. . . The glamor of distance enhances the interest that surrounds this story of frustrated passion. The increasing interest in medieval themes from the 1760's on may well have given added impetus to the Abelard and Heloise story. . . . "Eloisa to Abelard" and the "replies" to it were by far more popular during the decades in which the romantic point of view predominated in the literature of England than at any other time, and . . . with the decline of interest in romantic subjects this theme died out.' (Wright underrates the popularity of the poem in Pope's lifetime.)

The earliest printed reply seems to be that of John Beckingham in Curll's *Ten New Poems*, 1721 (I have not seen this). Later replies include those of William Pattison (1728), James Delacour (1729), James Cawthorn (1747),[1] Edward Jerningham (1792), and Landor (1795). Wright suggests that the reply, published in *Cupid Triumphant* (1747) and signed 'Mrs C—er', is interpreted in the table of contents as 'Mrs Centlivre' instead of as 'Mrs Cowper', i.e. Mrs Judith Madan (née Cowper), Pope's friend. He shows, however, that the poem is almost word for word that of Pattison. There are two MS. copies of the Pattison–Madan reply in the Brit. Mus.: (1) Add. MS. 4,456, ff. 92 ff. (following a transcript of Pope's poem); (2) Add. MS. 28101 [a 'Family Miscellany' belonging to the Ashley Cooper family], ff. 150 ff. This latter is headed 'By the same hand [i.e. Mrs Madan]—1720'. The poems by Mrs Madan in this collection are dated and placed in chronological order, which suggests that the dating has authority. On the other hand, the dating is not made in 1720, since poems by other writers and dated as late as 1741 precede it (the book appears to be as originally made up). If, however, 1720 is correct, Pattison is ruled out (he was not born till 1706). Certainly Pattison wrote *a* poem with this title (see the letter printed in his *Poetical Works*, 1728, i 41 f.). Perhaps his executor mistook Mrs Madan's poem for his.[2] Thomas Stewart published 'An Epistle from Abelard to Eloisa' in 1828, prefixing it with an epistle 'to Alexander Pope', which is interesting if only for this couplet:

But fled with thee is thy Augustan age,
Thy verse unsung, ev'n closed thy classic page.

The following works may be cited as indebted to Pope. (1) *The Preceptor. Or, the Loves of Abelard and Heloise. A Dramatick Entertainment . . . Dublin: Printed by S. Powell, for Abraham Bradley . . . M DCC XL.* [a ballad opera]; (2) *Eliza to Comus. An Epistle. In Imitation of Mr. Pope's Eloisa to Abelard. By Charles Augustine Lea . . . M DCC LIII*; (3) *An Elegy Written in An Empty Assembly-Room . . . M.DCC.LVI.* [The *Advertisement* reads: This Poem being a Parody on the most remarkable

1. See *The New Foundling Hospital for Wit*, ed. 1794, v 88 ff., for a lost dedication of Cawthorn's poem to a lady. The couplets are sown with phrases from Pope's poems.

2. John Whaley's *Collection of Original Poems and Translations*, 1745, contains on pp. 297 ff. a text of the Pattison–Madan poem (varying only slightly from Pattison's, and possibly identical with the text in *Cupid Triumphant*, which I have not seen). Whaley gives the poem as 'By a Lady'.

Passages in the well-known Epistle of *Eloisa* to *Abelard*, it was thought unnecessary to transcribe any Lines from that Poem, which is in the Hands of all, and in the Memories of most Readers'. The *Elegy* is included in vol. vi of Dodsley's *Collection* (1758)]; (4) *Eloisa en Dishabillè* [*sic*], *Being a new Version of that Lady's Celebrated Epistle to Abelard, done into familiar English metre* [anapaests], *by a Lounger* ... MDCCLXXX [often attributed to Richard Porson, but by John Matthews].

To these may be added 'An Epistle from Oberea, Queen of Otaheite, to Joseph Banks, Esq.' (*The New Foundling Hospital for Wit*, ed. 1784, v 237 ff.) and 'A Poetical Epistle ... from an officer at Otaheite' (*An Asylum for Fugitive Pieces*, ii (1786) 41 ff.), both of which echo Pope's poem in the midst of describing non-European sexual practices.[1]

1. 'Eloisa to Abelard' was translated five times into Polish in the later years of the eighteenth century and the first of the nineteenth, and during the same period it was edited fifteen times anonymously (see S. Helsztynski's 'Pope in Poland. A Bibliographical Sketch' in *The Slavonic Review*, vii, 1928–9, p. 738).

INDEX OF NAMES